The IMMORTAL PRINCE

JENNIFER FALLON

A TOM DOHERTY ASSOCIATES BOOK
NEW YORK

This is a work of fiction. All of the characters, organizations, and events portrayed in this novel are either products of the author's imagination or are used fictitiously.

THE IMMORTAL PRINCE

Copyright © 2007 by Jennifer Fallon

Originally published in 2007 by Voyager, an imprint of HarperCollins *Publishers*, Australia.

All rights reserved.

A Tor Book
Published by Tom Doherty Associates, LLC
175 Fifth Avenue
New York, NY 10010

www.tor-forge.com

Tor® is a registered trademark of Tom Doherty Associates, LLC.

ISBN 978-0-7653-5607-9

First U.S. Edition: May 2008
First U.S. Mass Market Edition: June 2009

Printed in the United States of America

0 9 8 7 6 5 4 3 2 1

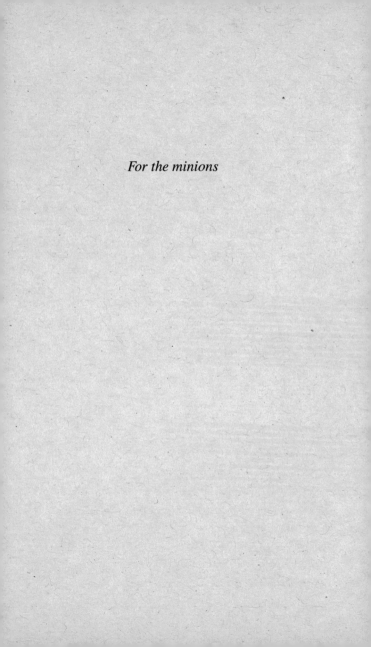

For the minions

The
IMMORTAL
PRINCE

Prologue

As the last of the stragglers stumbled into the cave, Krynan looked back over his shoulder at the end of the world, wondering vaguely why he felt nothing. He grabbed for the rocky ledge above, ignoring the pain of his burned hands, and pulled himself up, collapsing with relief as another bolt of lightning streaked the blood-red sky, thick with volcanic ash.

Propping himself on his elbows, Krynan felt, rather than heard, the ground rumble again. It had been shaking like this for days now, making it difficult to stand, let alone flee the carnage. Blinking back stinging tears, he shielded his eyes and turned to stare into the distance. There wasn't much left to see. The city of L'bekken was gone, and many of the outlying villages buried under layers of pumice and ash. Those structures that weren't swallowed by the advancing lava had been burned away earlier by the lightning thrown around with such abandon by the immortals who had brought this down upon them.

It was impossible to tell where his farm had once prospered by the river; impossible to pick one landmark from another. The river had boiled away, the land buried beneath the molten rock pouring from what had once been the fertile slopes of Mount Iriggin.

How many were dead was anybody's guess, what would happen to the survivors almost too frightening to contemplate.

"Krynan?"

He turned, barely recognising the woman who spoke to

him. His wife's face was blackened with soot and speckled with blisters gained fleeing the burning ash. Her fair hair was a dirty brown colour and her once-fine clothes in tatters.

She looked like a beggar.

We're all beggars now.

"What?" he asked, more harshly than he intended. It wasn't Alea's fault they were homeless, destitute and destined to die in this war between two gods who cared for nothing but their own desires.

"Your mother wants you."

Krynan sighed, knowing what his mother wanted of him; certain he wasn't ready for the thankless and probably futile task the Cabal had so desperately bestowed upon her only son.

"Tell her I'll be there shortly," he replied, turning to watch his world disintegrating before his very eyes.

Alea was silent for a moment and then nodded. "The Matriarch hasn't got long, Kry," she warned and then turned and headed back into the cave.

None of us have got long, Krynan thought, as another mountain farther to the east suddenly exploded, its peak boiling away in a ball of flame and ash, billowing into the sky like foaming ale spilling over the lip of a tankard. Still numbed by the magnitude of the destruction, he watched for a moment longer and then turned away.

His mother was lying on her side on a makeshift stretcher in the crowded cave. In the fitful light from the few torches they'd been able to salvage, he could see how badly she'd been burned. Her breathing was so laboured it was painful to listen to. Alea moved back when she saw him and allowed Krynan to kneel beside her.

"Mother . . ."

"Krynan. You're still . . . here."

"Where else would I be?"

With a blackened hand, his mother clutched at his tattered sleeve. "You have a job to do . . ."

"My job is to look after the survivors."

She shook her head painfully. "You are the Custodian of the Lore. Your job . . . your *only* job . . . is to protect the Lore. It's our only protection . . . against the Tide Lords."

"Fat lot of good it's done us this time," he retorted bitterly.

"All the more reason to . . . protect it, Krynan." His mother's face was etched with pain, but she seemed determined to ignore her own agony. For her, the Lore was everything; more important than any one person's fear or pain. "We might have . . . failed, but future generations can . . . they can build on what we've learned. The Cabal . . . is relying on you. Form another Pentangle. Protect . . . the Lore. It must . . . survive."

Her request, although he was expecting it, infuriated him. "You want me to walk away from my people? Let them suffer? Just to protect a few tattered pages of useless information?"

"Don't let your pain . . . cloud your . . . judgement, Krynan," his mother advised. Her voice was failing. She was fading fast. "You've known all along it might come to this."

That was the bitter truth. Ever since the Pentangle—the governing body of the Cabal of the Tarot—had appointed him Custodian of the Lore, Krynan had known it might come to this. But there was a vast difference between knowing you might be called upon one day to perform an onerous task, and the reality of being confronted by it.

He shrugged helplessly. "I fear the truth is that I never expected to survive."

"That you have . . . is a sure sign . . . this is your destiny, my son."

He shook his head. "I'm not strong enough for this, Mother."

"The Cabal thought you were, otherwise you would not have been made Custodian."

Krynan frowned, thinking he'd got the job because in the civilised parlours of L'bekken nobody really thought the Tide Lords would ever turn on each other so savagely. The humans weren't even sure what the fight was about, what altercation between the gods had escalated from a disagreement to the destruction of the whole world. Chances were they would never know, either, but like the countless civilisations before them who had suffered the same fate, it didn't really matter. All that mattered was saving the Lore, keeping it hidden out in the open, disguised as the Tarot. The Tide Lords were immortal but sooner or later, the Cabal believed, someone would find a way to destroy them. It was for that reason the Lore must be protected at all costs.

It just hadn't occurred to Krynan until now how high that cost might be.

His mother's breathing was thready, her voice almost gone. "Now promise me, Krynan . . . promise you'll . . . protect the Lore."

"I promise," he said, not brave enough to deny his mother's dying wish, despite how useless a task he thought it. "I'll see the wretched thing survives. Who knows, maybe in the future there *will* be humans smarter than us who can figure out a way to defeat the bastards."

She nodded and moved her hand, reaching for something tucked into her blouse. Seeing the pain the movement caused her, Krynan reached for it himself. It was a pitifully thin packet he extracted, wrapped in an oiled cloth to protect it from moisture. It wasn't fireproof, however. For that, Krynan's mother had used her own body, shielding the precious documents from the burning ash with her life.

Krynan didn't think he was nearly so brave. Or dedicated.

"The future . . . is relying on you, Krynan," his mother whispered painfully. "Don't . . . let it down."

"Protect the Lore at all costs," he quoted, trying to keep the scepticism from his voice because nothing else would ease her mind. "The Tarot must survive so humanity can survive."

"There *will* . . . come a time, Krynan," she promised softly, her eyes closing. "Just . . . not now. Not in our time."

"There will come a time," he agreed, surprised to taste

salty, sooty tears streaking his face. As he was speaking, his mother's raspy breathing slowed and then stilled. He waited for a moment, hoping it would pick up again, but between one breath and the next that never came, his mother's body had relaxed, her features no longer contorted with pain.

Alea came up behind him and placed a comforting hand on his shoulder.

"I don't have to leave," he said without looking back at her. "I could stay. Now she's dead, nobody cares—"

"The Tarot must survive so humanity can survive," Alea cut in. "You must fulfil your oath, Krynan. For all of us, not just your mother."

He stood up and turned to look at her. "Do you really believe that, Alea?"

"I *have* to believe it, Kry," she told him, leaning forward to kiss his tear-streaked face.

"Come with me then . . ."

She shook her head, smiling sadly. "We can't risk it. Go, my love, now, while the gods are still busy hurling mountains at each other. One man will slip through where a group might not. There'll be safer places to hide, other places where the devastation isn't as bad." She smiled with ineffable sadness, gently wiping away his tears with her thumbs. "Just think of us, sometimes."

"Alea . . ."

"You're the Custodian of the Lore, Krynan. It's your duty."

It seemed too heavy a burden, and probably a useless one. All they'd gone through to gather the information contained in the Tarot had proved futile. He reached down to the swell of her belly protruding from her tattered clothes. "I'll never see my son . . ."

"If you don't do this," his wife pointed out sadly, "it won't matter if your son is born or not."

"But—"

"I'm relying on you," she whispered, kissing his cheek. "*They're* relying on you."

He looked over his shoulder at the refugees crowded into the cave. There were scores of them, their faces blackened with soot and ash, their eyes blank pools of despair.

"You're their hope for the future, Kry," Alea reminded softly. "Their hope that humanity *has* a future."

The weight of responsibility felt enormous and he wasn't sure he had the strength to carry it, but the notion his unborn son might one day wear a look of such abject despair helped him find it. To be utterly without hope . . . to be so totally wretched. His son deserved better. He deserved to have a reason to hope, even if it ultimately proved a futile one.

Krynan pulled Alea to him and hugged her tightly, and then kissed her blackened lips, knowing if he didn't leave now, the despair might suck him down too and he wouldn't have the courage to go at all. He put his hand on her belly. "I love you, Alea. Make sure my son knows I loved him, too."

"He'll know his father was a hero," she promised. "Now go! Before the Tide Lords lose interest in hurting each other and start to wonder what has become of us."

He nodded and slipped the small packet into his shirt. "Is there anything you want before I . . ."

"Go!" she commanded.

Full of uncertainty, Krynan nodded and turned toward the cave's entrance, putting his back to the scores of pitiful survivors, his mother's corpse, his wife and his unborn child.

The Tarot must survive so humanity can survive, he reminded himself as he stepped out into the hellish night. *There* will *come a time. Just not now. Not in our time.*

PART I

Vanishing Tide

The tide never goes out so far but it
always comes in again.
—CORNISH PROVERB

Chapter 1

Hope seemed an odd emotion for a man about to be executed, but that was the only name Cayal could give the thrill welling up inside him as they led him up the steps of the platform.

Soon, one way or another, he told himself, *it will be over.*

He could see nothing with the black hood over his head, his other senses starved of input by the rough weave of the cloth. He gathered the mask was as much to spare the spectators as it was to offer a condemned man some semblance of privacy. It muffled sound, too, making the world outside seem remote, shrinking reality to only what he could hear and feel. The tall grim walls were gone, so were the overcast sky and the gloomy prison yard. He revelled in his sense of touch; relished the cold air on his bare chest and the musty canvas over his head that reeked faintly of other, successful deaths.

Cayal breathed in the aroma and hoped.

With luck, this might be the last thing he ever knew. Oblivion beckoned and Cayal was rushing to meet it with open arms.

"*What the . . . ?*" he exclaimed suddenly as a thick, heavy noose was tightened around his neck. He struggled against it, wondering what was happening. They should be ordering him to kneel, making him reach forward to the block.

He didn't want to hang. Hanging was useless. Futile. And likely to be very, very painful . . .

"No!" he cried in protest, but with his hands tied behind

him, his struggles were in vain. He could feel the hangman checking to make certain the knot was secure and in the right place, just under his jaw below the left ear, the place guaranteed to snap a neck as quickly as possible.

"Any last words?"

The gruff voice sounded disinterested, the question one of form rather than genuine consideration for a dying man's wishes. For a moment, Cayal didn't even notice the hangman was addressing him. Then he realised this might be his last chance to object.

In a tone that was anything but repentant, he turned his head in the direction of the executioner's voice. "What's going on here? You're supposed to behead me."

"The executioner's on vacation," the disinterested voice informed him. "Read the charges."

The order was directed at someone else. A moment later, a shaky voice announced from somewhere on his left: "Kyle Lakesh, citizen of Caelum. You are charged with and have been found guilty of seven counts of heinous murder . . ."

As opposed to any other sort of murder, Cayal retorted silently, his anger welling up. *The headsman's on vacation? Are they kidding me?*

". . . For this crime, the Supreme Court of Lebec in the Sovereign State of Glaeba has sentenced you to death."

Cayal cursed behind the hood, certain nobody would see the irony. He'd killed seven men to get here. Seven worthless humans to get himself beheaded. *And the flanking headsman's on vacation!* Still, there was a funny side to this, he thought, wondering what the venerable members of the Supreme Court of the Sovereign State of Glaeba would do if they knew of the seven odd million he'd killed before that.

"Is there any word from the Prefect regarding his grace's willingness to consider clemency?"

Another question of form, directed at the Warden. A last-minute reprieve could only come from the Duke of Lebec himself, an act that had only happened once in the past fifty years or so. Cayal knew that for a fact. He'd checked. When one was as determined to end their suffering as Cayal was, one did their homework.

Glaeban justice was harsh but surprisingly evenhanded, which suited him just fine. When you were deliberately setting out to be decapitated, there was no point in choosing a country known for its leniency toward killers.

The silence that followed the clerk's question put to rest any last-minute hopes Cayal had that they might not carry out his sentence. A moment later, he heard footsteps echoing hollowly on the wooden decking of the platform and felt a gloved hand settling on his bare shoulder.

"Ready?"

What if I say no? Cayal wondered. *What's he going to do? Wait until I'm in the mood?*

"I want to be decapitated," he complained, his voice muffled by the hood. "Hanging me is just wasting everybody's time."

"Do you forgive me?" the hangman asked in a barely audible voice. Cayal got the feeling that of all the questions the hangman asked of his victims, this was the only one to which he genuinely craved an affirmative answer.

"No point," Cayal assured him.

Blinded by the hood, he couldn't tell what the hangman's reaction was to his reply, and in truth, he didn't care. Cayal was beyond forgiveness. He was beyond despair. Just to be sure, he reached out mentally, wondering if there was any trace of magic left, but he could sense nothing, not even a faint residual hint of the Tide he once commanded. The magic couldn't save him from the pain he knew was coming . . .

Almost before he finished the thought, the platform dropped beneath him. He plummeted through the trapdoor without any further warning.

The rope tightened savagely, cutting off his breath. Cayal thrashed as the air was driven from his lungs, the knot under his left ear pushing his jaw out of alignment, snapping his neck with an audible crack.

Filled with frustration, Cayal jerked viciously on the end of the rope, choking, asphyxiating, hoping it meant he was dying. His eyes watered with the pain. His very soul cried out in anguish, begging for death to claim him. He thrashed about, wondering if the violent motion would complete the hangman's job. The agony was unbelievable. Beyond torture. White lights danced before his eyes, his heart was racing, lightning bolts of pain shot through his jaw and neck, he couldn't breathe . . .

Cayal cried out in a language nobody in Glaeba knew, pleading with the powers of darkness to take him . . . and then, with his last remaining breath, his cry turned to a wail of despair. He'd been thrashing at the end of the rope for far too long.

His cry had driven the remaining air from his lungs. His throat was crushed. His neck broken.

And still he lived.

They left him hanging there for a long, long time, waiting for him to die. It was the nervous clerk who finally ordered him cut down when it was clear he wasn't going to.

Cayal hit the unforgiving ground with a thud and lay there in the mud, dragging in painful breaths to replenish his oxygen-starved lungs as the noose eased, already feeling the pain of his dislocated jaw, broken larynx and neck beginning to heal of their own accord.

"Tides!" he heard the clerk exclaim as they jerked the hood from his head. "He's still alive."

The hangman was leaning over him too, his expression shocked. "How can it be?"

Cayal blinked in the harsh spring sunlight, glaring painfully up at the two men. Rough, unsympathetic faces filled his vision.

"I can't die," he rasped through his crushed larynx and twisted jaw, not realising that even had he been able to form the words properly, he still spoke in his native tongue; a language long gone from Amyrantha. Realising his error, he added in Glaeban, "I'm immortal."

"What did he say?" the clerk asked in confusion.

"Something about a portal?" the hangman ventured with a shrug.

Cayal took another deep breath, even more painful than the last, if that was possible, then lifted his head and banged his face into the ground, jarring his jawbone back into place.

"I'm immortal," he repeated in his own tongue. Nobody understood him. Even through the pain, with the failure of these fools to give him the release he craved, he found himself losing patience with them. "You can't . . . kill me. I'm a . . . Tide . . . Lord."

It wasn't until later—when the Warden came back down to see what was going on—that he'd recovered sufficiently to repeat his announcement in a language even these stupid Glaebans would understand.

"I'm . . . a Tide Lord," he'd announced, pushing aside the agony for a moment. He'd been expecting shock, perhaps a little awe at his news—after all, they'd just borne witness to his immortality—certainly not scepticism. "And as I've now proved . . . you can't hang me, I demand . . . to be decapitated!"

The Warden had been far from impressed. "A Tide Lord, eh?"

Ignoring the throbbing in his neck and jaw, trying to sound commanding, Cayal nodded. "You must . . . execute me again. Only this time, do it properly."

The man had squinted at Cayal lying on the ground at his feet in a foetal curl, smiling humourlessly. "I must do *nothing* on your command, my boy. I don't care who you think you are."

Cayal hadn't actually thought about what might happen if they didn't behead him. Not in practical terms, at any rate. He had wanted to end things so badly he hadn't allowed himself to consider the consequences, just in case it jinxed him somehow. Lukys would have called him a superstitious fool for thinking like that. But then, Lukys would have had quite a bit to say about this entire disastrous escapade if he'd known about it. Cayal wondered, for a moment, what had happened to him. It was a century or more since Cayal had seen any of his brethren. Perhaps, if he had, he might not have come to this, but finding the others was nigh impossible if they didn't want to be found. It was easy to get lost in a world of millions when there were only twenty-two of you.

So, alone and despairing, Cayal had waited until the lowest ebb of the Tide and then, quite deliberately and methodically, set out to put an end to his desolation.

And failed miserably; a problem he was only now—as he heard the Warden demanding to know what had gone wrong—beginning to fully appreciate.

"I am . . . Cayal, the Immortal . . . Prince," he gasped, between his whimpers of agony. The damage done by the noose and his anxious jerking about at the end of the rope was substantial. This wasn't going to heal in a few hours. Overnight, it might, but it was going to take time.

"You're a right pain in the backside, is what you are," the Warden muttered, turning to the guards who stood over Cayal, watching him writhe on the cold ground in agony as the healing progressed apace. "Take him to the Row while I decide what to do with him."

"Didn't you . . . hear me?" Cayal demanded as the Warden walked away, wondering if his inability to stand was somehow robbing his words of authority. The Warden seemed singularly unimpressed by the importance of his prisoner.

"I heard what you said, you murdering little bastard," the Warden assured him, glancing back over his shoulder at where Cayal lay. "And if you think acting crazy is going to save you from the noose, you can think again."

Crazy? Who's acting crazy?

"You don't know . . . who you're dealing with!" he tried to yell hoarsely at the Warden's back. The pain was unbelievable. Healing at an accelerated rate was a very nasty business.

"You've got a lot to learn about Glaeban justice yourself, old son," one of the guards informed him, hauling him to his feet. "Come on, your holiness. Your royal suite awaits you."

Cayal's legs hung uselessly beneath him, his shins banging against the stone steps as they dragged him up the narrow curving stairs to Recidivists' Row while they worked out what to do with the man who wouldn't die.

The man they refused to acknowledge as an immortal.

Chapter 2

Warlock could smell the danger from across the corridor, even in the darkness. It overrode all the other rancid aromas in this place, sharper even than the stench of mouldy straw, the reek of stale urine, human faeces and the sour tang of boiled cabbages that permeated the very stone of his prison walls. Even the smell of distant rain did nothing to mask it. The feeling of imminent danger tugged on a primal, ancestral memory beyond sense or reason, made more ominous somehow by the far-off rattle of thunder as a storm beat uselessly at these thick prison walls.

He knew what lurked across the hall; could taste the menace as surely as he could feel the rusty bars beneath his paws, as sure as he could hear the guards gaming far down the hall, so far away that not even the light from the guardroom reached his cell. He could hear the warders, though, his canine senses far sharper than mere human ears, even those belonging to the suzerain.

Warlock bared his teeth at the cell opposite. Although his moaning had not let up all night, the occupant was probably asleep, given the late hour. He would know nothing of the slight. He probably wouldn't care, either. But it made Warlock feel a little better. If he couldn't alleviate his discomfort, snarling in the face of his enemy made it a little easier to bear.

The danger he sensed had arrived last night in the form of the occupant of the cell across the hall. A foreigner, the guards informed Warlock as they waited for one of the orderlies to clean out the cubicle in anticipation of his arrival. A wainwright from Caelum convicted of murder. Yesterday he'd been awaiting execution.

And then, oddly, they'd brought him here.

"Here" was Recidivists' Row. At least, that's what the guards called this dank and dreary place. The residents had other names for it, the kindest of which was *hell*. Recidivists' Row was reserved for the worst criminals in Glaeba. Those the authorities had no intention of releasing but couldn't justify killing.

And why would they kill us, Warlock wondered, *when it's so much more fun to watch us rot?*

Warlock's crime was much less impressive. He'd only killed one man. That his victim had killed three of his older sister's cubs and been raping his younger sister when Warlock tore his throat out with his bare hands had meant nothing to the human magistrates who had stood in judgement of him. Warlock was Crasii. A slave. His crime was raising a hand in anger toward *any* human.

The only thing that had saved Warlock from the hangman was that his victim had been a criminal with no family to speak of. There was nobody willing to stand up and beg for justice at the trial. Had Warlock been human, that might have been enough to see him released without penalty. Glaeban justice was all about consequences, which meant the fewer there were the less severe the sentence was likely to be. The man Warlock killed was lamented by nobody and had his killer been human, the court might have dismissed the case out of hand. But a previous black mark— when Warlock was little more than a pup he'd accidentally hit a human in a bar fight and been charged with assault— had landed him here in Recidivists' Row. The Glaebans were just, but they weren't particularly tolerant. Attacking a human once could be considered an accident. Twice meant he was dangerous. So dangerous his threadbare prison uniform was stamped "never to be released."

And now, just when Warlock was beginning to come to terms with his incarceration, they'd caught a suzerain and tried to kill him.

Idiots.

The man across the hall had spent all night groaning in his sleep. He was still healing, Warlock guessed. Such was the price of immortality. Nature didn't like being tampered with. Without a doubt, the suzerain would live, but the accelerated healing process was unrelenting. This agony which made him cry out, even in his sleep, was the price one paid for immortality.

The prisoner screamed hoarsely again, and then began mumbling something in a language Warlock didn't understand. His knowledge of the suzerain was handed down orally through generations of Crasii, his fear and loathing of them as much instinct as it was reason. It was the same for all the Crasii. The nearness of a suzerain was enough to make them lose all semblance of independence, any vestige of courage or rebellion. Knowing he'd been bred to serve the suzerain, Warlock was surprised to discover he still had the capacity to hate one of them. He'd thought, given the proximity of the man, he'd be a gibbering mass of fawning submission by now. Oddly, he wasn't. He could feel the suzerain, taste his scent, but nothing in Warlock felt compelled to offer himself up to his master.

Maybe it wears off, he thought, *this need to serve the suzerain.* It was a thousand years since they'd been heard from last. Not since the last Cataclysm.

Or perhaps it's Low Tide. Warlock had no way of knowing the moods of the Tide Star. He was of a race created by magic, not one able to sense or wield it.

He was still pondering the mystery when another sound coming from the distant guardroom caught his notice. The faint scraping of a chair, the scuff of leather against stone, mumbled apologies, a promise to return . . . One of the warders getting ready to do his rounds.

Warlock glanced through the bars but there was no tell-tale flicker of torchlight heading his way yet. He took a step back, however, long experience having taught him how threatened the guards were by his mere presence, let alone any stance they judged to be overtly aggressive.

He didn't mind that they feared him. If anything, it gave him some small sense of self in this place designed to sap all trace of spirit from a creature's soul—Crasii or human. Knowing the guards considered him dangerous meant he was still alive; still capable of action. Warlock would rather have died than spend a lifetime cowering in the corner of his cell.

Booted footsteps against the flagstones alerted him to the approaching guard, even before he saw the light coming around the corner of the narrow stone passage. He could tell by the scuffing rhythm of his walk that it was Goran Dill, the garrulous, fat corporal fond of ale and collecting orchids. It was a strange hobby for a prison guard, the corporal readily admitted, but he was always willing to chat to his charges, as if by befriending them, he somehow lessened the danger to himself. Warlock had wanted to respond that it was a strange hobby for *any* man, but no sane prisoner upset one of the few even remotely decent guards in this hellhole, so he'd smiled and nodded and tried to sound interested as Dill explained about colours, variations and habitats of flowers he'd only heard about and never seen.

One does what one must to survive in this place.

The light grew steadily stronger as Goran Dill approached. Warlock smelled him long before he came into view. The man reeked of stale sweat, dirty leather and the faint perfume of the flowers he so adoringly tended.

When he reached the cells, Goran raised the hissing torch and squinted through the flickering light into the gloom.

"Can't sleep, eh, dog boy?" he remarked, when he caught the shine of Warlock's eyes in the torchlight.

"Not with that racket going on across the way," Warlock replied, jerking his head in the direction of the cell where the groaning suzerain was incarcerated.

Goran cocked his head and listened for a moment. The man was babbling incoherently again in some foreign tongue that neither the Crasii nor the guard understood.

"How long's he been groaning and mumbling like that?"

"All night."

The guard shrugged. "Should've died when he was supposed to. Then he wouldn't be having these troubles."

Goran's lack of sympathy was hardly surprising and Warlock knew exactly how he felt, but he needed to sleep and that wasn't going to happen with a man screaming in agony across the hall.

"Can't you give him something?"

"What do I look like? A flankin' pharmacist?"

"Knock him unconscious, then," Warlock suggested. "Better yet, let me in there for a minute or two. I'll shut him up."

Goran seemed amused. "Yeah . . . right . . . there's an idea. I'll let you at him, eh, dog boy? And how would I explain him being dead in the morning?"

"Trust me, Corporal Dill, of all the things that you may or may not have to explain in the morning, your friend across the hall there dying isn't among them."

"You buy his story then . . . about being immortal?"

"Is that what he's claiming?"

"Reckons he's a Tide Lord," Goran informed him. "Says that's why the noose didn't kill him."

"Then a short sharp blow to the head will either prove he's right or save the executioner the trouble of another hanging, won't it?" Warlock pointed out, trying very hard not to look surprised at the news. Not that it mattered. Given the dim light and Goran Dill's poor ability to read Crasii expressions, it was unlikely he noticed anything amiss. "Either way, if he's unconscious he'll shut up and I'll be able to sleep."

The suzerain cried out again, this time a tormented scream that echoed off the walls and made even the other prisoners stir in their sleep.

Goran sighed heavily, but nodded in agreement with the need to do something. "All right then. I'll see what I can do."

Taking the keys from his belt, he wedged the torch into the bracket set into the wall behind him and fiddled with the lock for a moment before throwing the door to the suzerain's cell wide open. Through the open bars, Warlock could tell the man didn't notice his visitor, either still asleep or too consumed by his pain to care what was happening around him. Goran Dill walked to the pallet and stared down at the writhing lump tossing and turning on the dirty straw mattress, and then, with little ado, withdrew his truncheon. One sharp blow to the temple and the man fell silent.

Warlock breathed a sigh of relief.

"Might be immortal," Goran joked as he relocked the cell, "but he ain't invincible."

"Thank you," Warlock said with genuine gratitude.

"All part of the service," Goran shrugged, lifting the torch out of its bracket. "You get some sleep now, eh, dog boy. Don't want you all snarly and growly in the morning when they give you a bath."

"A bath?" he repeated in surprise. "Why am I being made to have a bath?"

"Everyone in Recidivists' Row is gettin' a bath, lad. And fresh clothes. Gotta scrub the cells out, too. And change the bedding."

"Why?" he asked, unable to imagine any circumstance that would prompt such an unexpected burst of housekeeping.

"You've got an important visitor coming," Goran informed him as he headed back up the hall. "At least the Tide Lord does, 'cause he's coming to visit him. A real important man, he is. Can't have him getting offended by all you filthy scumbags, can we?"

"Who?" Warlock asked curiously. "What important man?"

"Declan Hawkes," Goran called over his shoulder. "The King's Spymaster his-self."

His announcement made, Goran headed back down the corridor, humming tunelessly, the flickering light and the smell of the corporal fading together with his shuffling footsteps, leaving Warlock alone in the blessed silence.

So the King's Spymaster is coming to visit the prisoners of Recidivists' Row. Warlock sat on his pallet, scratching himself idly behind his ear, wondering what would bring someone as important as Declan Hawkes to a place like Lebec Prison.

Then he glanced through the bars at the unconscious suzerain across the hall and thought he understood.

Chapter 3

The arrival of the King's Spymaster was an occasion of note at Lebec Prison although certainly not a welcome one. Although he had no authority here in Lebec—at least not officially—he was the eyes and ears of the King of Glaeba and that made him a man to be cautious of.

Looking down over the grim prison courtyard from the window of his office, the Warden watched his visitor dismounting in the drizzling rain. He chewed on his bottom lip as he tried to fathom the meaning of this most disturbing turn of events.

Am I to be held personally responsible for a botched hanging?

He had expected his report about the failed hanging to

cause problems—an investigation, perhaps, maybe even a reprimand to keep the Caelish Ambassador happy—but not this.

Not the King's Spymaster on his very doorstep . . .

Is Hawkes here to demand my resignation? Or worse?

Sweat beaded the Warden's brow. He'd heard rumours of men who'd never been seen again after crossing the King's Spymaster. Just as he'd heard the other, even more disturbing rumours about this common-born son of a whore who'd been appointed spymaster five years ago—at barely twenty-five—when the previous spymaster, Daly Bridgeman, retired. Everyone thought the king had taken leave of his senses when the announcement was made. Whatever his origins, however he had managed to get himself appointed spymaster, nobody doubted Declan Hawkes's ability to do what was required of him, ruthlessly, efficiently and without any qualms about removing anything or anybody he considered a threat to Glaeba's sovereignty.

The spymaster disappeared from view as he entered the building. Turning away from the rain-misted window, the Warden forced the last of his tea past the lump in his throat, put down the cup with a betraying rattle of china and glanced around his office one last time, just to make certain there was nothing there that might catch the spymaster's eye. The Warden had no idea what might catch the eye of a man like Hawkes, but that was one of the things that made him so dangerous. You just never knew what he was really after.

Although he was expecting it, the knock on his door—when it finally came a few minutes later—made him jump. He sat down and then abruptly stood up again, deciding to meet the man eye to eye, rather than be forced to look up at him. Even before he called permission to enter, the door began to open. The Warden had to force himself to resist the urge to mop the nervous sweat from his brow.

"Master Hawkes! What an unexpected pleasure!"

The spymaster eyed him curiously as he closed the door

behind him. "I sent a message two days ago saying I was coming to Lebec, Warden. Didn't you receive it?"

Declan Hawkes proved to be even more daunting in person than his reputation suggested. He was taller than the Warden by almost a head, and his damp hair was dark, as were his eyes . . . eyes that seemed to take in everything with a single glance.

"Well, yes . . . of course . . ."

Hawkes shook off his rain-splattered oilskin cape, shaking the raindrops onto the Warden's rug with little care for the damage he might be doing. "Then my arrival is hardly unexpected, is it?"

The Warden didn't know how to respond and Hawkes—curse his common-born hide—seemed happy to let the silence drag on for an uncomfortable length of time, waiting for a response.

The Warden cracked first. "Er . . . won't you have a seat, Master Hawkes?"

"Thank you."

Afraid his knees might give way, the Warden sat himself down abruptly as Hawkes lowered his tall frame into the chair opposite the remarkably bare desk. The Warden had been here half the night making sure there wasn't so much as a scrap of paper on the battered leather surface that Hawkes could catch a glimpse of.

"I . . . er . . . I take it you're here about the hanging?"

"And to think, there's a rumour getting about Herino that you're not very bright," Hawkes replied.

The Warden's eyes narrowed. He might have to put up with the King's Spymaster, but he didn't have to sit here and be insulted by him.

"What do you want, Hawkes? I'm a busy man," he demanded, dropping all pretence of cordiality.

Hawkes's dark eyes raked the empty desk and then he smiled. "Yes, I can see that. Why did you try to hang him?"

"Pardon?"

"You tried hanging this prisoner. I was under the

impression beheading was the normal method of execution in Lebec."

"It is," the Warden agreed. "But my executioner's mother died a couple of weeks back. He's gone back to Herino for her funeral and to sort out the family's affairs. As I didn't want to fall behind, I decided to proceed without him. Beheading is a fairly specialised skill, so we thought we'd hang the prisoners until he got back."

"I see."

"You'll want to interview the prisoner, I suppose?" the Warden asked.

"Eventually."

"Why eventually? Surely your first task is to find out how Lakesh managed such a trick?"

"After I've eliminated the possibility that it wasn't a trick."

The Warden smiled at the spymaster with all the condescension he could muster. "Just because you grew up in the slums with the Crasii, Master Hawkes, doesn't mean you have to believe everything you heard down there, you know."

Declan Hawkes didn't even seem to notice the Warden was insulting him. "I was referring to the possibility that one of your men was bought off by this Caelishman to botch the job, affording him a chance at a second trial."

"Impossible!"

"You think he won't get a second trial?"

"I think no man of mine could be corrupted in such a manner."

"You're probably right," Hawkes agreed with a perfectly straight face. "I'm sure the professions of hangman and prison guard attract only the most righteous and upstanding sort of characters."

The Warden bristled at the spymaster's implication. "Even if my men *could* be corrupted, they'd never allow themselves to be suborned by a Caelishman."

"You only hire patriots, too, I see."

This was getting too much. "I don't have to sit here and put up with this!"

"You're right, Warden, you don't," Hawkes agreed. "So why don't I wait here while you toddle off and find the hangman for me. I'll interview him first. Then I'll talk to the other guards in attendance at the hanging, the prison clerk and the guards Lakesh was dealing with on a daily basis prior to his miraculous escape from certain death."

"What about the prisoner? I would have thought the logical thing to do would be to speak to him first."

"Did you?" Hawkes let the question hang, as if he was waiting for the Warden to justify his position.

The Warden pretended not to notice. "I *can* arrange for you to speak with him first."

"Given the injuries you claim he sustained in your report, I doubt he's capable of speaking."

"He's recovered."

For the first time, Hawkes actually looked surprised. "Recovered how?"

"Other than a few fading bruises," he replied with a shrug, "the man is completely healed. In fact, by the following morning, he was fine."

Hawkes leaned forward in his chair, a gesture he managed to make threatening without any effort at all. The Warden wished he knew how Hawkes did that. Given the calibre of the people a man in his position was forced to deal with on a daily basis, it would have been a useful trick to know.

"You failed to mention this extraordinary recovery in your report."

"I didn't think it was important."

Hawkes was silent for a disturbingly long time before he replied. "Perhaps I will speak to the prisoner first, after all."

The Warden smiled in triumph. It was a small but significant victory.

"I'll have you taken to him," the Warden offered. *And you can damn well interrogate him there,* he added silently. If the King's Spymaster thought he could just march in here and take over his office without so much as a by-your-leave, he had another thing coming.

Disappointingly, Hawkes rose to his feet, as if he didn't even notice the Warden had won this small but significant battle of wills. "I want to see him now."

"Of course," the Warden agreed, ringing the small bell on his desk as he rose to his feet.

A moment later the door opened. The guard looked at the Warden questioningly. "Sir?"

"Escort Master Hawkes to the Row. He wants to speak to Kyle Lakesh."

"Thank you, Warden," Hawkes replied, heading for the door.

The Warden couldn't resist one last dig. "When you're done with him, perhaps you'd like to join me for tea?"

Hawkes stared at him for a moment and then, inexplicably, he smiled. "For *tea*?"

"It's a civilised custom, among men of breeding," he pointed out, with only the slightest emphasis on the word *breeding*.

Hawkes bowed with a surprising amount of grace for one born so low. "Thank you, Warden, but I fear I'll have to decline your . . . *civilised* offer. Once I'm done with this investigation I was planning to catch up with a few old friends while I'm here."

The Warden smiled. "Then far be it for me to keep you from your boyhood playmates, Master Hawkes. Of course, if you'd like to give me their names, I can check our register. I imagine a great many of your childhood friends finished up incarcerated in here for one crime or another."

Too lowborn to realise he was being insulted, Hawkes looked amused. "That might well be the case, Warden. Perhaps I should give you their names. There was one girl I was particularly close to when we were children . . . what was her name? Ah, that's right. Arkady Morel. She's married now. Did quite well for herself, they say. Perhaps you know of her?"

His minor victory over this insufferable man suddenly tasted like ashes in his mouth. The Warden paled. "Yes, of course I know of her."

"Excellent! Then when I'm done here, I'll give you the names of my other friends and you can send word if you find them. I'll be staying at Lebec Palace. With my old friend. Arkady."

Hawkes let himself out of the office, leaving the rest of it unsaid.

The Warden slumped down into his seat. Everybody in Lebec knew who Arkady Morel was. Tides, everybody in Glaeba knew it.

Only she wasn't Arkady Morel any longer. These days she was Lady Arkady Desean.

The Duchess of Lebec.

Chapter 4

Dinner at Lebec Palace was always an occasion; the exquisite decor, the mouth-watering menu, the faultless service, the sparkling company and the manifest lies—all of it unparalleled in any other stately home in the whole of Glaeba.

The hostess, Lady Desean, the Duchess of Lebec— Arkady to her closest friends, Doctor Desean to her colleagues at the university—presided over the dinner party with the ease and polish of long experience. With her high Glaeban cheekbones, rich dark hair and rare, sapphire-blue eyes, she was the jewel in Lebec's crown, her husband's prize trophy. It was an act, albeit a very good one. The Ice Duchess they called her. Arkady knew that, and didn't care. She was very good at ignoring snide remarks and envious glances.

High society in Glaeba was no place for the faint-hearted.

The twenty diners who had gathered here in the long, high-ceilinged dining room this evening were Stellan's friends, not hers, if "friends" was even the right word. Acquaintances, some of them; business and diplomatic associates, a few more. Others were here because they sought the Duke of Lebec's favour. One or two, like Etienne Sorell, the poet sitting at the centre of the long table—charming the rings off old Lady Fardinger—was here because he could be relied on to provide the riveting conversation for which the Duke of Lebec's dinner parties were so famous.

A few places to Etienne's right sat another regular guest: Lady Tilly Ponting, self-appointed clairvoyant to the rich and famous of Lebec. Larger than life, the Widow Ponting had a taste for bright, outrageous colours and was always good for a laugh. Rich enough to be considered eccentric rather than crazy, she was the sort of person who could fill an awkward silence with something inane and harmless. It made her priceless at a gathering such as this. She'd dyed her hair purple since they'd seen her last, too, and she'd offered to read everyone's Tarot after dessert, which should keep the political discussions to a minimum—a brilliant idea given the volatility of Glaeban politics lately.

Other guests, like the man sitting on Stellan's right—flirting across the table with her husband's niece, Kylia Debrell—were here for their own reasons and far more dangerous than Tilly. Arkady eyed him thoughtfully, while nodding absently in agreement with the woman on her right who was expounding loudly about the dire increase in the number of feral Crasii these days and how someone should do something about them. She sipped her wine and studied the young man through the forest of crystal and silverware separating the head from the foot of the table. Her husband's dinner companion must have felt her gaze on him. He glanced up, raised his glass mockingly in her direction, and then returned his attention to Lady Debrell.

Arkady frowned. Jaxyn Aranville. Lebec's Kennel Master. Distant cousin to the Earl of Darra. Scoundrel. Gambler. Troublemaker. Darkly handsome and arrogantly aware of the fact. And Stellan's lover, which made it impossible to be rid of him.

It couldn't last, Arkady knew. They never did. In that, she genuinely felt sorry for her husband. He was a gentle, forgiving man, but he was never going to be content because the one thing he wanted, he could never have.

But he kept looking. In all the wrong people, to Arkady's mind.

Jaxyn was toying with him, Arkady suspected. Young Lord Aranville's most recent lover before Stellan, if one believed the gossips, was a woman more than ten years his senior. If the looks he was giving Kylia Debrell were anything to go by, his next after Stellan Desean might well be a seventeen-year-old virgin. Not that her husband's niece was objecting to his attention, Arkady noted darkly. Perhaps it had been a mistake to seat them so close, although she'd had little option in the matter given Kylia was Stellan's heir, which meant protocol demanded she be seated at her uncle's right hand. This dinner was supposedly in Kylia's honour. The unexpected arrival of Stellan's niece several days ago called for nothing less than a full state dinner to introduce her to society. Still, Arkady had thought a frivolous girl would offer no attraction to a man like Jaxyn Aranville.

Then again, perhaps he'd guessed Arkady's intentions and was flirting with the girl for exactly that reason.

Jaxyn Aranville did things like that. It was how he amused himself.

"Don't you agree, your grace?"

Arkady felt, rather than heard, distant thunder rumbling in the background—the remnant of another spring thunderstorm—as she returned her attention to the man on her left. He was a balding man in his late fifties, one of the few people around this table Arkady considered *her* friend rather than Stellan's. An academic like herself, he was also working to uncover the lost history of Amyrantha, a

thankless task that saw them scorned, as often as not, for
their efforts. People didn't want to know what lay in the
past. Only what the future held.

It's what made Tilly Ponting and her wretched Tarot
cards so damned popular at parties.

"Forgive me, Andre. I'm afraid I was miles away."

"Doctor Fawk was just telling us we should pity the un-
indentured Crasii," Lady Jimison informed her through a
mouthful of truffles, sounding quite scandalised by the notion. "I mean, have you been through the slums lately? The
city outskirts are fairly crawling with the miserable, flea-
bitten creatures. They live like animals, copulate anywhere
they please, treat the streets like a public toilet. They're
disgusting. I say they should all be rounded up and put
down."

"A little drastic, don't you think?" Arkady asked, trying to
imagine Lady Jimison ever sullying her dainty satin slippers
in the muddy streets of the Lebec City slums. "The Crasii
living in our city slums—and every other city in Glaeba—
are desperately poor, have no income, no accommodation or
any of the other basic living requirements that indentured
Crasii enjoy as a matter of course. They have almost no
prospects for employment, and consequently, precious little
hope. I know these people, my lady. They deserve our pity,
not our enmity."

Lady Jimison frowned, but whether at her hostess's radical suggestion, or the unsubtle reminder of her common-
born background, Arkady couldn't really be sure. She took
a perverse pleasure in reminding snobs like Lady Jimison
that her duchess had started life in those slums she so despised. And it certainly wasn't fashionable to pity the
Crasii. Hadn't been fashionable for quite some time. Not
since Harlie Palmerston published his *Theory of Human
Advancement* about ten years ago, theorising that the Crasii
were a failed offshoot of humanity and living proof of his
conjecture that the human race had reached the top of the
food chain because of its superior intelligence.

Given the only other explanation about the existence of

the Crasii until that point had been the quaint notion that the mythical Tide Lords had blended human and beast magically, to create a slave race to serve them, Palmerston's theory had been welcomed with open arms by the scientific community of Glaeba. If the Ambassador of Caelum—who sat between Kylia and Etienne—was to be believed, the theory was well on its way to becoming accepted globally as the first logical and unified theory of human evolution. Of course, the science behind the theory meant little to the Lady Jimisons of this world. Bigots like her were just looking for an excuse to hate the Crasii.

"Frankly, my dear, I think if you spent a little more time being a wife, and a little less time doling out free meals to those mangy beasts in the slums, you'd gain a much better perspective on the matter of the lower races and the proper way to deal with them."

Lady Jimison's voice was shrill and her comment fell into a momentary lull in the conversation. It was followed by a long awkward silence.

Stellan came to Arkady's rescue. The duke smiled and leaned back in his seat, sipping his wine as he surveyed his guests. "I think my wife's efforts to help those less fortunate than us should be applauded, Lady Jimison. She sets an example we should all aspire to follow, don't you agree?"

Lady Jimison might be a bigot, but she wasn't a fool. She barely even hesitated before nodding apologetically in Arkady's direction and then smiling at Stellan. "Please, your grace, I meant no insult to your lovely wife. You're right of course. She is an example to us all."

"Well said!" the Caelish Ambassador agreed, his face flushed with a little too much wine for a diplomat to consume wisely. "But aren't you afraid of catching something in the slums, my lady? I mean, they're pitiable creatures to be sure, and they're not very . . . clean."

"Oh, the duchess has lots of experience in the slums," Jaxyn answered cheerfully before anybody else could say a word. "She's not afraid of catching anything. Besides,

Arkady's not really interested in the Crasii, are you, your grace? She just likes to dig up dirty little secrets about the long-lost Tide Lords, and apparently the Crasii know more about them than the rest of us."

"The Tide Lords? How quaint," the ambassador remarked. "Have you discovered anything interesting?"

"Like many others in my field, I'm working on the complete history of Glaeba," Arkady explained, silently wishing there was a way to have Jaxyn's drink laced with some terrible poison so she could watch him die a horrible, ugly death in front of the entire dinner party. "Not the Tide Lords, specifically."

"Like a growing number of our colleagues, Ambassador, we believe the Cataclysm that laid waste to the lost nations of Kordia and Fyrenne were not accidental," Andre clarified, coming to her defence. "The destruction seems far too specific to have been an accident of nature. Given the long oral history the Crasii have and that it predates our own written history by several thousand years, our hope is there is a clue to what really happened buried somewhere in their lore."

"But your theory is rather controversial, isn't it?" another voice added. "I mean, there's no real proof Kordia ever actually existed, is there?"

Arkady looked down the table to see who had spoken and sighed. Joal Dekerman. An old friend of Stellan's. One of the Herino Dekermans; moneyed, bored and jaded. He'd moved to Lebec with his equally bored and jaded wife about eighteen months ago to take up the role of Prefect. It was an honorary title. The Duke of Lebec was the real power in this prefecture and everyone knew it. But as the official representative of the crown, the title gave Dekerman social standing and the right to be heard, even if nobody was particularly interested in what he had to say.

"The idea that some almighty power brought down an apocalypse on Amyrantha," the Prefect sniffed, "is not only mildly offensive, it's absurd."

"But if we're right, someday we might be able to determine what really happened during the Cataclysm," Andre Fawk pointed out. "We may even be able to prevent it happening again."

Joal Dekerman studied Arkady curiously for a moment and then asked, "Do you think it was the Tide Lords?"

Arkady couldn't help but smile. "I deal in facts, Prefect Dekerman, not flights of fancy."

He smiled and raised his glass in her direction. "Then perhaps I have misjudged you, your grace. Please, forgive my ignorance."

In the brief silence that followed Dekerman's apology, Tilly Ponting clapped her hands loudly and announced, "Well, darlings . . . I can't tell if the Tide Lords caused the Cataclysm, and I can't tell a Crasii from a Scard, but I can certainly tell you what the future holds! Who's for having their Tarot read?"

With a relieved laugh, half a dozen of the diners indicated their willingness to have Tilly tell their fortunes and the conversation moved to much less dangerous ground as the more enthusiastic guests rose to their feet.

Dear Tilly, Arkady thought, idly moving her truffles and the rich cream in which they were smothered around her plate without actually eating them. She wasn't fond of truffles but they were a delicacy and expensive so, of course, they were a must for any meal served in the palace. *You're worth every one of those diamonds you're wearing.* This was the reason—purple hair and all—that Tilly Ponting graced so many tables in Lebec Palace. She could always be relied upon to shift the discussion back to something inoffensive.

At the other end of the table, Stellan smiled at her before turning back to his discussion with Jaxyn Aranville, who was looking decidedly smug. Arkady felt an unreasonable surge of hatred for the young man and the danger he represented, knowing full well there was nothing she could do about it.

But for the time being, the danger was past and Arkady was able to resume her perfectly proper smile as she presided over her perfect table, in her perfect palace with her perfect husband smiling at her fondly. She was the envy of every woman present, she knew, because the Duchess of Lebec—to outsiders at least—appeared to have a perfectly wonderful life.

A little later, when everybody had moved into the library to allow Tilly her chance to play fortune teller, Arkady followed her guests, having ordered supper to be served in another hour. She took a seat by the window and watched the fun. Surrounded by her admiring audience, Tilly was breathlessly informing a totally credulous Kylia Debrell that she would definitely marry a tall, dark and handsome stranger whom she would meet some time in the next five years.

There's a safe prediction, she thought, *given Kylia will undoubtedly be married off to some Glaeban lordling by the time she's eighteen.*

"I'm sorry about what Jaxyn said at dinner."

Arkady glanced over her shoulder to find her husband had come up behind her. Stellan Desean was only a little taller than Arkady, but he was a trim, attractive man, his caramel-coloured skin and dark, Glaeban eyes typical of his race and his class. They were a handsome people, the Glaebans; cultured, civilised, advanced . . . Not like the Caelum with their fondness for blood sports, or the Torlenians with their rigid morals, or even the Senestrans with their secretive religious rites. Arkady had only met a few people from places farther afield, so she couldn't comment on their character, but she knew her own people well enough. Stellan was one of their scions; the Deseans one of the True Families. His bloodline was precious.

Which, Arkady mused, *is at the root of most of Stellan's problems.*

"You don't have to apologise for him, Stellan," she said, turning to her husband. And then she smiled. "Make him come to me and apologise himself. Preferably on his hands and knees. That will do."

"Now, now . . . ," he scolded, good-naturedly. "Let's not be petty, my dear." A sudden burst of laughter from Tilly's audience drew his attention. He glanced at the crowd around the table and frowned. "Should I be worried about what non-sense Tilly is telling my niece?"

Arkady shook her head. "Apparently Kylia chose the Lovers, Cayal and Amaleta, when she dealt the cards. According to Tilly, it means Kylia will marry someone tall, dark and handsome."

"Well, as *tall, dark and handsome* describes more than ninety per cent of the likely candidates for the hand of someone as well connected as the Duke of Lebec's heir, I doubt Kylia will be disappointed," Stellan remarked. "But if you're sure she's safe in Tilly's hands for the foreseeable future—no pun intended—could you spare a moment, my dear?"

Arkady looked up at him, wondering at the request. "Is something wrong?"

He shook his head. "There's someone here to see you."

She raised her brow questioningly. "At this hour? Who?"

"Declan Hawkes."

Chapter 5

Declan was waiting for them in Stellan's study. It was a large, high-ceilinged room, built on the same grand scale as the rest of the palace, every surface gilded or painted by a master with scenes ranging from simple landscapes to stories attributed to the long-lost mythical *Book of the Tides*. The study was a work of art in its own right, each wall depicting the same scene painted at a different time of day. The west wall depicted sunset, the east sunrise, the north wall showed a bright and sunny aspect while the south wall was gloomy and overcast, the sky dark with storm clouds. Every piece of furniture had been chosen to complement the walls, even down to Stellan's opulent desk with its legs carved from solid ivory. Arkady had been overwhelmed by the magnificence of this place when she'd first come here to live after she married Stellan. Now she barely even noticed it.

"Lady Desean!" the spymaster exclaimed with a grin, turning from the fireplace to greet her. He'd been staring up at the stern countenance of Stellan's great-grandfather Rocard, larger than life and dressed in gilded armour in the portrait; a severed head lay at his feet while fires raged behind him, destroying what Arkady assumed was some sort of crude village. The Bloody Duke, they used to call him. He was the one credited with hunting the Scards of Lebec into virtual extinction.

Arkady hurried across the room and threw her arms around her old friend, hugging him tightly. "Tides, Declan, we haven't seen you for ages. What are you doing in Lebec?"

"Business brings me here. And your husband was kind enough to offer me a roof for the night."

"Why didn't you tell me he was coming?" she asked Stellan over her shoulder.

"I didn't know myself, until he arrived," Stellan informed her, taking a seat in one of the overstuffed leather armchairs facing the desk, which he moved to face the spymaster. Stellan tolerated her friendship with Declan Hawkes, but—for obvious reasons—her closeness with the King's Spymaster made him more than a little nervous. She'd told Stellan any number of times that she'd not shared his secret with her old friend, but he still worried about it. He'd never said or done anything to indicate he knew about her husband, but still, deep down, Arkady suspected Declan knew the truth.

Stepping out of his embrace, Arkady looked up at Declan expectantly. Rain pattered softly against the tall windows either side of the fireplace, not nearly as heavy as the earlier downpour that had come with the thunder and light-ning.

"Well, what *are* you doing here? It's too much to hope, I suppose, that you're simply here for the pleasure of my company?"

"Actually, I'm here for your expertise."

Arkady looked at him oddly.

"Do you remember a dreadful murder in the village of Rindova several months ago?" he asked. "A whole family—seven brothers—was slaughtered."

She was puzzled by the question. It certainly wasn't what she'd been expecting. "I remember. The killer was a foreigner, wasn't he? A Caelish tradesman of some sort? Didn't they catch him at the scene of the crime, standing over his victims, still covered in their blood?"

"They did," the spymaster agreed. "He was a wainwright. His name is Kyle Lakesh. He was tried and condemned for the murders, too."

"Is there some sort of problem with his trial?" Arkady glanced at Stellan. "Is that the reason you wanted the Cael-ish Ambassador invited to dinner this evening?"

"There is something wrong, Arkady," Declan informed her, "but the ambassador has nothing to do with it. Not yet, at least. You see, they hanged the criminal several days ago."

"And the ambassador is upset because we've executed one of his citizens?"

"He's got nothing to be upset about," Stellan remarked, brushing an imaginary fleck of dust from his trousers. "He didn't die."

"Who didn't die?"

"Lakesh," Declan said. "The murderer. They hanged him and he didn't die."

"You mean the hangman botched the job?" she asked, not at all certain she understood what they were telling her.

"No, as far as I can tell, the hangman did a fine job. The man just refused to die."

Arkady looked at her husband, hoping to detect a glimmer of amusement in his eyes, thinking this must be some sort of joke. But Stellan was quite serious. So was Declan Hawkes.

"How could he *refuse* to die?" she asked, looking from one man to the other. "Don't you people have some sort of arrangement where an officer delivers the fatal blow if an execution fails?"

"You're thinking of military executions," Stellan explained. "This is a civil matter. The man was hanged. It's ugly sometimes, but it's difficult to botch it completely. There are no alternate arrangements because they usually don't go wrong."

"So what happened in this case?"

Declan picked up his brandy from the marble mantel and took a long swallow. The rain on the windows behind him had almost stopped while they were talking, Arkady noticed out of the corner of her eye.

"According to Lakesh, his real name is Cayal and the reason he didn't die is because he's immortal."

Arkady laughed. "*Cayal,* did you say? As in *Cayal, the Immortal Prince*? The Prince of Tides? The legendary hero of ancient myth?" She shook her head, wondering if Declan had thought up this joke and her husband was just taking part in it to relieve the boredom. Maybe Jaxyn was behind it. It reeked of one of his pranks—except she couldn't envisage any circumstance that might entice Declan to do Jaxyn Aranville's bidding. "You don't need me, Declan; you need Tilly Ponting and her blessed Tarot cards."

"I'm just as sceptical of his claims as you, Arkady," Stellan agreed. "But this man's no fool. He's taken a lucky accident and turned it into a loophole."

"A loophole? But you said he's already been tried and convicted."

"And he *should* be already dead," Stellan agreed. "The problem we have now is that we can't hang him again without going back to court for another execution order."

"He's insisting he's a Tide Lord," Declan added, "and he's begging us to try again . . . to kill him again, that is."

"So he's suicidal? I wouldn't have thought that was a major dilemma given the man is slated for execution."

"But the state can only execute a sane man, Arkady," Stellan pointed out. "Master Hawkes suspects—and I agree—that this sudden bout of insanity is Lakesh's way of avoiding a second attempt. If the Caelish Ambassador gets wind of it, he'll start insisting the man be released."

"Why would he want a murderer released?"

"Because under Caelish law, if an execution fails a man is free to walk away with all his sins forgiven. I refuse to allow that to happen in this case. I'm certainly not going to let some Caelish wagon builder play us for fools by manipulating the law to suit himself."

"How could he do that?"

"If he's proved insane, we can't execute him."

Arkady shrugged. "I don't see what this has to do with me. Why not just lock him away in an asylum somewhere and be done with it? It's not as if you've never done anything unjust before."

"Well, for one thing," Stellan said with a disapproving edge to his voice, "I have no intention of letting it get about that one can escape the noose in Lebec by pretending to be crazy."

"For another," Declan added, "the Caelum Ambassador has been looking for an excuse to cause a diplomatic incident for almost a year—ever since the king refused the offer of a marriage between Prince Mathu and Princess Nyah. This mess is likely to give him one."

Arkady well remembered the incident Declan spoke of. While the idea of uniting Caelum and Glaeba in marriage had some political merit, the Crown Prince of Glaeba was a strapping young man of nineteen, who'd been more than a little disturbed at the prospect of being forced to accept an eight-year-old bride, particularly as Caelish law required proof of a consummated marriage within a month of the exchange of vows. The king had sent Stellan to

Caelum to explain—as tactfully as possible—that in Glaeba, such an arrangement was considered not just awkward, but actually immoral, however, if the queen would like Glaeba to consider the princess as a suitable consort for their crown prince at some point in the future, once she reached a more suitable age, then he'd be happy to consider the offer.

It was a testament to Stellan's skill as a diplomat that he had been able to refuse the proposal on behalf of the Glaeban king and walk away with both his head on his shoulders and Caelum still an ally of Glaeba. But there was still a degree of residual resentment among the Caelish who suspected King Enteny's refusal had something to do with their Princess Nyah not being good enough for a sodding Glaeban, rather than the stated cultural differences that made such a union untenable.

"And again I ask—what do you expect me to do about it?" she said, as it dawned on her that this was no prank, but a deadly serious matter.

"You work with the Crasii," Declan reminded her. "You know a lot about their lore and the Tide Lords."

"They're a myth," Arkady assured him. "There ends my knowledge."

"Your husband says otherwise."

Arkady glared at Stellan, wondering what else he'd told her old friend, before turning back to the spymaster. "Even if I knew everything there was to know about them, Declan—which I don't, incidentally—I still don't see what some child's fairytale—which I know for a fact you don't believe in—has to do with this madman."

It was Stellan, not Declan, who answered her. "Declan suggested you may be able to prove this man is lying, Arkady."

"And I'd very much like your expert testimony to that fact at his next execution hearing."

Arkady shook her head. "He's claiming he's a *Tide* Lord, for pity's sake. That sort of says it all, don't you think?"

"We can live with the lies, Arkady," Stellan assured her. "It's the insanity plea I'm trying to avoid."

Arkady was far from convinced. "There must be somebody else? What about Andre Fawk? He's far better qualified than me. Tides, Declan's grandfather knows more about the Crasii than any man alive. Why not ask him?"

"Andre doesn't live here in Lebec," her husband pointed out. "He has commitments in Herino that will be remarked upon if he neglects them. Bringing another expert from the capital will take days and alert the Caelish Ambassador to our problem. We can't risk that happening until we have proof this man claiming to be a Tide Lord is faking insanity to avoid the execution."

"As for my grandfather . . ." Declan hesitated for a moment and then shrugged. "You've much more credibility. You're the Duchess of Lebec and a historian in your own right. Pop is just an old man who lives in the slums."

Arkady frowned at the description, wondering what it would take to reconcile Declan and his grandfather. Then she smiled at him, mischievously. "I don't suppose you've considered the possibility that he's telling the truth?" she teased. "He might really be immortal."

Declan wasn't amused. "Please, Arkady, this is no joking matter. Will you do it?"

Arkady still hesitated. The decision wasn't an easy one. She had no particular desire to spend time with a cold-blooded killer who'd murdered a family he claimed he'd picked at random and then gave the reason for his crime when he was discovered standing over the bodies as "I envy their ability to die." Even Arkady knew about that. The case had been news, on and off, for months.

On a professional level, however, to have anybody recognise her as something other than the Duke of Lebec's wife was too good an opportunity to pass up. That might well be the reason Declan was offering her this job and not someone else more qualified. He knew better than anybody how hard she'd fought to be taken seriously.

She nodded slowly. "I suppose."

"How long will it take?" he asked.

Arkady shrugged. "That depends on what you want as proof. If I interview him for an hour and then stand up in court to announce that in my expert opinion he's faking insanity, his defence advocate will simply produce his own expert who'll claim with just as much authority that he's not, and if the Caelish Ambassador gets involved, you can bet he'll be far better credentialled than me. To do this properly, I'd need to trip him up, I suppose. Find the crack in his story and expose it."

"How long would that take?"

"Only a few minutes if he hasn't thought it through," she speculated. "Months if he's been working on his story for a while."

"This nonsense about him being a Tide Lord only started after the execution," Declan told her. "Up until then he was no different to any other prisoner. He certainly wasn't claiming to be immortal."

"Then it shouldn't take long," she suggested. "When did you want me to speak to him?"

"As soon as possible," Stellan advised. "We can't put the ambassador off much longer."

"I'll do it tomorrow, then."

"I'll have a carriage sent for you in the morning to take you to the prison," Declan offered, looking quite relieved. "And you'll be paid, of course. For your services."

Arkady couldn't hide her smile. "I recall you once referred to my 'services' as a quaint little hobby, Declan Hawkes. Now you're willing to actually pay for them. My, what a wonderful leveller desperation turns out to be."

"Arkady, please . . ." Stellan sighed.

"It's all right, your grace," Declan told him. "I probably deserved that. And the irony is not lost on me, Arkady."

"*Doctor* Desean," she corrected.

"Pardon?"

"When I'm working, Declan, I am Doctor Desean."

Declan glanced at Stellan, a little surprised. "You don't object to your wife using her academic title?"

"Should I object?" Stellan enquired. "You know as well as anyone that Arkady got her doctorate without any help from me."

Declan Hawkes didn't answer Stellan's question, but his silence spoke volumes. It was easy enough for Arkady to guess what he was thinking. *She might not have her doctorate because of you, Stellan, but she only keeps her job because without your support the University of Lebec would have to shut its doors.*

There was no point arguing about it, either. Arkady had learned that long ago. She and Declan had fought long and hard over her decision to wed Stellan Desean and barely traded a civil word for several years after the wedding. Declan had been furious with her when she told him who she was marrying. He accused her of selling her body for a title, a place in society and the Desean family fortune. It had taken Arkady a long time to forgive him for that. In fact, it was only since Declan had become spymaster that their friendship had slowly begun to resemble the closeness they'd shared as children.

"Certainly not, your grace. Forgive me for implying anything of the kind."

"Well, now that's settled, I suppose we should return to the party," Stellan suggested.

Declan bowed politely to Arkady. "I'll see you tomorrow, *Doctor* Desean. If you'll excuse me, your grace? There's some business I need to take care of in the city before I retire tonight."

"Are you going to visit your grandfather?" Arkady asked.

Declan stared at her for a moment and then shook his head. "No."

"You should. He misses you."

The spymaster ignored her comment and turned to her husband. "I'll see you in the morning, your grace. Goodnight."

"One of the Crasii will show you to your room, Master Hawkes."

A moment later Declan shut the door behind them, leaving Arkady alone with her husband.

Chapter 6

After the spymaster left, Stellan turned to Arkady curiously. "What was that about his grandfather?"

"Declan and his grandfather haven't spoken in years."

"Don't you think that's Declan's business, then, my dear, and not yours?"

Arkady shrugged. "I know . . . it's just . . . they used to be so close. His grandfather raised him. It pains me to see them like this."

"Stay out of it, Arkady. Nothing good ever comes from interfering in other people's family squabbles." Rising to his feet, he crossed to the sideboard and poured himself another generous splash of brandy before he turned to look at her. "I was surprised, though, when Hawkes asked if I'd mind your involvement in this rather delicate situation."

Arkady followed him with her gaze. "Why didn't you tell him it wasn't your place to decide what I should or shouldn't become involved in?"

He leaned against the sideboard, swirling the dark brown liquid in his glass. "Because we both know that's not how it works, Arkady."

She nodded, acknowledging the truth of his words. "I know. It'd be nice to think even an old friend like Declan Hawkes wanted my help because of who I am, not who I'm married to."

"*I* sought your help because of who you are," he reminded her.

"Which is actually the reason people don't take me seriously," she replied without rancour. "Still, I shouldn't be too upset. I wouldn't even have this much if it wasn't for being your wife."

"You see, my dear," he said, raising his glass in her direction. "We both benefit from this clever little sham."

"Which brings me to another problem," she replied with a frown. "How much longer is Jaxyn staying with us?"

"Why do you ask?"

"You said he'd be here a few days," she reminded her husband. "That was almost a year ago."

"He's earning his keep, Arkady. You can't deny that."

"I think he's going to be a bad influence on Kylia."

"You think he's a bad influence on *me*," Stellan corrected.

Arkady sighed, wondering why she bothered. This was an argument she had no hope of winning. "Just be careful, Stellan. Kylia is very young and Jaxyn can be very charming, as well as thoughtless. I don't want her getting hurt."

"I'll speak to him," Stellan promised.

"We should be getting back to our guests," she suggested. "People will start to wonder where we are."

Stellan smiled. "Maybe they'll think we snuck away for a romantic interlude."

"We've been married too long for people to think that," she assured him. "They'll probably think we're fighting."

Her husband finished his brandy and stepped forward, offering her his arm. "Well . . . what do we care about what people think, anyway, eh?"

A great deal, Stellan, my dear, Arkady thought. *Otherwise, you wouldn't have married a penniless physician's daughter to protect your family from the scandal of learning what you really are.*

Before she could say something aloud, however, the study door opened and Jaxyn Aranville's head appeared. "Ah! This is where you two are hiding."

"We were just about to return to our guests," Stellan informed him.

"You might want to hold off doing that for a moment,"

the young man suggested, opening the door fully. "Until you've spoken to your visitor."

Standing behind him was a young canine Crasii, one of the pups from the village. Dripping wet, he stood barely taller than Jaxyn's waist, and was covered in a pelt of reddish-brown hair, his big dark eyes wide with apprehension. He looked human from a distance, but for his distinctly canine head, with ears that twitched nervously in the presence of his masters, and his tail hung low and submissive. The pup was hopping from one foot to the other and wringing his hands, looking past Jaxyn anxiously, searching for something—or someone. His presence, Arkady knew, signalled that something was badly amiss. It was rare to see a pup here at the house. The elders usually didn't let them out of their sight, and certainly not at this time of night.

"Laddie?" Arkady asked. "What are you doing here?"

"Fletch sent me, your grace. He sent me to tell you to come right away."

"What's wrong?" Stellan knew as well as Arkady that the old dog wouldn't have sent a pup to the palace at this hour for anything less than a dire emergency.

"It's Boots, your grace," Laddie muttered, looking down at his feet.

"What about her?"

"She finally done it, your grace."

"Done what?" Stellan demanded impatiently.

"Done busted out of the compound," the pup informed them, raising his head. His eyes glistened and he was clearly distressed by the news he carried. "That's why Fletch sent me, your grace. 'Cause she near killed one of the felines gettin' away."

"I'll go," Arkady volunteered, after Stellan made Laddie repeat his startling news. It wasn't often a Crasii slave tried to escape, and certainly not from Lebec Palace, where they were treated better than on most estates, but the news didn't really surprise Arkady. Boots had been nothing but trouble since she'd learned how to talk.

"What about our guests?" Stellan asked, not questioning her decision. They both knew she was better at handling the Crasii than he was.

"Nobody will miss me. They're too busy with Tilly and her Tarot readings. If you put in an appearance, it's not likely they'll even notice I'm gone."

"I'll go with you," Jaxyn offered.

Arkady frowned but before she could object Stellan nodded in agreement. And with good reason, she supposed. He was the Kennel Master, after all. "Good idea. Things are likely to be a mite fraught down there if one of the felines is injured. Make sure you're armed."

Once again, Arkady opened her mouth to object, but it was Jaxyn who cut her off this time. "I won't need a weapon," he said.

She glared at him. "Planning to subdue the Crasii with the force of your winning personality, are you?"

"Of course," he replied. "What were *you* planning?"

"Fletch said to hurry, your grace," Laddie piped up, staring up at the human adults with a mixture of awe and fear. "Tipsy might be dying."

Jaxyn glanced at Stellan with a raised brow. "You named a fighting feline *Tipsy*?"

"What of it?" Arkady snapped, annoyed by his tone.

"It just never ceases to amaze me how you people manage to get any sort of work out of the Crasii at all, when you name them as if they were all children's pets."

"It never ceases to amaze me that after almost a year as Kennel Master, you didn't know we had a feline named Tipsy," she retorted.

"There's hundreds of them," Jaxyn reminded her with a shrug. "I can't be expected to know the name of every single slave on the estate now, can I?"

"Just go," Stellan ordered patiently, before Arkady could argue any further.

Jaxyn bowed mockingly first to Stellan and then in Arkady's direction and stood back, winking at her as she passed him. Arkady let out an exasperated sigh and headed down the broad carpeted hall with Jaxyn and Laddie in her wake, wondering what had provoked a young Crasii slave to throw away everything for the dubious notion of freedom.

The Crasii compound on the grounds of Lebec Palace was more like a cluster of small villages than traditional slave quarters. It was actually a series of three compounds radiating in a circular pattern around a central common, divided into three sections by tall brick walls designed to separate the occupants for their own protection, rather than confine them. The compound to the left nearest the lake housed the amphibians, the dark waters running underneath the wall to feed the birthing pools. The centre compound was home to the felines, while the largest enclosure on the right was home to the large canine workforce employed both at the palace and on the estate as agricultural workers. It was a radical design providing the slaves with an approximation of village life and not altogether successful. It was never a good idea to let the canine and the feline Crasii mingle too closely, and the amphibians were unsociable at the best of times. Fights frequently broke out between them and while the felines invariably won the confrontation, a canine bite could fester and turn gangrenous with remarkable speed.

There was an exterior wall surrounding the outer compound, but Arkady had thought it unnecessary. Crasii slaves didn't run away often, not if you treated them well. There were a few recalcitrants who bolted the first chance they got, but as a rule, Stellan was inclined to let the Scards—as the discarded Crasii were called—go when they ran away. It cost too much to mount a search party to hunt them down, and then when you finally caught them, you had to either restrain them or kill them. There was no point trying to make them work. Better to let them go, he said. Once a Crasii turned Scard, they were ruined anyway, and usually more trouble than they were worth.

But harming another Crasii in the process . . . well, that made things very awkward, Arkady knew. The natural animosity between the felines and the canines meant letting Boots leave without a fuss was simply no longer an option. The felines would demand retribution and failure to provide it would make them fractious and uncooperative. It was never a good thing to have an uncooperative army full of peeved felines capable of laying you open from neck to navel with a single swipe of their claws.

The rain had stopped completely by the time they arrived at the compound, although Arkady would have to change before she returned to her dinner guests. Her skirts were six inches deep in mud and her delicate evening slippers were ruined. She and Jaxyn were met by a delegation of canines on the central common in front of the walled compounds, many carrying torches that flared sporadically in the cool breeze, hissing occasionally as a stray raindrop landed on the oil-soaked wadding. The slaves looked concerned, as well they might, Arkady thought, as she stopped and waited for them to approach. Fletch was in the lead, his red fringed shawl—denoting his rank as the most senior canine in the village—as murky as fresh-spilled blood in the flickering light.

"My lord. Your grace," he said with a respectful bow. "Thank you for coming so quickly."

"Where is the injured feline?"

"In their compound. They've barricaded themselves in and posted guards. We tried to reason with them . . ."

"I'll talk to them," Jaxyn announced, pushing through the crowd. The canines parted for him without question.

"Jaxyn!" Arkady called after him, but he ignored her. The canines fell back for the young man as he headed toward the feline enclosure, bowing respectfully as he passed, something that always annoyed Arkady for no reason she could readily identify.

"We had no idea Boots was planning to run away again,

your grace," Fletch assured her, dragging Arkady's attention back to the canines.

"How did the feline get hurt?"

"She was on guard. She challenged Boots as she was leaving."

"Boots broke out of the confinement cell and ripped her throat out!" Laddie informed her gleefully. The animosity between the two Crasii species was legendary—fostered from an early age by the elders of both races, Arkady suspected—hence the delight Laddie was taking in the feline's injuries. His earlier nervousness at the palace was forgotten now he was back among his own kind.

"What was she doing in the confinement cell?" Arkady asked.

Boots was one of Fletch's many grandchildren, a good-looking creature with a reddish-brown pelt, big dark eyes and the almost-human facial features so prized among Crasii breeders. She was just sixteen, and only recently deemed ready to begin her formal training in the palace household.

"She was given her first tunic," Fletch said. "She and Lord Aranville had words about it."

It wasn't just the clothing, Arkady realised. Modesty was a foreign concept to the Crasii, as was privacy. Crasii of all breeds preferred their natural state—considering clothing a human affectation, a sign of status, rather than necessity. For most indentured Crasii, receiving their first tunic was an occasion of note, a rite of passage that signalled their acceptance into the ranks of adulthood. As the Crasii dressed only to please their human masters, being awarded her first tunic would have been akin to presenting the mutinous young canine with a ball and chain, Arkady guessed, and she had probably received a sentence of solitary confinement for her defiance. Boots had questioned her status as a slave since she was old enough to comprehend what it meant and had complained vociferously about it at every opportunity.

Arkady silently cursed the silly bitch for harming a fe-

line in her escape. Given Stellan's generosity toward runaways, the chances were good that she would have been
allowed to try her hand at freedom without hindrance, had
she slipped quietly away. But not now. Now they had no
choice but to mark her as wanted. And probably post a reward for her capture.

Privately, Arkady hoped Boots got away. Perhaps the
young rebel would find Hidden Valley, the mythical sanctuary the Crasii believed existed for all the Scards who
fled their masters and were never heard from again. The
reality was more likely that the fugitive Scards had perished in the mountains or become swallowed up in the
slums of the many city-states bordering the Great Lakes.
She'd seen plenty of absconding slaves over the years but
had never met one who'd had any luck finding sanctuary
among others of their kind. But the myth gave them hope
and that was something. Hopelessness could be more destructive to a soul—human or Crasii—than war.

Arkady glanced across the torchlit common in time to see
the felines open the gate to their compound with a squeal of
rusty hinges on a single word from Jaxyn. That surprised
her. Fletch was claiming they'd barricaded themselves in. At
the very least, she expected the felines to put up some sort of
resistance.

"Coming?" Jaxyn called.

Arkady turned to Fletch. "We'll talk in the morning,
Fletch. Right now, I need to see to Tipsy."

"Of course, your grace."

The old dog bowed as Arkady hurried toward the feline
compound where Jaxyn was waiting by the gate, beyond
which the mirror-like eyes of the felines caught the flickering torchlight like pinpoints of malevolence.

Unlike the canines, whose village consisted of several long,
dormitory-style buildings, the feline compound was made
up of scores of smaller cottages, and two larger residences
with caged yards at the far edges of the complex, where
the males were housed. Arkady followed Jaxyn toward a

cottage near the western edge of the compound through a
corridor of silent, angry glares. With their flat faces, wide
noses and slanted, almond-shaped eyes, many humans
found it hard to read the expressions on feline faces. Arkady
had grown up around them, however, and knew what those
twitching tails signalled. Although no feline stood much
over five feet tall, she and Jaxyn were in danger, she realised, quickening her step to catch up to her companion.
Slaves they may be, but the feline Crasii were warriors, first
and foremost. If they considered the justice dealt out by
their human masters over this attack to be less than satisfactory, there was going to be trouble.

The hut where Tipsy was being treated was dark, the
only light in the single-roomed cottage a small candle on
the low table beside a pile of furs on the floor. It was a typical feline abode, dark, warm, small and cosy—just the
way they liked it. In the darkness it was hard to tell where
Tipsy ended and the furs started.

"We need more light," she whispered to Jaxyn.

"Bring another lantern," he ordered the female kneeling
over Tipsy's limp body, not nearly as considerate of the
felines' feelings as Arkady.

The black-and-white Crasii rose to her feet and hurried
out of the hut. Arkady scowled at him. "How do you do
that?"

"Do what?" the young man asked.

"Get the Crasii to jump to your orders like that?"

"It's all in the tone of voice," he told her, turning his attention to Tipsy. He looked down at her unsympathetically, studied the wounded feline for a moment and then
shrugged. "You might as well put it out of its misery."

A hiss of anger, or perhaps distress, behind them on the
cottage steps was the only objection Jaxyn received to his
callous pronouncement. Arkady glanced over her shoulder
at the score of felines gathered outside in the darkness and
then shut the door on them before she turned back to
Jaxyn. "You haven't even had a close look at her."

"Don't need to." He shrugged. "Can't you hear it breathing? The pup was right. Your escaping bitch all but ripped its throat out."

"Her name is Tipsy," Arkady corrected, annoyed at the way Jaxyn treated the Crasii as things rather than living creatures with minds and feelings of their own.

"Her name is *dead*," Jaxyn retorted. "You really shouldn't get so attached to them, you know."

Pushing past him, Arkady squatted beside the piled-up furs, reaching cautiously forward to stroke Tipsy's head, acutely conscious of the feline's potential to react violently to the slightest provocation. Although the creature's shape was outwardly human, the feline was a tabby, her grey fur matted around her throat, which glistened with fresh blood in the candlelight. Her human-shaped hands curled in pain, the claws exposed and ready to shred anyone who got too close. Jaxyn was right about her breathing. The air rasped in and out of her lungs, bubbling around the wadded bandage her companions had used to stanch the bleeding. Boots had probably done exactly what Laddie claimed, which made Arkady wonder what injuries the young canine had sustained in the altercation.

Much as it pained her to admit it, Jaxyn was probably right about the likelihood of survival, too. Arkady was a physician's daughter. She knew a fatal wound when she saw one.

"Is there anything I can do to ease your pain?" she asked softly.

Tipsy shook her head, ever so faintly, her eyes wide with fear.

"We *will* avenge you," she vowed, thinking it a useless promise. The chances were good Boots would never be seen again, and if she was, it was unlikely anyone would bother with a trial to address the issue of one slave killing another. But it would give the dying Crasii some comfort, she supposed, as she drifted into death.

"Once upon a time, she'd have been able to avenge herself," Jaxyn remarked.

Arkady glanced over her shoulder at him. "What are you talking about?"

"Doesn't Crasii legend claim that if a feline died in battle, the Tide Lords would bring them back over and over again, to keep on fighting? Nine times was the limit, wasn't it, before they couldn't revive them any longer?"

"Please don't mock their beliefs, Jaxyn," she asked, wondering how he'd learned of that particular legend. The Crasii didn't share their lore with humans readily. But Jaxyn had a habit of surprising her with little snippets of information like that. Things she'd taken years to coax out of the Crasii, even those who trusted her.

"I wasn't mocking anything," he protested. "I was just wondering why you can never seem to find a Tide Lord when you need one."

Arkady cursed his callous flippancy under her breath, turning her attention back to the dying feline. Moved by the Crasii's silent fortitude, she stroked Tipsy's forehead gently, feeling the cold settling under her soft pelt. Tipsy's breathing was increasingly laboured. Arkady feared she would be dead before Mitten returned with another lantern.

"It would be kinder to put it down," Jaxyn repeated behind her.

"That would be murder."

"Do you think it's more humane to watch it suffer?"

Arkady rose to her feet and turned to face the young man, wishing Stellan was here now. This was the Jaxyn Aranville her husband never saw. He was all sweetness and light when his lover was nearby, but this side of him, this cruel, unfeeling wretch, was something only Arkady knew. Jaxyn probably realised she saw through him and figured there was no point in pretending otherwise.

"Get out!"

"Temper, temper, my lady. You'll upset your patient."

"So help me, Jaxyn, I'll do more than—"

Arkady never got a chance to finish the sentence. The door banged open in a flare of light just as Tipsy's strangled breathing fell silent. Jaxyn forgotten, Arkady dropped to her knees beside the Crasii but it was too late to do anything. It had been too late before they got here. Mitten, the feline who'd brought the extra lantern, raised it high, glaring at Arkady, as if she was personally responsible for the death, a low growl building in the back of her throat.

Choking back a lump, inspired by fear as much as grief, Arkady pulled the covers over Tipsy's still form and rose to her feet. "Your blood-sister will be avenged, Mitten," Arkady promised, trying to ignore the Crasii's unsheathed claws and threatening stance. "Tell your sisters I'll have Boots declared outlaw. She'll be found. And made to pay for what she's done."

Mitten said nothing, her twitching tail the only indication of her mood. Her silence was enough to make Arkady sweat. An angry feline was something to be feared and once word spread of Tipsy's death to the other warriors, the problem would only get worse. It was a long way from this hut to the gate, with several hundred angry felines between them and safety.

"Back off!" Jaxyn warned.

To Arkady's amazement, the Crasii lowered the lantern, bowing her head in acquiescence. "Forgive me, my lord."

"Now thank the duchess for her concern," Jaxyn ordered. "And for her consideration in coming all this way—in the middle of a dinner party—to see to a mere slave."

"Thank you, your grace. We appreciate your sacrifice and I'm sure you'll see to it that Boots is made to pay."

"Now leave," Jaxyn added. "And tell your friends out there to return to their quarters."

Without question, the feline did as the young man ordered, her tail twitching violently as she left the tiny hut, taking the lantern with her. Arkady stared at Jaxyn in the gloom, not sure what disturbed her most—his arbitrary

orders or the fact that the Crasii had followed them without question.

"They're not *your* slaves, Jaxyn," she reminded him.
"You have no right to order them about like that."

"I'm Kennel Master here, your grace. It's my job to see
they behave." When Arkady said nothing in reply, he
shrugged. "I'll just let them attack you next time, shall I?"

"I'm in no danger from the Crasii," she declared gamely,
determined not to let this man think she owed him any
favours.

He stared at her thoughtfully for a time, so long that
Arkady thought he might argue the point with her, but then
the moment passed and he smiled, the sly, facetious Jaxyn
she knew so well back in force. "Well, you know them best,
your grace. Shall we return to your dinner guests? They must
be wondering where we are."

Chapter 7

Cayal woke to the first faint rays of dawn slicing
through the darkness in his cell, wondering if his
dream had woken him. He couldn't recall the details and
didn't want to in any case. Cayal's dreams were something
he could well live without.

He sat up slowly, sighing. *Tides, what's it going to take?*

Glaeban justice, being what it was, had little interest in the
facts, only what *appeared* to be the facts. On the face of it,
the wainwright from Caelum had attacked and killed seven
men without provocation, left seven widows and twenty-six
orphaned children, not to mention a village without a leader
and seven families without a breadwinner.

His sentence was so predictable Cayal wondered why
they'd bothered with the cost of a trial.

But they had and they'd brought him, guilty as charged,

here, to the Lebec Prison, fed him a last meal of baked fish, soggy cabbage and foaming ale, and then put a noose around his neck, when by every circumstance imaginable, they should have decapitated him.

The headsman was on vacation, *for pity's sake?*

Until Cayal repeated his assertion that he was a Tide Lord, it never really occurred to him just how completely his kind had been forgotten. The Warden and the prison guards didn't fall to their knees, as they would have done a thousand years ago. They'd actually laughed at him, even accusing him of trying to fake insanity in order to escape the noose.

If only they knew how he longed for it.

"So the suzerain awakes. Feeling better, are we?"

Cayal looked up at the remark, not sure what surprised him most, the contempt with which it was spoken or the fact that he'd been referred to as a suzerain. The name was an ancient insult, used only among the Crasii, a feeble attempt to spit in the eyes of their masters.

The creature who had uttered the words was leaning against the bars of the cell across the corridor. Although they'd been separated by nothing more than a corridor for several days now, this was the first time the creature had spoken. He was a huge beast, easily six and a half feet tall. His features were human enough at first glance, his dark eyes large and intelligent, his ears pert and pointed, his forearms displaying a disturbingly well-defined musculature lurking beneath his ragged prison shift. He was covered in a fine pelt of brown hair and his fingernails were more claws than nails. A Crasii, then, Cayal decided. One of the canines. He knew the type. Dumb as a plank, strong as an ox and pathetically eager to serve.

Obviously, something this one had forgotten.

"Bow in the presence of your master, gemang."

"Look around, suzerain. You're not the master here."

"I'm *your* master, Flea-trap," Cayal responded. "Something you'll never be able to change."

The Crasii smiled, baring his pointed canines at Cayal.

"Don't be too sure of that, suzerain. The Tide can be a long time turning, and you wouldn't be here if it was on the way back."

Never a truer word was spoken, Cayal lamented silently. The Crasii was right. It was the long drought caused by the Vanishing Tide that had brought him to this desperate pass and there was still no hint of when the Tide would begin to turn, and with it, his fortunes.

"When it does turn, you'll be on your knees, begging for the scraps from my table, gemang," he predicted, leaning on the bars to study his companion more closely. He really was a magnificent specimen. From Tryan's kennels, if Cayal guessed correctly. He'd bred his Crasii for their size and strength. "Enjoy your moment of rebellion. It won't last long."

The Crasii wasn't given a chance to answer. At that moment, several guards rounded the corner of the corridor, shoving a trustee and a water cart ahead of them, yelling at the prisoners to step back from the bars so they could open the cells.

Cayal did as the guards asked, watching the big Crasii across the hall as they shackled his hands and feet, thinking that if he decided to make a break for it, he'd need the Crasii to aid him. Until the Tide turned and Cayal's power with it, he was helpless. Perhaps, with the aid of a beast specifically bred by his kind to serve the Tide Lords, he had a chance of escaping this place.

Then, with luck, he could resume his quest to find a way for a tormented immortal to commit suicide.

Several hours later, with his cell reeking of bleach and clean ticking on his straw-filled mattress for the first time, Cayal suspected, in at least four generations, he lay down to wait for the historian they were sending to interrogate him.

It was gratifying to learn the Warden had taken his claim of being a Tide Lord seriously. Seriously enough that the King's Spymaster had been to see him and now they were sending a historian to speak to him, too.

The Duchess of Lebec herself, no less.

He was surprised they were sending a historian. He'd been expecting a doctor; and one armed with a straight-jacket and a vial full of laudanum, at that.

Not that he held much hope any human scholar would be able to verify his claim. And this one was female, to boot. Given the low opinion the men of Glaeba held of educated women, Cayal imagined either this duchess must be some spoiled heiress playing at being an academic to while away the long hours of her leisure time—which was bad enough—or worse, she took herself seriously and would question him endlessly on facts she had no way of checking.

He wasn't sure which would be more painful.

This Glaeban duchess might well prove a worse torment than the noose.

That was the trouble with hiding for a thousand years. People forgot about you. Or they twisted your story around so much they turned you into a myth; they scorned your very existence until you began to wonder if you were real, or just a figment of your own imagination.

Cayal folded his hands behind his head and closed his eyes, still cursing his own stupidity. It had been foolish to think this might work; sheer lunacy to imagine the Vanishing Tide would release him from his hellish sentence. He'd tried it before, to no avail. And it wasn't as if he didn't have proof of the futility of trying to die. Even with everything they had done to each other over the years, no Tide Lord had yet succeeded in killing another.

But Cayal still hoped for an escape. It amazed him a little that he was still able to do that.

Or maybe not. Before the relentless drudge of immortality had worn him down, Cayal had always been an optimist. Even in the most dire circumstances, he'd always believed things would go his way, sometimes to the point of idiocy. It was a trait he'd brought with him into immortality; something he'd been guilty of long before fate had taken a hand in his future and made it endless.

Perhaps it was with him still. Only an optimist would think it possible for an immortal to find a way to die.

Cayal dozed eventually, something he suspected he would be doing a lot in the coming days and months. There was little else to do in Recidivists' Row. The Glaeban prison system was punitive, not remedial. They made no pretence about reforming criminals here. They were only interested in keeping them off the streets. If the criminals suffered in the process of their incarceration, so much the better.

As he dozed, Cayal dreamed of places long gone and people he could no longer name. Thousands of years of memories vied for his attention when he slept, sometimes coming in broken snatches, other times unravelling with startling clarity, as if he was reliving the moment all over again. Sometimes he couldn't bear to close his eyes. Other times, he sought refuge in sleep. Sometimes faces from his past spoke to him in his dreams. Often he couldn't put a name to them, or even recall how he'd known them.

And some faces had stayed with him through eternity, their memory too strong to fade, even with the passage of endless time.

Today was one of those times. Gabriella came to visit him again. In the back of his mind, Cayal knew she wasn't real. He had known her—loved her—long before he was made immortal. Gabriella had been his future once. Now she was so far in his past all that remained of her was this infrequently recurring dream.

Nobody alive remembered Gabriella. Only Cayal could recall her long, rich brown hair, her devastating eyes, her flawless fair complexion, her throaty laughter, her stunning body. She was a nobleman's daughter and if the fine weave of her clothing hadn't given that much away, her bearing certainly did. She was proud, Gabriella was—proud and tall and beautiful. A fit consort for a prince.

And she knew it, too.

Gabriella spoke to him in words he couldn't make out. Cayal wasn't sure he wanted to hear what she had to say, anyway. They had not parted friends. Gabriella's promise to stand by him through adversity and pain until the end of time had lasted right up until the first time Cayal found himself in serious trouble.

But he missed her in his dreams. Or the idea of her, at least. Cayal remembered that much. He remembered what it was to be in love, to love and be loved. He lamented the loss of it, even if the memory left a bitter taste in his mouth that eight thousand years of distance had never been able to completely dispel.

Maybe that's the true torment of immortality? he wondered. *To be tortured by the memory of true love while knowing it will forever elude you.*

Longing can be more painful than grief, if it never ends.

Was that what Gabriella was saying to him? Her lips were moving, those luscious, soft lips he remembered so well, almost as well as he remembered how her lithe, naked body had felt in his arms, her soft breast, the taste of her skin, the moist warmth of her forbidden places . . .

And then he was jerked rudely out of his dream by a loud metallic banging. Cayal's eyes flew open and he turned his head, his vision colliding with reality as he looked at her . . . standing on the other side of the bars . . . Gabriella . . . the same hair, the unmistakable bearing . . .

He met her eyes and stared, dumbstruck . . .

And then the guard banged his truncheon against the bars again and Cayal realised he'd been dreaming. This wasn't Gabriella. He was in a Glaeban prison for murdering Rindova's butcher and his six stupid brothers. And when he looked at her more closely, stunning though she was, other than the same hair colour, this woman was nothing like his long-dead lover.

This was the Duchess of Lebec.

And simply by the way she was staring at him, Cayal realised she wasn't here to help him. She was here to prove he was a madman.

Chapter 8

The ride through Lebec to the prison had taken the better part of an hour, during which Arkady got very little out of either Timms or Flanel—the two men Declan
Hawkes had sent to escort her—about Kyle Lakesh. All
they would tell her was that she would see for herself what
he was like when she met him, so Arkady turned her attention to the scenery rolling past the rain-splattered windows of the carriage and let her mind wander.

It was early spring and the countryside was in full bloom,
the lush fields bursting with new life, the trees glistening
with traces of last night's thunderstorm that had washed the
world clean. On her left, the silver waters of the Lower Oran
glittered in the broken beams of sunlight that managed to
pierce the clouds, white sails dotting its mirror-like surface,
set against the hazy blue outline of the Caterpillar Ranges in
Caelum on the distant shore of the lake. The most impressive of the Great Lakes, the Lower Oran boasted the largest
freshwater body on the entire Glaeban continent, not to
mention the highest concentration of population.

Twelve of the nation's most powerful city-states fronted
the Lower Oran, although few were as rich or powerful as
Lebec. Stellan's ancestors had expanded their territory well
into the mountainous regions to the east of the Great Lakes
and claimed the vast mineral and timber wealth that came
with it. As they passed through the crossroads leading to
Clyden's Inn and the mines beyond, Arkady wondered how
many people toiled in the mountains to produce the wealth
she enjoyed. It made her feel a little guilty.

Arkady had seen the mines of Glaeba. Her father used to
take her there sometimes, when she was a small child, as he
tended to the miners who might never have access to a
physician in the normal course of events. The tall, forested
slopes held little mystery for Arkady.

It was the existence of the Waste which kept Arkady and

her fellow historians awake at night. There seemed no logical reason for such places to exist. There were many of them. She'd received a number of letters from a colleague in Torlenia who was investigating the same phenomenon in his country where vast tracts of land had been rendered uninhabitable during the Cataclysm. Nobody knew what had caused the Cataclysm or why the effects had been both widespread and yet so localised. Millions of people had died—later generations had found the mass graves to prove it—and yet even the skeletons they'd dug up gave no hint of how they'd perished. All the historians knew was that more than a thousand years ago a great many people had died, and that there had been enough survivors left to bury them. Other than that, their fate and what had devastated so much of every continent on Amyrantha remained a complete mystery.

Of course, it was such mysteries that gave the Tilly Pontings of this world all the ammunition they needed, Arkady lamented. It was people like her who fed the rumours and the appetites of fools who'd settle for any explanation that involved the supernatural.

Arkady, being a rational and logical person, considered such beliefs to be utter nonsense and it was part of the reason she was looking forward to meeting Kyle Lakesh. The more Arkady thought about it, the more she realised how dangerous this man was, and not simply because he was a cold-blooded murderer. If word got out that the hangman had failed and the survivor was claiming to be immortal, every crackpot in Glaeba—and beyond—would be lining up to shout "I told you so."

That wouldn't happen if Arkady Desean had anything to say about it.

The carriage finally rattled through the forbidding gates of Lebec Prison, forcing Arkady to concentrate on more immediate concerns. Flanel—or Timms, she couldn't tell them apart—handed her down from the carriage where the prison Warden was waiting to greet her.

"Your grace!" he exclaimed, bowing excitedly. He obviously wasn't in the habit of entertaining such a noteworthy guest. "Lady Desean! You honour us beyond words!"

Arkady shook her head, wishing—not for the first time—that she'd married a man nobody had heard of. "You needn't bow to me, Warden, or address me so formally. I am here in an academic capacity. You may call me *Doctor* Desean."

The Warden seemed a little taken aback by her suggestion but nodded anxiously in agreement. "Of course, your . . . Doctor. As you wish. Please . . . come in, come in . . . I have refreshments waiting for you in my office . . ."

"I'd really rather speak to the prisoner first, Warden. Can that be arranged?"

Again, he nodded anxiously, desperate to impress. "Of course. Timms! Flanel! Escort Lady Desean to the Row."

Arkady raised a curious brow. "The *Row?*"

"Recidivists' Row," the Warden explained. "It's where we confine the worst offenders. I'm sorry . . . perhaps you'd rather have the prisoner brought to you in a place somewhat less . . . intimidating?"

"No, it's all right, Warden. I'd like to speak to the prisoner in a place where he feels comfortable. Are you expecting Master Hawkes this afternoon?"

"Any moment now, your . . . Doctor Desean."

"Then I'll see you both when I'm done. Perhaps then I might avail myself of your generous offer of refreshments?"

"Whatever you desire, your grace."

Arkady bit back a snarl at the man's fawning inability to address her by the title she'd earned, rather than the one she'd married, and followed Timms and Flanel up the weathered flagstone steps of the prison. Darkened to an even more ominous shade of grey by the recent rain, the walls loomed over her so oppressively she found it hard to breathe. It was as if the architects of this building had set out to rob all who entered here of any hope of redemption.

As they approached, another guard opened the heavily

studded door for them, revealing a gaping maw from which Arkady imagined she could almost feel the misery emanating. She knew she was being foolish; she knew the darkness of Lebec Prison could not harm her, but she hesitated before crossing the threshold.

Her father had taken a step like this once, and never returned.

"Doctor Desean? Are you all right?" one of her escorts enquired.

"I'll be fine," she assured him, and taking a deep breath Arkady followed the men inside.

Recidivists' Row was located on the fourth floor of Lebec Prison. To get there, Arkady had to climb four flights of cold, steep, narrow, winding stairs, pass through a cluttered guardroom reeking of stale cooked cabbages and then down another long hallway which bent at a right angle some fifty feet from the guardroom, opening up into a long narrow corridor with open-barred cells on either side. There were a dozen cells, six on each side, lit by narrow barred windows. Too small for a man to crawl through, the windows let in enough light to see the occupants of the cells, but not enough to remedy their pallor.

The prisoners stared at her, some with curiosity, and some with total apathy. They were uniformly wretched, but she hardened her heart to their plight. There might be other men incarcerated elsewhere in Lebec Prison who were less recalcitrant, but no man without a past filled with other people's misery finished up here, confined in Recidivists' Row.

"Are the prisoners allowed out at all?" she asked, as she walked slowly between the cells.

"Not this lot, Doctor Desean," Flanel assured her.

"Not even for exercise?"

"What good would exercise do?" Timms asked, as if genuinely puzzled by Arkady's question.

She braced herself as they approached the last two cells. Both were occupied. On the left, the prisoner was a

Crasii; a huge canine who looked as if he should be muzzled as well as confined. He seemed to be none the worse physically for his confinement. The beast watched her curiously but made no threatening gestures.

In the cell on the right, Arkady assumed, was the self-proclaimed Tide Lord, Kyle Lakesh.

The young man was dozing, she noted, as she stopped outside the bars flanked by her escort. Timms banged on the bars with his truncheon, jerking the prisoner awake. He sat up, staring at Arkady oddly, as if he was either shocked to see her, or confused by something. Timms banged the bars again. The prisoner frowned, rubbing his eyes, and then pushing the fugue of sleep aside, he rose to his feet. He was taller than Arkady was expecting, clean-shaven, with shaggy dark hair. But his eyes were remarkable, a clear piercing blue that shocked her with the intensity of his gaze.

"Well, well, well . . . ," the prisoner remarked, eyeing Arkady up and down with an insolent smile. "They sure don't make historians like they used to."

Timms belted the iron bars with his truncheon again, making Arkady jump.

"You keep a civil tongue in your head, scumbag."

"Or you'll what?" the prisoner taunted. "Kill me? Tried that already. Didn't work."

"Because you're immortal?" Arkady suggested, wondering if the man was willing to repeat his allegation when confronted with genuine scepticism. She knew Declan didn't believe his wild claim any more than she did, but men like Timms and Flanel would be wondering if maybe . . . just maybe . . . this man was what he claimed to be.

"*You* didn't take much convincing, did you, precious?" Kyle Lakesh smiled at her, revealing a row of unnaturally perfect teeth. In a world where most adults—particularly in the lower classes—had lost a few permanent teeth by the time they reached thirty, his were even, white, and showed no sign of wear or staining.

"I doubt there is anything you could say to convince me

of your claim, Master Lakesh. And my name is Doctor Desean, not *precious*."

"My name is Cayal, not Lakesh."

"The Warden says your name is Kyle Lakesh."

"The Warden is wrong."

"What would you prefer to be called?"

"Your royal highness."

Despite herself, Arkady smiled. "What's your second preference?"

"Call me Cayal."

"And you're a Tide Lord, so you claim?"

"That's right."

Arkady nodded thoughtfully. "Very well, then. Prove it."

"Excuse me?"

"Prove it," she ordered. "You claim to be an immortal, a sorcerer, a wielder of elemental magic. So wield something. Make the bars melt. Have the walls grow flowers. Give us a demonstration of your power, O Mighty One."

"Ha!" the Crasii in the opposite cell chuckled. "She's got you there, suzerain."

Arkady turned to study the big Crasii. She had no idea what he was incarcerated for, but he looked strong enough to part the bars with his bare hands. His fur was short, the rich brown colour favoured by the more discerning breeders. His ears were pointed and twitched with interest. His tail, however, remained still. He wasn't friendly, this beast, neither was he afraid. He was intelligent, too, she judged. He spoke like an educated human. This Crasii wasn't a stray. Someone had gone to a great deal of trouble to housebreak and train him.

"What did you call him?" she asked the Crasii.

"He called me a suzerain," Lakesh said. "It's an insult. The Crasii thought it up because they were too stupid to think of anything more creative." He looked past Arkady and her escort and glared at the Crasii. "Go sit in the corner and lick your balls, gemang."

Timms bashed the bars of Cayal's cubicle with his

truncheon again for his crudeness as the Crasii lunged at the bars of his cell opposite, making Arkady take an involuntary step backwards. The step brought her dangerously close to Lakesh's reach, unnoticed by either Flanel or Timms, who were concentrating on the snarling Crasii.

"Get rid of the guards," he whispered urgently. "Then I'll prove anything you want."

Arkady almost admired his gall. She stepped away from his reach and smiled. "Oh yes, *that's* going to happen. Anything else you'd like, while I'm at it? The keys to your cell, perhaps?"

Cayal smiled suddenly. "Are you offering?"

Arkady didn't bother to reply. Instead, she turned around to look at the Crasii again. He had backed off, but she suspected it was because he was trying to appear nonthreatening, not because Flanel or Timms had scared him away with their truncheons.

"What's your name?" Arkady had dealt with a great many Crasii, both the slaves who now served her and her husband and the poor, sick and desperate ones who had sought out her father's help when she was a child. They held little fear for her, which made her a rarity among her class, most of whom were quietly terrified of the beasts who served them so loyally.

"Warlock," the Crasii answered after only a brief pause. "Out of Bella, by Segura."

He knows his pedigree, which means he isn't a stray, Arkady thought. "You're housetrained."

"I served in Lord Ordry's household," the Crasii confirmed. "As his steward."

Arkady knew Lord Ordry. He was a harmless old man, scatterbrained certainly, but not known for brutalising his Crasii. Whatever the reason Warlock had wound up here, it wasn't because Ordry mistreated him.

"Why do you call this man a suzerain?"

"That's what he smells of."

"That's the name your people give the Tide Lords in your legends, isn't it?"

"What makes you so sure they're legends?" Warlock asked.

"See!" Lakesh called out from across the corridor. "Even the fleabag agrees with me!"

"I'll shut him up, Doctor Desean," Timms offered with an impatient sigh, raising his truncheon as he turned.

"If the hangman couldn't take me, what makes you think you and your little stick are going to fare any better, fool?" Lakesh challenged, nimbly skipping backwards out of reach of the truncheon.

This is ridiculous! Arkady thought, wondering what she ever thought she might achieve here. There was no way to prove or disprove what this man claimed short of killing him again, and she certainly wasn't qualified to ascertain how sane he may or may not be.

The trouble was, the Crasii intrigued her; or to be more precise, the Crasii's reaction to Kyle Lakesh intrigued her. She'd never seen a slave react to a human so strangely before. Certainly not one as well trained as Warlock had obviously been.

Filled with uncertainty, she turned to study the wild-eyed young man claiming to be a Tide Lord, and then turned her gaze on the huge canine Crasii who swore his cellmate smelt like one.

Not for a minute did she think Kyle Lakesh was actually what he claimed, but she was dangerously inquisitive and that, Arkady knew from long experience, meant she probably wouldn't rest until she had sated her curiosity about both of them.

Chapter 9

Declan Hawkes was waiting for Arkady when she returned to the Warden's office, sipping tea from a delicate floral tea service that seemed wildly out of place in this dank, depressing prison. The room was surprisingly comfortable, furnished with dark, wooden furniture of a quality not normally seen in any establishment furnished out of a Warden's stipend. A small fire kept the chill out of the air, the book-lined wall opposite the fireplace a silent testament to the Warden's surprisingly good education. Arkady noted some of the book titles with interest—including a leather-bound copy of Harlie Palmerston's *Theory of Human Advancement*—as she accepted a cup of tea from the Warden and took the chair he offered opposite his desk, taking an appreciative sip of the lemon-scented brew before she spoke.

"You have some interesting inmates, Warden," she remarked, as she lowered the cup onto the saucer.

"That's one way of describing them," the Warden replied. With Declan in the room he seemed much more nervous than he had when she first arrived, although thankfully appeared to have gotten over his need to call her *your grace.*

"What was your opinion of Lakesh?" Declan asked, placing his cup on the Warden's remarkably empty desk. The spymaster might give the impression he had nothing better to do than sit here sipping tea, but she knew him well enough to sense that he wasn't pleased about the wait.

"Ah," Arkady sighed, quite deliberately drawing out her answer. "Kyle Lakesh. Or Cayal, the Immortal Prince, if you believe him. Interesting fellow."

Declan scowled at her. "I'm glad he piqued your academic interest. But what did you find out?"

"In the bare fifteen minutes I was allowed with the prisoner, absolutely nothing," she replied, taking another sip of tea. "And what piqued my academic interest wasn't our would-be immortal, Declan. It was the Crasii's reaction to him."

"The Crasii?"

"You mean Warlock?" the Warden asked. "Did he give you any trouble?"

"Not really. But he and Lakesh seem to despise each other. Or rather he seems to despise Lakesh and Lakesh seems to look down on him as if he's some kind of animal."

"The Crasii are animals," the Warden pointed out with a shrug. "I see nothing unusual in that."

"How long have they been in opposite cells?" Arkady enquired.

"A little more than a week," the Warden informed her. "The first hint we had of any trouble between the two of them was the night of the hanging. The watch reported Lakesh kept the rest of the Row awake half the night with his moaning."

"He seems to be in no pain now."

The Warden shrugged, unable to explain it. "The man does appear to be a quick healer."

"Enough to make him immortal?" Declan asked, clearly sceptical about the whole notion of Tide Lords.

Arkady shook her head. "I'm suggesting nothing of the kind. Have you questioned the hangman about how this man survived? I gather it's not a common occurrence."

Declan nodded. "There seems to be nothing amiss."

"Did they speak before the execution?"

The Warden shrugged. "It's traditional for an executioner to request the forgiveness of the man he's putting to death. My understanding is that Lakesh didn't grant the executioner forgiveness for his hanging so much as complain that we should have beheaded him."

"Maybe your Caelishman offered something else—like a substantial bribe?" she suggested, not able to imagine any other way a man could have survived the noose and recovered so quickly from his injuries.

"I can assure you, Doctor Desean, as I did Master

Hawkes—my men are above reproach. The man acting as hangman the day of the execution has held his job for nigh on ten years. If he was the easily corruptible sort, he'd have proved it long before now."

"I'm sure you believe that, Warden," she replied, and then turned to Declan. "I thought we beheaded criminals in Lebec."

"Apparently the headsman was on *holiday,*" Declan informed her in a tone she knew well.

Arkady covered her smile with her teacup and turned to speak to the Warden. "I'd like to speak to the prisoners again tomorrow."

"Prisoners?" he asked, looking a little confused. "I was given to understand that you are here only to speak with the Caelishman."

"I would also like to keep the Crasii nearby."

"For what purpose?" Declan asked.

"His reaction to the presence of Lakesh is intriguing. He called him a suzerain."

The Warden seemed quite puzzled. "What's that?"

Declan answered before Arkady could. "It's an insult. A name the Crasii—in their legends, at any rate—had for the Tide Lords."

"I don't see the problem," the Warden said, leaning back in his chair. "The man's calling himself a Tide Lord and the Crasii insulted him accordingly. There's no mystery there."

"But how did Lakesh know what a suzerain was?" Arkady asked. "He knew *exactly* what it meant. The Crasii are very protective of their oral history and their legends. As far as I know, the only people who know what a suzerain is are the Crasii and those few humans who have managed to gain their trust."

"Like you, for instance?"

Arkady met his gaze evenly. "That's why I was asked to come here, isn't it? Because I study the Crasii and they're the only ones with any sort of knowledge of the Tide Lords."

"Having knowledge of the Tide Lords would imply they're real," the Warden reminded her.

"To the Crasii, they are."

"The Crasii are animals, Doctor." The Warden shrugged. "Any intelligent man knows their fairy stories are just that . . . stories made up to explain things they don't have the wit to understand."

Declan shook his head. "That still doesn't explain away Warlock's reaction to Lakesh. I sensed it too, when I spoke to the prisoner."

Arkady nodded in agreement. "If they've only been opposite each other for a week, they haven't had time to develop the animosity that's already built up between them."

"So you think Lakesh really is a Tide Lord because some big dumb animal doesn't like the smell of him?" The Warden rolled his eyes.

Arkady glared at the Warden. "What I think, sir, is that it won't take long for word to get about that your Crasii prisoner thinks Lakesh's claim is genuine. Add that to his miraculous escape from the noose and it won't be the Caelish Ambassador we have to worry about. Even if every rational person in Glaeba thinks it's nonsense, the Crasii—for whom the Tide Lords are quite real—may start to believe it. Do you really want every slave in the country thinking his ancient masters have returned and they are no longer required to serve *us*?"

Not surprisingly, the Warden didn't have an answer to that.

"What do you recommend?" Declan asked, in the awkward silence that followed.

"If Lakesh has enough knowledge of the Crasii to know what a suzerain is, then he's done his homework. I doubt this is a spur-of-the-moment plan. He's thought this out, and very carefully."

"For what purpose?" the Warden asked, clearly not convinced.

Arkady shrugged. "There could be any number of reasons." She turned to Declan. "You asked me here because we're still having problems with Caelum, didn't you? Maybe in revenge for the insult of refusing Princess Nyah they've come up with a way to destabilise the very foundation of Glaeban society by making our Crasii believe the Tide Lords have returned. Maybe it's a scam cooked up by Lakesh himself for some nefarious purpose of his own. Whatever the reason, this man needs to be exposed as a fraud before you execute him again. If anything went wrong a second time, it would be calamitous. He's already survived the noose once. If he's trying to convince the Crasii he's immortal, he's probably clever enough to find a way to beat it again."

"I'll have the bastard run through!" the Warden declared. "That should cure his delusions of immortality."

"And then *you* can explain his death to the Caelish Ambassador," Declan reminded him. "I'm sure he won't object to us killing one of his citizens out of hand because we felt the prisoner needed to be disabused of his delusions of immortality."

"But how do you intend to prove the man is lying, your grace?" the Warden asked, pretending Declan hadn't spoken.

"I want to talk to him. At length. And without any watchdogs hovering over me."

Declan frowned. "That would be very dangerous."

"If Lakesh stays in his cell and I stay out of reach, I'll be safe enough." She smiled. "Surely you don't think he really has magical powers, Declan?"

"No, I suppose not." He thought about it and then nodded. "Can you have him moved to somewhere more accessible for her grace's visits, Warden?"

"Actually, Declan, I'd rather speak to him where he is. Where Warlock can overhear the conversation. His knowledge of the Tide Lord legends and his reactions to Lakesh's answers should help my work considerably."

"Let me see if I understand this, your grace," the Warden said. "You plan to prove to the Crasii that this Tide Lord is a fake by allowing one of them to sit in on your discussions while the man verifies his claim?" The Warden smiled at the spymaster, shaking his head. "There's an example of incomprehensible female logic for you."

"You don't think I might actually succeed in exposing Lakesh?" she enquired, ignoring his snide condescension. "That in the process of exposing his lies, the Crasii would come to believe the man was faking?"

"Assuming you *can* expose his lies," Declan countered.

"If you think I can't, Declan, then my work here is done. You obviously don't need me. Thank you for the tea, Warden."

Arkady rose to her feet as she placed her teacup on the desk. She turned for the door but had only taken two steps before Declan stopped her.

"Arkady . . . please."

She looked back at him, surprised he had addressed her by name in front of the Warden. "Oh, so you do need my help?"

"You know we do. Too many people know about this already."

"Then let me help you. *My* way."

"*Can* you expose him, though?"

Arkady nodded, hoping she appeared a lot more confident than she felt. "Unless he really is a Tide Lord, then yes, I believe I can."

Declan Hawkes hesitated but finally he nodded and turned to the Warden. "Give Doctor Desean whatever she needs; whatever she wants."

The Warden nodded. "As you wish, Master Hawkes."

They left the prison together, Declan taking the time to hand Arkady into her carriage before taking charge of his own mount. "Don't let me down, Arkady," he warned as she took her seat.

"Don't patronise me, *Declan*," she responded impatiently.

He seemed more amused than annoyed by her reply. "You're looking very well, by the way. I meant to tell you that last night," he added, as he closed the door, "but I wasn't sure what your husband would think of such an observation. Being a duchess suits you."

"You don't seem to be suffering too badly, yourself," Arkady replied through the open window.

He smiled at her the way he used to when they were children looking for mischief in the backstreets of the Lebec slums. "We've done all right for ourselves—you and I. For a couple of slum brats."

"Does this mean you've forgiven me?" she asked, eyeing him curiously. "For . . . what was it you called it? That's right . . . for *whoring myself for the sake of a fortune and an empty title*?"

He shook his head apologetically. "You're never going to let me forget that, are you?"

"Not anytime soon," she agreed.

"He seems to be fond of you," her old friend conceded with some reluctance.

"Who? Stellan? Why would you assume my husband was anything less than fond of me, Declan? Tides, you can't believe he married me for my money?"

"Actually, I'm still puzzling that one out."

"Well, it's nice to know the King's Spymaster is doing something useful with his time. Why can't you just accept that Stellan married me for love?"

"Dukes marry for property or political advantage. You brought him neither." He smiled at her. "I'm suspicious by nature, Arkady. You know that."

She studied him for a time, thinking he wasn't the only one with a suspicious nature. It was a sixth sense you developed in the slums if you intended to survive. "Why did you really ask me here, Declan?"

"You know Crasii lore better than anyone I know."

"Even better than you?"

"What do you mean?"

"You knew what a suzerain was," she pointed out. "Do you really need my help to break this man?"

He was silent for a moment and then he shrugged. "You want an honest answer?"

"No, Declan, I was hoping you'd lie to me."

He leaned a little closer. "I can't stay here in Lebec. I have to get back to Herino. I shouldn't really be here at all, truth be told. This is a provincial problem, not a matter for the crown. I want you to do this because you know Crasii lore, I trust you, and I suspect Kyle Lakesh will tell a beautiful woman things he won't tell a male interrogator because he'll let down his guard in your presence."

His answer made sense. And it didn't surprise her. She had long grown accustomed to the notion that Declan Hawkes wasn't above using anybody he needed to achieve his goals, his best friends included. Interesting, too, she thought, that Declan thought she was beautiful. He'd never once commented on her appearance before and she'd known him since she was eight years old.

"You dress better these days, Declan, but you're still the same wretched boy I knew as a child."

He grinned. "You say that like it's a bad thing."

She frowned at him, not amused. "I'll help you, Declan, but you have to do something for me in return."

"Name it."

"Leave my husband alone."

Declan eyed her curiously. "Is he involved in something I *should* be interested in?"

"Whatever you think my reasons were for marrying Stellan Desean, he's a good man. I don't want you doing anything that might endanger his position with the king."

Declan's smile faded. "While ever you remain child-less, Arkady, he's doing that without any help from me."

That was a topic she had no intention of discussing with Declan Hawkes, no matter how good a friend he might be. "I mean it, Declan. Promise me you'll leave Stellan alone."

Without answering, he stepped back from the carriage and signalled the driver. The carriage jerked into motion, carrying Arkady away from the gloom of Lebec Prison's walls and back toward her gilded palace. She leaned out of the window to stare at him but as soon the carriage moved off, he turned his back on her to mount his horse.

Frustrated and more than a little annoyed by his manipulation, Arkady slumped back in her seat. Her thoughts weren't on Declan Hawkes for long, however. As the carriage trundled through the prison gates, Arkady was surprised to find that all she could think of was a pair of vibrant blue eyes and the mystery of a Crasii who addressed a common murderer as suzerain.

She wondered if Warlock even knew what the word meant.

My lord. That's what suzerain meant.

Without even understanding why, the Crasii, Warlock, had instinctively addressed Kyle Lakesh, however scathingly, as *my lord.*

Chapter 10

Jaxyn Aranville was bored and boredom invariably meant he went looking for trouble. Jaxyn knew this, much as he might have once wished it was otherwise, he couldn't seem to help himself.

It was Stellan's fault he was bored. He'd been called away to the capital on business; something to do with the king. That was the trouble with being a cousin of the king, particularly one far enough down the line to actually feel the need to earn his keep. Stellan was a natural peacemaker, a born diplomat. Whenever there was a problem, King Enteny called on his cousin, Stellan Desean, to fix it.

That meant Stellan was on his way to Herino City and Jaxyn was stuck here in Lebec with nobody but Stellan's niece and his intimidatingly intelligent wife for company.

Fortunately, the intimidatingly intelligent wife was out at present, which left only Kylia to amuse him.

And she did entertain him. For reasons nobody in this household could imagine, Jaxyn took a great deal of interest in the antics of Kylia Debrell.

Kylia had been at the palace for more than a month now, arriving without warning with the announcement that she'd had enough of the ladies' college Stellan had abandoned her to when she was barely twelve. Apparently, now she had reached an age where she was no longer required to obey him slavishly, she intended to have some fun. Arkady had persuaded Stellan to let her stay, not send her packing—which was the course of action Jaxyn had counselled—so now they were stuck with her. Jaxyn had resigned himself to her presence, and to her uncle's vast relief, she still hadn't questioned why Jaxyn—who as Kennel Master ranked little better than one of the hired help—was living in the palace.

Stellan was easily convinced the girl hadn't noticed what was going on when she'd stumbled over Stellan and Jaxyn sharing an intimate embrace in the library last week, believing it was her provincial upbringing that made her so blind to the reality of her uncle's situation. Maybe—Jaxyn had persuaded Stellan—in Kylia's innocent, black-and-white world, there was no room for anything but a man and a woman falling in love and living happily ever after.

Fortunately for all of them, Stellan had been satisfied with Jaxyn's explanation. All that remained now was for Jaxyn to get young Lady Kylia alone. There were a few things he intended to ask Lady Kylia about exactly what was really behind her sudden appearance in Lebec.

He found one of the Crasii in the halls, young Tassie, a canine pup of about seventeen. Loyal, eager to serve and covered with a fine pelt of white fur under her simple white-and-gold shift, she was still being trained, hence the reason she was working the morning shift and not the evening events in the more public areas of the palace. But she was keen to learn and always responded well to a kind word and a bit of encouragement. As usual, as he approached, she instinctively cowered away from him, her tail drooping, a reaction that always amused him.

"Good morning, Tassie," he said pleasantly as she stopped before him, the teacups on the tray she carried rattling softly as she trembled.

"My . . . my . . . lord."

"I'm looking for Lady Kylia."

"She's in the m-m-morning room, sire."

He smiled. Nameless fear was a delicious thing to behold. "Is something wrong, Tassie?"

"N-n-no, my lord."

"Are you afraid of Lady Kylia?"

"N-n-no, my lord."

"You're not afraid of me, are you?"

The young Crasii hesitated and then, somewhat to his surprise, she nodded. "A little bit, sire."

He raised a brow at her. "Only a little? I must be slipping."

"To serve you is the reason I breathe, my lord," she assured him, bowing her head in submission.

Jaxyn smiled. "Then the world is as it should be. In the morning room, you say?"

"Yes, my lord."

Jaxyn watched her silently for a moment longer, until the Crasii realised he was waiting for her to step aside, and then he continued down the hall toward the morning room, leaving Tassie staring after him, her tray softly rattling with her fear.

As it turned out, Jaxyn didn't need directions to find his prey. He could simply have followed the sound of Kylia's laughter. Tilly Ponting was with her, the two of them giggling over something laid out on the table. Jaxyn turned on his best smile as he entered the morning room.

"I hope I'm not interrupting anything, ladies?"

"Jaxyn!" Tilly declared. "What a delight! Of course, you're not interrupting! Come join us!"

Jaxyn crossed the elegantly furnished room to the table

where Tilly and Kylia were sitting. Sunlight streamed in through the tall bay windows, the morning bright and clear after the storm last night. They had the Tarot cards out again. Kylia seemed quite taken with the idea someone could predict her future.

Stellan's niece smiled coyly as he approached. Her dark hair and dark eyes set off against her caramel skin made her a pretty enough prospect, although not the devastating beauty Arkady was. But she radiated a kind of leashed lust that seemed more than a little out of character in an innocent girl. Maybe it was the idea that underneath that modest posture and coy smile was a virgin vixen straining to be let loose. Kylia could say all that and more with a mere glance in his direction. She certainly hadn't learned such a thing at a respectable ladies' college. It was fortunate her charms didn't seem obvious to other women and that her uncle was quite immune to them, otherwise young Lady Debrell might find herself being asked more questions than she was prepared to answer.

"Kylia, you grow prettier every day you spend here in Lebec," he declared when he reached the table. He took her hand, kissing it gallantly. "I swear, if you don't stop it, I will have to tell Stellan to place a guard on your room at night to protect you from my uncontrollable lust."

Kylia snatched her hand away, appearing both mortified and thrilled at the same time. Jaxyn smiled. *Damn, she's convincing.* He turned to Tilly and kissed the old lady's cheek. "Of course, the only thing that keeps me in check is my unrequited love for you, Lady Ponting."

Tilly pushed him away. "Jaxyn Aranville, you're a scoundrel. Don't listen to him, Kylia. This boy leaves a trail of broken hearts wherever he goes."

Kylia looked up at him, but still didn't say anything. Apparently his presence tended to strike her dumb unless she had a few wines in her.

"What are you doing?" he asked, as he took a seat opposite. The small table in the morning room was round, meant for intimate breakfasts and informal card games.

Sitting opposite Kylia, Jaxyn's leg was touching hers under the table. She might seem too overwhelmed to speak, but she didn't move her leg.

"We're going through Kylia's Tarot again," Tilly explained. "It's more accurate when you don't have an audience."

"Then I *am* interrupting," he concluded. He made to rise, adding, "I'm sorry. I shall go and leave you in peace."

"You can stay, Lord Aranville," Kylia told him. "Tilly just meant a big audience, like we had here last night."

Jaxyn resumed his seat. "You honour me with the secrets of your future, Lady Kylia."

Kylia smiled at him but didn't answer. Tilly rolled her eyes at his words, however, perhaps more aware of how contrived they were. Jaxyn made a mental note to remember that Tilly Ponting wasn't quite as silly as she seemed.

"Take another card, dear," she instructed the girl.

Kylia did as Tilly ordered, turning over a card that looked like the knave from a more traditional deck of cards.

"The Page of Tides," Tilly announced, pursing her lips thoughtfully.

"Is that bad?" Kylia asked, looking a little worried.

"This card is bringing you a message of love or perhaps romance."

"There!" Jaxyn declared. "That's nothing to worry about!"

"But it also comes with a warning," Tilly added ominously.

"What sort of warning?"

"This love you seek," the old woman said, pointing to another card that lay face up on the table. "It may end in heartbreak."

Jaxyn turned his head to study the other card. It was the Lovers again, Cayal and Amaleta. Bordered in gold, the card depicted a man—the Immortal Prince, he supposed—and a woman, probably Amaleta, his legendary one true love, standing at a crossroads caught in a *very* intimate embrace.

"But you said drawing the Lovers means I should trust my instincts," Kylia reminded the clairvoyant, obviously confused.

Jaxyn smiled, knowing full well—as Kylia doubtless did, too—that the whole wretched Tarot was nonsense. *To look at her, though,* he thought, *you'd swear she was completely taken in.*

"I think you *should* trust your instincts, Lady Kylia," Jaxyn agreed. "The Page of Tides might not even apply to you. For all you know, it may mean your uncle's marriage to Arkady might end in heartbreak."

Kylia frowned as she thought about it. Tilly Ponting, on the other hand, was unimpressed by his interpretation. "Something you've been working on, perhaps, dear?" she enquired with a raised brow.

Jaxyn smiled at her. "Come now, Lady Ponting. You know me."

"Which is why I pose the question," Tilly replied evenly.

The old bird was definitely much smarter than she looked, Jaxyn thought. If Tilly took an active dislike to him, his plans for securing his immediate future could be in serious danger.

Kylia was frowning, obviously worried her uncle and his wife might be having marital problems. "You don't think it means that, do you, Lady Ponting?"

"What? That Stellan and Arkady have had a falling out? Don't be absurd. There were never two people more in love."

"Are you certain?"

"Have you ever seen them fighting?" Tilly asked. "Ever heard them exchange so much as a harsh word?"

"Well . . . no . . . I don't suppose I have, now that you come to mention it."

"Then what are you worried about?"

"Listen to Lady Ponting," Jaxyn advised, deciding it might be prudent to show the old hag he was on her side. "She knows about these things. Your uncle is in love and has never been happier. I can vouch for that myself."

Tilly spared him an odd look, but said nothing to contradict him. She obviously knew the lay of the land; either knew or suspected Jaxyn's real role in this household. But she was too old and too wily to comment on it.

It made Jaxyn wonder, for a moment, how many other people suspected the truth. He was certain the king was ignorant of his cousin's sexual preferences. Stellan and Jaxyn both had Arkady to thank for that. The King of Glaeba's feelings on the matter of men who fancied other men were well known. Stellan would have been banished long ago if Enteny suspected, even for a moment, that one of his most trusted advisors—his own cousin, no less—took his pleasure on the wrong side of the bed. Jaxyn's own fate would be just as dire, he knew. It was the reason he flirted so flagrantly with women. Everyone knew about his affair with Lady Carver. Even Arkady was convinced he had his sights set on Kylia. Very few people knew, however, that he was Stellan Desean's lover.

Tilly Ponting was clearly among the very few.

"Jaxyn's right, my dear," Tilly assured the young girl, patting her hand. "Your Uncle Stellan has never been happier."

"Arkady *is* very protective of him," Kylia agreed.

Too damned protective of him, Jaxyn silently amended. *And not bad at protecting herself, too.*

Despite all his attempts to find out the identity of Arkady's lovers, either she was exceptionally good at keeping them hidden or she had none. As Jaxyn couldn't comprehend the latter—not for a woman as beautiful as Arkady Desean—he was still searching for evidence of the former.

Jaxyn's original plan for Arkady Desean had been quite clever, he thought, when he conceived of it a few days after he'd first met the Duke of Lebec. Here was a situation just begging to be exploited—a marriage of convenience between a powerful man and a very desirable woman, to hide a secret that would see a cousin of the king and an heir to the throne destroyed if it became public knowledge. Jaxyn had planned to become the lover of both Stellan *and* Arkady, which would have seen him well taken care of—in the manner to which he was accustomed—for quite some time.

From a distance, it had seemed a brilliant idea. But that was before he'd met Arkady. Before he discovered she despised him, mistrusted him and had probably guessed what he was planning within moments of first meeting him. Stellan was far more trusting, but Arkady was never going to believe a word Jaxyn uttered. He'd spent much of the past year trying to find a way to blackmail her instead, hoping extortion might work where seduction had failed.

Just as he was beginning to completely despair of ever finding anything even remotely embarrassing on his lover's wife, everything changed.

Kylia Debrell had arrived at the palace.

Orphaned since the age of five, Kylia had been raised—out of sight and out of mind—on her late parents' estate near Venetia by various nannies and servants until being sent to the very exclusive college for young ladies from which she had so recently escaped. Her presence here was a thorn in Jaxyn's side he would give a great deal to be rid of.

"Arkady loves your uncle more than life," Tilly assured Kylia. "Don't you think so, Jaxyn?"

"Absolutely!" he agreed with a smile. "Have you drawn my card yet?"

"Your card?" Kylia asked with an odd look.

"Jaxyn, the Lord of Temperance. My father's idea of a joke, I think, to name me after the most boring Tide Lord of them all. Or perhaps it was wishful thinking. Doesn't appear to have worked, though," he chuckled.

"I'll say," Tilly agreed with feeling. "I'm surprised you even know what temperance means, Jaxyn."

" 'Moderation and self-restraint'," Kylia quoted, speaking directly to Jaxyn. " 'In one's behaviour or expression, specifically showing restraint in the use of, or abstinence from, alcoholic liquors'." She smiled then and turned to Tilly. "We had to learn that definition at school. They harped on about it a lot."

"I suppose that's why you escaped from those staid old hags and came here to the palace, where you can have some real fun."

"I think you'd benefit from a bit of discipline from a few staid old hags, my lad," Tilly suggested with a frown.

He grinned at the old woman. "Only if you promise to tie me down first, Lady Ponting, and tell me I've been a very naughty boy." Before she could respond to that, he turned to Kylia. "You know what I think? I think you and I should take a punt out on the lake. After the rain last night it's as flat as a piece of smoked glass."

Kylia's face fell, as she realised she couldn't just walk out on Tilly without being considered rude. "I can't, Lord Aranville. Tilly came out here specially to give me a private reading this morning. I couldn't possibly abandon her to go boating."

"No, she couldn't possibly," Tilly agreed, but not because she was likely to be offended. Jaxyn wondered if Arkady had been in the old lady's ear, warning her to keep him away from Kylia.

"I think perhaps, if you ask her nicely, Tilly won't be offended," Arkady remarked from the door. "Not now that I'm here to keep her company."

Jaxyn leapt to his feet, not sure what surprised him more: that Arkady was standing there pulling off her gloves, or that she'd just sanctioned his outing with her husband's niece.

Although he knew she'd gone out this morning, he didn't know where she'd been. She'd obviously been working, dressed in the clothes she usually wore when she attended the university: dowdy, buttoned up high, grey and unattractive. She tried to play down her appearance, Jaxyn knew, as if dressing plainly would somehow give her credibility. But nothing Arkady Desean did could disguise her beauty. Stellan had married her for that reason, Jaxyn was certain. He might not be attracted to women sexually, but he did like to look at beautiful things.

Pity she's such a frigid bitch.

Kylia was quite flustered by Arkady's unexpected suggestion. "Would you . . . really not mind, Tilly?"

"Well . . . I suppose . . . if your aunt doesn't mind . . ." Clearly, Tilly Ponting was just as puzzled by Arkady's uncharacteristic approval.

"You run along, Kylia," Arkady ordered, as she placed her gloves on the side table. "Just make sure you take a hat. And a shawl. It can be quite chilly out on the lake at this time of year."

Kylia rose to her feet, curtseyed quickly to Tilly and then hurried out of the morning room, stopping only long enough to plant a hasty but grateful kiss on Arkady's cheek as she raced off to find her hat and shawl. Jaxyn also stood up and headed for the door. When he drew level with Arkady, she turned to him, her expression stern.

"Jaxyn."

"Yes, your grace?"

"She'd better come back a virgin."

Jaxyn stared at her for a moment and then smiled. The one thing he did admire about Arkady was that she wasn't afraid to say exactly what she meant when the occasion called for it.

"You know I'd never harm anything Stellan loved," he reminded her.

"I also know what you're after, Jaxyn Aranville. So let me assure you of this. If you expect to spend another night under this roof, you'll return Kylia home at a decent hour, whole, unharmed and preferably not betrothed to you."

Jaxyn smiled. "Spoilsport."

"Try seducing Kylia," she suggested frostily. "If you want to discover how much of a spoilsport I can be."

Jaxyn decided not to answer that. He turned and bowed to Tilly. "Lady Ponting." Then he turned and bowed to Arkady with an insolent smile. "Your grace."

"I mean it, Jaxyn."

"You're very attractive when you're being domineering, did you know that?"

"I'm also a heartbeat away from revoking my permission for Kylia to go anywhere alone with you," she warned.

"Then I'll be gone, your grace, while I'm still ahead in the game. You ladies enjoy the rest of your morning now, won't you?"

He left before Arkady could respond, certain he had aggravated her enough to count himself the winner of this particular encounter, but not enough to have her do anything to evict him from the palace.

It was a fine line Jaxyn Aranville walked with the Duchess of Lebec. Sooner or later, one of them would have to go.

Jaxyn was working hard on making sure it wasn't him.

Chapter 11

"Was that wise?" Tilly asked as she began to gather up her cards.

Arkady rang the bell on the side table to summon a slave and walked across the morning room. It was quite stuffy in here with both fireplaces alight. She undid the button at the waist of her jacket and loosened the top few buttons on her blouse as she walked.

"Probably not," she admitted, taking the seat so recently vacated by Kylia. "But I wanted to talk to you. It seemed as good an excuse as any, to get Kylia out of the way. Have you been reading her Tarot again?"

Tilly nodded. "She's very interested in the identity of her future husband."

"Could you please tell her it's *not* Jaxyn Aranville?"

"I could," Tilly agreed, "but that might not be what the cards say."

Arkady picked up the nearest card and studied it for a moment. "You don't really believe a card can tell you anything about the future, do you, Tilly?"

"I don't *not* believe it."

"That's not an answer."

"I tell fortunes, darling," Tilly chuckled. "I'm supposed to be cryptic."

"Do you believe the Tide Lords really existed?"

Tilly leaned back in her chair and looked at Arkady. "There's a question I never thought I'd hear from you. What's brought this on?"

"I'm curious, that's all. You know I'm working on the history of Glaeba prior to the Cataclysm."

"By trying to get the Crasii to tell you their legends, so I'm told," Tilly said.

"There's usually a grain of truth in most legends, Tilly."

They were interrupted by the arrival of a slave answering Arkady's summons.

"You rang, your grace?" the Crasii enquired, after bobbing awkwardly in a curtsey, her tail wagging eagerly. Until she learned to control it, she wouldn't be allowed anywhere near the public areas of the palace that housed any number of priceless—and importantly breakable—antiques and artefacts.

"Could you bring us tea, Tassie?" she asked.

"Of course, your grace, is there anything else? Anything at all I can do for you? Anything?"

Arkady smiled. "Settle down, Tassie. Just tea will be fine."

Tassie bobbed another awkward curtsey and hurried away to fetch the tea.

"She's a nice-looking beast," Tilly remarked as the Crasii left the room.

Arkady nodded in agreement. "We bred her in-house. She's one of Fluffy's pups."

"You got another litter out of Fluffy, then?"

"Stellan probably could have bred her a few more times, but she was worn out, poor thing. Twins every year for the past eight seasons. Tassie was out of her last litter. We covered Fluffy with a sire named Rex we purchased from Lady Jimison, actually. I hear she was furious when she realised what she could have made in stud fees if she'd thought to hang on to him."

"That stupid woman wouldn't know a canine Crasii from a hunting dog," Tilly agreed. "But we're getting off the topic. Why this sudden interest in the veracity of the Tide Lord legends?"

"I met a man today who claimed he was one."

Tilly laughed. "Have someone kill him for you, darling. That should settle his claim fairly smartly."

"Well, they did, actually. That's the problem."

Tilly's smile faded. "You can't be serious!"

"Funny, that's exactly what I said."

"You mean they tried to kill a man who claims to be a Tide Lord and he didn't die?" Tilly looked quite shocked.

"Don't get too excited," Arkady warned. "This man's a confidence trickster, Tilly. I'm certain of it. But I need to prove it."

"How?"

"Well, that's what I've spent the last hour on the way back from Lebec Prison wondering. This man has really put some thought into it. He's beaten the noose. He knows things about the Crasii that even I've had trouble getting out of them, and I've more trust among them than most. He's going to be hard to expose."

"Kill him again," Tilly suggested. "If he's not immortal, that will settle the argument one way or the other."

"It's not that simple, I'm afraid," Arkady sighed. "The man's Caelish, not Glaeban. We can't attempt the 'let's settle this once and for all' solution until we've exhausted every legal avenue, or there'll be hell to pay. If the man is proved insane, on the other hand, we'll never get to execute him for committing seven cold-blooded murders to which he willingly confessed."

"If he's claiming to be a Tide Lord, darling, I'd be going with the insanity option myself," Tilly chuckled.

"Only if he genuinely believes he is a Tide Lord. My instinct is that this man is faking."

"Get him to do something magic, then."

"I tried that. Apparently, it's *Low* Tide, so he's powerless until the Tide turns."

"How convenient."

Tassie came back with a small cart before Arkady could answer. They waited while she served them, bowed three or four times more and then headed for the door.

"Tassie!" Arkady called on impulse.

"Your grace?"

She looked over her shoulder at the young Crasii, watching her curiously. "Would you know a Tide Lord if you met one?"

Tassie's ears flattened and she looked away, wringing her hands, suddenly very self-conscious. "The Tide Lords are gone, your grace."

"Yes, I know that. But suppose they came back? Your people believe the Crasii were magically bred to serve the Tide Lords. Don't you think you'd know one if you saw him?"

The Crasii shrugged. "I couldn't say, your grace."

"Very well," Arkady sighed, turning back to her tea. "You may go."

"She's lying," Tilly noted, as Tassie closed the door behind her. "Not something you see the Crasii do often."

"It's more likely she didn't know the answer," Arkady surmised. "We may disagree with the Crasii about their origins and whether or not the Tide Lords ever actually existed, but we agree they're no longer around. The Crasii believe the Cataclysm destroyed the Tide Lords."

"Or so they tell us," Tilly amended. "Still, you must give me all the gossip on this Tide Lord of yours. Is he handsome?"

"I suppose," she said, remembering the intense look he gave her the first time their eyes met. Arkady discovered she couldn't recall his features, just those soul-piercing eyes.

"Which one is he claiming to be?"

"Cayal. The Immortal Prince."

Tilly nodded, unsurprised, as she spooned a good helping of honey into her teacup. "Well, that would make sense, I suppose."

Arkady picked up her tea, took a sip, studying Tilly over the lip. "Why does it make sense?"

"Well, there's more written about Cayal than any of the others. If you're going to take on a Tide Lord's persona, why not the one you can learn the most about?"

"What do you mean, there's more written about him than any of the others? Where, Tilly? The only people who know anything about the Tide Lords are a few crusty academics—and I know *all* of them personally—and the Crasii. I've spent a lifetime working with *them* and I've barely gained their trust. Believe me, I've seen the way this man treats Crasii. And the way the Crasii react to him. He didn't get *anything* from them. Not willingly, at any rate."

"Then perhaps he reads his Tarot."

She smiled sceptically. "You think he had *supernatural* help?"

Tilly put down her teacup and picked up the cards. She began laying them out on the table, discarding all but the major cards and placing them out in an order that made no sense at all to Arkady.

"What I mean," the widow explained, as she continued to separate the cards, "is that the Tarot tells the story of the Immortal Prince."

"I thought it told the future?"

"Well, it does," the old lady agreed. "But the cards tell their own story. See?"

Arkady studied the cards, no more enlightened than she had been before Tilly showed them to her. "See what?"

"The story of the Immortal Prince! You see this first card here . . . the picture . . . that's Cayal, the young man, off to seek his fortune. The next card depicts his meeting with Arryl, the Sorceress, who is possessed by the spirit of the

Tide Star. She's the one who convinces him to become immortal. In the next card, he meets Diala, the High Priestess, who teaches him what he needs to know . . . and on it goes. If your boy is pretending to be a Tide Lord, Arkady, and the Crasii didn't take him into their confidence, then I'm guessing this is where he got his information."

Arkady shook her head, unconvinced. "But surely he'd know anybody with access to a deck of Tarot cards would see through his ploy?"

"Not if he was using the Tarot to back up his claim."

"You mean lacking any other source of information, he can say, *If you don't believe me, just check your Tarot*?"

"Exactly!" Tilly declared. "If he's learned it well enough, he'll have an answer for anything you throw at him."

"And if he doesn't?"

"Then he's surely not a Tide Lord, darling."

Arkady studied the cards for a moment, nodding thoughtfully. "You know, it would be interesting to see his reaction when he realises I'm on to him. Can I borrow these?"

"Be my guest," Tilly offered. "But they're not much good to you if you don't know what each card means."

"That's a good point."

Tilly leaned forward, with a conspiratorial smile. "So, when you visit your Tide Lord again, I could come with you . . ."

Arkady shook her head. "Absolutely not, Tilly."

Tilly leaned back in her chair, throwing her hands up. "Oh! Come on, Arkady! Jaxyn was right! You're a damned spoilsport."

"I'm also not supposed to be discussing this with anyone. This is an extremely delicate situation. I can just *imagine* the Warden's reaction if I roll up with one of my noble friends tomorrow, to give our Tide Lord a Tarot reading." Tilly reached for the deck but Arkady lifted it out of her grasp and began shuffling through the cards. "You'll have to teach *me* what they mean, Tilly."

"Will you promise to tell me every word he utters?"

"Will you promise to mention this to nobody?"

"I suppose," Tilly sighed.

Arkady began laying the cards out on the table. "Then tell me the legend of the Immortal Prince, so I can keep us both entertained."

Chapter 12

Herino City was located some fifty-five miles south of Lebec, which meant the journey took two days if one travelled by coach. Stellan could have travelled by boat on the lake, but that meant involving a lot more people and no way of slipping into the city quietly. By leaving at dawn and riding a fast horse and changing mounts twice along the way, however, with only a two-man escort, Stellan Desean was in the capital about two hours after sunset on the same day.

Despite what he'd told Jaxyn and Arkady, it wasn't the king who had summoned Stellan to Herino City. It was the King's Private Secretary, Lord Karyl Deryon, who'd sent the message. Stellan probably wouldn't have pushed so hard if the summons had come from King Enteny himself. The Duke of Lebec was required at court often enough, but with another month or more before the Privy Council was due to sit, it was doubtful Enteny was even in the capital at present. More likely he was still relaxing on his winter estate south of Herino, just outside of Jokarn.

A summons from Lord Deryon, on the other hand, invariably meant there was trouble. The sort of trouble that needed to be kept in the family. The sort of trouble Stellan was particularly good at taking care of.

Usually trouble that involved a young man named Mathu

Debree, who was, rather awkwardly, the Crown Prince of Glaeba.

The palace sat on the peak of a small hill and, like every other building on the island-city of Herino, was built on a massive scale. He dismounted in the torchlit courtyard and gave his horse and his escort into the care of the palace grooms. Over the top of the wall he could just make out the lights of the city stretching all the way down to the lake shore. Behind him, the tall marble columns at the palace entrance loomed like a threat over the whole island. The rare white marble had been cut from the mercilessly hot quarries on Torlenia, brought to Glaeba by ship, and then painstakingly shaped by countless Crasii craftsmen.

When he was younger, Stellan would study the columns, with their bases taller than a man and their intricately carved double rows of acanthus leaves, thinking that if you scrunched up your eyes and squinted at them from a distance, the columns looked like bars. It was a fitting analogy in Stellan's mind. Being a member of the royal family was as good as being a prisoner at times.

Stellan was expected at the palace and hurried through the broad halls behind a canine Crasii page who was under instructions to show him straight into the presence of Lord Deryon no matter how late he arrived. The King's Secretary was waiting in the atrium, located in the middle of the labyrinthine palace, its centrepiece a large bronze fountain depicting several nymphs carrying water jars to a large and undoubtedly flattering statue of Agranella, the first of their family to assume the title of Queen of Glaeba some three hundred years ago.

"Lord Stellan!" Lord Deryon exclaimed with relief when the page announced his guest. "Thank you for coming so quickly." The King's Private Secretary was older than Stellan by nearly thirty years, but his back was ramrod straight, and his face unnaturally smooth, despite his white hair.

"Would it be too much to hope that Torlenia has declared

war on us, and that's why you summoned me?" he enquired, as he shook the other man's hand.

Lord Deryon smiled thinly. "Likely as that is to happen if we don't sort out something about who actually owns sovereignty over the Chelae Islands, your grace, our Torlenian cousins are quiet, at present. I believe the Imperator has a new wife and she's keeping him distracted."

"How long can that last?"

"Not long enough, I fear. We'll have to do something about it soon."

"Well, Jorgan's a competent fellow," Stellan said, recalling the ambassador charged with keeping the peace between Glaeba and Torlenia.

"I suspect not as competent as you, my lord," the secretary said with a slight bow. "Lord Jorgan has a temper, which is hardly an asset in the art of diplomacy."

"I appreciate the compliment, old friend," Stellan replied. "However undeserved it might be."

"You are too modest, your grace."

"Perhaps." He sighed as he pulled off his riding gloves. "I suppose if we're not at war, then it's our *other* little problem again."

"I'm afraid so, your grace."

"Do you know where he is?"

Deryon motioned for the page to leave before he answered. Once he was certain they were alone, the old man let out a heavy sigh and turned to face Stellan, indicating he should rest on one of the many couches arranged in small groups about the atrium. "He's in a brothel near the docks, best we can tell. Your timing is impeccable, as usual. Hawkes only located him a few hours ago."

"How long this time?" Stellan asked, taking a seat. He didn't bother getting too comfortable, certain he would have to leave again shortly.

Deryon shrugged and took the couch opposite. "Four or five days is our best guess. Did you want something to drink? You must have damn near foundered your horse to get here so quickly."

"I'd better sort this out first," he suggested with a frown. "I thought he was supposed to be in Venetia with Reon? Learning the finer points of provincial government, wasn't it?"

"Apparently Venetia's provincial delights aren't enough for our Mathu."

"I suppose the king knows nothing of this?"

"Of course not."

Stellan studied the secretary, shaking his head in wonder. "I never cease to be amazed at your ability to keep Mathu's excesses from the king, Lord Deryon."

"I keep a lot of things from the king, your grace," Deryon remarked. "It's part of my job, you know . . . keeping secrets from him."

Stellan met his gaze, waiting for Deryon to add something further, but his secretary seemed content to leave it at that.

"Can you have someone take me to him?" he asked, rising to his feet before the silence dragged on long enough to become uncomfortable.

"I'll have someone take you to Hawkes," Deryon offered. "From there you'll probably be able to hear our noble young prince and his drunken friends making fools of themselves from half a mile away."

"Save that drink for me," Stellan suggested. "I think I'm going to need it by the time I get back."

"I'm sorry to put this on you again, your grace. You've been having an interesting time of it lately, that's for certain."

"What do you mean?"

Deryon smiled sympathetically. "First there was that business with the botched hanging. And then that escaped slave who killed another Crasii in their haste to depart?"

"That only happened the other night," Stellan pointed out, a little concerned by the speed with which the news of his domestic problems had reached Herino.

Lord Deryon shrugged. "Declan Hawkes mentioned something about it. Bad luck comes in threes, they say."

Stellan shook his head with a thin smile. "Then I dread to think what's next."

He turned for the entrance but Deryon called him back. "Lord Desean!"

"Was there something else?" he asked over his shoulder.

"I meant what I said about keeping secrets."

The duke hesitated and then nodded, turning back to face Deryon. They were no longer talking about the wild behaviour of Glaeba's heir. Both men knew that. "I appreciate your forbearance, old friend."

"Then take an old friend's advice, your grace. Don't leave the question of your own heir in doubt much longer."

"Kylia Debrell is my late sister's only child," he reminded the secretary. "She is currently, and quite legally, my heir."

"A stopgap heir, at best, my friend. Particularly given you have a wife perfectly capable of bearing a child. It's been six years since you married your physician's daughter, and I still remember your elegant and persuasive arguments when you petitioned Enteny to allow the marriage. All those passionate speeches about how the True Families would benefit from the injection of new blood; how your beautiful, clever, common-born wife would bring much needed vitality to the Desean line . . ." Deryon sighed and opened his hands in a gesture of helplessness. "The king loves you like a brother, Stellan, and he adores your wife—you know that—but he grows impatient."

"There *will* be an heir, Karyl," Stellan assured him.

"You are a scion of the True Families, Stellan. If Arkady doesn't give you a son soon, the king will do one of two things. He'll assume Arkady is barren and force you to put her aside so you can take a more fertile wife, or he'll start to wonder if there's another reason why you haven't gotten her with child."

Deryon wasn't threatening him, Stellan knew that. But it was a timely reminder of his responsibilities. "I'll speak to Arkady, Karyl. As soon as I get home. I promise."

"Please understand, I only mention this out of concern for you, Stellan. And your lovely wife."

The duke nodded in agreement, not doubting the man's honourable intentions. "I appreciate your discretion."

Karyl Deryon smiled tiredly. "Speaking of discretion, you will try to get Mathu back here as quickly and quietly as possible, won't you?"

"Don't I always?"

"The king will reward your loyalty someday, Lord Desean."

"I'd rather he didn't learn of it, actually," he replied with a wry smile. "For all our sakes."

Declan Hawkes was waiting for Stellan on the waterfront in the Sailors' Friend, a tavern across the street from the brothel where Glaeba's crown prince was currently ensconced with a number of his friends. Still a couple of hours before midnight, the taverns near the lake were in full swing, laughter, music and the sound of revelry spilling out from every open door and window along the waterfront.

"Behold the delights of the Friendly Futtock, your grace," Declan announced, as Stellan slid into the seat opposite the spymaster in a booth facing the street. Declan signalled for ale and a moment later, a frazzled-looking wench dumped a foaming wooden tankard in front of the duke. Stellan left it untouched. Ale was not his beverage of choice. Through the grubby window, he could just make out the run-down building across the street where the house of ill repute was located.

"The Friendly *Futtock*?" Stellan repeated, shaking his head. "Mathu doesn't think about how his little adventure is going to sound when his mother hears about it, does he?"

"I believe the idea is for his mother *not* to hear about it," the spy reminded him, and then he smiled. "Besides, futtocks are just the timbers that fasten together to make the ribs of a ship, you know, so it's really not as bad as it sounds."

Stellan smiled. "I'm impressed that you know that, Declan."

"I'm surprised you don't, your grace."

Stellan turned and studied the street outside. There were quite a few people wandering about, but as the night grew colder, the Lower Oran began to steam and a mist started to rise off the lake. In another hour, Stellan guessed, the fog would be as thick as a goose-down blanket.

"How many men have you got?"

"Three in here," Hawkes informed him. "Two outside. And a Crasii in the brothel itself, keeping an eye on our boy."

"How'd you get a Crasii in there?"

"She's a chameleon Crasii," Declan explained. "Tiji, her name is. Spookiest thing I ever saw. She just stands still in one spot and a few moments later, you can't tell her from the wall. Gives me the shivers every time she does it," the spy added. "Damned useful, though, to have her around."

"Do we know who's with him?"

"The usual troublemakers. Osdin Derork. Leam Devillen. And a new playmate, Wale Aranville."

"One of the Darra Aranvilles?" Stellan asked in surprise.

"He's Jaxyn Aranville's cousin, I believe, your grace."

The spymaster said nothing more on the subject, but the mere fact he'd even mentioned Jaxyn's name told Stellan a great deal. He shouldn't be surprised, he supposed. If Karyl Deryon's job was to keep secrets from the king, it was Declan Hawkes's job to find out those secrets in the first place. And this man was one of Arkady's oldest friends. Who knows what secrets the two of them had shared . . . ?

Stellan forced his attention back to the matter at hand. "What're they doing in Herino?"

Declan shrugged. "Perhaps Mathu's practising for the day he becomes king."

"Let's hope that sorry day remains a long way off," Stellan sighed. "How long before this fog thickens, do you think?"

Hawkes stared out into the night for a moment and then shrugged. "Not long now."

"Good. The fewer spectators the better. Can you get a carriage down here? A closed one?"

"People will notice a carriage on the waterfront at this hour, your grace."

"Unavoidable, I'm afraid, and the reason I'd like to wait for the fog to thicken up a bit. I doubt our boy will be in any fit state to ride. I'd like to get the other young gentlemen out of there at the same time, if I can."

"You're not here to save every errant noble son in Glaeba from scandal, your grace," Hawkes reminded him.

"And given a choice, I'd leave every one of the little sods to drown in his own vomit," Stellan agreed. "But if any of them is seen down here, all he has to do is say who he came here with for *him* to be off the hook and the prince to be exposed."

"They don't have to go back to the palace, though, do they?" Hawkes suggested, a glint in his eye that made Stellan frown suspiciously.

"I suppose not. Why?"

"Well . . . your grace . . . ," the spymaster ventured, "if somebody took these poor misguided lads aside—into a nice dark alley, perhaps—and pointed out the error of their ways . . . subtly of course, but in a way that will more than likely make them shit their fancy highborn trousers . . . I was thinking . . . maybe the next time your boy decides to play, he won't be able to round up quite as many willing playmates?"

Stellan stared at the younger man in amazement. "You're asking me to sanction you and your thugs roughing up three sons of the most important families in Glaeba?"

Hawkes smiled. "It sounds so tawdry when you say it like that, your grace."

It did sound tawdry, but Stellan nodded, wishing he'd

thought of it himself. "It also sounds like a grand idea. Will it work, do you think?"

The spy shrugged. "We've tried everything else."

"Promise you'll not leave any marks."

"Not so much as a love bite."

"In that case," Stellan said, "I think I'll pay a visit to the Friendly Futtock myself, and see if I can't coax our little friends out of there voluntarily."

"You be careful now, your grace," Hawkes warned. "All those whores . . . and you with a fat purse . . ."

"I'll try to resist the temptation," he assured the spy wryly. "Can you arrange to have the carriage out front? In a quarter of an hour?"

"I'll be there," Hawkes promised. "And I'll have the rest of the lads with me if you need help."

"Hopefully, it won't come to that."

Hawkes shook his head. "You should know better than to think that, your grace. We've done this dance together before, you and I."

"You know me, Declan," Stellan replied with a thin smile. "I live in hope."

"That you do, your grace," the spymaster agreed. "That you surely do."

Chapter 13

The interior of the Friendly Futtock was everything the dilapidated exterior promised it would be. It was little more than an abandoned warehouse divided into curtained-off cubicles across the back for the pleasure and, presumably, privacy of the patrons. In the centre of the room the floorboards had been ripped up, exposing the earth beneath, and a rough fireplace had been built in the hole. The room was lit by a number of thick tallow candles in wrought-iron stands. Lacking a proper chimney, the fire smoked quite badly, the smoke seeking any escape it could through the rough and draughty planking of the warehouse walls.

There were perhaps a dozen women lounging about the dimly lit room, ranging from the very young to the disturbingly old, all in various stages of undress. Stretched out across the laps of two of the whores near the fire, he noticed the unconscious form of Osdin Derork, eldest son of the Duke of Altarnia. His face was buried between the naked, pendulous breasts of one of the whores, who was chatting unselfconsciously to her companion while her patron slept and seemed quite content to leave the comatose young man where he was. Stellan didn't blame her really. These girls were paid by the quarter hour. Osdin's little nap would end up costing him a fortune. There were a few undecided patrons in the room, as well, who paid Stellan little attention. Of Mathu and the other two young men there was no sign.

He had barely stepped through the door before he was approached by a large woman wearing an emerald ball gown that had definitely seen better days. She eyed him up and down, taking in his expensive, albeit travel-stained, clothes, pursing her lips thoughtfully.

"You're either lost, desperate or lookin' for someone in particular," the madam observed. And then she added after a moment, "My lord."

"Guess," Stellan suggested, looking around for the prince. Mathu had to be here somewhere. Osdin Derork didn't stray far from his friends on excursions such as this.

The old whore smiled knowingly. "Figured someone'd come looking for him, sooner or later. You gonna pay his bill?"

"I'm almost afraid to ask how much it is."

"Two hundred gold fenets, near enough."

Looking around at the shabby interior, Stellan raised a curious eyebrow. "He bought the place, then, did he?"

"Oh, you're a wit, you are."

"More a good judge of property values. Where is he?"

"What about my money?"

"You'll get your money. Where is he?"

The woman planted her hands on her ample hips and glared at him in the dim, smoky light. "I want it now."

Stellan looked down at her with all the condescending disdain he could muster, which was considerable. "What you will get, madam, if you don't take me to him right this minute, is the City Watch tearing this place up, and you run out of the city. If you don't believe I have the power to arrange that, pop over the road to the Sailors' Friend for a moment. Declan Hawkes is there, right now, waiting for me to tell him whether or not I want this place raided."

The old whore paled. There wasn't a man or woman in Glaeba who hadn't heard of the King's Spymaster. Or doubted how dangerous he was. She jerked her head toward the back of the room. "The one with the green curtains."

Stellan thanked the woman and pushed his way through the lounging whores to the cubicle in question. He shoved the curtain aside and discovered Glaeba's crown prince sprawled face down and naked across the body of a partly dressed girl who appeared no older than Kylia. She looked up as he entered, frowning.

"I don't do freesomes," she announced petulantly. In the light of the single candle burning in a copper holder on the floor, with her long fair hair and unusual green eyes, the whore seemed pretty enough, Stellan thought, in a rough, unwashed sort of way. But that wasn't why Mathu had chosen her, he knew. This boy could have any woman in the kingdom at the crook of his little finger. Mathu's predilection for inappropriate bed-partners was a form of rebellion, a feeling Stellan was very familiar with, albeit for entirely different reasons.

"Leave us," Stellan ordered the girl. He tossed her a gold fenet for her troubles. She snatched it out of the air, pushed Mathu off her and scrambled over the pallet to the curtain before her unexpected bounty could be taken from her.

There was a small stool in the cubicle, besides the filthy

mattress. Stellan pulled it up to the side of the pallet and sat down, waiting for Mathu to notice he had company. The whore had woken him in her haste to be gone.

The prince raised his head and peered myopically at his visitor.

"Tides!" he said as his head flopped onto the mattress. "What are you doing here?"

"Hello, Mathu."

The prince lifted his head again, pushing his dark hair from his face. "How did you find me?"

"Hawkes found you," Stellan told him.

"*Imagine* my surprise," he groaned into the dirty pillow.

"I'm surprised at *you,* Mathu. You should know better than to try anything in Herino City and not realise that Declan Hawkes will eventually find out about it."

"And good old Uncle Karyl sent you down here to rescue me, I suppose?"

"I can't think why. It's not like you ever listen to me when I drag you out of these places."

With a groan that hinted at a mighty hangover, Mathu turned over and pulled himself up into a sit, running his hands through his ragged hair, trying to concentrate. The boy was normally quite a presentable young man. He was nineteen, fit, tall, dark-haired and very charming when the mood took him. Right now, though, he was a dreadful mess. He smelled of sour wine, cheap perfume, hadn't shaved or bathed for days and looked as if he'd never slept in a real bed. And the Tides alone knew what creatures he was sharing that filthy mattress with.

"Well, seeing as how you're here, cousin . . . care to sample the entertainment? My treat."

"No, thank you."

Mathu drew up his knees and rested his head on them. "You're a real prude, Stellan, you know that?"

"I have Arkady waiting for me in Lebec," Stellan reminded him, well practised in such evasions. "What whore could tempt me when I have such beauty waiting at home?"

"Fair enough." Mathu shrugged. With his forehead still

resting on his knees, he turned his head and studied Stellan. "Are you going to tell my parents about this?"

"I should."

"But you won't?"

"Not if you come quietly."

Mathu sighed heavily. "Tides, I envy you."

"*You* envy *me*?" he echoed in surprise.

The prince sat up a little straighter. "You know who you *are*, Stellan. You know exactly what your job is. You know exactly how to go about it, too. You do everything right. I wish I had even an ounce of your certainty."

Stellan smiled at Mathu's sorry misconceptions about his life. "You have no idea what you're talking about, lad. And you do have a job."

"My *job*, cousin, is to sit around and wait for my father to die," the prince pointed out. "That wouldn't be so bad, I suppose, if I hated him. Trouble is, I actually quite like the old stick. I don't want him to die."

"Not a sentiment one could deduce from your current behaviour, your highness. Your father *would* have a stroke if he knew you were down here whoring around the Herino docks when you're supposed to be in Venetia with Reon."

"Reon's an old woman. You know that."

"That doesn't make his counsel any less valid."

The prince reached for his shirt and pulled it over his head, perhaps awake enough by now to realise he was conducting this conversation while still naked as a Crasii pup. "Don't make me go back to Venetia, Stellan," he begged, as his head appeared through the neck of his vomit-stained shirt. "*Please.*"

"It's not up to me, Mathu."

"You have influence with Karyl Deryon," the prince reminded him. "If you speak to him, he'll listen to you."

"What do you expect me to say to him?"

Mathu thought about that for a moment and then smiled brightly. "Tell him I'm going back to Lebec with you."

"The hell you are!"

"But it's a perfect solution, don't you see?" he exclaimed. "Father has me studying provincial government with Reon because he's my cousin. Well, so are you. Lebec's not that different from Venetia. And you manage a provincial government just as efficiently as Reon Debalkor."

"The king chose Reon Debalkor as your mentor for a reason, your highness."

"The king chose Reon Debalkor as my mentor because the shyster paid my father ten thousand gold fenets for the privilege," the young prince corrected sourly.

"That's a dreadful accusation to make."

"Can I come back to Lebec with you if I promise not to repeat it?" Mathu asked with a hopeful grin.

Stellan shook his head. "And what happens the first time you get bored?"

"What do you mean?"

"Are you going to run away from Lebec the way you have from Venetia?"

The prince grinned impishly. "I'll have to rely on you to make certain I don't *get* bored, won't I?"

"In that case, you can stay right here and rot, your highness," Stellan told him, rising to his feet. "I'm not prepared to gamble my entire province on your contrary whim."

"Stellan, wait!" Mathu pleaded, scrambling off the pallet. "Don't be like that."

The duke studied the scruffy, disreputable-looking young man for a moment and then sighed. "Get dressed. We need to get out of here. And I have to settle your debts."

"Are you mad at me?"

"I've been up since before dawn and had to ride fifty-five miles just so I could drag you and your drunken friends out of a Herino brothel, Mathu. What possible reason could I have to be angry with you?"

"I'm sorry . . . ," he said, lowering his eyes, genuinely remorseful for once. "I never think these things through."

"That's the Tide's honest truth."

"Will you think about me coming to Lebec, though? If I promise to behave?"

"You've made that promise before."

"But I mean it, this time. I swear."

"I've heard *that* before, too."

"Don't send me back to Venetia, Stellan," he begged. "Reon is such a bore. He serves watered-down ale instead of wine at the dinner table."

"Ale won't kill you."

"But I might end up killing Cousin Reon. You don't want that on your conscience, do you?"

Stellan smiled. Despite the young man's recklessness, he liked Mathu. And he sympathised with his dislike of Reon Debalkor. Even the man's own wife and children complained about him.

"I'll think about it," he agreed reluctantly. "But I'm not promising *anything*. Now finish getting dressed. Where do I find Leam Devillen and Wade Aranville?"

"With Epatha, probably."

"Who?"

"Epatha the Man Maker," Mathu explained a little sheepishly, as he tugged on his trousers. "That's why we came here to the Friendly Futtock. She has a reputation for making boys into men, you see, and as young Wade was still a virgin . . ."

Stellan rolled his eyes. "Tides!"

"It was just a bit of harmless fun, Stellan."

"I doubt the Duke of Darra will see it that way, if he finds out you took it upon your royal self to have some whore called *Epatha the Man Maker* make a man out of his grandson. I hope the boy doesn't catch anything."

"I swear, I'll never do anything like this again, Stellan," the prince promised earnestly. He climbed to his feet, hopping from one foot to the other as he pulled up his tangled trousers. When he was done, he straightened up with a grin and added hopefully, "Not if you let me come to Lebec. Perhaps I could study with Arkady at the university."

"Be careful what you wish for, Mat," he warned, wondering what Arkady's reaction would be to such a notion. "You might get more than you bargained for. Now let's get out of this filthy place. Do you think you could manage that much without embarrassing the crown any further this night?"

Mathu gripped Stellan's shoulder and smiled at him. "You're a good friend, Stellan."

"No, I'm not," he corrected, picking up Mathu's discarded boots and thrusting them into the boy's arms before pushing him out into the smoky main room ahead of him. "A good friend would stop bailing you out every time you get yourself into strife and make you face up to the consequences of your stupidity."

"Then you're a bad friend," the prince amended. "And I'm grateful for it."

You ought to be, Stellan thought, as Declan Hawkes appeared in the main doorway of the brothel. That meant the carriage was here. The man nodded when he saw Stellan and the barefoot young prince, and then waved another couple of his men inside, ignoring the objections of the other patrons, with orders to extract the unconscious Osdin Derork from between the breasts of the patient whore who was still nursing his head. He then sent another four men to hunt up Wade Aranville and Leam Devillen.

As they were leaving, a movement to his left caught Stellan's eye. He turned and watched in amazement as the wall appeared to waver and then, where a moment ago there had seemed to be nothing but old planking, a shape detached itself and resolved into the body of a naked female Crasii. Slender and hairless, her skin covered in fine silver scales, without a word the Crasii unselfconsciously followed Declan and the others out of the brothel, nodding politely toward the duke as she passed him.

A few moments later, and two hundred gold fenets poorer, Stellan Desean was on his way back to the palace with the prince. The others, including the remarkable chameleon

Crasii, disappeared in the opposite direction, presumably to
find a nice dark alley where three inebriated young men
were about to have the error of their ways pointed out to
them—subtly, of course—by the most dangerous man in
Glaeba.

Chapter 14

Despite an intriguing day spent learning the legend behind the major cards of Tilly's Tarot, Arkady left
them behind the next time she visited the prison. The academic in her couldn't quite bring herself to consider a set
of Tarot cards as a historical text. The Immortal Prince's
story, by Tilly's account at any rate, was a simplistic morality tale, laden with cumbersome, heavy-handed parables
and, Arkady suspected, would make her the laughing stock
of the entire academic community of Glaeba if it ever got
about that she was taking it seriously.

Now that Declan was back in Herino and the entire responsibility for exposing the prisoner lay in her hands, she
decided instead to question Kyle Lakesh on the subject of
his alleged immortality. Denied the obvious option of simply running the man through to see if he survived, this was
the weakest part of his story. The logistics of immortality
were such that it was, to Arkady's scientific mind, quite an
absurd and impractical concept. To this end, she had com-
piled a list of questions she was sure would put an end to
his charade, sooner rather than later.

It was raining again, as it had almost every day for the
past week, when she travelled to the prison along the same
route, the fields burgeoning with new growth, their Crasii
attendants seemingly oblivious of the inclement weather,
as they toiled on, tilling a field here, planting a late crop
there, weeding another crop farther beyond the road. She

wondered idly if the weather didn't bother the Crasii, or if it was simply another assumption humans made about them, thinking that because they were animals, they lacked the same depth of feeling real people possessed.

This time only Timms came to collect her and the Warden didn't bother to meet her when she arrived at the prison, although there was a message telling Arkady he looked forward to her company for afternoon tea once her interview was done. She followed Timms up the long winding staircase to Recidivists' Row, almost gagging on the rank prison smells, wondering how anybody got used to this place.

When they finally reached the fourth floor, she discovered a chair waiting for her in the corridor between Warlock's cell and Kyle's cell opposite. She got another shock when she drew closer to the cells. Kyle Lakesh was clean, and looked like a different man. He appeared much younger than he had the day before, perhaps twenty-six or twenty-seven. His skin was pale, much paler than Glaeban skin, and he was more than presentable, he was actually good-looking. Arkady stopped abruptly, shocked to discover her first reaction to seeing him looking so respectable was far more visceral than she expected.

He smiled when he noticed her surprise. "The Warden seemed to think I offended your highborn sensibilities, your grace," Kyle explained, leaning on the bars as she approached. "Thanks to you, I get to bathe every day now. For that, I will continue with this absurd charade, provided you promise to keep visiting me."

Arkady eyed him warily, and then turned to peer into Warlock's cell. The Crasii was sitting on the floor in the corner, his chin on his chest, apparently asleep.

"Good afternoon, Warlock."

"Your grace," the big canine replied in his deep voice.

"Why waste your time talking to the flea-trap?" Kyle asked. "Isn't it me you came to visit?"

Arkady turned to face the Caelish prisoner. "Very well, I thought you might like to tell me about being immortal."

"It's a nightmare," Kyle replied. "Next question."

"A *nightmare*?" she repeated curiously.

"That's not actually a question."

"But your response intrigues me, Mr. Lakesh."

"I told you to call me Cayal."

"Very well, Cayal, why is being immortal a nightmare?"

"Because it's endless," Cayal replied, as if the answer was self-evident.

"I would have thought it quite the opposite," Arkady said. "I mean, it's one of those things that everyone secretly dreams of, isn't it? To have all the time in the world . . . to be able to learn any language, master any skill, achieve any goal. To never grow old. If I'm to believe what you're telling me, you've discovered the fountain of youth. Yet you seem to be wallowing in self-pity because of it."

"Self-*pity*?" he asked, looking more than a little offended.

"Do you have a better word?"

"You don't understand what it's like," he said. "You *can't* understand."

"Then help me to understand. That's what I'm here for."

He studied her suspiciously for a moment. "What happened to the other fellow?"

"You mean Declan Hawkes?" she asked. "He's returned to Herino. To take care of more important matters."

Cayal scowled at her. "More *important* matters?"

She smiled. "I'm sorry, Cayal, does that bother you? The fact that you're not the most important thing in the world?"

Cayal's face suddenly broke into a knowing grin. "You're pretty good at this, aren't you?"

"You have no idea," she assured him. "Tell me about the drawbacks of immortality."

"The killer is boredom."

"But to have no fear of dying . . ."

". . . is to experience the *true* meaning of boredom, Arkady. Can I call you Arkady?"

"No, you may not. How old are you?"

The young man shrugged. "I don't know. I've stopped keeping count."

Convenient, Arkady thought. "Make a guess."

Cayal looked away for a moment, obviously calculating something in his head, then he looked across the corridor at Warlock. "Hey, gemang!" he called. "What year is this by Crasii reckoning?"

The Crasii looked to Arkady, not sure if he should answer the question.

"It's all right, Warlock," she assured him.

"It's the year six thousand four hundred and sixty-seven," the Crasii replied. "According to our histories."

Cayal shrugged and looked to Arkady. "There you go! Add fifteen hundred years or so to that," he suggested. "We started experimenting with Crasii after the first Cataclysm. So I guess that makes me eight thousand years old, give or take."

Ignoring his absurd claim about his age, Arkady was fascinated by something else entirely. "The *first* Cataclysm? Are you saying there's been more than one?"

"Half a dozen, that I know of."

"But that's impossible."

"So's the notion that humans could ever rule Amyrantha while my kind lived, yet here we are."

"Your kind?"

"The Tide Lords."

She eyed him sceptically. "You look human enough to me."

"I am human . . . or I was . . . once."

Arkady smiled. "So what, Cayal, you just woke up one day and decided to become immortal?"

"It seemed like a good idea at the time, but that's another story. Ask the gemang if you don't believe me. He knows what I am."

Arkady looked across at the Crasii. "Is that right, Warlock? Do you believe Cayal is immortal?"

"He smells like a suzerain," Warlock agreed with a low growl. "Like rancid, rotting, decaying, putrefying flesh."

"See what happens when you don't domesticate them properly?" Cayal remarked. "They get all snarly and learn too many adjectives."

Arkady ignored his attempt to be witty and took her notebook and pencil from her satchel instead. "Why do you call him a gemang?"

"He calls me that because I call him suzerain," Warlock answered before Cayal could. "Gemang means *mongrel.* In one of the ancient languages, I think."

"Kordian, fool. It means *mongrel* in Kordian."

Arkady looked at Cayal in surprise. "You *speak* Kordian?"

"I was born there."

"Kordia is a legend. There's no proof it ever existed."

"Well, it didn't after the first Cataclysm," Cayal pointed out with a shrug. "And its correct name was Kordana, not Kordia."

"You told everyone in Rindova you were from Caelum, didn't you?"

"If I'd told them I was from Kordana, they might have been suspicious," he replied with a shrug.

"And not without cause, given what you did to them," she retorted.

"They'll get over it." He shrugged. "Truth is, I probably did them a favour."

"There're seven widows in Rindova who would disagree with you, I suspect."

"Are you sure about that?" he asked, not in the least bothered by her disapproval. "Maybe you should ask them."

Arkady looked away, pretending to make a few notes in her notebook before answering. "Convenient, don't you think, that you just happen to come from a country that nobody can prove ever existed? A country where nobody can check on the veracity of your claims?"

"Actually, Doctor, I find it quite *inconvenient* that everything I once knew and loved was destroyed by Tryan just because he's . . . well . . . a prick."

"Tryan?" Arkady asked, recalling the name from Tilly's Tarot. "You mean Tryan the Devil?"

"Is that what he calls himself these days?" Cayal shook his head. "Pretentious bastard."

"And you believe it was the Tide Lord Tryan who caused the first Cataclysm which destroyed Kordia and Fyrenne?" Arkady reminded him, trying to keep the conversation on track.

"I don't *believe* it, I *know* it," Cayal corrected. "I was there, remember? By the way, Fyrenne wasn't destroyed until years after Kordana. And it was Elyssa, not Tryan, who wiped that inoffensive little population off the face of Amyrantha." He turned his back on her, leaning against the bars of his cell. "Tides, don't give Tryan any *more* credit than he deserves! He's insufferable enough without it."

Arkady found herself admiring the prisoner's nerve. He spoke with real conviction, not as if he'd studied these mythical characters, but as if he actually knew them. This was no simple criminal. He was far more intelligent than his current predicament might indicate.

Which begged another question: *What's the real reason he is here in Glaeba?*

Is it possible, she wondered, *this man really is a Caelish agitator?*

If the Queen of Caelum was looking to avenge the insult to Princess Nyah, why not train a man for the job? Pick some handsome and personable young fellow with a sharp mind and have him pose as a Tide Lord. Teach him Tilly's Tarot. Throw in a few unverifiable facts to give the story the ring of authenticity. Pepper it with enough Crasii folklore to make it seem plausible, and then sit back and watch the fun.

It was certainly cheaper than declaring war.

Her reasoning also brought her back to her original line of questioning. Cayal's claim to immortality was the weakest part of his story, and probably the easiest way to expose him. She almost admired the complexity of the plan as she realised the last thing they could do now was attempt to kill this prisoner again. If he died, it might debunk this man's claim to immortality, but it would also rid them of their proof of a Caelish agitator in Glaeba.

This man might not be immortal, she mused, *but he's surely found a way to avoid dying.*

"Let's get back to your alleged immortality," Arkady instructed, taking a seat on the chair the Warden had provided for her. "How does it work?"

"I don't die," Cayal said, turning his head to watch her. "That's what immortal means, Doctor. You're supposed to be educated. I thought you'd know that already."

"So you . . . what? . . . can't be hurt . . . can walk through fire . . . break every bone in your body, and you'll just walk away unscathed?"

"I *wish*!" Cayal exclaimed with feeling. "I can be hurt just as much as any other man. I just heal up, afterwards."

"What if you lose a limb?"

"It grows back."

Arkady smiled. "Really."

"Really," Cayal assured her. He turned and put his right hand through the bars. "See here. Krydence cut my right hand off once. Grew right back, good as new."

Arkady wasn't foolish enough to get within reach of his hand, and there was no point, anyway. There would be no scars, no telltale marks to prove his claim. That's what made this swindle so effective.

"How long did it take to grow back?" she asked, wondering how far through he'd actually thought this.

The young man shrugged. "Couple of hours, maybe. The pain was indescribable. For some reason bones grow quicker than flesh, so the more tissue damage the longer it takes to heal and the more painful it is."

"And what if someone cuts off your head?" she enquired, certain this was where his story would begin to crumble. She looked at him curiously, not attempting to hide her scepticism. "Does *that* grow back too?"

"It surely does," Cayal agreed.

His reply took Arkady by surprise. She wasn't expecting that. "You're telling me that if I cut off a Tide Lord's head, it grows back?" she repeated, to make sure she'd heard him right. "That's impossible."

"In your world, lady, not mine."

"But that would require . . ."

"Magic," Cayal finished for her. "Something you appear to have trouble coming to grips with." He pushed off the bars and walked to the back of his cell, taking a seat on the straw pallet. "If you don't believe me, ask poor old Pellys."

"Pellys the Recluse?" she asked, naming another card in Tilly's Tarot.

"The *Recluse*?" Cayal chuckled, folding his hands behind his head and leaning back against the rough stone wall. "Wouldn't you want to be a recluse, too, if someone chopped off your head and after a few of hours of intense agony it grew back and you discovered you had no idea who you were, because your memories dropped into the basket under the headman's block along with the rest of your old head?"

"Is that what you're claiming happened to Pellys? Someone chopped off his head?"

"That's what happens when you piss off another Tide Lord," Cayal warned. "Some of us have absolutely no sense of humour."

"Why did a Tide Lord decapitate Pellys?"

He stared at her with those piercing blue eyes that seemed to have a light of their own, even in the gloom of his cell. "Why should I bother telling you? You don't believe a word of this."

"I'm actually more interested in whether or not *you* believe it."

Cayal seemed genuinely surprised by her accusation. He stood up abruptly and walked back to the bars. "Do you think I'm faking insanity to avoid another execution?"

"I'm interested in how a man claiming to be a simple wainwright from Caelum knows enough about Glaeban law to understand that's an option open to him."

Cayal frowned, obviously annoyed. "Let's get something straight, your *ladyship*. For one thing, I'm not claiming to be a wainwright; I'm claiming to be a Tide Lord. That I happen to know how to mend a wagon is not the point. I've been alive for eight thousand years; I know how to do a great many things. And for another, I probably know more about your laws than you do. I'm something of an expert when it comes to various Amyranthan legal systems. The Tides know I've been tried by enough of them."

"You've been arrested before?"

"Torlenia put me on trial once. After the third Cataclysm. Of course, I didn't actually attend the trial—I was still getting over the Tide turning so quickly—but as I heard it, a rollicking good time was had by all. And they sentenced me to death, too, which is pretty stupid, given I'm immortal. I mean, look what happened when your people tried it."

This man is really very, very good, Arkady thought. It was no wonder the Caelish thought they could get away with using him this way.

"What did they charge you with?" she asked, playing along with him to see how far he was willing to go. The more he told her, the more chance she had of exposing his lies. The more complex his story, the more detail he provided, the more likely she would eventually trip him up. Nobody could lie that well.

"It was over a little incident that happened to the Great Inland Sea."

Arkady frowned. She'd never heard of such a place. "Torlenia has no inland sea. It is an arid continent. Don't you mean the Great Inland *Desert*?"

"Well, it used to be a sea . . . you see . . . that's what the trial was about."

"Are you telling me you turned a sea into a desert?" she enquired, making no attempt to hide her amusement.

"I'm glad you think it's funny," Cayal sniffed. "At least I didn't make half a damn continent uninhabitable. Well, I suppose that's not strictly true . . ."

Arkady couldn't hide her smile. "And you performed this remarkable feat with magic, I suppose? Magic that comes from the Tide Star?"

"Naturally."

"And where is this powerful magic that allows you to lay waste to entire continents now, O Immortal Prince?" she asked, rising to her feet.

"It's Low Tide." He shrugged. "It'll come back eventually. It always does."

"And then we can witness the full might of the Tide Lords for ourselves?"

Cayal's smile faded. "You might want to hope you're not around when that happens, lady," he suggested. "The Tide's been out a long time. When it comes back next time, it's going to be a howler."

"I'll keep that in mind," she assured him, stowing her notebook in her satchel. She picked up her bag and glanced across at Warlock who had barely made a sound during the whole interview. "What about you, Warlock? Do you expect the Tide to return soon?"

"I can't tell." The canine shrugged.

"Do you think Cayal is lying?"

He looked up at her with his big dark eyes and bared his teeth. "You should never trust a word a suzerain tells you, your grace. Even when he's telling the truth."

"You know, come the next High Tide, gemang," Cayal called across the corridor, "the first Crasii I'm going to have licking my arse will be you!" He turned to Arkady and added, "That's why we bred them, you know. We liked being grovelled to and nothing else we ever came up with grovelled better than the canines. That's why we bred them for house slaves. All that boundless enthusiasm . . . that pitiful need to please their masters . . . Tides, they were pathetic then and they don't appear to have improved much over the last six thousand years."

This man is too convincing, Arkady realised, *to be an amateur.*

Arkady was guessing he was an actor or performer of some kind, recruited by the Caelish queen or one of her agents to wreak havoc in Glaeba. He was too good—and too good-looking—to have passed through Caelum or even other parts of Glaeba, unremarked.

She wasn't going to let him get the last word in, however. Pushing her chair aside, she shouldered her satchel and turned to face Cayal. "Odd, don't you think, your immortal highness, that your loyal Crasii here—the one bred to serve your kind so faithfully—doesn't seem in the least bit interested in grovelling to anyone, least of all you."

"There's nothing wrong with old fleabag over there that can't be remedied with a horsewhip and a good strong collar," Cayal replied. He eyed Arkady up and down quite deliberately and then added with a wink, "A remedy which, I suspect, might work just as effectively on you, my lady."

Arkady had spent much of her adult life being leered at like that, but rarely did it bother her the way it did when this man looked at her. Defiantly, she lifted her chin. Cayal Lakesh was sadly mistaken if he thought he could intimidate her, or make her feel uncomfortable with nothing more than a seductive leer.

"Careful, Cayal," she warned. "You're giving me ideas. I could decide to have you prove your immortality by chopping off one of your extremities, now I come to think of it, just so I can watch it grow back." She looked down at his groin and added with a cold smile, "All that's left to decide really is which extremity to chop off."

Before Cayal could respond to that, Arkady turned on her heel and headed down the corridor toward the guardroom and the stairs, thinking that if worse came to worst, she had her way to prove this man was lying.

How long will your story hold up, Cayal, the Immortal Prince, she wondered, feeling a little smug, *if I bring out the butcher's knives?*

Arkady smiled grimly as she descended the stairs to join the Warden for tea. Cayal probably wouldn't be nearly so arrogant, she suspected, with a cleaver poised over one of his hands.

After all, Arkady's father had been a physician and she'd acted as his assistant right up until he was arrested.

The Duchess of Lebec knew how to amputate a finger.

Chapter 15

I t was four days after his heroic dash to Herino that Stellan Desean returned to Lebec with the Crown Prince of Glaeba in tow, wondering why he'd allowed himself to be talked into such a potentially disastrous arrangement. Despite all Stellan's objections, somehow Mathu had managed to convince not only him, but the notoriously intransigent Karyl Deryon as well, that if he were allowed to study in Lebec, he would behave himself; that under Stellan's guidance, he would suddenly blossom into the studious and responsible young man that everyone hoped he would become.

They arrived after dark, the return journey having taken twice as long as Stellan's mad ride south because of the size of Mathu's retinue. Not that the young man insisted on anything extraordinary. Given a choice, Mathu would probably have saddled up his horse and ridden back with Stellan on his own, but Lord Deryon insisted that if the crown prince was going to Lebec, he was going to do it properly, and that meant Crasii slaves, servants, guards and a luggage wagon.

Impatience got the better of Mathu as the sun set over the Lower Oran near the village of Rindova, turning the lake into a sheet of molten gold. Almost as anxious as

Mathu to be home, Stellan found himself agreeing to leave the remainder of their retinue behind while the two of them, with only the two-man escort Stellan had taken to Herino originally, went on ahead. As the silhouette of the palace came into view on the rise beyond the city, he halted their small troop and pointed to the palace, ignoring the misty rain.

"There it is," he said. "Lebec Palace."

"It's smaller than I remember," Mathu remarked, shaking the raindrops from his oiled cloak.

"Things always seem bigger when you're a child. I remember being totally overwhelmed by the Herino Palace when I was small."

"That's something I still haven't gotten over," Mathu chuckled. "Have you ever noticed how the big columns out front look like bars if you squint at them?"

"I thought I was the only one who imagined that."

Mathu's smile faded as he studied the palace on the horizon. Twilight was all but done, the sky rapidly losing colour as the little light remaining disappeared, the air chill with the rain and the loss of the Tide Star. Pinpoints of light were beginning to appear in the darkness, as the palace stirred for the evening meal. "Are you sure Arkady won't mind my coming?"

Stellan smiled. "No."

The prince looked at him earnestly. "I'll try not to let you down, Stellan."

"Don't let yourself down, Mathu," he advised his young cousin. "That's more important."

For once, Mathu didn't seem to have a glib answer at the ready. After a moment, Stellan gathered up his reins, and with the Crown Prince of Glaeba at his side, urged his mare forward toward home.

"Stellan!" Arkady exclaimed in surprise when he walked unannounced into the dining room. She smiled with genuine pleasure, always glad to see him. "Why didn't you send word you were coming home?"

"I would have beaten it," he told her, walking the length of the table to kiss her cheek. "Besides, I wanted to surprise you. Good evening, Jaxyn," he added with a nod across the table to his lover. The young man did nothing but incline his head in acknowledgement of the greeting, too practised at hiding their relationship to do anything that might give them away. Then Stellan turned to his niece. "And how's my girl this evening?"

"I'm very well, Uncle Stellan," she assured him, as he kissed her cheek. "You're all wet, is it still raining? I swear, it hasn't let up for days. Not since Jaxyn took me punting on the lake the other day."

"Then it must have stopped for a short while at least." Stellan kissed her again, on the top of her head, and then turned toward the door. "I have a surprise for you."

"For me?" Kylia asked, her eyes lighting up.

"For all of you," he corrected. "Mathu!"

At his call, the crown prince stepped into the dining room and began walking the long length of the table to the other end where Arkady, Jaxyn and Kylia had been taking their evening meal.

Arkady jumped to her feet when she saw him. "Your royal highness!"

"Lady Desean. You're looking stunning as always."

"What the . . . I mean . . ." She looked at Stellan for an explanation, clearly shocked. "I mean . . . This is an unexpected pleasure, your highness."

"Very unexpected," Jaxyn agreed as he rose to his feet, also giving Stellan a questioning look. Then he bowed to Mathu. "Your royal highness."

"Lord Aranville," Mathu replied with a short bow. "My cousin mentioned you were here in Lebec. He says you're his Kennel Master. Claims you have a true gift when it comes to handling the Crasii." He addressed Jaxyn but the young prince's gaze was fixed on Kylia.

"His grace is too kind," Jaxyn replied, giving Stellan a look that spoke volumes. Fortunately, Mathu had eyes only for Kylia, which was something Stellan hadn't anticipated.

He still thought of Kylia as a child. He forgot sometimes that she was all but grown and certainly old enough to attract the attention of a young man like the prince.

"This must be your lovely niece?" Mathu exclaimed as he reached her chair. Kylia had remained seated, apparently not at all pleased by the new arrival. "You probably don't remember me, do you, my lady?"

Kylia nodded, scowling. "I remember you. You pushed me into the lake at the New Year's party in Herino when I was nine."

"The correct way to address the crown prince is *your royal highness,* Kylia," Arkady reminded her gently, as Jaxyn choked on his wine.

They all looked at him with concern, but he waved away any assistance.

"Truly, I'm fine," Jaxyn gasped. "Just went down the wrong way." He sat down, burying his face in his water glass.

Arkady turned back to Kylia, who seemed more amused than worried by Jaxyn's condition. "I'm sure his highness regrets any unfortunate misunderstanding that might have occurred when you were both children."

"It's all right, your grace," Mathu assured Arkady. "I was a little monster back then. Still am, if you listen to my cousin Reon." He turned his attention back to Kylia. "Did I really push you into the Lower Oran, Lady Kylia?"

"Yes, your highness, you did."

He took her hand and kissed it apologetically. "I don't recall doing such a dreadful thing, but if you say so, then it must be true. If I'd known you would grow up to be so charming, my lady, I might not have been so hasty to give you a dunking."

"That will be quite enough of that, my lad," Stellan warned, as Kylia smiled at the young prince in a manner just a little too alluring for Stellan's peace of mind.

Where had she learned to flirt like that? Surely not at an establishment devoted to teaching young noblewomen the finer points of etiquette? *Perhaps, when the school proudly advertised that all their students made good marriages, it's because their students are being taught more than the classics,* he mused.

Stellan was beginning to regret leaving his orphaned niece in the care of others for so long. To his eternal shame, he'd not even recognised Kylia when she arrived at the palace and the more he got to know her, the less he understood about her. She'd gained a great deal of confidence at the school, however, as her chastisement of the prince proved. Kylia was nothing like the shy young girl he'd handed over to the care of a ladies' college when she was twelve.

With a stern look, he extracted Kylia's hand from Mathu's and then turned to his wife. "Could you arrange something to eat, Arkady? We decided to forgo dinner in favour of speed I'm afraid. I don't know about Mathu, but I'm starving."

"I could eat a Crasii, I'm so hungry," the prince agreed with a laugh, ignoring Stellan's warning and taking a seat next to Kylia, who was fluttering her eyelids at the young man.

"Then if you will excuse me, your highness," Arkady begged graciously. "I'll see what I can arrange. Stellan? A moment?"

It needed no great leap of intuition to guess what Arkady wanted to talk to him about. With Jaxyn watching them curiously and Mathu oblivious to anything in the room other than Kylia, Stellan followed his wife out of the dining room and into the hall where she hailed Tassie and ordered the young canine to tell cook they had a royal visitor and to have more food sent up. She then headed along the corridor to his study, leaning against the door with a heavy sigh when she closed it behind them.

"What in the name of the Tides is Mathu Debree doing here?"

"He got himself into trouble again," Stellan explained,

turning to face her. "Karyl Deryon asked me to keep an eye on him."

"I thought the king sent him to Venetia?"

Stellan shrugged. "You know what Reon's like. He had no hope of controlling Mathu."

"So *you* volunteered?"

He shrugged helplessly. "I didn't really have much choice, Arkady. What was I supposed to do? Tell Mathu he couldn't come to Lebec because I didn't want him to learn the truth about me?"

"Then you must send Jaxyn away, Stellan," Arkady advised. "First thing tomorrow."

"Jaxyn won't be a problem," he assured her, taking her gently by the shoulders. "He's very good at being discreet."

She frowned, unconvinced. "I'm glad *you* think so."

"Kylia has no idea . . ."

"Kylia is barely more than a child, Stellan. Your particular predicament doesn't exist in her world. She doesn't understand what she's seeing, even when it's right in front of her. Mathu is not nearly so innocent. One accidental look from Jaxyn across the dinner table could give you away."

"I'll be careful, Arkady. I promise."

"It's not you I'm worried about."

"Jaxyn's as much at risk as I am, my dear. He won't betray us."

His wife remained unconvinced. "The danger is too great, Stellan."

He pulled her close and held her for a moment. "You're generous to worry so much for me."

"I've allied myself with you, Stellan," she said, hugging him briefly. Then she pulled away and looked up at him. "For better or worse. If you go down, I'll go down with you." She kissed his cheek and stepped out of his embrace. "But I still think you should send Jaxyn away while Mathu's here."

"I'll speak to him. But I don't think things are quite as drastic as they seem."

"Then you're far more optimistic than I am."

"Lord Deryon sends his regards, by the way," he told her, wondering how he was going to broach a subject he considered much more problematic than the fear Jaxyn Aranville might inadvertently let on that he and Stellan were lovers. "And he asked . . . when we might be expecting an heir."

Arkady raised her brow questioningly. "Isn't that rather up to you?"

He sighed. "I know. But it's not as easy as . . . perhaps we should . . ." Stellan wasn't sure what to say. He admired Arkady, loved her even, in his own way, but not once during six years of marriage had he ever desired her. He'd never desired any woman. The thought of making love to a woman physically repulsed him. One of the things that made Arkady such a rare treasure for a man like Stellan Desean was that she seemed to understand that.

Arkady took his hand and squeezed it encouragingly. "I appreciate your dilemma, Stellan, truly I do. But I can't fulfil my part of our agreement without your help."

He hesitated, and then gave voice to the only other solution he could think of. "You could take a lover."

The suggestion seemed to amuse her. She raised a brow at him. "Did you have anyone in mind?"

"Well, no . . . of course not . . . I was just thinking . . ."

"Suppose I chose someone you didn't like?"

"I rather think the point of the exercise would be what *you* like, wouldn't it?"

"That's not what I mean, Stellan. This has consequences beyond me having an affair. Could you really pass off another man's bastard as your own son? Could you love him like your own? Not watch him constantly, waiting for him to betray his ancestry? Could you stand up before King Enteny—your own cousin—and lie about who fathered your heir?"

"My whole life is a lie, Arkady," he reminded her. "What's one more?"

Arkady wasn't so easily deterred, certainly not by

maudlin self-pity. "And what of the child's father? Wouldn't he have the right to know he had a son? And if he did know—which I imagine any man who can count would be able to work out—how do you trust a man willing to sleep with another man's wife to keep the secret of your son's true paternity? And suppose I have a daughter? Do we choose another candidate and try again or do we go back for seconds?"

"You are far too analytical," he complained, as she presented him reason after reason why this was a bad idea.

"Thank the Tides I am, Stellan," she suggested. "Left to your own devices, you'd sink us all."

"Will you give the idea some thought?"

"About taking a lover? Absolutely not. It's far too dangerous."

"Then I guess we're back where we started . . ."

She studied him curiously for a moment, obviously sympathetic, but puzzled nonetheless by his reluctance, even for something as important as the continuation of his line. "Would it be *so* intolerable to touch a woman, Stellan? We could try again . . . With my back to you . . . if I made no sound, perhaps . . . if the lights were out . . ."

He shook his head. "I can't explain it, Arkady."

"Then I'll think about it," she promised, albeit reluctantly. "But I still think we should consider involving a third person as a last resort, not our first option." She glanced at the clock on the mantel and turned for the door, smiling apologetically. "I should be checking on our crown prince's dinner. And you need to get out of those wet clothes. Can we talk about this later?"

He looked at her standing there in her exquisite, elegant green-silk gown, her hand on the latch, tall, beautiful, fiercely intelligent and ferociously independent, wishing—for a rare moment—that he was the sort of man who could appreciate what he had in Arkady, physically as well as intellectually. She deserved so much more than he could offer, and she asked so little of him in return. It seemed a very unfair arrangement.

He smiled. "If only you were a man, Arkady."

"If only *you* were, Stellan," she replied, leaning forward to kiss his cheek, and then she left him alone in the study to ponder the cruel twist of fate that had put the soul of the one person on Amyrantha who truly understood him in the body of a woman he couldn't bring himself to touch.

Chapter 16

J axyn waited until he was certain the rest of the palace was asleep before he made his way silently through the wide palace halls to Stellan's room. He desperately wanted to talk to the duke. The unexpected arrival of Mathu Debree disturbed him a great deal. Kylia's arrival had been bad enough. There was no room in Jaxyn's plans for any more competition for Stellan Desean's affections, no matter how platonic. He needed to find out the reason behind the crown prince's arrival, certain there was something sinister in it.

"Arkady was right," Stellan remarked, looking up as he heard Jaxyn locking the door behind him. "You really don't think, do you?"

"She said that about me?" he asked, crossing the rug to the bed. Stellan was stretched out on the cover reading by lamplight. It was his habit to catch up on the business of the estate late at night, when he was unlikely to be disturbed. Rain pattered softly against the windows, the earlier shower having settled in for a good long soaking. It would rain all night again, more than likely, a common enough occurrence in Glaeba at this time of year but one Jaxyn had a little trouble getting used to. The Glaeba of his youth had never been this soggy.

"She wants me to send you away while Mathu's here," Stellan added, putting aside the document he was reading.

I'll just bet she does, Jaxyn thought. But he'd learned the hard way not to malign Arkady to her husband. Stellan was irrationally protective of his wife. "She worries about you too much."

"A not-unreasonable fear, I'm forced to concede, given that you've just sneaked into my room in the dead of night."

"I locked the door."

"Making your visit even more suspicious."

"Why did you marry her, anyway?" Jaxyn asked, sitting on the bed and swinging his boots up on the coverlet. He leaned back against the bedpost, picked up one of Stellan's stockinged feet and began massaging it.

Stellan closed his eyes, murmuring appreciatively. "We were in a position to do each other a favour."

"And how did she take the news on your wedding night that your interests lay . . . elsewhere?"

"Arkady knew about me long before we married. She caught me, actually, in the arms of a rather handsome young troubadour who'd been staying at the palace. His troupe was moving on. We were saying goodbye in the library when she burst in on us, demanding I release her father."

"So she blackmailed you into it?"

"Hardly," Stellan said, lifting his other foot so that Jaxyn could massage that, too. "She didn't care. She was more worried about her father. It wasn't until later that it occurred to me that Arkady had seen what she had and not said a word. She didn't express disapproval. She didn't try to use the information against me—and the Tides know she had reason enough to. She just shrugged it off. I'd never met anybody—man or woman—who'd reacted to learning my true nature like that before."

"So out of gratitude you married the first woman who didn't condemn you?"

"You have very little compassion in your soul, Jaxyn."

He smiled. "That's what makes me so irresistible."

"It's what makes you so damned dangerous," Stellan corrected, but to Jaxyn's relief he didn't say it with much conviction. "We'll have to be very careful while Mathu's here."

"And how long will that be?"

"At the very least, until the king returns to Herino at the beginning of summer. Can you contain yourself for a month or so?"

"Aren't I always discreet?"

The duke frowned. "This will require more than discretion, I fear. As my wife so astutely pointed out earlier this evening, Kylia is an innocent and Mathu far from it. We mustn't give him any reason to suspect the truth."

"Then we'll tell him I'm your masseuse, shall we?"

"Oh yes, Jaxyn, what a marvellous idea. That's not in the least bit suspicious."

Jaxyn chuckled softly. "Your secretary, then?"

"That would involve you doing actual work, Jaxyn."

"Ah, we can't have that now, can we?"

"There's really nothing wrong with telling him the truth, you know."

"A novel suggestion."

"You *are* Lebec's Kennel Master," Stellan reminded him, a little impatiently. "There's nothing suspicious in that."

"I thought you were the master here." Jaxyn smiled at him and pushed Stellan's feet aside, leaning forward, moving the massage farther up his leg.

Stellan pushed him away distractedly. "Not tonight."

Jaxyn leaned back against the bedpost with a frown. "Well, I can see having the crown prince as a houseguest is going to be a barrel of laughs, isn't it?"

"It's nothing to do with Mathu," Stellan assured him.

"What is it then?"

"I've got a lot on my mind."

"Anything specific, or are you just worrying for the fun of it?"

Stellan hesitated and then sighed. "The same old problem. My heir. Or to be more specific, my lack thereof."

"Kylia's your heir." *Clever little minx that she is.*

"By default, only. I'm a scion of the True Families, Jaxyn. I'm expected to produce a son."

"And Arkady won't oblige?"

"The problem is mine, not hers."

Jaxyn nodded, feigning sympathy, although in truth, he didn't really understand Stellan's dilemma. He had been attracted to members of both sexes at various times. For Jaxyn it wasn't the gender, but the person—or what they could do for him—that he found attractive. If he'd been Stellan, he would have just closed his eyes, thought of Lebec and been done with it.

But that wasn't in Stellan's nature. He was an odd combination of a man who at once lived a terrible lie for the benefit of others while being unable to lie to himself.

"Perhaps you could prevail upon Arkady to seek aid . . . outside the marriage bed?" he suggested carefully, not sure of the reaction he was going to get. His concern that Stellan produce a viable heir was genuine. Jaxyn was almost as anxious as the king to see Arkady pregnant, horrified by the idea of Kylia as Stellan's successor.

Stellan merely shook his head, not in the least bit offended by the idea. "She's adamantly opposed to it. She fears we'd never be able to trust the man involved to keep our secret."

"Unless it was someone you already trusted," Jaxyn pointed out.

"Who did you have in mind, Jaxyn? *You?*"

He smiled. "Why not?"

Stellan actually laughed aloud at the notion. "For one thing, Arkady despises you."

"Are you sure about that?"

"Yes."

He shrugged. Jaxyn refused to believe Arkady was completely indifferent to his charms. "Women sometimes use one emotion to disguise another, Stellan. Even the practically perfect Arkady isn't above that."

The duke remained unconvinced. "Arkady feels many things for you, Jaxyn, I'm sure, but I seriously doubt any one of them is desire."

"That's not really the point, though, is it?"

"What do you mean?"

"I mean it's not really her decision. She agreed to give you an heir. If you're not able to perform the task yourself, then you should be able to nominate a proxy, and she should accept your decision."

"Forcing Arkady to accept a man she doesn't want just so I can have a son would be tantamount to rape."

"Don't be so melodramatic," he scoffed. "I'm not talking about raping anybody. Of course, she'd have to agree to it. But you have to *make* her agree to it."

Stellan shook his head. "I know what her reaction would be."

"I don't think you do, Stellan. Arkady might act as if there's snowmelt running through her veins, but I suspect you'll find it's an act she puts on to protect herself as much as it is to protect you."

"And you'd do this selfless thing for me, would you, my love? Sleep with my wife?"

There was an edge to the duke's voice that set alarm bells ringing in Jaxyn's head. "I'd give you the son you crave, Stellan," he corrected. "And I'd do it because of what I feel for *you*, not your wife."

"Then perhaps you should speak to her yourself."

"*Excuse* me?"

"Speak to Arkady," Stellan repeated. "Put your eloquent case to her. If you can convince my wife of the nobility of your selfless offer and she agrees to it, then you have my blessing."

"Are you serious?"

"Absolutely," the duke assured him. Then he smiled. "Of course, I'm almost certain what her reaction is going to be, but I will enjoy watching you try."

"You're *challenging* me to seduce your wife?"

"I suppose you could look at it like that."

"You're insane!"

"Probably," Stellan agreed. "But at the very least, you'll have to stop flirting with Kylia for a bit and while you're pursuing my wife you'll give Mathu something else to worry about. The king is far more understanding about adultery between a man and a woman, after all, than he is about the same sin committed between two men."

"You really are losing your mind, you know, old boy."

Stellan shrugged philosophically. "Ironic, don't you agree, that insanity is acceptable in our world, Jaxyn, and yet us loving each other is not?"

"You know me. I'm far too shallow and venal for such deep thoughts. Still, I do promise not to make things any harder on you," Jaxyn assured him. He swung his legs onto the floor and stood up from the bed, adding with a wicked grin, "No pun intended. Don't stay up too late, eh? You've had a long day."

"Yes, Mother."

"Being rude to me won't help your cause, you know."

Stellan smiled tiredly. "Go to bed, Jaxyn. Your *own* bed."

"Goodnight, Stellan."

"We'll talk again tomorrow."

"Perhaps. If I have time," Jaxyn sighed as he headed for the door. "I may be too busy seducing your wife."

"She'll say no," Stellan called after him. "And if you're really lucky, she won't leave any marks."

"We'll see."

Jaxyn opened the door and glanced up and down the hall outside before he turned and looked back at Stellan. The duke had picked up the document he'd been reading when Jaxyn came in, a solitary figure wrapped in the warm yellow glow of the lamp beside his bed; a single puddle of light in the otherwise dark room.

"I suspect you don't know Arkady as well as you think, Stellan."

With that final prediction, he closed the door behind him and made his way down the hall, back to his own room, whistling softly to himself.

Things were back under control, Jaxyn Aranville mused. *Kylia would soon be made redundant.*

And Arkady Desean was officially fair game.

Chapter 17

It took another week and several more frustrating interviews with Kyle Lakesh before Arkady was able to pin down her husband to discuss what she considered the fastest and most effective way of bringing this farce to an end. She wanted to call the prisoner's bluff, and needed the approval of the Duke of Lebec to do it.

Arkady couldn't say why she was so anxious to bring her visits with Cayal to an end. At first, she thought it might be simply her dislike of Lebec Prison. After all, her father had died there, so she had little affection for the place. However, as she rode out to the prison each day with the silent and watchful Timms as her escort, her heart beating a little faster in anticipation of seeing her prisoner again, Arkady began to realise it was more than dislike for the building. It was Cayal himself who disturbed her and she couldn't—for the life of her—understand why.

That the young man was a consummate actor was beyond question. His story was flawless. He had an answer for everything and never once hesitated before providing one. He had not attempted to avoid her interrogation, never dodged a question. He was suspiciously anxious to cooperate, in fact, arrogantly insisting that once the Glaeban authorities recognised what he was, they would have no choice but to release him.

Warlock's reaction to him was equally disturbing and was the reason Arkady was becoming more and more convinced this man's story needed to be discredited urgently. From across the gloomy prison passage, the Crasii listened closely to her interrogation of the Caelishman, and although he clearly despised him, every word the would-be Tide Lord uttered, rather than expose his lies, seemed to reinforce the Crasii's opinion that Cayal was what he claimed.

Arkady didn't believe for a moment that Kyle Lakesh was really Cayal, the Immortal Prince, but she knew how much Crasii folklore centred on the Tide Lords; how critical the immortals' existence was to the Crasii understanding of their place in the world. The Tide Lords, according to their oral history, were the Creators. The Mother, the unnamed Tide Lord they believed responsible for their very existence, was spoken of in hushed and reverent tones and rarely mentioned to outsiders. The Tide Lords were the Crasii gods who had fashioned their race by blending humans and animals; the gods who had—according to legend—instilled them with the irresistible compulsion to serve. The relationship between the Crasii and their gods was ambivalent, however. They despised the Mother while worshipping her; resented the Tide Lords while being unable to refuse their commands . . .

Or they would be unable to refuse them if the Tide Lords were actually real, Arkady reminded herself, as she knocked on the door to Stellan's study and let herself in without waiting for an answer. It was warm in the office, the fire blazing in the carved marble fireplace not really necessary on such a mild day. The rain had let up for the past day or so and the whole world seemed brighter for it.

Stellan was sitting behind his ivory-legged desk in his shirt sleeves going through one of the large, leather-bound estate ledgers, with Mathu leaning over his shoulder. The prince was still on his best behaviour and had done nothing, thus far, to embarrass either his father or his host.

"Good morning, Lady Desean."

Arkady curtseyed elegantly to their guest. "Your royal highness. How are you this morning?"

"Bored senseless," he complained. "I can't believe how tedious it is learning about tax collecting."

"Tedious but necessary, I'm afraid," Stellan reminded him. "We could do with a break, though. What can we do for you, Arkady?"

"I wanted to talk to you about Kyle Lakesh."

The prince looked at them questioningly. "Who's Kyle Lakesh?"

"A Caelish prisoner currently incarcerated in Lebec Prison, your highness, who's claiming to be a Tide Lord," Arkady informed him, figuring there was no point in trying to hide the details from Glaeba's crown prince.

"Really?" he said, resting on the back of Stellan's chair with his arms crossed. "How bizarre! Why would any man claim such an absurd thing?"

"It's not so absurd if the Crasii believe him," she replied, taking a seat opposite the desk on one of the exquisitely carved and embroidered chairs Stellan's grandmother had commissioned to match the rest of the room.

"*Do* the Crasii believe him?" Mathu asked.

"The one in the cell opposite him does," she told them. "And he's not very happy about it."

"I'm surprised at you, Arkady," Stellan said, leaning back with a smile. "I thought you'd have this chap on the run within a few hours of meeting him."

"To be honest, so did I," she admitted. "He's proving to be a much better liar than I anticipated. Suspiciously so."

"You think there's something more sinister going on here than a simple attempt to avoid the noose?" her husband asked, frowning.

She shrugged. "I wish I knew. The man's Caelish, which might have something to do with it. He certainly has an answer for everything. It wouldn't surprise me in the slightest to learn he'd been coached."

He nodded thoughtfully. "If he's a spy, it would account for the ambassador's interest in him."

Mathu's forehead creased in a puzzled frown. "Surely if this man's claiming to be immortal, your grace, then the quickest way of deciding the issue would be to kill him, wouldn't it?"

"Tried that," Stellan said, glancing over his shoulder at the prince. "Which is the reason we're having this discussion."

"You *killed* him and he didn't *die*?"

"We hanged him and he survived," Stellan corrected. "We thought he was faking insanity to avoid a second—and more than likely successful—attempt."

"So hang him again. That should settle it."

"With the Caelish Ambassador taking an interest in his case?" the duke asked, shaking his head. "I think not."

"There might be another way," Arkady suggested carefully. She couldn't say why, but she wanted to be done with Cayal as quickly as possible and she had the means, if only Stellan would let her use it.

"I'm listening."

"Cayal . . . that's what he calls himself . . . insists he has an unlimited ability to regenerate. He claims to have had a limb amputated that grew back. He even claims a Tide Lord named Pellys was decapitated and grew another head."

Stellan looked at her, a little puzzled. "So . . . what do you want of me?"

"I need you to speak to the Prefect. And the Warden. Do you think they'll let me amputate something?"

Silence descended over the study. It was the prince who broke it. "Lady Desean, you can't be serious!"

"I'm quite serious, your highness."

"But that's . . . barbaric!"

"It's also liable to be very effective. This man is very likely a Caelish spy, sent here to cause trouble as some sort of retribution for our refusal of Princess Nyah as your consort. As it was Stellan who delivered news of the refusal to the Caelish queen, it makes sense that any attempt at evening the score would start here in Lebec. But as well rehearsed as this man is, I suspect his story will change fairly quickly if he thinks we're serious about cutting off a few fingers so we can observe his immortality in action."

"And when we have to give him back?" Stellan said, a little less shocked than Mathu. But then, he knew her better. "How do we explain away his missing fingers?"

"Why do we have to give him back?" Mathu asked.

"Because if he's a spy, we can trade him for one of our spies the Caelish are holding."

The prince's eyes lit up. "We have *spies* in Caelum?"

"We have spies in a lot of places, Mathu," Stellan assured him.

Arkady sighed when she realised what Stellan was telling her. Mathu was still looking a little confused, however. "I don't understand."

"What my husband is saying is that if this man really is a Caelish spy, whatever we do to him, the same, or worse, will be done to our prisoners in Caelum."

"You mean, we beat their spy, they beat ours?"

"We amputate a few fingers, they do the same," Stellan confirmed with a nod.

"I'm sure it won't come to that, Stellan," Arkady assured him with more hope than conviction. "Can I at least threaten to do it?"

"What purpose would it serve?"

"If he thinks he might lose a few fingers, I fancy the Immortal Prince's story will change very smartly."

"And if he calls your bluff?"

"Then he loses his fingers." She shrugged.

"Which means you're not really bluffing, are you, your grace," Mathu pointed out with a grin. "I must say, I never realised how deliciously brutal you could be, Lady Desean. No wonder Stellan toes the line so diligently."

Arkady glanced at Stellan with a puzzled look. He smiled. "Mathu is a little surprised I had the strength of will to refuse the offer of one of his ladies of the night in Herino."

"I'm shocked you would even make such an offer, your highness," she declared in mock dismay. "Stellan is a married man."

"So I discovered, Lady Desean," he chuckled, finding nothing amiss in the situation. "And a very faithful one, too, I'm happy to report."

"Nonetheless, it was very naughty of you to suggest such a thing. Perhaps I should threaten to chop off a few of *your* fingers."

"I believe you'd do it, too," Mathu laughed. "But let's get back to this immortal of yours. Why not have him prove he's a magician by doing something magic?"

"Ah, now that's the true genius of his deception. According to our immortal, it's Low Tide."

"And Tide magic was supposed to be tidal, wasn't it?" Mathu said. "So until the Tide turns . . ."

"He's helpless," Arkady finished for him.

"Clever."

"But surely you can trip him up in other ways?" Stellan asked. "Declan Hawkes asked you to speak with him because of your knowledge of the Tide Lords, Arkady."

That news caught Mathu's interest. "Declan *Hawkes* is involved in this?"

Stellan glanced over his shoulder at the prince. "There's not much that goes on in Glaeba Declan Hawkes isn't involved in, Mathu. It would serve you well to remember that the next time you feel like doing something foolish."

"My knowledge is gleaned from Crasii legends," she explained. "Their histories don't relate to specifics about individual Tide Lords. It's sad to think so, but Tilly Ponting's wretched Tarot gives more detail about the Tide Lords themselves than anything in the Crasii legends I've been able to drag out of the few willing to share their oral histories with me."

"Isn't that where your Caelish Tide Lord would have learned it too?" Mathu asked.

Arkady nodded. "That's what Tilly suggested."

"Then perhaps you should check Cayal's story against

her Tarot first, Arkady," her husband suggested, "*before* we start torturing and mutilating prisoners?"

"Chopping off his pinkie will be quicker, dear."

Stellan smiled. "Mathu was right. You *are* a barbarian."

Arkady wasn't amused. "I'm more worried for my professional reputation. I find the notion of confronting our prisoner with a Tarot card I borrowed from an eccentric widow with purple hair more than a little disturbing, not to mention so scientifically unsound it doesn't bear thinking about."

"Nevertheless, Arkady, I'd rather you eliminated that option before you take to him with a scalpel."

Stellan had that intransigent look about him that Arkady knew well. She had no chance of winning this argument. She sighed in defeat. "Then I shall drag this charade on for a little while longer, shall I? Quiz our immortal with that unimpeachable historical record, the Tide Lord Tarot, as my only resource? I'm certain to trip him up *that* way."

"Sarcasm does not become you, my dear."

"If it's any consolation, I'm on your side, Lady Desean," Mathu assured her cheerfully. "Chop off his filthy Caelish digits, I say!"

"Fortunately, you don't have a say in this, Mathu," Stellan remarked, frowning up at the young man.

"Pity," Arkady said, rising to her feet. "I have to go, I'm afraid. If I'm going to rip our clever spy's story to shreds using nothing but a deck of cards, I'm going to need to speak to Tilly on the way to the prison this morning."

"And you won't be amputating *anything* without my express permission, will you, dear?" Stellan said in a tone that displayed a disturbing lack of trust in her intentions.

Arkady hesitated before answering, and when she finally did agree, it was with a great deal of reluctance. "If you insist."

"I do."

She smiled at Mathu. "And you thought Reon *Debalkor* was a bore?"

"You can leave us *now,* Arkady," Stellan suggested, his good humour starting to fade.

"Yes, dear."

"Will you tell us all about it at dinner, your grace?" Mathu asked.

"Every riveting word of his confession, your highness," she promised. She glared at Stellan. "The confession I plan to scare out of our devilish Caelish spy with the judicious use of a Tarot card."

"Good*bye,* Arkady."

"Stellan," she said with an elegant curtsey. "Your highness."

Her husband made no further comment as she left the room, slamming the door ever so slightly on the way out, the only outward expression of her irritation.

Chapter 18

Warlock had discovered that, among the less obvious drawbacks of incarceration, he wasn't allowed— for obvious reasons—a file with which to trim his nails. Left unattended they would grow and curl until his fingers became all but unusable. Out in the wider world, he'd always been able to file his nails down whenever they began to grow too long. Lacking a rasp, however, he was left with no choice but to use the rough granite wall to keep his nails trimmed. It was a slow and laborious process and he spent hours at it every other day, slowly wearing down his claws against the stone in a rhythmic, hypnotic motion that left his mind free to wander. And wander it did, usually outside these dreary prison walls to a place and time much happier than here.

"Tides, how long can you keep up that infernal scraping!" Cayal complained from across the corridor.

That was the other advantage of filing his nails against the stone. It drove the suzerain to distraction.

He glanced across the hall and bared his teeth in the gloom. "Long as I have to."

The suzerain was sitting on his pallet, leaning against the wall. He glared balefully at Warlock. "Come High Tide, I intend to do something about you, gemang."

"Would that be before or *after* I've licked your arse?" Warlock enquired.

"If you *don't* do what I command," Cayal warned, "I'll have your filthy Scard corpse fed to the ravens."

"You think I'm a Scard?" Warlock asked, abandoning his nail filing to squint at the suzerain curiously. The word was slang, short for "discard." The discarded Crasii who didn't work out the way the Tide Lords planned, their foremost fault being the lack of any compulsion the suzerain had instilled in all their magically wrought slaves to obey their masters blindly and without hesitation. Of course, they'd killed any Scards they found without mercy, but there were some who'd escaped, smart enough not to let on that their obedience was merely a way of disguising their true natures until they had a chance to break free.

He was planning to ask Cayal more, ask why the suzerain thought he was a Scard, when he caught a whiff of perfume. Long before they heard her footsteps on the flagstones, Warlock knew Lady Desean was coming for her daily interrogation of Cayal. He could smell the strange human scent of her—jasmine soap mixed with clean sweat mixed with a hint of musky perfume mixed with a whisper of fear.

And desire.

The duchess probably wasn't even aware of *that* emotion, but Warlock could tell. On some level, certainly not a conscious one, something about the suzerain called to the baser side of Arkady Desean. *Cayal is a mystery and perhaps she finds that enticing?* Or maybe it was simply human weakness. The Tide Lords were very good at manipulating people. Even without Tide Magic to aid him, Cayal had had eight thousand years to polish his seduction technique.

"Your visitor is here."

Cayal sat up straighter. "How can you tell?"

"I can smell her."

"What does she smell like to you?" the suzerain asked as he climbed to his feet.

"A human," Warlock replied unhelpfully.

Cayal smiled. "A canine with a sense of humour, eh? There's something they didn't plan to breed into your line, I'll wager. What's your pedigree, anyway?"

"Why do you care?"

"I'm curious." Cayal shrugged, leaning on the bars to stare at him across the hall. "Besides, if you turn out to be a Scard, once the Tide turns, I'll be rooting out every pitiful bastard pup in your line and destroying him."

"I am Warlock, out of Bella, by Segura," he informed him proudly. "And there aren't enough of you to destroy my line, suzerain."

"Don't be too sure about that," Cayal warned. "It could take some time, granted, but we suzerain are quite fond of ventures that take a lot of time. Helps alleviate the boredom, you see."

Warlock couldn't help himself—he smiled. "Is *that* why you're here rotting in a Glaeban gaol? To alleviate the boredom?"

"I've done stranger things for lesser reason." Cayal shrugged.

Their visitor's footsteps were audible now, even to someone without the benefit of canine hearing. Cayal and Warlock waited for a few moments and then she appeared, bringing with her the only bright spot in the day of both the Tide Lord and the Crasii.

Arkady was wearing much the same as always, a long grey skirt and matching jacket, cinched at the waist and trimmed in velvet, over a high-collared white blouse adorned with delicate pintucking and small pearl buttons down the front. She was—as usual—carrying the battered leather satchel where she kept her notebook.

This woman dresses to hide her beauty, he thought.

Warlock knew quite a lot about women's fashion. His mother had been a seamstress of some note in the service of Lady Bellobrina when he was a pup. He knew what women—particularly human women—wore when they were trying to attract a mate. The Duchess of Lebec dressed as if she was trying to drive them away. And yet he could smell the latent lust on her and it didn't match her outward appearance at all. She was a puzzle, this duchess who knew about the histories of the Crasii; this well-educated noblewoman who seemed to care about his kind far more than the average human. He wished, sometimes, that she were here to interrogate him and not that arrogant suzerain across the way.

"Good morning, Cayal. Warlock."

"Your grace," the Crasii replied politely. "Is it raining again?"

"Yes, it is," she informed him. "Can you hear it in here?"

"I can smell it."

She nodded and turned to look at Cayal. The suzerain was still leaning against the bars, watching her like a cat watches its prey while it debates the most entertaining way to torment it.

"Lady Desean."

"Cayal."

"What trick questions do you have for me today?" he asked. "Did you want to know what we do for fun? What immortals eat? Why we even bother to eat, given we're never going to die of starvation? Or thirst."

"Do you know that for certain?" Arkady asked, curiously.

Cayal nodded. "Even tried it once. I got hungry and I got thirsty, but nothing much else happened. Didn't even lose weight. Did you know there are no fat immortals?" he added. "There're no skinny ones, either. Arryl speculates it's because immortality forces one's body into its optimum configuration and keeps it there. More efficient, that way, you see, and if nature is anything, it's efficient."

"Arryl," Arkady said, opening her satchel. "Arryl, the Sorceress. She's the one who convinced you to become immortal, isn't she?"

"*Convinced*?" Cayal repeated. "Don't know that I needed much convincing. Immortality seemed like a rather attractive prospect once, but no, she wasn't instrumental in my transition from mere mortality to this . . . higher plane of existence."

"You'd think," Warlock remarked from the gloomy depths of his cell, "that your higher plane of existence might have come better equipped than this."

Arkady glanced at him with a smile. "I was thinking much the same thing, Warlock."

Cayal's expression soured. "Oh, the world is just full of jesters this morning, isn't it?"

"If you think that's funny, wait until I show you this." She put down the satchel and moved the chair a little closer to Cayal's bars, before taking a seat. She had something in her hands that at first glance, Warlock thought was a small book. Then she began to fan the pages out and he realised it wasn't a book, but a deck of cards.

"We're going to play cards?" Cayal asked, obviously as puzzled as Warlock.

Arkady shook her head. "These aren't playing cards."

"What are they, then?"

"The Tide Lord Tarot."

Cayal burst out laughing. "You're kidding!"

"This is all that's left of you and your kind, Cayal," she mocked. "This is it. The historical record of the immortals. Quite pitiful, don't you think, to realise how the mighty have fallen so low?"

"Those cards are a load of superstitious old twaddle," the suzerain scoffed.

"You're familiar with them, then?"

"I've been around for a long time, Arkady. There's not a lot I *haven't* seen."

"My friend . . . the one who's expert in such things, says these cards tell the true story of the immortals."

"Your *expert* friend is an idiot, if he thinks that."

Arkady held up one of the cards for Cayal to see. "The first card of the Tarot, I'm led to believe. This is Cayal, the Immortal Prince. Here he is dressed in his colourful but ragged clothes, carrying a magnifying glass, a cat at his heels, a palace on a mountain in the background, a sun . . ."

"None of it is true," Cayal objected.

The duchess was undeterred by his scorn. "According to Tarot legend, Cayal, the Immortal Prince, travelled the world endlessly in search of happiness and fulfilment. What was the magnifying glass for by the way? Tilly couldn't answer that."

"It's all nonsense," Cayal insisted.

"The second card is the Sorceress," Arkady continued. She seemed amused by Cayal's reaction, rather than discouraged by it. "According to the Tarot, the next person you meet on your journey is Arryl." The duchess consulted her notebook in her lap and began to read from it. "Possessed by the spirit of the Tide Star, Arryl raises one hand to the sun, and pointing the other at the ground, the Sorceress calls upon the power of the Tide Star. Magically, the ground opens up at Cayal's feet. In front of the Immortal Prince are all the possibilities in the universe laid out before him; all the directions he can take, every alternate reality . . ."

"What are you trying to prove?" Cayal cut in impatiently.

"That you're immortal," Arkady replied pleasantly. "I thought you'd be glad to help."

"This is ridiculous!"

"And claiming you're immortal *isn't*?" she countered with a raised brow. "Let's look at the third card, shall we. Diala. The High Priestess."

"Spare me!" Cayal groaned, turning his back on her.

"Continuing his journey," Arkady read from her notes, "the Immortal Prince comes upon a mysterious veiled lady lying on a bed set between two pillars and illuminated by the Tide Star. She is the soul sister of the Sorceress . . ."

"She's a slut," Cayal corrected sourly.

". . . seductive rather than persuasive, enticing rather than convincing. She uses her body where the Sorceress uses her mind to entrap the unwary . . ."

"As I said: a slut."

Arkady kept on reading. Warlock was certain she was doing it to aggravate him. *What strange games these humans play.*

"She is the High Priestess," the duchess read on, "and she amazes Cayal by knowing everything there is to know about him: his thoughts, his hopes, his dreams *and* his sins. *'Since you know all my innermost secrets, my lady, perhaps you can guide me?'* he asks, sitting beside her on the bed. *'The Sorceress showed me the myriad paths to infinite possibilities, but I don't know which road to take.'* In answer, the High Priestess produces an ancient scroll. *'Everything you need to know is contained in this scroll, but you must give me something in return.'* *'What do you want?'* Cayal asks. *'Your undivided attention.'* So, seating himself at her feet, the Immortal Prince listens to the High Priestess as she reads to him by the light of the Tide Star. When she is done, Cayal understands which path he must take—"

"Oh, for the Tide's sake, will you stop!" Cayal cried.

Arkady looked at him in surprise. "Why, Cayal? I thought you'd be delighted to know your history has been so diligently preserved."

"That's not my history!" he snapped. "It's a fairytale. It happened nothing like that!"

"*It* being you becoming an immortal, I suppose?" Arkady asked. "How *did* it happen, then, if the Tarot is so wrong?"

He turned to glare at her, his blue eyes blazing. From his cell across the hall, Warlock rose to his feet, sensing a danger in him that he hadn't previously felt. Even Arkady could feel it. When she spoke again, her voice was gentle, conciliatory, soothing . . .

"Tell me the truth, then, Cayal."

"What would be the point? You don't believe me."

"I'll believe the truth."

Cayal paced his cell, debating something within himself, and then suddenly he turned and grabbed the bars. "You really want to know, do you? *Really*? The truth?"

Arkady nodded. "The truth."

"Then you'd better get comfortable," he warned. "It's a very long story . . ."

Chapter 19

I f I had to point to a single incident—the one deed that set me on this path—it was the moment I killed Orin, son of Thraxis, in a duel defending the honour of some girl I'd never met until a few hours before and whose name, to this day, I still don't know.

I remember what caused the fight well enough. We'd been sheltering from a blizzard in Dun Cinczi on our way to Lakesh, me and two of my older brothers. We were on our way home for a wedding. My wedding. I was twenty-six years old and only two days away from marrying the love of my life, Gabriella of Kippen, and I resented every moment of the damned blizzard that forced us to break our journey.

Dun Cinczi was tucked into a small valley in the Hotendenish Mountains in northern Kordana. It belonged to a vassal of my sister, Queen Planice. The lord of the dun, Thraxis, was happy to open his hearth to travellers caught by the storm, particularly to those related to his queen. I was only a younger brother—there were eight older siblings between me and the throne—but we were near enough to the seat of power for Thraxis to treat us as honoured guests.

Thraxis's only son, Orin, and I had been friends since childhood, so we settled in for a pleasant evening around a blazing hearth quaffing vast quantities of mead with my brothers and the other men of the dun while the blizzard raged outside. From what I remember of it, the night turned into an impromptu bachelor party. Everyone was in fine spirits, boasting of their hunting triumphs and bragging about their conquests—highly exaggerated, I'm sure—of the opposite sex.

Orin was in the midst of one such lengthy and highly improbable boast when the last of the night's travellers blew in. I remember looking up as a gust of icy wind announced the arrival of a nervous young couple, bundled up in ragged furs.

Tides, it could get cold in Kordana . . .

The chilly blast was cut off as the door was slammed shut and we all turned to study the newcomers. They looked tired and wary of a hearth full of drunken strangers. The husband seemed particularly protective of his wife, who was unmistakably in the late stages of pregnancy. With a belly almost swelled to bursting and clearly fatigued from her journey, we made room for her around the fire as Thraxis's wife hurried in with a bowl of venison stew and a tumbler of what was—most likely—fermented mare's milk.

She ate her meal hungrily, the pregnant woman, sitting next to Orin, who studied her curiously for a moment and then placed his arm around her shoulder. We all thought he was just being kind, you know . . . offering her the warmth of his body to aid the fire in taking the blue from her lips. The woman might have been pretty; probably was, I suppose, given Orin's interest in her, but I couldn't say. I only remember her belly. And the furs.

Odd, isn't it? After all this time, how the little things still stick in your mind.

Anyway, the stories continued. The night wore on. We got drunker and the blizzard showed no sign of letting up. The young husband—I never learned his name, either—drank very little. He spent most of his time glaring at Orin, who was starting to act as if the wife was *his* woman.

Things came to a head when the young man rose to his

feet and announced he and his wife would retire for the evening. I think the pregnant woman made to rise, but Orin pulled her down again beside him. He made some drunken declaration about her knowing a *real* man when she saw one. And then he announced she'd decided to spend the night with him.

Thraxis, who was probably more inebriated than all the rest of us put together, laughed uproariously at the proclamation. It was proof, he bellowed drunkenly, of what a great man his son was. *Look at him!* the old drunkard chortled. *Her belly's already starting to swell, and he's only been sitting next to her!*

I must have been too drunk to notice the tension in the hall, at least until things had gotten completely out of hand. I still can't say what made me take notice. Perhaps it was the panicked look on the face of the young pregnant woman. It might have been watching Thraxis's wife trying to coax the girl from the fire, a move Orin thwarted by dragging the girl onto his lap as soon as he realised what his mother was doing.

It was at that point the husband tried to intervene.

Laughing at his objections, two of Thraxis's men held him back as he cried out, protesting Orin's possession of his wife. The young woman struggled, trying to get away, but she was held fast, despite her best efforts.

"*Help* me!" she begged, looking straight at me, as Orin pushed her down and began to tear at the furs in which she was swaddled. "For pity's sake, is there nobody here who'll help me?"

She screamed as Orin pushed the furs aside and ripped apart the laces on her shift, laughing as her heavy breasts were exposed.

Even with eight thousand years to wonder why, to this day, I still can't say what prompted me to intervene. I didn't know the girl and Orin was a lifelong friend. In hindsight, I doubt it was out of a sense of chivalry; in those days chivalry was a concept still foreign to humanity, something they took another few hundred years to think of. And it wasn't because

I considered taking a woman against her will to be particularly wrong. Although my fiancée had been lucky—my engagement to Gabriella was a love match that suited both families so it had been allowed to proceed—there weren't many wives in Kordana who'd gone willingly to their marriage bed. Stealing the woman of your dreams and taking her by force passed for a national sport in the country of my birth. There wasn't even a word for rape in the Kordian language.

But something in the voice of the pregnant woman struck a chord. Before I knew what I was doing, I was on my feet. "Leave her alone, Orin."

Orin took his mouth from her breast long enough to laugh at me. "Wait your turn, you greedy sod."

"I mean it, Orin. Let her be."

He looked up at me, astonished to realise I was serious. "Do you *challenge* me for her?"

"She's not yours to give or take, Orin," I remember saying, or something like it. I'm sure it sounded terribly noble to my mead-fogged mind.

Whatever I said, it was enough to infuriate Orin. He pushed the woman aside and staggered to his feet. Everyone scrambled clear as his mother dragged her out of the way while the other women started removing anything that might break—the inevitable result of two men disagreeing about anything around Thraxis's hearth.

"You want her . . . you're going to have to get past me first!" Orin declared, shaking his fist at me. Even then, I don't think I appreciated how serious he was.

Or how serious I was, too.

"I don't want her," I tried to explain, beginning to wonder—somewhere in the dark recesses of my addled brain—what I'd started. "And she obviously doesn't want you, either. Just let her be."

"You can't tell me what I can and can't have in my own father's hearth!"

"Orin, this isn't worth fighting over . . ."

Famous last words, I've often reflected in hindsight.

The details of the fight are still unclear. I was drunk. There were fists at first and not much damage being done, I think, given the amount of leather and fur we were both wearing . . .

And then I got in a lucky hit, belting Orin on the nose. I remember the spray of blood, Orin's howl of pain and outrage, the cheering circle of men, and the flickering light from the huge hearth, the smell of greased leathers, smoking timber and poorly cured furs . . . odd things like that. I remember Orin's furious bellow as he charged . . .

But I can't . . . not for the life of me . . . remember how the knife came to be in my hand.

Or how it finished up buried to the hilt in Orin's unmoving chest.

Shocked silence descended over the dun's hall when Orin fell. It wasn't as if nobody had ever shed blood on this hearth before. In winter, with the men cooped up and feeling fractious, it was almost a nightly occurrence in Dun Cinczi. But it was all in good fun. There were rarely any weapons involved.

Until tonight. I'd crossed that unspoken boundary, even if I couldn't recall exactly how I'd managed it.

My poor recall meant nothing to Thraxis. As Orin's mother fell to her knees beside her son, keening with despair, Thraxis roared out with the agony of his loss. The next thing I knew, I was being dragged from the hall and thrown into the icy meat store, the only door in Dun Cinczi with a lock on it.

I stayed there for three whole days, certain my punishment was freezing to death.

Solitude is an interesting companion. It is both enemy and friend, comforter and tormentor. I spent a lot of time in Dun Cinczi's meat locker trying to decide which. Fortunately, when I tired of solitude, I had guilt to keep me company. Guilt is an even more interesting acquaintance than solitude, let me tell you. Solitude is a harsh but essentially benign attendant. Guilt, on the other hand, is a living, breathing creature, cruel and remorseless. It eats you from the inside out; devours what little hope you have left. It feeds on you, growing stronger with every accursed replayed memory, every useless recrimination.

My guilt was a tangible thing, tinged with inescapable grief, Orin was my friend and I had killed him over some woman. What was I thinking? I didn't know her. There weren't words to describe how little she meant to me. Yet Orin was dead because I had leapt to the defence of a complete stranger. My stupidity was breathtaking, my guilt overwhelming, my future uncertain, every day spent in this icy meat locker another day closer to dying—I was convinced—either at the hand of Thraxis or of hypothermia, the former almost a welcome prospect given the nature of my confinement.

But death would have been too easy. The Tides had a far crueller fate in store for me, although it would be a while yet before I discovered it. The ultimate irony, of course, is that I would welcome it when it finally came, too foolish to recognise the danger.

So I froze, and I paced the small space between the hanging carcasses, and I fretted endlessly and on the fourth day, the door opened.

When I saw the silhouette standing there, I knew my life was in mortal peril. My guilt meant nothing. My remorse meant even less.

Orin's death would be avenged with mine, I was certain, and there was probably nothing I could do to prevent it.

Chapter 20

"Your grace?"

Arkady started at the unexpected interruption. She glanced over her shoulder to find Timms standing behind her.

"The Warden would like to see you, your grace."

It took her a moment to register what Timms was saying. Arkady stared at him blankly, still caught up in Cayal's tale. "Um . . . er . . . of course . . ."

"Your grace?" Timms asked, looking rather concerned.

"Her ladyship seems a little confused," Cayal noted.

Arkady forced herself to concentrate. Unbelievably, it was almost sunset. She rose to her feet, stuffing her notebook back in her satchel before Timms or Cayal had any chance to see it. The notebook was a waste of time anyway. She'd stopped taking notes about the time Cayal rose to defend the young pregnant woman, but didn't want either the prisoner or his guard to know that. So she smiled condescendingly at the prisoner and said, "You missed your calling, I suspect, Cayal. You should have been a bard."

Leaning on the bars, he eyed her curiously. "You didn't believe a word of that, did you?"

"It's certainly a fantastic tale," she conceded.

"Why not ask your living lie detector over there," he suggested, jerking his head in Warlock's direction. "Ask *him* if I'm lying."

Arkady didn't want to ask Warlock's opinion, because she was fairly sure she knew what it would be. "A five-year-old could tell you're lying, Cayal. But you do weave a magical tale. Perhaps tomorrow," she suggested, pushing the chair to one side after she'd put Tilly's Tarot cards away in the satchel next to the almost empty notebook, "we can hear the rest of your remarkable story."

"I've been around a very long time, Arkady," he reminded her. "It's going to take more than a couple of leisurely afternoons to tell you about *my* life."

"Then let's hope the hangman is patient," she suggested frostily. It made her uncomfortable when he addressed her by name, but she usually ignored it, certain remarking on his rudeness would only give him more ammunition. It was a subtle if silent battle she was engaged in with Cayal, the Immortal Prince. She had no intention of arming him with anything he might use against her.

"I'll see you gentlemen tomorrow, shall I?"

"You tell us," Cayal replied, studying her closely, almost as if he could tell what she was thinking. "You're the one with the freedom to come and go as you please."

"Then I *will* see you tomorrow," Arkady assured him, and then she turned on her heel and followed Timms as fast as she was able without actually breaking into a run.

As instructed by the Crown Prince of Glaeba, Arkady was required to repeat the essence of Cayal's tale over the dinner table that night. There was no dinner party this evening, but Stellan, Jaxyn, Mathu and Kylia were all in attendance, so she gave them an abbreviated version. She told herself she was censoring the story for the sake of a good narrative, but she wasn't. Arkady didn't really want to share the details. Cayal had told his story to her. It wasn't meant for strangers' ears.

"So," Stellan concluded when Arkady had finished telling her story. "He tells you just enough to make it seem real, without giving you anything you can verify or even deny. Our spy has been well coached."

"A little too well, I fear," she replied, frowning as she sipped her water.

"What do you mean?"

She shrugged, not sure how to put her concerns into words. "If this man is a Caelish agent—if he's been sent here to stir up the Crasii—you'd think his tale would follow the known histories more closely."

"I thought the problem was that we don't actually *have* any proper histories of the Tide Lords?" Mathu said.

"Which is exactly my point, your highness," Arkady agreed. "The Crasii oral history doesn't deal in specifics, so given the dearth of factual information, if he wanted to prove his claim, logically, his story *should* follow the Tarot—the only known record besides the Crasii—as closely as possible. But it doesn't. There's a seed of truth in his tale, perhaps, but nothing more. And he speaks as if it really happened to him. It's unnerving."

"Have you considered the possibility that he's insane?" Mathu asked. "Perhaps it sounds so real because he truly believes it?"

"Or the Caelish are more sophisticated than we give them credit for," Stellan suggested. "Perhaps our spy is spinning a somewhat different tale to make it seem real, knowing any other path would be suspect."

"Do you think he's handsome, Arkady?" Kylia asked.

Mathu glanced at her curiously. "Why do you assume he must be handsome, Lady Kylia?"

"Well . . . he's a Tide Lord . . . or claiming to be one. I thought they were all supposed to be outstanding beauties."

"He's obviously outstanding at something," Stellan chuckled, dabbing his mouth with his napkin. "But I'm not sure it's his looks that deserve the credit."

"What would you know, Uncle Stellan?" Kylia said dismissively. "You're a man. You don't know what handsome is."

Jaxyn laughed aloud at Kylia's declaration. "You're absolutely right, my lady. What would a big, ugly brute like your uncle know about what makes a man attractive, eh?"

It really should be legal to murder someone like Jaxyn Aranville, Arkady noted darkly. Everybody laughed, of course. Kylia—and fortunately Mathu—had no idea that Jaxyn meant anything other than exactly what he said.

Completely oblivious to his double meaning, the young woman turned to her, grinning broadly. "Well . . . what do you say, Arkady? Is this Caelishman handsome enough to be a Tide Lord?"

Arkady shrugged. "I suppose."

"You mean you haven't noticed?" Jaxyn gasped in mock alarm. "How unobservant of you, your grace! And here you are doing all this remarkable intelligence work for the King's Spymaster and you haven't even taken the time to notice what our Caelish spy looks like? I'm shocked."

Arkady smiled. "You're right, Jaxyn, I should pay more attention. And now I come to think of it, he is very handsome. Compared to you, at any rate."

Everyone laughed at Arkady's retort, even Jaxyn, but she could tell he was less than amused by it. Their eyes met across the table for a moment, the look he gave her one of pure venom.

Don't try engaging in a battle of wits with me, Jaxyn Aranville, she warned him silently as she smiled at him just as poisonously.

"Are you going to visit him again, Arkady?" Kylia asked, entranced by all this talk of mystery and espionage.

"I must, I'm afraid, Kylia." She looked up at Stellan and added with a smile, "Your uncle won't let me chop one of our immortal's hands off to see if it grows back, so I'm going to have to do this the hard way."

"Eeeuw!" Kylia exclaimed. "That's revolting!"

"Your aunt can be very revolting," Jaxyn agreed, toasting Arkady mockingly with his wineglass. "Don't you agree, Stellan, that you find some things about your lovely wife revolting?"

"You're right, Jaxyn," Stellan replied, refusing to be drawn into Jaxyn's idiotic game. "I only like revolting women."

Kylia frowned. "Does that mean you think I'm revolting, too, Uncle Stellan?"

"Of course I don't, Kylia," he assured her. "I was just making fun of Jaxyn."

"It sounded more like you were making fun of me. And Arkady."

"Would I make fun of my favourite girl?"

Kylia looked surprised. "Isn't Arkady your favourite?"

Stellan shook his head, smiling at his niece. "She wants to chop people's limbs off. You're much better company."

Apparently Kylia wasn't the sort to stay depressed for long. She smiled and looked across the table at Arkady. "Do you mind that Uncle Stellan says I'm his favourite, Arkady?"

"Of course I mind," Arkady replied calmly, reaching for the cream. "I shall have to wait until he's asleep tonight and chop off one of *his* limbs unless he begs my forgiveness immediately."

"You'd better apologise, cousin," Mathu warned with a chuckle. "I think she's serious."

Everyone laughed again and the conversation soon moved on to safer topics. Arkady didn't really notice, eating her dessert without registering what it was, her mind still swirling with the images Cayal had evoked of a daring young man, noble and honourable enough to risk his life to defend the honour of a woman he'd never met before and would never meet again.

Chapter 21

Much later that evening, Stellan went looking for his wife, finding her eventually in her bedroom, sitting cross-legged on the large carved bed, squinting in the lamplight, the quilt covered in scraps of paper. She had let down her long hair, her blouse was open at the neck, there was a pencil stuck behind her left ear and she was frowning over something she was reading.

She glanced up when he let himself in, smiling distractedly. "Come for your regular conjugal visit, husband?"

"Let's hope that's what the servants think," he said, locking the door behind him out of long habit.

"Then you'd better stay awhile," she suggested, returning her attention to her papers. "To make it look plausible."

He walked across the room to the bed and sat down on the end of it, leaning back against the heavily carved pillar holding up the rich brocaded canopy, careful not to disturb her carefully laid out notes. "What are you doing?"

"Going through my notes on Cay . . . our prisoner. I didn't have time earlier."

He studied her curiously. "This man disturbs you, doesn't he?"

She hesitated, put down the paper she was reading and looked at him. "More than I'd like to admit, actually. How did you know?"

"I know *you,* Arkady."

"Then maybe *you* can tell me why he bothers me so much."

"Is it really because you think he's a Caelish agent?"

She shrugged. "I'm starting to hope he is."

"Why?"

"Because the alternative is too horrible to contemplate."

Stellan laughed. "Surely you're not starting to believe he's actually immortal?"

"Of course not!" she said. "But Mathu raised a very good point at dinner. Cayal might just be insane."

Stellan shrugged, not sure he understood her problem. "Then we'll have it made a legal judgement, confine him to an asylum and that's the end of it."

"Cayal doesn't belong in an asylum, Stellan. I'm not sure where he belongs, mind you, but he doesn't deserve anything so brutal."

"He killed seven people, Arkady. Surely you haven't forgotten that?"

"No," she snapped, a little too defensively. "I haven't forgotten that."

He looked at her in concern. "Perhaps you should stop visiting the prison. It's obvious this is upsetting you. I'll tell Hawkes to find someone else to do his dirty work for him."

She shook her head, smiling, probably in an attempt to reassure him. "For the sake of Glaeba, I must get to the bottom of the mystery that is Cayal, the Immortal Prince," she said. "Besides, I won't sleep well again until I figure him out, I'm quite certain."

He leaned forward and picked up the stack of gilt-edged cards sitting on the covers near the edge of the bed. "Tilly's Tarot?"

"The very same."

"Does the prisoner seem familiar with the cards?"

"He seems familiar with the people they represent," she corrected. "That's what makes him so scary. I wish you could speak to him."

Stellan shook his head. "It's bad enough Declan Hawkes got involved. Until we're certain he's not been sent here by the Caelish queen, I don't want to be seen paying Kyle Lakesh any more attention than he deserves. The prisons are the Prefect's direct responsibility, not mine, and if people think I'm taking more than a passing interest in them, it will be . . . noticed."

"But still, if you could speak to this man . . ."

Stellan shook his head firmly. "You can visit him and it seems odd. *I* visit him and there'll be rumours flying all over Lebec within hours. Hawkes is still on the case, if it's any comfort. He's making enquiries in Caelum. We should know something in a few weeks."

"A few *weeks*?"

"You can stop seeing him any time you want, Arkady."

She shook her head. "No, it's all right. I'm tougher than some madman who thinks he's immortal."

Stellan smiled. "I've no doubt about that. Do you think I've stayed long enough to satisfy the downstairs gossips?"

"I'm more concerned about the upstairs ones. You really must have a word to Jaxyn, Stellan. He was behaving like an idiot at dinner."

"He doesn't mean any harm, Arkady."

"Oh, yes, he *does*," she disagreed, returning her attention to her notes.

"I'll speak to him," he promised, wondering if there would ever come a time when Arkady would accept Jaxyn. She'd never reacted to any of his other lovers in such a fashion. Maybe fear inspired her angst. He'd had lovers before, but they'd come and gone without disturbing the equilibrium. Jaxyn was different; he'd lasted longer, been more a part of their lives than any of the others. Stellan knew, as Arkady did, that Jaxyn was trading on their relationship to keep himself in the manner to which he had become accustomed, but unlike his wife, he felt he could see the good in the young man, and had hopes that love would prevail. "Has he said anything to you?"

"About what?"

"I was talking to him about my lack of an heir."

"Was that wise?"

Stellan shrugged. "It's not like Jaxyn doesn't know my deep, dark secret, dear."

"True enough."

"He suggested *he* might be willing to father an heir for me."

Arkady didn't even look up from her papers. "I hope you told him I'd rather have rusty needles stuck in my eyeballs."

"Actually, I told him to go ahead and try."

This time she did look up at him. "You *cannot* be serious."

He smiled. "I told him he'd have no chance with you, of course." His smile faded, and he added quite seriously, "But with Mathu in the house, I thought it might be prudent if Jaxyn had his attention fixed on you for a while."

Arkady raised a brow at him. "You set your lover onto me to avert suspicion from you? There's a marriage vow I don't remember making."

"Mathu would be displeased, my dear, but it would not cost us the duchy if he thought you were having an affair with Jaxyn Aranville. I doubt he'd be as understanding if he learned of my indiscretions."

"Then send Jaxyn away, Stellan. That's the logical solution."

"Love is never logical, Arkady."

"A truism you seem determined to prove."

He smiled at her hopefully. "Will you be nice to him? For me?"

"Define *nice.*"

"No slapping his face or kneeing him in the groin if he makes a pass at you. No chopping off limbs . . . that sort of thing."

She hesitated, making a great show of considering her answer.

"Arkady. . . ."

"Oh, very well," she agreed with ill grace. "If I must."

"You must."

She sighed heavily. "Then I shall allow your lover to make eyes at me and amuse myself with bloodthirsty thoughts of what I'd *like* to do to him, rather than putting them into practice."

"You really are the perfect wife, you know," he told her, rising to his feet.

"Just keep telling yourself that, dear."

He smiled, and leaned down to kiss the top of her head. "I'll see you in the morning."

"Are you going somewhere?"

"Mathu's found a Scard fight going on in town. It starts at midnight. Not my idea of entertainment, but at least if I'm with him, he's less likely to get into trouble."

"He's been here barely a week!" she exclaimed. "How does he find out about these things?"

"I think Jaxyn had a hand in it."

"There's a surprise."

"Goodnight, Arkady."

"Goodnight, Stellan."

He left Arkady on the bed, closing the door softly behind

him, her attention already back on her notes so completely that she didn't even look up when he left the room.

The Scard fight that Jaxyn and Mathu had found in Lebec was in a lakeside warehouse disturbingly reminiscent of the Friendly Futtock in Herino. In the centre of the torch-lit building was a rough wooden enclosure constructed to contain the fighters, with a floor covered in sawdust. Stellan looked around the crowded warehouse and then studied the arena where a post was set in the ground in the centre of the pit. The bear would be chained by the leg when it was brought out, Stellan knew, which enabled it to reach almost, but not quite, to the edge of the arena. The much smaller Crasii would then be let loose and would stay in the arena until one of them was dead.

The fight organisers had arranged tiered seating, giving everyone a clear view. The seats were filled to capacity, the lesser bouts having started earlier.

When the doorman realised the three noblemen seeking entry were the Duke of Lebec and two of his friends, less worthy patrons were shoved aside to make room for them ringside. Nobody recognised Mathu, but Jaxyn was certainly well known here, returning more than one cheerful greeting from among the exclusively male audience. The bookmakers were particularly pleased to see them. With noblemen came the prospect of far larger wagers than usual, from men who could afford to gamble.

"Who's fighting?" Mathu asked, leaning over the chest-high barricade to examine the arena. The sawdust was clumped in places, Stellan noticed, no doubt the result of blood spilt during previous bouts this evening. They'd arrived in time for the main event, rather than come earlier. Even Jaxyn bored easily when the only things on offer were fighting cocks and rabid dogs.

"The main event is a Jelidian snow bear against a feline Crasii," Jaxyn told them. "I'm wagering fifty silver fenets on the bear."

"Hardly seems a fair fight," Stellan remarked. Jelidian

snow bears were uncommon in Glaeba. Prized as much for their stark white fur as their entertainment value, the beasts were huge, standing eight feet tall on their hind legs. The largest feline Crasii Stellan had ever seen was barely five feet tall.

He didn't think it would be much of a battle. Feline Crasii were common enough, and this one was probably a criminal of some description, no doubt sold by the courts to make reparation for her crimes. A Jelidian snow bear, on the other hand, was a very expensive investment. Stellan doubted there was much risk involved for the bear.

"Are we wagering on the outcome or how long the fight lasts?" Mathu enquired, obviously of the same mind as Stellan.

"Whichever you prefer," Jaxyn assured them. "The bookies will give you odds on either."

Mathu looked at Stellan, shaking his head. "I wager a minute flat before the bear is chewing on the Scard's thigh bone."

"That long?" Stellan chuckled, as the master of ceremonies began to ring the small brass bell near the barred entrance across the arena, which presumably led to the cages out back. The crowd sat forward in their seats in anticipation as a ferrety little man with an avaricious gleam in his eye hurried across the sawdust to where Stellan, Mathu and Jaxyn were sitting, to enquire about their wagers.

"May we inspect this Scard before we decide who has the better chance?" Stellan asked.

"She is a fearsome creature, your grace," the man assured him. "You can wager on her with every assurance of collecting on your winnings."

"But I can't see her until *after* I've placed my bet?"

"Those are the house rules, your grace."

"With rules such as those, it's a wonder you can't afford a better house."

The man smiled, revealing a row of broken, brown teeth. "One has to make a living, your grace."

"Something you need to remain in my good graces to

do, sir, if you intend to continue making this living of yours in *my* city," the duke pointed out pleasantly.

The man wasn't stupid. He bowed his head and pointed to the barred gate. "Perhaps for you, my lord, a private showing might be arranged, yes?"

"I thought you'd see things my way."

"But *only* you, your grace," the man added, looking pointedly at Jaxyn and Mathu. "Not your friends."

It was dim in the rooms beyond the arena, stinking of stale urine and fear. The ferrety little bookie led him past cages full of fighting dogs and cocks wounded from the evening's earlier fights. The place set Stellan's teeth on edge. Animals whimpered as they passed the cages, in pain and fear, or snarled at them for the same reasons. Finally, Stellan and the bookie reached two much larger cages in the back of the warehouse. The one on the left housed a magnificent snow bear, easily the largest creature Stellan had ever laid eyes on. It prowled back and forth across the wheeled cage as if it couldn't wait to be unleashed, the chain around its leg rasping metallically against the bars. The handlers were getting ready to release the beast, manoeuvring the cage toward the arena. He studied the snow bear for a moment, frowning, wondering what hope any living creature had against such power.

"They've been starving it for days," a female voice informed him from the cage on the right.

Stellan turned to look at the Crasii, shocked at how human she appeared. Feline Crasii usually looked more cat than any other creature, but this one's pelt was ginger and so fine that from a distance it seemed no different from tanned human skin. Her body was unmistakably that of a human female, her green eyes were slanted, her nose flat, her ears pointed, but her fingers and toes ended in retractable claws that could open a man from throat to belly in a single swipe. She had two pert, human-like breasts that showed no sign of ever having borne milk, the line of fallow nipples beneath them under her fur invisible in the dim light. As she stepped up to the bars, he noticed her slender, muscular tail whipping back and forth impatiently. She was tall for a feline, perhaps five foot two, and there was no fear in her demeanour, even though she clearly knew what she was about to face.

"Can you defeat it?" he asked her, wondering if she was as confident as she seemed.

The Crasii shrugged. "What would be the point?"

"To go on living?" Stellan suggested.

"So that weasel can make me fight again in a month when I'm recovered?" she asked, glaring at Stellan's companion. "I'd rather be put out of my misery now."

"Everyone is wagering on the bear."

"Then they'll win," she replied, apparently unconcerned.

"What's your name?"

"Chikita," she replied proudly. "Out of Kamira, by Taryx."

Stellan's eyes widened in surprise. This Crasii's pedigree was impeccable. Not the sort you'd expect to find in a place like this. "You're one of Taryx's cubs?"

"You've heard of him?"

I own him, Stellan was tempted to reply, but he wasn't sure how she would react to such news. Instead, he nodded. "I have several of your siblings in my service."

Chikita shrugged. "Tell them I said hello. Just before a snow bear ripped me to shreds."

"It's time to go, your grace," the bookie insisted. "The other patrons grow impatient."

"Let them wait," Stellan told the man, and then turned back to Chikita, intrigued how such a pedigreed feline had fallen so low. "If you had sufficient incentive," he asked curiously, "could you take him?"

"That stupid bear? In three minutes flat," Chikita assured him.

It was an unlikely boast, but the feline's confidence might

not be misplaced, Stellan thought, given her line. "I'll wager a hundred gold fenets on the Crasii," he told the bookie.

"The odds on Chikita winning are one hundred to one, your grace," the man informed him with a frown. "If she wins, that would break the house."

"No need to break the house," Stellan said. "If she wins, I'll take her off your hands. A feline Crasii, even one able to take down a Jelidian snow bear, isn't worth anything near a thousand gold fenets. You'd be getting the better end of the deal."

Given that Stellan had the power to shut him down and run him out of the city on a whim, the man had little choice but to agree. He didn't seem too worried about the deal, however. He could only lose the bet if this feisty little Crasii defeated a snow bear. There was a sound reason the odds were a hundred to one *against* that happening.

"As you wish. It's your loss."

"There," Stellan announced, turning back to the Crasii. "If you beat the bear, you will belong to me and you won't have to fight in the arena again. Is that sufficient incentive for you?"

The Crasii looked him up and down with a disparaging glare. "I don't have to fight again, eh? Why? So you and your friends can sate your noble curiosity with a little bit of bestiality? Thanks, but I think I prefer a quick death at the hands of the bear."

This Crasii was lucky, Stellan thought, that he was married to a woman like Arkady, who'd taught him tolerance of the Crasii in a manner rare among his class. Any other man in his position would have had her run through for her temerity.

"Do you know who I am?"

"You keep slaves, so you're rich, that much is obvious. You're probably highborn. You may even be important."

"I am Stellan Desean. Duke of Lebec."

She seemed unimpressed. "Then I guessed right, didn't I?"

He sighed patiently. "If you win this fight, you will enter my service. As I have no interest in bestiality, that leaves me with little option but to place you in my guard, a position you are uniquely suited to and where I already have in excess of two hundred other feline Crasii slaves—some of which are members of your own family—all of whom seem quite content in my employ. Of course, if you'd rather die at the hands of a hungry snow bear for the entertainment of a warehouse full of bloodthirsty human gamblers, be my guest."

Stellan turned away. He had barely taken two steps before she called him back.

"Are you really the Duke of Lebec?"

He turned to look at her. "I am."

"Do you mean it? About joining your guard?"

"Yes, I mean it."

She thought about his offer for all of thirty seconds before she turned to the fight master, her ears, suddenly all smiles. "You'd better rethink your odds, you old swindler. I think I just found an incentive to go on living."

The man jerked his head in the direction of the snow bear, who was being wheeled toward the arena. He smiled knowingly. "It's not me you have to convince, kitten." He shrugged. "It's the bear."

Chapter 22

When it wasn't raining, Arkady often took breakfast on the terrace at the rear of the palace, overlooking the gardens. She loved the view of the lake, the crisp breeze that blew in off the water early in the day and the feeling that over all this, she was queen.

The day they married, Stellan had brought her out here on the terrace at sunset, after the guests had all left and they were finally alone. "You're effectively the Queen of Lebec, now, you know," he'd told her, putting his arm around her. "You're not going to make me regret this, are you, Lady Desean?"

"No," she assured him, still not used to her new title. "You've kept your end of the bargain, Stellan. I'll keep mine."

Stellan's end of the bargain had been a pardon for her father and his release from Lebec Prison as soon as they were married. A messenger had been dispatched with the appropriate paperwork from the wedding reception by her new husband as soon as the formalities were over. They were still waiting on word from the prison that he had been released. Arkady's side of the bargain had been to provide Stellan the appearance of a happy family life and eventually an heir.

As it turned out, neither of them had been able to fulfil their promise to the other.

Arkady's father had died before the messenger could deliver his release papers and six years later, through no fault of Arkady's, Stellan still had no son to inherit his title.

But they'd remained friends through all of it.

Two misfits with only the other to understand us, Arkady often thought. *Strange how these things work out.*

"All alone, your grace?"

Startled by the unexpected interruption, Arkady jumped to her feet as Mathu Debree climbed the steps leading down to the lawn, glad the young man couldn't read her thoughts. He was dressed in riding boots and a crumpled shirt and had obviously been out and about for some time this morning.

"Your royal highness!"

"Please," he urged, "don't get up on my account. I don't mean to disturb your breakfast. May I join you?"

"Of course," she said, pointing to the wrought-iron chair opposite hers on the other side of the small table. "Would you like something to eat?"

"I've eaten already," he assured her, taking the offered seat. "I was up early with your husband, riding around the estate. He had something else to check on so he asked me to meet him before we head down to the slave pens to see how his new Crasii is settling in."

"Stellan has a new Crasii?"

"He won her last night at the fight."

"Must have been an interesting fight."

"It was disturbingly quick, actually," the prince remarked with a frown. "Do you think we should worry about how vicious the Crasii are?"

"In my experience, they're only vicious when you mistreat them."

Mathu smiled. "Ah yes, I've heard about you, Lady Desean. Champion of the weak, the downtrodden and the disenfranchised. The common-born daughter of a bleeding-heart physician who scandalised the entire nobility of Glaeba by appearing out of nowhere and somehow snagging one of the most eligible bachelors in the country. You're the wrong person to ask about the savagery of our slave races, aren't you?"

"You sound as if you disapprove of me, your highness."

"Far from it," he laughed. "I think you're a breath of fresh air. And please, you've welcomed me into your home, Arkady. I really would prefer it if you called me Mathu."

"If you insist . . . Mathu. But I'm more interested to know why you think the Crasii are so vicious?"

The prince's smile faded. "Last night I saw a feline Crasii kill a Jelidian snow bear twice her size with nothing other than wits and claws. Have you ever seen a bear baiting? They chain the bear in the middle of the pit and then let the Crasii loose. She has to dodge it, kill it or die. Only this one didn't even try to dodge it. She tricked it into looking away, ran up its back and then ripped its jugular open with her claws."

Arkady frowned. "Thank you, Mathu, for sharing that image while I'm eating."

He grinned sheepishly. "Sorry. It's just it occurred to me last night that if they ever took it upon themselves to revolt, we'd be in a lot of trouble."

"Then perhaps you should prevail upon your father to make cruelty to the Crasii a crime, Mathu, rather than a hobby for jaded noblemen."

He studied her curiously for a moment. "I'm surprised to hear you defend them so staunchly, Arkady. Weren't the Crasii the reason your father died in prison?"

"My father was arrested for being part of an underground movement helping wounded and terrified slaves escape brutal masters. It's the fault of the men who terrorised their Crasii into fleeing that my father was forced into such a role, and their fault he died in prison. The Crasii are the victims, not the aggressors."

"But they were Scards . . ."

"A Scard is any slave who refuses to obey his master, Mathu. At least by our definition. That doesn't make them inherently evil."

"By *our* definition?"

"To the Crasii, it's quite a different thing. A Scard is actually a Crasii not compelled to follow the orders of the Tide Lords. It has nothing to do with their human masters. The inability to worship their creators was a flaw the Tide Lords sought to eradicate, according to Crasii lore, which is why the Tide Lords discarded them, hence the slang reference to Scards. They obey us because they choose to, Mathu, not because they have to."

"How do you know so much about them?"

She shrugged, seeing no harm in telling the tale. It wasn't as if it was a secret. And the key to any successful lie, she knew well, was to stick as closely as possible to the truth. "I wanted to be a physician like my father, but they wouldn't let me study medicine at the university because I'm a woman. The only course open to me was history, because it's common—even acceptable—for women to research their own or their husband's family background to prove how well connected they are. With my father sheltering runaway Crasii, I had to pretend I was studying them to remove suspicion about why there were so many seen coming and going from our house. My feigned interest became a genuine one."

"Until your father was arrested."

Arkady shook her head. "I'm not the only human in Glaeba interested in the Crasii. There's a whole department dedicated to researching their origins at the University of Herino. Harlie Palmerston, the author of our much-lauded *Theory of Human Advancement,* is among its leading lights."

"You're the only one who's had a family member arrested over it, though."

"There've been plenty of other people arrested for aiding runaways," she assured him. "And many more the authorities prefer to ignore. You just don't hear about them in polite society."

"Because their daughters usually don't marry into the Glaeban royal family?" Mathu asked with raised brow.

"Exactly!" Arkady declared with a smile. "That's how Stellan and I met, you know. After they arrested my father, and I'd had no luck getting him released through normal channels, I came charging up here to the palace to demand the Duke of Lebec do something about it."

"I always thought you and Stellan were childhood sweethearts."

She smiled, shaking her head. "Not exactly. I'd met Stellan before when we were children. My father was sometimes called to treat his father, when the old duke was still alive, if the palace physician was away. I decided our previous, albeit tenuous, relationship was all the invitation I needed to barge into his library to inform the Duke of Lebec exactly how I thought he should run his duchy."

"Fortunate for you that Stellan has a sense of humour, I suspect."

"Indeed," Arkady agreed. The rest of the story she left to Mathu's imagination, quite sure he would fill in the romantic details for himself, no matter how far removed from the truth they might be.

It was at that moment that Stellan himself appeared on the terrace from the dining room behind them with Jaxyn. He waved both the prince and his wife back into their seats when they made to rise, kissed Arkady's cheek and then helped himself to one of the pastries on the table. "So, I turn my back for a moment and find you working your devious wiles on my wife, eh, Mathu?" Stellan joked.

"To no avail," Mathu lamented. "Arkady seems more interested in educating me than entertaining me, I fear."

"Ah . . . but what an education it would be," Jaxyn suggested with a wink, making both Stellan and Mathu laugh.

"And one we don't have time for," Stellan warned. "Did you still want to come down to the barracks and meet Chikita, Mathu?" He turned to Arkady and added by way of an explanation, "I won myself a feline Crasii last night."

"So Mathu informs me. Is she breeding stock?"

"A bit early to tell. She's a fighter, though, that's for certain. One of Taryx's line."

"Then don't let me keep you, dear. And don't let this new Crasii of yours work out unless she's up to it. I imagine she didn't escape a Jelidian snow bear without some injuries."

"A few, but nothing too serious," he agreed. "Are you coming, Jaxyn?"

"Tides, no!" he exclaimed, collapsing into one of the vacant chairs. "My head is still pounding. You go on ahead. I'll stay here and see if my devious wiles are any more effective on your lovely wife than Mathu's."

Stellan kissed her cheek again, smiling. "Sorry, darling. It seems to be the morning for it. Will you be in for lunch or are you heading back out to the prison?"

"I thought I'd pay another visit to our immortal."

"Then I shall look forward to another entertaining anecdote at dinner tonight. Come on, Mathu."

The duke and the young prince headed down the steps and across the lawn toward the slave quarters. Jaxyn helped himself to a cup of tea from the pot sitting on the table and then turned his attention to Arkady.

"Don't bother," she told him, before he could utter a word.

"Pardon?"

"Don't bother trying your 'devious wiles' on me, Jaxyn Aranville. Stellan told me about your offer. And I can promise you, there is more chance of Kyle Lakesh proving to be immortal than there is of me *ever* sharing a bed with you, no matter how noble the cause."

"I'm disappointed in you, Arkady."

"I'll just bet you are."

"No, seriously. I thought you genuinely cared for Stellan."

"I do care for him. That's why I'm counting the days until you tire of him and move on to something more enticing."

"Stellan loves me."

"Something I'm sure he'll live to regret."

Jaxyn leaned forward on the table, looking at her earnestly. "Stellan would love a son of mine like it was his own."

Sad, but true, Arkady thought, although her expression betrayed no hint of what she was thinking. "You'll have to come up with a better argument than that to convince me," she told him.

"Are you a virgin, Arkady?"

"I *beg* your pardon?"

"Are you a virgin?" he repeated, curiously. "I mean, there was no hint of any previous lovers before Stellan, or the king would never have allowed the marriage. And there's never been as much as a whisper of scandal since the wedding, which means either you're discreet beyond imagining, or there's been nothing to be discreet about."

"You have some nerve, Jaxyn . . ."

"You know, I think you might be," he said, relaxing back in his chair as if astounded by his own brilliant deduction. "Tides! That would explain so much!"

Arkady smiled serenely, refusing to dignify his accusation with a reply. "You truly are a fool, Jaxyn Aranville."

"And you're afraid," he retorted, sounding very certain of himself. "You're a twenty-six-year-old virgin who's terrified of men."

"Am I?"

"Of course you are! That explains why you married Stellan. I mean what could be safer than marrying a man who will never, ever, want you? No wonder you're so damned frigid."

"And shouting this accusation out across the terrace is going to make me melt into your arms to correct this deplorable state of affairs *how,* exactly?" she enquired.

Jaxyn glanced around guiltily for a moment and then fixed his gaze on her with a sly smile. "You're a cool one, Arkady, I'll grant you that."

"Far cooler than you," she advised, rising to her feet. "You'd be wise not to forget it, too."

Arkady turned for the dining room door, but she stopped on the threshold, certain that if she didn't put an end to Jaxyn's speculation, she was never going to hear the end of this. "And for your information, I haven't been a virgin since I was fourteen years old. That the king doesn't know about my past is merely proof that given the right incentives, even the King's Spymaster will hold his tongue."

She left Jaxyn sitting on the terrace, staring after her in surprise, smiling to herself as soon as her back was turned. *Living a lie is getting easier by the minute,* she mused. Or maybe it was because she'd been taking lessons from the master of all liars lately: Cayal, the Immortal Prince.

Chapter 23

Mathu looked around with interest as they entered the Crasii village, quite taken with this innovative method of housing slaves. In Herino, as it was in most other places in Glaeba, their slaves were confined in cells or locked barracks. The idea of letting them coexist in a village setting was something he'd never encountered before.

"I'm guessing this was Arkady's idea?" the prince remarked as the word spread through the canine village that their lord and master had come to visit. Crasii pups had appeared on the common the moment they arrived, bounding around their ankles, barking excitedly, while their more reserved parents tried to call them back.

Stellan bent down and picked up the nearest pup. The size and shape of a small human child, he was black and white, his pelt so soft Stellan couldn't resist the need to stroke it. "This is Bounder," he told Mathu. "One of Tassie's many siblings."

Mathu smiled at the pup and reached out to pat him. "Hello, Bounder."

Bounder barked excitedly, licked Mathu's hand and then wiggled out of Stellan's grasp and jumped to the ground.

He let the pup go with a smile. "He's only about two or three, I think. He'll be five or so before he stops barking and starts learning to speak."

"And you let them live like humans?" Mathu asked, looking around at the neat row of dormitories lining the single street of the village.

"They're part human, Mathu. Mostly human, if you believe Harlie Palmerston's theory. We have them in our homes, we let them cook for us, we entrust our children to their care and we let them fight our battles for us. Why are you surprised they have the ability to live like civilised human beings?"

The prince considered the matter for a moment and then

shrugged. "I don't know. I guess I never thought about it much."

"You should think about it," Stellan suggested. "You'll be king someday. The Crasii are your subjects, too."

Mathu smiled. "I think my father would shudder to hear you suggest such a thing, Stellan."

"You don't have to rule the same way as your father, Mat."

"Isn't it a little treasonous to suggest you don't like the way he's ruling now?" the young prince teased.

"Ah!" Stellan exclaimed, raising his hand to his forehead dramatically. "You've discovered my dreadful secret!"

Mathu laughed as they continued across the common. "Yes, well, I shall have to report this, you know. Can't have seditious activities like treating the Crasii humanely going on in the kingdom! What will our neighbours think?"

"For the sake of Crasii everywhere, I hope they're impressed, your highness."

The two men stopped before the slave who had answered Mathu's question, an old Crasii wearing a knitted shawl fringed in red over his shaggy tan shoulders, indicating he was the most senior Crasii in the village. A hunting Crasii, now retired to a life at stud, he bowed politely to Stellan and Mathu, waiting for Stellan to formally introduce them.

"Your royal highness, this is Fletch, the village mayor."

"You let them have their own government?" Mathu asked in surprise.

Fletch nodded. "Lord Desean allows us to manage our own affairs, your royal highness. Up to a point."

Stellan smiled. "We disagree about where that point lies, occasionally, but generally, it works well. It's less work for me and the Crasii appreciate a little autonomy, don't they, Fletch?"

The old canine nodded, his lips curling back from his teeth in a smile, although it looked rather more like a snarl to the uninitiated. But Stellan was used to the old dog, and they got along well enough, given the inequitable nature of their relationship.

"There are a few areas of contention," Fletch informed the prince. "For example, his grace won't let us chase the felines, even for exercise."

"It's for your own protection," Stellan reminded him. "You know that."

"It's a risk we're willing to take, your grace."

"But one *I'm* not willing to take," the duke replied. "You're too valuable, all of you, canine *and* feline alike, to risk anybody getting hurt or possibly killed in a pointless game."

"It's only humans who think chasing felines is pointless, your grace. We think it's a noble and worthwhile pastime. Not to mention, well, fun."

"The felines think fishing for tadpoles is fun too," he pointed out. "I don't let them indulge in that game, either."

"As always your wisdom is exceeded only by your concern for our welfare, your grace," the old Crasii replied respectfully. He bowed low and stepped to one side. "Please, don't leave it so long before you visit us again."

"The Tides protect you," Stellan replied, using the formal Crasii salutation that few humans bothered to remember.

Fletch smiled and bowed even lower. "The Tides protect you also, your grace."

"Tadpoles?" Mathu asked in surprise, as they resumed their walk toward the feline compound. "You have amphibian Crasii?"

"You've never heard of Lebec's freshwater pearls?"

"Of course I've heard of them."

"Where do you think they come from?"

The prince pondered the question for a moment. "I never really thought about that, either."

"We farm the pearls in the lake just north of the estate. The amphibians do most of the work."

"I heard they were notoriously hard to keep in that sort of setting," Mathu remarked. "Rumour has it the minute you put them in the water, they're gone."

"You have to give them a reason to come back," Stellan told him.

"Well, you certainly seem to have the canines eating out of your hand."

He smiled and glanced over his shoulder at the old Crasii who watched them walking away with an unblinking stare. "If you're referring to Fletch's grovelling admiration of my animal husbandry skills, just now, don't be fooled. He was a hunter in his day and he's wily as they come. He knows the right thing to say. It's the canine need to please their masters. It can be dangerous to mistake it for what they really feel."

"Which is what?"

"Ah, now for *that* you would have to ask Arkady. She knows much more about the Crasii than I do."

They reached the end of the common and the first of the high brick walls dividing the villages from each other. There was a wooden gate set into the wall, with a small round window cut out at about four feet off the ground. Beside the gate was a brass bell with a small metal ball hanging from a short length of rope. Stellan rang the bell a couple of times and then bent down to peer through the hole in the gate.

A few moments later the sound of a bolt sliding back was followed by a metallic screech as the gate was opened by a black-and-white feline who bowed when she realised her visitor was the duke.

"Your grace! Welcome!"

"Hello, Mitten. We've come to visit our new arrival."

"Of course," she said, stepping back to let them enter.

The gate screeched closed again, making Stellan wince. "Why don't you oil those hinges?"

The feline shrugged. "Because the noise drives the canines crazy."

"I could rescind the order about them chasing you anytime I wanted," Stellan warned with a frown. It was just like the felines to find something that annoyed their canine neighbours.

"We have no problem if they chase us." Mitten shrugged. "And they have nothing to fear unless we let them catch us."

Mathu seemed amused. "There's a reason we confine the

Crasii to pens back in Herino, you know, Stellan. We're not confronted with any of these discipline problems you have to contend with."

"You get less than half the productivity out of them, too, I'll wager," he countered. "This is Mitten, by the way. Mitten, this is Prince Mathu."

The feline bowed just low enough to be respectful. "Your highness."

She held out her arm, indicating they should follow her toward the largest building at the back of the compound. Off to the left, against the outer fence, were two separate residences. There were armed feline guards standing outside and caged yards surrounding the cottages.

"It's where we keep the males," Stellan explained, noticing the direction of Mathu's glance.

"How many do you have?"

"Four at the moment," he replied. "The three younger males share the larger house. Taryx lives in the other pen on his own."

"Taryx? The sire of the Crasii you won last night?"

Stellan nodded. "Named for the Tide Lord. He's been a very profitable and prolific sire."

"Did you tell her that her sire was here?"

He shook his head. "It wouldn't have made much difference if I had. The felines don't pay much attention to familial ties. If they do, it's usually because they're bragging about their lineage. The felines like to brag."

"Why do you keep him separated from the others?"

"Because he's old and cranky. Did you want to meet him?"

Mathu nodded. "Is he dangerous?"

"Not if you stay out of reach."

Stellan changed direction and headed across the compound to the smaller cottage with Mathu beside him. Mitten took another few steps before she realised her visitors were no longer behind her, and then turned to find out why, obviously displeased when she saw the direction they were headed.

"Your grace," she called after them. "Please. Don't encourage him . . ."

Stellan and Mathu ignored her call and kept walking toward the bars of the enclosure behind the cottage on the right-hand side of the compound. Inside, a figure reclined on a battered sofa, soaking up the sunlight that broke through the clouds. It would rain again before the day was out and the old cat was making the most of the sunshine. He was a huge beast, outwardly human from the chest down, but his tawny fur was black streaked with silver and grew in a thick mane that completely encircled his neck and reached partway down his back and chest. He made no attempt to rise as they approached; instead, he rolled on his back and tucked his hands behind his head, exposing his impressive genitalia to his visitors.

"That's Taryx for you," Stellan remarked. "The king of good manners and civilised behaviour."

"He's fairly impressive," Mathu agreed, sounding a little uncertain.

Stellan laughed. "For the Tides' sake, don't let him know you think that. He's insufferable enough without you feeding his narcissism. Be nice to him, though. He fancies himself king of the pride." They stopped at the bars. "Good morning, your highness," Stellan called.

"Good morning, your grace."

Stellan waited and after a moment, the Crasii deigned to rise from his couch and wander over to the bars where Stellan and Mathu waited.

"What's this then?" Taryx asked, as he leaned on the bars, eyeing Mathu up and down curiously. "Lunch?"

"This is his royal highness, Prince Mathu Debree, Crown Prince of Glaeba."

"Dinner, then," the Crasii corrected.

Stellan smiled. Crasii felines no more ate humans than the canines did, but Taryx enjoyed perpetuating the myth. "Mathu, this is Taryx, the king of the Lebec Pride."

"Your reputation precedes you, your highness," Mathu

informed him, playing along with the notion that the Crasii had some sort of royal rank. "You've sired half the fighting Crasii in Glaeba, I believe."

"More like two-thirds," the feline corrected, a little miffed. Then he smiled suddenly and turned to Stellan. "I hear one of my cubs took out a Jelidian snow bear last night."

Stellan nodded. "She certainly did."

"Damn, I'm good," he preened.

Stellan was used to Taryx's arrogance. As far as the Crasii tom was concerned, he was directly responsible for anything impressive his descendants did, while being in no way responsible for their mistakes. Sometimes, Stellan envied this uncomplicated creature, kept in comfort, fed on demand and required to do nothing more than mate with the females of his pride. If his pelt was a little scarred these days, it wasn't all from fighting. A feline in heat was a ravenous beast and intercourse between any two creatures with retractable claws capable of tearing the throat out of a Jelidian snow bear was bound to be dangerous.

"You tell her I'm proud of her," Taryx instructed.

"I will," Stellan promised. "And you take care, eh? Those young bucks aren't ready to take your place yet."

"They'll never be ready," the tom predicted confidently.

"Your grace," Mitten reminded them, a little impatiently. "Did you want to see Chikita or not?" She was standing behind them, her tail lashing back and forth with annoyance.

"Of course," Stellan agreed and they turned to follow Mitten. As they walked away, Mathu glanced over his shoulder at the old feline and then looked at Stellan. "How will you know when one of the other males is ready to take his place?"

"The felines have an annual festival. They call it the Passage of the Tide. Part of the celebrations is a chance for the younger males to take on the head of the pride."

"And the winner becomes the new leader? That must make for a rather peeved loser."

"The loser is usually dead, Mat," he told him. "So it's not a problem we've ever had to deal with."

The prince looked shocked. "You let them fight to the death?"

"Their idea, not mine. But I can see the logic behind it. Taryx would be dangerous and unmanageable if he was deposed by a younger male. We'd end up having to put him down, anyway. At least this way he'll get to go out in a blaze of glory."

Mathu shook his head, sighing. "And I thought you were trying to be more humane in your treatment of the Crasii."

"But they're feline Crasii, Mathu," he pointed out as they entered the longhouse. "The object is to let them live by their rules, not ours."

Chikita was confined to a cage at the back of the longhouse, normally reserved for felines on heat that Stellan didn't want mating with any of the males. They walked the length of the empty dormitory behind Mitten, past rows of narrow beds piled with furs and blankets, as if each Crasii was trying to own more bedclothes than their neighbour did. Stellan always found it intriguing that the Crasii slept on top of their bedclothes, rather than under them, even in the dead of winter. It was a feline thing, he guessed. They didn't like to be covered. Even in battle they eschewed armour or any other sort of protection, preferring the freedom of movement that came with fighting in nothing but their own skin.

The Crasii jumped to her feet as soon as she spied Stellan and Mathu approaching, grabbing at the bars of her cage, her tail whipping back and forth angrily as she growled at them.

"You lied!" she accused, before Stellan could utter a word.

"I beg your pardon?"

"You told me if I won the fight I'd be free!"

"Actually, I believe the duke told you that you could enter his service," Mathu corrected, obviously alarmed by the feline's aggressive tone. "Crasii weren't meant to be free."

"Step a little closer, human," Chikita suggested with a snarl. "Then we'll see who was meant to be free."

"Settle down, kitten. You're in here for your own protection," Stellan assured her, putting his arm out to prevent Mathu from doing exactly what the feline suggested. In her current mood, she'd rip him from neck to navel if he got in reach of those claws. "It'll take a few days before the others get used to your scent. Once they do, you'll be free to join your comrades. Until then, and until you've recovered from last night's fight, you're better off where you are."

Chikita glared at him for a moment and then looked past him. She hissed at Mitten, growling low in her throat.

"And you won't be going anywhere until *that* stops, either," Stellan warned.

"I am a fighter," Chikita announced. "You would have me acting like a house cat."

"Which is marginally better than being torn to shreds by a bear for the entertainment of a room full of bored humans, I would have thought."

Chikita's eyes flashed with defiance, but her tail slowed and she seemed to calm down a little. "I will wait then, until my lord commands me."

Stellan frowned, thinking her capitulation a little quick. "That's a much better attitude to take."

"Will I be permitted to meet him soon?"

"Meet who?" he asked. He had no idea what the Crasii was talking about.

"Chikita is just nervous because she's new," Mitten explained, glaring at the young female. "She is pleased to meet both her lord and her prince. She doesn't mean anything else."

"But I can smell—," the feline objected, but Mitten cut her off impatiently.

"She can smell Taryx, your grace," the Crasii told them with a shrug. "It's making her a little jittery."

"Everything will be fine once you're used to the place," Stellan assured her. "Mitten will see to it you have anything you need."

"Of course, your grace," the older Crasii agreed with a subservient bow.

A little unsettled, but at least satisfied that his new slave was well in hand, he turned and headed back out into the sunlight. Mathu followed him, stopping on the top step of the porch to look out over the Crasii village.

"Is it my imagination, or was there something very odd going on just now," he asked, "between those two Crasii?"

"No," Stellan replied. "You weren't imagining things."

"So who do you think she can really smell?"

Stellan shrugged. "I have no idea. Maybe she's coming on heat."

"I met a man once," Mathu told him, "who decided to find out what a feline on heat was like."

"That'd be a rather dangerous game to play."

Mathu nodded. "It was. I mean, she looked human enough—if the light was low and you didn't mind the idea of fur instead of bare skin—but those claws . . ." The young prince shuddered. "He said it was amazing. Trouble is, he damn near bled to death finding it out."

Stellan grimaced. "Never seen the attraction in fornicating with another species, myself. Even an almost human one. There's something innately repulsive about the very idea."

Mathu clapped him on the shoulder, amused rather than surprised. "You really are a staid, unadventurous old prude at heart, aren't you, cousin?"

Stellan smiled. "I guess I must be," he agreed, idly wishing the rest of the world was as easy to convince of that as Mathu Debree.

Chapter 24

Tilly Ponting's house in Lebec was set at the end of a cul-de-sac not far from the lake's edge in the more exclusive part of Lebec City. It had been her town house before her husband's demise; her family seat being located some forty miles northeast of the city. After her husband died, she'd moved into the city full time. Tilly was a social creature and while she enjoyed the wealth that came with being one of the landed gentry, she wasn't all that interested in spending time on the land.

A well-trained canine Crasii showed Arkady through the house to the morning room, where Tilly was indulging her latest hobby. The widow had decided several months ago that she had some talent as an artist based, apparently, on a passing comment an art tutor made to her when she was a girl. Now that she was free to pursue whatever hobbies she desired, she had decided to discover the hidden artist within, who had been—she'd assured Arkady—stifled by years of repressive marriage and suffocating conformity. When Arkady arrived at the house, Tilly was staring pensively at her latest canvas, paintbrush in hand, and appeared to have been in that position for some time. A large ginger cat slept curled on the table beside the easel, the tip of its tail resting in a pot of blue paint.

"What do you think, Arkady?" Tilly asked, turning to greet her guest. "Should I call this *Mist on the Lake* or *Ocean at Rest*?"

Arkady considered the painting for a moment. "How about *Big Blue Blob*?"

"You are cruel beyond imagining, Arkady," the older woman replied. And then she smiled. "Although a little more tactful than my son, I have to say, who suggested naming it the *Ode to My Complete Lack of Talent*."

Arkady laughed and took a seat at the table. "How is Aleki? I haven't seen him in ages."

"He's fine," Tilly sighed, putting down her paintbrush and taking the seat opposite Arkady. "He loves being a farmer. I despair of him ever finding a decent wife."

Arkady smiled. Only Tilly Ponting would consider her son's dedication to his family's massive estates *farming*. "I thought you were trying to arrange a union between him and Davista Brantine?"

"It was a disaster," Tilly lamented. "My son is a bore and Davista is a silly girl. Don't suppose Stellan's interested in marrying Kylia off, is he? Would you like some tea?" she added, indicating the silver tea service on the table.

"Thank you, I would." She accepted a cup that Tilly poured with her own hand, and took a sip, before she answered her hostess's first question. "Even if Stellan was looking for a husband for his niece, Tilly, I doubt Aleki is in the running. He's more than twice Kylia's age."

"Tides, he's not going to let her marry for love, is he? It would be just like that fool man to do something so stupid."

"You think marrying for love is stupid?" Arkady asked curiously.

"Don't you?"

She hesitated before answering. "Actually, I hadn't really thought about it."

"I've thought about it a lot," Tilly told her. "If I'd had my way when I was seventeen, I'd have married one of my father's grooms. His name was Neron. I was so in love with him, I thought I would die when I was told I couldn't have him."

"Did he feel the same way?"

The widow shrugged. "I like to imagine he did, but the truth is, about three months after my father found out about us and forbade him to see me again, he married a girl from his village, moved back home and that was the last I ever saw of him." She sipped her tea and smiled. "Hardly the stuff of epic romance."

"Do you ever regret it?"

Tilly shook her head. "Not a moment of it. I don't regret falling in love with a groom any more than I regret marrying Aleki's father. I've had a good life, Arkady, and I've lived every moment of it in the style to which I'm sinfully habituated. Even better, my dear husband had the decency to pass away while I was still young enough to enjoy being a widow, but not so young that I needed to remarry. I have a decent, hardworking son, determined to keep me in the manner to which I'm accustomed, and delightful, terribly well-connected friends like you to keep me on every reputable invitation list in town. It's all worked out rather swimmingly, in fact."

"You're an evil old cynic, Tilly," Arkady laughed.

"Better to be an evil *old* cynic than a cynic at your age," she scolded. "You need to fall in love, my girl. Hard. It would do you the world of good."

"What makes you think I'm not in love with Stellan?"

"Hmmm . . . ," Tilly said, feigning deep thought. "I think it comes down to two words . . . Jaxyn Aranville."

"You really *are* an evil old cynic," Arkady accused, frowning.

"I'm right though. You need to have an affair, girl. And I don't mean some discreet little assignation once a week, all done in good taste and decorum. I mean something that makes you foolish. Something so consuming you'd throw your whole life away for it. I'm talking passion. A screaming, tear-my-clothes-off-and-take-me-now-you-brute sort of fling. Preferably with someone totally inappropriate."

Arkady shook her head. "And exactly what would that achieve?"

"You'd know you're alive, Arkady."

"I'm content with other, less dangerous indicators that I'm alive," she replied. "You know: breathing. A pulse. That sort of thing."

"They're just proving you're not dead," Tilly corrected. "That's a whole world away from being alive, my girl."

Arkady smiled. "I don't know why I listen to you, Tilly Ponting. You're a shameless meddler and you give the worst advice of anybody I've ever met."

"But that's why you love me," Tilly chuckled, patting

Arkady's hand across the table. "So tell me, dear. If you didn't come for my advice on matters of the heart, what are you doing here?"

"I came to talk to you about the Tarot."

"You want to know more?"

"About the characters on the cards, yes."

"How did your last interview go?"

"It was . . . interesting."

Tilly looked at her cannily. "But your immortal is not so easily tripped up?"

She shook her head. "Not so easily."

Tilly rose to her feet and crossed the room to the sideboard. She opened a drawer and pulled out another deck of cards similar to those she had loaned Arkady and then came back and began laying them out on the table.

"Engarhod," she said, as she dealt the cards. "Emperor of the Five Realms. His wife, Syrolee, the Empress. Elyssa, the Maiden. Tryan, the Devil. Pellys, the Recluse. Lukys, the Scholar. Rance, the Hanging Man. Krydence, the Judge. Taryx, the Warrior. Sometimes they call him Tyrax—"

"Slow down!" Arkady begged. "I'm not going to remember all of this. He mentioned Pellys, though."

"The Recluse?"

Arkady nodded. "Cayal claims Pellys was a recluse because someone had him decapitated. His head grew back afterwards, but without his memories. That's *why* he was a recluse."

Tilly looked at her in surprise. "He actually *told* you an immortal's head grows back?"

"It's apparently one of the benefits of immortality."

"Did he tell what else happens?"

Arkady looked at Tilly with a raised brow. "Is something else *supposed* to happen?"

Tilly laughed. "There's the legend that it'll destroy the world, but I guess we got lucky. Good thing our headsman was away, eh?"

Arkady smiled at the very notion. "I tried to get Stellan to let me chop off one of Cayal's fingers to see if it grew back so we could settle the matter once and for all, but he won't let me do it."

"How inconsiderate of him," Tilly agreed.

She looked at her friend oddly. "You think I'm a barbarian, too, don't you?"

Suddenly the widow smiled again, although it seemed a little forced this time. "No, I think I was right about you needing to have an affair. You really have cut yourself off from normal human emotions, haven't you, dear?"

Arkady shook her head and pointed to the cards. "Just stick to the Tarot, Tilly, and stop trying to fix things that aren't broken."

The old woman dealt out another card. It was a picture of two lovers entwined in an intimate embrace. "The Lovers. Cayal and Amaleta." Tilly laid it down quite deliberately, studied the card for a long, meaningful moment and then looked at Arkady with a raised brow. "If I was superstitious, Arkady Desean, I'd say there's an omen here."

Arkady rolled her eyes. "For the Tides' sake, you read *Tarot* cards, Tilly. You think there's an omen in everything."

"Could be I'm right."

"Well, I'm sure your Tarot lovers are the very embodiment of happily-ever-after, but they're not going to help me much. Maybe you should tell me about this Emperor of the Five Realms," Arkady suggested. "I'm quite sure the omens can take care of themselves."

"The Lovers represent tragedy, not happiness," Tilly corrected. "The legend goes that Cayal had already discovered the secret of immortality by the time he met Amaleta. After he fell hopelessly in love with her—according to the Tarot, at least—he took her up into the Shevron Mountains and there he asked her to marry him, promising her immortal life as proof of his eternal love. She was understandably nervous about making the transformation, but he begged her to trust him. Eventually, she agreed, and he set about making her immortal so they could share their eternity in perfect bliss."

"Well, yes, Tilly," Arkady said, smiling. "I can see what a tragedy that must have been."

"It *was* a tragedy. Cayal got it wrong. Instead of giving Amaleta eternal life, he killed her."

Arkady was having a hard time keeping a straight face. "That must have been rather awkward for him."

Tilly was clearly not pleased Arkady wasn't giving her Tarot the respect she felt it deserved. "They say his grief was inconsolable. According to legend, the Great Lakes are the result of the Immortal Prince's tears."

Arkady could no longer hide her amusement. "Odd, if we're talking about the same Immortal Prince we have locked up in Lebec Prison. He doesn't strike me as the weepy type."

Tilly leaned back in her chair and stared at Arkady. "If you're not going to take this seriously . . ."

"I'm sorry, I shouldn't tease," she said, patting Tilly's hand, realising she was very close to offending her old friend. "Please, tell me more. I don't mean to scorn your Tarot. It's just the academic in me has trouble dealing with the notion I'm being forced to rely on a deck of cards used for telling fortunes as my only dependable resource, that's all. Tell me about the others. I'll not laugh again, I promise."

Tilly frowned, deliberating the sincerity of Arkady's apology, before nodding and dealing out the rest of the cards. "The Tarot deserves respect, you know."

"Of course it does."

"People died to protect it, during the last Cataclysm."

Arkady nodded solemnly. "I'm sure they did."

Tilly glared at her. "Some of us go to a great deal of trouble to ensure this record of the true nature of the Tide Lords never fades from memory, Arkady. It's a solemn trust that we take very seriously. If you're going to scoff at it, you can find someone else to tell you about the Tarot."

"Some of *us*?" Arkady asked with a smile. "Tides! You make it sound like you're part of some giant conspiracy to keep the knowledge of the Tide Lords alive."

Tilly continued to glare at her. "Some secrets are worth protecting, Arkady."

"*Secrets?*" This was starting to get a little bizarre and it was certainly the first time Arkady had ever seen Tilly so serious. While she knew Tilly deliberately cultivated the idea that she was nothing more than an eccentric widow, Arkady had always believed it was all part of her plan to avoid another marriage. It never occurred to her that Tilly might be doing it for any other reason. And certainly not for something as trivial as a deck of Tarot cards.

Picking up the nearest card, Tilly handed it to Arkady. "I've said too much already. Let's get on with this."

"Tilly," Arkady asked curiously, "do you actually believe the Tide Lords are real?"

The old woman was silent for a moment and then she shrugged. "It doesn't matter what I believe. You're the one supposedly interrogating an immortal. I think what you believe is rather more important at this stage."

Her answer surprised and disturbed Arkady a little. She'd never seen her old friend like this before. "I'm sorry, Tilly," she said. "I don't mean to mock you or your beliefs."

"Let's start then," Tilly said, rather more frostily than Arkady was expecting, "with the Emperor of the Five Realms . . ."

It was past lunch by the time Arkady arrived at the prison, the day overcast and gloomy. She was led through the depressing halls to Recidivists' Row without ceremony, the guards so used to her visits by now they addressed her by name as she passed by.

When she reached the Row, she was surprised by how pleased both Cayal and Warlock were to see her. Cayal's smile in particular was rather unsettling. He seemed disturbingly eager and, for a moment, Tilly's suggestion about indulging in a screaming, tear-my-clothes-off-and-take-me-now-you-brute sort of fling with someone totally inappropriate flashed through her mind.

Idiot, she told herself sternly. It was easy to forget she was their only contact with the outside world other than the guards. For these prisoners, she was a window into a realm from which they were excluded, probably for the rest of their lives. That was why they were so glad to see her, she reminded herself. If Cayal seemed to eagerly approach the bars whenever she arrived, it was just because she was the only respite he had from the boredom of his incarceration. If his eyes widened when he looked at her, if his gaze lingered longer than it should, if his smile seemed a little too familiar, it meant nothing—no more than her own quickening heartbeat meant simply that she despised being in this place where her father had perished.

"Good afternoon, gentlemen. Sorry I'm late."

"You have no need to apologise to us, my lady," Warlock informed her gravely.

"Oh . . . I don't know," Cayal disagreed. "I kind of like the idea myself."

"You would," the canine rumbled, retreating to the back of his cell.

Cayal turned his attention to Arkady. "So, what *is* your excuse for being late, then?"

She frowned at his impudence. "Don't push your luck."

"I don't really care, anyway." Cayal seemed distracted. "But I've been thinking."

"How nice for you."

"I think we should trade."

"Trade for what, exactly?"

"The rest of my story, in return for a bit of fresh air. I'm going crazy locked up in here."

"I thought that was the whole point of your claim to be immortal, Cayal? To prove you're crazy?"

He shrugged. "That's your idea, not mine. I want out of here. Even if only for a few hours a day. Tides! Even the gemang wants out of here. You arrange it for us, and I'll tell you anything you want to know."

It seemed an unlikely offer, but she wasn't sure it was one she could refuse. It was hard to avoid the feeling this man was manipulating her. "Will you tell me who sent you here? Who you work for?"

"I'm a Tide Lord," he reminded her. "I don't work for anybody."

Her eyes narrowed suspiciously. "Very selfless of you to include Warlock in your request for fresh air and exercise."

"Maybe I'm planning to escape and I need the gemang to help."

"If you want to enlist my help to escape, suzerain," Warlock remarked from the cell across the way, "not calling me gemang would be a good start."

Arkady couldn't help but smile. "Your magically created race of adoring slaves really isn't performing to specifications, is it?"

"Wait 'til the Tide turns," Cayal suggested. "Then you'll see."

"I'm breathless with anticipation," she assured him. "Tell me about Diala. In the Tarot she is the High Priestess."

"Arryl was High Priestess."

"What was Diala then?"

Cayal smiled sourly. "We used to call her the Minion Maker."

"The *what*?"

"The Minion Maker," he repeated. "That's what she did, Arkady. Diala sought out likely minions for the Tide Lords and then trapped them into an eternity of servitude."

Arkady's brow furrowed. "Minions? I don't understand."

He stared at her for a moment and then smiled. "You don't seriously think every one of those names in your pathetic Tarot was actually a Tide Lord, do you? How many cards have you got there? Twenty or more? No world could survive that many jaded lunatics looking for ways to entertain themselves."

"Who are they then, if they're not immortal?"

"Oh, they're immortal," he assured her. "They just can't manipulate the Tide very well. Mastery over the Tide is a skill only a few of us have."

"You mean some of them have no magical power."

"Some power. Not a lot. And it varies."

"Will you tell me about them?"

"Will you speak to the Warden about us getting out of here for a bit each day?"

"That depends on how cooperative you are."

Cayal smiled. "Then pull up a chair, Arkady. As I told you before, it's a very long story."

Chapter 25

W here were we? That's right—freezing to death in the meat locker at Dun Cinczi. The door had opened . . .

Squinting in the painfully bright light, I really began to worry when I realised the silhouette in the doorway was my sister, Planice, the Queen of Kordana.

You may wonder why I wasn't sighing with relief, thinking rescue was at hand, given I was the queen's brother. Planice was a good fifteen years older than me. We'd never been close. I think her resentment of me was because it was *my* birth that had finally killed our mother. She was only fifteen when our mother died and along with her title, Planice had inherited a clutch of nine siblings that included a newborn babe needing care and attention. As she lacked any real maternal instinct, I'd been a nuisance she was forced to deal with most of her life. And it wasn't as if I'd been a particularly easy child. In fact, my only real use had proved to be as a convenient groom for the daughter of a much-needed ally, once I'd grown.

Until now, that is. Until I'd unwittingly given her the excuse she was looking for to be rid of me, something that only just occurred to me as I warily stepped toward her.

"Planice . . . thank the Tides you've come . . ."

She responded by backhanding me, her royal signet tearing the frozen skin from my cheek. The blood was warm on my face as I fell backwards against the hanging carcasses, hurt more by her reaction to my plight than her blow.

"Idiot!"

I staggered to my feet, only just starting to appreciate the trouble I was in. It wasn't that I didn't understand the consequences of killing a man. And it wasn't as if I expected no cost for my actions. But to anger Thraxis was one thing. To annoy the Queen of Kordana was another thing entirely.

"I can explain . . ."

"You killed Thraxis's only son over some woman you've never laid *eyes* on before?" she screeched, almost as angry as Thraxis himself. "Two days before you're to marry the daughter of one of our most tenuous allies? Do you have any idea what you've *done*?"

"It was an accident . . ."

"I ought to hang you, you dangerous little fool!" she shouted, her face red with fury.

I *ought* to hang you, she said, giving me a glimmer of hope. Given the mood she was in, I'd been expecting her to say: I'm *going* to hang you.

"So why don't you?" I asked, dabbing at my bloody cheek.

"Because Thraxis is demanding it," she informed me. "And I can't afford to have any dun lord in my kingdom telling me who I should and shouldn't kill."

"But Planice . . ."

"Shut up, Cayal, I'm not interested in anything you have to say. Much as it grieves me, you'll get to live." Before my relief at this reprieve had time to register, she added coldly, "But only because I'm making a point here, not because I care one scrap about you. And even if it *does* suit me to let you go on breathing, nothing says I have to put up with you at my hearth. You are banished, Cayal of Lakesh," she decreed, assuming a formal air. "You may take the clothes on your back and a weapon to defend yourself and leave the borders of Kordana by sunset tomorrow. If you are still within my borders by then, or if you ever attempt to return, you will be hunted down, like the vermin you are, and killed without mercy. Do you understand?"

I nodded, too surprised by her decree to think about what it meant. I don't think, at that moment, I understood the emotional impact of exile. I just knew it meant I'd keep on breathing. That was something to be grateful for.

Planice stood back from the door. "Let him go."

"What about Gabriella?" I asked.

Between my bouts of guilt and remorse over Orin, I'd spent much of the past three days clinging to the image of Gabriella. We used to joke about how life would be so much easier if I wasn't a prince, if the hopes and ambitions of Gabriella's father didn't rest so firmly on her shoulders. Always the optimist in those days, even after my sentence had been pronounced, I still dared to hope. Perhaps this would be our chance.

Perhaps, out of this nightmare, something good might happen.

Gabriella loved me, after all. I never doubted that for a moment. With her by my side, I had no fear of anything.

Planice seemed less sure of my fiancée's undying devotion. She even smiled at my naivety. "Even if she'd still have you after this fiasco, do you really think I'd still let the wedding go ahead?"

Her scorn worried me. "Don't you think that should be Gabriella's decision?"

Planice stared at me for a moment, as if debating something, and then she shrugged and stepped back from the door. "Fine. Ask her. Ask your beloved if she's willing to go into exile with you and become a pauper's wife."

I emerged into the sunlight blinking, the snow's reflection hurting my eyes, which had grown used to the darkness of the meat store. Everyone had gathered in the dun's yard. Thraxis was there, glowering angrily. Several of my brothers were standing beside the dun lord; the two brothers who had arrived in Dun Cinczi were there, too, in addition to several others who must have accompanied Planice from Lakesh. They looked ready to hold Thraxis back if the need arose, although there was nothing sympathetic toward me in their demeanour.

And Gabriella was there, her face pale. I stepped toward her.

She spat on the ground in front of me.

"Gabriella?"

Her dark, devastating eyes blazed angrily. "Don't come any closer, you unfaithful cur!"

"What?"

"Was the child yours?"

I stared at her in confusion. "Child? What child?"

"She means the pregnant woman you claim you didn't know that you killed your best friend to defend," Planice said behind me.

I glanced over my shoulder at my sister, as it dawned on me that somewhere between the young couple seeking shelter in Thraxis's hall a few nights ago and now, the child the pregnant young woman was carrying had apparently become mine.

"No!" I protested. "It wasn't like that . . ."

"I can't believe you had to gall to arrange for your whore to follow you to Lakesh for our wedding," Gabriella spat. There was nothing in her eyes but hatred, nothing in her words but scorn.

"I swear on the Tide Star, Gabriella, I never saw her before—"

"So you killed the heir of Dun Cinczi over a perfect stranger?"

I realise now how it must have sounded, but what can you do when the truth is so unbelievable?

Gabriella's scorn was acidic. "How noble of you, Prince Cayal. Is this something you do often? Were you planning to tell me of your hobby of rescuing damsels in distress *after* the wedding?"

"Gabriella . . ."

"She doesn't want you anymore, Cayal," Planice pointed out, taking more than a small degree of pleasure from my pain. I wasn't surprised. She'd set out to deliberately hurt me often enough when I was a small child for me to have no doubts on that score.

"Shut up, Planice." I had no reason, any longer, to keep the peace with my sister. And at that moment, I couldn't have cared less what she thought.

I turned to look at Gabriella, unable to comprehend how easily she was abandoning me. I was young and naive enough to think love could conquer anything. In truth, even then, as she made a mockery of every whispered declaration of our undying devotion to each other, a part of me was looking for a sign, looking for some secret indication that this was an act put on for the benefit of our large audience.

If there was a sign, it was too subtle for me to find.

"Go, Cayal," Planice advised behind me. "Before I change my mind."

As if to emphasise the queen's rejection, Gabriella turned her back on me and walked the short distance to where Orin's mother stood off to the left with the other women of the dun, their eyes swollen and bloodshot from crying. A sea of faces surrounded me, all full of accusation, but the only one that still stands out clearly in my mind—after all this time—is Gabriella's.

There was no word for my hurt, no scale large enough to measure it, no vessel great enough to contain it.

One of my brothers drawing his sword prompted me to move. Blindly, numbly, I turned toward the gate. The crowd parted for me, leaving a corridor of muddy, trampled sludge pointing to the snow-bound countryside beyond the dun. I walked without thinking, my pain a gaping wound that should have left bloodstains on the snow, it felt so real. As I reached the open gates, a woman began to keen, the cry soon taken up by the other women of Dun Cinczi.

To the wail of unrelenting grief, my own as much as of the women of the dun, I stepped out onto the rutted road and turned to face the accusing audience who were watching my disgrace, several of them with a degree of malicious satisfaction. Of the young woman for whom I'd thrown away my entire life, there was no sign.

But *she* was there, witnessing my banishment with no more emotion than someone watching an ill-behaved dog being locked out of the hall on a stormy night.

Gabriella. My beautiful, magnificent, cruel Gabriella.

"Set foot in Kordana again," Planice called after me, "and you'll be sorry, Cayal."

"You're the one who's going to be sorry," I shouted back. And then I added thoughtlessly, "Curse your wretched kingdom, Planice, and everyone in it!"

I said the words to Planice, but it was Gabriella I couldn't tear my eyes from.

Gabriella for whom I meant the curse.

She didn't seem to care. Spitting contemptuously into the mud again, Gabriella turned her back on me once more and put her arms around Orin's grieving mother.

It wasn't until later—after Tryan had laid waste to Kordana—that I would remember my unthinking curse and wonder if I wasn't to blame, after all.

I'll spare you the details of the next few months after I was thrown out of Kordana. Other than my complete and utter humiliation, not much happened, really. I was ill equipped for a life on the road. I'd no skills to speak of, other than my ability to hold a weapon competently and hunt well enough to keep myself fed, but those were skills owned by every man in Kordana and any of the score of nameless kingdoms that populated the land of my birth eight thousand years ago. Cayal, the Exiled Prince, had nothing with which he could barter. I had no trade or craft to fall back on, no money to speak of and no notion of how one went about earning a living.

After traipsing alone and friendless with my heart ripped to shreds by Gabriella's betrayal, across first Kordana and then north through Senestra, I grew weary of the continent of my birth, and the rumours that followed me. Rumours that lingered like a clinging fog and refused to go away. I heard in Harkendown that Gabriella was betrothed again—less than three months after I was banished—to Daryen, one of my older brothers. I was shattered by the news.

Love had little to do with marriage in Kordana. I understood that. The alliance my wedding to Gabriella would have brought was still important to Planice, I appreciated that, too. I tried to tell myself I couldn't have cared less. She was my past. She was my lesson hard learned. A memory turned sour by bitter reality.

I fled north, thinking distance would dull the pain.

It took me eight months to reach Magreth.

In hindsight, I suspect my journey northwest was prompted by the desire for warmth as much as any real yearning to visit the fabled country. In Magreth, at least sleeping outdoors didn't mean risking frostbite.

The truth was I was running away, trying to find somewhere my pain might be eased, but it's easier and so much more "manly" to blame the weather.

Survival demanded I move on, although my heart wasn't listening. No matter how much I told myself otherwise, I still missed Gabriella like an amputated limb. News of her betrothal simply drove home how badly I wanted my life back. I was hungry and desperate enough by then that I didn't care if Planice hated me. I just wanted to go home and the only way I could do that was to somehow redeem myself in my queen's eyes.

In my heart, I didn't accept Gabriella no longer loved me. I had turned her rejection of me into something far more noble and selfless. By then, I'd managed to convince myself she'd spoken so cruelly to protect my sister's holdings from her father's wrath. In my lovesick blindness, I began to imagine there was some hope for us. *Perhaps,* I lay awake at night telling myself, *if I can find a way to re-*

store my reputation in Planice's eyes, I will be allowed home.

I'm sure a part of me realised I was clutching at straws. But desperation can blind a man better than a hot poker, which might have been less painful.

But my hopefulness meant I had begun to look for something noble to do; some great act of heroism to prove my worth to my heartless sister and my poor, misguided Gabriella.

Tides, what a naive fool I was in those days.

Such a quest wasn't easy to find. Delusion, misery and desperation brought me to Magreth. Being a hero without a cause is a depressing state of affairs. Magreth, on the other hand, was the home of the Eternal Flame. The High Priestess of the Tide resided there. Perhaps there was some task I could undertake for her. Perhaps the High Priestess of the Tide needed the services of a well-intentioned, albeit disenfranchised, prince.

I'm not sure who put the notion in my head to go to Magreth, or where I got the idea such a quest were even possible, but with nothing better to do with my time, it seemed as good a plan as any.

I managed to find a berth on an oared sailing galley making the perilous voyage across the Jade Ocean. As manning an oar required brute strength rather than any particular skill, I was able to play down my lack of experience with the ship's master and convince the man I could do the job. An hour out of port, my shoulders burning from the unaccustomed exercise, I was already regretting my decision. Two days later, so sick I could barely stand, my hands rubbed raw by the oars, I was ready to throw myself overboard.

By the seventh day, I was convinced I was about to die. My hands were blistered and bloody, my body wretched, thin, worn out and dehydrated from the constant vomiting. My back was a slab of raw meat exposed by the lash of the oar-master who had no sympathy for any man who couldn't take the pace. My life blurred into such a litany of pain, misery and woe that even the memory of Gabriella's rejection seemed less painful in comparison.

I doubted I had the strength to go on, not even for another day. Unfortunately, Magreth was a couple of thousand nautical miles from Senestra and I came to this conclusion several hundred miles from the nearest coastline, so there wasn't much I could do but endure.

The voyage took another thirty-seven endless, nightmarish days.

Somehow, I made it. It would be an exaggeration to claim I began to enjoy the cruise, but by the time we docked in the island harbour of Taal, I'd come to terms with the notion of hard physical labour. My hands were calloused, my back scarred from the oar-master's lash, and I was quite determined never to set foot on an ocean-going vessel ever, ever again.

I soon learned another valuable lesson in Taal. One could, I discovered, run away from their problems, but one could never really escape them. I was just as unemployable in Magreth as I had been in Senestra, only now I had the added complication of not speaking the language.

Magreth was a breathtakingly beautiful place. A cluster of volcanoes had grown up out of the ocean floor over the eons until they formed a small island continent, the rich soil fertile enough for seasoned timber to take root. Surrounded by treacherous reefs, startlingly white coral sands encircled the continent, stretching for miles with pristine beaches shaded by tall palms and populated by laughing, naked, brown-skinned children who thought the tall, pale stranger sleeping on their beach was quite a novelty.

The children poked fun at my fair, sunburned skin and told me I'd never survive the heat. They also taught me enough of the language to discover that even getting in to see the High Priestess was next to impossible.

I scoffed at their warnings about the High Priestess, but they were right about the heat. I soon abandoned my Kordanian leathers for the sensible local custom of wearing a wrap. The only difference between the male and female mode of dress in Magreth, in fact, seemed to be the place at which one tied on their garment. The women wore theirs tied just above the breast. The men wore them tied around their waists. They were bright and colourful, but most importantly, they were cool. I felt ridiculous and self-conscious at first, wearing nothing but a scrap of cloth tied around my middle, and it was a stolen scrap at that, but common sense and the risk of sunstroke won out over fashion sense. I decided I'd rather be cool than care if anybody noticed my lash-scarred back or my pitifully protruding ribs.

The Temple of the Tide was located in the foothills of the Hanalei Mountains, a fabulous place built of marble and gold, some two hundred miles from Taal, no distance at all given how far I'd already travelled. By the time I reached it, I was tanned almost as brown as the beach children, thin to the point of emaciation, but healed from my ordeal on the galley, although I still bore the scars on my back and the calluses on my palms.

And I was driven. Driven by the thought that every day I spent as an exile was another day closer to Gabriella marrying my undeserving brother; another day closer to the end of hope. I had no idea if the High Priestess was even in residence, certainly little hope she would agree to see me, but such is the power of self-delusion that still I dared to dream.

After ten days on the road, within sight of the Temple of the Eternal Flame, I was set upon by bandits.

I never understood why they attacked me. Perhaps it was because I was a foreigner. I had nothing of value. Anything I had ever owned worth selling was long gone, sold or bartered in exchange for food.

But attack me they did, and when the bandits realised I had nothing worth taking, they beat me some more, as if that somehow made ambushing this weary traveller worth the effort. I tried to resist, but the fight had gone out of me by then. Months of lonely exile and near starvation had left me a mere husk of my former self. As I lay on the ground, blows raining down on me, I was certain I was going to die and for the first time in my short life, the prospect didn't bother me unduly. As I was battered, punched and kicked without mercy, even the pain faded into the distance after a time. I barely felt the boot that ruptured my kidney, or the punch that burst my spleen.

I did see the foot coming that ended it all, however. A boot in the face is a memorable thing, even for a man in the process of being beaten to death.

I felt nothing after that, convinced I was dead, a feeling that only got stronger when I felt gentle arms lifting me from the road. The pain receded. Oblivion beckoned. I opened my eyes to find a woman leaning over me. She was smiling. Dressed in a white wrap, her fair hair glinting like gold in the sunlight. She was more than beautiful. She was exquisite.

"Rest easy, young traveller," she murmured in a voice woven from silk. "You are safe now."

"Who . . . who are you . . . ?" I managed to stammer through my broken jaw. I remember tasting the metallic tang of my own blood, the jagged feel of my broken teeth, the odd thickness of my swollen tongue, but I was in no pain—a sensation (or lack of it) which merely exacerbated the feeling that I had died and crossed into the afterlife.

"A friend," she assured me in a silken whisper, smiling, smoothing the blood-matted hair from my forehead.

"I am Cayal . . . ," I must have told her.

"And I am Arryl," she said. "The High Priestess of the Tide."

Chapter 26

Once again, the spell of Cayal's story was broken by the appearance of Timms, come to escort the duchess from Recidivists' Row. Arkady acknowledged him with a nod and rose to her feet. Cayal watched her closely, as if he was trying to gauge her reaction to his tale.

"Well?" he asked, when she offered no comment.

"Well, what?" she asked, putting away her notebook. Once again, she had only pretended to take notes, Cayal's hypnotic voice distracting her from her purpose. Once again, the pages were almost blank, her scientific objectivity forgotten as she became engrossed in the world he created with his fabulous tale.

"Do you believe me yet?"

"I believe you've studied the Tarot. Your tale says exactly what the cards say. The Immortal Prince travelled the world looking for adventure."

"You don't allow for the fact that your wretched cards are based on my truth and not the other way around?"

"Not for a moment."

"Then more fool you, my lady."

Arkady turned away, afraid he'd read her uncertainty. It was gloomy in the cells. She shivered a little as the temperature dropped with the setting sun, wondering idly how these prisoners got through the night with nothing but a thin blanket for warmth.

"I'm curious about one thing," she said, shouldering her satchel and turning to face him, composed once more.

He raised a brow at her curiously. "Only one?"

"If you truly are immortal, then you've known all along, if I understand this correctly, that you can't die?"

Cayal nodded. "Well . . . yes."

"And yet you committed a heinous crime in a place where you knew the only punishment is likely to be execution. You must have known your hanging wouldn't work. Why bother?"

"Because they weren't supposed to hang me. Lebec usually beheads their criminals."

"What good would that do you? You told me Pellys was decapitated and his head grew back. Why didn't you say something when they tried to hang you?"

"I did try. My pleas of I'd rather you didn't hang me because I can't actually die didn't seem to impress the hangman overly much."

With that, Cayal turned his back on Arkady and walked to his pallet. She stared after him and then glanced across at Warlock and Timms, wondering if the Crasii or the guard had any idea what Cayal meant.

"The suzerain grows weary, I think."

Arkady looked over her shoulder at the big Crasii. "Weary of what?"

"Living."

"What do you mean?"

"Decapitation would have taken his memory away, if not his life."

Arkady turned to look at Cayal. "Is that true?"

He lay back on his pallet, arms folded behind his head. "Truth is an illusion."

"It is in your world," she agreed, a little annoyed that he had retreated behind his veneer of disdain and contempt once more. The Cayal who spoke so eloquently of his long-forgotten world seemed a different man entirely to the one incarcerated in Recidivists' Row.

"Will you speak to the Warden, your grace?" Warlock asked, approaching the bars. Timms drew his truncheon with a threatening scowl, warning the Crasii back.

Arkady looked at the canine blankly. "About what?"

"About being allowed out for exercise. As the suzerain requested."

She glanced across at Cayal, whose gaze was fixed determinedly on the rough ceiling of his cell. She hesitated and then nodded. "I'll see what I can do."

"Thank you, your grace."

Timms ordered the Crasii away from the bars, but Cayal made no attempt to echo the Crasii's gratitude. More than a little peeved by his moodiness, she shouldered her bag a fraction higher, pushed the chair aside, and then, on impulse, as Timms headed back down the corridor assuming she was behind him, she stepped up to the bars of Cayal's cell.

"Something else about your story intrigues me," she said.

"How nice for you."

"You speak of Magreth as a continent. You talk of a temple dedicated to this Eternal Flame of yours."

"So?"

"Well, what happened to it? Magreth is nothing more than a series of uninhabited islets, surrounded by reefs and riddled with volcanoes. Where did your temple go? There are no ruins on Magreth that I've ever heard of, and I'm a historian, so I would have heard something about them, if they ever actually existed. Where are they? What happened to the people? Did they just vanish, too?"

"Pellys happened to them."

"What do you mean?"

Cayal was silent for a moment and then sat up abruptly, rose to his feet and walked back to Arkady, stopping so close only the pitted iron bars separated them.

Before she could stop him, he took her hands in his. His touch startled and surprised her. There were no calluses on his hands, as one might expect on a labourer. They were smooth, unmarked and unscarred, which was odd for a man claiming to be a tradesman. Even Stellan's hands were calloused from holding the reins after a lifetime on horseback.

"You really are too curious for your own good, Arkady."

She refused to react to him, pretending she didn't notice he was holding her hands.

"You're avoiding my question, Cayal." She'd never been this close to him before. It alarmed her to realise her heart was pounding. She knew this man unsettled her, but she hadn't expected she might be afraid of him.

"No," he said, massaging her hands gently. "I'm not."

"Then tell me what happened to Magreth." She wanted to step back, but was afraid the movement would betray her uneasiness, or attract Timms's attention. She couldn't understand why she wanted to protect Cayal from Timms's truncheon. This man was a liar, a murderer and probably a spy. He had no business making her pulse race with fear.

And it is *fear,* she told herself sternly. She wouldn't allow herself to contemplate the notion that it might be for any other reason.

"Magreth was destroyed," he told her, studying her face closely, as if he could read every conflicted emotion lurking behind her eyes.

"In the Cataclysm?"

"In a fit of pique."

"I don't understand." Arkady was no longer even certain they were talking about the same thing.

"When Pellys's head grew back," Cayal told her softly, forcing her to focus on what he was saying rather than what she was feeling, "he was a blank slate, just a whole lot of power and no memory of how to control it. The gemang has that much right. Pellys split the continent asunder with a stamp of his foot."

"He destroyed the temple?"

"He destroyed everything. The immortals survived, naturally—or unnaturally, I suppose would be more accurate—but the rest of Magreth's population wasn't nearly so fortunate. Diala and Arryl were able to protect the Eternal Flame, but Lukys estimates nearly half a million people died that day."

Arkady searched his face, certain that this close, she should be able to detect some hint that Cayal was lying. But all she could see were a pair of startlingly blue eyes that seemed to devour her very soul. "So you tried to get yourself executed for what, Cayal? Were you trying to *erase* your memory?"

"More or less."

"Why?"

"If I can't die, then oblivion will suit me just as well."

Arkady smiled faintly, thinking that at last she'd found a chink in his story. "If that was your purpose, Cayal, why kill seven people? You could have found someone . . . paid someone . . . surely, to chop your head off . . . if that was really your intention."

"I wanted my head *chopped* off, Arkady, not hacked off. The job needed a professional to do it properly. It's a somewhat specialist profession, you'll find. And it takes a decent axe to do it painlessly. Why didn't I just pay someone? Because headsmen don't tend to advertise their occupation. Too many pissed-off relatives to deal with, I suppose."

"So you did something that would bring you to the headsmen," she concluded, thinking, yet again, that either Cayal was the most gifted liar on Amyrantha or he really was telling the truth.

"For all the good it did me."

"And the power you claim such an event would unleash? What about that? If I'm to believe this sorry tale, your beheading might well have destroyed Glaeba."

He shrugged. "I would have survived it."

His callous disregard for human life broke the spell. She snatched her hands away and stepped back from him, more rattled than she was prepared to admit.

"How do you know so much about what happened to Pellys?"

"Because I'm the one who decapitated him."

Arkady recovered her composure quickly, certain now that he was mocking her. "You really must take me for a fool."

"I'm not the fool here, Arkady," he warned. "Word will reach the others, eventually, that I'm here. And when it does, they'll come looking for me."

She raised her brow sceptically. "The other immortals can't be coming to kill you, surely?"

"I have immortal enemies aplenty and we have other ways of taking vengeance on each other," Cayal assured her ominously. "They're much more effective than death. Mostly they involve destroying things you think your enemy cares about."

Far from being intimidated by his warning, Arkady was genuinely amused. This story of Cayal's immortality was getting wilder by the day. "Oh, so now you're suggesting we should release you to protect Glaeba from the wrath of your immortal brethren?"

He smiled crookedly. "There's a thought."

"I think you really are insane, Cayal."

He shrugged. "Can't hang a man for asking."

"No," she agreed. "We save that punishment for murderers."

"Now you're trying to hurt my feelings."

"A tactic that might work, if I thought you had any."

Arkady turned away, satisfied she had gotten the last word in, but she was still too close to the bars and Cayal was quicker than she anticipated. He snatched at her arm and held it tight, pulling her closer with bruising force, until his lips were next to her ear, the cold bars pressed against her side. Across the corridor, Warlock lunged at the bars of his cell, growling, but there was little he could do to aid her.

"You know *nothing* of my pain, Arkady," Cayal hissed, his hot breath burning her ear, sending shivers down her spine. "Your narrow, wretched, shuttered, *mortal* mind can't conceive of the true agony of immortality."

"Let . . . me . . . go," she ordered stiffly, afraid of this dangerous man for any number of reasons, few of which—she was only just beginning to appreciate—were his potential for anger or violence.

"If only you understood," he added in an agonised whisper, "that release from this hell in which I reside is all I crave."

He released her then and retreated to the back of his

cell, refusing to look at her again, leaving Arkady rubbing her bruised arm, wondering what he meant.

Of one thing, Arkady was certain. When Cayal spoke of the hell in which he resided, he wasn't talking about Lebec Prison.

Chapter 27

Once a year, the King of Glaeba came to Lebec.

It was a tradition as old as the nation of Glaeba itself, although the reasons for the annual ball were lost in antiquity. Tilly Ponting claimed it had something to do with one of Stellan's ancestors saving a Debree's royal hide in some obscure battle fought long ago, and the annual visit was to acknowledge the family debt.

Being rather more cynical than his wife's friend, Stellan thought it probably had more to do with the king keeping on the good side of the one branch of his family with the wealth, the resources and the right bloodline to topple him, if the mood ever took them. The Deseans were loyal supporters of the king, but it would only take one Duke of Lebec to get a little greedy for the whole royal house to start trembling.

That, Stellan knew, was the reason Mathu had originally been sent to Reon Debalkor and not here to Lebec, when it came time for his lessons in government. Enteny wished to keep his cousin onside. He didn't particularly want him *in*side.

Despite that, Enteny and Stellan got along quite well, helped, no doubt, by the difference in their ages. The king was already a young man by the time Stellan was born. In fact, he was closer to Mathu's age than the king's age. They had never been rivals—Stellan and the king—or even particularly close friends when they were younger. It was only since Stellan had become Duke of Lebec that the king had begun to fully appreciate what a loyal servant he had in his cousin, and maybe even now, he didn't fully understand how good a friend Stellan was. Karyl Deryon knew, but it was in the best interests of both men that the king remained in ignorance of some matters.

The king's visit, however—politics aside—was easily the most important social event of the year, marking the beginning of summer and end of the court's winter recess. Everybody who belonged at court, many who wished they did, and quite a few who were out of favour, flocked to Lebec for the King's Ball and then retired to their town houses in Herino for the rest of the summer, where they could attend court on a daily basis if they wished to. Or if the king wished them to.

An invitation to the King's Ball in Lebec was a guarantee of favour for the coming court season. Exclusion might mean something as simple as an oversight, or it might herald the downfall of an entire House. One advantage of hosting the ball, Stellan thought as he descended the grand sweeping stairs that led down to the ballroom, was there was no danger he wasn't going to be invited.

"The flowers are all wrong! That's not what I ordered at all!"

Stellan smiled at Arkady's irritated exclamation as he reached the bottom of the staircase. The vast ballroom was empty, but for his wife and the score of Crasii slaves loading up the tables and placing gilded, velvet-upholstered chairs around the walls.

"Should I fall on my sword now, or wait until the king arrives?"

"You mock me at your peril, Stellan," she warned.

He kissed her cheek fondly. For a common physician's daughter, she had a remarkable eye for the finer details of staging a royal event. He studied the flowers in question, which were being held by a nervous canine Crasii whose face was lost amid the foliage of the large arrangement. "They look fine to me."

"That's because you're a complete ignoramus about anything floral. You can't tell the difference between a petunia and a pine tree. Fuchsias are in this year. Royal Cerise fuchsias, to be precise. These are Noble Scarlet fuchsias."

"They look like pretty red flowers to me."

"Laugh at my flowers one more time, Stellan Desean, and trust me, you won't need to fall on your sword. I'll give you a push."

"I wouldn't dream of questioning your floral expertise," he assured her, forcing his features into a very serious, albeit entirely false, expression. "You look quite stunning, by the way. Is that the dress you beggared me for?"

She nodded distractedly, dismissed the Crasii who'd brought her the flower arrangement to inspect, and then turned to look at him. She was wearing the family rubies, an elaborate choker encrusted with deep red stones interspersed with freshwater pearls that had been in his family for generations and was probably worth as much as some entire noble estates. The ball gown was red beaded silk, the same colour as the rubies (and Arkady's questionable fuchsias), cut low at the front, even lower at the back, designed to entice as much as conceal. Her dark hair was caught up in a matching ruby and pearl clasp on the right side, but allowed to tumble over her bare left shoulder in a cascade of perfectly arranged curls. *She has an eye for more than the appropriate flowers, this wife of mine,* he thought.

"Do you like it?"

She was beyond beautiful. She was breathtaking. But Stellan knew how annoyed she could get when he reminded her of the fact. He shrugged. "Actually, I'm a bit disappointed. Given the price of the damned thing, I was expecting it to be encrusted with hand-sewn virgin mermaid scales, at the very least."

Arkady spared him a brief smile, ordered another one of the Crasii to move the punchbowl on the main table and then turned back to him. "It's the quality of the workman-ship, Stellan. The stitching is so small you can barely see it. No, Tassie," she called suddenly, "put the cups by the punchbowl, not by the hot food platters!" With a sigh, she turned her attention back to her husband. "Have you seen Kylia yet?"

"No. Why?"

"No particular reason. Just be certain to make a fuss of her when you do see her, particularly if Mathu's around. This is her first official outing as an adult. She needs to know she's beautiful."

"Is Mathu suggesting she isn't?"

Arkady smiled. "Just do it, Stellan. Don't try to figure it out. Be impressed by her. And don't ask what the dress cost."

He sighed dramatically. "If you're so determined to ruin me, Arkady, I could arrange for you to stand at the gates and throw all my worldly wealth to the passers-by, you know."

"I'd never be able to lift the antiques," she replied blandly. "This is much more fun."

Shaking his head, Stellan smiled. "I'll bet she looks a treat. As do you, I might add. Are you planning to flirt with the king?"

"Don't I always?"

"You know he thinks you're the only woman in Glaeba he can't have."

Arkady seemed amused. "That's only because he doesn't get out much, Stellan. Do you think they'll be on time, this year?"

"As they haven't made it on time once in the past decade, I'm not certain it would be wise to count on it this year, your grace."

Stellan and Arkady both turned at the unexpected an-swer to find Declan Hawkes standing at the entrance to the ballroom, cutting a surprisingly elegant figure in his unac-customed finery. It must be raining again, Stellan noted. The spymaster's hair was damp, although obviously he had taken the time to comb it before entering the palace ballroom. Hawkes stepped forward, bowed politely to

Stellan when he reached the foot of the staircase and then turned and bowed with equal respect to Arkady. "You look lovely as always, your grace."

"Thank you, Declan. It's nice to see you again."

"As always, it's nice to be home," he replied, raising her hand to his lips.

Stellan frowned. The friendship between Declan Hawkes and his wife made him more than a little uneasy. He frequently told himself there was nothing sinister about it. They'd grown up in the slums of Lebec together. Their friendship was almost as old as they were, but it disturbed him, nonetheless. Perhaps it was because he was never certain just how much Arkady had shared with her best friend, or indeed if Declan Hawkes wasn't secretly jealous of him for marrying Arkady and simply biding his time, waiting for the right moment to bring the whole world crashing down upon his rival. Stellan had no proof, or even the slightest evidence that was the case, but the possibility niggled at the back of his mind every time he saw his wife and the spymaster together.

And then another thought occurred to him. Arkady knew Stellan would not object to a lover. If she took one, would it be this man? For that matter, had she already chosen him? Was that what she meant when she'd warned a lover was too dangerous? Did she mean all lovers in general or was she specifically referring to Declan Hawkes?

"Is the rest of the royal party following you?" Arkady was asking, as Stellan forced his growing paranoia away to concentrate on Declan's reply. *You worry about nothing,* he assured himself. *Hawkes would die before he allowed anything to hurt Arkady and I trust her implicitly.*

"The king and queen were an hour or so behind me," he was assuring Arkady. "I rode on ahead so you can tell me of your progress with our would-be immortal."

Relieved there was a rational explanation for Hawkes's early arrival, Stellan smiled. "Arkady has been quizzing him quite diligently. She wanted to chop his pinkie off."

Declan's face creased into a smile. "That sounds like

something Arkady would suggest. As for proving his immortality, for all we know, it could be true."

"What do you mean?"

"The Caelish have never heard of him. Or if they have, they're denying it."

"Then he's *not* a Caelish agent?" Arkady asked, with a glint in her eye that made Stellan wonder if she was still planning to dismember their prisoner.

"There's a question about whether or not he's even from Caelum," Declan told them. "According to my sources, the only reason the Caelish Ambassador hasn't denied it officially yet is because his government is still trying to decide if there's some sort of profit to be made by claiming him."

"If he's not Caelish, what is he then?" Stellan asked. "Tenacian, perhaps? Senestran? He's too fair-skinned to be Torlenian."

"He says he's Kordanian," Arkady informed them, clearly sceptical of the claim.

Declan shrugged. "That's convenient. Claim to come from a nation that no longer exists. Who decided he was Caelish, anyway?"

"I believe that's what he said when he first arrived in Glaeba," Arkady informed them. "Or they assumed it. It doesn't surprise me to discover he's lying. Cayal lies about everything."

Stellan shook his head. "Are you sure we're not just dealing with a madman?"

"Not entirely," Arkady conceded. "But I suspect not. His story is too well thought out to be the ravings of a lunatic."

"Well, you're the one interrogating him," Declan told her, "so I'll leave you to be the judge. Just be careful."

"We can't be faulted on this, Declan," Stellan assured him, a little surprised to hear the spymaster issue such a warning. "We've done everything according to the strictest letter of the law. The fear this man might be a Caelish agent left us no other choice."

"Don't be too sure of that, your grace," the young man

warned. "To an outsider it looks as if you have your wife interrogating a potential spy, instead of executing him again or handing him over to me officially. Someone is bound to read something into that."

"You know the reasons we can't execute him again as well as anybody, Master Hawkes. And it was your suggestion Arkady become involved."

"Yes," the spymaster conceded. "But that was before Prince Mathu invited himself here. It's not what I believe that counts, my lord. It's what the king believes. And right now, you have another cousin suffering intense embarrassment because the king's heir would rather be in Lebec with you than in Venetia with the mentor his father chose for him."

Arkady glanced at her husband with an expression that spoke volumes, but she was too polite to say *I told you so* with Declan Hawkes looking on.

"Mathu hasn't put a foot wrong since he's been here," Stellan reminded him.

"A situation that simply makes Duke Reon look even more incompetent."

"Am I in trouble with the king?" Stellan asked, a little sick of Hawkes's instinctive need to hedge around the real issue.

Hawkes shrugged. "Let's just say that both the king and the Duke of Venetia are acutely aware of the crown prince's presence, not to mention his exemplary—and quite out of character—behaviour, in Lebec."

"Enteny only had to say something and I would have sent Mathu back to Reon in Venetia," Stellan reminded him.

It was Arkady, as usual, who saw straight to the heart of the problem, even before Hawkes could answer.

"You should have known, Stellan," she told him. "That's what the king will be angry about. He's mad at you because he shouldn't have had to say anything about it at all."

Chapter 28

Jaxyn Aranville waited a good long time before he attempted to speak with Arkady at the ball. There was no point going near her early in the evening. As Stellan's hostess, either she was too busy organising the legion of Crasii slaves on duty for the occasion or she was occupied greeting their guests with her husband, Mathu, and the King and the Queen of Glaeba. Either way, she had no time to spare for a houseguest whose only function this evening was not to draw attention to himself.

He watched her from afar, thinking the Duchess of Lebec was going to be a real challenge. It wasn't just her physical attributes that attracted him. Arkady offered a challenge the likes of which he hadn't enjoyed in a very long time. She genuinely despised him. What's more, she despised him for the purest and most admirable of reasons. She could see through him.

And that, to Jaxyn's mind, meant that she understood him.

To understand him, Jaxyn figured, she must be able to think along the same lines. To fully appreciate the depth of his ambition, she must have a similar ambition of her own. It was that which Jaxyn found so enticing. The idea that in the perfectly proper Arkady there might lurk a soul mate was like dangling a piece of shiny string in front of a kitten. Even if she didn't realise the truth in herself, the fun would come from peeling away those protective layers she had drawn about herself, exposing the darkness lurking underneath.

It was more than enticing, Jaxyn decided. It was nigh on irresistible.

Corrupting innocence is easy, after all; corrupting the self-righteous . . . now that is infinitely more satisfying.

Jaxyn had watched the party rather than taken part in it. He had a very comfortable life here in Lebec and wasn't about to ruin it by embarrassing Stellan. He kept to the fringes, smiling, drinking and nodding to the few people he wished to acknowledge and avoiding those friends of the family likely to ask awkward questions about his activities, or worse, actual members of the Aranville family. It was close to midnight before he deemed it safe to approach Arkady. By then everyone had consumed enough alcohol that he could count on hazy memories tomorrow, if need be—including his own.

Not that it mattered much. Nobody was really watching him. All eyes were on the crown prince, the room talking of nothing but the attention the young man had paid to Kylia Debrell all evening. And what was Prince Mathu doing in Lebec anyway? Hadn't the king sent him to Reon in Venetia?

Kylia was wearing a much more demure gown than Arkady. Dressed in layers of pale green silk so fine they were almost transparent, she wafted around the ballroom, her gaze only for the crown prince, ignoring every other person in the room.

The prince's obvious attraction to her didn't surprise Jaxyn. She might have Stellan believing she was an innocent, but Jaxyn knew better. The girl was a born seductress. What remained to be seen was how her machinations would impact on Jaxyn's plans. He hadn't decided yet if Kylia was going to be a problem, partly because he wasn't entirely convinced she had the skills to snag herself a prince, which was clearly her intention, and the reason the gossips were so busy. He watched her looking into Mathu's eyes as they danced, her face alight with happiness, and shook his head.

Poor Mathu didn't stand a chance, really.

Putting aside the dilemma of Kylia, Jaxyn turned his attention to his own, more immediate problem. As the evening wore on he worked his way surreptitiously around the ballroom, nodding a greeting here, smiling there, even taking the time out to partner Lord Devalon's decrepit old wife through the quadrille. When he finally got near Arkady, he hesitated, content to just admire her from a short distance. She was addressing a number of slaves, issuing more orders, and the canines listened eagerly, determined to please. True, that was the nature of canine Crasii. The eagerness of dogs to please their masters was the reason the Tide Lords chose to blend dogs and humans into household slaves in the first place, Jaxyn knew. Arkady had a way of dealing with them that went beyond simple inbred loyalty. The Crasii actually loved her. They *wanted* to be her slaves.

"Did you wear that dress for me?" Jaxyn asked, sidling up to Arkady as she finished ordering the last few slaves to bring out another platter of pastries for the dessert table, and they'd hurried off to do her bidding. "You certainly didn't wear it for your husband."

The party had thinned a little, but still had a way to go before it was done. The king and queen hadn't retired yet, and most of the guests would not dare leave before they did. Arkady turned to Jaxyn, smiling, far too aware of the need to publicly maintain her gracious posture to react to his taunt.

"Lord Aranville," she replied. "How nice of you to join us this evening."

"Wouldn't have missed it for the world," he assured her, slurring his words a little. "You look stunning, by the way. But you know that already, don't you. Want to know how I can tell?"

She sighed in annoyance, but her smile never wavered. Anybody watching them from a distance would be unable to determine the nature of their discussion unless they could lip-read. "I'm sure you're going to tell me."

"It's because you're never surprised when a man tells you how beautiful you are. You accept the compliment like it's your due."

"Then consider your dues paid and get out of my way," she told him pleasantly.

He moved a little closer, running his fingers lightly down her exposed back. He felt her stiffen with shock under his touch, but she couldn't do anything about it without draw-

ing attention to them both. "Can I come to your room tonight?"

"Only if you fancy being castrated."

"I'm serious, Arkady."

"So am I, Jaxyn," she assured him, stepping away from
his hand.

Jaxyn's smile widened. The more he had to do with
Arkady Desean, the more convinced he became that she
was just like him. "Stellan wouldn't mind."

"I would."

"Only until you came to your senses." He cast his gaze
over her enticing cleavage. "And I could arrange for that
to be *days* from now."

Arkady surprised him by laughing aloud. "No wonder
you've turned to your own sex for gratification, Jaxyn. No
woman over the age of fourteen would fall for that line."

Jaxyn glanced around, surprised she had made such a
statement so openly. There was nobody within earshot, fortunately, and even if there had been, with the music and the
level of conversation going on in the ballroom, she probably
wouldn't have been overheard. Still, Arkady was proving
herself far more willing to take risks than he first suspected.

"You like living dangerously, don't you?"

"Unlike you," she retorted, "who likes living like a
well-kept pet."

He raised a brow at her and grinned. "Jealous?"

"Not in the slightest."

"Ah, that's right . . . I'm a profligate parasite, but you
have your noble academic work to keep you occupied,
don't you?"

"Don't be so hard on yourself, Jaxyn," she scolded
sweetly, her smile dripping venom. "You have important
work, too. Whoring can be a real challenge, I'm told."

"Have you broken Cayal yet?"

His question took her by surprise, shaking her out of
her smug condescension. "What?"

"The Immortal Prince?" he reminded her. "Cayal of
Lakesh. Have you broken him yet? Proved his mortality."

"What's that got to do with you?"

"Just curious."

"It's none of your business, Jaxyn, whether I have or not."

"I bet you'd wrap those gorgeous long legs around a real Tide Lord if you were given half a chance."

She glared at him. "You should retire now, Jaxyn, while I'm still in the mood to dismiss your remarks as the drunken ramblings of a small-minded fool."

"And you should learn to quit while you're still ahead of the game, Arkady. You're playing with fire and you don't even realise they've tied you to the pyre."

She shook her head, clearly puzzled by his warning. "What are you babbling about?"

He almost told her, but stopped himself at the last moment. She wasn't ready yet and this game had a long way to go before it was done. "Nothing. You were right. It's just the drunken ramblings of a fool. Care to dance?"

"Don't be absurd!"

"Then I and my drunken, foolish ramblings shall retire, your grace. This is your party, after all, and this well-pampered *pet* doesn't fancy having to find a new home anytime soon."

She stepped back from him, obviously confused by his erratic behaviour and more than a little disturbed by it. "Goodnight, Jaxyn."

"Your grace." He bowed to his hostess, wobbling a little on the way down, and then headed off across the ballroom leaving Arkady staring after him, clearly concerned.

With his back to her, he smiled, not nearly as inebriated as Arkady thought he was. He hadn't gotten any closer to seducing her, that was true, but he had worried her enough that it was unlikely she would think about much else for the rest of the evening.

Any night Arkady couldn't get her mind off him was a success, Jaxyn believed. Every worried frown, every nervous sip of wine she took while wondering what he was up to, who he was speaking to, who he might be offending, who he might be sharing Stellan's dangerous secret with . . . every one of them was a moment spent thinking of *him* and that, Jaxyn knew, was half the battle.

The first rule of seduction was to make your victim aware of you.

Forcing them to think of little else was the touch of a master.

Chapter 29

The morning after the ball, Stellan and Enteny Debree, the King of Glaeba, took a turn by the lake before breakfast, their first chance to speak in private since the king had arrived in Lebec. Although nothing had been said so far, Stellan knew his cousin was displeased, and wondered if the consequences were going to be anything more dire than a telling off. Enteny was not an unreasonable man, but neither was he particularly flexible. Nor was he very tolerant of his son's peccadilloes. Or of those who appeared to condone them.

Enteny was tall and well built, the muscle of his youth softened with age. His hair was completely grey now, his face lined by a lifetime of worries few normal men ever had to deal with. They walked beside the water's edge in silence for a time, the ground squelching underfoot, and when the king finally spoke, it was of inconsequential things. It took him some time to get to the real reason he had asked for this stroll along the shore. The sun was still low on the eastern horizon, a faint mist hovering over the lake. The rushes whispered softly on Stellan's right, the rustling caused by the birds that nested in the tall reeds. There was no wind. With the overcast sky just waiting to burst, the air felt so still it was as if the world was holding its breath.

226

JENNIFER FALLON

"Mathu seems to have enjoyed his time here in Lebec," the king remarked finally. "Unexpected though it was."

"I'm sorry, Enteny," Stellan replied. "I should have consulted you before bringing him here."

"You should have sent him straight back to Reon," the king scolded. "It was not Mathu's choice where I sent him and certainly not your role to override my wishes. I'm still not even sure how he wound up here in Lebec. Reon's claiming you engineered the whole thing with the express purpose of throwing my son and your niece together."

The duke shook his head. "If I was planning a union between Kylia and Mathu, I would have come to you long before now, Enteny, and proposed the damn thing formally. I've nothing to gain by throwing them together and hoping they fall in love."

"Well . . . are you?"

"Am I what?"

"Planning to approach me about Kylia and Mathu?"

"No."

"Why not?" the king grumbled. "Isn't my son good enough for a Desean?"

Stellan smiled. "I was under the impression you had Reon's eldest daughter, Sarina, in mind for Mathu's consort. Hence the reason you sent him to Venetia in the first place."

Unexpectedly, the king sighed. "Tides, is everything I do so damned transparent?"

"Speculating about who will marry your son is a sport that's been popular since Mathu drew his first breath. It'll just get worse until he's finally off the market."

The king didn't seem surprised by the news. "Karyl Deryon tells me the same thing. Was I the subject of so much intense conjecture when I was his age?"

"Probably," Stellan agreed. "I'm too young to remember it myself. You were already married by the time I first came to Herino Palace."

Enteny stopped walking and looked out over the lake, squinting a little as the rising sun gilded a narrow path along the still water. He was silent for a time and then turned to his cousin. "Reon's very angry, Stellan. He's angry with Mathu for leaving Venetia without so much as a by-your-leave. With you for bringing him here to Lebec instead of sending him back. With Lord Deryon for seeking your help when the boy turned up in Herino, instead of sending word to Venetia. With me for not *insisting* you send him back . . ."

"Why *didn't* you write to me the moment you learned Mat was in Lebec and demand I send him back to Reon?" Stellan asked. "I was half-expecting you to."

Enteny shrugged. "Because Reon's a fool and a bore and in Mat's place I probably would have wanted to do the same thing. Not that you're to ever let him know I said that. Right now, my son thinks I'm planning to have him dismembered. I intend to let him continue thinking that for a few more days at least. Not only will it do Mathu good to sweat for a bit, but it makes Reon think I'm suitably outraged as well."

"And what punishment have you in mind for me, your majesty?" Stellan enquired with a raised brow. "That will satisfy the Duke of Venetia?"

"I'm thinking of sending you into exile."

Stellan glanced at the king a little worriedly. It was impossible to tell from his tone if he was serious. *"Exile?"*

"Of a sort. Things have been rather strained in Torlenia since the new Imperator came to power. Lord Jorgan—whom we both know is not renowned for his patience—finally lost his temper with him a few days ago over this business of who has sovereignty in the Chelae Islands. He's been thrown out of Ramahn. I need a new ambassador. Reon's suggesting—very loudly—that it should be you."

"And you're actually considering it?"

Enteny shrugged. "The idea has merit, Stellan. After Caelum, Torlenia is the most contentious ally we have and you are—without question—my most accomplished diplomat. You were high on my list of suitable contenders anyway. Placating Reon Debalkor is just a bonus, really."

"Will the knowledge that I have no wish to leave Lebec, especially for a place like Torlenia, do anything to influence your decision?"

"It might have once," the king replied with a scowl. "Before you brought Mathu here and caused all this fuss."

Stellan shook his head, unable to believe what he was hearing. "But there's the estate to consider and I would have to speak to Arkady. She may not want to leave . . ."

"You have plenty of staff and an efficient estate manager," the king reminded him. "He never had any trouble in the past looking after your affairs while you've been away. As for Arkady—she is your wife, Stellan; she will go where you do. In fact, she's half the reason I'm tempted to send you to Torlenia, anyway. I adore the girl, you know that, but you allow her far too much freedom. You've been married six years. You should have half a dozen brats running around the palace by now. In Torlenia, with no university to distract her, Arkady can get on with the prime function of her gender, which is to bear the next generation."

Stellan was glad Arkady wasn't here to witness the king's declaration, quite certain she would not have been able to hold her tongue. As it was, he could imagine her reaction when he informed her of this disastrous turn of events. Although the king had said he was only *thinking* about sending them to Torlenia, the more he spoke, the more certain he seemed, almost as if he was talking himself into it. Karyl Deryon had warned Stellan the king was displeased with their childless status, although he certainly hadn't hinted at a foreign posting as a solution.

"It would be awkward," Stellan suggested carefully, "for me to leave Lebec at the moment."

"Why?" the king demanded.

"Well . . . for one thing, we have this business with our Caelish agent . . ."

"Declan tells me the Caelish have never heard of him."

"They're claiming that now," Stellan agreed. "But Arkady is convinced he's been sent here to stir up the Crasii. Until we've gotten to the bottom of it—"

"Hand the prisoner over to Hawkes," the king ordered. "A few days with his boys and a red-hot poker should settle the matter one way or another."

"Your majesty, we can't torture the prisoner. If the Caelish learn of it, we have people in their prisons who will suffer a similar fate."

"But they're denying he belongs to them, so they can hardly object to the way we're treating him, can they?" The king waved his arm dismissively. "No. Let's be done with this nonsense. It's simply more proof of what I was saying about your wife, anyway. She shouldn't be getting mixed up in things like this. She should be at home, having babies like a proper wife."

Stellan sighed, wondering how he was going to break the news to Arkady. Even if she took it well—which was unlikely—he was convinced this was a terrible idea.

"Enteny . . . ," Stellan began.

"I'll sweeten the deal," the king offered, before Stellan could object any further.

"How?" He couldn't imagine any circumstance that was going to make this untenable situation easier to bear.

It's odd, he thought. *You spend all your time worrying about one thing, and when the axe finally falls, it comes from a totally unexpected direction.*

"I'll agree to a betrothal between Mathu and Kylia."

Stellan was speechless.

The king smiled. "Aha! You didn't know about that one, did you?"

"Know about *what*? I never suggested . . ."

"No. But Mathu did."

"Mathu?"

Enteny nodded. "He was in my ear about it the moment I arrived in Lebec. And his mother's ear, too, and you know how she can never say no to him. He wants to marry your niece and I'm inclined to let him, because although I think Reon has a right to be angry, the idea of strengthening the family ties between Venetia and Herino doesn't seem all that attractive any longer." The king let out a short, sceptical laugh. "If this business has achieved anything useful, it's reminded me how dreadful it would be to have the Debalkors as in-laws. Reon's bad enough when I only have to put up with him a few times a year at court. Imagine what it would be like to have him as a close member of the family."

"I thought you were resolved to have Mathu remain unmarried for a while longer? At least until the Caelish have gotten used to the idea that he's never going to marry Princess Nyah?"

"You took care of the Caelish, didn't you? You told me they'd accepted the reasons for our refusal of Nyah as a viable wife for the Glaeban crown prince."

"I said they *appeared* to have accepted it. Until we have proof this Lakesh fellow isn't one of their agents . . ."

"Oh, for pity's sake, stop with this spy nonsense, cousin!" the king ordered. "You've no more proof he's a Caelish spy than I am. Declan will settle the matter once and for all and that will be the end of it."

Stellan wasn't going to give in so easily. "Kylia's only seventeen."

"Plenty old enough to marry. And I gather she's very favourably disposed to the idea."

"She's too young to understand the consequences."

The king frowned. "Are you refusing my offer?"

He shook his head. "I'm just pointing out that Kylia may not understand what it means to marry the crown prince."

"You underestimate your niece, Stellan. Take some of the credit for raising her well. Her breeding is impeccable, her education ideal, her family beyond reproach, and she's young enough to be guaranteed a virgin, something I'm not completely convinced of, by the way, about Sarina Debalkor. In fact, it couldn't be more perfect. You take care of Torlenia for me, I'll take care of your niece, and we've effectively taken care of Reon Debalkor and thumbed our noses at Caelum in the process. It's a grand idea, don't you think?"

"Does it actually matter what I think?" Stellan asked.

Enteny gripped Stellan's shoulder and smiled encouragingly. "Don't be like that, Stellan. I'm offering your girl the chance of a lifetime. Your niece will rule Glaeba someday."

The unfairness of it left Stellan feeling as if he'd been winded. "Even assuming I wanted that for her—which I don't—you're sending me into exile to placate a man you can't abide!"

The king shook his head. "I'm sending you to Torlenia because I need you there, cousin. The Chelae Islands are too strategically important to leave in the hands of an enemy and not strategically important enough to go to war over. There's nobody I trust better than you to point this out to the Torlenians. Cheer up! Reon may think I've exiled you, but his triumph won't last long once I announce the engagement between Mathu and Kylia."

Stellan sighed dejectedly, the futility of arguing with the king when his mind was set something he'd learned long ago. The mist was starting to lift from the lake, he noticed out of the corner of his eye, the sun piercing the clouds like lances of light. If the rain held off and the king had not just destroyed his entire world with a few simple words, it might have been a beautiful day today. "Can I ask one boon, your majesty?"

"If it's a reasonable one."

"Don't make the announcement yet. Let me speak to Arkady, first. And to my niece. I want to be certain Kylia appreciates what she's getting herself into and isn't just caught up in the throes of some fleeting girlish crush which may vanish as soon as the reality of her situation sinks in."

"You can speak to them at breakfast."

"Arkady may have already left for the day."

The king thought about it for a moment and then nodded. "You have until the end of the week, then. I will make the official announcement at dinner on the last night we're here in Lebec."

"I was hoping for a little more time than that."

"You're lucky I'm willing to grant you that much. I am

still more than a little vexed with you, cousin, for causing me all this grief."

"As you wish, your majesty," Stellan agreed unenthusiastically.

Tides, how did this happen? he wondered as they turned and headed back across the lawn to the palace. An hour ago, he had control of his life and the lives of those for whom he was responsible. Suddenly, it had all slipped from his grasp. *Kylia is going to marry Mathu Debree, while the rest of the household is being sent into the brutal, scorching deserts of Torlenia because I committed the crime of saving the king and queen from a scandal.*

Stellan wondered who was going to take the news worst.

His wife, Arkady, who would be required to give up everything for which she'd worked so hard?

Or Jaxyn Aranville, the lover he was going to have to leave behind?

Chapter 30

"I'm honoured, your grace," Cayal announced with a mocking bow when Arkady arrived at the prison for her interview.

"Honoured by what?" she asked, as Timms placed her chair in the corridor between the cells. She was tired after the ball last night and knew there'd be consequences resulting from her absence at the palace for breakfast, but for some reason, she couldn't stay away. Although she told herself the urgency of her mission had increased tenfold due to the king's visit and the news that Cayal had been disowned by Caelum, the truth was much more straightforward. Despite telling herself over and over that she didn't believe a word of it, Arkady wanted to hear the rest of Cayal's story.

She wanted to know how he became immortal.

"The king is here in Lebec," Cayal reminded her. "And yet you've eschewed his royal company for mine. I'm flattered."

"Don't be."

"Wasn't the famous King's Ball held last night?"

"How did you hear about that?"

"We're not completely cut off from the outside world in here," he said, leaning against the bars. "Are we, gemang?"

"The guards spoke of the king's annual visit," Warlock informed her, rising to his feet. He was such a huge beast, easily one of the largest canines Arkady had ever seen. But he seemed so gentle. So civilised; even under the constant provocation of his aggravating cellmate. Arkady found it hard to believe Warlock was here because he'd killed a man with his bare hands. "They spoke of the ball held in the king's honour each year."

"What else do the prison gossips say about the king?" she asked curiously.

"They say he's a right old bore," Cayal replied. "And that you were wearing quite a stunning red dress."

Arkady's eyes widened in surprise.

Cayal smiled. "You look worried, your grace."

"I am, a little," she admitted. "I can't imagine how you know what I was wearing last night."

"Same way I heard about the king. Magic."

Arkady smiled suddenly. "Magic, eh? I think there's a far more likely explanation." She glanced over her shoulder at Timms, who for once was showing no inclination to reach for his truncheon. "Your wife is a seamstress for Lady Kardina, isn't she, Mister Timms?"

"Yes, your grace."

"And she was undoubtedly on hand last night to sew Lady Kardina into her gown, and still there when her ladyship returned home in the early hours of this morning, when her extremely fashion-conscious mistress would have described every dress she'd seen last night in great and glorious detail, including mine. I imagine the news travelled from her, to her husband to you. Hardly magic, Cayal. Just good, old-fashioned gossip."

"Tides, are you such a killjoy about everything?"

"It's one of my more endearing traits, I always thought."

He smiled at her as Arkady realised with alarm that she was all but flirting with him. *Idiot,* she told herself sternly. "So, are you willing to tell us more of your tale?"

"Have you spoken to the Warden about us getting some fresh air?"

"I'm meeting with him after we're done here this morning."

"So you want the next instalment on credit."

Arkady sat down and opened her satchel, the act of searching for her notebook giving her an excuse not to meet his eye. "I suppose you could say that."

"Why should I trust you?"

"Why shouldn't you trust me?" she asked, looking up. "You expect me to take you at *your* highly suspect word. It's only fair, don't you think, that you return the favour?"

Cayal thought on that for a moment, and then he shrugged. "Fair enough. I'll take you at your word."

"That's very big of you," she couldn't stop herself from retorting.

"Don't take your sore head out on me, your grace," he chuckled, amused for no reason Arkady could explain.

"I do not have a hangover."

"No," he agreed thoughtfully. "I don't suppose you do. You probably never drink to excess. You probably don't do anything to excess, do you?"

"Whether I do or not, it's hardly any of your business."

"Is it hard work, being so perfect all the time?"

She met his eye evenly. "Actually, I find it's no work at all."

Cayal held her gaze without flinching. "Good answer. You really are quite the clever one, aren't you?"

"Yes, I am."

"Modest, too."

She sighed impatiently. "Are you actually going to tell

me anything this morning, Cayal, or just stand there trading insults?"

"Why? Have you someplace better to be?"

"The King and Queen of Glaeba are currently guests in my home," she reminded him. "Believe me, there are *plenty* of other places I could be."

Plenty of other places you should *be,* an accusing voice in her head reminded her.

Cayal bowed dramatically. "Then we are *truly* honoured by your presence, your grace."

"As you should be. You were telling me how you met Arryl, the Sorceress," she reminded him, her pen poised to take notes. "Please continue."

Cayal turned his back on her, leaning against the bars. "I told you already—Arryl wasn't a sorceress. She can barely sense the Tide, let alone wield it."

Arkady sighed, wondering if he would ever falter, even slightly, in the telling of this wild tale. She'd been hoping to shake his story, trip him up in a lie, but he never seemed to miss a single detail. "Can't all Tide Lords use magic?"

"Arryl is merely immortal. That doesn't make her a Tide Lord."

"It does according to the Tarot."

"And haven't I spent hours trying to convince you that your precious Tarot is about as useful as tits on a melon, Arkady? We've had this discussion before. You don't listen very well, do you?"

She ignored the jibe, still hoping to expose a crack in his story. "So all Tide Lords aren't immortal?"

"All immortals aren't Tide Lords," he countered.

"What are they, then?"

He shrugged. "Just immortal."

Arkady raised a brow curiously. "*Just* immortal."

Cayal looked over his shoulder at her. "It takes all kinds, Arkady, and even immortals need friends. That's what Diala used to do, you know, although she'd deny it if you accused her of it—make new friends."

"You called her the Minion Maker."

"Minion . . . friend . . . in Diala's world there's not a lot of difference."

"Is that how you became immortal? Are you one of Diala's minions?"

Cayal snorted contemptuously. "She wishes . . ."

"Then how *did* you achieve immortality?"

He pushed off the bars and turned to look at her. "You mean other than having my name enshrined in the annals of everlasting superstition and stupidity by being named as the first card in your wretched Tarot?"

"Yes," she agreed with a faint smile. "Other than that."

"I asked for it."

"Why?"

"Immortality's a bit like a sure bet at the races, my lady. It seems like a really good idea at the time. It's not until you've lost everything you ever owned that you start to wonder about the wisdom of gambling."

"So you've rethought your position?"

"I've had eight thousand years to rethink my position."

"Too much reflection can be a dangerous thing," she warned.

Cayal nodded solemnly in agreement. "More dangerous than you know, my lady."

"Then how about a little less reflection and a little more information?" Arkady suggested. "You were telling me how you travelled the world looking for redemption."

"Did I say that?"

"Words to that effect."

"Then I suppose you'll want to hear the rest of it . . ."

Chapter 31

It took time, but I healed completely from the attack, even my teeth were restored. I knew it was the result of something the priestesses had done to me. I'd felt them working their magic, even in the semi-conscious depths of my pain, but every time I questioned Arryl about it, she simply smiled and told me to thank the Tide for my blessings.

Strange, don't you think, that it never occurred to me—or Arryl, for that matter—that there was anything unusual in the notion I could feel the magic? In hindsight, I'm certain she said nothing to Diala about it. I would never have been offered the chance to become immortal by Diala if she thought for a moment that I might one day be a threat to her.

Diala was after minions, not masters.

Arryl, on the other hand—the one you insist on calling the Sorceress—was the very definition of sweetness. She and her sister, Diala, kept vigil over the Temple of the Tide. It was an impressive white marble edifice perched on a cliff top overlooking a dazzling waterfall that tumbled endlessly into a narrow lake, on the shore of which the emperor's palace was built. She'd been on her way back to the temple with her entourage when she found me lying on the road, left for dead by my attackers. Her men had lifted me into her litter while she walked the rest of the way back to the temple, so I could rest.

Arryl and Diala are like night and day. The eldest by seven years, Arryl is sweet, pure even. When I first met her, I wondered if she'd taken a vow of charity, or some such thing, which seemed the only way to account for her generosity. She cared for me, nursed me back to health with herbal poultices, her silky voice and one or two miracles.

In contrast to her sister, Diala is a seductress. I'm sure

you've heard the Crasii claim bitches give off a particular scent when they're on heat that male Crasii can smell. I'm here to tell you those who claim it aren't mistaken. She only had to be in the room for me to start thinking of her, even when I was still drifting in and out of consciousness.

This was in those long-distant days, remember, when I was still ignorant of the true power of the Tide—naive as a newborn fool for all that I had killed a man.

In Kordana we'd never embraced the worship of the Tide Star very enthusiastically, although we'd certainly traded with those who did. We Kordians were a pragmatic lot and worshipped little other than our own ingenuity. Even so, every nation on Amyrantha I have ever visited has worshipped the Tide in some form, at some point in their history. Some nations prayed directly to the sun itself, others have had much more formal church hierarchies and referred to the Tide as God. They've even worshipped us on occasion, sometimes as Tide Lords, other times naming us gods, which some among us find rather gratifying. But one way or another, the people of Amyrantha have always understood that all life comes from the Tide Star. At least they did back then. You shun the worship of the Tide as ignorant superstition now, but in those days people knew they owed the Tide Star their allegiance and they behaved accordingly.

In Magreth, however, they claimed a closer connection than most. They claimed to hold a piece of the Tide Star, which was the reason I had come here.

The Eternal Flame, a small fire that was never allowed to go out, burned on the white marble altar of the massive Temple of the Tides. The flame came from the Tide Star itself, Arryl told me, retrieved from a burning fragment of meteorite which had fallen into the frozen wastes of Jelidia more than a thousand years before, brought to this land by Engar. He had established the Empire of Magreth and then built a temple to house the holy flame, awarding it credit for his victory. The current Emperor Engarhod and his wife Syrolee, the empress, were his direct descendants, according to Magrethan folklore, and worshipped as demi-gods because of it.

I paid little attention to what Arryl was telling me, mostly because halfway through her tale, Diala had come into my room to replace the flowers with fresh ones and my attention immediately fixed on her.

I couldn't understand my fascination with the younger priestess. Arryl was by far the prettier and kinder of the pair, and I was still pining for Gabriella. She was the reason I was here, after all. I was looking for a noble quest, not a sexual conquest. But it was Diala, not Gabriella, I dreamed about; Diala whose face haunted my increasingly erotic dreams; her sinfully voluptuous body beckoning with every slight movement, no matter how innocuous. It was Diala's smouldering green eyes, filled with the promise of indescribable passion, that I yearned to see fixed on me with the same craving as my eyes fixed on her.

Arryl was not unaware of my attraction to Diala and considered her sister to be the one at fault. I discovered this when I stumbled across them arguing about me in one of the long corridors that encircled the main hall of the temple, several months after Arryl had rescued me from the side of the road.

"I'm sick of this, Diala," I heard Arryl complaining to her sister, just before I rounded the corner.

"Sick of what?" Diala asked, sounding full of wounded innocence.

I stopped, wondering at her response, trying to imagine about what the sisters might be arguing.

"You know what I'm talking about."

"No, sister dear, I don't. Among all the great powers the Tides have bestowed upon me, telepathy doesn't seem to be among them."

"Neither does common sense," Arryl retorted. "And you know exactly what I'm talking about. I don't want it to happen again."

"I haven't done anything to him. And I haven't done anything *with* him, either."

"But you're thinking about it constantly, and he's affected by your lust. Tides, even the mice around here are probably breeding more prolifically, with the heat you're giving off."

"Now you're exaggerating."

"I wish I was!"

Diala laughed. "Oh, come on, Rilly. I can have a bit of fun, can't I? And he's very pretty, don't you think? Now that I've fixed him up."

"You shouldn't have done that either," Arryl scolded. "He hasn't stopped asking questions since he woke up. Broken bones might heal, Diala, but teeth aren't supposed to grow back and scars don't miraculously disappear. Are you *trying* to give away our secret?"

"Actually, I'm still trying to figure out why we're keeping it a secret at all, but that's an argument for another time. What is it you wanted of me, sister?"

"I want you to leave the boy alone."

"He's a man, not a boy."

"By our standards, Cayal is a boy," Arryl corrected.

"By *our* standards?" Diala sneered. "He's twenty-six, Arryl. In that hovel you and I were born in, that would make him a village *elder*."

"And you the village idiot," Arryl shot back. Then she added in a more conciliatory tone, "Please . . . just let him be, Diala. You know the rules."

"Oh, and if I *break* them? What are you going to do? *Tell* on me? Now I'm really frightened."

I heard Arryl sigh patiently. "Syrolee has good reason to insist on her rules. You agreed to them when you became a Priestess of the Tide."

"That was before I realised she was using the Tide to create her own personal empire. Forever is a long, long time, Arryl. She can't think she's going to be allowed to dictate to us for that long."

"Talk to Syrolee yourself, if you disagree with her," Arryl suggested. "In the meantime, leave Cayal alone. Let him heal and let him leave. He's not for you because he's not one of us. And please, don't call me Rilly. You know how much it irks me."

I heard footsteps on the tiles, heading away from me after that. Guessing the conversation was over, and intrigued by what it might mean, I was about to move off when I heard Diala add in an irritated voice, obviously not meant for anyone but herself, "He's not one of us, eh, *Rilly*? Well, I can remedy *that* minor inconvenience easily enough."

I heard her footsteps fading into the distance a moment later, but I stood in the shadow of the great pillars for a while longer, wondering what they were talking of. I should have seen the danger signs, but I fear the greater part of me was basking in the knowledge that the priestess Diala—the desire for whom filled my every waking moment as well as my dreams—was lusting after me, almost as much as I was lusting after her.

The atmosphere in the temple changed subtly after I overheard the sisters arguing. It might have been because I was now acutely aware Diala was paying attention to me, or it might have been the undercurrent of tension that flowed back and forth between the two women. Meals became tense, the conversation laden with double meaning. If Arryl noticed something amiss, she said nothing, perhaps content her warning had been enough.

But I hadn't been warned about anything, I reasoned, and I couldn't take my eyes off Diala. I took to following her around the temple—surreptitiously, I thought—even when she climbed down the rocks near the cliff to wash her long dark hair, her body outlined in exquisite, tormenting detail by the folds of her white wrap, which was all but transparent when it was wet.

I thought I might go mad, I wanted her so badly. I had never wanted any woman, not even Gabriella, the way I desired Diala, which is odd, because somehow, I still believed my mission in life was to perform some great task that would see me restored in the eyes of my sister and my beloved.

Strange how a man can find room in his heart for such diametrically opposed beliefs, but I managed it, and without ever noticing the conflict.

As is usually the case with eavesdropping, though, I was left with more questions than answers. I didn't understand what Arryl had meant by breaking the rules or the relationship between the empress and the temple. No member of the Imperial family came to worship. Never even sent so much as an offering, for that matter. In fact, the only contact between the palace and the Temple of the Tides, that I was aware of, in all the months I'd been there recuperating, was the day Arryl returned from the palace and found me lying on the road and a visit some months later from Engarhod's son, Rance. He'd just returned from Senestra and stopped by to deliver some spices Arryl had requested he find for her in his travels.

I didn't understand much of anything, really, but I did think I'd worked out the "he's not one of us" remark. It wasn't a racial thing. With Arryl's blonde hair and Diala's green eyes, neither woman was a native of Magreth—that much was certain. I assumed she meant I wasn't a follower of their religion. I didn't understand their ways. As a priestess, Diala had a responsibility to the Tide Star, after all, and I was little more than a foreign pagan.

But time was passing and even through my lusting for Diala, I knew the day was fast approaching when Gabriella would marry my brother and be lost to me forever. I know you'll think me strange for still believing I had any right to her affection. There I was, panting after Diala like a dog after a bitch on heat, imagining I had a future with Gabriella. I can't explain it and I have no intention of trying to justify it. That is how it was.

I never, not even for a moment, imagined anything could go wrong with my grand plan to redeem myself and be allowed to return home. By then, you might think I'd begun to learn the stupidity of such a blind optimism, but I hadn't. Maybe that's why the Tide made me immortal. Perhaps it knew it would take an eternity for me to learn that bitter lesson and was determined to see I had the time in which to do it.

Diala didn't laugh at me when I broached the subject of a noble quest with her. I'm sure, knowing her as I do now, she must have burst something internally trying to stop herself from exploding with mirth when I went to her so full of earnest hope, but to my face, she nodded and smiled and made all the right noises in all the places I expected to hear them. I explained my case most eloquently, I thought, putting forward all my well-thought-out arguments about finding a task that would prove to the Queen of Kordana that I was a worthy subject, and to my beloved Gabriella that I was worthy of her love.

Diala barely hesitated before agreeing to help me.

"The Emperor of the Five Realms would welcome such a worthy supplicant," she informed me gravely. "And I'm sure he can aid you in your quest. But you'll have to go through the cleansing ceremony first before you can be admitted into his presence."

"What does that involve?"

"We'll have to do it in the main temple," she said, rising to her feet. There was no sign of Arryl. I wasn't sure where she'd gone but she was nowhere to be found. Later—much later—I realised her absence was the only reason Diala agreed to my request. Had Arryl been anywhere in the vicinity of the temple, she would have stopped Diala and my life would have followed a much different—not to mention infinitely shorter—path.

The temple was empty—tall, cavernous and majestic; its walls open to the gentle Magrethan climate. Only the burning vessel on the altar was shielded from the wind. As we entered the temple, Diala took my hand and led me to the altar.

Unafraid, and with no inkling of what was about to happen, I followed her, expecting a sermon about the spirit of the Tide Star or some such thing, perhaps even a repeat of the story of Engar bringing the Eternal Flame back from Jelidia. But when we reached the altar, Diala didn't say a word. She stopped and turned to me. Smiling, she slipped her arms around my neck, stood on her toes and kissed me with all the wanton abandon of a well-paid Lakeshian whore.

I was too stunned to question the reason for such a blessing. Without a thought, I pulled her to me, kissing her as if I might be able to devour her whole. I'd been lusting after her for so long I wanted to throw her down on the temple floor and take her, there and then. But Diala had done this before—so I discovered later—and knew precisely what she was doing. With the mere touch of her velvety and dangerously knowledgeable mouth, the press of her body against mine . . . that alone gave her all the power over me she needed.

In a matter of moments Diala had me right where she wanted me.

"Will you be mine, Cayal?" she breathed as her hands worked at the knot holding the wrap I wore around my waist.

"Tides! What a stupid question, woman," I muttered, wishing I was as adept at undoing knots as Diala. If only I'd known what she was really asking, I might have been less concerned about her wrap and more concerned about my future, but she was clever, Diala was. She knew how easy it is to distract a young man with promises of love.

"You have to want this, Cayal. Otherwise, I'll be in trouble for breaking the rules."

Rules? I vaguely recalled something about rules, but was too engaged in what her hands were doing to care about it. "Of course I want this."

After a couple of futile attempts between kisses to undo Diala's wrap, I abandoned the knot and instead pushed aside the thin white fabric, my hands groping for any part of her body I could reach. She let me fondle her breast, moaned with pleasure when I bent down to suck on it, but the moment my hand strayed to the moist cleft between her legs, she pushed me away.

"You're not ready yet," she announced, her eyes bright,

her face flushed with what I assumed was desire. It was, I suppose, but not for my body.

Diala wanted my soul.

At some point, she had managed to divest me of my wrap. I stood naked before her. Glancing down at the obvious evidence of my need, I took a step closer. "Trust me, Diala, I'm ready."

"First, you have to be cleansed."

She turned from me and stepped up to the altar, plunging her hand into the flaming bowl without warning. Before I could cry out in horror, she turned back to me, her hand alight.

I jumped away from her, afraid, but curiously, the sight of Diala's hand on fire did nothing to dampen my desire.

Diala noticed that, too. She smiled even wider. "I want you to burn for me, Cayal."

"Literally?" I enquired, staring at the flame with a great deal of concern.

"It doesn't hurt," she assured me, stepping so close I could feel the heat of the flame. "This is the Eternal Flame."

"Why doesn't it burn you?"

"Because I'm immortal." She moved even closer, the flame beckoning. "Do you want redemption, Cayal? *Really* want it? Do you want your sister to bow down before you? Your beloved Gabriella to worship you? Do you want to be like me? Forever young? Forever beautiful?"

"I don't understand."

"How old do you think I am?"

Eyes still fixed on her burning hand, I shrugged, wondering about the wisdom of answering such a question. "Nineteen, maybe."

"I am six hundred and fourteen years old," she announced. The flame still burned in her hand. I was entranced by it.

And I was entranced by the notion of immortality.

It seems such a wonderful idea when you don't stop to think about it for too long.

"I was eighteen when I stepped into the eternal flame," Diala coaxed. "Arryl was twenty-five. We did it together."

"Why doesn't the flame burn you?" I asked again, mesmerised by the sight of the fire licking at her unsinged flesh, seduced as much by the flames and the promise of immortality as I was by her physical presence.

"The Eternal Flame likes me." She stepped closer. "It likes you, too."

"How can you tell?"

"Because *I* like you."

Diala moved close enough for me to feel the heat from her right hand. With her left, she reached out to touch me, running her fingers lightly down my chest. I closed my eyes in anticipation of where her hand would stop, but she hesitated, stepping even closer. "I briefly can save you, Cayal," she insisted in a breathy voice that spoke of endless bliss. "Everything you ever wanted could be yours . . ."

My gaze locked on the flames, the anticipation more anguish than pleasure. It never really occurred to me that she was offering me an eternity of torment. At that moment, I couldn't see past the next few minutes. At best I had some vague notion that I might return home a hero someday. Infinity didn't even factor into it.

"I need to hear you say it, Cayal," she whispered softly, her breath on my neck teasing me with the wordless promise of even more delights to come. "I want to serve the flame."

"I want to serve the flame," I repeated mechanically, paying no attention to what I was saying. I was far too distracted by what Diala's free hand was doing to worry about it. I let the pleasure wash over me, staring at the green flames, as seduced by them as I was by Diala.

That was enough, it seemed, for Diala. It was certainly enough for the Eternal Flame.

No sooner had the words left my mouth than Diala was kissing me again. This time, when she slid both arms around me, my hair ignited. Within seconds, we were both engulfed in flames.

In a panic, I broke off the kiss, the agony of immolation putting an instant end to any other desire I might have been harbouring. I didn't know how long it lasted. Later, I learned, it was no more than a few minutes, but it felt like a lifetime. The Eternal Flame consumes only unworthy flesh, you see. For a soul who wanted what the flame had to offer, for them the magic was much kinder.

I want to serve the flame, I had told Diala, meaning every word of my passionate declaration with every fibre of my being.

Unfortunately, we were talking about two entirely different things. The fact that Diala knew that—had manipulated me into promising it—and still let me burn was the reason I grew to despise her.

In a few moments, the flames had died down and the pain began to fade. I was on the floor of the temple, curled into a foetal position. I might have cried from the sudden end to my agony, but the heat of the flames had dried all trace of my tears.

Diala knelt down and gently gathered me into her arms, holding me, muttering soothing nonsense words. I didn't know what had happened. All I knew was that the pain was gone and Diala was here, holding me to her breast.

"What . . . what happened?"

"You survived," she said simply.

I looked up at her, even now, feeling the need for her, but understanding for the first time that my desire wasn't natural. I don't know how I knew that, but I did.

Before I could ask her about it, however, Arryl stepped into the temple.

"Tides, Diala," she said, when she saw us. "You've done it again, haven't you?"

When Diala immolated me, she was already over six hundred years old. She'd been trying that particular trick every few years pretty much since she realised immortality would be a lot more fun if she had her own minions. At least every five years or so—and I think it was more often than that—she'd find some dupe like me and set him alight. She'd already burned her way through a hundred or more candidates by the time I came along. Unfortunately, Diala's success rate wasn't all that impressive. Her failures wound up as fertiliser on the temple gardens, in case you're wondering.

The rules I'd overheard Diala and Arryl speaking of had to do with the potential of Diala's minions to become Tide Lords. Syrolee was very protective of her children's power and feared anybody else able to wield it. She insisted Diala present any potential immortals to her first, so she could determine their likelihood of being able to wield magic— as if she could tell—a rule Diala flagrantly ignored. There is no way to tell beforehand if a man or woman will be able to wield Tide magic until they're made immortal. That was the danger, you see. The thing the others feared most.

But the implications of being immortal didn't occur to me immediately. In part, it was because the idea was too abstract to grasp, and partly because I was still convinced the quest I assumed I had been immortalised to perform was my ticket home. I didn't understand there was no place I could ever call home again. Until you've survived a few too many close calls with death to call it luck, you don't fully grasp the idea that you're immortal, either.

It took me many years to even fully appreciate what I could do, let alone work out *how* to do it. There's no written guide about how to control Tide magic; no spells to learn or incantations to recite. It's very simple really. Once one emerges unharmed from the Eternal Flame, a conduit to the Tide opens in the survivor. For some, like Arryl, it simply gives them immortality—a body that will heal itself over and over, no matter how devastating the injury sustained, and in Arryl's case, the ability to accelerate healing in others. But for a rare few of us, it opens all the way and gives us the power of a god.

You think I'm exaggerating? At High Tide, I can make a flower bloom early or a volcano erupt. I can change the weather patterns of an entire continent on a whim or crush a piece of coal into a diamond in my bare hands, simply by willing it into being. I can make the wind carry me across the world, calm the sea until it's so solid I can walk on water. Lukys knows the secret which enables him to cleave the smallest particles of matter in two, destroying everything in the vicinity, and if you think I'm exaggerating, visit the Waste sometime and take a look for yourself . . .

But I digress. Learning all that was years away. In the days and weeks following my immolation, I didn't understand any of it. I was too excited about my upcoming quest and the possibility of returning home to appreciate my predicament.

I did sleep with Diala—in case you're wondering. Our affair petered out after a couple of months. I'm not sure who tired of whom first, but unlike my first love, this one died of apathy rather than a blazing row. Not long after we stopped sleeping together, Diala found another young man to play with. This one kept her amused for almost a year before she immolated him. Unfortunately, for the lad in question, his will to live wasn't as strong as mine and the Eternal Flame was a demanding mistress. There are no half measures. Either you desired it with every fibre of your being or you died. Diala's new plaything ended up a pile of ashes on the temple floor. She sulked for months about it afterwards too, I heard.

At the time Diala immolated me, there were a score of other immortals, but only eight true Tide Lords. I wasn't the last immortal, but I was the last Tide Lord.

And for good reason.

You see, I am the one who extinguished the Eternal Flame.

Chapter 32

N ews of Kylia's betrothal to Mathu Debree beat Arkady back to the palace. She learned of it from Queen Inala, who took her hostess aside as they were sitting down to dinner to enquire if she was absolutely certain Kylia was still a virgin. Still distracted by her earlier interview with Cayal, she was taken completely aback by the queen's blunt enquiry.

"Er . . . yes, your majesty," Arkady stammered, making no attempt to hide her shock at being asked such a thing. "As far as I know. Why do you ask?"

"One has to be certain about these things," the queen replied with a look that hinted Arkady would know such things if she were highborn. "One can never be too careful with the future of one's line and Jaxyn Aranville *has* been a houseguest here for quite some time." She leant forward and added in a low voice, "Knowing the young man's reputation, one has reason to be concerned, don't you think?"

Arkady glanced across the room at Jaxyn, who was gallantly seating Kylia at her place at the dinner table. He looked up, feeling her gaze on him, and smiled languidly as he took his own seat.

"Jaxyn has no interest in my husband's niece, your majesty," she assured the queen quite truthfully. "But you still haven't told me why you're so interested in Kylia's maidenhead. Or what it has to do with the royal line."

"She's to marry my son," Inala replied, as if everybody else in the room already knew it and Arkady was simply behind the times. "Enteny and Stellan are hammering out the details as we speak. Didn't your husband or his niece inform you?"

"He was probably hoping to keep it a surprise," Arkady replied with admirable calm.

"And I've spoiled it for him," the queen sighed, patting Arkady's arm. "How thoughtless of me."

Arkady forced a smile. "I'll just have to pretend to be surprised when he tells me."

"And what of your houseguest?"

"Pardon?"

"What is keeping him here so long, dear, if he's not pursuing your niece?"

His parasitic desire to be kept like a pampered house cat, Arkady was tempted to reply. "He's been working on the estate as our Kennel Master."

"Is that right?" the queen asked, glancing at Jaxyn with a raised brow, clearly sceptical of the notion.

Arkady nodded, indicating that the queen should take her place at the table. "It's true," she confirmed, as they walked back to the table. "In fact, only a few days ago, Jaxyn found another fighter for us at a bear baiting, isn't that right, my lord?"

Jaxyn nodded, rising from his own seat as the queen took hers, smoothly picking up Arkady's lie and running with it. "It's true, your highness. The duke has me scouring the countryside for Crasii. Particularly fighting felines." He laughed then, and added to the rest of the company, "Sign of a misspent youth, I fear, this ability of mine to spot a good fighter from a mile away in bad light."

Mathu, who had taken a seat on the other side of Kylia, laughed at Jaxyn's confession. "I can vouch for that, Mother. He has a real way with them too. I swear the Crasii fairly cower when he glares at them."

"And is there any particular reason why the Duke of Lebec feels the need to bolster his fighting forces?" the queen enquired with a frown. "Is he planning something?"

Mathu grinned at his mother. "That must be it, Mother. Stellan Desean is gathering an army in secret because he has his eye on the crown."

"Don't be an idiot, Mathu," his mother scolded. "I merely enquire why, in this time of peace and plenty, any duke needs to increase his army?"

"I believe we're having trouble with the miners up in Lutalo," Arkady explained, as the Crasii slaves hurried to serve their masters' wine. "The Scards are becoming quite unmanageable in the mountain regions around the Valley of the Tides. Stellan is keen to increase the protection for his miners and the ore wagons on their way to the smelter."

"I liked the whole 'plotting to take the crown' scenario better," Mathu chuckled.

"Who's plotting to take my crown?" the king demanded as he entered the dining room from the terrace with Stellan by his side.

Everybody at the table rose to their feet, but the king waved them back into their seats. As Arkady sat down, she frowned at the look on Stellan's face. *Something is amiss.* Seriously amiss, she guessed, by his expression, although given he'd walked into dinner at the king's side, it might not be too dire.

"I was just trying to convince Mother that Stellan was raising a Crasii army against us," the young prince joked, resuming his seat.

As Stellan reached Arkady's chair he bent down to kiss her cheek. A little of her concern must have been reflected on her face.

"Later," he whispered through the kiss, and then smiled and took his place opposite her. With Enteny here, Stellan had relinquished the head of the table to his king.

"And are you?" the king asked of his cousin, as he took his own seat.

"What? Planning to overthrow you?" Stellan asked with a smile. "Of course I am, Enteny. That's all I do all day, you know—plot evil schemes against my king. I thought Declan Hawkes would have mentioned something about it in passing?"

"The young devil must be asleep on the job," the king laughed, not in the least bit disturbed by the bizarre nature of the conversation. Whatever was bothering Stellan, it didn't seem to affect his standing with Enteny. Kings didn't joke about plots to overthrow them with their dukes unless they trusted them implicitly. "Let's hope he can redeem himself on our immortal, eh?"

Arkady looked up sharply. "I *beg* your pardon?"

"You shouldn't be bothering yourself with criminals, Arkady, so I've ordered your husband to hand our would-be immortal over to Declan Hawkes," the king informed her. "A few days of my spymaster's less-than-subtle methods of persuasion should settle the matter, don't you think? At the very least, it'll save you the need to visit that dreadful prison, my dear." He glanced at Stellan, oblivious to the effect his news was having on his hostess. "It is a dreadful place, this prison of yours, I hope? Wouldn't do for the criminal element to have too easy a time of things during their incarceration."

"Rest assured, it's dreadful," Stellan agreed, his eyes turning to Arkady. He was willing her to remain silent, she knew; praying she wouldn't embarrass him by arguing with the king.

Gripping the stem of her wineglass so hard her knuckles turned white, she nodded in agreement. "I must concur with my husband's appraisal, your majesty," she said, forcing herself to smile. "It's quite the most dreadful place I've ever been."

"Then you should thank me for sparing you further discomfort, Arkady," the king announced, obviously quite pleased with himself. "Besides, you'll have plenty of other things to keep you occupied in the coming weeks," he added with a conspiratorial wink in Stellan's direction. "You won't have time for all this academic nonsense. Will dinner be long, do you think? All this talk of criminals has quite piqued my appetite."

She caught Stellan shaking his head opposite her, almost imperceptibly, silently begging her to say nothing. Out of the corner of her eye, she noticed Jaxyn smiling, as if he found something amusing about all of this.

Seething with anger, but unable to do anything about it, she rose to her feet. "Would you excuse me then, your majesty? Dinner should have been served by now. I'll see what's causing the delay."

Without waiting for the king's permission, Arkady fled

the dining room, furious over the king's arbitrary decision about her visits to Lebec Prison and frustrated at her helplessness to do anything about it.

"Arkady!"

Stellan had followed her out of the dining room.

"Stellan! What the Tides is—"

"Not here," he warned, jerking his head in the direction of his study.

Acknowledging the wisdom of his warning, she followed him into his private sanctuary, turning on him the moment Stellan closed the door behind them and they were alone.

"I won't have time for all this *academic nonsense*?" she repeated incredulously. "What did you say to him, Stellan?"

"It was more what he said to me," her husband replied, leaning against the door. "Reon's been in his ear, demanding reparation because Mathu came to Lebec."

"I warned you no good would come of bringing Mathu here."

Stellan nodded in agreement. "It's worse than you think. We're being exiled, you and I, my dear. To Torlenia."

Arkady stared at him, aghast. *"What?"*

"Oh, it's disguised as a diplomatic posting, so our family honour is intact, but it's exile, sure enough. And because he feels bad about it and Mathu is a romantic fool, the king has decided Kylia can stay and marry his son, as some sort of compensation."

Shaking her head in disbelief, Arkady began pacing the rug, certain she must still be asleep in her room upstairs and that at any moment she would wake to discover this was nothing but a very bad dream. "Inala told me about the engagement just before you and Enteny arrived. I thought she was joking. It's an insane idea. They barely know each other."

"They know each other well enough for Mathu to fancy he's in love with her. And I suspect Kylia feels the same way."

"She's seventeen," Arkady scoffed. "She doesn't know what she feels. And Mathu . . . Tides, you were rescuing him out of dockside brothels in Herino a little over a month ago. And now he wants to settle down? I hardly think that's likely."

"I did try pointing that out to the king, Arkady."

She threw her hands up in despair. "This is a nightmare!"

"Jaxyn won't take the news well," Stellan agreed.

She frowned at him. "Words cannot describe how little I care about what Jaxyn Aranville will make of this change in our fortunes, Stellan. What I want to know is how Cayal became involved?"

He shrugged. "Declan Hawkes isn't in the business of working behind the king's back, Arkady. You know that. Once he got involved, there was no chance the king wasn't going to be informed about our condemned prisoner who didn't die."

"You can't let them torture him, Stellan."

"I can't stop them, Arkady, and neither can you."

"You could pardon him," she suggested, not sure what prompted her to suggest such a thing.

He looked at her in surprise. "On what grounds? You're the one who keeps telling me how dangerous he is."

"I know, but . . ."

He sighed and walked to her, blocking her path to stop her pacing. Taking her hands in his, he studied her closely for a moment. "Arkady, there is nothing we can do about your Caelishman. Let Declan have this criminal. The Caelish are denying he's theirs, so our people can't be hurt in retaliation."

"Torture is barbaric."

"You wanted to chop his pinkie off not so long ago yourself."

She sniffed indignantly. "That was different."

"How?"

"I wasn't planning to torture him."

"Maybe you should appeal to your friend the spymaster, then." Stellan smiled reassuringly. "Kyle Lakesh is no longer our problem, Arkady. Forget your Immortal Prince. Our problem is Torlenia. And Kylia."

"Can I see him again?"

Her husband frowned. "Why would you want to?"

"I can't bear to leave a job incomplete. Please. Let me have one more stab at this? I know you trust my judgement. This man is important. I'll get much more out of him than Declan will."

"The king wants you to drop it, Arkady."

"Then don't tell him."

He hesitated, clearly torn with indecision, and then he nodded. "All right. But just this once. And you'd best do it first thing tomorrow, before Hawkes gets his orders officially."

Arkady kissed his cheek. "Thank you."

"Don't thank me, Arkady," he warned, dropping her hands. "If the king catches you visiting the prison, I'll deny I know anything about it."

"He won't catch me," she promised. "And if he does, I'll stand there, meek as a lamb, while you publicly berate me for defying you. I'll even try to cry, if you think it might help."

"Just don't get caught," he begged. "That would be the best thing for all concerned."

"And what about Kylia?"

Stellan sighed helplessly. "I'll speak to her. Not that I think it will do much good."

Arkady smiled wistfully. "And to think, I used to fear Jaxyn Aranville seducing her was the worst thing that could happen to your niece."

Her husband frowned. "Your well-known animosity toward Jaxyn aside, Arkady, it's not actually the end of the world to find yourself engaged to the Crown Prince of Glaeba. He's quite a decent young fellow, actually."

"He has more of his father in him than you realise," she warned. "And he holds with most of his father's opinions, too. Your lot won't improve when Mathu becomes king, Stellan, even married to your niece."

"Do you think she can handle becoming a queen?"

Arkady was doubtful. "Kylia can be a little . . . spoiled, Stellan."

"She's still a child." He shrugged. "We don't know what she'll be capable of when she's grown."

"So maybe we should wait until she's grown before we thrust her into the bed of a young man whose education regarding women seems to have been acquired almost exclusively in the brothels of Herino."

Stellan obviously wasn't pleased with her assessment of the situation. "Go say goodbye to your immortal, Arkady, and let me take care of my niece."

She stepped back from him, a little hurt at his tone. "Perhaps you should have listened to Tilly after all. She did predict Kylia would marry soon, remember? And that he'd be tall, dark and handsome. And that he'd break her heart."

"Tilly and her Tarot are nonsense," he said, impatiently. "So go. Have your immortal tell you another fabulous tale. And then get back here and start packing, my dear, because a couple months from now, you'll be twiddling your thumbs with boredom and confined to the *seraglium* like a good Torlenian wife, while my niece moves into the Herino Palace and begins her education in the art of statesmanship."

He headed for the door, leaving Arkady staring after him. She was so overwhelmed by the news about the betrothal and Cayal's impending torture, she had not thought what exile to Torlenia would mean to Stellan.

"Is there no way the king will change his mind?" she asked.

He hesitated, and then turned to look at her. "I doubt it."

"What will Jaxyn do when you tell him?"

"I have no idea."

"I don't suppose he'll be allowed . . ."

"In Torlenia?" Stellan asked with a short, bitter laugh. "I believe extra-marital relationships attract the death penalty in Torlenia, Arkady. Jaxyn loves me, I'm sure, but perhaps not that much."

"I'm sorry, Stellan."

"No, you're not."

"Not for Jaxyn," she agreed. "But I am for you. You don't deserve this."

"Maybe I do deserve it." He shrugged. "They say a man's sins have a way of catching up with him."

"Your only sin was to save the king a great deal of embarrassment."

He smiled sadly. "Ironic, don't you think, that we might have avoided being sent to Torlenia if you were pregnant?"

He wasn't accusing her, merely stating a fact. "Is that what you want, Stellan? I'll do it. If it will save us from exile."

"I fear it's too late for that, Arkady. But I do appreciate the offer." He placed a sympathetic hand on her shoulder. "Shall I chase up dinner while you compose yourself before rejoining us?"

"If you wouldn't mind."

Stellan smiled at her before leaving the room, leaving Arkady alone in the study, wondering if there was anything she could do to save Stellan from exile, or Cayal from Declan Hawkes.

Chapter 33

After stewing on it all through dinner, forcing herself to be pleasant to the king and her other guests, Arkady realised Stellan's suggestion that she appeal to Declan Hawkes regarding Cayal's fate—however glibly suggested—really was the only course left open to her. Petitioning the king was useless, and given the king had just effectively exiled them, Stellan was going to be no help at all, either. Declan, however, had it in his power to see that Cayal was treated humanely, at the very least, and for no reason she could readily name, she was prepared to risk quite a bit to ensure his safety.

Declan wasn't at dinner. She finally found him, later that night, saddling his horse in the stables. Although he had the authority to order any slave on the estate to perform the task for him, Declan preferred to take care of such things himself. Arkady suspected it was his instinctive lack of trust in others, honed over years of all but living on the streets of the Lebec slums, that kept him so grounded and not any particular love of the task.

"A bit late for an outing, don't you think?" she asked, shaking the raindrops off her cloak as she entered the stables. They were alone. Outside the rain beat a soft tattoo on the shingles. It hadn't let up all day, the relentless downpour starting to wear on the fortitude of even the most patient soul.

Declan didn't turn at her approach. Instead, he kept pulling on the girth strap of his saddle. His reluctant gelding was clearly resisting the notion of an outing this late, particularly when it meant leaving a warm, dry stable.

"I have business in town."

"At this hour?"

He glanced over his shoulder. "The King's Spymaster never sleeps."

"You spread that rumour yourself, don't you?"

He smiled. "Among others. Reputation is everything in this game, you know."

She didn't return his smile. "So the reputation you have these days as a ruthless monster who'll do anything to get what he wants is just a rumour then?"

Declan stopped trying to saddle his horse and turned to study her curiously. "What did I do to deserve *that*?"

Arkady glared at him without apology. "The king wants you to torture a confession out of Cayal."

"I know. He actually told *me* before he mentioned it to your husband."

Arkady's heart skipped a beat. *Is that where Declan is headed now? To collect Cayal? To begin his torment?*

"And do you intend to?"

He shrugged. "I am known for my partiality for following the king's orders, you know. It's one of the most effective ways to keep my job as his spymaster."

Arkady wasn't amused. "The boy I grew up with would never deliberately hurt another creature."

"The girl I grew up with despised women who married for money. So it seems we're both doomed to be disappointed, your grace."

Arkady stared at him, saddened to realise Declan still hadn't forgiven her for marrying a Desean. *Tides! What is it going to take?* It had been more than six years since they'd first argued about this and it still stood like an invisible wall between them. "I didn't marry Stellan for his money."

"You sure as hell didn't marry him for love."

"Don't you dare judge me, Declan Hawkes," she retorted, a little surprised to realise how much his censure still hurt. "I married Stellan to help my father."

"Your father died while you were dancing the night away in a palace, toasting your good fortune with your royal in-laws, Arkady," Declan reminded her heartlessly. "Not sure how you figure that was meant to help him."

"Stellan agreed to release my father . . ."

"*After* the wedding," he pointed out. "Was that your idea or his?"

She shook her head, knowing he was trying to anger her and annoyed at herself for letting him. "I don't have to stand here and listen to you berate me for something you don't understand, Declan Hawkes."

"Then go back to the palace and your husband, your ladyship. I was just leaving, anyway." He turned back to his horse and picked up the girth, pulling it so hard the gelding grunted in protest.

"Are you going to visit your grandfather?"

With his back to her still, Declan hesitated for only a fraction of a second before he answered. "No."

"You condemn me for trying to help my father, yet you've

turned your back on the only family you've got. Rather hypocritical of you, don't you think?"

Declan's voice was tight when he answered her. "My grandfather knows why I don't want to see him."

"Everyone in the Lebec slums knows why."

That did spark a reaction in him. He turned to her, his dark eyes full of anger. "You have no idea what you're talking about."

"Don't I?"

"No."

"You broke his heart, Declan," she told him, as if pointing out his mistakes would somehow ease the pain of her own. "He spent his whole life trying to help people and you ran off and joined the king's service so you could make a mockery of everything he ever taught you. Instead of helping those less fortunate, you're paid to hunt them down. What's more, you actually seem to enjoy it."

"Arkady, you should stop now . . . while we're still friends."

"*Friends?* Tides! Your *job* is to arrest and torture the very people—like my father and your grandfather—who try to make this a better world. Your grandfather is weighed down by the shame of who you are, Declan; of what you've become."

That seemed to amuse him. "What *I've* become? All I did was find myself a job that didn't involve working myself into an early grave or starving on the streets of the Lebec slums. You're the one I have to address as *your grace.*"

She shook her head sadly. "I don't understand you anymore, Declan."

"I'm still the same person, Arkady. Just better dressed, and much better paid."

Arkady frowned at his flippant reply. "The friend I knew as a child would have shed blood to protect those weaker than himself. In fact, I can recall several times when he did."

"This king you're so censorious of happens to be *your*

husband's cousin," he reminded her. "And yet somehow you still manage to sleep at night."

"I use my position to help the Crasii."

"How very noble of you, your grace."

She sighed. She hadn't come here to fight with Declan. "Look . . . I know it's probably none of my business—"

He turned back to finish saddling the gelding. "You've got that much right."

"But couldn't you just visit him once? He'll have heard you're in town. Would it kill you to take an hour out of your busy schedule to make an old man happy?"

Her reasonable tone seemed to strike a chord in him. The tension faded from his shoulders and he shrugged. "I'll think about it."

"And Cayal?"

"What about him?"

"Can you . . . ?" Arkady didn't finish the sentence. It suddenly occurred to her that she had no rational explanation for wanting to save Cayal. Certainly none that would satisfy Declan Hawkes.

"Can I what?" he prompted, glancing over his shoulder at her, perhaps guessing her intentions. "Go easy on him?"

"He doesn't deserve to be tortured, Declan."

"As I recall, you were quite prepared to dismember him."

Arkady frowned, wishing people would stop reminding her of that. "The surgical removal of a finger is hardly torture."

"Tell that to the owner of the finger," he shot back.

Arkady wanted to scream at him with frustration, but knew it would just make things worse. Taking a deep breath, she tried to sound as reasonable and detached as possible. "Cayal is deluded, Declan, and quite possibly insane. I doubt torturing him will achieve anything. It certainly won't get him to change his story."

"Then I'll just have to use him for practice."

Arkady didn't rise to that. She knew he was taunting her. "You'll be wasting your time. He's depressed, probably suicidal and definitely delusional. For all you know you'll be giving him exactly what he wants."

"And you called me a ruthless monster . . ."

"I'm serious, Declan."

"I know." He finally lowered the stirrups and turned to look at her. "I'm sorry."

"For what? Torturing Cayal?"

"For involving you in this. If I'd known you were going to get so . . . emotional about this man . . . I would never have asked for your help."

"I'm still wondering why you did," she said. "Given that you're now totally ignoring my advice."

"Your advice comes a poor second to the king's orders, Arkady."

That was the bitter truth. "Is there nothing I can say that will stop you doing this?"

He stared at her, shaking his head in bewilderment. "Are you serious? Think about what you're asking me to do, Arkady. You want me to defy a direct order from the king because you're afraid a condemned murderer—one you are the first to admit is probably a Caelish spy—might suffer a little in the pursuit of information we might need to protect Glaeba."

She knew how it sounded, and with sick certainty that nothing she could say would change Declan's mind. "You're right; it was foolish of me to expect any compassion from the King's Spymaster."

"You can't make me feel guilty about doing my job, Arkady," he warned. "I'm surprised you'd even try."

She searched his face for a moment, hoping to find even a glimmer of compassion there, but it was a waste of time. Declan had chosen his path a long time ago and it was no longer the path she trod.

"I'm sorry. You're right. I shouldn't have bothered you."

Arkady turned on her heel and headed back out into the

rain. As she pulled the hood up against the downpour, she thought she heard Declan calling her back, but she chose to ignore it.

There was nothing her old friend could or would do to help her.

Stellan wasn't in his study when Arkady got back to the palace. Having exhausted all other possibilities, she figured one more appeal to her husband might be worth a try. She had no idea what she was planning to say to him. She had already tried every argument she could think of, to no avail.

But she had to do something. Tomorrow Declan Hawkes's men would collect Cayal from Lebec Prison and take him back to Herino, where he faced days, perhaps weeks, of agonising torture, unless he died or was prepared to change his story of immortality and confess the real reason for his presence in Glaeba. Arkady knew it would never happen. Either insanity or sheer pig-headed stubbornness would make Cayal stick to his story just as Declan wouldn't stop until he'd broken him. It was a game where there were no possible winners.

With a sigh, she leant against the desk, glancing down at Stellan's unfinished correspondence. He'd been writing to the mine manager in Lutalo, by the look of it. Reading it upside down, the letter had something to do with sending more felines to guard the ore shipments coming down from the mines. Next to the letter lay a stick of wax and Stellan's ducal signet, a ring so heavy and cumbersome that he rarely wore it, except on official occasions.

Arkady stared at the ring. It symbolised everything about the duchy, was the ultimate proof of the duke's authority in the province.

I might not have the power to save Cayal, she realised, *but as Duke of Lebec, Stellan—if he was prepared to defy the king—certainly does.*

And the instrument of that power lay before her on the desk.

Without thinking about what it might mean if she was caught forging her husband's signature, Arkady hurried around to the other side of the desk and pushed aside Stellan's letter to the mine manager in Lutalo. Taking a deep breath, she picked out a clean sheet of paper and began to wield a little ducal power of her own.

Chapter 34

Sunlight smells different, Warlock decided, taking another deep breath, as if it would somehow last beyond the meagre hour they had been allocated in the open air.

As she promised she would, the Duchess of Lebec had arranged for the inmates of the Row to be allowed out of their cells once a day for exercise. Not wishing to appear as if she favoured either Cayal or Warlock, the duchess had apparently insisted all the prisoners should be included. The Warden, for his own reasons, agreed to accommodate her request, so the prisoners of Recidivists' Row had been allowed out of their cells for an hour. It seemed a gift more precious than gold.

For a wonder, the sky was clear this morning; the sun shining brightly, even here beneath the shadowed walls of the prison yard. Until he took his first breath of unfettered air, Warlock hadn't realised how much his confinement was affecting him. Although the walled yard wasn't that large and was surrounded by a wall-walk patrolled by human guards armed with crossbows and leashed feline Crasii who seemed anxious to test their claws on any prisoner foolish enough to make a sudden movement, the ability to take more than four steps before hitting a wall felt almost like true freedom.

The suzerain reacted curiously to his liberty, Warlock observed. Although he had been confined in the Row for weeks, Cayal showed none of the ill effects that afflicted the dozen or so other inhabitants. His skin colour remained good, his weight hadn't changed, despite his poor diet; his hair wasn't falling out or growing in corkscrews, a sure sign of scurvy. His muscle tone remained healthy, his eyes clear. There was no sign of swollen, bleeding gums or loosened teeth and he moved fluidly and easily, apparently not afflicted by the soreness and stiffness of the joints that affected many of the other human prisoners who shuffled around the yard, trying to make their tired limbs work.

But then why would he? Warlock thought. *The suzerain are immune to the diseases that plague normal men.*

"What are you staring at, gemang?"

Breathing hard, Warlock rose to his feet as the suzerain approached. He'd paced a circuit of the yard a dozen times now, and was resting before he repeated the exercise, appalled by how weak he was becoming through forced inactivity.

"Nothing."

"I'll wager I know what's bothering you," Cayal suggested, jerking his head in the direction of the nearest guard above them.

This close, Warlock could smell the Tide Lord. His scent filled the air, strong and dangerous . . . a blatant warning to anybody who knew the signs. And Warlock wasn't the only Crasii who sensed the danger. He glanced up at the wall-walk. It seemed the guards were having trouble with their felines this morning; had been ever since Cayal had entered the yard. Only Warlock and Cayal understood the reason. The humans just thought the felines were being fractious.

"Your presence disturbs them," Warlock remarked.

The suzerain smiled and looked up at the wall-walk. "Want to have some fun?"

"Exactly what do you mean by *fun*?"

"I mean how much fun would it be to give one of those felines a run around the yard?"

Despite himself, Warlock bared his teeth in a grin. The suzerain was right. It would be a great deal of fun to chase a feline. "You'd have to get her down here first."

"That's the easy part."

Warlock's smile faded. "And the moment I made a move in the direction of a feline, one of the guards would probably put a crossbow bolt through me."

"How about that?" Cayal said with an ingenuous smile. "A game where everybody has a good time."

Warlock turned his back on the Tide Lord. "Find another way to entertain yourself, suzerain. One that doesn't involve killing me."

"Don't you dare turn your back on me, gemang."

Warlock stopped dead in his tracks, as Cayal's order sent a shiver of fear through him. It wasn't what he'd said, so much as the way he'd said it. And the ancient language he'd spoken. It reverberated through Warlock as if his body was a harp string that had just been plucked.

Before he knew what he was doing, Warlock turned back to face Cayal.

"My lord," he found himself saying.

The Tide Lord nodded with satisfaction. "Better. Now bow to me, gemang. Show the whole world who is really the master here."

Warlock shook his head, shocked by how little effort it took to defy the order. According to everything he'd been taught, every instinct he owned, he shouldn't have been able to refuse a Tide Lord anything. He shouldn't have even been able to contemplate the idea.

"You are the past, suzerain," he declared defiantly. "You have no power over me or my people any longer."

"I *can* make you," Cayal warned in a low voice. Nobody was paying any attention to their confrontation. The other prisoners were too involved in their own exercise and the guards on the wall-walk were busy trying to calm the restless Crasii.

"Not at the moment, you can't," Warlock said, growling low in his throat, his confidence growing with every moment he defied the instinctive Crasii urge to blindly follow Cayal's instructions. "It's Low Tide. If you had any power, you'd not be here. You'd be looking for a way to enslave the entire world, not trying to get yourself killed in some grubby Glaeban gaol, or playing along with these humans you think you're so much better than. Your time may come again, suzerain, but it's not now and until it does come again, I will bow to no one, especially not you."

The Tide Lord's eyes flashed dangerously, but he made no move toward Warlock. Perhaps he understood the futility. Attacking another prisoner would just mean a beating, and given there were a half-dozen testy felines not ten feet above them, it would probably mean being ripped to shreds into the bargain. Knowing one could survive such an attack didn't lessen the pain of it and Warlock guessed Cayal wasn't fool enough to bring that down upon himself, just to take a swing at a gemang.

"You'll live to regret saying that," Cayal warned, instead.

"Not as long as you will, suzerain."

If the Immortal Prince had a response, Warlock never got to hear it. At that moment, the gate into the yard swung open with a squeal of rusty hinges and another guard appeared with the news that the Duchess of Lebec was here to visit the prisoners.

They were not led back to their cells, but to the Warden's office, the variation in routine a worrying departure from the norm. There was no reason Warlock could think of that would require either his presence or Cayal's in the Warden's office. Neither of them had done anything to incur the wrath of the Warden, and the duchess had seemed happy enough when she left the prison yesterday. He glanced at Cayal as they were escorted through the dank, labyrinthine halls but the suzerain's expression was unreadable. He might not even be worried. Cayal hadn't been here long enough to know when something was amiss.

When they were shown into the Warden's office, Lady Desean was waiting for them. Warlock looked around with interest, the smell of furniture polish and old leather sharp in his nostrils, reminding him of home.

Only I have no home now, he told himself harshly, *other than a small cell on Recidivists' Row.*

Warlock hadn't been in this office since the day he first arrived in Lebec Prison and was introduced to the Warden, who made a point of greeting all his charges personally, to inform them of the perils of making trouble while a guest in his establishment. The room seemed unchanged, it certainly smelled the same, but Arkady Desean reeked of fear, although she was outwardly calm and the Warden gave no indication that he thought anything odd about her demeanour.

"I have news for you both," the Warden announced, watching the prisoners closely as they stood to attention before him.

"You've finally seen the light, so you're going to release me?" Cayal suggested.

Lady Desean rose to her feet, and held out a folded document, sealed with the ducal signet of Lebec. Oddly, it was to Warlock that she offered the document, not Cayal. "Close, but it's not you who's been pardoned, Cayal. It's your companion."

Warlock stared at her, certain he must have misheard the duchess. He took the document warily, reading it through twice to assure himself it really was what she claimed, then he looked at her, slack-jawed with shock.

Arkady smiled. "Don't look so surprised, Warlock. Your assistance has been most valuable these past few weeks and after I brought your case to my husband's attention, he reviewed the details of your sentence. In light of the extenuating circumstances of your crime, he decided to pardon you."

"You pardoned the gemang?" Cayal exclaimed in disgust. "For what? Not growling at you?"

"You're not doing much for your own chances of a pardon," the Warden pointed out with a frown.

Cayal looked at Arkady. "But I'm not getting a pardon, am I?"

The Duchess of Lebec shook her head. "Quite the opposite. You're to be handed over to the King's Spymaster, Cayal. His majesty believes you'll be rather more forthcoming under torture. I am here merely to escort you back to the palace where Declan Hawkes awaits your arrival." She turned to the Warden. "Have him chained, would you, Warden, before we leave? I have a squad of felines with me, but I don't want to take any chances."

"Of course, your grace." The Warden hurried to the door to organise it. Cayal glared at Arkady, but she paid no attention to him, turning her gaze on Warlock, instead.

"You have a great opportunity to make a better life for yourself, Warlock," she told him. "Don't waste it."

"I won't, your grace," he promised, still not really believing she had arranged a pardon for him. "Nor will I forget your kindness." There was no doubt in his mind that this unexpected bounty was due entirely to her. "I cannot thank you enough for your intervention with the duke."

"Oh, *please* . . . ," Cayal muttered beside him.

The duchess turned to him then, looking somewhat amused by his reaction. "You disappoint me, Cayal. I thought you'd have something more to say about Warlock's pardon. The gemang is released while the Tide Lord remains a prisoner? Doesn't that irk your immortal little heart, even a tiny bit?"

Warlock liked Arkady Desean for many reasons, not the least of which was the disdain with which she usually handled Cayal. Unfettered by the instinctive need to obey, she was free to turn her back on him. And she did. Frequently, despite the undercurrent of tension that ran between her and the Tide Lord.

He wondered if Arkady realised that to a Crasii, whenever she went near the suzerain she smelled like unbridled lust. Warlock wasn't sure if the suzerain could actually smell it on her, or even consciously sense it, but he could tell it affected Cayal. He could see it in the way he looked at the duchess. The self-conscious way their body language echoed each other's movements, even though neither seemed aware of it.

What strange creatures humans are, he thought. *They give off a scent they don't even have the ability to detect. What's the point of that?*

"What irks me is that you're freeing a Scard," Cayal replied, his lips curling in disgust. "We used to put them to death."

"Well, when the Tide Lords are ruling the world again, Cayal, you can execute all the Scards you like," Arkady told him. "Unfortunately, my husband is in control of the world you inhabit at the moment, and he's about to hand you over to the king. So say goodbye to your cellmate, Cayal. The King's Spymaster awaits you."

The door opened and a guard came in carrying legirons, which—on the Warden's orders—he proceeded to clamp around the suzerain's ankles before Cayal could come up with a suitable reply.

Still clutching his precious and totally unexpected pardon, Warlock stood back and watched as they chained the Immortal Prince, hand and foot, and then led him away, wondering how long such a creature would allow himself to be treated like a common criminal.

Not much longer, he guessed. *The novelty of incarceration has long worn off. He's getting impatient.*

Arkady turned to Warlock to say goodbye. He wanted to warn her, feeling he owed her that much. He wanted to tell her to be careful. He wanted to tell her chains were useless against a man who had the power to break a continent in half when the Tide was at its peak.

But he knew there was nothing to be gained by delivering such a warning. She was human. Her kind had very short memories, unlike the Crasii who guarded their oral histories to be sure they would never forget. She didn't even believe the Tide Lords were real. There was no point trying to warn her of the danger of something she didn't think existed.

Besides, he consoled himself, *chances are we'll all be long dead before the Tide turns again; long dead before Cayal and his brethren emerge from hiding.*

Warlock clung to that thought as Cayal met his eye one last time.

"We'll meet again, gemang," he promised ominously.

"Only if *your* luck runs out, suzerain," Warlock replied.

Cayal was led away, after that, followed by the duchess and the Warden, leaving Warlock alone in the office, a ducal pardon in his grasp, still getting used to the idea that he was suddenly and unexpectedly free.

Chapter 35

Arkady sat opposite Cayal as the coach jerked into motion, her expression blank, her heart pounding so loud it was a wonder he couldn't hear it over the rattling of his leg-irons. She wasn't sure how much longer her courage would last; surprised it hadn't let her down yet. It was vital she give the appearance everything was normal, and more importantly, that her arrival at Lebec Prison with orders to escort the prisoner to the King's Spymaster was the express wish of her husband, the Duke of Lebec.

Arkady had tried—within the limits of the king's orders to hand Cayal over to Declan Hawkes—to arrange things so that later, when she was questioned, her actions might be dismissed as the amateurish meddling of a woman. Arkady knew how the men of Glaeba thought. Although she doubted Declan would be fooled, she knew the king would be outraged, but she was gambling on him believing her when she announced she'd simply been trying to help.

It would set her cause back years, she knew, to admit such a foolish thing, but it seemed worth it for the greater good.

No man deserved to be tortured for any crime. Despite the danger she was certain he represented, she refused to be a party to this man being broken. Arkady couldn't say why, exactly, but she felt more strongly about this than any other cause she had championed since she forced her way into the palace all those years ago to demand Stellan release her father after he was arrested.

She'd been unable to save her father, in the end. She didn't intend to let another man die for no good reason.

Warlock's pardon had almost been an afterthought. As she was sitting there at Stellan's desk, the ducal signet heavy in her hand, it had seemed a pity to waste the opportunity. She couldn't risk defying the king's orders by trying to pardon Cayal, but Warlock meant nothing to Enteny Debree. If things went wrong, some good at least, she consoled herself as she forged Stellan's signature, would have come from her interference.

She wished she could be as clear on her reasons for aiding and abetting a confessed murderer to escape. Although she was silently listing the justifications in her head, she knew there was no acceptable reason for doing this. She was defying her husband, her king, even her own common sense.

Well, Tilly had told me I needed to take a risk . . .

"You look worried," Cayal remarked, dragging her attention back to the jolting carriage and alerting her to the fact that she was letting her concern reflect on her face. "Surely the duchess is not troubled over the fate of a convicted murderer?"

"You could tell me the truth about who you really are, Cayal. Then there wouldn't be a need for me to worry."

"So you admit you're worried."

"Yet again you dodge the question."

"I don't mean to, truly," he told her, shifting to a more comfortable position with a rattle of chains. He looked very out of place against the carriage's plush red leather upholstery in his rough prison uniform and leg-irons, and his eyes seemed even bluer and more piercing away from the gloom of Recidivists' Row. "But I do resent the accusation that I've lied to you, Arkady."

"Of course you do. How heartless of me to not believe your perfectly reasonable tale of how you survived being burned alive without a mark. What *did* you do after you realised Diala had immortalised you, by the way? We never did get to that part."

"It didn't really occur to me I was immortal at first."

She raised a sceptical brow at him. "The whole 'I survived being burned alive' incident didn't give it away?"

"You really are a terrible cynic, aren't you?"

"Did you know hesitation and avoidance are the two main indicators that someone is lying?"

"Who told you that? One of your brilliant academic colleagues?"

"My father, actually. He was a physician. You'd be surprised how often people lie to their physicians." Despite herself, Arkady smiled at the memory of him. "He used to say that three months after the King's Ball there were more pregnancies in Lebec caused by holding hands than there were during the rest of the year from actual intercourse."

"So at least *one* member of your family has a sense of humour, then?"

"Had," she corrected. "My father is dead."

"He's lucky."

"I'm glad you think so."

"Death is a gift, Arkady. Don't mourn your father, rejoice in his mortality."

Arkady frowned. "Rejoice?"

"You really don't know how lucky you are, having the ability to die."

"I can't imagine why you think dying is lucky."

"Then let me give you an example. Not long after I was made immortal, Lukys came to see me . . ."

"Lukys the Scholar?" she asked.

Cayal wasn't amused. "Tides, woman, can't you forget your wretched Tarot even for a moment?"

No purchase necessary.
Hastings.
WONDERLAND OF FORTUNE
Reveal only 3 coins. If 3 match, reveal the prize box.
Play to win up to $250,000
VOID if more than 3 coins are fully or partially revealed.
Every ticket is a potential WINNER!
PRIZE BOX
4 02142 35687 6
3BH041400D5

"It's my natural cynicism," she explained as the carriage jolted along the road toward Lebec. "Every time you name another character from the Tarot, you do nothing but reinforce the absurdity of your tale."

"The absurdity is your refusal to believe me," he replied. "But that's beside the point. You asked why I said you should rejoice for your father. I was going to tell you about Lukys. And Pellys."

"The one who had his head chopped off?"

He nodded. "Even *before* he lost his head, Pellys was a little strange. He used to hang around the temple in Magreth a lot. It was the only way he could be close to Syrolee and his children, I suppose. I mean, he wasn't exactly welcome at the palace."

"Why not?"

"He was married to Syrolee when she was made immortal, a circumstance our future empress found more than a little awkward once she realised the opportunities fate had suddenly presented her with. She set him alight with the Eternal Flame and went off and married Engarhod, thinking that would be the end of him."

"But he survived it?"

"Obviously."

"What did he do about Syrolee?"

"Not much he could do, by the time he worked out what had happened to him. Remember, I first met Pellys a little over a thousand years after he was immolated. He was still hopeful, I think, back then, that Syrolee would come to her senses, dump Engarhod and return to him."

"But she didn't?"

"And is never likely to, either, but he doesn't remember much of it these days, so it's not the problem it was back then."

Arkady couldn't help but smile. "That's right, you decapitated him, didn't you, and his head grew back without his memories?"

"Tides, you were actually listening, for once. Will wonders never cease?"

She frowned. "What has any of this to do with the ability to die?"

"I was getting to that. You see, Lukys came to visit the temple not long after Diala had immolated me. I was watching Pellys in the temple gardens trying to catch the goldfish in the fountain."

"Well, yes, I can see how *that* must have changed your perspective on things."

"You'd be surprised," he said, impatient with her sarcasm. "Lukys and I were talking on the terrace. He's a real Tide Lord, by the way, not just immortal. And one of the few I respect . . . but that's another story. Lukys was the first immortal who took the time to warn me about what I'd gotten myself into. I believe that day was the first time anyone suggested I might be one of the few who could fully manipulate the Tide. Diala certainly wasn't going to tell me magical power was one of the side effects of the Eternal Flame, particularly as she didn't have a lot of it herself. I hadn't even *tried* to do anything magical, at that point. I'd only just been informed of the quest she had in mind, which would restore me in the eyes of my family."

"Your stalling isn't achieving anything, Cayal. Every mile takes us closer to Lebec Palace and Declan Hawkes."

"I'm not stalling; I'm trying to explain something to help you, Arkady."

"Oh . . . my mistake . . . *do* carry on."

He scowled at her, but continued his tale. "Lukys and I were talking when suddenly Pellys cried out: 'I got one!' I looked over and there he was, dripping wet, grinning like a fool, holding up a fish in his left hand. It was gasping its last few breaths, then finally went limp, either from suffocation or the strength of his grasp—I can't say which. Pellys studied the fish for a moment, and then with a gentleness that shocked me, he kissed the dead creature and tenderly placed it on the ground beside the fountain. It sent shivers down my spine, watching him do that. He stroked it for a moment longer, smiling beatifically, and then he forgot all about it and plunged his hand back into the pool to resume his game.

"It made my blood run cold, watching him with those fish. I don't know how long he'd been at it, pulling fish out of the pond, but there was quite a pile of carcasses on the ground. In the end, I turned to Lukys and asked, 'Why is he doing that?' "

"What did he say?" Arkady asked before she could stop herself, a little annoyed at how easily Cayal could pull her into his imaginary world.

Cayal leaned forward a little, his gaze holding her in thrall. " *'Because he's immortal,'* Lukys told me. *'Pellys can't experience it for himself, so he likes to watch things die.'* "

Arkady stared at him for a long, silent moment and then she laughed. "So what you're telling me is that you're *all* psychotic killers, you immortals? Not just you?"

Cayal leaned back in his seat, turning to look out the window, clearly annoyed with her. "How long until we reach this palace of yours?"

Arkady glanced out of the window at the budding spring pasture rolling past the carriage. The lake shimmered in the distance, a silver smudge on the horizon in the bright sunlight. "A while yet."

Leaning his head against the side of the carriage, Cayal closed his eyes, feigning sleep. Arkady studied him for a time, at war with herself over this man's future. She need do nothing, she knew, and all would be well. She could deliver him to Declan, suffer him telling her off for being a fool, for taking such a risk by transporting the prisoner herself with only an escort of a dozen Crasii, but that's all that would happen. Life would go on. She and Stellan would take up their post in Torlenia and forget all about the man who claimed to be immortal.

Or she could rely on her gut instinct, something that didn't come easily to Arkady. Even as a child, Declan was the one who trusted his instincts. Arkady had always been the one who wanted proof. Taking risks was something she resisted. Perhaps that was why they had complemented each other so well, when they were younger. Declan was the adventurous one, Arkady the voice of reason. She'd kept him out of trouble and he'd coaxed her out of the cocoon of her father's tiny, comforting house and into a world of which she was terrified. Declan's grandfather used to call her the sensible one, the one who tempered his beloved grandson's recklessness. The trait had followed her into adulthood. She was a scholar, now. She gathered facts, evidence, proof, before she came to a conclusion. This feeling that all the evidence was wrong, that her dependence on logic might let her down, was an alien sensation, one that left her almost physically ill.

Suppose Cayal really is immortal? that annoying, illogical voice in the back of her mind teased. *Suppose the Crasii legend of their creation by the Tide Lords is more than a myth? Suppose the Tarot is actually based on fact? Was it even possible?* Her last conversation about the Tarot with Tilly suddenly leapt to mind. *Some of us go to a great deal of trouble to ensure this record of the true nature of the Tide Lords never fades from memory,* Tilly had told her. *It's a solemn trust that we take very seriously.*

Are the Tide Lords real? A discovery of such magnitude would dwarf anything that insufferable misogynist Harlie Palmerston had come up with, including his much-lauded *Theory of Human Advancement.*

"What was the quest?" she asked abruptly.

Cayal opened his eyes and stared at her blankly. "What?"

"You said you were given a quest," she reminded him. "Something to restore you in the eyes of your sister. Something that would convince her to revoke your exile and allow you to return to Kordana to marry Gabriella. What was it?"

He looked away. "You think I'm a liar. Why should I tell you anything?"

"Pretend your life depends on it."

Cayal thought on that for a moment and then smiled sourly. "If only you knew how much I wish it did."

She shrugged, as if it didn't matter to her, one way or the other. "It'll be a while yet, before we reach the palace. We might as well pass the time pleasantly."

"You think hearing about my life is pleasant?" He seemed amused by the notion.

"Well, it's certainly entertaining."

Cayal smiled. "I'm going to miss you, Arkady."

Somewhat to her surprise, Arkady managed to stop herself from replying: *I'll miss you too, Cayal.*

Chapter 36

"We charge you with bringing the Eternal Flame to Kordana. That is your quest, Prince Cayal of Lakesh. You must bring the full knowledge of the Tide to your people."

"We" turned out to be the Emperor and Empress of the Five Realms.

I first met the self-appointed Imperial family a few days after my immolation. I'd met Pellys by then. And I'd already met Engarhod's youngest son, Rance, when he'd visited the temple while I was recuperating.

Immolated in his early thirties, Rance was—still is, for that matter—a humourless man with fair skin and reddish hair who accepted my admission into their ranks with little more than a heavy sigh in Diala's direction. Rance wasn't unfriendly so much as apathetic. He had his own issues to deal with, mostly to do with his siblings, although Arryl offered no further explanation about the sibling rivalry in Engarhod's clan. When I asked Diala about it, she was even less forthcoming, so I didn't bother to pursue it. I had my own problems, too. There wasn't much room left for worrying about what the other immortals might be up to.

It didn't take me long to learn the folly of such a blasé attitude.

Unfortunately, by then, Kordana had been destroyed.

It was several days after my fateful assignation with Diala and the Eternal Flame that they took me to meet the emperor. News had reached the palace that Diala had introduced another minion to their ranks and the emperor was planning to throw a party to welcome me, Arryl explained. Of course, she didn't use the word *minion,* she made it all sound very polite and civilised. I soon learned quite the opposite was true, but I was looking forward to it at the outset.

The palace was built on the shores of the crystal volcanic crater lake by a family of ignorant fools with endless time and resources on their hands and was constructed on a scale commensurate with their immortal status. Designed and decorated mostly by Syrolee, the palace was a shrine to ostentatious vulgarity. Syrolee had been a whore once, and the palace was proof—in my opinion—that good taste is an inherent trait and not something one learns over time. Syrolee is immortal, after all, but even after nine thousand years, she still thinks the only difference between class and crass is a single letter of the alphabet.

Your much-feted Herino Palace? The one that overawes visitors eight thousand years later? It's small and mean by comparison. You can't imagine what this building was like. Columns of gold-flecked marble thicker than six men standing close together dominated the entrance. The columns were gilded around the base and finials—the whole palace took several thousand slaves and fifteen years to construct. Arryl told me all about it as we entered it, with a touch of irony in her smile that hinted I was likely to hear the story often.

I couldn't help but gape as they led me inside. The endless floors were made of several different-coloured marbles laid out in a complicated geometric pattern, interspersed with gold-flecked travertine, inlaid with silver edging. The halls were vast caverns designed to impress, the ceilings so high they made me dizzy. Some of the rooms were there for no other reason than to be gaped at, I'm sure. The entire complex was designed to intimidate all lesser mortals—and other immortals for that matter—who happened to step inside.

There was a throne room—naturally—in keeping with the scale of the rest of the palace. Open to the elements along one side with a vaulted ceiling tiled in mother-of-pearl, this one room was roughly the size of Dun Cinczi. Diala led the way with Arryl and me a step behind, stopping before the podium, which held two ornate jewelled thrones that looked suspiciously as if they were constructed of solid gold.

Engarhod occupied the throne on the right. A tall, angular man, he looks about fifty. His dark hair is grey at the temples and in those days he wore it tied back and held down with a golden circlet. His face is weathered by the time he spent as a mortal, and if he doesn't open his mouth, he looks regal enough, I suppose. That day he was wearing a cloth-of-gold wrap, his chest a canvas tattooed with an intricate scrollwork, beneath his greying chest hair. Every time I see Engarhod, the tattoos are different. He has them drawn on his skin these days, because real tattoos won't take—his body keeps healing them, you see.

On Engarhod's right sat his queen—Syrolee, Empress of the Five Realms. The whore elevated to empress. Both Arryl and Diala had warned me about Syrolee, but I wasn't prepared for the reality. She wore a golden wrap matching Engarhod's, but I could barely make it out under the weight of the golden chains she wore around her neck. Her hair was fixed in an elaborate nest of braids, her face painted white, her thin lips defined with a blood-red paste and her eyes heavily shadowed with kohl.

I tried not to stare, but it was a challenge. Great beauty might draw the eye, but ugliness enhanced by bad taste is impossible to look away from.

Diala stepped forward, bowed to the emperor and empress and then held out her hand to indicate her latest minion—me. "Your imperial highnesses, allow me to introduce the newest member of our company, Cayal of Lakesh, Prince of Kordana."

Syrolee studied me for a time before she spoke. "Diala informs us you seek a quest that will take you home."

Strictly speaking, I was looking for a quest that would see me *welcomed* home, not one that would take me there before my exile was revoked, but I didn't argue the point. I was being offered the quest I sought. It would have been rude, I thought, to argue semantics.

It was Engarhod who made the announcement that ended up costing so many lives. "We charge you with bringing the Eternal Flame to Kordana. That is your quest, Prince Cayal of Lakesh. You must bring the full knowledge of the Tide to your people."

I had my quest. It wasn't what I was expecting— proselytising didn't strike me as being a very adventurous occupation, but it meant returning to Kordana with the sanction of the Temple of the Tides. Even Planice would have trouble denying me entry with the weight of an entire religion behind me.

I was still pondering the emperor's words when Syrolee's eyes narrowed suspiciously. "Arryl tells us you're a *real* prince."

I nodded uncertainly, a little alarmed by her tone. I'm not sure what I expected, but it certainly wasn't such animosity or distrust. "My sister is Queen Planice of Kordana."

"I suppose you think that puts you above us, eh?"

The question took me by surprise. And I had no idea how to answer it. After a moment, I shrugged. "I never really thought about it."

"That'll change," a wry voice suggested from behind me.

I turned to see who had spoken, but Arryl answered my

question before I had a chance to ask it. "Lukys! Welcome home!"

The man smiled as he approached across the vast expanse of the throne room, stopping long enough to kiss Arryl's cheek as he passed her. He was dressed in loose linen trousers and a sleeveless shirt with bare feet that made no sound on the white marble floor. As he drew nearer I noticed a mottled grey creature sitting on his shoulder which turned out to be a tame rat, of all things. "Hardly the place I call home, Arryl, but I do appreciate the sentiment."

"Nice to think there's *something* you appreciate," Diala remarked sourly.

He ignored the younger priestess and turned to study me, instead. "Kordana, eh? You're a long way from home, lad."

"It's a long story," I told him, trying not to stare at the rat perched on his shoulder.

"You'll have plenty of time to tell us the details, won't he, Syrolee?" Lukys glanced up at the podium and then he looked back at me, with a sardonic expression. "That's one thing we immortals have in abundance, you'll discover, my young immortal prince. Time."

"Immortal?" I asked.

Lukys turned to Diala. "You didn't tell him?"

"I asked him if he wanted to be like us," she replied, more than a little defensively. "It wasn't as though I didn't tell him how old I was."

"Ah, but did you explain your ceremony and what it would do to him?"

"What did it do to me?" I shudder, even after all this time, when I remember how naive I was.

"It's made you immortal, son," Lukys informed me.

"How can you tell?"

"Because the only other outcome is death. You're standing here arguing about it, ergo, you must be immortal." While I was still trying to take that in, Lukys turned to Diala. "Must have really tickled you, Diala, to think you could make an eternal minion out of a *real* prince, this time."

"Minion?" I echoed stupidly.

"Ah! Forgot to explain that bit too, did she?"

"Ignore him," Diala advised with a frown. "Lukys finds it amusing to denigrate the emperor's mission to bring the worship of the Tide to all the peoples of Amyrantha."

"Not at all," Lukys disagreed. "If I thought for a moment that's actually what these two were up to, I'd be out there banging a drum alongside the rest of you." He laughed suddenly and turned to me. "But, who am I to interfere with the plans of the Emperor and Empress of the Five Realms? Diala is right. Pay no attention to me, Cayal, our Immortal Prince. I am a cynic and a bore."

Lukys is nothing like the wise and wizened old figure in your wretched Tarot. He's a good decade younger than Engarhod to look at and much darker skinned, almost as dark as a Magrethan. The rat—whose name is Coron, by the way—is his constant companion. It's immortal, too, the only animal I've ever heard of that survived the Eternal Flame. But I was describing Lukys, wasn't I, not his wretched pet? His eyes are blue, his hair so blond it's almost white. Even if his personality wasn't so beguiling, the combination of light hair and eyes against that dark skin, and the rat frequently perched on his shoulder, is unusual enough to leave a lasting impression on everyone who meets him.

"Cayal, the Immortal Prince, eh?" Engarhod echoed. "Tides, if we start calling him that, everyone will want a title."

"If anybody is going to be known as the Immortal Prince," Syrolee declared petulantly, her golden chains clinking softly as she folded her arms across her breast. "It should be *my* son, Tryan."

"Why?" Lukys asked dryly. "Is somebody else using *Lord of the Witless Wonders*?"

Jumping to her feet, Syrolee raised her hand angrily,

obviously intending to strike Lukys down where he stood, but before she could do anything, she was slammed back against her throne by Lukys's invisible grip, gasping with indignation.

I was stunned. This was the first time I had witnessed anybody using Tide magic. The first time I even knew it was possible. What made it even stranger was I had *felt* Lukys manipulating the Tide. Until that moment, I wasn't even aware I could sense it.

But the others had no hint yet that I might have the ability to wield the Tide, and ignorance stopped me from revealing myself. I didn't know if what I'd felt was common to everyone present, so I said nothing.

"Don't even think about it, Syrolee," Lukys warned in a voice that chilled me to the core. "I can't kill you, but I can surely mess that face of yours up enough to keep you out of my way for a few days." He let her go and she slumped in her throne, glaring at him, sulking but no longer defiant.

I watched the exchange in astonishment, a part of me noting that Lukys was probably not a man I'd like as an enemy. Lukys must have noticed my expression because suddenly he laughed again. (He laughs a lot, Lukys does. Nobody else has such an eye for the absurd as him. Or is so willing to mock it.) "Bit of a shock to realise what a happy little family we are, isn't it, Cayal? Just wait until you meet the rest of us."

"You shouldn't speak to my wife like that, Lukys," Engarhod scolded belatedly. "She's the empress."

"She's a flanking fool," Lukys corrected absently, his attention still on me. "A trait common among our kind, I've noticed. Did Diala trick you the same way she tricked Taryx and Brynden?"

I glanced at Diala, not sure who Taryx or Brynden were. The priestess shrugged and looked away. "They wanted it."

"Pity they didn't understand what 'it' was." When Diala refused to rise to the bait, Lukys shrugged. "On the bright side, you'll have an eternity to wonder whether 'it' was worth the price you've paid, son. Have they taught you anything yet?"

I shook my head. "I've sort of been . . . feeling my way."

"That's what got you into this mess, wasn't it?" he asked with a raised brow. "Hope you're not the squeamish sort."

"Squeamish?"

"Ah, haven't met the rest of the family yet, have you?"

"He'll meet them soon enough," Syrolee announced, sitting a little straighter on her throne. "And my daughter, too. Are you married, Cayal?"

The sudden change of subject took me by surprise. "Ah . . . no . . ."

Syrolee smiled. "Good." Her predatory smile made me shudder. Still does, when she looks at me like that.

Lukys noticed it too. "Tides, Syrolee! Don't you think you should give the boy a chance to catch his breath before you start marrying him and Elyssa off?"

"I suggested no such thing!"

"You'd better watch your step, Cayal," Lukys warned. "That royal blood of yours makes you almost acceptable enough to be a consort for the maiden princess."

"Lukys, do you think you could try to go more than five minutes without insulting my family?" Engarhod complained.

"And then what would I do for entertainment?"

Ever the peacemaker, Arryl headed off the argument. "Is that lunch I catch on the breeze, Syrolee? It smells wonderful."

I couldn't smell a thing and suspected Arryl couldn't either. But even Diala seemed anxious to move on. "I think you're right, Arryl. It does smell wonderful and I'm starving."

"Then we should lunch," Syrolee agreed with ill grace. The empress offered her hand to Engarhod and together they rose to their feet. "Lukys, get rid of that disgusting creature. You're not bringing him to the dinner table. It's time," she added, looking down on me, "for our prince to meet his immortal brethren."

Between them, Syrolee and Engarhod have four children, all of them born of their marriages to other people. There was a rumour, Diala told me once, that the count had once been much higher but the immolation process had eliminated the weaker members of their family, leaving only the strongest to carry on into eternity. I've never been able to determine the accuracy of the rumour, but I'm inclined to think there might be a grain of truth in it. Syrolee strikes me as the sort of mother willing to immolate any number of her family members if it gets her what she wants.

Lukys put Coron down and he scurried off across the marble tiles to look for entertainment elsewhere as we headed across the vast throne room, chatting about inconsequential things. Lukys asked me about Kordana and my general impressions of Magreth. It was innocuous enough until we reached the banquet hall, where the remaining offspring of the Emperor and Empress of the Five Realms awaited us.

The first of them to step forward was Syrolee's daughter Elyssa. I'll never forget our first meeting. I stared at her in surprise. Like Diala, she was only eighteen or nineteen when the Eternal Flame made her immortal, but she wasn't exactly preserved in the first blush of womanhood. Despite the rumours that persist down the centuries about the beauty of the Tide Lords, immortality does nothing to improve what nature has naturally endowed one with. Ugly mortals become ugly immortals, and that applies equally to their personality and their physical appearance. Scars might heal, pockmarked skin might recover, but nothing can create beauty where it doesn't already exist.

Although her complexion is as flawless as any immortal's, with teeth as crooked as a shoreline and lashless eyes set so far apart they seem to have been placed there by mistake, she's hardly the matchless beauty your Tarot speaks of. Elyssa curtseyed, eyeing me off like a piece of raw meat. She was wearing thick white powdered makeup like her mother, but it had creased into unsightly clumps along the line of her chin.

"Oooh . . . ," she squealed, clapping her stumpy fingers together gleefully. "Fresh meat."

Lukys noticed my alarmed expression and leaned in close to my ear. "And now you understand the reason she's still the *maiden* princess," he chuckled.

"What was that, Lukys?" Syrolee snapped, rightly guessing his comment was less than complimentary.

"Nothing, Syrolee. Just remarking on the weather." He smiled at Elyssa. "You're looking lovely today, my dear. Have you lost weight?"

"My weight never changes, Lukys," she replied, looking a little puzzled. "Nobody's does. You know that."

"He's teasing you," Engarhod told her, scowling at Lukys. "This is Diala's newest recruit. Cayal."

"The Immortal Prince," Lukys added with a smirk in Syrolee's direction.

Elyssa smiled at me coyly. "Are you really a prince?"

I nodded. "I was. I'm not sure if I still am. I was banished."

"Why did they banish you?" the young man standing behind Elyssa asked.

"Cayal, this is Tryan," Lukys informed me. "Elyssa's brother."

Tryan was as beautiful as his sister was unattractive. Tall, dark-eyed and exquisitely formed, it's as if Mother Nature spooned all the beauty into one basket and all the muck into another and then created brother and sister out of them. The handsome young man stepped forward, offering me his hand.

"Welcome to eternity," he said.

Tryan was smiling as he said it, but there was something a little too contrived in his welcome and it set my teeth on edge. Would that I had listened to my first instincts about him, Kordana may have seen out the year, but this was all too new and I hadn't learned to rely on my gut feelings yet. Foolishly, I was still at that point in life where one trusts in others and believes some good will come of it.

"And these two troublemakers," Lukys added, indicating the two men standing behind Tryan, "are Krydence and Rance, Engarhod's sons."

"I've already met Rance," I explained, with a nod of greeting to the younger brother.

The older man eyed me speculatively. "So, what *did* you do?"

"Pardon?"

"To get yourself banished from Kordana?" Krydence clarified.

"Got into a fight."

"Did you kill someone?" Tryan asked.

I hesitated, not sure how they would take the news, and then I nodded. There was no point lying about it. If my mission was to return to Kordana to bring word of the Tide, there was no way they weren't going to learn of my disgrace, sooner or later.

Krydence seemed amused. "This one should fit right in."

"Don't you find it interesting," Lukys remarked, "that Diala never seems to find innocent little doves with pure hearts and unsullied pasts to join our ranks? That says something about immortality, don't you think?"

"Brynden fancies himself pure of heart," Diala reminded them with a glare at Lukys. "In fact, he's quite obnoxious about it."

"Brynden?" I asked in confusion.

"Another of Diala's recruits," Rance explained. "First thing he did was run screaming from Magreth with no notion of how he was going to handle immortality." He glanced around at his siblings. "Then the stupid fool came back here a couple of hundred years later, trying to tell us we'd been immortalised for some noble religious purpose and should start wearing hair shirts and doing charitable works for the greater good of mankind. Has anybody seen him recently?"

"I saw him about forty years ago," Krydence told them. "He was living in a cave in the Caterpillar Ranges. I believe he's now trying to resolve his dilemma with meditation."

"Better than drinking yourself into a perpetual state of oblivion like Jaxyn, I suppose," Rance suggested.

"Is Jaxyn another immortal?" I asked. This was all happening far too quickly for me. I couldn't sort out who was who here in the palace dining room, let alone who the others were.

"Jaxyn was Diala's first successful immolation," Lukys told him. "Quite a moment for celebration, it was."

"Jaxyn certainly thought so," Syrolee agreed, obviously not happy with discussing the missing immortals. "Jaxyn's like you," she added in my direction. "Highborn. Thinks he's a cut above the rest of us."

"I never said that!" I objected.

"Good," Elyssa said with her uneven smile, taking me by the arm. "In that case, you can come sit by me. I want to hear all about Kordana."

Elyssa's attention on me seemed to mollify Syrolee somewhat. With the first hint of serious misgivings about what I might have gotten myself into, I allowed Elyssa to lead me to a chair at the long table. As I took my place, I glanced around, catching Lukys's eye as the older man sat down. He winked at me and mouthed the word *later,* then turned his attention to something Krydence was saying on his left, and paid me no more attention for the rest of the meal.

Several days later, Lukys came by the temple to speak with me. That was the day Pellys killed all those goldfish.

Pellys spotted Lukys first, looking up and grinning broadly when he saw him approaching. "Lukys!"

"Hello, Pellys. You look like you're having fun."

"I'm showing Cayal how to catch fish. He's my new friend," the big man announced, slapping me on the back so hard that I staggered under the force of the blow. "My *best* friend."

"Lucky Cayal," Lukys replied, smiling.

Pellys grinned and pointed at Coron, perched—as usual—on Lukys's right shoulder. "Your best friend's a rat."

"Which says a lot about me, don't you think? May I borrow your new best friend for a moment? I just need to ask him something."

Pellys thought on that for a moment and then nodded. "Only as far as the railing," he warned, pointing to the marble balustrade some thirty paces away that separated the temple gardens from the waterfall and the lake below.

"Not a step further," Lukys promised. "Cayal?"

Curiously, I followed him across the garden to the balustrade. I remember glancing down at the sheer drop for a moment with a queasy feeling and then turning to Lukys. "I suppose I should get over my irrational fear of heights, now that I can't die in a fall."

To my surprise, Lukys shook his head. "Tides, no! Cling to every one of your phobias, lad. It's what makes you human."

"Am I still human?" I asked. I still don't know the answer to that question, by the way.

"I haven't really worked that out yet. Do you have any plans?"

I looked at him in confusion. "Plans for what?"

"For what you intend to do with the rest of this long life you've been granted after you've brought the Tide to your people, or whatever nonsense Engarhod was spouting the other day. Eternity is a very long time, Cayal. Your worst enemy is no longer a flesh and blood entity. It's boredom."

"I haven't really thought about it." That was the Tide's own truth. I was still rejoicing in the knowledge that I was heading home. The wider implications of immortality beyond that hadn't even occurred to me.

"Then consider this," Lukys suggested. "There are nearly

a score of other immortals out there, my lad, and most of them are already starting to get restless. It's going to lead to trouble, you mark my words, and given that some of them have the power to manipulate the elements on a rather impressive scale, it could get rather nasty, too."

"I'm not sure I follow you."

Lukys turned to the waterfall and raised his arm. A moment later silence descended over the gardens as the waterfall abruptly stopped. Crystal beads of water hung in midair, waiting for permission to continue on their way. I could feel Lukys warping the Tide around the drops of water like something crawling on my skin; could feel the strain as his control over the elements warred with the natural inclination of all liquids to settle on the lowest possible surface.

"The water is resisting you," I remarked without thinking.

He seemed surprised. "You can feel that?"

I nodded, unaware there was anything unusual in it. After all, I'd just been made immortal. Nothing seemed impossible after that.

He dropped his arm and the waterfall resumed its interrupted tumble down the rocks to the lake below, the air once again filled with the cooling spray and the ever-present sound of rushing water. Lukys studied me thoughtfully, but said nothing.

His silence worried me. "Can all immortals do things like that?"

"Surprisingly few of them, actually. Have you mentioned this to anyone else?"

"Mentioned what?" I asked.

"That you can sense the Tide? Feel others manipulating it?"

I shook my head. "Is that a bad thing?"

Suddenly, Lukys smiled. "I'd not mention it to anyone around here until you're certain, lad. And worked out how to deal with it. Such ability is bound to be considered . . .

threatening . . . to those who lack the same sort of power. You may have noticed the emperor and his clan aren't exactly endowed with an over-abundance of magical ability, just an endless desire for power and conspicuous wealth."

"You speak so disparagingly of Engarhod, yet Diala tells me you two were once friends." I turned and leant against the balustrade. "She told me you and Engarhod discovered the Eternal Flame and brought it back here to Magreth."

"That's true enough, I suppose," he agreed, "if you strip the story down to its bare bones. But we certainly weren't friends. Far from it, in fact. I wasn't even a fisherman by trade. I was an astrologer who wanted nothing more than a quiet life spent studying the heavens, but I was also an eldest son and my father was a merchant with very clear ideas about what an eldest son should do with his life. He'd bought Engarhod's fishing boat the year before we found the flame and sent me along on the trip because he thought Engarhod was trying to cheat us."

"Then how did you find the flame?"

"The flame found us, actually. We were chasing a catch around the icebergs of Jelidia, praying we'd find something worth selling before the ice closed in and we were stranded there for the next eight months. Being so far south, we were accustomed to the strange lights in the sky at night, but one night, the sky itself seemed to catch fire. It was a magnificent sight. I was actually enjoying myself for the first time since being forced aboard that wretched ship. I stood there watching flames streak the sky for hours, realising too late that the shooting stars were getting much too close for comfort. One of the meteorites hit us square amidships."

"And you survived," Cayal concluded. "With Engarhod."

He nodded. "And Coron here," he said, scratching the rat under the chin. "We named him Coron after the boat, by the way. Anyway, when the meteor struck I remember thinking: *It can't end like this!* We were the only three who lived through the explosion, at any rate, which was the most remarkable thing of all, because we'd been standing closest to where the meteor hit."

"Did you realise what had happened to you?"

"Not at first. And to be honest, we only kept the flames alive because we were stranded on an iceberg, it was freezing and all we had left was the remnants of the boat, a fair bit of which was still on fire. It took a while to realise something had happened to us. I think those first few nights we really thought we were going to die, either of starvation or exposure. But the flames kept on burning, neither of us got sick, or even very hungry, and we began to wonder why. By then my friend Coron here was hanging around a fair bit, so we caught him and tried to kill him for food. When that didn't work we tried to kill each other. Eventually, it dawned on us that we were immortal but I don't think we comprehended it fully for a long time after we were rescued. Immortality is not a concept easily grasped by a fragile human mind."

"How long were you stranded down there?"

"Eight . . . maybe nine months. Plenty of time to come to the realisation that we weren't the same people who'd sailed out of Cuttlefish Bay the previous summer." Lukys turned his pale eyes on me. "Nine months is a long time to be stuck on an iceberg with a man you don't like. You learn a lot about each other. And when you're starting to suspect you can't die, you spend a lot of time making plans for the future, too."

"Did Engarhod's plans include becoming Emperor of the Five Realms?"

Lukys rolled his eyes. "Isn't it a dreadful title? Syrolee thought it up when we got back from Jelidia. It has something to do with having command over the five elements, which is rather optimistic of them. Engarhod can't command anything, not even his wife. He just wanted to be rich. His wife is the one with the delusions of grandeur."

"Wasn't she Pellys's wife back then?" I'd been at the temple for several months by then. I wasn't totally ignorant of the story about him and the empress but this was the first time anybody had offered any sort of detail to fill in the gaps.

"Ah, now that was a sordid little affair that rebounded rather unfortunately on everyone involved." Lukys sat himself on the edge of the balustrade and pointed to Pellys, who was still on his knees, splashing happily about in the fountain trying to catch the goldfish. "Poor old Pellys. He's not very bright now, but I don't remember him being much brighter back then, either. He was the bouncer in the brothel where Syrolee worked. She married him because it meant he'd bounce the customers she didn't fancy before he'd help any of the other girls. Didn't hurt that he used to hand over all his pay to her each week, either. Although strangely enough, given their ability to wield the Tide, I think he really is the father of both Elyssa and Tryan."

"Where does Engarhod come in?"

"He was a fishing boat captain, which in the social strata of the Cuttlefish Bay wharf district in those days made him pretty close to royalty. She latched on to him like a barnacle the first time he wandered into that Tide-forsaken brothel and never let go."

"And Pellys knew about it?"

Lukys jerked his head in Pellys's direction. "You did notice that he's not the sharpest hook in the tackle box, didn't you?"

I nodded, wondering at the dark truths lurking behind Lukys's tale. He spoke as if he was relating an anecdote about a particularly amusing hunting trip, but what he was telling me was much more important. I probably didn't appreciate how important at the time, but I was starting to get a sense of the danger. Or maybe I just think that now, because I can't abide the notion that I might have once been such a blind fool. Whatever the case, I'd been warned. That I didn't listen, that I allowed Tryan to return with me to Kordana . . . well, that's a decision I've learned to live with.

Regret and immortality are sorry companions at the best of times.

"So what happened when you got back from Jelidia?" I think I asked, or words to that effect.

Lukys seemed happy to tell me the rest of the story. "We'd made a pact, Engarhod and I, when we were stranded on that iceberg, to keep our immortality a secret. We swore an oath on the lives of every person we cared about. Naturally, the first thing Engarhod did after we were rescued by another fishing boat the following spring was visit Syrolee. The second thing he did was blab the whole story to her, including the secret of the Eternal Flame. She was on fire about ten minutes after he got back to Cuttlefish Bay. Burned the whole damned brothel down in the process."

"That was a huge risk, wasn't it?"

"We didn't fully appreciate the subtleties back then," he told me. "I'm not sure Syrolee understands them, still. But once she was immortal, she had much bigger plans. First and foremost, she wanted to be rid of Pellys. For want of a better explanation, we'd come to the conclusion by then that the desire to live seemed to be the determining factor in who survived and who burned. What we hadn't discovered was that there's simply no way of telling who has the stronger will to live. Some people claim they have it, and they're toast within minutes. Others—and they're few and far between—have a will that even the flames recognise and respect. Turns out, Pellys was one of them. Syrolee immolated her husband, thinking he was too stupid to understand what was going on and that he'd probably die in the process."

"But he lived."

"Worse, he can wield the Tide with almost as much power as I have, which gets up Syrolee's nose no end, let me tell you."

I crossed my arms against my body, gripped by an indefinable chill. Lukys can have that effect on you. He has a way of delivering the most dire news in the most conversational tone. "Tides! It all seems too fantastic to be real."

I remember he smiled sympathetically. "Sometimes I *still* feel that way."

His camaraderie surprised me. More than a little suspicious of it, my eyes narrowed as I studied my surprisingly forthcoming new friend. "Is there a reason you're telling me this?"

Lukys nodded. "You're heading back to Kordana with Tryan to fulfil this quest of yours. I just wanted to make sure you realise exactly who you're dealing with."

"You think I shouldn't go?"

"I think you're in for a rude awakening, my friend," he corrected. "But if I've learned one thing since becoming immortal, it's that the only lessons that really stick are the ones you learn for yourself. Go back to Kordana. Bring your people to the Tide. And when you're done, look me up. You and I will have a great deal to talk about by then I suspect."

Chapter 37

By the time Cayal finished speaking the carriage had reached the crossroads outside the city. Arkady was jerked back into the present—quite literally—by the coach turning right, taking the road that led into the mountains. The main road through the city to the palace dwindled into the distance. It was still possible to reach the palace by this route, but it was much longer.

Arkady had given the coach driver her instructions before they left the palace this morning. The destination she had in mind was an inn some two miles along the road, favoured by miners on their way to or from the mines located in the Valley of the Tides, as well as prospectors who scoured the nearer mountain streams around Lutalo for alluvial gold.

Cayal had fallen silent, his gaze fixed on the passing scenery. Although she wanted to hear more, Arkady was glad of the chance to gather her thoughts. What she was planning was at best foolish, at worst an act of treason against the crown. Far from saving Cayal from torture at the hands of Declan Hawkes, she might well bring the same fate down upon her own head.

"Lebec Palace is rather less salubrious than I imagined," Cayal remarked, as the coach rocked to a halt in the yard of the run-down inn.

The inn was owned by a one-armed man named Clyden Bell. Arkady's father had amputated the old miner's left arm after he was caught in a cave-in and in danger of half a mountain falling on him. Clyden had never forgotten her father's courage that day. Nor had he forgotten he owed his life to a passing physician, heading home from a visit to Fioma, with his ten-year-old daughter in tow. Arkady still remembered the lantern trembling in her hand as she stood by her father's side in the dark mine, listening to the creaking timbers threatening to collapse on top of them. She had handed him his bone saw and the other instruments he needed to free the young man, wiping the sweat from the brow of the trapped and terrified miner, pretending she wasn't scared witless.

Clyden hadn't forgotten it, either. If there was anywhere in Lebec Province Arkady could be sure of complete discretion, it was at the inn belonging to Clyden Bell.

Nobody came to open the carriage door. As instructed before they left the palace, the Crasii escort surrounding the carriage remained mounted. They would not move until they were ordered to.

It was the question of who would give the order that Arkady had brought Cayal here to settle. That's what she intended to tell Stellan, at any rate. *I was trying to force him to admit he was a Caelish spy,* she planned to say when she was questioned. *I never thought he'd make a run for it . . .*

Arkady took a deep breath. *One step at a time,* she reminded herself.

"I asked permission once, to amputate some of your fingers," she informed Cayal, surprised at how steady she sounded.

Cayal eyed her askance. "Is that a particular hobby of yours?"

"You claim to be immortal; that your limbs can regenerate. I thought it the fastest way to establish the veracity of your claim."

"But you didn't," he pointed out.

"My husband wouldn't permit it. He was afraid if we mistreated our Caelish spy, then the Caelum government would mistreat our prisoners in return."

"How terribly civilised of him."

She ignored his sarcasm and continued with what she had to say. It wasn't difficult. She'd rehearsed it mentally all the way to Lebec Prison. "Your problem, Cayal, is that the Caelish are denying they know anything about you. It seems you're not a Caelish agent, after all."

"I don't recall ever claiming I was."

"Then who decided you were from Caelum?"

He shrugged. "I lived there for a time before I arrived in Glaeba. I probably mentioned it to someone in Rindova. Maybe that's where they got the idea."

"Where exactly in Caelum did you live?"

"In the capital. In Taerl."

"So you had plenty of time to be recruited and trained by the Caelish as a spy."

"In theory," he agreed with a thin smile. "But that doesn't mean I was."

"No. You claim to be a Tide Lord."

"So you *were* listening . . ."

"I've no time for your games, Cayal. I'm offering you a chance."

"To escape?" He seemed amused. "I saw our escort, Arkady. You're not planning to let me go anywhere."

"Our escort is Crasii. There are no humans among them. Even the coach driver is Crasii. If you are who you claim, they'll follow your orders over mine. They won't be able to help themselves."

"But you don't believe my kind exists," he accused.

"The Crasii do," she reminded him.

Cayal shook his head. "This is just an excuse to kill me, because they won't let you hang me or chop off one of my limbs." With a rattle of chains, he folded his arms across his chest and leaned back in the seat, obviously not planning to go anywhere. "Don't do me any favours, Arkady. Take me to this spymaster of yours. Let him torture me. Believe me, he'll tire of the game long before I do."

"I don't need to kill you to prove you're not what you claim," she pointed out. "Surrounding this carriage is a score of Crasii who've never heard of Kyle Lakesh. They don't know who you are, or why you're here, only that you're my prisoner and we're on our way to the palace to hand you over to Declan Hawkes. Our Crasii are loyal and well trained, Cayal. Nothing short of a command from a Tide Lord would make them defy their orders. So do it. Prove you're a Tide Lord. Step out of this carriage in leg-irons and command your slaves to obey you. Order them to set you free."

"And if they do?"

"If they do, then you're free to go."

"Really?" he asked sceptically. "And what about you?"

She shrugged, unconcerned. Of this entire, ill-conceived plan, she was sure about this one thing. "I'll go back to the king and my husband and tell them the truth. I'll say I agreed so wholeheartedly with the need to torture a confession from you that I personally undertook your transfer from the prison. They'll believe me. I was the one who wanted to cut off your fingers, after all. I'll tell them we stopped at the inn on the way back from the prison to water the horses and you commanded my Crasii to release you. Unaccountably, they followed your orders. Stellan will suspect I was involved, and so will the King's Spymaster, but my husband can't implicate me without implicating himself and Declan Hawkes is a very old friend. The king will just think I'm a fool for letting you get the better of me, but what do you expect of a woman?"

"Why?"

"Because misogyny is a national sport in Glaeba."

"No . . . I mean why are you willing to let me go?"

"I don't condone torture."

"You seem to be just fine with treason, though."

She didn't answer his accusation, partly because she wasn't really sure of the answer herself. There were a thousand reasons why she shouldn't be sitting here, giving Cayal this opportunity to escape the king's justice, and very few good reasons why she should.

Cayal studied her closely and then he smiled, as if he could see her dilemma and it amused him. "I'm curious, my lady. If you're right, and I'm not a Tide Lord, then the Crasii will ignore me, and we'll continue on our way. I'll end up in the hands of this torturer of yours anyway, and you'll have gained nothing."

"I'll have proof you're not a Tide Lord," she pointed out. "In which case, Declan Hawkes can do his worst, because I think you're here in Glaeba to cause mischief, Cayal, and I suspect your target is the Crasii. I won't let you hurt the Crasii for some nefarious purpose of your own, when it's within my power to stop you."

He smiled. "I wish I was even half as complicated as you think I am, Arkady."

"Prove you're not," she challenged. "Open that door. Go out there and order your slaves to release you."

"You think I won't?"

Arkady smiled. "I think you will if you want me to believe you're mad, Cayal. For the sake of your story, you have no choice but to go out there and try to bluff your way past my Crasii. On the other hand, if you're the agitator I suspect you are, you'll sit here and smile condescendingly, all the while trying to give the impression you couldn't possibly dignify this ridiculous charade by participating in it."

Cayal studied her for a moment, smiling at something Arkady could only guess at, and then he shrugged. "Very well. Let's prove I'm a madman, shall we?"

His answer didn't surprise her. She nodded and leant forward to open the door. As soon as she did, one of the felines hurried forward to lower the step, and helped her down into the inn's muddy yard. Surrounding the coach, mounted on sturdy Glaeban ponies, sat her contingent of Crasii guards, waiting patiently for the order to dismount. Arkady turned to the nearest feline. She was new, Arkady realised, when it occurred to her that she didn't know the young female's name.

"You're the Crasii from the bear fight, aren't you?"

The feline nodded. "Chikita, my lady. Out of Kamira, by Taryx."

"Help the prisoner out of the carriage, Chikita," she commanded. "Those leg-irons will trip him up, otherwise."

"As you wish, your grace." The feline dismounted, handing the reins of her pony to the Crasii beside her, and then hurried to the carriage to carry out her orders. As she did, Clyden emerged from the inn, wiping his one good hand on his beer-stained apron, smiling broadly.

"Arkady!"

"Hello, Clyden," she replied, smiling at the big man.

He bowed gallantly. "You honour my humble inn with your presence, your grace." Unlike Declan, Clyden was impressed with the marriage she had made, and that she had remained his friend in spite of it. It didn't hurt that Stellan took a detour via the inn occasionally, to partake of an ale he didn't particularly want, just to improve business for an old friend of his wife's with a bit of ducal patronage. "To what do I owe the honour of this unexpected visit?"

"We're just on our way back to the palace, Clyden. I thought my escort might like some refreshment."

He nodded and opened his mouth to invite them inside, but he fell silent at the sight of the chained prisoner being helped from the carriage. Arkady turned to watch Cayal curiously, wondering if he would try to order the Crasii to release him.

And what he would do when they refused.

If he really were mad, then he'd probably rationalise away their disobedience with tales of it being Low Tide or some such nonsense.

It would be interesting to watch, regardless of the outcome.

Cayal jerked the chains as he jumped to the ground, and then straightened up and glanced around at Arkady's escort. The felines sat rigid in their saddles, a few of the ponies nickering nervously as they waited.

He hesitated and then fixed his gaze on Arkady.

"Are you sure about this?" he asked, as if it were Arkady who might want to reconsider their deal.

She smiled at his audacity and waved her arm to encompass her escort. "Be my guest, Master Lakesh."

"Don't say I didn't warn you," he replied, but despite her invitation and his own brave words, he hesitated still, confirming her suspicion it was for making mischief and not madness that had prompted Cayal's claim to immortality. A part of her was a little disappointed. Although she'd never for a moment believed he might actually be a Tide Lord, a part of her had hoped that his delusions were real—to him at least—and not a callously fabricated web of lies.

She waited a few moments longer, and then shaking her head, Arkady sighed, wondering why she'd expected any other outcome. "Put him back in the carriage, Chikita."

"Actually, I think I'd rather you got rid of these chains, gemang," Cayal said calmly, never taking his eyes from Arkady.

She smiled, glad he'd made at least a token effort to confirm his madness.

"To serve you is the reason I breathe, my lord."

Arkady stared at the Crasii in shock as she did exactly as
he ordered. Cayal shook free of the chains as she dropped
to her knees before him, her head bowed. Silently, and without so much as a whimper of protest, the rest of the escort
dismounted and followed her lead.

Cayal rubbed his wrists, glancing around the yard, and
then he fixed his eyes on Arkady, who was standing in the
yard of Clyden Bell's inn, stunned into immobility, surrounded by a squad of a dozen well-disciplined Crasii on
their knees in the mud, paying homage to a Tide Lord.

Chapter 38

Cayal knew, almost as soon as he ordered the Crasii to
unchain him, that he shouldn't have done it. Long
and painful experience had taught him the perils of being
immortal in a world full of people afraid of death. It was
different when the Tide was high and he could wield the
power of a god. But to reveal himself now, when he had no
power, was simply asking for trouble.

Arrogance invariably caused the downfall of the Tide
Lords. Lukys had warned Cayal of as much within the first
few days of meeting him. With immortality came the misguided belief that one was infallible, Lukys claimed. They
weren't infallible, of course, but it seemed to be a lesson
quickly forgotten by even the most self-effacing of their
kind.

He didn't even want to think of the consequences if
word escaped Glaeba that the Immortal Prince was abroad
once more, something he'd been secretly dreading since
blurting out that he was a Tide Lord while lying under the
gallows the day they tried to hang him. It would reach one
of the others for certain. For that matter, there may be others of his kind already hiding in Glaeba. He had no way of

knowing if there were. He had as many enemies as he had friends among his own kind and when the Tide retreated, they all slithered under the nearest rock to await the return of their power.

But he'd ruined it now. To impress some overeducated, sexually repressed, glorified librarian, he'd revealed himself to a whole squad of Crasii.

And a one-armed barkeep, he noted.

Arkady was looking quite pale. He ordered the felines to stand back, speaking in the ancient tongue, a little surprised they reacted to it in much the same way Warlock had this morning when he'd tried it out on him. Except these Crasii didn't question him. There were no Scards among this lot.

"What did you say to them?" Arkady demanded.

"I told them to back off. I'm a bit surprised they understand me, actually. Nobody's spoken that language in more than three thousand years."

"Where did *you* learn it?" she demanded, apparently still not willing to concede he might be what he claimed. *Tides, this woman is stubborn.*

"It was the language we all spoke back then."

"Back when?"

"Back when we first created the Crasii."

Arkady's eyes flashed angrily and, for a moment, Cayal actually felt sorry for her. In Arkady's world, there was no room for Tide magic. No room for anything that couldn't be explained away by a theory or a mathematical formula. He suspected she would cling to her rationalisations long past the point of logic.

"Can't you, just once, speak the truth, Cayal?"

He sympathised with her distress. The truth, he suspected, was much more than Arkady Desean had bargained on. It wasn't that she didn't believe him, Cayal realised. She didn't *want* to believe him.

"We had a deal," he reminded her. "If the Crasii obeyed me, I was free to go. Are you planning to keep your end of the bargain? Or did losing never actually cross your mind?"

She didn't answer him, which Cayal took to mean the latter. It would never have occurred to Arkady that he could do what he claimed. In fact, he was quite certain she considered this just another trick he had engineered to fool everyone into believing the impossible.

"Well, I'm going to give you the benefit of the doubt," he told her, "and assume that you did mean it."

Arkady shook her head, but seemed unable to speak. Her one-armed companion was much more forthcoming. He took a step forward, shaking his fist threateningly.

"You'll not speak to the duchess like that!" he declared. "Stand down now, you villain! Surrender, before I take you apart with my one good arm!"

With a sigh, Cayal turned to the nearest Crasii. "Kill him."

The feline rose to her feet without hesitation, baring her claws.

"No!" Arkady cried, when she realised the young female intended to do exactly what he ordered.

"Hold!" Cayal commanded the Crasii and then he turned to Arkady. "And to think, I thought you had nothing to say."

"Cayal, don't kill this man," she begged. "Please. You're in enough trouble . . ."

"Arkady, Arkady, Arkady . . . ," he said, shaking his head. "I'm not the one in trouble here. Haven't you noticed that?" He took a step toward her, half-expecting her to back away. But she held her ground. "You're the one suddenly confronted with the unthinkable."

"You won't get ten miles out of Lebec before they hunt you down," she warned.

"Which is a damned shame, really," he agreed. "But nothing we can't deal with." He turned to Chikita. "That carriage is too conspicuous. Find me something to ride. And for her ladyship, too. She'll be coming with us."

Chikita hurried off toward the stables on the other side of the muddy yard. Cayal ordered several more Crasii to set a perimeter, thinking that if one was going to steal a dozen Crasii, it was a damned good thing he'd managed to find a squad of well-trained, military-minded felines. The one-armed innkeeper had moved closer to Arkady, putting his only arm around her protectively.

If I had any sense, I'd kill him before we leave, Cayal thought, *just to be on the safe side.*

Arkady had value as a hostage, but the innkeeper was a witness to his identity, and Cayal had no doubt this incident would be talked about for months around the taproom of his ramshackle inn. But the secret was out now and surely the Tide was due to turn again soon.

And if it didn't . . . well, Cayal could lose himself again. That was something the Tide Lords were particularly good at.

"You!" he demanded of a smallish feline with a grey pelt, still on one knee by her pony. "What's your name?"

"Misty, my lord. Out of Sooty, by Kosta."

"Go with the innkeeper. Find me some food. Real food. I haven't had a decent meal in months. And if he gives you any trouble, Misty," he added, looking pointedly at the old man, "disembowel him."

"My lady . . . ," the man began nervously, apparently fearful for his duchess.

She smiled reassuringly. "I'll be all right, Clyden. Go. Do as he says."

Reluctantly, the old man headed back into the inn with Misty on his heels. Cayal watched them leave and then turned to face Arkady.

"Taking me hostage will only intensify the search for you," she predicted, before he could say a word. "And killing Clyden won't help, either. It will just seal your fate when they catch you."

"If only I thought dying were that easy," he replied, wondering if she'd read his thoughts somehow. "But give me a little credit. You're my safe-passage out of Glaeba. Your husband isn't going to know that if I kill the messenger now, is he? You really should learn more about me before you jump to conclusions, you know."

"What more is there to learn?"

"That I'm much more restrained than you think, for one thing. Tides, with a dozen well-trained felines, if the Tide was up, I could take over the whole damned country, if I was in the mood."

"But it's Low Tide, isn't it? Hence the reason for all this arrogance and no actual magical power to back it up?"

He smiled. "You know, Lukys would like you."

"Cayal, you don't have to keep up the charade," she sighed. "Whatever it is you're up to in Glaeba, I've played right into your game, I can see that now. But at least spare me your tales. I've had all the Tide Lord nonsense I can take from you."

If she was getting fed up with the stories about him, he was more than a little fed up with Arkady's blind faith in the infallibility of her own opinion, even when she was confronted with undeniable evidence that threw doubt on everything she believed. But then, maybe she didn't see the truth at all. However improbably, she had a point. With an accomplice or two, he might have somehow bribed the hangman and subverted the Crasii.

Life would be so much easier for Cayal if she believed him. She might even want to help. She'd certainly do whatever she must to keep him free long enough to answer her questions. Cayal was sure of that. The academic in Arkady and her insatiable curiosity would allow no other course of action. Cayal had been around Glaeba long enough to know what it must be like for any woman with ambition and intelligence. And he had laughed himself senseless when he heard about Harlie Palmerston's pretentious *Theory of Human Advancement*. To be the one who debunked *that* theory, Arkady would probably be prepared to take quite a risk.

She might even aid him if she thought he was just sadly deluded.

He was fairly certain, however, she would do nothing to aid or abet a man she believed to be simply a cold-blooded Caelish murderer.

Glancing around the yard, he spied a large stump by the woodpile, a sturdy axe resting beside the chopping block. He grabbed Arkady's hand and dragged her to the pile, and then picked up the axe. Instinctively, she cowered away from the weapon, but he wasn't planning to harm her. Instead, he handed her the axe.

"Prove it."

"What?" She almost dropped the blade on her own foot.

"You want proof, don't you? Here's your chance." He placed his hand on the chopping block. "Do it. Cut it off. Then we'll see if it grows back, shall we, and decide whether or not I'm truly immortal?"

Rather than look repulsed by his offer, Arkady hefted the axe thoughtfully and met his eye, apparently more suspicious than disturbed by his suggestion.

For a fleeting moment, Cayal lamented the loss of the Eternal Flame.

Arkady Desean, he suspected, might well have survived it.

"You're bluffing."

"Try me."

She glared at him doubtfully. "You're just going to stand there and let me cut your hand off with an axe?"

"I was hoping you'd settle for a couple of fingers," he corrected. "But if your aim's not that good, a hand will grow back just as well, I suppose, although it will take a little longer and it'll hurt like hell."

"If you're trying to prove you're insane, Cayal, this is a very good way to convince me."

"Quite the opposite. I'm trying to prove I exist. Do it."

She hesitated, testing the weight of the axe. "You think I won't."

"I think you're stalling."

"I *will* do it, Cayal . . ."

"Tides!" he exclaimed in exasperation. "Give it here!"

He snatched the axe from her grasp.

"No!" Arkady screamed.

Ignoring her protests, Cayal braced himself against the pain, and then—before he could change his mind—brought the weapon down sharply across the fingers of his left hand. Blood gushed across the stump, leaving the tips of three fingers behind.

Cursing the blinding agony, Cayal dropped the axe and jammed his wounded hand under his right arm, clamping down on it with all his might, bending almost double in the hope that pressure would ease the pain. At Cayal's agonised bellow, the Crasii rushed to investigate. More than a few of them bared their claws as they approached Arkady, thinking she was the one responsible for his injury.

"Leave her!" he managed to bark through tear-filled eyes when he realised the Crasii might harm her in retaliation. "Go!"

Looking concerned, the felines obeyed him, nonetheless, and returned to their positions around the inn. Cayal collapsed against the stump, cursing in every language he knew. The healing had already begun and that was almost as painful as the axe blow.

Arkady rushed to his side and helped him to sit. "You maniac! You didn't have to prove . . ."

He managed a thin smile when he realised that far from proving his immortality, he'd simply confirmed her opinion that he was insane.

"I'm not crazy."

"I know," she agreed soothingly. "Now let me look at that . . ."

"Arkady . . ."

"Cayal, please. It could become infected . . ."

"It won't."

She glared at him impatiently. "I can't help you, Cayal, if you won't let me."

"You can't help me at all, Arkady," he countered, "if you don't believe me."

Without waiting for her answer, his eyes watering with the agony of his severed fingers, he held his hand up for her inspection. It was bloody and shockingly clean cut, only a few minutes since he'd struck the blow, but already the bleeding had stopped.

"Now," he gasped painfully, while Arkady watched in wide-eyed terror as the flesh of his fingers slowly reconstructed themselves before her very eyes, "will you finally accept that I am who I claim to be, and that I am immortal?"

Chapter 39

The most difficult thing about Stellan's appointment as the Ambassador to Torlenia was the knowledge he must leave Jaxyn Aranville behind. In Jaxyn, Stellan had found a companion, as well as a lover, a contrast to his own personality that he found almost irresistible.

Jaxyn could be reckless; he could be irresponsible, even dangerous, at times. Stellan knew this, but could never explain—certainly not to Arkady—that this was the attraction of him. He was everything Stellan was too well-bred, too self-conscious and too restrained to be. Jaxyn was a window into a world where Stellan didn't have to lie, where he could announce openly who and what he was and not give a hang about the consequences. The attraction of such freedom was seductive and even when Jaxyn was flirting with disaster, rather than frighten Stellan, it often aroused him, which made it almost impossible to let Jaxyn go.

There was no question that Jaxyn would be permitted to accompany them to Torlenia, however, no matter how attractive the prospect. It was one thing, here in Lebec, where Stellan was the master of all he surveyed, to tempt fate by keeping a lover, quite another to tempt fate in a country where adultery was a crime punishable by death.

In the arid deserts of Torlenia, any sort of sexual relationship outside the marriage bed (regardless of the gender of the lovers) was considered a mortal sin.

But philosophical differences aside, Stellan knew well that no foreign diplomat was allowed into Torlenia without his wife beside him. Even if Stellan could have thought up a reason to include Jaxyn in his entourage, as an unmarried male he would not be granted entry into the Torlenian capital in the first place.

Jaxyn, it seemed, was fully aware of that, given his reaction when Stellan broke the news to him just after lunch. He'd called Jaxyn into his office on the pretext of discussing additional training for the Crasii. The king and queen had excused both the duke and his companion, while they and Mathu, Kylia and most of their entourage had gone boating on the lake. This was likely to be the only chance Stellan would have in the next week for a private discussion with his lover.

"You're abandoning me," Jaxyn accused, as soon as Stellan told him of his new appointment.

"If there was any way . . . ," Stellan began, wishing he could have broken the news more gently. "But we're talking Torlenia here, Jaxyn. These people stone women for falling pregnant out of wedlock."

Jaxyn grinned. "Suppose I promise not to get pregnant? Could I come with you then?"

Stellan smiled. "I wish it were that simple."

"But if I was part of your household . . ."

"You would still have to be married, Jaxyn. You know the Torlenian edicts about foreigners as well as I do. Where are you going to find a woman—"

"Like Arkady?" he cut in, a little impatiently.

Stellan shrugged.

"So what . . . that's it? It's all over between us?"

"Of course not! It's just going to be . . . difficult . . . while I'm away."

"And what's to become of me?"

"You can stay here."

"For how long?" Jaxyn asked. "Until the king decides Reon Debalkor is sufficiently appeased to let you come home again? How long will that be?"

"I have no way of knowing," he admitted. "But if we found something useful for you to do, here on the estate in addition to your duties as—"

"Oh, so now I'm useless? Is that it?"

Stellan would have denied Jaxyn's accusation, but at that moment, the door flew open and Tassie hurried in, bowing excitedly. "Your grace! Your grace!"

"How many times have I warned you about entering a room without waiting for permission, Tassie?" he snapped.

The young canine's bottom lip quivered at his tone, and her ears flattened against her head, but she held her ground. "Your grace, there's someone here to see you."

"Tell them I'm busy."

"But it's Master Bell. From the inn."

"Then tell Lady Desean he's here."

"But she's not back yet from the prison, your grace."

"Then he'll have to wait."

Tassie was not so easily deterred. "He said it's really, *really* important, your grace."

He wasn't going to get any peace until this was dealt with. "Oh . . . very well." Stellan sighed, glancing at Jaxyn. "I'm sorry, this shouldn't take long."

The young man rose to his feet. "Fine. Talk to your innkeeper. I'll go find something useful to do, shall I?"

"Don't be like that. Please. Stay."

Jaxyn sank back down into his seat looking decidedly unhappy, but he didn't say anything further. Wishing he'd handled the whole thing differently, Stellan turned to Tassie. "All right. Show him in, Tassie. And next time, knock first."

"Yes, your grace," she promised, backing out of the room.

A moment later, Arkady's old friend, the one-armed innkeeper from Clyden's Inn, entered the study, looking around in awe. He'd never been inside the palace before and it obviously overwhelmed him. Jaxyn crossed his arms petulantly, his expression dark.

Stellan forced a smile he didn't feel, hoping whatever business Clyden Bell had, it wouldn't take long. "Master Bell! What brings you to the palace? Arkady's not here, I'm afraid, but I could ask her to visit when she—"

"It's about Arkady that I've come, your grace," Clyden said, snatching his hat from his head self-consciously as he stood before the duke's large desk. "I know your wife's not here, because I've just seen her, not three hours ago."

Stellan frowned. "Has something happened to her, Clyden?"

"She's been taken, your grace."

"Taken?" Jaxyn asked, suddenly interested. "Taken *where*?"

"Into the mountains," the old man told them. "Least that was the direction they was headed when they left the inn. Her ladyship, that maniac with the axe and a whole squad of felines. I don't know what was going on, your grace, but those Crasii of yours weren't paying no mind to Lady Arkady's orders. If he's one of your men, he seems to have struck out on his own, if you take my meaning, and he took m'lady with him as a hostage."

Stellan stared at the one-armed man, certain he was telling the truth, but unable to imagine what bizarre circumstance had led Arkady to Clyden Bell's inn with a squad of feline Crasii.

"I thought Arkady went out to the prison before lunch?" Jaxyn said, clearly as baffled as Stellan.

"She did." Stellan closed his eyes for a moment, as a dreadful possibility dawned on him. Then he opened his eyes and looked at Clyden. "Did this man . . . this maniac with an axe . . . have a name?"

"Kyle? Lyle? Something like that." Clyden shrugged. "He was in chains when they arrived, but then he ordered the Crasii to release him, and they all fell down on their knees like he was a god, or something. And then after that business with the axe, he stole some horses and—"

"What business with the axe? Was Arkady hurt?"

Clyden shook his head. "I don't think so. Didn't see it all, but I saw the blood and after they left, I found . . . well . . . these . . ." Reaching into the pocket of his vest, Clyden produced a small parcel wrapped in a square of bloodstained linen, which he placed on the desk in front of Stellan.

With a great deal of trepidation, the duke unwrapped the cloth, staring at the bloody contents with a growing sense of dread. Jaxyn leaned forward curiously, then jerked back, his hand over his mouth.

"Tides!" he exclaimed in horror. "Are they what I think they are?"

Stellan nodded bleakly. "Human fingers."

"Whose fingers?" Jaxyn asked in alarm.

"Not Arkady's," Stellan concluded with relief, thinking them too broad to have come from a female hand. And lacking retractable claws, they certainly weren't Crasii. "Damn!"

Jaxyn looked at him oddly.

"Arkady wanted to establish, once and for all, that our Immortal Prince wasn't immortal," he explained in response to Jaxyn's questioning look. "She suggested we chop a few fingers off to prove it."

Jaxyn was stunned. "You think *Arkady* did this?"

Stellan didn't answer him, certain Jaxyn would see through his denial. Instead, he turned to Clyden. "How long ago did they leave the inn?"

"Be three, maybe four hours, by now," the innkeeper told him with an apologetic shrug. "I'd have gotten here sooner, your grace, but they took all the horses, even the ones pulling the carriage. I had to wait until someone else came by so we could borrow a mount to bring you word."

"You did your best, Clyden," Stellan said, thinking that with a four-hour head start they would be well into the mountains by now. "And I thank you for bringing the news. You say this man was in chains when they arrived?"

Clyden nodded, but it was Jaxyn who pointed out the obvious. "She had your Caelish agent with her."

"How could she? Without a direct order from me, the Warden would never . . ." His voice trailed off, as he realised there would be time later to figure out how Arkady had managed to have Kyle Lakesh released into her custody.

"Let me go after them," Jaxyn offered, rising to his feet.

"*You?*"

"I need to appear useful, you said," he reminded him. "So let me do this. You stay here and entertain your guests, while I take another squad of felines and a couple of canine trackers into the mountains. I'll have them back by morning."

Jaxyn's suggestion made a great deal of sense. Much as Stellan would like to go charging off into the mountains to rescue his wife, he wasn't entirely convinced she'd actually been kidnapped. The bloody fingertips on his desk spoke of something far more sinister afoot.

"Do you really think you can find them?"

The young man nodded. "I'll find them, Stellan. You can't leave now in any case. Not with the king and queen here. And the last thing you want is Enteny or Mathu deciding they'd like to help. Let me do this. For you *and* Arkady. I can have them back before the king learns anything about it."

Torn with indecision, Stellan turned to Clyden. "How was Arkady when they left the inn? Was she distressed? In fear for her life?"

The one-armed man shrugged. "To be honest, your grace, she looked stunned, much as anything. I'm not sure she went willingly, but he didn't drag her off kicking and screaming, if that's what you're asking. And them felines . . . don't know what this Lyle chap promised 'em, but they were fairly purring every time he looked at one of 'em."

"All the more reason to handle this quietly, Stellan," Jaxyn added with infuriating common sense. "If your felines have gone Scard on you, we can't afford it to become public knowledge. It'll affect every Crasii in Lebec, not to mention the damage it will do to the resale value of your other Crasii."

"I'm actually more worried for Arkady, Jaxyn, than the resale value of my slaves," Stellan informed him, a little annoyed that Jaxyn would think of the slaves' value first, before Arkady's welfare. Sadly, he had a point, however unpleasant it might be to admit it. "You might be right about keeping this quiet, though. Would you say nothing of this for a time, Clyden, if I ask it of you?"

The old man nodded. "If you're going after her, your grace, I'll keep your confidence as long as you need me to."

Stellan nodded and turned to his lover. "Then go, Jaxyn. Find Arkady and this Caelish criminal. And don't worry about bringing him back alive. He's an escaped convict now, as well as a kidnapper. Even if Caelum wasn't denying they own him, he lost any protection of the law he might have had the moment he stepped outside of it."

"I'll find them, Stellan," Jaxyn promised, more confident than the duke had ever seen him. And then he added with a dangerous smile, "And trust me, when I do find them, I'll see the Immortal Prince gets exactly what he deserves."

Chapter 40

Shaken to the very core of her being by what she had witnessed at the inn, Arkady rode blindly behind Cayal and the escort of Crasii that she had once believed her own, too traumatised to even think of trying to get away.

They rode into the mountains, she registered that much, but even once she began to feel a little more in control of her situation, the question of escape didn't really occur to her. She had just witnessed the impossible and until she had some satisfactory explanation for what had happened when Cayal hacked off the fingers of his left hand with an axe and for the inexplicable behaviour of her Crasii, Arkady wasn't going anywhere.

They travelled in a cold, fitful rain; north for the most part, on narrow roads Arkady was unfamiliar with, finally turning off, just before dusk, onto a track that even the Crasii had trouble following. Cayal seemed to know where he was headed, however, and ordered the felines to ride on, which they did without question.

Riding behind Cayal, cold, wet and numb, Arkady fretted at her Crasii's willing subservience and spent her time imagining ever more complicated plots to explain away their behaviour—plots involving Caelish agitators and highly organised foreign spy rings—not because she didn't believe what she'd seen, but because the truth was too terrifying to contemplate. She wondered what her colleague at the Lebec University, Andre Fawk, would think when she told him what she'd witnessed. They'd spent so many hours researching the Crasii; trying to document their oral histories, smiling indulgently at the innocent simplicity of their myths.

Only they weren't innocent, Arkady knew now, or perhaps even myths.

She wished Andre were here now. She wished *anybody* but her was here now . . .

Cayal brought their small column to a halt just as the clouds resting on the tops of the mountains to the west were turning crimson. The damp air had cooled rapidly with the onset of night and Arkady was shivering as she dismounted, looking around to find a small cascade tumbling down the rock face behind her, probably snowmelt from higher in the mountains.

"We'll stop here for the night," Cayal instructed the Crasii. "Make camp."

"Aren't you afraid they'll catch us?"

He turned to look at Arkady and shrugged. "I know these mountains pretty well."

"You've been here before then?" she asked, clutching at any hope that this was some sort of swindle he was running, that the Crasii were cleverly trained plants sent among them to await the arrival of their Caelish master. She knew she was losing her mind. The chances that anybody had suborned their Crasii, had planted spies among them, and that she had, at random, selected every one of them to accompany her to the prison this morning was beyond improbable.

The trouble was, if she didn't believe that version of events, the only alternative was to believe that Cayal really *was* an immortal, and that wasn't improbable. It was impossible.

"I've been alive for eight thousand years, Arkady. I've been everywhere before."

"How did you suborn my Crasii?" she demanded, shivering in the cold air as they made camp around her.

"Blind obedience to the Tide Lords was bred into them," Cayal told her, as he turned to unsaddle his mount. "They can't help it."

"Warlock never did as you ordered."

"That's because your pet canine is probably a Scard. Pity, actually. He was a good-looking brute. Would've made prime breeding stock back in the old days." He hefted the saddle from the back of his mount and dropped it onto the ground. Arkady watched him closely; looking for some sign his injured hand was causing him difficulty. Cayal noticed the direction of her gaze and smiled, holding it up before her face, wiggling his fingers. "See? All better?"

She could see that his hand was completely healed. Were it not for the blood he'd not had a chance to wash away, she wouldn't have believed his fingers had ever been damaged, let alone amputated with a woodsman's axe.

"That was just a trick," she insisted, trying to convince herself, as much as him. "You didn't really . . ."

"Yes, Arkady, I did. You hungry?"

"Er . . . I suppose," she replied, too overwhelmed by the events of the last few hours to think about food. "Do you need to eat?"

"Not really."

"What happens if you don't?"

"I get a little hungry." He turned from her and called Chikita over to him. "Do you hunt, gemang?"

She nodded. "Yes, my lord."

"Take two others. Find us something to eat."

"Of course, my lord." Chikita bowed and hurried off to do Cayal's bidding.

He smiled at Arkady's expression. "You're not dealing with this very well, are you?"

"You're a liar, Cayal. This is just some complicated plan you've cooked up to subvert the Glaeban Crasii into believing the Tide Lords have returned."

"Is it?" he asked, rather annoyed, it seemed, by her stubborn insistence that what she had witnessed in the yard of Clyden's Inn couldn't possibly be real. "I really do wish I was as clever as you imagine."

"I think you are."

"I think, if I was that clever, I would have let you hand me over to this spymaster of yours, had him escort me back to Herino, escaped along the way somewhere and disappeared into legend."

"But you didn't. Why not?"

He shrugged. "I like you."

"You *like* me?" she gasped. "You chopped off three fingers because you *like* me?"

"I didn't say it was a particularly well-thought-out decision."

She shook her head, still denying the evidence of her own eyes, trying to tell herself they must be playing tricks on her. "I think I was right the first time. You're insane!"

"Then explain this," he suggested, holding up his hand again. "Ah! That's right. It didn't really happen, did it, because Arkady Desean doesn't believe in magic?"

"It wasn't magic!"

"Then what was it, Arkady? Do you think I somehow arranged to have your friend at the inn replace his real axe with a fake one? That I carry spare fingertips around in case of emergencies? Or do you really think that of all the Crasii you could have brought to the prison this morning, you just happened to pick the ones I had somehow cleverly arranged to infiltrate your estate?" He waited for a moment, but when she didn't respond, he turned to the girth straps on her mount. "And you say *I'm* the crazy one."

"It's just, I think . . ." She stopped, not at all sure what she thought. He was right, of course. The absurdity of clinging to the belief this was a bizarrely complex plan concocted by Glaeba's enemies, simply because the facts presented her with something she didn't want to confront, was almost as crazy as believing such a plan might actually exist. "Tides! I don't know what I think . . ."

"You deny *my* reality yet you name the Tides as a curse," he pointed out, lifting her saddle to the ground. "Don't you ever wonder why?"

She sighed, exhausted by her doubts. "I'm sure you're going to tell me."

"Not if you're going to be like that."

"I'm in no mood to entertain you, Cayal. I'm your hostage, remember? Your safe-passage out of Glaeba?"

"Then you have no choice but to humour me."

She frowned. "Humour you how, exactly?"

"You could start by admitting you believe me."

"Very well, I believe you."

"Don't patronise me, Arkady."

She threw her hands up impatiently. "What do you expect, Cayal? Respect? Admiration? Do you want me to bow down to you the way the Crasii do?" Her frustration and fear were making her angry, at herself, as much as Cayal. "And I still want to know how you're doing that, by the way. These are the best-trained felines in Glaeba. I don't believe they're simply following you out of instinct."

"It's more than instinct. It's a compulsion. I'm not sure

of the details. Crasii farming was never my particular passion."

"Crasii *farming*?"

"They didn't just come into being by magic, you know." Cayal smiled. "Actually, that's not entirely true. They *were* created by magic. But it wasn't just one of us waving their arm to create a new race of slaves, Arkady. It took a lot of time, effort and Tidewatchers to get it right."

Wrapping her arms around her body against the cold, Arkady found herself drawn into the argument against her better judgement. "What's a Tidewatcher?"

"The half-breed offspring of an immortal and a mortal," he explained as he led her mount to the cascade to drink its fill.

"You have children?" she asked in surprise.

He rolled his eyes impatiently. "No, Arkady. I took a vow of chastity and haven't been with a woman for eight thousand years."

Ask a silly question . . . , she scolded herself silently. "So, in fact, you might have immortal children, and you just don't know about them."

He shook his head. "There are no immortal children. Immortality stops the body ageing from the moment it takes hold of you. Two immortals can't create new life because the new life would be immortal, which means it can never progress beyond the instant it was created."

Strangely, that made sense to Arkady. But the rest of his tale was more than a little disturbing. "And these Tidewatchers? These half-breed offspring? Out of your own flesh and blood, you created your slaves?"

"You say that like you're surprised, Arkady."

"But that's . . . well, it's cruel. It's inhuman."

Cayal shrugged. "That's what it is to be a Tide Lord," he said.

Chikita and her companions returned with a small hind just as the last hint of daylight faded into night. Mercifully, the rain held off as Cayal expertly butchered the deer with a knife he'd apparently had the foresight to steal from Clyden's Inn. The hind's throat had been ripped out, and her withers were scored by a series of deep scratches, but Arkady was so hungry by then she didn't care. The venison tasted as good as anything she'd ever been served in the palace.

After dinner, she wandered toward the edge of the ledge and glanced at the sky. The clouds had dissipated enough to allow a few stars to shine through. Below her somewhere was the rift valley and the Great Lakes that filled it, but the trees blocked her view, leaving her no option but to guess where Lebec might be located.

"You can't see it from Kordana," Cayal said, making her jump as he came up behind her.

"See what?" she asked.

He pointed at the brightest star just above the horizon, which shone faintly red against the velvet blackness of the moonless night. "The planet, Playnte."

"I thought that was a star, Trudini."

He shook his head. "You might call it that now, but we used to call it Playnte when I was a child. And it's a planet, not a star. So is that one," he added, pointing left to the next brightest star, which had risen above the mountain tops while they ate. "That's Carani. Although the inhabitants might call it something else."

Arkady shivered, but smiled at his words. "The inhabitants?"

"Sure. Why shouldn't there be inhabitants? Do you think we're the only living creatures in the universe?"

"I never really thought about it."

"Shame on you," he scolded. "And you call yourself an academic?"

Arkady glanced at Cayal, surprised to find he wasn't joking. "How do you know they're worlds like ours?"

"Lukys has been there."

"Really?"

"So he claims."

"How did he get there?"

Cayal shrugged. "I'm not sure exactly how he does it. It has something to do with rifts and thunderstorms, I think. He needs one to create the other, or something like that. He did try to explain it to me once, but I wasn't really paying attention."

"Someone was explaining a way to travel to another world to you, and you weren't paying *attention*?" Arkady shook her head in disgust. "No wonder you want to die. For that you *ought* to."

He glared at her, rather put out by her lack of sympathy. "I was rather preoccupied at the time."

"With what?" she asked. "What could possibly be more important than learning something like that?"

"I was busy," he explained, a little defensively. "Busy doing a friend a favour, actually."

"Must have been some favour."

"It was," he agreed. "And I wish I'd never done it."

"Because you missed your chance to travel to another world?"

He shook his head and turned to stare at the distant planets. "Because it led—eventually—to something far, far worse."

Arkady looked at him, wondering at his strange tone of voice. "What happened, Cayal?"

"Are you sure you want to know?"

"Yes."

So he told her.

Chapter 41

Like a great many other innovations that changed civilisation, the Crasii were an accident.

The story I heard was that Elyssa was responsible. The Immortal Maiden wasn't a maiden any longer by then, but immortality hadn't done much for her love life, either. Irritating and shrill, even in her most benign moments, there are few men willing to commit to Elyssa for any length of time; certainly no immortal is going to promise her his heart until "death us do part."

The only immortal who's ever made the mistake of getting seriously involved with her is Taryx. He was another of Diala's recruits; a Senestran sailor who considers immortality, and its attendant immunity to disease, a licence to spend eternity getting laid. I swear, he's spent most of his time since surviving the Eternal Flame trying to sleep his way through every brothel on Amyrantha.

Lukys used to joke that Taryx turned to Elyssa because she was the only female between the age of fourteen and eighty-four left on the planet that Taryx hadn't slept with yet.

Their relationship didn't last long, only a few months, by all accounts. And it was very one sided. Taryx was amusing himself. Elyssa was painfully in love, and given that her paramour was immortal, she was quite convinced her happiness would last forever. Taryx didn't see things in quite the same romantic light. He left the palace one morning a few months after he moved in and never bothered to go back.

They were living in Tenacia at the time. After Pellys destroyed Magreth, the Tide ebbed for a long time and we had once again faded from human memory. When the Tide returned, Engarhod and Syrolee looked for something a little less unstable than a continent formed from a chain of volcanoes to re-establish their empire, and finally settled on Tenacia, the continent north of where Magreth used to be.

Being powerless when the Tide was out doesn't sit well with Engarhod and his clan, and there's always a scramble when they feel the first glimmering of the returning Tide to reclaim their dominion over the world they believe they rightfully own. At the risk of mentioning your dreaded Tarot again, for the most part you have the names of the immortals right. I could introduce you to a few of them. You may even like some of them. On his own, Taryx is harmless enough, although Jaxyn's a sleazy little opportunist. You should meet Kinta, too. You'd like her, I suspect, although Brynden can be a bit of a bore. Kinta's a trifle tetchy, but compared to Elyssa, she's a real lady. And then there's Ambria. She's Krydence's wife. The two of them had a falling out about four hundred years after they married and they haven't spoken since. For that alone, I like the woman. Lina and Medwen are fine, too, provided you keep them away from Engarhod's boys. Lina's a survivor of the brothel fire in Cuttlefish Bay, Medwen the result of a nasty little accident that happened in Magreth.

Anyway, Tenacia filled their requirements for a base quite comfortably, in that it had a temperate climate, plenty of natural resources and a large population with no central government to get in their way.

Such are the raw materials from which empires are fashioned.

Using the reliable fallback of religion, the Emperor and Empress of the Five Realms were busy gathering followers at an impressive rate among the unsophisticated rural folk, while Elyssa and Taryx engaged in their affair. The new palace wasn't quite as impressive as the last one. The people of Tenacia weren't the builders the Magrethans of old had been. But it was impressive enough, and Elyssa was having a high old time playing house with Taryx until he wandered off, looking for something more titillating.

It took a while for Elyssa to accept that Taryx wasn't

coming back and perhaps another year for her to work herself into a frenzy over it. She must have been quite a piece of work by the time her brothers decided to go looking for her missing lover. Syrolee told me later it was her brothers' love for their jilted sister which prompted them to seek out the recalcitrant immortal and return him to Tenacia. I'm more inclined to believe Lukys's version of the affair, which was that Krydence, Rance and Tryan finally tired of Elyssa's whining and went looking for Taryx so he could wear the brunt of their sister's displeasure and spare them.

They found him, eventually, playing house with a mortal woman in a small village on the coast of Senestra. The woman, to add insult to Elyssa's calamitous injury, was heavily pregnant, and even though the Tide was nearing its peak, Taryx seemed happy to indulge her fantasy that he was likely to be a good husband and father to her child.

It was no secret among our kind by then that immortals can only reproduce with mortals. Ambria and Lina had both borne mortal children, but neither of them had particularly enjoyed watching their children wither and die while they remained ageless, so they took precautions, these days, to avoid falling pregnant.

As for how many bastards we immortal males have left in our wake over the past few thousand years—that's anybody's guess. Lukys puts the number in the hundreds, possibly the thousands. He reckons that between the two of them, Jaxyn and Taryx alone are probably responsible for the entire population of Caelum.

Whatever the number, Taryx's child by a mortal woman was nothing unusual. We'd even thought up a name for our half-breed offspring—Tidewatchers—as if that somehow made their existence morally acceptable.

Children of the immortals are human in every respect, a few rare ones inheriting our ability to sense the Tide. Except in extremely rare cases, they wield no magical power of their own. For those born at Low Tide, they live and die without realising they have the gift. For those born when the Tide is rising or ebbing, the effect ranges from mild discomfort for those who can't understand what they're feeling to a fully conscious ability to make the most of their talent.

The Tide was well and truly up when Krydence finally tracked down his sister's missing lover. Rather than confront him, however, he returned to Tenacia to collect Elyssa, figuring she would prefer to deal with Taryx herself.

And deal with him she did. Furious beyond words by Taryx's betrayal, she waited until he'd left the cottage he was sharing with his mortal lover, and then confronted the young woman.

It would have been pointless, of course, to attempt to hurt Taryx physically. She can't kill him. Any physical injury heals within a few hours—at worst, he'd be whole again in a matter of days. But she could cause his woman a world of hurt and she could damage his child, leaving him with a living reminder of the folly of rejecting her.

The unsuspecting young woman was in the small pigsty out behind the stables feeding scraps to a large sow who was nursing a hungry litter of newborn piglets when Elyssa and Krydence found her. It was the squealing piglets that gave Elyssa the idea, apparently. Screeching something about her rival being a fat, ugly old sow, driven by equal measures of anger and jealousy, Elyssa picked up a piglet, held it against the mortal woman's abdomen and magically forced it through her skin, into her womb and then finally into the child she was carrying.

"We'll see how much he likes you and your disgusting mortal spawn now, you filthy pig!" Elyssa announced when it was done.

It's a testament to the young woman's strength that the shock of Elyssa's savage attack didn't kill her outright. Perhaps Elyssa healed her magically as part of Taryx's punishment, more interested in the monstrosity she was now doomed to carry than in killing her.

Whatever her reasons, Elyssa's bizarre revenge left Taryx's pregnant lover traumatised but alive and a month later she gave birth to a creature who was to become the very first Crasii.

It's a measure of how far removed from humanity we had become that rather than react with abhorrence to the horror inflicted upon his lover, Taryx was fascinated by the creature Elyssa created in her anger. Taryx isn't a particularly gifted magician, but he's pretty good at spotting an opportunity when he sees one. More than anything, he wanted to know *how* she had created it, and hurried to Tenacia as soon as the child was born, to show the others the results and learn the secret himself.

I never heard what happened to Taryx's unfortunate lover, or saw the first blended creature. Lukys told me the half-piglet child didn't live long beyond its first few months. But the immortals had a new hobby—once they ironed out prickly little details like the human mothers' tendency to die at a prodigious rate.

The production of Crasii slaves requires only two raw materials, you see: any animal whose characteristics we wanted blended into a human, and all the fertile mortal women we could get our hands on. It wasn't a pleasant business. In fact, it was almost a century before Elyssa hit on the successful method of blending the species and leaving the mothers alive to breed a second or third time, but eventually she found the right formula and the Crasii were born.

All of this happened while I was out of Tenacia, mind you. I put together the story from various other sources, and by the time I ran into Engarhod, Syrolee and their clan again, the Crasii were a well-established fact, farmed and bred in quantities sufficient to establish them as a whole sub-species in their own right.

Of course, not all of us used Crasii slaves. Some of the immortals actively despise them. Were it not for Medwen— Medwen the Guide your silly Tarot calls her, although the

Tides know why—I wouldn't have become involved with them, either.

By the way, it was Brynden of Fyrenne who first coined the name Tide Lords.

Immolated by Diala several hundred years before me—and in the same fashion—Brynden was a soldier, a mercenary hired to protect the gold shipments from the barbarian mines in Glaeba that Engarhod and Syrolee brought to Magreth to gild their palace. Diala spied him on the wharves and took a fancy to him in much the same way she'd fixed her attention on me.

It doesn't surprise me that Brynden survived the flames. By the age of twenty-eight, he'd already lived through a near-deadly stab wound and numerous other potentially fatal nicks and cuts gained in the course of his perilous employment. What sets Brynden apart from the rest of us, however, is his innate sense of nobility. If there is a single Tide Lord who deserves the title of Lord, in my opinion, it's Brynden.

Tall and fair-haired, he's a native of Fyrenne, which used to be a nation located in the far reaches of the distant northern continent north-west of Tenacia. Although they were competent seafarers and much sought-after fighters, it was rare for his people to venture into the far south, which is probably why he caught Diala's eye.

It wasn't until several hundred years after I left Magreth that I finally met the Fyronnese immortals. Like me, Brynden didn't stay on Magreth after his immolation, although he was smarter about leaving than I was. Shocked and disturbed though he must have been, he didn't ask for a quest that would ultimately destroy his homeland. He was—still is—convinced our immortality has been granted to us for some noble purpose, so he set out to find out what it was. Brynden left Magreth and went looking for his destiny. With him went Kinta, another Fyronnese warrior—she was made immortal by Brynden not long after Diala had immolated him—and a number of other immortals including Krydence's former wife, Ambria.

I think ideology drew the others to him, but it was more than ideology keeping Brynden and Kinta together. They were lovers, even before they'd joined the ranks of the immortals. In fact, it was Brynden who burned Kinta to prove the Eternal Flame was real and not just a wild reason he'd thought up to excuse his affair with a Priestess of Magreth.

They settled in Torlenia eventually, on the shores of the Great Inland Sea. Bryn built himself a palace—as austere as Engarhod's palace was ostentatious—and set out to seek the knowledge he believed immortality meant us to gain. With Kinta at his side, they couldn't help but adopt their Fyronnese warrior ethic and, almost by default, the Torlenians began to first revere, and then finally worship the two immortals living in their midst. The strange ideas they have about women being seen in public, the battle forms practised by Torlenian soldiers to this day . . . they're direct descendants of ideas Brynden introduced. They still prefer chariots in a world where sprung coaches are the norm in other lands. Even though they don't remember it, the whole nature of Torlenian society is influenced by the memory of the god-like warrior and his queen.

The others drifted away after a time, but Kinta stayed and acquired the title of the Charioteer in your Tarot, probably because that was how most people remember her, driving her chariot along the shores of the Great Inland Sea, going to and from their palace near the northern city of Acern. Brynden eventually acquired the nickname of the Lord of Reckoning, but that was later, during the Scard Wars. It's an apt description of his righteous wrath. Brynden in high dudgeon is a sight to behold. And not something you want to be the focus of.

But if Brynden is noble and incorruptible, Kinta isn't. While she agreed with his vision in principle, even back then, I think she privately leant more toward Engarhod and Syrolee's method of achieving it. But at the height of the

Crasii farming era, Kinta was still staunchly by Brynden's side, still certain the Tide Lords had been created to help mankind rather than enslave them, and willing to stand up and be counted.

Boredom drove me to visit Acern to seek out Brynden and Kinta, as it did most things I did by then. Immortality seems like such a gift at first. But here's the real problem: you can, given enough time, master any skill, acquire any knowledge and once it's done, there is nothing more. It's the journey that makes life worth living. Getting there is merely a stop along the way, a place to catch your breath until you start something new.

Such notions make mortals pray for more time.

Such notions make immortals go mad.

I was already easily bored by then, something which only gets worse with each passing year, of which I've seen far too many. There are a finite number of things to be done and learned in this world and infinite time in which to do them.

And then what? What is left when you speak every language known to man fluently? When you can paint like a master as easily as you can shear a sheep, milk a cow or construct a palace?

Man wasn't meant for eternity.

I heard from Maralyce that Lukys was in Torlenia. Maralyce is the strangest of the immortals and the only one I can't pin down on who made her immortal. She was in her late forties, I guess, when she was made, but if she was a crotchety old loner before she became immortal, or has simply become that way after thousands of years of friendless boredom, I don't know. She has little or no time for the rest of us, with the possible exception of Lukys, and lives no differently when her powers are at their peak than she does when she's helpless.

I'd run into Maralyce by accident while I was visiting Glaeba looking for something to distract me. It was a dry, hilly place back then. The old girl had made a home for herself in the mountains surrounding the vast rift valley that separated your ancestors in Glaeba from the Caelish barbarians on the other side. Maralyce looks for gold. She was a miner before she was immortalised and considers her gift simply the Tide's way of handing her unlimited time to look for it. Even then, she'd already dug a vast network of tunnels all through your mineral-rich mountains, hoarding her gold in a hidden cavern that is still the stuff of legend to this day.

Anyway, it was Maralyce who begrudgingly informed me that last she'd heard, Lukys was headed to Torlenia. She wasn't being helpful, I suspect, just trying to get rid of her unwanted guest.

I shared one last meal with my reluctant hostess in her cabin high in the Shevron Mountains and then took the hint and left Maralyce's questionable hospitality and headed south.

"You could not have come at a better time, Brother Cayal," Brynden informed me gravely, when I finally arrived in Torlenia. I was welcomed amicably enough, but after greeting my hosts, I received quite a shock to discover Medwen was also a guest at the palace. She kissed me on the mouth by way of greeting, smiling wanly. Despite the warmth of her welcome, there was a fragile quality to her demeanour that made me wonder if something was wrong.

Lukys—his pet rat, Coron, perched on his shoulder as always—appeared later that day. Over a glass of wine on the battlements, the two of us set about catching up, filling each other in on the highlights of our last eight hundred years. That evening, I was treated to an austere meal in Brynden's austere dining hall with only Kinta, Medwen and Lukys for company. No servants wait on the Tide Lords at Brynden's table. Brynden thinks them an unnecessary extravagance.

Brynden's comment about my timing when I first arrived intrigued me, but it remained unexplained. It was dinner that evening before I finally got a chance to ask why he—who had never shown more than a passing interest in anything I did—was suddenly so glad to see me.

"When I arrived, Bryn, you mentioned something about coming at a good time. Is there something going on?" I enquired, as I broke apart my bread. Black bread, of course, and it seemed to be at least a week old.

"Why do you assume something is going on?" Kinta asked, tucking into her meal with a warrior's zeal.

I smiled. "You actually seem glad to see me."

Kinta is a statuesque blonde who favours leather over cloth, even in the temperate climate of Torlenia. I'm not surprised she's a warrior in your deck of Tarot cards. I consider myself a competent swordsman, but I've never fought Kinta, something I consider a prudent decision, because I'm really not sure who'd win.

Brynden frowned at my question. "There are evil times afoot, Cayal. It behoves us to take action to free the mortals of this world from the tyranny of our less-than-scrupulous peers."

I forced my smile away. In all the years I've known him, Brynden's wordy turn of phrase hasn't changed at all. Krydence and Rance tease him unmercifully about it. It's much of the reason, I suspect, that Brynden set himself up in opposition to the Emperor and Empress of the Five Realms and their obnoxious offspring in the first place.

"What he means," Lukys explained, reaching across the table for the wine jug, "is that Engarhod and Syrolee are at it again."

"What have they done this time?"

"They're making Crasii," Kinta explained unhelpfully.

I looked at her blankly. "What's a Crasii?"

"Blended creatures," Medwen replied, her bitterness surprising me.

Raven-haired and dark-skinned, Medwen looks no older than the seventeen years she had been when Krydence burned her alive. She'd been working in the palace on Magreth when she'd caught Krydence's eye, hundreds of years before I was made immortal. Their affair lasted a little over a year, she told me once. Then Ambria had caught her husband in bed with the young serving girl and ordered him to be rid of her. Krydence assured Ambria he would and, with sweet words and quite malicious intent, had set Medwen alight, promising her immortality, expecting her to die.

When she survived, it was debatable who was more shocked—Krydence, Medwen or Ambria. She'd drifted since then, like me, never really settling in one place for more than a decade or two.

"Blended with what?" I asked. There was an air of ineffable sadness about Medwen that I found quite disturbing.

"Humans," Lukys informed me before Medwen could reply.

I stared at them around the table, not sure if they were playing a jest on me. "How is that possible?"

It was Brynden who answered. "As best we can tell, they take a human woman, have an immortal impregnate her, and then when the foetus has developed sufficiently, they ram an animal foetus through the wall of her uterus and force it to magically blend with the child, creating a half-human half-beast creature they can use as a slave. Apparently, the emperor's boys are applying themselves with great zeal to their new role as stud stallions for the Crasii farms."

Oblivious to her pain, I pulled a face and winked at Medwen. "Tides, I wonder what the poor girls think is worse, giving birth to a beast or sleeping with Krydence?"

Feeding titbits to Coron, Lukys smiled thinly, but Kinta was not amused. "There's nothing voluntary in this, Cayal. This is institutionalised rape with the express intention of polluting the human race to create a sub-species of slaves."

The silence that followed Kinta's declaration was tense. She's a formidable woman, as fair as Brynden, her eyes icy blue, her flaxen hair so pale it's almost white. She can be very intimidating when she wants and now seemed to be one of those times. I looked around the table, frowning. "And what is it you expect me to do about it?"

"We'd like you to go to Tenacia and find out what's really going on."

I turned to my host. "Why doesn't one of *you* go to Tenacia and ask?"

"It would be more believable if you were to go," Medwen suggested. "Engarhod doesn't like Brynden. Or Lukys."

"I'm not exactly his favourite person, either," I reminded them. "Does anybody remember Pellys and a certain ruined palace in Magreth they still blame me for?"

"But you are young, foolish and male," Kinta pointed out, which I thought a bit rude given I was over sixteen hundred years old by then. "Even Engarhod will believe you heard what they were doing and couldn't resist the opportunity to stand at stud."

I looked at Kinta askance, wondering if she was simply being thoughtless, or deliberately trying to offend me. Telling me I was foolish seemed an odd way to elicit my cooperation, never mind the implication that I had nothing better to do with my time than satisfy my carnal needs.

I shook my head. "I can't help you. Syrolee and Engarhod are still mad at me over what happened in Magreth with Pellys."

"That was almost a thousand years ago." Medwen shrugged. "They'll be over it by now."

"I'm sorry. I'm not buying into this. Besides, if Syrolee and Engarhod are involved then Tryan will be around, and it will be better for everyone on Amyrantha if I don't have to deal with him."

"You can't hide from him forever," Lukys suggested, cutting a slice of cheese for Coron and placing it on the table in front of him. The creature picked it up in his paws and began to nibble the cheese. Nobody at the table seemed bothered by Lukys sharing his meal with a rat.

"Actually, Tryan is hiding from me." I looked around the table, wondering why I'd been chosen for this mission. As you may have gathered, I was well and truly over my fascination with noble quests by then. "Why doesn't one of you go?"

I could understand why Brynden and Kinta weren't welcome in Tenacia. Even why Lukys might prefer not to go, but Medwen, last I heard, had no particular argument with Syrolee and her family. I'd been surprised to find Medwen here in Torlenia, in fact. With no magical power to speak of or territorial ambitions of her own, she usually gravitated to wherever the greatest concentration of immortals was during High Tide, and that was often the Emperor and Empress of the Five Realms and their kin.

"I *was* in Tenacia," Medwen announced flatly. "I left."

I looked at her curiously. Medwen and I shared a cottage once—for about eighteen years during a Low Tide—posing as a married couple in a smallish village on the opposite shore of the Great Inland Sea. It had been a pleasant enough time. Like me, Medwen had taken Lukys's advice to learn a trade or two that would see her through the hard times, and she'd become a glassmaker of some note by then. In the old days, before glassblowing became popular, core forming was the most common method of producing glass and Medwen was very good at it. As livelihoods went, it was among the most benign that I've ever known. I kept the forges hot and watched over the annealing process as the glass cooled, while Medwen created her delicate vessels around a mud-and-dung core she later broke up . . . you probably don't need the details. But I'll tell you one thing—those cores stank like a midden heap when they were heated . . .

Such peaceful serenity never lasts, though. People started to remark on how the pretty, dark-skinned glassmaker and her nice young husband hadn't changed a bit in all the years they'd lived in the village. Women who'd purchased gifts for the birth of the first child were coming back to us to purchase gifts for their grandchildren and they remembered things like that. You can't spend your whole life among mortals, never looking older than seventeen or twenty-five, without attracting attention.

Medwen and I went our separate ways when the speculation began to get a little too intense, with a vague promise to do it again sometime, even in another country, perhaps, where everybody had forgotten us. Medwen was keen to try her hand at faïence, you know . . . making ceramic glazed tiles. She needed someone to grind the quartz for her, but we never followed through with our plans. That pleasant interlude faded into memory, we'd both become involved in other things, and then the Tide returned and all bets were off.

But I still had a soft spot for Medwen and she was one of the few immortals I'll go out of my way to help. Her flat tone of voice when she spoke of leaving Tenacia was something I knew well. There was more going on here, I thought, than Brynden, Lukys and Kinta worrying about the fate of some unknown Tenacian mortals currently being tortured to create these Crasii.

"What happened?" I asked Medwen.

"Rance convinced me to have a child."

I didn't answer immediately, wondering how Medwen could ever be foolish enough to let Rance convince her of anything, least of all to bear a child. That the father must have been mortal was a given. We all knew by then that there was no such thing as an immortal offspring.

"I wasn't raped, if that's what you're thinking," she added, taking my silence to mean—rightly enough—that I was afraid to ask *how* she'd fallen pregnant.

"I didn't assume that you had been," I assured her. "It's High Tide." Even without any significant magical power, no mortal man was going to lay an unwelcome hand on an immortal woman during High Tide and live to tell of it.

"The name of the father is irrelevant," Lukys added. "Suffice to say he was a slave in Engarhod's palace, Medwen mentioned in passing that she thought he was handsome, and that gave Rance the idea. He said she could have him if she agreed to have a child by him."

I stared at Medwen. "And you said *yes*?"

Medwen smiled faintly. "He was *very* pretty, Cayal.

Even prettier than you." Then her amusement faded. "You don't have to look to me like that. I know how stupid it was, but I did it, anyway. You should know being immortal hasn't imbued a single one of us with any more common sense than we were born with."

There was no arguing with that. I shook my head in despair. "So what happened?"

"In my eighth month, Rance came to me and suggested that if an immortal man could impregnate a mortal woman and blend an animal into the Tidewatcher foetus to create a Crasii, it should work the other way, too. He wanted me to allow him to blend a cat foetus with my unborn child. They'd been trying to perfect a part-feline warrior caste. I don't know the exact details, because I didn't hang around long enough to find out."

"You refused?"

She glared at me. "Of course I refused!"

"So . . . what happened to the child?"

"She was born human," Medwen assured me. "I made sure of that. And then Syrolee took her." The pain in Medwen's eyes was real, as was the despair in her voice. It was typical of Rance though, and most of the immortals. *If you can't hurt your enemy, hurt those they love.*

Kinta picked up the tale when it became obvious Medwen was too upset to continue. "Syrolee refused her access to her child, so Medwen fled Tenacia and chanced into Lukys. He brought her here while we decide what to do. Your arrival has been most fortuitous."

"You want me to find Medwen's child?"

"I want her back," Medwen declared.

"Oh . . . you want me to *kidnap* Medwen's child."

"It'd be handy if you found out whether or not they've managed to perfect that warrior caste of feline Crasii they were working on, too," Lukys suggested. "The Emperor of the Five Realms armed with an army of warriors with the killing capabilities of a cat and the ability to think like a human is a rather disturbing prospect."

"A caste of warrior *cat* people?" I asked, shaking my

head. It seemed such an absurd concept in those days. "What does one do with an army like that, anyway?"

"We think he has plans for them beyond Tenacia," Kinta replied.

Brynden nodded in agreement. "We think Syrolee has her eye on the title of Empress of Amyrantha."

"Why stop at a continent?" Medwen added sourly. "When you can rule the whole world?"

"But why bother?" I asked. "It's High Tide. If they want to rule the world, there's really nothing stopping them. Both Tryan and Elyssa can wield the Tide as well as Lukys or Bryn or I can. What do they need an army for?"

"To control the human population afterwards, perhaps?" Lukys suggested.

"It's easy enough to scare any human population into doing what you want when the Tide's up." I shrugged, unconvinced. Then I glanced at the others and added, "We've all done it."

"Not *all* of us," Brynden corrected stiffly. "But I believe Lukys has the right of it. Respect inspired by fear is only effective when the reason for that fear is reasonably close by. Immortal they may be, but there aren't enough of Engarhod's clan who can actually use Tide magic effectively and they can't be everywhere at once."

"Build yourself a loyal army, however," Lukys agreed, "one that is magically compelled to obey you, and you're halfway there. A hierarchical power pyramid based on fear with the Tide Lords at the top and a willing army of killers at the bottom. Very efficient method of controlling a world, based on the well-documented mathematical principle that shit flows downhill."

I couldn't help but smile. "You always did have a way of putting things in perspective, Lukys."

"Perspective being one thing sorely missing among our kind," he agreed.

I rolled my eyes. "This from the man who thinks he can find a way to travel between the stars."

Lukys stared at me, his blue eyes bright against his

dusky skin. "You waste your immortality on trivial things, my lad. I've no interest in ruling a world when there might be a chance I can rule a whole galaxy." He tickled the rat fondly. "Isn't that right, old son?"

I looked at Brynden. "And what do you think, Bryn? Is there room, somewhere in your noble warrior ethic, for the notion of ruling a galaxy?"

"One cannot presume to rule others until one has total command of oneself," the Fyronnese Tide Lord replied.

"One can redress an injustice, however," Kinta added impatiently. "Even without achieving such a state of purity."

Her comment gave me the first hint of the split that would eventually drive Kinta and Brynden apart, but I didn't realise it then. Instead, I turned my attention to Medwen. "How long ago did you and Rance have your . . . unfortunate encounter?"

"Almost eleven years ago, now."

"And nobody's done anything about it yet?"

"We were waiting for the right time," Medwen explained.

"And the right person," Lukys amended. He raised his cup to me with a mocking smile. "The time has come I suspect, Cayal, our Immortal Prince, for you to do something useful."

Much later that evening Medwen came to my room, sliding silently into the hard narrow bed beside me. We made love—out of habit, as much as desire—not saying a word until after we were spent. Medwen lay beside me afterwards, her head resting on my chest, and spoke idly of the years we'd spent apart, of things she'd done, places she had seen, people she had met. She said nothing of Tenacia, or the loss of her child. She didn't have to. The fact that she was here in my bed was proof enough of her pain.

"Why?" I asked eventually, when she'd run out of things to say.

"Why what?"

"Why did you go anywhere near Tenacia?"

"I was bored." She shrugged. "And regardless of what you think of them, you have to admit Syrolee and her clan know how to live in style."

"You're immortal. You could set yourself up as a goddess anywhere you wanted if you feel the need to be worshipped so badly."

Medwen sighed in the chilly darkness. "But it's so much work. And I'm not like you and Lukys. I can barely light a candle, even at High Tide. It's much easier, don't you think, to ride in the wake of someone who enjoys doing that sort of thing?"

I smiled faintly, glad for the warmth of an extra body. The thin blanket Brynden provided for his guests did little to ward off the cold. Although our bodies regulate themselves so we don't really feel the cold much anymore—and I suspect that without immortal protection, we might well have died of hypothermia in Brynden's icy castle—I still felt the cold grip of something. Perhaps it was my imagination, but I was glad of Medwen's warmth, nonetheless.

"Why a child?"

I felt her shrug beside me. "I was lonely. I knew the child would die of old age eventually, but I wanted someone to love me, Cayal, even if it was only for a little while."

"I love you, Medwen. You know that."

"Only because I'm here in your bed. You'll have forgotten about me by morning."

Sadly, that was probably a fair comment. "But a child? Surely you didn't think a baby would bring you anything but pain?"

"You had to be there, Cayal. It's not that easy to explain."

"What did the others say when they learned Rance had taken it?"

"Nothing much," she told him. "At least not in my hearing. Engarhod was singularly unsympathetic. And Elyssa suggested it was my own fault."

"So who gave birth to this cat creature Rance wanted?"

"Elyssa. I found out later that she'd birthed most of the first generation. I think she was tired of being pregnant, which is why Rance asked me."

"Did someone finally *order* a mortal slave to sleep with her?"

I felt, rather than saw, Medwen smiling against my chest. "That's a cruel thing to suggest."

"But probably true."

She turned in my arms, and looked up at me, her dark eyes glittering in the gloom. "Will you go, Cayal? Will you do as Brynden asks?"

"I want to talk to Lukys again first."

"Why?"

"As I said at dinner, he has a way of putting things into perspective. You know . . . that skill we immortals sadly lack?"

"Do you trust him?"

I looked at her in surprise. "Don't *you*?"

She laid her head down again so I could no longer read her expression. "I sometimes think he's the most dangerous one of us all."

I laughed softly. *"Lukys?"*

"He wants to rule the whole galaxy."

"Every immortal needs a hobby, Medwen."

She slapped my bare chest impatiently. "I'm not kidding, Cayal. This is serious. We point at Syrolee and Engarhod and roll our eyes at the way their family scrabbles for power every time the Tide turns. We even think Brynden and Kinta are a little odd for setting themselves up as gods in this dismal abbey, making a virtue out of grim austerity. But think about it for a moment. What does Lukys do with his immortality? He's as powerful as any of you who can wield the Tide and yet he disappears for centuries at a time. He never stops trying to test the limit of his power. He doesn't care about lording it over the mortal population, and he makes a point of helping every other immortal find their way, so we all end up thinking of him as our best friend. Why? Because he's nice? Because he has a pet rat? Or because he wants immortal minions the same way Syrolee and Engarhod want their army of feline Crasii?"

"Lukys only cares about his astrology," I disagreed. "He doesn't want to rule us."

"He's trying to find a way to *reach* the stars," she reminded me. "Not just study them. We have forever, Cayal. Eventually he may discover it, and then we'll no longer be equals because while Tryan and Jaxyn and the rest of you with more power than sense are causing cataclysms on Amyrantha to amuse yourselves, he'll be realigning the planets to suit his whim and there won't be one of us with the knowledge or the ability to stop him."

I tightened my arm around her gently, bending my head forward to kiss the top of her head. "What are you saying, Medwen? That I should forget Rance and your child and try to take down Lukys and his wretched rat instead?"

She shook her head, sighing. "No. I'm not sure what I'm saying. I just think we all put far too much store in Lukys's opinion."

"I'll bear your warning in mind when next I speak to him, my lady."

"Now you're patronising me."

"Sorry."

"No, you're not." After a moment, she turned to look at me again, her expression fierce. "Bring me back my baby, Cayal."

"If I can."

"If you can't, will you make Rance suffer?"

"It'll be my pleasure."

"How?"

"I haven't the faintest idea."

"He took my baby, Cayal."

"I know."

"He has to suffer."

"I'll make him suffer," I promised, trying not to seem impatient with her demands. I knew Medwen was hurting, but she was wallowing a little too comfortably in her pain. *Tides, it happened eleven years ago,* an unsympathetic voice in my head was complaining. *Get over it.*

I said nothing aloud, however, and soon Medwen laid her head against my chest again, her dark hair tickling my nose. She was silent for a time—so long, I thought she must have drifted off to sleep. When she finally spoke, her question stunned me.

"Cayal," she asked softly in the darkness, "do you ever wish you could die?"

I hesitated before answering. "I've never really given it much thought."

"I never thought about it much, either. Not until Rance took my baby."

There was no answer to that, so I said nothing. But it set me thinking as I lay there in the icy darkness, Medwen's body curled into mine, her deep even breathing lulling me to sleep.

It was the first time I was forced to confront the notion that if I ever actually wanted to die, I had a serious problem.

Chapter 42

It was the early hours of the morning before Cayal finished speaking. Their fire had burned down to embers and both Arkady and the Crasii had listened to his tale entranced, heedless of the bitter wind that howled through the mountains.

It was Chikita who broke the silence, her tone awestruck. "You have spoken to the Mother, my lord?"

Cayal nodded. "Who, Elyssa? Of course."

Arkady stared at Chikita in surprise, forcing herself to focus on what the Crasii was saying. She'd heard the Crasii refer to "the Mother" plenty of times, but the identity of the goddess the Crasii considered their maternal figure was one of those closely guarded secrets they refused to share, even with an outsider as trusted as Arkady. Confronted with such a startling revelation, she was disturbed to discover how much effort it took to concentrate on the disclosure. It was proving rather difficult to banish the image of Medwen lying beside Cayal while she slept with her head resting on his naked chest.

"Did you do it?" Arkady couldn't help but ask.

"Do what?"

"Find Medwen's child?"

Cayal hesitated and then shrugged. "Not exactly."

Cayal leaned forward, poking at the embers of the dying fire. It was impossible to read his expression in the darkness, but she could sense his reluctance to go on. "If I've learned one thing since becoming immortal, Arkady, it's that it is far easier to destroy a friend than an enemy."

"And much easier to be cryptic than give a straight answer, too, I've noticed."

"I just meant I hung around with Rance and Krydence for a time," he told her, throwing another branch on the coals. "Probably longer than I should have, truth be told. Fact is, it wouldn't have made a difference to Medwen. By the time I got there, her child was already dead."

"So how did you get revenge?"

"I helped put a stop to Crasii farming, for one thing. Eventually."

"But not the Crasii," Arkady remarked, glancing around at the felines surrounding them. Although the rain had stopped and the fire had dried her off, Arkady was still freezing and she envied them their fur coats. Their eyes shone in the darkness, watchfully, warily, as if they were waiting for her to try something. She wondered what they thought of Cayal's story. If he was telling the truth—and the felines obviously believed he was—he must be shattering a few of their illusions about his kind. In Crasii legend, the Tide Lords were gods. There was no mention of a Tide Lord who refused to be a party to their creation. Or of other Tide Lords who might have actively opposed their creators.

The fire flared, sparks vanishing into the night, as Cayal coaxed it back to life. If he was worried about the effect his tale was having on the Crasii, he gave no sign of it.

"By the time we were done, there were enough Crasii around to continue the species without magical help," he continued. "Actually, they'd reached that point long before I got there. When I arrived in Tenacia, Krydence, Taryx and Rance were well on their way to building their army. It was Syrolee and Elyssa who kept on experimenting."

"With blending the races?"

He nodded. "They got really creative there for a while. I even had a talking horse called Bevali, once."

"A *talking* horse?" Arkady smiled, certain he was teasing her now. "What happened to these remarkable talking horses? I mean, we still have the felines you claim the Tide Lords created, and canines and amphibious Crasii, even reptilian Crasii, although they're rare. Can't say I've ever been spoken to by a horse, though."

"They were never really viable." He glanced across the flames at her with a shrug. "Too hard to make and too difficult to manage when we did. The horses were Rance's idea, but the others experimented with a lot of crazy mixtures, and not all of them logical. Some blendings worked and some didn't. I don't think the equines were infertile, but once you give an animal a chance to voice its feelings, you've overridden a large part of their natural instincts and in some species that's just asking for trouble. I heard they wouldn't breed because they were so attached to their human masters, they started to think *they* were human, too. The equines weren't interested in their own kind. Not even for sex. Did you know we're the only species that has sex for fun?"

"Do you include all the Crasii in that sweeping generalisation?"

"Yes."

"But if they're part human as you claim . . ."

"Chikita!" Cayal barked in reply. "Why does a female feline copulate?"

"Because she can't help it," the feline replied without hesitation. "The need comes on her with the heat and she must fulfil it. We must go on. We must breed. It is the way of things."

"And feline males? Why do they mate?"

The young woman spat on the ground in contempt. "It is their function and they desire nothing more because they are animals."

"There," Cayal said, turning back to Arkady. "You heard her. It is the way of things. They must breed."

Arkady was silent for a time, wondering why she had never thought to question Crasii sexual practices before. And why she was buying into this nonsense in the first place. She smiled. "You nearly had me there."

He looked at her in surprise. "Pardon?"

"You nearly had me believing in magic."

Cayal shook his head with a sigh. "I marvel at your ability to ignore the evidence of your own eyes, Arkady. You're so set on what you *think* is real, you can't accept the truth, even when it has its fingers chopped off, right before your very eyes."

Cayal was wrong. Arkady wasn't ignoring anything. She knew she was clinging to a myth, but she wasn't ready to let it go just yet. Admitting the truth about Cayal would mean stepping through a door Arkady Desean wasn't sure she had the courage to open. No matter how absurd, in light of all she had witnessed this day, it just seemed easier to hold on to her old reality rather than deal with the new one.

"If you're telling the truth, Cayal, then I have to confront the notion that my world is based on a lie," she admitted eventually.

"That's not actually my fault," Cayal replied with a shrug, and then without offering her any other opinion, he lay down, turned his back to the fire and promptly went to sleep.

The following morning, in a steady downpour, Cayal turned their party south, taking them even deeper into the mountains. The track they traversed was so faint, Arkady wondered if Cayal was imagining it. They were frequently required to dismount in order to get past the narrower, more dangerous sections of the slippery game trail he followed, but he kept onwards and upwards relentlessly, with the confidence of a man who knows exactly where he is going and what to expect when he arrives.

Protected by their pelts, the felines seemed unbothered by the icy rain that soaked Arkady's skirts, finding every vulnerable seam with wet, icy fingers. She wasn't dressed for trekking in the mountains. Her coat was a summer-weight, decorative garment, not meant to protect a body from the relentless rain or the harsh winds that whipped around the peaks of the Shevron Mountains, and her high-heeled boots were ill-suited to riding, even less appropriate for walking over rough ground, or climbing across narrow ravines.

Exhausted, her feet blistered, her thighs rubbed raw, her lips blue, her fingers numb, Arkady took a moment or two to register they had stopped, when Cayal finally called a halt to their progress just on dusk.

It was three days since they'd left Clyden's Inn. Arkady had stopped trying to reason her way through her predicament. Survival demanded more of her attention now than idle philosophical arguments. She was too tired and too overwhelmed to worry about it any longer. Immortals existed, she decided as she sank to her knees on the rocky plateau Cayal had chosen for their campsite, and Arkady couldn't have cared less.

"Tides!" Cayal exclaimed, as Arkady collapsed. "Look at you! You're frozen through! Why didn't you say something?"

She looked up at him through eyes blurred with wind-driven tears. "Would you have stopped?"

Cayal didn't answer her. Instead, he cursed impatiently and ordered the Crasii to care for the horses and make camp while he helped Arkady up and led her into the lee of the cliff behind them. There was a shallow depression in the rock face, not deep enough to be called a cave, but enough to offer some small relief from the rain. He drew her close and began rubbing her upper arms briskly, to stimulate the circulation.

"Your hands are so warm," she remarked in surprise through chattering teeth, glad of the little bit of heat he was able to provide.

"Another advantage of immortality," he shrugged.

"More of your body regulating itself?" she asked. "Like not getting too fat or too thin?"

Cayal stopped rubbing her arms for a moment and shook his head. He seemed amused. "You're on the verge of passing out from exposure, Arkady. Don't you ever stop trying to analyse things?"

She shrugged. "Sorry. I can't seem to help myself."

In reply, he pulled her close, wrapping her in his warm embrace. She closed her eyes and tried not to think about the cold. It was disconcerting to be held so intimately but she was too grateful for the unnatural warmth of his body to question its source. Over the top of her head, she could hear Cayal issuing orders to the Crasii to get a fire going.

When he was done with the Crasii and her teeth had stopped chattering, she looked up at him. "Where are you taking me?"

Cayal glanced down at her, still holding her close. "Why?"

"I have a right to know, don't you think?"

He thought on that for a moment and then shook his head. "Not really."

A part of Arkady wanted to push him away angrily, but the part of her that was just starting to thaw out resisted the temptation.

"They'll find you, you know. My husband will already have his scouts out, scouring these mountains. We've left a trail a mile wide. The Crasii are not attempting to conceal our progress. A blind man could follow us."

Cayal shrugged, unconcerned. "I'm not actually trying to hide, Arkady. Just find a place of strength from which to negotiate."

She stared up at him, a little surprised at how much she wanted to believe him. "They won't let you go, Cayal," she warned softly.

He smiled down at her, supremely confident. "We'll see."

Arkady shivered as the numbness began to fade a little. Unconsciously, she tried to bury herself even deeper into Cayal's embrace. She felt his arms tighten about her. Soaking up his unnatural warmth, Arkady closed her eyes again, letting his solid strength envelop her, and tried not to think about anything other than surviving this nightmare so she could return to her husband and her perfectly constructed life full of lies, as if, after what she'd done, there was even a slim chance such a circumstance was possible.

Chapter 43

At first, Warlock had no real destination beyond the city in mind. His release had been too sudden and unexpected to allow him time to make plans. He had taken his pardon and his few possessions and all but run from the high, bleak walls of Lebec Prison the moment they closed the gates behind him.

Despite the persistent, misty rain, the first thing he did was shed the prison uniform they'd made him wear these past two years. Clothes were a human foible, required because their hairless skins could not protect them from the elements. The Crasii rarely wore them, unless required by their masters to denote which house they belonged to, or in some cases, merely to match the decor. But Warlock was free now. He need wear clothes for no man.

Once he'd stashed his rough linen shift behind a rock on the side of the tree-shaded road, Warlock turned toward the distant city. As he walked, he wasted little effort trying to fathom the actions of the Duke of Lebec, or his unaccountably generous wife.

It wasn't his problem.

Warlock's problem now was that he was free in a country where his kind was only truly accepted as slaves. There was perhaps some small measure of shelter for him on the rough streets of Lebec, but no real chance of a future there. Even if he didn't get into trouble directly, it wouldn't take the authorities long to discover some unsolved crime looking for a suspect and find a way to pin it on the stray canine wandering the streets of Lebec for no other reason than his very existence disturbed them.

There was really only one thing for it, he decided after several hours as the city gradually resolved out of the rain in the distance. He was going to have to either leave Glaeba entirely or try to find Hidden Valley.

All his life, Warlock had heard rumours of a valley to the west of the Great Lakes, where the Scards of Amyrantha had found a home. When he was a pup, the threat of being denied entry to it had been used to frighten him into obedience. As an adult, he'd begun to wonder if the stories of a place where the desperate and dispossessed could find succour were true. Before they'd thrown him into his solitary cell on Recidivists' Row, he'd heard other Crasii speak of it in the prison. Legend or no, Hidden Valley was the place to which they all dreamed of escaping. The belief was so pervasive, so universal, even among the other Crasii races, that Warlock had begun to believe it might—even in some small measure—be true.

He even had the name of someone they claimed could lead him to the Valley. *Shalimar,* the prison Crasii had whispered in awe. *He knows the way. Find Shalimar,* they hissed in the shadows. *Get out of this place and find Shalimar.*

He will lead you home.

Trouble was, nobody knew where to find this Shalimar character. He was nothing more than a name. Rumour had it, he lived in Lebec.

Not much to go on, admittedly, but a start.

A start that never got any further than Warlock wondering about it. He was in Lebec City for a mere four hours when they caught him again.

"Halt!"

Warlock froze and glanced about. The slums of Lebec were a crowded and filthy place, filled with people seeking work—qualified to do nothing the city desired but the most menial jobs—or those interested in not working at all. Used to the order of Lord Ordry's household, even the severe but regulated loneliness of Recidivists' Row, Warlock was overwhelmed by the chaos, by the noise, the smells and the fugue of unrelenting poverty that permeated the stinking streets of the city's outskirts. Effluent flowed freely in the rain-filled gutters while human and Crasii children alike splashed in the puddles and dodged between the legs of their elders, ragged and thin, but strangely happy in their games.

It amazed Warlock how some people, particularly children, could find amusement, even glee, in the basest circumstances. Perhaps it came from never knowing any better.

It was almost sunset when they hailed him, the teeming streets filled with people returning home from their decent jobs while others headed out to partake in less savoury employment. People scurried by holding oiled cloaks over their heads against the downpour, others dressed in the faded finery so common among the whores and thieves of the city pushed past him as if he wasn't there, trying to ignore the brewing altercation between the huge canine and the City Watch.

Slowly, Warlock turned to face the men who had hailed him, not doubting for a moment that he was the focus of their attention.

He'd suspected his inexplicable pardon was too good to be true.

The City Watchmen looked smart and extremely out of place here in the slums in their blue-and-green tunics. There were six men in the squad, all of them conspicuously armed with daggers and swords, one of them pointing a loaded crossbow directly at Warlock. It was a stupid thing to do, Warlock noted in some corner of his mind not afraid of death. A wild shot could easily take out an innocent bystander.

"Yes?" he enquired, with a calmness he didn't feel.

"On your knees, dog!" the officer of the squad commanded, stepping up beside the man with the crossbow.

"I have done nothing," Warlock pointed out, looking around. He wiped the rain from his face and wondered what his chances of escape were. They appeared slim. The guards were expecting him to make a break for it, the streets were crowded and nobody here, human or Crasii, owed him any favours.

"Who is your master?" the officer demanded.

Warlock carefully extracted his precious pardon from the belt pouch slung over his shoulder. He'd not let it go since Lady Desean had awarded it to him. "I am a free Crasii."

The officer stepped forward, snatched the document from Warlock's hand and then stepped back again, so the bowman had a clear shot. He unfolded the paper, read it through and then looked up, frowning.

"Warlock," he said, "out of Bella, by Segura. You're the one we're looking for, I'd say."

"But I have done nothing," he protested as a matter of principle. Warlock knew the futility of resisting, but he felt compelled to protest his innocence, nonetheless. And he wanted to reach for his pardon. The rain was falling on

it, blurring the ink in large spatters. If he stood there holding it long enough, his freedom might easily be washed
away.

"Sure, you've done nothing," the officer agreed sceptically, folding the pardon and slipping it into his coat.
"That's why we were sent to find you, I suppose?"

"And having found me, what do you intend to do with
me?"

Warlock's sharp hearing caught a hissed intake of breath
at his insolence from one of the onlookers. He glanced sideways, catching sight of a female canine clutching a large
woven basket to her chest, standing off to his left, watching
the proceedings with intense interest. She was a well-
formed creature with a reddish pelt under a simple linen
shift—common attire among the city Crasii—from out of
which a bushy tail hung low and unthreatening. She was
hardly more than a pup, he judged, as her dark eyes filled
with concern on his behalf. He barely had time to register
that much before the squad moved in to surround him and
the pretty canine Crasii was gone, replaced by an officer of
the City Watch.

The man moved a little closer, his hand resting on the
hilt of his sword, and looked up at Warlock.

"You can walk with us, or we can drag your unconscious carcass through the gutters," the officer informed
him matter-of-factly. "The choice is yours, dog boy."

Warlock *really* hated being called "dog boy," almost as
much as he despised the name gemang. He had to force
down the snarl that leapt to his lips.

"I will walk."

"Wise decision," the officer agreed.

"Where are you taking me?"

"The Watch-house."

"Am I under arrest?"

"Not if you come quietly."

Warlock glanced at the Watchmen surrounding him and
nodded slowly, unable to avoid the feeling that he was con-

senting to his own death, all for the sake of not making a scene. Perhaps it was the crossbow he feared. Not so much for himself, but the fear of that dangerous quarrel ending up buried in some innocent onlooker like the young female who'd gasped at his audacity. Warlock couldn't really say.

"As you wish."

"There's a good doggy," one of the guards muttered behind him, giving him a shove.

Slipping on the wet, greasy cobblestones, Warlock stumbled forward, growling softly under his breath. But he let the comment pass and fell in behind the officer as they made their way through the rapidly darkening streets toward the Watch-house.

There was a time and a place to take care of men who made comments like that, and this was neither.

Besides, he had to survive this unexpected detour first.

The City Watchmen who escorted Warlock to the Watch-house proved to be gentlemen compared to the men who took over his custody when the squad resumed their patrol. As soon as Warlock stepped inside, he was bashed across the shoulders with a truncheon until he fell to his knees on the hard stone floor. It was dark by then, the Watch-house lit by guttering torches. He was beaten, cajoled and threatened into a cell not far from the main entrance, and then left with an escort of two guards to watch over him. Neither man spared him so much as a look once the door closed behind the others, provided he did not attempt to get up from the floor.

Warlock wasn't sure what was happening, but he was certain of one thing: agreeing to come quietly to the Lebec City Watch-house was possibly the dumbest thing he'd done in his entire life.

He was left to dwell on his monumental stupidity for the better part of an hour. Then the door opened finally and a man stepped into the cell. Hurriedly the guards stood to attention. Their visitor wasn't a particularly tall man—few humans were tall compared to Warlock—but he carried himself proudly, his face handsome in the way of humans, clean-shaven and olive-skinned, and he was dressed more finely than any man Warlock had met since he'd left the service of Lord Ordry's household. The man smelled of expensive soap, of hidden fears. And of power.

"Leave us!"

The guards did as the man ordered without question. Whoever he was, his scent of command was not misplaced. He had authority here. A great deal of it.

"You are the canine they call Warlock?" In contrast to his barked orders to the guards, when he spoke to Warlock, his voice was cultured, his tone nonthreatening, although it was clear he expected an answer. Fortunately, unlike the City Watchmen, he didn't seem to feel the need to beat his prisoner to get one.

Warlock nodded warily, daring to climb to his feet. The human showed no fear. He didn't even flinch when Warlock rose to his full height, forcing the man to look up at him to meet his eye.

"Who wants to know?"

The newcomer held up a piece of paper that Warlock recognised as his ticket to freedom, so recently handed to him by Arkady Desean, even more recently surrendered to the City Watch. It was spattered with raindrops, the ink blurred in places, but it was still legible. "This pardon you carry bears my signature and my seal."

Warlock's eyes narrowed. "You are the Duke of Lebec?"

"I am."

"Then you have my eternal gratitude, your grace," he said with a low bow.

The duke frowned. "If only I'd actually done something to warrant it."

"Sir?"

"The seal on this pardon is mine, Warlock," the duke informed him, holding the paper a little higher. "The signature isn't."

This wasn't likely to be good. "I . . . I don't understand."

"Neither do I," Stellan Desean admitted. "I was hoping you might be able to enlighten me."

Confused, the Crasii shrugged. "I cannot explain it, your grace. The duchess—your lady wife—visited the prison a few days ago with the intention of escorting another prisoner back to the palace, so she informed us. And to award me a pardon. I cannot say why."

The duke nodded, as if this confirmed what he already knew. "Tell me about this other prisoner."

"Cayal?"

The Duke of Lebec nodded, clearly unhappy about something. "Arkady's Immortal Prince."

It was obvious the man had no faith in Cayal's claim. *Foolish humans.* They had no idea of the peril the suzerain represented. The Crasii remembered. They made a point of it. But humans . . . their pride was too strong, their memories too short, to be even remotely aware of the danger. "Cayal was not lying, your grace. He is who he claims to be."

"Arkady . . . my wife, didn't seem to think so." There was nothing snide or condescending in his tone. To Warlock's amazement, the Duke of Lebec was almost respectful of Crasii beliefs, enough not to scoff at Warlock's insistence that Cayal was the Immortal Prince, at any rate.

"She may learn, to her peril, that she was wrong, your grace."

The duke looked worried by that. "Do *you* think she's in danger from this man?"

Warlock hesitated as it occurred to him his detention might have nothing to do with his unexpected release at all, but was a part of something much bigger. "Has something happened, your grace? To her ladyship?"

Stellan Desean hesitated and then nodded, as if admitting the truth could do no harm. "While she was escorting this would-be immortal back to the palace, he escaped and took my wife hostage."

Somehow, the news didn't surprise Warlock. "I don't

think he'll harm her, your grace," Warlock found himself saying, not sure why he felt the need to reassure the man directly responsible for his incarceration. He owed the Duke of Lebec nothing, it seemed, not even his release.

"How can you be sure?"

Because I could smell it on them, Warlock wanted to reply, but knew he couldn't say it aloud. You didn't tell a man with the power of life or death over you that you could smell lust simmering between his wife and another man. Cayal was nothing more than an escaped murderer to Stellan Desean. Telling him he suspected Cayal wouldn't hurt his wife because it was obvious he desired her would hardly set the man's mind at rest.

"The Immortal Prince is renowned for many things, your grace, but wanton cruelty is not among them."

"You keep insisting he's immortal. Arkady thought he might be a Caelish spy. Or a madman."

"It matters little which one, sire," Warlock pointed out. "If Cayal is really an immortal or if he has simply assumed the persona of the Immortal Prince, he is bound by the legend he has claimed and if he wants to keep up his fiction he must therefore act as the real Cayal would act. In Crasii legend, Cayal is known as an adventurer, a scoundrel, even a champion of lost causes at times, but he has never been known for being deliberately malicious. Nor is this man a fool. If he has your wife, she will be alive, because he intends to trade her safety for his escape."

The duke studied him for a time. "You've thought this through, I see."

"It requires very little thought, your grace. I would have thought the evidence spoke for itself."

The duke smiled thinly. "Arkady said you were intelligent."

Warlock didn't return the smile. "She also said you granted me a pardon, your grace."

The duke glanced down at the document he was still holding. "A circumstance which presents me with something of a dilemma, I fear."

Warlock could see the duke's problem. It was obvious, now, that his wife had forged the pardon, which meant she'd probably forged Cayal's release papers, as well. Whatever game Arkady was playing, whether it was aimed at embarrassing her husband or something more sinister, Warlock was caught in the thick of it. His life now hinged on the willingness of this man to overlook his wife's active participation in the release of two convicted murderers.

His lordship didn't appear happy about it, either. "If I honour this pardon, I become complicit in her crime."

"And if you don't honour it, her crime becomes public, your grace," Warlock reminded him, guessing that was the reason the duke hadn't called the guards in yet, or had Warlock dragged back to Lebec Prison in chains. *His wife's defiance is not something he wants to advertise,* Warlock guessed, *not with the king and queen in Lebec.*

"Where were you headed?" the duke asked abruptly. "When they apprehended you?"

"West," Warlock told him honestly. "To Caelum. I was hoping to find Hidden Valley."

The duke seemed amused by his admission. "The legendary sanctuary of the Scards? Do you think it really exists?"

"I believe the Immortal Prince exists, your grace. Why shouldn't I believe there is a home for my kind out there somewhere?"

"My wife's colleagues at the university—the ones who fancy themselves smarter than the rest of us—insist the Crasii belief in magic is one of the things that make you less than human."

"And yet, by Crasii reckoning, it's what makes us *more* than human."

The duke had no answer for that. He turned and knocked on the door behind him, his expression apologetic. "I wish we had time to become better acquainted, Warlock, out of Bella, by Segura. You strike me as an interesting man."

It wasn't often a human referred to a Crasii as a "man."

Warlock appreciated the gesture, certain though he was that it was simply the duke's way of expressing his regret for what he was about to do. Four hours, Warlock had been free.

It wasn't long enough.

It would have to be.

"You could come visit me in prison and we can talk again," Warlock suggested. "I've nothing much else to do with my time."

Before the duke could answer, the door opened. Another City Watch officer stepped through the door, saluted sharply and then glanced at Warlock.

"What are your orders concerning the Scard, your grace?"

Stellan Desean hesitated for a fraction of a second before he answered, handing the pardon to the officer. "Release him," he ordered, his voice much more certain than his eyes. "This isn't the Scard we're looking for."

"But . . . your grace . . . ," the officer argued. "He fits the description perfectly. He has the pardon . . ."

The duke's tone changed. So did his uncertain expression. "Are you questioning me, sir?" All trace of his earlier doubt was gone. This was the voice of a man who wielded the power of life and death over the citizens of Lebec and he would clearly brook no interference from an underling.

The officer backed down with alacrity, bowing to his lord and master. "Of course not, your grace."

"This particular canine aided my wife in one of her academic projects and was pardoned for his assistance. He is not to be harassed while in my city, is that clear?"

"Yes, your grace."

"You are free to go," the Duke of Lebec informed Warlock. "I wish you luck in your quest, however futile it might prove to be."

"Finding a place one can call home is never futile, your grace," Warlock replied.

"No," the duke agreed, "I don't suppose it is."

With that, the Duke of Lebec turned on his heel and strode from the cell, leaving Warlock staring at the City Watch officer, who was holding the precious pardon and making no attempt to hide his disgust at the notion of having to let this Crasii murderer go free.

Chapter 44

Jaxyn handpicked the Crasii he intended to take into the mountains. There were a dozen he chose—all felines except for one, a canine named Chelby, Stellan's best tracker and the only male in the group. He chose the Crasii for their stamina, their fighting skills and, most importantly, their unquestioning obedience. It would be too late, once he found Arkady and her escaped murderer, to discover he had any Scards among his escort.

They left Lebec Palace the day after Clyden Bell reported Arkady taken. Stellan would have preferred him to leave sooner, but with the king in residence, such a thing was not so easily achieved. Jaxyn might be making a heroic dash to save his good friend's wife, but they didn't particularly want anybody knowing about it, or worse— tagging along for the ride. Jaxyn and Stellan had made a great show at dinner the night before he left, about hunting down an escaped Crasii, and even more time trying to discourage Mathu from joining the hunt. They were saved in the latter by the queen herself, who objected loudly at the very notion of her son riding off into the mountains in pursuit of some filthy Crasii runaway.

Stellan covered Arkady's absence by claiming she was ill and, with the queen's help, they finally convinced Mathu he'd be better served preparing for the formal announcement of his betrothal to Kylia in a few days' time than traipsing through the mountains after a slave. It had been an altogether harrowing time for the conspirators and Stellan was quite pale by the time the matter was settled and the dinner table discussion moved on to other things.

Their caution was justified. Jaxyn knew that if the king got wind of what had happened to Arkady, it wouldn't be one nobleman and a dozen Crasii heading off in pursuit of the Immortal Prince. Enteny would bring the entire Glaeban army down on Lebec to avenge the insult to his crown. Arkady Desean was more than just a woman the King of Glaeba found beguiling. She was a cousin by marriage. A member of the extended royal family. She was married to the man third in line for the throne. There were consequences for endangering such an important person.

Something Cayal has obviously not considered, Jaxyn thought, as they made camp a few days later, the bitter mountain wind tugging at his cloak. The rain had let up for a time, thankfully. He took in the view, the magnificent vista laid out before him, not really seeing it, no longer impressed by the tall, darkly forested Glaeban mountains, no longer impressed by much of anything, for that matter.

The days when Jaxyn Aranville could stand on the peak of a mountain and be overawed by the majesty of his surroundings were long past.

They had followed Cayal's trail easily enough for the first day, always climbing higher but inexorably heading northeast. The escapee and his errant Crasii made no secret of their passage. It was as if Cayal was taunting his pursuers by leaving such an obvious trail, something Jaxyn wouldn't put past him. Earlier today, however, the trail had faded to almost nothing and Chelby was ranging out ahead of them even now, making the most of the available light, still looking for some hint of the fugitives' direction.

Jaxyn was certain the Crasii would find it eventually. And if he didn't, well . . . perhaps, if they couldn't follow Cayal, they could figure out where he was headed. This was a spur-of-the-moment plan, this kidnap of the Duke of Lebec's wife. Cayal would have had no time at Clyden's

Inn to plan anything else, no time to consider the effect of his actions. His only concern would have been escape. The Immortal Prince's lack of forethought would work in his enemies' favour.

Cayal hasn't thought this through very well at all. "How typical."

"Sire?" the nearest feline asked. She'd been setting up his small oiled-silk tent, but stopped when she thought he'd spoken to her. "Did you say something, my lord?"

"Just thinking out loud," he replied, tugging his cloak closed against the wind. "Get a move on with that, would you? I want to rest."

The feline nodded and hurried back to her work. Jaxyn smiled at her obsequiousness. Some things about the Crasii never seemed to change.

"My lord."

He turned to find Chelby coming up behind him. The canine wasn't as big as some Jaxyn had seen, but he was an excellent tracker. His pelt was tri-coloured, the white fur covering his hands and feet stark against the black and brown patches that covered the rest of his body. His almost-human face was drawn into a frown, wide nostrils flaring.

"Did you find any sign of them?"

"About a half-mile to the south of here, my lord," Chelby informed him, pointing in the direction of which he spoke. "I've marked the place. We can pick up their trail in the morning."

"You've done well." Jaxyn wasn't being nice to the Crasii out of sentiment. He just knew, from long experience, that it never hurt to praise a canine. They thrived on it. And worked harder for it.

Chelby bowed low, his tail wagging. "Thank you, my lord. Thank you, thank—"

"Where are they going, do you think?" Jaxyn asked, cutting off the Crasii's stream of gushing gratitude.

"They seem to have turned higher into the mountains, my lord," the canine replied, a little chastened. "If he's looking to escape Glaeba—the Immortal Prince—you'd think he'd move in a more southerly direction."

Jaxyn was surprised the Crasii had thought of such a thing. He supposed he shouldn't have been. Stellan encouraged his Crasii to think for themselves.

He wasn't sure why. Jaxyn had never seen the point of intelligent Crasii, really.

"Who told you we were in pursuit of the Immortal Prince?" Jaxyn asked, a little concerned. These creatures worshipped the Tide Lords, were bred for their blind obedience to them. If they thought they were chasing one down, there was no telling what they'd do when they found him.

"Before Clyden Bell spoke of the events at his inn to the duke, my lord, he was required to relate his tale to the Crasii doorman to gain entry to the palace. It was common knowledge even before you arrived at the village to select your escort that you would be seeking to find the Immortal Prince and bring him to justice."

Jaxyn snorted at that. *Bring Cayal to justice? Chance would be a fine thing.*

"So, where do you think he's headed?" he asked, curious how much lore of the Crasii the canine knew. If he'd been well-schooled by his dam, Chelby would know the legends. He might even be smart enough to put two and two together and come up with the right answer.

The Crasii dropped his eyes and lowered his tail and refused to answer.

Jaxyn grasped the young male's shoulder reassuringly. "You can tell me, Chelby. I promise, I won't be angry with you."

The Crasii hesitated for a moment longer before he spoke. "I was just thinking, sire . . . if this man we pursue . . . if he really is the Immortal Prince . . . might not he be headed for Maralyce's Mine?"

Jaxyn frowned. *So the legends are still told among the Crasii.* That was both a good and a bad thing, he mused, and not altogether convenient.

"And do you know where to find it?" Jaxyn asked, curiously. "This legendary mine of Crasii lore?"

The young canine shook his head, looking very disappointed. "No, my lord. Our legends tell of the mine's existence; of the fabulous treasure buried within. But other than the mine being hidden in the Shevron Mountains east of the Great Lakes, they do not speak of a specific location. I thought perhaps . . . you . . ." The canine's voice trailed off, as if he feared the consequences of his presumptuousness.

Jaxyn let the silence draw out, enjoying the Crasii's discomfort.

"You thought I might, what, gemang?" he asked eventually.

"I thought *you* might know . . . my lord . . ." Chelby looked ready to chew his own foot off out of mortification.

"You think *I* should know?"

"I'm sorry, my lord . . . I should not have presumed . . ."

Chelby's fawning was starting to irritate Jaxyn. "You're right, gemang. You should not presume. Still, you're not incorrect in your assumption. I do know where Maralyce's Mine is."

Around him, Jaxyn could feel the feline Crasii go still, even those behind him he couldn't see. "You seemed surprised, gemang? Why? Did you think I would forget?"

"Of course not, my lord," one of the felines assured him. "You are omnipotent."

He smiled. "That's a big word for a little cat. Stellan really does overeducate you lot, doesn't he?"

The feline bowed. "If you say so, my lord."

Satisfied the Crasii were still his to command, he turned his back on them, lifting his face to the sky so he could feel the setting sun on his face, the bite of the wind, the icy chill of the oncoming night. The air was thin and smelled of rain and old snow at this altitude and he was feeling a little light-headed as his body adjusted to the change.

But it wasn't just the air making him feel strange. Underneath the tingling of the brittle atmosphere against his skin, there was something else, he realised. Something tickling at his awareness, something pulling at him, like an indefinable itch.

A slow smile crept over Jaxyn's face. A score of times he'd felt this. A score of times he'd welcomed it. Jaxyn forgot about the Crasii and closed his eyes. He held his arms out wide, letting the sensation whisper over him like the tender kiss of a secret lover.

Jaxyn knew what it was.

It was power. Life. Eternity. There . . . on the very edge of his awareness, something he hadn't felt for a thousand years.

The Tide was coming in.

PART II

Low Tide

I must go down to the seas again,
for the call of the running tide
is a wild call and a clear call
that may not be denied.
—John Masefield
(1878–1967)

Chapter 45

It was dark by the time the City Watch let Warlock leave the Watch-house, located at the entrance to the older, walled part of the city, and it was clear he would not be permitted entry at this hour. Not that he had any business in the city proper. Now he was free again—at least until the next time the City Watch thought up a reason to arrest him—Warlock really only had one purpose in mind.

Find Shalimar. Get out of this place and find Shalimar. He will lead you home.

The sky was low and overcast, the night misty, although the rain had finally stopped. Warlock turned away from the gates and the suspicious stares of the Watchmen on duty and headed back into the slums outside the walls, where he'd been arrested earlier. His stomach growled with hunger as he walked, wondering if he could find the street he'd been looking for again. Shalimar, according to what little Warlock knew of him, was some sort of healer. The logical place to look for him then, the Crasii figured, was down Curing Street where most of the healers working the slums had their shops. It was hardly the most scientific approach to finding a person who might well be a figment of the collective Crasii imagination, but he had nothing better to go on.

Warlock was two or three streets from the Watch-house when he realised he was being followed. At the next corner, where the soft yellow light and cheerful music of a pub spilled out into the street, illuminating pockets of the muddy road while plunging other parts of it into shadow, he stepped back against the wall and waited. Holding his breath, his pulse pounding in his ears, Warlock flattened himself against the rough weatherboards. The music from the pub continued unabated, the place smelling of beer and overcooked meat, making his hunger that much sharper.

He forced himself to concentrate on the creature following him. Sure enough, a few moments after Warlock vanished from sight, his pursuer stepped cautiously into the lane. He was small for a canine, although unmistakably that's what he was. Shadowed by the irregular light from the pub, Warlock could make out little more than the silhouette of a small canine with a thick bushy tail. Warlock held himself still, waiting for his pursuer to get closer. Unaware he had turned from hunter to prey, the canine walked deeper into the alley.

The beast was two steps past Warlock when the big Crasii struck, crashing into him, forcing him to the ground. Instinctively, he bit down on the creature's throat, ready to rip it out if the canine gave him any trouble, but to his surprise, the creature went limp beneath him and made no effort to fight back.

Warily, he let go of the throat and, still astride the beast, Warlock knelt back on his heels, growling. The young canine rolled on his back and raised his shift, exposing his belly to his enemy in a gesture of submission.

It was then Warlock realised that his pursuer wasn't male at all.

It was the female who'd watched him being arrested. The one who'd gasped in horror when he answered back.

"Why are you following me?" he growled.

She glared up at him, her dark eyes full of suspicion, but she wasn't afraid of him. "Why did they let you go?"

"Who are you?"

"Your worst nightmare, farm dog, if you harm a single hair on my tail and expect to get out of Lebec City afterwards." Her complete lack of fear surprised Warlock a little. He was twice her size and she was in a very vulnerable position, but he couldn't smell anything that reeked of fear. If anything, her scent was musky. And enticing. As if she was about to come on heat and was oblivious to the fact. It made their current position all the more dangerous. For both of them.

He leaned back and studied her more closely in the fitful light. She was ginger-haired and well-formed, long lashes framing large dewy eyes so brown they were almost black. And her scent was beginning to drive him crazy.

Conscious of the risk of staying so close to a female who smelt like that, Warlock slowly climbed off her and stood up warily. She didn't move, her submissive stance at odds with her fearless demeanour.

Warlock held his hand out to her. The female stared at his outstretched arm for a moment, and then, with some reluctance, accepted his aid. He pulled her to her feet, surprised to discover she was taller than she'd seemed when she'd been tracking him.

"Why are you following me?" he asked, in a much less threatening tone.

"We saw your arrest."

"It was a misunderstanding," Warlock informed her. "Who is *we*?"

She shrugged. "Just some concerned citizens who want to know what a canine Crasii is doing roaming the streets of the Lebec slums without a collar or a shift, or any sign of a master. And why the City Watch would arrest him, and then let him go a few hours later after a visit from the Duke of Lebec."

They'd been watching him the whole time, he realised. "I have no master."

"You're a *freed* Crasii?" she asked sceptically.

"I just got out of prison," he told her, figuring there was no benefit in lying. It was not a skill that came easily to canines, anyway. "I came here to look for someone."

"Who?"

"A healer named Shalimar."

The girl didn't react, or give any indication she knew anybody by that name. He was a little disappointed, even though he understood the unlikelihood of the first canine he spoke to in Lebec being in any way connected with the male he was looking for.

"Did you find this Shalimar?"

"I was arrested before I could find anything."

"Which brings us back to why you got arrested, farm dog. And why they let you go."

"The City Watch thought there was something amiss with my pardon," he explained. "The duke came down to verify it was legitimate and then they let me go. There's nothing suspicious about it."

The girl seemed unconvinced. "If you know the Duke of Lebec well enough to score a pardon from him, farm dog," she informed Warlock, as she straightened her shift and brushed off the dust and debris of the laneway that had attached itself to her ginger tail, "then *suspicious* doesn't even begin to describe you."

He shook his head. "I don't know the duke at all. I was able to perform a service for his wife and she rewarded me by arranging a pardon." The story Duke Stellan had told the City Watch was plausible enough. Better yet, it sounded like the truth because he didn't have to hesitate before offering an explanation.

"What sort of service?"

"Excuse me?"

Her eyes narrowed. "What sort of *service* did you perform for the duchess?"

It took him a moment to realise what she was implying. Warlock was shocked. "You think I . . . and the duchess . . . that's disgusting!"

The young canine seemed anything but shocked by the notion. "Happens more often than you'd think, farm dog. There're whole brothels down here in the slums dedicated to selling dog meat to the masters who like to play a bit rough."

Warlock couldn't believe any canine could be so blasé about such a thing. "I have never done anything of the kind!" He squared his shoulders proudly. "I am Warlock, out of Bella, by Segura, and I would never shame my line!"

Unaccountably, the girl smiled. "My name is Boots," she said.

He glanced down at her, waiting for her to offer her lineage, but she seemed disinclined to reveal her family names.

"Where are you staying?" she asked, instead.

"Nowhere, really," he told her, a little puzzled why she hadn't volunteered the information about her sire and dam. Where Warlock came from, such a thing was considered the height of bad manners.

"I suppose you'd better come with me, then," she suggested, turning for the entrance of the lane. "You can stay at my place. Did you want something to eat? I could hear that stomach of yours rumbling from across the street."

Given how hungry he was and the musky scent of her, Warlock couldn't think of anything else he wanted more, but the offer was too casually offered to be genuine. Or maybe they just did things differently here in the city. The peaceful order of Lord Ordry's estate seemed very far from this alien place.

When she realised he wasn't following her, she stopped and looked at him over her shoulder. "What? My place not good enough for you, farm dog?"

"Why do you keep calling me that?"

"Because it sticks out a mile." She grinned suddenly. "And I don't just mean your rather impressive stud tackle, farm dog."

Warlock glanced down at his pelt in confusion. *"What?"*

"You're not wearing clothes." Boots rolled her eyes at his ignorance. "It might be all right to strut around his lordship's country estate in nothing but the coat the Mother gave you, but here in the big city, my naive friend, our masters aren't nearly so accommodating. To be honest, that's why we thought you were arrested."

"You followed me because I don't dress as you do?"

"You don't actually dress at all," she reminded him. "And for the record, I followed you because I was told to."

"By whom?"

"Someone who wants to meet the Crasii with the ear of the Duke of Lebec."

"I told you, I don't know him. I never met him before today."

"Which, at the very least, makes you one up on the rest of us, farm dog."

He frowned. "My name is Warlock."

"Out of Bella, by Segura," she finished for him with a smile. "I know. I heard you the first time. A word of advice, my friend. Around here, we're not so enamoured of our pedigrees as you are."

"It is who I am."

"Which is all well and good if you know who you are. Some of us don't have that luxury."

Warlock stared at her, shocked to realise she hadn't offered her line when she introduced herself because perhaps she didn't know it.

"I'm sorry . . . ," he stammered awkwardly. "I . . . I . . . didn't mean to draw attention to your . . . misfortune . . ."

Boots laughed. "*Misfortune?* Oh boy, they are just going to *love* you at the Kennel."

"What's the Kennel?"

"It's where I live," she told him. "Me and the other strays in the city."

"You have no master?"

"I'd hardly be roaming the streets of Lebec at this hour following you if I did, would I? You coming or not?"

Warlock hesitated, not at all sure if he could afford such a detour. He wanted to find Shalimar. He wanted a way out of Lebec City, not a home here. A slum kennel full of strays was about as far from that ambition as he could get.

Still, Boots was right. He was hungry and homeless and knew so little about the city he had left his clothes lying on the side of the road.

Besides, the smell of her was almost enough to make him forget any other purpose he might have. It irked Warlock a little to think that no matter how much education or breeding he had, he was still a canine Crasii and this female offering to take him back to her place was only days away from coming on heat.

Slowly, almost reluctantly, Warlock nodded. She turned toward the entrance of the lane again, glancing down the street each way before stepping out of the shadows. Warlock followed her, telling himself that going with Boots wasn't a bad idea.

Maybe someone at the Kennel had heard of Shalimar.

Chapter 46

The Kennel of the Lebec City slums proved to be to an old warehouse, originally intended as overflow grain storage, which had fallen into disuse when the northern part of the city had been expanded about eighty years ago to include a newer industrial sector. The building smelled musty and even now the cracks in the floorboards were filled with ancient mouldy grain dust. Warlock could hear rats scurrying out of their path as Boots led him through the darkness to the main hall, where the majority of the strays had made their home.

The hall reeked of other canines, gathered in small groups scattered all across the large warehouse in no discernable order. Suspicious stares followed them through the dim hall, and more than one male bared his teeth in Warlock's direction as they passed.

Finally they reached the centre of the warehouse where a large group of Crasii were gathered. At first, Warlock wondered if there was some sort of meeting going on, then he noticed the pups and the large number of nursing females in the group and realised this was just another family pack, although a remarkably large one.

"Rex?" Boots called, when they stopped on the edge of the pack. "I've someone I want you to meet."

A head appeared out of the gloom, looking around with bright, curious eyes. He spotted Boots and smiled, rising to his feet. The Crasii was small for a canine, not much bigger than a feline, and ugly, too. Warlock tried not to stare. He came from a world where short hair was preferred, pelts so smooth that from a distance humans couldn't tell if you had skin or fur. Rex was quite the opposite. Brown and black with no obvious pattern, he was shaggy to the point of being disreputable. His tail was stubby and almost hairless. It was no wonder he was living here in the slums as a stray. No human household would have kept on a Crasii with such an obvious deformity.

"Whoa!" he chuckled when he spied Warlock. "Boots has found herself a big new bone to play with!"

"He's the one you sent me to follow," she told Rex patiently.

"So you brought him *here*?" the Crasii asked as he disentangled himself from several pups clinging to his shins and stepped out of the circle of canines. "He's probably a plant sent here by the Watch to spy on us."

"I am no spy," Warlock objected, baring his teeth.

Rex smiled up at him. "Settle down, big fella. If Boots thinks you're all right, then you probably are. Although," he added thoughtfully, turning his attention to the young female, "given the way she smells at the moment, it might be the wrong end of her doing the thinking."

"He has a ducal pardon," Boots informed Rex, ignoring his crude suggestion. "He says the Watch pulled him in and called the duke down to the Watch-house to verify it."

"And how is his grace?" Rex enquired with a raised brow. "Been a while since he and I have had a chance to catch up."

"I never met him before tonight. I only knew his wife."

Rex frowned. "Seems Boots isn't the only one who found herself a big bone to play with."

"Lady Desean would never do something like that," Boots told Rex emphatically.

Warlock looked at her in surprise. "That's not what you implied when we first met. You made it seem you believed she and I—"

"I was checking your story," she cut in. "Any Crasii claiming to know the Duchess of Lebec would know she's on our side. Tides, she arranges for food to be served to the poor in the slums and actually comes here herself to help, sometimes. If you'd claimed you knew her because she was using you for favours, you'd be dead by now."

"But how could you possibly know if I was telling the truth?"

"Because I grew up at Lebec Palace," Boots informed him. "I know Lady Desean. And Duke Stellan."

Clearly, Warlock had underestimated this female. "What are you doing here?"

"Knowing them, liking them even, doesn't mean I want to be their slave."

Warlock nodded, thinking he understood the sentiment, even if he didn't really agree with it. He'd not left Lord Ordry's estate by choice. Had things worked out differently he'd still be there, probably the head steward by now. To think Boots had thrown away a prime living on an estate like Lebec Palace . . . it just didn't seem logical.

"So, what did you do to earn a pardon from the Duke of Lebec?" Rex asked.

"There was a suzerain incarcerated in Lebec Prison. Lady Desean was interrogating him. She wanted to know if the suzerain was telling the truth."

All about him, the Kennel stilled, as he spoke. Rex's eyes narrowed. "There was an immortal in Lebec Prison? Which one?"

"Cayal."

"The Immortal Prince," Rex spat, cursing softly. "Tides, how long has he been here?"

"In Glaeba? A couple of years, I gather. He was trying to get himself hanged, I think."

Boots laughed sourly. "What good would that do him? He's immortal."

"And not very happy about it, either," Warlock added, remembering the suzerain's depression. "I'm not sure what's going on with him. It's still Low Tide, I believe. Maybe he's bored and hadn't spent time in a prison before? Who knows?"

"That makes seven of them we know of," Rex remarked.

"Seven of what?"

"The suzerain," Boots explained. "We've been able to place seven of them, now. We don't know where the rest of them are."

Warlock studied his new friends in confusion. "You keep track of the Tide Lords?"

Rex nodded. "Of course we do. When the Tide turns a goodly portion of us are likely to fall under their influence again, my large and ignorant friend. If we know where they are, we can be elsewhere when it happens."

Suddenly, it all made sense.

"Hidden Valley," Warlock said.

"Pardon?"

"Hidden Valley," he repeated. "That's what it is. It's not a myth at all, is it? It's a place where Crasii can take refuge the next time the Tide turns and the immortals rise again."

"Your dam told you too many bedtime stories, son," Rex chuckled.

"Perhaps," he agreed. "Will you take me there?"

"To Hidden Valley?" Rex turned to Boots, highly amused. "You might need to keep this one on a leash, Boots. He's got the stud tackle to make a good mate, clear enough, but he's going to embarrass you in company if you let him open that big mouth of his."

Boots smiled. "I'll take care of him."

Rex reached up and patted Warlock on the shoulder. "There! You're all set now, lad. Boots will look after you.

And find you something to wear. We don't like to draw attention to ourselves down here, although, if I was built like that . . ." He let the sentence trail off, chuckling to himself as he turned back to his family, clambering over the females to get back to his place in the centre where he'd been playing with his pups when his visitors arrived.

"Come on," Boots said, tugging on Warlock's arm. "I'll show you where you can sleep."

He looked down at her with a frown, not in the least bit interested in sleep. "Do you know where Hidden Valley is?"

"We'll find you something to eat, too," she offered.

"You do, don't you?"

"Do you eat anything, or just meat?"

"Tell me about the suzerain then," he insisted. "Where are they?"

Boots sighed. "Let's go back to my box. We can talk there."

Realising that was as good an offer as he was likely to get, Warlock nodded and followed Boots deeper into the dark, reeking, cavernous warehouse to the ragged pile of furs she called home.

"We always know where Maralyce is," Boots explained once they were settled on her furs. She had some jerky tucked under a floorboard, which she shared with him, the leathery texture tasting like prime beef, he was so hungry. "She never moves and never causes us trouble. She's up in the mountains around the Valley of the Tides, somewhere, looking for gold, no doubt. Do you think she'll ever decide she's got enough wealth and start spending some of it?"

Warlock shrugged. "I don't know."

"Anyway, we think Brynden is in Torlenia, still. There's a monastery in the desert near Elvere where they still worship the Tide Lords and we think he's hiding there, posing as one of the monks."

"Is Kinta with him?"

Boots shrugged. "We don't know where she is, but she

might be nearby. They always seem to go together those two, regardless of whether the Tide is in or out."

"What of the others?"

"Medwen is in Senestra, living quietly in a village on the coast. And we think Krydence and Rance are hiding out in Caelum. There's a pair of brothers there running a circus, of all things. All the performers are Crasii and they'll perform some pretty amazing, not to mention absurdly dangerous, stunts, all on a simple word from the ringmasters. It's hard to be certain, because any one of us who gets too near them runs the danger of falling under their thrall, but we're pretty sure it's them."

"That's five," he reminded her. "You said you knew where seven of them are."

"Well, thanks to you, we know where Cayal is, now. Jaxyn is currently residing at Lebec Palace, posing as a member of some obscure Glaeban noble family."

Warlock was horrified. "But . . . Lady Desean said nothing . . ."

"How would she even know?"

"You knew, though," he concluded. "You said you came from there."

She nodded. "It's why I left. Jaxyn justifies his position at the palace by claiming he's an expert in handling the Crasii, so he got himself hired as the Kennel Master. It's really just because we were compelled to obey him that he looks so good at it. Couple of months ago the duke's niece unexpectedly arrived. Jaxyn sent for me, threw a tunic at me and announced I was going to be trained as Lady Kylia's housemaid. Instead of thanking him for the honour like a good little lapdog, I told him where he could shove his tunic and Lady Kylia with it. I'm not sure who was more surprised, him or me. I think it occurred to both of us at the same time that I must be a Scard."

"What did he do?"

"Well, nothing at the time. He couldn't afford to risk his position with the duke by killing a Crasii out of hand. He threw me in the confinement cells, of course, and I knew he'd come after me as soon as the duke or his wife weren't around to interfere. If it wasn't that day, it'd be another. So I ran away. It means there's a price on my head now, but better that than trapped in the power of a suzerain like Lord Jaxyn, even if it is Low Tide."

"Then the City Watch is looking for you?"

"Probably," she agreed, suddenly very cagey. "But they have a lot on their minds, so if I don't draw attention to myself . . ."

She let the sentence hang, leaving Warlock to wonder if she had paid off some corrupt Watchman to be left alone, or if there was something more sinister afoot. He sympathised with her need to escape the clutches of a suzerain, however. Having spent time across the hall from Cayal, he could imagine how terrifying it must be to find yourself in the power of a Tide Lord like Jaxyn. And Jaxyn *was* a Tide Lord, not just an immortal. His wrath was something to fear.

"Do you think the Tide will turn in our lifetime?" he asked, thinking it a safe enough question. Her scent was still driving him crazy but focussing on the danger the Tide Lords represented helped to distract him.

"Tides, I hope not."

"Cayal accused me of being a Scard, too," he told her.

She seemed pleased by the revelation. "Do you think he was right?"

"I'm beginning to hope so," he replied.

She smiled at him coyly, wrapping her gorgeous bushy tail around her legs, which did little to aid his self-control. There wasn't much point, he knew, making a move on her before she was ready. He'd seen males with their throats ripped out when they'd let their impatience get the better of them and tried to mate with a female who wasn't ready.

But Tides, the scent of her . . .

"Did you want some more jerky?"

He forced himself to concentrate on what she was saying. "Isn't this your only food?"

"We can find some more tomorrow outside the city

taverns," she assured him. "Someone your size should be able to scare away the competition easily enough."

"You rummage in *garbage* piles for food?" Even in Lebec Prison, he'd not been reduced to that.

"We do what we must to survive, Warlock," Boots told him, a little annoyed at his censorious tone. "You're not a house dog anymore, but . . . if you think you can do better without our help . . ."

"I'm sorry," he said hastily, anxious not to alienate her. "I don't mean to judge you."

"I should think not."

"Are we still friends?" What he was really asking was: *Do I still have a chance with you when you come on heat?* He wasn't fool enough to think Boots had befriended him solely out of the goodness of her heart. With her mating time approaching, it was likely her instincts were overriding her common sense. She couldn't help but seek out the most likely male partner, any more than he could resist the smell of her.

She scowled at him for a moment and then nodded. "I suppose."

"You won't regret it," he promised.

She smiled. They both knew he was talking about a great deal more than friendship.

Chapter 47

Arkady awoke, cold and stiff from a night spent on the ground, to discover Cayal standing on the rim of the ledge on which they were camped, his face turned to the sun, his arms outstretched, as if he could soak up the creeping dawn by sheer force of will.

Who are you really, Cayal? she wondered, as she watched him standing there, oblivious to her scrutiny. It was rare to catch him in such an unguarded moment. In the deepest recesses of her soul, Arkady knew she was close to admitting the truth about him. It was just so hard to let the dream go. Lies were such familiar things. Something you could control. The intricate web of falsehood surrounding Arkady was so familiar she didn't *want* to let it go. Lies were oddly comforting. A world she had constructed for herself, rather than dealing with the one she had been given.

How skewed has my world become, she asked herself, rubbing the sleep from her eyes, *when I would rather believe this man is a liar and murderer than admit he might be something I don't want to accept?*

"You're awake."

He lowered his arms and turned to look at her, his piercing blue eyes alight, as if he really had been soaking energy directly from the sun. Arkady grimaced. Immortal or not, nobody had a right to look so healthy first thing in the morning after spending the night on a wet, rocky, windswept ledge.

"Awake, am I? I rather thought I'd died and discovered there really is a hell."

Cayal shrugged. "I wouldn't know."

"Where are we going today?" she asked, pushing herself up painfully. She had a stone bruise under her right hip, her bladder felt set to burst and she was quite sure she'd never be truly warm or dry again as long as she lived.

"Same place we've always been going," he informed her. "We may even get there, if the weather holds."

"Can't you do something about the weather? Ah, that's right . . . ," she amended, answering her own question. "It's Low Tide. The magic's all gone."

"Strictly speaking, it's a Vanishing Tide," he corrected. "Low Tide is when it starts to come back."

"And when is that likely to happen?"

Cayal looked away. "Sooner than you think."

"But conveniently not in my lifetime, I suppose." Climbing to her feet, Arkady glanced around, looking for a suitable tree behind which she could relieve herself. She was far too civilised these days to feel comfortable about her need to perform perfectly normal bodily functions in the view of her fellow travellers, a reticence which, she feared, amused the feline Crasii no end.

"Not if you're lucky," Cayal told her with a frown. "But I fear you won't be. Over there."

"Pardon?"

He pointed to the small copse of trees clinging to the ledge behind her. "There's a tree over there where you can relieve yourself. And never fear, my lady, I'll make sure the Crasii don't disturb you."

Arkady felt herself blushing. "Oh . . . Thank you."

"You're welcome." Cayal smiled, but mostly because he was trying not to laugh at her, she suspected. "Let me know when you're ready to leave. I'd like to press on. I want to reach our destination in daylight."

"And what is our destination?" she asked for perhaps the hundredth time since he kidnapped her, resisting the undignified temptation to cross her legs.

To her astonishment, he answered her this time. "I'm going to take you to meet a friend of mine."

She raised her brow. "You actually have *friends*?"

"One or two."

"Does this friend have a name?"

"Maralyce."

She'd heard that name before. In Tilly's Tarot. "Isn't she part of the Tarot?"

Cayal sighed the same way he did whenever she mentioned the Tarot. "Actually, she's a person, but do be sure to tell her you thought she was a playing card when you meet her. That should amuse the grumpy old bitch no end."

Arkady glared at him. "You deliberately misunderstand me . . ."

He shrugged unrepentantly. "I know. I know. I'm a bastard. Why don't you go find a tree before you burst? I'll get the Crasii to rustle up some breakfast."

The urgent call of nature won over Arkady's desire to

argue about it. Turning rather more stiffly than she would have liked in order to maintain her dignity, she strode into the copse of trees, putting Cayal, the Crasii and the impossibility of her situation out of mind in order to concentrate on more mundane, but far more urgent, necessities.

About two hours after midday, the almost invisible track they'd been following suddenly widened into a navigable road. The road was well-concealed amid the tall, ubiquitous pines that blanketed the Shevron Mountains, in the shelter of which lurked countless small pockets of unmelted snow, clinging determinedly to the shadows of the hidden nooks and crannies, defying the persistent rain. From a distance, Arkady mused idly as they rode ever higher, it looked as if someone had split a giant feather pillow over the mountain and scattered the contents beneath the trees. She smiled privately at the mental image, wondering what had become of her hard-won academic scepticism.

Once I refused to even contemplate the idea an immortal might exist. Now I'm imagining giant pillow fights.

She glanced at Cayal, riding slightly ahead of her, wondering if it was the Immortal Prince who had wrought such a change in her, or something she'd done to herself. Now they were on the wider path, they no longer rode in single file. Cayal had fallen back a little and rode on her right. She could see him in profile, but guessed she was just beyond the edge of his peripheral vision, which meant she could study him without being observed herself.

He's still clean-shaven, she realised, even though they'd been on the road now for more than five days. There was no shadow of stubble on his face. She wondered what that meant. *Had he shaved the day he became immortal, and that was how he was preserved?* Given everything else he had told her about immortality, it seemed the most likely answer. *Fortunate too,* she mused, *that he was immortalised in his prime.* There might not have been a divine hand at work in his selection, but nature had surely chosen

well, if she was looking to save a sample of her work.
Such symmetry of form was rare and even Arkady, who
lived surrounded by beautiful things, was forced to concede that Cayal would stand out wherever he went—
immortal or not.

Such musing had a dangerous side effect, however, and
Arkady tried to push away the thoughts, once she started
to dwell a little too intensely on Cayal's physical attributes. For all that she'd spent much of her life keeping her
emotions firmly in check, Arkady was a woman in her
prime. She still remembered the first time she saw Cayal.
It wasn't the reek of Recidivists' Row, the chill of the
stonework, the gloom of the cells that stuck in her mind.
What she remembered most vividly was Cayal opening
his eyes and turning to look at her.

That look had shocked her, it was so intense, so openly
wanting, so full of naked desire she'd almost recoiled in
shock. It had only lasted a second or two, and then he'd
blinked and awoken fully and the moment had passed.

Arkady had lain awake at night, wondering what it
meant, cursing herself for a fool, wishing she were still
naive enough to believe any man would ever gaze at her
like that in this lifetime and mean it. Arkady knew the
look wasn't meant for her. Cayal had been dreaming. That
look, that desire, was meant for someone else, someone in
his dreams.

Amaleta, perhaps? The lover spoken of in the Tarot?

Arkady wished she knew. She wished she were game
enough to ask him about it.

After perhaps three miles or so, the road widened again,
for a short time and then narrowed once more. It was at
this point that Cayal called a halt to their progress. The
path ahead led into the trees, then curved away to the left,
disappearing amid the dense foliage.

"Is something wrong, my lord?" Chikita asked as Cayal
dismounted.

"The duchess and I will proceed on foot from here," he
announced. "You'll be our escort, Chikita. The rest of you,

set a perimeter and don't let anything come up this road behind us unless I order it, is that clear?"

The felines nodded, and began to dismount. Arkady stared at them, still not certain she believed this unswerving obedience of her Crasii to a perfect stranger.

"You up for a walk?" Cayal asked, turning his back on the felines.

"Where are we going?"

"To meet Maralyce."

Arkady swung her leg over the pommel of her saddle and let Cayal help her dismount. His hands were strong as he lifted her down, his face so close to hers she could count the fine pores on his skin. Blushing, she looked away. Cayal held her for a moment longer than absolutely necessary and then let her go, turning to issue more orders to the other felines about organising their camp.

After another half-hour on foot, Cayal, Arkady and Chikita reached their destination, which proved to be a small but sturdy miner's cottage built into the lee of a small cliff, over which the snow-capped peak of a mountain loomed. They smelled the wood smoke before they rounded the last bend, so Arkady wasn't surprised when they finally arrived. The encampment spoke of long habitation, numerous bits of broken mining equipment Arkady couldn't name lying discarded in the trampled, muddy yard.

The cottage on the left, with two shuttered windows, faced the yard and a forge beside it. On the right was the entrance to a mine, shored up by wooden planking that looked set to topple at any moment. Coming from the forge was the rhythmic sound of metal banging on metal, which echoed off the cliff behind the house, making the mountain air ring with its metallic song.

Arkady looked around, wondering why anybody would live voluntarily in such an isolated place as Cayal stopped and waited, motioning her and the Crasii to do the same. He said nothing, and did nothing, content to wait until they were noticed. Chikita seemed unaccountably nervous, the hair on her neck standing up, her claws unsheathed, her tail twitching uneasily.

After a time, the banging stopped, and a moment or two later, a figure emerged from the forge. At first glance, it was hard to determine gender, but as she stepped into the yard, a small sledgehammer in her right hand, it was clear the figure was female. Her leather apron was stained with scorch marks, her unruly salt and pepper hair braided impatiently and tucked behind her ears. Her face was streaked with soot and her demeanour was anything but welcoming.

"Hello, Maralyce," Cayal said.

The woman studied the three of them for a moment and then shook her head. She seemed to be in her forties, but it was mostly her hair that created the impression. Her skin was unlined, her body straight and lithe under her shapeless miner's clothes.

"Well, well, well. Look what the cat dragged in." Maralyce stared at Chikita and added with a frown, "Literally."

"Is that any way to greet an old friend?"

Maralyce shrugged. "Dunno. Bring me an old friend and we'll see how it goes."

Cayal seemed unsurprised by this less-than-enthusiastic welcome. "It's good to see you too, Maralyce."

"What do you want, Cayal?"

He smiled ingenuously. "Would you believe nothing more than the pleasure of your esteemed company?"

Maralyce's eyes narrowed suspiciously as she glared at them, the lengthening shadows and the chilly breeze eating into the little warmth Arkady had managed to engender with the walk here. Whatever gripe Cayal had with Maralyce, Arkady hoped he resolved it quickly. That cottage looked very cosy.

"Just a coincidence, I suppose," the old woman remarked sourly, "that I felt a glimmer of the Tide this morning for the first time in a millennium and then miraculously, you turn up?"

"I felt it too," Cayal admitted. "And oddly enough, yes, it is nothing more than a coincidence."

"Then you're in trouble again, aren't you?" Maralyce snorted. "Who's after you this time?"

"Why do you think that's the only reason I came to see you?" Cayal put his hand over his heart. "You wound me, Maralyce."

"If only I could," the old woman grumbled, turning for the cottage. "Get rid of that Crasii abomination, and I might let you inside for some tea. You'll have to make your own, mind you. I have work to do."

Cayal turned to Chikita. "Return to the others. Send word the moment you sense any sign of pursuit."

The Crasii saluted and turned for the road, obviously pleased to be getting away from this place. Arkady watched her leave, shivering a little as the sun sank below the trees.

"And who are you?" the old woman demanded of Arkady.

"My name is Arkady Desean."

Maralyce paid her no further mind as she pushed the door to the cottage open. It was dark inside but much warmer out of the wind. The old woman dropped the sledgehammer on the rough-hewn table, fetched a lamp from the mantel over the banked coals and then struck a flint and lit it, filling the small cabin with a warm yellow glow.

Then Maralyce turned and squinted at Arkady in the lamplight. "You're not his lover, are you?"

Arkady shook her head, more than a little taken aback by the question. "No!"

"Good," the old woman exclaimed grumpily. "The last time he got excited over a girl, the whole damn world suffered for it."

"Shut up, you old hag," Cayal told her pleasantly.

"Shut up yourself, Cayal," she retorted. "You'd better stir the fire up. Your little friend there's so cold she looks like she's freezing her tits off. You'll be replacing any firewood you burn, though," she added, "so don't get too good a blaze going in here unless you plan to spend the next few days chopping wood."

Cayal smiled. "Go dig for your wretched gold, you grumpy old hag, and leave us in peace. And never fear, I'll chop your wood for you, if you're too feeble to manage it yourself."

There was a note of affection in Cayal's banter that even Arkady could hear, and Maralyce, for all her brusque and unwelcoming manner, was obviously aware of it. She wouldn't admit it though, at least not in front of a stranger. Instead, Maralyce grunted something unintelligible, lifted the sledgehammer from the table and left the cabin, slamming the door behind her.

Arkady watched her leave and then turned to Cayal. "What did she mean?"

"What did who mean?"

"Maralyce," she told him, as he began to stoke the fire, certain he was deliberately misunderstanding her. "When she asked if I was your lover?"

"Nothing."

"Are you actually capable of telling the truth?" she asked, curiously. "Is mendaciousness one of those 'unexpected side effects of immortality' you're always telling me about?"

"I've never lied to you, Arkady." Cayal continued to work on the fire, refusing to look at her. "I just don't happen to want to talk about it, that's all."

"Was it so painful?"

This time he looked up, but he seemed vaguely amused, rather than angry. "Do you fancy sharing the intimate details of all your relationships with a virtual stranger?"

Arkady hesitated. She'd never actually been in love, not the way Cayal meant. But she'd had her share of sexual encounters and in that respect he was right. She didn't want to talk about them.

"I'm sorry. I shouldn't pry. I can't help myself sometimes."

"I noticed," Cayal agreed. "Hungry?"

"A little."

"Let's see what sort of larder Maralyce keeps, shall we? I have to warn you, it may not be much. She forgets to eat, sometimes for years at a time."

As it turned out, Maralyce had been eating quite well of late and there was more than enough for an ample meal in her larder. Cayal cooked up the last of the venison hanging in the pantry, chopping it into a stew, adding carrots and parsnips and a few other root vegetables Arkady hadn't eaten since she was a child.

The small miner's cabin was cosy, lit by brass lamps and the cook fire. Several thousand years was plenty of time to find and plug all the possible draught sources in a two-roomed cabin that would fit comfortably inside the dining room of Lebec Palace, she supposed. Her eyes heavy, Arkady could feel the cold seeping out of her as the hot food and snug cabin enveloped her in their simple, homely comforts.

"Go to bed, Arkady, or you'll fall asleep in your stew."

It was dark outside, a soft rain pattering against the shutters. Her limbs felt weighed down with fatigue. "I suppose I should. You cook very well, by the way."

"Years of practice," he reminded her. "When you're immortal, eventually you get good at everything."

"Is there anything you've yet to master?" she asked. It was so much easier not to argue about it.

"Death," he replied unsmilingly.

"Besides that."

"I've nothing left that I want to do."

"Except die?"

"You're mocking me now."

"I'm too tired to mock you, Cayal. I'm too tired to think."

"Then go to bed. Maralyce won't mind your sleeping in her bed. She doesn't use it much."

Too exhausted to argue, Arkady rose to her feet, weary beyond imagining, and stumbled into the other room, collapsing onto the fur-covered platform with relief. She took the time to unlace her boots and kick them off, discarding her jacket too, thinking the furs looked warm enough to keep her snug, even if she were naked. Closing her heavy eyes, strangely secure in the tiny cabin, Arkady pulled the furs up to her chin and drifted off to sleep.

Arkady wasn't sure what woke her. It was still dark, and although she was tired, the crippling fatigue she'd experienced earlier was gone. Silently, she pushed off the bed and wandered barefoot back into the other room. The lamps were extinguished and the fire had burned down low. Cayal was sitting on the floor by the hearth, staring into the flames. Carefully opening the door that separated the two rooms, she stopped and watched him for a time, his profile painted gold by the firelight.

"Is he handsome?" Arkady remembered Kylia asking once.

Kylia would not be disappointed by Cayal, the Immortal Prince, Arkady thought.

She must have moved, or made some sound that alerted him to her presence. He glanced up, hurriedly wiping his eyes.

Arkady was stunned to realise Cayal had been weeping.

"Cayal? Are you all right?"

He looked away, knuckling his eyes with his fists, embarrassed to be caught in such a moment of weakness. "Go back to bed, Arkady."

She crossed the small room to the fire, squatting down beside him. "Cayal . . ."

"Leave me alone."

"Is something wrong?"

To her surprise, Cayal laughed bitterly. *"Wrong?* Is something *wrong*? You really don't understand what happens when the Tide turns, do you?"

"Then explain it to me."

"I have explained it to you, Arkady. You don't believe me."

"I don't *want* to believe you, Cayal. There's a difference."

"You're afraid," he concluded, in a tone that struck Arkady as odd.

She nodded. "Is it that obvious?"

"In you? Not really. But it's the main thing that separates you and me, Arkady. You are able to fear."

His arrogance was so predictable it was almost amusing. "And you're not afraid of anything, I suppose?"

"What is there to be afraid of?" He shrugged. "I'm immortal and all human terror has the fear of dying at its root."

"That's an absurd generalisation!"

"Is it? Think about it for a moment. A person isn't afraid of heights as such—they're actually afraid of falling to their death. And nobody is really frightened of spiders, they're afraid of being bitten and dying from the bite. Even a child lying to his mother over the smallest little thing isn't lying out of fear he'll be caught. It's because he's afraid—deep down—of angering a parent. When your very survival depends on your mother's goodwill, losing her protection can be fatal."

"And if you're *not* afraid of dying, you're not human anymore. Is that what you believe?" She studied his profile in the firelight, a little surprised to realise he was serious. "Do you think you're not human?"

"I know it," he replied with bitter certainty. "Hell! I can even pinpoint the moment when the last shred of humanity I owned deserted me. Immortality doesn't confer forgetfulness on you, unfortunately."

"And when was that?"

He shook his head. "It doesn't matter."

"Yes, it does matter. You want me to believe you. So tell me something I *can* believe, not something you think I want to hear."

"Like what?"

Arkady wasn't expecting that. She thought on it for a

moment, as she sat beside him on the floor, and then remembered Maralyce's earlier comment about being
Cayal's lover.

"Amaleta," she said. "Tell me about Amaleta."

"Why do you want to know about her?"

"Wasn't she supposed to be the great love of your life?"

"No."

"But the Tarot says . . ."

He smiled wanly. "I thought by now we'd established
that your Tarot cards are a load of flanking old manure,
Arkady."

"Then how did the story come about?"

He leant forward to stoke up the fire, the flames grabbing at the fresh firewood as he exposed the underbelly of
red-hot coals to the air. "Same as all the others, I suppose.
Someone took a grain of truth, passed it on to a dozen
other people who got it arse-about and turned it into a legend."

"Will you tell me what really happened?"

He eyed her sceptically over his shoulder. "Will you believe me?"

She nodded slowly. "Yes, Cayal. I think I will."

He sat back on his heels. "Why do you want to know
what happened to Amaleta?"

"I want to understand you."

"Even if it means you may not like me after you hear
that particular story?"

Arkady smiled. "What makes you think I like you
now?"

Cayal studied her in the firelight for a moment longer.
And then he said something that took her completely by
surprise. "You remind me of someone I knew once, you
know."

"Someone you loved?" she asked, wondering why she
would even think such a thing, let alone say it aloud.

Fortunately, Cayal didn't seem to think the question
odd. "It was someone who betrayed me, actually."

"Oh."

With the fire blazing, Cayal sat himself down on the floor beside her again, smiling at her expression. "If it's any consolation, Gabriella was very beautiful."

"But ultimately treacherous?"

"Yes."

Arkady raised a brow at him. "I remind you of Gabriella?"

He nodded. "To a disturbing degree."

She frowned. "I'm not sure how I feel about that."

"Neither am I." There was an uncomfortable moment of silence between them and then Cayal turned to stare at the fire.

Certain she'd gotten too close to something painful, she smiled apologetically, hoping to make a joke of it. "You were going to tell me about Amaleta. She didn't betray you too, did she?"

"Quite the opposite," he said, looking into the flames. "I betrayed her."

She wasn't expecting that. Gently, Arkady reached out and put her hand over his. "Tell me what really happened, Cayal."

So he did.

Chapter 48

You want to know if I loved Amaleta? I hope it's not going to disappoint you too much if I tell you I didn't. Tides, I never even slept with her. She was caught up in events that resulted in your wretched legend, surely enough, but she was the sideshow, not the main event.

My first meeting with Amaleta and its dire consequences began with another event, which at the time seemed far more important. It began with a proclamation, bland and heartless, made in the great hall of the rebuilt palace in Tenacia.

"The child has to die."

I think I flinched when Syrolee spoke, closing my eyes, as she finally said aloud what everyone else in the hall was undoubtedly thinking. A whimper of protest escaped Arryl's lips, but the Empress of the Five Realms remained unmoved. Syrolee's bright, bird-like eyes fixed on each of us present in the vast hall, daring us to defy her.

By then, Syrolee had dispensed with the white powdered make-up she'd favoured when I first met her. These days her eyes were the focus of everyone's attention. Outlined in kohl and shaded with a glittering shadow made of crushed beetles' wings, they looked like two deep orbs of malevolent darkness set in a cruel, sallow face.

Funny the things you remember about the past. I recall the air in the hall was heavy with the scent of jasmine, making it hard to concentrate, which might be why it sticks in my mind.

"You'd kill an innocent child for the crime of being able to touch the Tide?" Diala asked.

I turned in time to see Diala appear at the other end of the hall. I remember what she was wearing, perhaps because she was dressed in the formal, flame-red robes she and her sister adopted for their order around that time. Her dark hair was caught up in a jewelled coronet, and bracelets of garnet and carnelian encircled both wrists. A surge of unreasonable resentment always wells up in me at the sight of her, which surprises me even now.

You'd think I'd be long past feeling anything for Diala.

"I don't recall anyone asking your opinion on the matter," Rance remarked, as Diala strode the long length of the hall toward the empress and the small gathering around the throne dais. "Or inviting you to intrude upon a family gathering." His voice echoed faintly off the marble pillars supporting the gilded dome high above us, giving it a resonance it didn't deserve.

"But I *am* a member of this unique little family, Rance," Diala replied with a venomous smile. "We're all in this together. 'Til the end of time. I'm entitled to my opinion."

"It's the irritating assumption that everyone *else* is entitled to it that seems to be the issue here," Krydence remarked sourly.

Diala ignored him, stopping in front of Syrolee's throne. Engarhod was absent, but then the emperor often is when there are awkward decisions to be made. Somewhere between my immolation, the destruction of Magreth, and several peaks and ebbs of the Tide, the priestesses responsible for the Eternal Flame and the Empress of the Five Realms had had a falling out. I don't know the details, but there's no love lost between the women these days. Their animosity was such that Arryl and Diala had even gone so far as moving to another continent by then, taking the Eternal Flame with them. They were settled in Glaeba; their temple and the precious flame they guarded perched on the edge of a small hill overlooking the Great Valley.

Ironically, it was their presence in Tenacia that had precipitated this current crisis. A Scard attack on the caravan bringing Arryl and Diala to the palace via their grand tour of the major cities of Tenacia had been thwarted by magic, wielded not by a Tide Lord, but by one of our own—one of our mortal offspring. Given the carelessness with which we Tide Lords spilled our seed back then, it was anybody's guess whose child Fliss actually was, but that didn't lessen our problem. If anything, it made the decision to be rid of the child even harder.

Any man in the room might have fathered her.

Her parentage was the least of Diala's concerns. "On the contrary, Syrolee, this issue concerns my sister and me a great deal. We were there, remember."

"An unfortunate accident I would have done a great deal to have prevented."

Diala smiled, an edge of malice in her dark eyes. "How awkward for you, Syrolee. If the child had been killed in the attack, you'd never have discovered there was something wrong with her. The poor child survives it, and now you're going to kill her anyway."

Arryl let out another wordless cry of protest. She looked haggard. Distraught. The only one among us displaying any obvious emotion, Arryl was perhaps the last of us left with any human compassion.

"We have no need of your help, Diala," Elyssa declared. "Or your counsel."

Poor Elyssa . . . I know she was responsible for the Crasii. I know she's a whining, vindictive little bitch, but you can't help but feel sorry for her. Even with all her power she never gets it right. That day, as I recall, she was dressed like her mother, somehow making the elegant drape of her gown look awkward and ungainly. Neither had she mastered Syrolee's trick with eye make-up. Her eyes just looked as if someone had blacked both of them with a fist.

But she'd gained a lot of confidence since the Crasii were created and now fancied her opinion held significant value.

"Don't you, Elyssa?" Diala asked, no more able to stand Elyssa than the rest of us who weren't actually related to her. "How many more have slipped by, I wonder? How many more of these abominations do you unknowingly harbour in the palace creche?"

"Fliss is not an abomination!" Arryl objected.

"She's actually quite talented," Jaxyn remarked, from his seat on the edge of the dais. "It would be a shame to just destroy her out of hand."

I frowned at Jaxyn's comment. Hearing that sleazy little reprobate defend the girl in question was vaguely ominous. Jaxyn had no interest in the child that I knew of. No more than any other man in the hall, at any rate.

"Syrolee is right, though," Rance agreed. "If anything, knowing how strong Fliss might be merely reinforces the argument that the child should be destroyed."

"What say you, O Immortal Prince?" Syrolee asked.

She looked across the hall at me. "What do you think we should do with the child?"

I was listening to the argument from the balcony, hoping nobody would include me in the discussion. A futile hope, it proved. I turned to face them. "I think it would be foolish to kill her."

Arryl stifled a whimper of relief at my words.

"Why?" the empress demanded.

"Because she can't actually harm us . . . not in the long run. Your fear is for your political position here in Tenacia, not that she might represent some sort of threat to the Tide Lords. Besides, this is the first time we've discovered a mortal child actually able to wield Tide Magic; one that we know of, at any rate. I think you should find out why, not just destroy her out of hand because she's different."

"Her death can be made to look like an accident," Rance suggested calmly. "It would certainly be better for all concerned if those pompous fools in Torlenia never found out it was deliberate."

"Rance . . . *no!*" Arryl cried. "How can you even suggest killing a child in cold blood?"

"She's a mongrel, Arryl. The sooner you accept that, the better for everyone."

Syrolee turned to her eldest stepson, looking for his support. "Krydence?"

He shrugged uncertainly. "I don't know what to advise. If the child really can wield Tide magic, then maybe Cayal is right. We ought to learn something about how this odd thing happened, I suppose."

I didn't like the sound of that. Not only was it rare for Krydence to agree with me, the last time the Tide Lords had decided to "learn something about how an odd thing happened," it resulted in the Crasii.

"If we're going to kill her, it'll have to be dealt with quickly and quietly," Tryan suggested, leaning on the side of his mother's throne. Given a choice, he'd be sitting in Engarhod's empty place, and often did when his stepbrothers weren't around. We'd come to a sort of uneasy

truce by then. I still hadn't forgiven him for what he did in
Kordana, but there was now a chain of unstable islands
where Magreth and their wretched palace had once been,
so I figured we were pretty much even. "Krydence is right,
Mother. We can't risk news of this reaching Torlenia."

And Medwen, was my unspoken addendum. We Tide
Lords have long memories and this was a mere decade or
two after Medwen's child was taken from her. The child
was long dead, of course. She'd been impregnated with a
Crasii as soon as she was old enough and died in child-
birth. I'd been able to establish that much since arriving in
Tenacia.

What I hadn't done was tell Medwen about it.

It was cowardly of me, I know, but how do you tell a
mother something like that? It was easier to keep up the
charade with Syrolee and the others that I'd heard about
the Crasii and was interested enough in having a slave
race to cater to my every whim to donate my seed. They
believed me, too.

I suppose when you're essentially without morals of
your own, it's easy enough to believe others are like that,
too.

Did I sleep with numberless slave girls while I was in
Tenacia with the sole aim of impregnating them so the
Crasii farms could blend their unborn children with ani-
mals in Elyssa's bizarre experiments?

Certainly.

Could I tell you their names?

Not a one.

Did I rape them?

Probably, although I'm vain enough to think I'm a considerate lover and that I was able to make it a less traumatic experience than the others might have done. Besides, taking a
woman by force strikes me as being far too much effort for
the reward involved.

I don't know if it made the slightest difference to the
women they sent me—none of whom was a volunteer—
other than not being sent back to the farms covered in

bruises, but it allowed me to live with myself, which is an important consideration when there is no alternative.

Regardless of how I've managed to justify what I did to myself since then, the fact is, when one is in Tenacia, one does as the Tenacians do. I was a spy, after all, and my cover included having to give the impression I fully supported this bizarre plan to create blended animal slave races and was willing to do whatever it took, to help the cause.

I did warn you this wasn't a particularly noble time in my life, didn't I?

I understood why they feared the news reaching Torlenia, all too well. Over something like this, Medwen's grief at the disappearance of her long-dead child would stir to anger and probably stir Brynden and Kinta along with it. Brynden is as powerful a Tide Lord as any of us, prone to championing noble causes and not too concerned about the cost in ordinary human lives in order to set things right. While I'm not suggesting for a moment that Syrolee or any of the others gave a fig about saving mere human lives, wars are messy, expensive and disruptive. Don't mistake our reluctance to fight for anything other than what it is—expedience.

We go out of our way to avoid wars because they're impractical.

I had my own reasons for hoping news didn't filter back to Torlenia, not the least of which was the fact that I'd come here two decades ago to gain intelligence for my friends and never actually returned with the information they wanted.

"We?" Arryl echoed. "When did this become *our* problem, Tryan? You're the ones who caused this calamity, you and your sick experiments—messing with nature just to see what sort of beasts you can make." Suddenly, she turned on me. "What about you, Cayal? Are you just going to stand by and let them kill an innocent child?"

I shrugged, wishing I'd had the sense to stay out of this argument. I could have ignored Syrolee's summons to the throne room. In hindsight, I probably should have. "Been to a Crasii farm lately? What's one more dead mortal, give or take?"

"But this isn't Crasii magic!" Arryl insisted. "Fliss isn't a deliberate blend of two species. She's a Tidewatcher! The only crime this child is guilty of—this child who happens to be the daughter of one of you, incidentally—is trying to do the right thing."

"This child killed thirteen people, Arryl," Syrolee reminded her.

"They were Scards, and she saved the life of every mortal in our entourage, too, don't forget that!"

Syrolee shook her head impatiently. "The mortals Fliss saved are of no consequence. The child threatens to undermine everything we've worked for. Cayal is right about that much. People believe the Tide Lords, and *only* the Tide Lords, can manipulate the Tide, and our power over them rests firmly on that premise. If word gets out a mortal has the same ability, our authority will be seriously eroded."

I was tempted to point out the mortal belief that all immortals could manipulate the Tide was likely to be far more damaging if it got about that they couldn't, but decided to hold my tongue. I was a fool for coming here in the first place. No need to compound the error by getting caught up in the argument.

"Even if you think it foolish sentiment," Jaxyn added, "if we *don't* kill this accursed child, Arryl, what in the name of the Tides are we supposed to do with her?"

"We *will* kill her," the Empress of the Five Realms announced. "And then we test all the other children in the creche and kill any others who might display the same ability. Let that be the end of it."

Syrolee looked at each one of us in turn, until we all nodded our agreement. Even Arryl agreed in the end. A trace of compassion she might have, but she still inevitably bows to Syrolee's wishes when it comes to the crunch, and probably always will. Diala's reasons for agreeing were somewhat different, I suspect. In truth, she probably cared little for the fate of Fliss. She just enjoyed the chance to argue with Syrolee whenever the occasion presented itself.

"Then that just leaves the question of who's going to do it?" Tryan said.

"I will!" Elyssa volunteered. "Never could stand the little brat, anyway."

"No," I said heavily, not sure why I volunteered. "I will."

"You?" Tryan asked, clearly sceptical of the offer.

I shrugged and met his gaze without flinching. "Like I said, Tryan, what's one more dead mortal, give or take?"

"Cayal!" Arryl called, falling in beside me on the shaded path as I was heading back toward the palace guest quarters. The air was warm and the magnificent gardens in full bloom. I can't tell you what flowers they were, but I do remember they were blooming. Syrolee likes her flowers and many of the plants that crowded the carefully tended walkways were magically encouraged to flower, despite the fact that beyond the walls of the palace the rest of Tenacia had, until recently, been caught in the grip of a particularly savage winter.

"Arryl."

"Are you really going to do this?"

"Syrolee was right, you know," I told her, deciding avoidance was better than confrontation. "You should go back to Glaeba. This is none of your concern." Refusing to be drawn any further on the matter, I kept on walking.

Behind me, Arryl folded her arms stubbornly. "That's not what I asked you, Cayal."

I stopped and turned to look at her. Arryl and Diala have the same eyes, although there the similarity between the sisters ends. It's a pity really, that I was at odds with her. I have none of the animosity for Arryl that I have for her sister. "Look . . . I agree it's not very fair . . ."

"But you're still going to kill her, aren't you?"

I shrugged. "Somebody has to. At least I'll do it cleanly

and I won't gain any particular joy from the act, which is more than I can say for a few others around here."

She studied me for a time, her expression puzzled. "What are you doing here, Cayal?"

"What do you mean?"

"It's a straightforward question. Why are you here in Tenacia? You don't like Syrolee and Engarhod. You can't stand Elyssa. You're perpetually at odds with Krydence and Rance and I'm certain you'd nail Tryan to a wall if you thought you could manage it. You and Jaxyn haven't traded a civil word in a hundred years, and I'm damn sure they still haven't forgiven you for what happened after you decapitated Pellys. So why are you here?"

"This place is no better or worse than any other place," I said. "And as someone pointed out to me once, it's a lot of work being a deity. It's much easier to ride in the wake of people who enjoy doing this sort of thing."

"You never used to be such a cynic."

"We're all cynics, Arryl. Every one of us."

Arryl didn't disagree with me, but she wouldn't easily concede the point, either. "Cynic or not, Cayal, Fliss is just a baby. Even if you're callous enough to stand by and watch the Crasii being made without being sick, how can you kill a baby in cold blood?"

"Babies don't wield Tide magic and kill people with it," I pointed out. I didn't really want to fight with Arryl but there was no point in her harbouring false hopes for the child. For once, I thought Syrolee was right. A mortal able to wield Tide magic was just too dangerous. "It's bad enough that some of us can influence the Tide. Do you really want mortals to be able to do it, too?"

"Would they be any less dangerous than us?" she asked.

"Probably worse," I replied. "We, at least, don't have to worry about running out of time."

She shook her head obstinately. "I don't see the difference. We're not gods."

"To mortals we might as well be."

"More's the pity."

She wasn't going to let this go, I realised with despair. "Have you any idea how strong that child is? Forget the fact that she killed more than a dozen Scards, and she's only—in your words—a baby. She can swim almost as deep into the Tide as I can. I dread to think what she'll be capable of when she matures. Throw in a bit of mortal impatience with that mix and the safest thing for everyone on Amyrantha might be to kill her now and to hell with the consequences."

"Fliss can't help what she is, Cayal."

"She could be the biggest threat this world has faced since *we* came along," I warned.

"Or she might be our salvation," Arryl retorted.

I shook my head, convinced that, however unpalatable the act, killing this six-year-old girl might be the most sensible thing I'd done in years.

"What do you want, Cayal, not to do this thing?"

"Arryl, if I don't kill her, I'll never hear the end of it. And one of the others would simply do it instead."

She glared at me. "What's more important, Cayal? Your reputation or your daughter's life?"

I shook my head, smiling at her. "You can't play the guilt hand on me, Arryl. You don't know whose child she is."

"Yes, I do."

"It won't work," I warned, turning my back on her. "Nice try, though."

"Elyssa keeps records," Arryl informed me as I walked away. "She doesn't tell you or the others about them for precisely the reason we're standing here now."

Suddenly filled with trepidation, I stopped and turned to stare at her.

"Fliss is your child, Cayal. Alita was fathered by Krydence. Nilaba was fathered by Jaxyn and Travus is Rance's son. Tryan hasn't fathered a Tidewatcher in years, but Elyssa's waiting for the most opportune time to tell Syrolee. I don't think she's annoyed enough at her brother right now, to do anything about it."

"How do you know she keeps records?" I asked, hoping

Arryl was wrong, even while knowing she probably wasn't. Arryl isn't the liar among us. She's the one who picks beaten travellers up off the road and nurses them back to health.

"I've seen them."

"I don't believe you."

"Yes, you do," she said, stepping a little closer. "That's why you volunteered to do this dreadful thing yourself."

"Now you really *are* imagining things."

"Even if you don't see the physical resemblance in the child, I still believe you offered to do this, Cayal, because in your heart, you suspect the truth."

"We're Tide Lords, Arryl. We no longer have hearts."

"That's not true."

"Visit a Crasii farm sometime," I suggested. "That should convince you."

She reached out to touch my face. "I'm only trying to help you, Cayal."

"Why?" I demanded, jerking away.

She lowered her arm, studying me intently. "Because you're one of the few who's not totally lost."

"Really? How can you tell?"

"You take no pleasure in killing."

"Are you sure about that?"

"Yes."

"You're wrong, Arryl," I said. "You're wrong about everything. Fliss isn't my child and I'm no better than any other fool in this Tide-forsaken place. Don't make me out to be something you'd like me to be, rather than what I am."

She studied me for a moment longer and then shrugged, clearly disappointed by my response. "Then I apologise, Cayal, for my mistake in thinking you had some shred of humanity left in you. I suppose you're not interested in my plan for saving Fliss, either. Do have fun murdering your own child, won't you?"

She turned on her heel and headed back along the brick

path, but had only taken three steps before I sighed, shaking my head.

"*Arryl!*".

"Yes?" she enquired, glancing over her shoulder, as if she had no notion as to why I was calling her back.

"What plan?" I asked.

Chapter 49

"Are you going to tell me you actually killed that poor child?" Arkady asked when Cayal's voice faltered just on dawn. The fire had burned down to coals again, but she was warm enough, sitting close beside him on the floor near the hearth. At some point, she'd rested her head on his shoulder and closed her eyes, listening to his hypnotic voice as it transported her back to a place and a time that couldn't possibly exist.

"No, I didn't kill Fliss."

"Then why did you warn me that I'd like you less once I'd heard the tale?"

"Because you haven't heard it all yet."

Arkady lifted her head from his shoulder, rubbed her eyes and glanced around the cabin, not sure that she wanted to hear the rest of it. She'd been expecting to be told about the great love of Cayal's life but, as he suggested when he began his tale, Amaleta was almost a footnote, rather than the focus of the tale. She yawned and stretched luxuriously. "It's almost dawn. Did Maralyce not come back?"

"We may not see her again for days," Cayal told her. "She's not all that fond of company."

Stiffly, Arkady moved a little, only to discover her backside had gone to sleep on the rough wooden floor. She rubbed it painfully as pins and needles shot down her legs, frowning. "What's for breakfast?"

"Are you hungry *again*?"

"We poor, insignificant mortals have to eat, you know."

He looked at her curiously. "Does that mean you're finally ready to admit that I'm *immortal*?"

"Tides, no!" she exclaimed, climbing to her feet, stamping them to banish the tingling from her numb buttocks. "That would mean admitting I'm wrong. I'm never wrong. Just ask my husband."

"Do you love him?" Cayal asked, looking up at her.

"Of course I do."

"Then why are you here with me?"

"You kidnapped me, remember?" Stretching again, Arkady glanced around the small cottage with a frown. "It would be too much to hope, I suppose, that this place has internal plumbing?"

"It's a miner's cabin, Arkady."

"I feared as much. Will you put the kettle on while I answer the call of nature?"

He nodded and Arkady turned for the door, gasping as the icy dawn slapped her awake when she opened it. Hopping gingerly from one bare foot to the other, she spied the outhouse on the other side of the muddy, equipment-strewn yard and hurried across to take care of business. By the time she returned, Cayal had the fire stoked up again and the water sitting over it, the large black kettle hanging on the hinged metal hook attached to the side of the fireplace for just that purpose.

She shivered as she closed the door and hurried back to the fire. "Tides, it's cold out there."

"It's the altitude," Cayal explained. "Did you want the last of the bread?"

Arkady nodded, helping herself to the remains of the bread lying discarded on a wooden platter beside last night's meal, which sat congealing on the table. The bread was stale but she was ravenous enough not to care.

"You're common-born, aren't you?"

Arkady stopped chewing mid-mouthful and stared at Cayal. "You can tell that just from the way I eat?"

He shook his head. "I can tell from the way you do everything. Your manners are far too perfect for one raised with them. You've learned to be a duchess, Arkady. You weren't born one."

"Did something happen while I was gone?" she asked, looking around the cabin. "Why the sudden need to insult me?"

"I wasn't insulting you. I was complimenting you."

"Then I'd rather you didn't do me any more favours, thank you."

"How *did* you become a duchess?"

"I married a duke."

He smiled thinly. "You know what I mean."

"I don't see that it's any of your concern," she replied, taking a seat at the table.

"You expect me to tell you every little intimate detail of my life," he reminded her, as he spooned the tea leaves into Maralyce's chipped teapot. "Don't you think it's fair you tell me something about yours?"

"No," she stated flatly. "I don't."

"Let me tell *you* about it, then."

She rolled her eyes and looked away, knowing there was little she could do to stop him. "This ought to be good."

Cayal set out the teacups and turned to the fire, lifting the heavy kettle from its hook with his bare hands. If he was burned by the scorching metal, she couldn't tell. He poured the water as if it came straight from a cool mountain stream, rather than bubbling over a fire. "You don't love your husband, Arkady. You might like him. You may even respect him, but you don't love him. I'm guessing you have your own bedroom at the palace and he has his. He probably takes lovers, now and then, but he's the king's cousin, so he knows how to be discreet. You married him because you gained something from it—wealth, certainly, although you don't strike me as the avaricious type—and he gained a very nice table ornament to trot out at dinner parties." Cayal replaced the kettle over the fire and turned back to the teapot. "You'll have to give him an heir, someday, I suppose, but you've time yet, before you reach the danger years for childbearing, so he doesn't mind you playing at being an academic for a while longer. How am I doing?"

Swallowing the last of her bread, which had suddenly turned to ashes in her mouth, Arkady made no attempt to deny his accusations. Nor was she impressed by them. "You could have found out all of that from any guard in Lebec Prison."

"They told me your father died there."

"Then you know everything about me."

He smiled humourlessly and began to pour the tea into a couple of mismatched cups he'd found on the mantel. "I have a feeling we could be acquainted for a thousand years and I'd never get to know you, Arkady Desean. You're far too practised at concealment. I doubt you'd even recognise yourself, if you were ever forced to confront the truth about who you really are."

Arkady looked away. "I believe we're rapidly approaching that 'you'll like me less when I'm done' point you spoke of."

"Why was your father arrested?"

"He was caught helping escaped slaves."

"He'd been doing it for years, I heard." Cayal handed her the tea, which she accepted gratefully as she nodded in agreement, much more comfortable talking about her father than the direction the conversation had been heading a few moments ago.

"He was betrayed by a colleague at the university," she told him, sitting at the table opposite him. "Someone he trusted. They arrested him, took him to Lebec Prison and interrogated him for days without respite. My father was a sick old man before they took him away. He was dead before I could find a way to have him released."

"What happened?"

"I just told you what happened."

"No, I mean what happened to make this trusted friend suddenly betray your father?"

Arkady hesitated for a long moment before she answered, not sure, even as she did, why she was confiding in this man. "Because I refused to sleep with him any longer."

Cayal said nothing, but neither did he look particularly surprised.

"Aren't you going to say something?" she asked in the awkward silence that followed her announcement.

He shook his head. "Is there anything I could say that would make a difference?"

His question surprised her a little. "I . . . I don't know. Probably not."

"Did your father know?"

Arkady shook her head. "My father's betrayer was a man named Fillion Rybank. He was the head of the School of Medicine at Lebec University. He and my father had been the best of friends since their student days. It would have killed him if he'd known."

"It killed him anyway, I'd say," Cayal pointed out a little heartlessly.

"Ironic, isn't it?" she agreed. She wasn't angry. Cayal said nothing she hadn't tormented herself with for the past seven years. And it surprised her now how easily the tale came out. "It started when I was fourteen. Fillion came by to visit my father late one night on some pretext or other and caught him treating an escaped feline in the basement."

"Did he confront your father about it?"

"No," she said. "He didn't know Fillion was there. But I saw him and I begged him not to say anything. He agreed on the condition that I come to his rooms the next afternoon to . . . 'take care of some important business for me' I believe was how he put it." She sipped her tea, not surprised at how distant the memories seemed. Arkady had partitioned off that part of her soul many years ago. "I soon learned what sort of business he had in mind, and that it mostly involved me on my hands and knees, begging him to punish me for being a naughty girl, and then thanking him afterwards for having his way with me. I think I must have cried for two days after the first time. And he kept making me come back, week after week, for the better part of six years. I was so frightened of Fillion. So frightened for my father. I couldn't tell him what was going on. At first I thought I was protecting him. When I got older, I realised he'd die of shame and mortification if he discovered I'd suffered such abuse to save him, when he believed so fervently that it was his job to protect me."

"But you put an end to it," Cayal said. It wasn't a question.

Arkady shrugged. "I got older. And a friend discovered what was going on. He threatened to kill Fillion himself if I didn't put an end to it. Odd, don't you think, that it was the threat of his death that helped me finally get the courage up to tell Fillion Rybank it was time he started taking care of his own business? Mind you, I was more concerned for my friend than for my tormentor, because he was quite serious about killing him. I didn't want him punished for my foolishness. Anyway, Rybank didn't take the news well and three days later, they arrested my father."

"And yet despite these setbacks, you somehow came out of this calamitous mess married to a duke," Cayal remarked.

Arkady remained calm, displaying no emotion. She'd had almost six years of weekly visits to Fillion Rybank's rooms to practise that particular skill and had mastered it long ago. "I've known Stellan Desean since we were children. When I'd exhausted every legal avenue to have my father released, I petitioned him directly." She might be feeling unusually garrulous, but there were some secrets she wasn't prepared to surrender quite so easily.

"And what?" Cayal asked with a raised brow. "One look

at your matchless beauty and he took you to wife after promising to release your father?"

"More or less."

"You're a good liar, Arkady."

"It takes one to know one," she retorted. "Tell me the rest of it."

"Why should I bother? You think I'm a liar."

She smiled. "I enjoy watching a master at work."

Chapter 50

We left the palace—Fliss and I—in the early hours of the morning, taking the ferry across the mist-shrouded waters of the river. The walls surrounding the royal palace were little more than a pale blur in the predawn greyness as we slipped through the fog, creeping across the meandering river like thieves escaping in the night.

She was a good-looking child, long-limbed and tall for her age, with dark hair tucked carelessly behind her ears and eyes the colour of polished sapphires. Other than the fact she had wielded Tide magic and lived to tell about it—despite what Arryl claimed about her parentage—there was nothing about her physically that separated Fliss from the rest of her kind, no strong family resemblance to any of her "uncles" which might indicate whose child she was.

Our departure was arranged with indecent haste. Arryl made certain Fliss barely had time to say goodbye to her cousins, or farewell to the Crasii who had attended her since she was born, before she found herself shivering on the pier, Arryl fussing over her anxiously as we waited for the ferryman to load her baggage.

Fliss looked up at me as the ferry slid across the fog-bound water toward Libeth on the eastern side of the river. The world felt still. Paused on the brink. Only the rhythmic suck and splash of the ferryman's pole disturbed the silence.

"Where are we going, Uncle Cayal?" she asked.

Aware that anything I said might be reported to Syrolee by the ferryman, I avoided the question. "Away."

"Are we going away so you can teach me, Uncle Cayal?"

I looked at her in surprise. *"What?"*

"Isn't that why we're going away? So you can teach me all about the Tide so I don't hurt anybody again? How to do stuff."

"How to do *stuff*?" I repeated, glancing across at the ferryman. Did he know I was escorting this child to her death?

I forced a smile I didn't feel and looked down at the little girl, wondering if Arryl was right. Was Fliss my own flesh and blood, or was Arryl simply lying to elicit my cooperation? I didn't know. I had no inkling of what it might be like to feel paternal, and no way of knowing if that's what I was feeling now. My unease might simply be a reaction to the inclement weather.

But whatever the ferryman reported back to Syrolee, I wasn't going to frighten the child unnecessarily. "Yes, Fliss, I suppose I'll have to teach you how to do *stuff*."

"Will it be hard?"

"That depends on you," I told her.

"Will you teach me Crasii magic?"

I frowned. "You should learn how the Crasii are made before you decide you want to follow that particular line of study."

"Will you show me a Crasii farm?" she asked eagerly.

I debated the matter for a moment and then nodded, realising it made little difference what the child believed at this point. "Perhaps we can take a detour on our way."

Fliss slipped her small hand into mine. "This is going to be so much more fun than living in the palace."

I looked down at her with a dubious frown. She had dark hair like mine and the same blue eyes, but then so did half the population of Tenacia. It proved nothing. "I hope you still think that in a few days' time, Fliss."

"I have to keeping thinking it, Uncle Cayal," she replied solemnly. "Otherwise I'll cry."

By the time the ferry reached the dock on the other side of the river, the fog had lifted, revealing a crisp blue morning and the towering white walls of Libeth, a town famous for its tapestries and fine linen. Shivering in the cool air, Fliss stared up in wonder as we approached.

"Don't gape," I ordered, as the ferry bumped against the long pier. "You're a Tide Lord, remember? You need to cultivate an air of jaded cynicism."

"What's that, Uncle Cayal?"

"The worst advice you're ever likely to get," an amused voice answered from above us.

We looked up to find someone waiting for us on the pier. He was young, barely twenty, in fact, although he was hundreds of years older than me, with dark hair braided back in the fashion of the day, dressed in leather breeches and a linen shirt, with a finely embroidered jacket over it. I frowned when I saw him, wondering how he'd known where we would be this morning.

"Uncle Jaxyn!" Fliss exclaimed happily. "What are you doing here?"

"Exactly what I was going to ask," I remarked with a scowl, as the ferryman tied the barge to the pylons.

Jaxyn looked down at Fliss and offered her his hand. "Heard you were going on a little trip, Fliss. Thought I'd invite myself along."

"That's so wonderful!" she cried, allowing him to help her up onto the dock. I followed them up, carrying Fliss's smallest bag and my own pack. I turned and tossed a coin to the ferryman.

"Take the rest of the baggage back to the palace," I ordered, pointing to the towering pile of "essentials" that

Fliss's nanny had sent along with her charge. "Tell them it wasn't required."

"But that's all my things!" Fliss protested.

"You won't need them where you're going, Fliss," Jaxyn assured her, looking over her head at me. "Isn't that right, Uncle Cayal?"

I refused to be baited by him. Instead, I turned my back on the ferry and Fliss's possessions and fell in beside Jaxyn as he headed back along the jetty, our boots sounding hollow on the damp, slatted wood.

Probably afraid we planned to abandon her with the same ease I'd disposed of her luggage, Fliss hurried after us, squeezing her way in between the two of us. The white walls of Libeth loomed over us, but there was no sign of a welcoming party. I was mightily relieved, having chosen this early hour to leave the palace for just that reason.

"Why has nobody come to greet us, Uncle Cayal?"

"Because I didn't tell them we were coming."

"You told Uncle Jaxyn we were coming, didn't you?"

I glanced across at Jaxyn with a frown. "Apparently."

"You don't seem pleased to see him, Uncle Cayal."

"Oh, my!" Jaxyn chuckled. "I almost wish I was going to have a chance to watch this one grow up."

"Are you leaving, Uncle Jaxyn?" Fliss asked.

"In a while." He shrugged. "I've got things to do. In other places. But don't be too upset, precious. I doubt your Uncle Cayal will miss me."

"Why?"

"Fliss, are you actually capable of uttering a sentence that doesn't start with 'why'?"

"I think so, Uncle Cayal. Why?"

I rolled my eyes, but Jaxyn laughed and took her small hand in his. "Fliss, I think I'm really going to enjoy having you around until Uncle Cayal . . . takes care of you."

"Will you show me stuff, too, Uncle Jaxyn?"

"Stuff?"

"That's Fliss's all-encompassing word for the mysteries of Tide magic," I explained.

"I suppose I'd better show you something, Fliss. You'll not learn much otherwise with Uncle Cayal as your instructor."

"Will you teach me Crasii magic? Uncle Cayal's already promised to show me a Crasii farm, but I don't think he wants to show me anything else."

"He *has*?" Jaxyn asked, looking over her head at me.

"I thought Fliss might want to see how the Crasii are made before she decides she really wants to have anything to do with them."

"Does she really need to know, though?" he asked with an ingenuous smile. "I mean, given your . . . um . . . *plans* . . . for Fliss, do you even have the time for such a detour?"

I glared at him, wondering if Jaxyn had invited himself along because Syrolee had sent him—which is what I'd first assumed—or if he was here because he was actually entertained by the idea Fliss was to be killed and wanted to be around to watch.

We travelled south-west, avoiding Libeth and the inevitable pomp and ceremony that accompanied any of our kind appearing at the city gates. It was just on sunset when we reached the village of Marivale, located about halfway between Libeth and Lorenvale. A pall of wood smoke choked the air, trapped in the small stony hollow where the village was located on the very edge of the flax farms bordering the river. We could see warm yellow lamplight illuminating the crackled glass windows of the shops as we rode into the village.

I dismounted in the paved courtyard of the village's only inn. Fliss yawned, rubbing her eyes. The little girl had chattered happily to us for most of the afternoon, asking question after question about life in the world outside the palace, finally falling asleep slumped in my arms about an hour ago. I'd slowed our pace and held her while she slept, a remarkably paternal act that I never imagined myself capable of.

"You're planning to stay *here* tonight?" Jaxyn asked in surprise.

"I don't think Fliss is quite ready for a night in the open. Not at this time of year."

"Good plan," Jaxyn agreed as he dismounted. "I mean, we wouldn't want to risk our girl catching pneumonia and dying, would we? That'd be tragic." Before I could respond, Jaxyn glanced around and added, "It's going to cause a riot, you know, a couple of Tide Lords arriving in a village this size without warning, demanding rooms."

"Can't be helped." I shrugged.

As Jaxyn predicted, the unannounced arrival of two Tide Lords in the small village precipitated something akin to a riot. We were well known in Tenacia, so within moments of our appearance, the courtyard was swarming with people, most of them prostrating themselves at our feet, gushing with the need to serve their gods' every desire.

Their devotion didn't surprise me. The Tide had been up for several hundred years by then and Engarhod and Syrolee are very good at what they do. All mortals living in the shadow of the Emperor and Empress of the Five Realms reacted the same way to our kind. At least they did in Tenacia. Daresay with the Tide out as long as it has been this time, they're left with little more than your wretched Tarot cards to remember us by, these days.

"To serve you is the reason I breathe, my lord!" a woman blubbered, falling to her knees before me as I emerged from the inn after speaking with the owner. I stepped back before she could kiss my feet—that's a really disgusting sensation, you know, having a perfect stranger slobber all over your feet. She was an older woman, the innkeeper's wife, I guessed. In her wake several other young women pushed through the crowd, no doubt the daughters of the house. They fell to their knees beside their mother, too afraid to look us in the eye. Behind them were even more people, unwashed and uncivilised, all wanting to gape and grovel at the feet of their gods.

Fliss pulled her cloak a little closer, clinging to Jaxyn for security in the face of the swarming humans who had increased in numbers so quickly I figured the whole village must be here by now. A few of them carried torches, their flickering light poking holes in the rapidly falling darkness. They looked more like a mob than a congregation.

"Clear this place!" I ordered.

The crowd hurried to comply until only the innkeeper's wife and her daughters remained. The rest of them gathered in the street, straining to see what was happening inside the courtyard walls.

"Are you deaf, woman?" I snapped at the prostrate mortal and her daughters.

"My husband . . . this is his . . . our inn," the older woman mumbled into the paving stones.

"Then stand up, for the Tide's sake!"

The woman scrambled to her feet, followed by her three daughters. They ranged in age from about fifteen to the eldest, who looked to be about twenty. She was a pretty girl with wavy dark hair and clear blue eyes lined with thick dark lashes.

"You! What's your name?" I asked her.

"Amaleta, my lord," she replied, blushing crimson at being singled out. She was nervous, but I could sense no fear in her—unlike her mother and sisters, who radiated their terror like an open fire.

"This is Fliss, favourite of Syrolee, Empress of the Five Realms. You will take care of her."

Fliss glanced up at me in confusion. "Am I Syrolee's favourite, Uncle Cayal?"

"You are tonight, Fliss."

She accepted that and turned to Amaleta. "Can you show me where the latrines are? I'm busting."

I bit back a smile as Amaleta shyly approached the little girl and held out her hand. "Come with me, my lady. They're not the golden ones you're used to, I'll be bound, but I reckon they'll do the trick."

The call of nature overriding any other concerns the

child had about being handed into the care of a complete stranger, Fliss let Amaleta lead her into the inn. Relieved of that responsibility, I turned my attention back to the innkeeper's wife.

"Our horses require food and stabling."

Expecting nothing less than her blind obedience to my orders—I might find being worshipped irritating, but that doesn't meant it isn't useful at times—I turned on my heel leaving the woman staring nervously after us and headed in the direction that Fliss and Amaleta had disappeared.

Jaxyn was one step ahead of me. I found him inside, warming his hands at an iron brazier of glowing coals where it was obvious he'd already ordered our dinner. The younger daughters of the house were hurriedly laying out our meal on the table set up between the couches, glancing fearfully over their shoulders at us watching them work.

The inn was quite grand for such a small village. Built in a poor imitation of Magrethan architecture, it was constructed of the local grey stone, its windowless walls offering protection from the outside world. There was a small and rather paltry atrium in the centre of the building with a broken fountain. Surrounding the atrium were a number of small alcoves, as I recall, the sort you find in far more salubrious establishments, offering couches and low tables for patrons to relax and drink their dark warm Tenacian beer, which I have always thought tastes much the same as horse piss would taste. I guess the tavern had been hastily emptied of all its mortal patrons to make way for us.

"Where's Fliss?" Jaxyn asked, as I came to stand beside him.

"Answering the call of nature."

Jaxyn seemed amused. "I'll bet you never thought of that. In fact, you don't seem to have thought about much at all, regarding this child. What in the name of the Tides possessed you to take her from the palace? Couldn't bring yourself to do the job with an audience? Or did you plan to have a little fun with her before you finish her off and were afraid that Arryl might object?"

I shook my head in wonder. There is no limit to the perversions Jaxyn can imagine. "Were you this sick before you were immortal, Jaxyn, or is it something you've been working on since then?"

"Bit of both," he replied cheerfully, not in the least bit offended. "What *are* you going to do with this wretched child? Even if you're merely planning to make her last few days moderately pleasant ones, what do you know of children? You have no servants to care for her. Are you planning to look after her yourself?"

"I'll work something out," I assured him. The plan had been to get Fliss to the coast where Arryl would meet us. Obviously, that wasn't going to happen now—not with Jaxyn in our company. And much as it irked me to admit it, he was right. I knew nothing about children. Still don't know much. Despite my boast that eventually we get good at everything, that's one area of responsibility I've deftly managed to avoid for the past eight thousand years.

"You need to do something *now,* Cayal."

"What do you suggest?"

"I *suggest* you do what you promised Syrolee you'd do, and put an end to her. Failing that, find her a nurse. A human one if you must, given your apparent aversion to Crasii."

"You might have made this brilliant suggestion while we were in Libeth. We could have visited the slave markets before we left."

"Had I realised you weren't planning to do the job immediately, I would have."

"Then I'll find someone else to look after her."

"Well, whatever you do, do it soon, Cayal. Neither you or I know anything about the care of little girls."

"Which brings me to another problem."

"What's that?"

"Who invited you along anyway?"

Before Jaxyn could answer, Fliss skipped into the room

with Amaleta close behind her. She headed straight for the table and stared at the food doubtfully.

"Is it safe to eat, Uncle Cayal?" she asked.

"I'm quite sure it's perfectly safe," I assured her.

Satisfied that she wasn't about to be poisoned, Fliss began piling her plate with all the enthusiasm of a famished six-year-old. Amaleta coughed politely and then dropped into a deep curtsey when we turned to her.

"Will that be all, my lords?"

"You live here?" Jaxyn asked, eyeing the young woman curiously. She wasn't that tall, but her skin was very fair against long dark hair tied back in a loose braid. What I remember about her most is her eyes. They were dark . . . the colour of late twilight . . .

"My parents own this inn, my lord," I think she must have replied . . . or something along those lines. I was too entranced by those eyes to pay much attention to what she was saying.

"Would you like a job, Amaleta?"

That question put an abrupt end to my idle musings.

"My *lord*?" she gasped, almost as shocked as I was by Jaxyn's suggestion.

My companion laughed softly. "A job. You know—paid employment. My good friend here needs a nurse to take care of his charge."

Amaleta fell to her knees, lowering her head with humble gratitude. "To serve you is the reason I breathe, my lord. If my gods wish me to serve them, then of course, I cannot refuse . . ."

"Oh, get up!" I ordered impatiently, glowering at Jaxyn.

"I don't think he wants your adoration," Jaxyn told her, grinning at me as if he found my irritation amusing. "I believe he's rather more interested in knowing if you're capable of caring for Fliss."

"I think she's nice," Fliss offered through a mouthful of apple from across the room.

"There!" Jaxyn announced. "What better recommendation could we ask for? Well, do you want the job or not?"

Amaleta stared at us, clearly confused. "You mean . . . you'd pay me?"

"Unless they've redefined the nature of employment recently, then yes, Lord Cayal will pay you. I suppose he'll have to compensate your parents for the inconvenience, too, but that shouldn't be a problem. He's a Tide Lord. He can afford it."

"This is too great an honour, my lord!"

"I doubt you'll think so in a few days' time, Amaleta. Fliss can be quite a handful, and Cayal's a right pain in the arse. Do you want the job or not?"

"Jaxyn!" I objected. "I think we should—"

"Indeed!" Jaxyn agreed before I could finish. "I think we should too, but seeing as how you appear to be too gutless to do the job without working yourself up to it, we're going to need a nurse in the meantime. Well, Amaleta? What's your answer?"

"I couldn't possibly refuse such an offer!"

"Then get off your damned knees and go tell your parents you'll be leaving with us in the morning. And send your father in. Lord Cayal will need to arrange to purchase another horse. I'm sure he doesn't plan to dawdle at a walk all the way to wherever it is we're going because you're traipsing along behind us on foot. Can you ride?"

"Yes, my lord," Amaleta assured him, scrambling to her feet.

Jaxyn beamed at me. "See! Already she's proving her worth. Off you go then, girl."

Amaleta fled the room, leaving me glaring at Jaxyn. "You just hired some girl you know nothing about who's probably never been more than five miles from her village."

Jaxyn shrugged. "I'm making do. Of course, if you were planning to do what you promised you'd do anytime soon, a nanny for your little friend over there wouldn't really be necessary, would it?"

There was no answer to that . . . or if there was, I couldn't think of one. So I said nothing, irked to realise I was left with no other course but to play along with Jaxyn, pretend I was still planning to murder Fliss and drag Amaleta into a drama that would end up costing her far more than she would ever earn as the servant of a Tide Lord.

Chapter 51

His stomach rumbling with hunger woke Warlock the next morning. Curled on a scrap of fur loaned to him by Boots, he shivered and pushed himself up stiffly, glancing around the Kennel. In daylight it fared even worse than it had by firelight. The building was shabby, the high raffers draped with age-old cobwebs thick with dust, most of the light coming through cracks in the walls where the boards had slipped off as the nails rusted away. The warehouse was all but empty now, only a few females, mostly the mothers of young pups, still hanging around.

Warlock climbed to his feet, wondering where the nearest exit was. By the smell of this place, he could tell that soiling one's sleeping place was frowned upon, which relieved him a great deal. After Boots telling him it was common for the strays to hunt food in the city's garbage, he'd feared the worst. But Rex kept a surprisingly tidy Kennel, all things considered, and when one of the females from the leader's pack noticed he was awake, she jerked her head toward the right, guessing what he was looking for. He followed the direction she was indicating and spied a small door. With a nod of thanks, he hurried outside and discovered proper latrines had been dug against the fence in the small yard at the back of the warehouse.

"We're not animals, you know," Boots remarked as he

emerged from the small cubicle, which didn't have a door, but rather a sack hanging across the entrance to provide some semblance of privacy.

"I never said you were."

"But you have that look," she accused. "I think you're a bit of a snob, Warlock, out of Bella, by Segura."

Warlock frowned. He'd never thought of himself that way. But then, he'd never been in a situation like this before, either. "I . . . I just never saw myself living like this."

"What? *Free*?"

"I was going to say unemployed."

She smiled, and stepped a little closer. Not even the smell of the latrines could mask her scent. If it had been hard to concentrate yesterday when she was nearby, today it was damned near impossible. Any day now, he knew, perhaps any hour, she would be fully in heat and would finally choose a mate. Only good manners and a heroic amount of self-control stopped Warlock from throwing himself at her this very moment and begging her to choose him as her partner.

"Unemployed, eh?" she chuckled. "Never heard freedom referred to like that before."

He might desire this female more than air at this moment, but that didn't give her the right to mock him. "You say you grew up at Lebec Palace. You surely can't be happy living like this? Rummaging through garbage to eat? Sleeping in a den with dozens of different packs and no idea what their pedigree is . . ."

"I was right, you really are a snob."

"I'm concerned for you."

"You needn't be," she assured him. "I can look after myself."

"If that's what you call living like this."

"Come see me when you haven't eaten for a week," she suggested. "You might find your opinion somewhat less inflexible. In the meantime, you've gotten lucky."

"Lucky how?"

"Shalimar wants to see you," she said. "He'll feed us when we get there."

"Normally, we'd wait awhile before bringing you here," Shalimar informed Warlock as they sat down to the largest breakfast he'd seen since leaving Lord Ordry's estate. "But given your news about the Immortal Prince, I deemed it worth the risk."

Shalimar was human, which surprised Warlock. He'd been expecting a Crasii at the very least, and probably a canine at that. He wasn't expecting this sprightly old man with bright, pale eyes that seemed oddly out of place against his dusky skin. Warlock couldn't tell what race he was or place his accent, which bothered him a little, but he seemed happy enough to welcome them into his cluttered little apartment, and lay on a feast that distracted Warlock almost enough to make him forget the scent his companion was giving off.

Boots had refused to answer any questions about Shalimar as she led Warlock through the crowded slums. She'd found a worn but serviceable cotton tunic for him to wear, so he blended in with the rest of the slum dwellers, and led him via a roundabout route to Shalimar's home. He was certain she'd done so simply to confuse him, making sure he was completely disoriented before finally ending up here in this attic above a physician's shop surprisingly close to where he'd been arrested yesterday.

"I am not a risk to you," Warlock assured the old man through a mouthful of thick sausage. It was so long since he'd eaten this well, it could have been perfectly roasted pork drowned in rich brown gravy and not tasted any better.

"You've been here a few days, lad, and in that short time have been arrested, released without penalty, met the Duke of Lebec and been inexplicably pardoned for murdering a human. Stop me when I get to the part that isn't suspicious, won't you."

Warlock looked to Boots for help but she was too busy tucking into her breakfast to care what Shalimar might be

accusing him of. Her impending mating time was undoubtedly making her ravenous. Perhaps that's part of the reason
she'd brought him here. If Shalimar regularly set a table
like this, any excuse to visit him would have been prefer-
able to rummaging through piles of garbage.

"Do you think I'm some sort of spy?"

"I think there's a lot of human masters out there who'd
give a great deal to find their runaway slaves." Then he
smiled. "But Boots seems to think you're far too guileless
to be a spy. Apparently even agents of evil know better
than to wander the slums wearing nothing but a belt pouch
and the pelt the Mother gave him."

"If you fear I'm a spy, you must have something to
hide," Warlock concluded.

"Perhaps."

"Then Hidden Valley really does exist?" he asked, hoping he didn't sound quite as excited as he felt at the
prospect.

"Let's talk about Cayal first," Shalimar suggested,
pulling up a chair opposite the heavily laden table. "Then
we'll see if you've a need to know anything about Hidden
Valley."

Warlock speared another sausage with his fork and
shrugged. "What is there to tell? He was in Lebec Prison,
he was taken the same day I was pardoned to be handed
over to the king's men for interrogation. There isn't much
more I can tell you."

"How did he seem?" Shalimar wanted to know, leaning
forward, his pale eyes intent and hypnotic. "Happy, sad,
smug . . ."

"They're all smug," Boots remarked, reaching for an
apple.

"Cayal seemed depressed," Warlock told them, after
thinking about it for a moment. "Suicidal, even."

"That must be frustrating for him," the young female
chuckled. "A suicidal immortal."

"It was," Warlock agreed. "I think that's what he was
doing in prison. It's Low Tide and he thought a beheading

might work, so he killed seven people to make sure they'd try, but they hanged him and screwed up all his plans."

Shalimar sighed. "Typical. The Tide Lords only ever think of their own pain. They never spare a thought for what it might cost the mortals they tramp all over to get their way."

"It didn't work, obviously," Warlock continued. "I met him the night after the hanging. He kept the whole of Recidivists' Row up, moaning and groaning with the pain. Next morning he was as good as new and calling me a filthy gemang. Not long after that, the King's Spymaster and then the Duchess of Lebec came to interview him."

"What did he tell them?"

"The truth," Warlock replied, "although nobody believed him. I saw the spymaster once, but Lady Desean visited us every day and every day Cayal would tell her more about himself, and every day she grew more suspicious of him." He left out the bit about smelling the lust on them both, mostly because he didn't want to give Shalimar the wrong idea. Lady Desean had conducted herself without fault while she was interviewing Cayal, showed Warlock nothing but respect. And then she'd freed him. He owed her something. Not giving the impression she was in cahoots with a Tide Lord was the least he could do for her.

"Do you think Jaxyn sent her?" Shalimar asked.

"What are you suggesting?"

"Jaxyn's at the palace," Boots reminded him. "Been living there for the better part of a year. You can't honestly believe it's just an amazing coincidence that suddenly Cayal turns up in Glaeba too, and Lady Desean starts visiting him in prison?"

"Lady Desean doesn't even accept the Tide Lords exist!" Warlock objected. "She's human. Worse, she's a historian. She thinks we're an accident of nature, that humans have explained everything about our existence away with their wretched 'theory of human advancement.' Trust me,

Arkady Desean wasn't there to find out if Cayal was really the Immortal Prince. She was there to prove he was a liar, a Caelish spy or something like that. She certainly wasn't trying to help him."

"If she's Jaxyn's agent," Shalimar corrected, "she'd not be trying to help him, she'd be doing her damnedest to make him suffer. There's no love lost between the Immortal Prince and the Lord of Temperance."

"Do you think they know about each other?" Boots asked Shalimar.

He shook his head. "Cayal may not know that Jaxyn is nearby, but I'd wager my left foot on Jaxyn knowing about Cayal." He sighed and leant back in his chair. "It's a pity we have no way of knowing what's happening inside the palace since Boots left."

"At least it's Low Tide," she pointed out. "I mean, without their powers, how much damage can they do?"

"Not much," Shalimar agreed. "But the Tide is turning. We don't have long before they start to get restless again." Then he glanced at the clock on the mantel and shook his head. "Tides! Is that the time, already?"

Warlock stared at Shalimar in shock. "You can feel the Tide?"

The old man shrugged as he rose to his feet, but didn't deny the accusation. "I'll see you again, won't I?"

Warlock was too stunned to notice they were being tossed out. "Then you are the child of an immortal?"

"Probably."

"Which one?"

"I have no idea," Shalimar told him walking to the door. "I was raised in a brothel. My mother was probably a whore, which means she didn't even know which of her customers sired me. She certainly didn't check with any of them to see if they were immortal."

"But that's . . . ," Warlock began, shocked into speechlessness by the old man's casual acceptance of his heritage. "Have you never tried to discover who he was?"

"To what purpose? They're all as bad as each other. Truth is, I don't really care which one it was. Do come and visit me again."

Despite the fact Boots was pushing him towards the door, Warlock wasn't willing to let this go so easily. "So Cayal or Jaxyn could be your father?"

"Or Tryan," he agreed. "Or Lukys. Or Brynden. Even Pellys. Like I said, it doesn't really make a difference to me. Same time tomorrow, shall we say?"

Boots had a hold of his arm and was tugging on it quite forcefully, trying to get Warlock into the hall. But this was too important. "Is that why you help Scards?"

Shalimar smiled. "Call it my puny attempt to thumb my nose at the monster who fathered me."

That was a motive Warlock could understand, even sympathise with. He shook free of Boots and studied Shalimar in the dim light of the narrow stairwell. "And you say the Tide is turning?"

The old man nodded. "Been able to feel it coming back since I was a child. It won't be long now. And it's going to be a clanger."

"How can you tell?"

"The Tide's been out for over a thousand years, son," Shalimar explained, with a grim expression. "The longer it's out, the faster it comes back and the bigger it is when it gets here. We may be in for a King Tide this time, and that's not good news for anyone on Amyrantha—human, Crasii or Scard."

With that, Shalimar shut the door, leaving Warlock to stare after him, not sure what disturbed him most—that the Tide was turning or that an old man living in the Lebec slums seemed to be the only one who knew or cared about it.

Chapter 52

N o sooner had Shalimar closed the door of his loft on the big Crasii and his bushy-tailed companion, another figure emerged from the shadows behind him. The figure waited for a moment until the old man sensed his presence, and then smiled when, unsurprised, Shalimar locked the door and turned to face his visitor.

"I thought I heard you sneaking in the back way."

"Surprised I still fit through that window, actually."

Shalimar smiled fondly at his grandson. "You always were good at getting in and out of odd places. And turning up when you're least expected. I heard you were in town."

"One of the many joys of being infamous. It's getting harder and harder to sneak around."

The old man grinned and embraced Declan warmly before pushing him down into the chair so recently vacated by Warlock. Declan smiled and took the seat without protest. Since he'd shot up to over six feet tall at the age of fourteen, his grandfather had been complaining that it hurt his neck to look up at his grandson when they were talking.

"So . . . how much of that did you hear?"

"Most of it," Declan replied, surveying the table with interest. He hadn't eaten all day, yet Shalimar had put on quite a spread for his Crasii guests.

"Do you think Boots is right?"

"That Arkady Desean is in league with the Tide Lords? Hardly." Declan helped himself to what was left of the chicken as his grandfather began to clear away the dishes. "I was the one who sent her to speak with Cayal, remember. That female who was with Warlock. Is she the missing slave who killed that feline at the Lebec Palace a few months back after giving Jaxyn a mouthful of lip?"

Shalimar nodded as Declan picked at the leftovers. "Why do you ask? You're not planning to arrest her, are you?"

"Not if she's a genuine Scard."

"I'm pretty certain she is," his grandfather assured him. He stacked the dirty dishes on the bench under the window. The cleaning woman—the one Declan had arranged and paid for—would come by later to take care of them. "Warlock's probably a Scard, too, given his reaction to the Immortal Prince."

"I gathered as much from what Arkady told me about him. Will you keep an eye on them for me?"

The old man shrugged. "Don't I always?"

Tossing aside the chicken bone he'd sucked clean, Declan looked up at the old man. "You know, Arkady thinks I'm a heartless fiend," he said, snatching a slice of ham from the platter before his grandfather could take it away. "She gave me quite a telling off about you the other day."

"That's because every time she brings me a food parcel, I ask after you with a tear in my eye and a catch in my voice. It's quite a moving performance, actually. She thinks we haven't spoken in years." He turned from the bench and frowned at Declan. "It pains me to lie to her, Declan."

He remained unmoved by his grandfather's disapproval. "It's necessary."

"Are you so sure we shouldn't think about bringing her into the Cabal?"

Declan shook his head. "We've had this discussion before, Pop. We can't risk it."

"But we know her . . ."

"I thought I knew her," he corrected. "Right up until she announced she was marrying Stellan Desean. And don't tell me you weren't floored, too, when she told you."

"However misguided, she had her reasons," Shalimar pointed out, saddened by Declan's intransigence on the matter. "You must know her loyalties are with us."

"She's married to the king's cousin," he reminded his grandfather, a little annoyed they were having this discussion again. He wondered, for a moment, what Arkady would do if the next time she asked why he wouldn't visit his grandfather, he told her it was because he was sick of hearing about how he should trust her more.

Truth was, he hadn't really trusted Arkady since he'd found out the reason behind her weekly visits to Fillion Rybank.

Declan had been shattered to discover Arkady was keeping such a dreadful secret from him; even more disturbed that she'd suffered in silence for six years and hadn't come to him for help. Worse—she'd actively concealed her torment from him; lied about it to everyone, in fact, even her father. Now he was older, he understood her fear of his reaction but Declan still hadn't completely shaken off the hurt her decision not to confide in him had engendered. The feeling she no longer trusted him only got worse when she married the Duke of Lebec. When Arkady calmly announced that she'd done a deal with Stellan Desean to have her father released, and that her side of the bargain required her to become his wife, he felt like he'd been punched in the gut.

Although he'd been able to forgive her for not asking for his help with Rybank, even after six years he still found her willingness to trade herself for a favour—no matter how selfless—more than he could fathom.

"I'm not entirely sure where Arkady's loyalties lie these days, Pop," he said. "And I'd rather not risk the Cabal by finding out the hard way."

Shalimar seemed disappointed by his stubbornness. "She's still one of us, lad."

Declan shook his head. "She married the Duke of Lebec."

"And you're the King's Spymaster," the old man pointed out. "You're hardly the one to point fingers."

"You know why I do what I do," Declan replied, a little irked by his grandfather's reproachful expression. "In fact, as I recall, it was your idea that I join the king's service, and it was the strings Tilly Ponting pulled that got me the job as spymaster. Don't blame me for doing what the Pentangle asked of me."

"Never occurred to me you'd be so damned good at it, though," the old man grumbled. And then he smiled. "I swear poor Lord Deryon still hasn't gotten over being told he had to recommend the common-born grandson of a Tide-watcher as spymaster to the king."

"That's what he gets for underestimating Tilly Ponting. King's Private Secretary or not, even another member of the Pentangle daren't deny the Custodian of the Lore."

"Have you seen Tilly since you've been in Lebec?"

Declan nodded. "I spoke to her a couple of nights ago. I was on my way there when Arkady told me off for being such a bad grandson, actually. Tilly's been trying to instruct Arkady in the Tarot, but she didn't want to reveal too much because she's more than a little concerned Arkady might be falling under Cayal's spell."

"Do you think she is?"

Declan shrugged, wishing he knew the answer. "Hard to say. She's quite obsessed with proving he isn't immortal, but that might just be Arkady being Arkady. She can be fairly stubborn when the mood takes her."

Shalimar shook his head, looking at Declan as if to say: *she's not the only one who's stubborn.* "It was dangerous, sending her to interrogate him."

"There was nobody else in Lebec who wouldn't instantly raise suspicion. She's not a member of the Pentangle or even the Cabal, so she couldn't accidentally give anything away. Besides, Cayal's got a weakness for beautiful women. There was always the chance she'd get something out of him you or I, or even Tilly, wouldn't be able to discover."

Shalimar was unconvinced. "Tilly would have been the better choice. She's the Custodian of the Lore. She knows the Tarot—and all the precious Lore that goes with it—inside out. She would've been able to get some *useful* information out of the Immortal Prince, not the flights of fancy he's been telling Arkady."

"And how would I explain sending an eccentric, purple-haired widow to Lebec Prison to interrogate a murderer, Pop?"

His grandfather shrugged. "Why are you asking me? You're the professional liar in this family."

Declan grinned at his grandfather, knowing his remark was meant as a compliment. The lies he told protected more than Glaeba's sovereignty; the deceptions he was involved in had more to do with the survival of humanity than one single nation. "Interesting how Cayal paints himself in such a noble light, don't you think?" he remarked, helping himself to the last of the bread. "It's all just a big mistake, according to the Immortal Prince. Destiny has been unkind and he's simply an unfortunate, misguided dupe swept along on the tide of fate."

His grandfather frowned. "And yet the true Tarot, the one we don't roll out at parties, paints quite a different tale. You should have warned Arkady of the danger."

Declan shook his head. "That would have meant admitting I knew Kyle Lakesh was probably the immortal he was claiming to be. Arkady isn't ready for that."

"Very few people are."

Declan knew that to be a bitter truth, one he'd learned at his grandfather's knee. The legacy of the Tarot and the protection of the Lore was left to so few of them since the last Cataclysm, mostly because there were so few who actually believed anymore. Unlike the Crasii, who trusted their instincts far more than humans, men were more likely to scoff at the legends of the past instead of embracing them. That's why their task was so important. Sooner or later the Tide Lords would rise again and it would be left to the Cabal and the five members of the Pentangle—of which Shalimar, Lord Karyl Deryon and Lady Ponting were members—to face the danger.

"Does he use the name of Lakesh to taunt us, do you think?"

"More likely he doesn't care," Shalimar suggested. "He probably thinks the Cabal of the Tarot was wiped out in the last Cataclysm."

"Let's hope the rest of the immortals think the same." Declan stood up from the chair. "I really should get going before anyone realises I'm here. Do you need anything?"

His grandfather glanced down at the remains of his

impressive table with a smile. "I somehow manage to struggle by."

"I can see that." He embraced the old man. "You take care, all the same. I'm not sure how long it'll be before I'm back in Lebec so it may be a while before I see you again."

"I'll get a message to Tilly if I need anything."

Declan glanced at the table for a moment and then turned to his grandfather. "Don't your Crasii friends ever get suspicious at how well you live?"

"Most of the poor sods down here are too hungry to question their luck."

"Well, you need to be careful," he warned. "You don't want some fool deciding you've got a fortune stashed in here and turning the place over."

"I *can* look after myself, Declan."

"I know you can, Pop," he assured the old man. "But I worry about you, all the same."

The old man patted Declan's shoulder, shaking his head. "You've got other things to worry about, lad. The Tide is turning and the Immortal Prince has reemerged. My fate comes a poor second to that."

"The king has ordered me to torture a confession out of him."

Shalimar's expression darkened at the news. "Then you be very, *very* careful, my boy. Any day now, Cayal's powers will return. You don't want that happening while you're waving a hot branding iron under his nose."

"Maybe I'll get a tale out of him," Declan suggested. "Like the ones he's been telling Arkady. She went out to the prison yesterday, so I'm told, to hear the rest of his story before she has to surrender him to me. In fact, she was gone again this morning, even before I left."

Shalimar seemed unsurprised. "Cayal should have posed as a bard, not a wainwright. Even the Lore says he spins a good yarn."

"I wonder," Declan mused, "what tale he's telling her now . . ."

Chapter 53

That night we spent in Marivale turned out to be quite important, but only in hindsight. I didn't realise at the time, of course—one never does—that I was witnessing the precursor to a pointless death for which I actually felt, for a time at least, quite guilty.

The only other incident of note that night happened when I went out to the stables to check on my horse. As I approached the arched entrance of the stables, my breath frosting in the crisp air, I heard voices. I stopped in the shadows near the entrance. From where I was standing, I could make out only a male figure—presumably the stableboy, given he was brushing down Jaxyn's chestnut gelding.

". . . and it's not as if you haven't been looking for an excuse to leave Marivale since you were . . . oh . . . five years old . . . ," the lad was complaining.

A moment later, Amaleta stepped into my line of sight, leaning on the rail, watching the young man at work. They were of an age, I guess, and more than friends, given the late hour. The lad seemed angry. I could tell that even from where I was standing.

"Don't be mad at me, Ven."

The young man brushed the horse with hard, even strokes, venting his rage in the mundane, repetitive action. "Who says I'm mad at you?"

"You have nothing to worry about . . ."

"I see. You *want* to go with them. That's what all this is about, isn't it? You'd rather be enslaved by the Tide Lords than stay here and marry me."

"That's not true!"

"You think you'll do better as a Tide Lord's whore than you will as my wife? Is that it?"

"No!"

"Don't you know what will happen to you, Amaleta?"

Ven warned. "They'll use you as their plaything and then one day, when you fail to please them any longer, they'll toss you aside and you'll end up a pitiful breeding cow on a Crasii farm somewhere, carrying abominated animals in your womb. You'll be raped and impregnated time and again, just so the Tide Lords can have animals who'll talk to them."

"They offered me a *job*," Amaleta retorted, clearly angered by his lack of understanding. She pushed off the rail and glared at him. "They want me to look after the little girl. I'm nobody's whore, Ven Scyther. Not the Tide Lords' and not yours, either. Besides," she added, crossing her arms defensively, "if I . . . insist on certain conditions—"

"Conditions!" Ven snorted. "You don't put *conditions* on the Tide Lords, Amaleta! Slave or freeborn, they own us, body and soul. The best you can hope for on this world is to avoid coming to their attention."

"What was I supposed to do, Ven? Refuse them?"

"If you're so sure they truly want to hire you, not enslave you, then yes, that's exactly what you should have done."

"You make it sound so simple."

"It is simple. And you've made your choice. Them or me. You chose them."

"I love *you*, Ven."

He stopped brushing the horse and turned to look at her. "Cast me aside if you must, Amaleta, but don't add to the insult by lying to me."

"I'm *not* lying to you, Ven! I don't want to leave. I want to stay here and marry you and grow old and die here in Marivale."

"Then go back in there and tell them you've changed your mind."

"I can't. Not now. If I refuse, we don't know what they'll do." She smiled tentatively. "Anyway, I won't be gone for that long. They just need someone to mind the little girl. After they reach wherever it is they're going, I'll come home and it will be just like it was before. We can still be married.

It might only be a few days that I'm gone, maybe a few weeks . . ."

"And if one of them wants more of you than your services as a nursemaid?"

"Then I'll close my eyes and pretend it's you," she told him with a mischievous smile. I had to stop myself from laughing out loud. Whatever else this girl was, she clearly had a sense of humour, even if her boyfriend didn't. Perhaps Jaxyn had done her a favour in offering her work. This girl hadn't jumped at the opportunity out of fear, I realised. She was looking forward to the adventure.

As if his anger wearied him, Ven tossed aside the brush and walked over to the rail. He leant on it with a sigh, touching his forehead to hers. "I can't bear the thought of losing you."

"And I can't bear the thought of going. But it won't be long . . ."

He kissed her, cutting off her assurances. Amaleta slipped her arms around him and pulled him even closer. When they finally came up for air, Ven buried his face in her thick dark hair. "If you ever need me, I'll come for you," he murmured, so low I could barely hear him. "If it means killing an immortal, I won't let them harm you."

"Don't say that, Ven. You can't kill them and I can't fight them. We just have to make the best of things."

"But you *must* fight!" he insisted, taking her by the shoulders, his eyes boring into hers, demanding a pledge she clearly did not intend to give him. "It's what they really want of you, Amaleta. They're predators. You must fight them with every last breath in your body!"

Amaleta shook free of him, raising a brow curiously. "You'd rather have me raped?"

"That's not what I meant . . ."

"Isn't it? Suppose one of the Tide Lords does decide he wants me, and I try to fight him off? What do you think will happen to me then, Ven? Is that what you want? To see me broken, or even killed, just to keep your male pride intact?"

He bristled at her tone. *What an arrogant young fool,* I thought.

But Ven was just getting warmed up, it seemed. "If you really loved me, you'd not even think of letting another man touch you! Mortal or god! You'd die first."

"If *you* really loved *me,* you'd tell me to do whatever I must to survive!" Amaleta retorted. "And then you'd promise to keep on loving me, no matter what I had to do to ensure that I returned to you whole and unharmed!"

"She has a point, you know."

Amaleta jumped back from the rail in fright as I stepped out of the shadows. The poor girl looked shocked, but the look on Ven's face was priceless. I hadn't intended to become involved, but I was getting a little fed up with Ven's insistence that I was some sort of evil rapist roaming the countryside looking for young girls to corrupt, when in fact I was nothing of the kind.

That I was actually roaming the countryside looking for a quiet place to murder a six-year-old child made Ven's suggestion quite ridiculous, but the irony was lost on me at the time.

"My . . . my lord! We didn't see you there!"

"That much is obvious."

"This is my betrothed, Ven," she said, glancing at her beloved with a look that begged him to hold his tongue. Not that it was likely to do much good. I got the distinct impression that once Ven was riled, it was impossible to reason with him.

I looked the stableboy up and down. "It really *would* be foolish of your girl here to refuse one of us, if we took it into our minds to have her," I said, walking up to the rail of the stall where my mare was stabled. The beast moved to the rail and nuzzled my shoulder. "On the other hand, at the risk of shattering your rather sordid little fantasy, my friend, there are surprisingly few of us who entertain themselves raping peasant girls. Our pleasures are far more sophisticated and a great deal more complicated these days."

"He meant no offence, my lord," Amaleta mumbled, hanging her head in fear. Understandably, I thought. Krydence and Rance had killed men for less.

I looked at Ven curiously. "Why do you mortals flatter yourselves so much thinking that we have nothing better to do than lust after your women?"

"I've seen a Crasii farm," Ven said. He probably figured he was already dead. Unlike the felines, you can only kill an ordinary human once.

I shrugged, knowing there was no defense against such an accusation. "If we indulged in even half the atrocities ascribed to us we'd barely have time to eat."

Ven took umbrage at my patronising tone. "When the Tide turns someday, you'll eat those *words,* my lord," he predicted angrily.

"Then let's hope they're well-seasoned," I replied. "Now, if you're quite finished cursing the cruelty of me and my kind, do you think you could arrange a blanket for my horse? She doesn't like the cold."

Without waiting for either of them to answer, I patted the mare, and then turned and left the stable.

Just before dawn the following morning, I slipped from my bed and made my way through the sleeping inn, my footfall preternaturally loud on the slate floors of the villa. I stepped outside into a light mist spreading from the river a few hundred yards to the north. The edges of the fog were tinted pink as the dawn bled into the sky. The night before, I'd spied a narrow staircase on the left that gave access onto the flat roof of the inn. I took the steps two at a time, anxious not to miss the sunrise.

From the rooftop, I could just make out the flat, red tiled roofs of the rest of the village, many of them, like the inn, with decks that served as extra living space during the long, hot Tenacian summer. Feeling dawn approach, I turned my back on the village and faced the east.

The Tide Star was just beginning to inch its way over the

horizon, a fact I could feel, rather than see. Even without consciously touching the Tide, I could sense it stirring with the rising of the Tide Star. The Tide Lords and the Tide Star are inextricably linked in a manner that few—even among the immortals—understand. Lukys taught me to appreciate that.

And to acknowledge it, once in a while.

Without the Tide we're helpless. It's the ability to use the Tide—not immortality—that makes a Tide Lord superior to other immortals. The ability to touch it, manipulate it and thrive on it . . . to bend the Tide to our will.

That's what it is to be a Tide Lord.

The Tide Star was rising quickly, drowning out the night. With a faint smile of anticipation, I closed my eyes and took several deep, calming breaths, and then I plunged into the Tide.

It's hard to describe swimming the Tide. Swirling colours always fill my mind at first; a kaleidoscope of confusion that it takes me a moment to sort out. During High Tide there are always dangerous eddies in the current to trap the unwary, too. Diving in without being certain you're grounded in reality is a dangerous mistake. So I waited and let the waves of magic subside, slowly resolving themselves into some semblance of order before I cast my senses out further. Surfing the Tide, coasting over the waves of magic that emanate from the Tide Star, is something I knew how to do by instinct. From the moment I first felt Lukys manipulating the Tide the day he slammed Syrolee back against her throne, I'd been aware of it.

"What does it feel like?"

I opened my eyes. Fliss was staring up at me, shivering in her nightgown.

"What are you doing up here?"

"I heard you sneaking out. Are you surfing the Tide?"

"I didn't *sneak* out," I said. "I was trying not to wake anyone. And yes. I am surfing the Tide. At least I was until you interrupted me."

"What does it feel like?" Fliss repeated curiously.

"I'm not sure I can describe it," I replied. "You're a Tide-watcher, aren't you?"

"I suppose," Fliss agreed with a nod. "But I could never do it properly. Aunt Elyssa used to tell me I was too stupid to do it right."

Probably, I thought, *because while other Tidewatchers were skimming the Tide, only able to sense it, but not affect it directly, you were actually in contact with it.* It was no surprise to discover she'd never been able to master the skills her Tidewatcher cousins had learned. "Aren't you cold?"

"Freezing," the little girl admitted, crossing her arms and rubbing them briskly.

"Then go back inside."

It may have been that I was touching the Tide when I spoke to her, but for the first time, I sensed the Tide swirling around Fliss and what I saw chilled me to the core. She was a dark speck in an ocean of light and her presence seemed to draw every lurking shadow to her. I'd never seen anything like it. Never felt anything so terrifying.

Unaware of my thoughts, Fliss slipped her hand into mine and squeezed it. "I don't care what Syrolee says about you. I think you're nice."

I stared at the child, shaking my head. "You know, I'm not surprised the empress wants to be rid of you. She probably got sick of you repeating her every word."

"Does the empress want to be rid of me?" Fliss asked.

Tides, sometimes I just open my big mouth without thinking . . .

I smiled. "I'm joking, Fliss. Let's go find that new nurse of yours and get you dressed. We've a long ride ahead of us today."

"But didn't you want to keep watching the Tide?"

"I think the Tide is safe enough for now."

Fliss smiled up at me trustingly. "I'm glad you're my friend, Uncle Cayal."

"So am I," I said with a smile.

You can add hypocrisy to skills I've mastered over the years, too.

Later that morning, as I was saddling my mare for the journey south, I turned to find Amaleta on the other side of the stall, clutching a small leather bag. She seemed smaller than she had yesterday, and nervous. Her dark hair was neatly braided and she wore a rough woven cloak over practical woollen trousers and a plain linen shirt. I looked around, but there was no sign of her belligerent young fiancé.

"All ready to go?"

"Yes, my lord."

"Where's your betrothed?"

Amaleta's nervousness deepened into tangible fear at my question. "I . . . I'm not sure, my lord. Did you want him for something?"

"He's not planning to make a scene when we ride out this morning, is he?"

"He won't be a problem, my lord," she promised. I knew she was lying, but didn't know what else I could do. Silently, I cursed Jaxyn. He should have made some enquiries about the girl before hiring her. Perhaps then, he might have learned about her passionate and rebellious fiancé.

I was in no mood for passionate and rebellious fiancés, either.

"Then it's time we got moving. We've already wasted half the morning. If you've any more goodbyes to say, you have about five minutes to get them done."

Amaleta curtsied inelegantly and hurried from the stable.

Ven was there to see us off, but the young man did nothing more than lean against the wall of the inn with a sullen glare as he watched his beloved ride away. The chill of the morning had softened into cool sunlight, the cloudless sky pale and washed out by the muted colours of winter. I led the way into the narrow village street. Jaxyn rode beside me. Amaleta came last, with Fliss perched in front of her saddle, waving to her family and the villagers who had come to see us off. The crowd was much smaller than the previous evening. Many of the villagers were out in the flax fields at this time of day. The economic necessity of earning a living outweighs even the chance to look upon a god, I suppose.

"You don't need to pay her, you know."

I looked at Jaxyn blankly as we moved off. "What?"

"The girl. You don't actually have to pay her."

"Why not?"

"Because to do this job right, my reluctant and squeamish old friend, you're probably going to have to kill both the nurse *and* the child," he pointed out in a conversational tone. "When you finally get around to it, that is."

"I wasn't the one who hired the nurse," I reminded him. "Maybe you should kill her yourself. Just don't get any other ideas about her."

He looked at me in surprise. "What makes you think I'd be interested in a rustic, ill-educated innkeeper's daughter?"

"Leave her be."

"Why? Have you staked a claim already?"

"I mean it, Jaxyn."

"And what are you going to do if I ignore you, Cayal?" Jaxyn asked. "*Kill* me? You're starting to amass a bit of a backlog, old son."

I grinned as a much more entertaining revenge leapt to mind. "Touch Amaleta and I'll do worse than that. I'll destroy your reputation. I'll start a new religion in your name. Better yet, I'll have Brynden do it. He's good at that sort of thing. I'll have him add you to his list of worthy deities in Torlenia. I'll have him declare you the Lord of Reformed Drunks and Virgins."

"Is there such a thing as a reformed virgin?"

"I mean it," I threatened, really warming to the idea. "I'll have him make it a virtue to abstain from anything smelling remotely of pleasure in your name. By the time Brynden is done with you, Jaxyn, virgins the world over will be taking oaths of celibacy in your honour. You'll go down in history as the most boring immortal of them all."

"That's cruel, Cayal."

"Then don't cross me, Jaxyn."

"When are you going to kill the child?"

"I don't need to kill her," I said. "She's dying anyway."

The Tide was never meant for mortals.

Until I felt the Tide around Fliss that morning, I don't think I truly understood that. But the darkness I'd seen there, the dangerous eddies, the malevolent whirlpools . . . they were the dangers from which immortality protected the Tide Lords. Fliss didn't have that protection.

She was mortal, vulnerable.

And the Tide was killing her.

How she'd grown this old was something of a mystery. Perhaps she hadn't waded into the Tide often enough to do any real damage. Perhaps growing up believing she had only the ability to sense the Tide rather than enter it protected her. It wasn't until the Scard attack on Arryl and Diala's caravan that she'd opened the conduit fully and now the Tide had a hold of her, it was threatening to swallow her whole.

The danger was what might happen as she drowned. A dying man will gasp for air; reach for anything, to save himself.

A child drowning in the Tide might reach for anything. Fliss might slip away, drawn under the Tide to fade away in peaceful slumber, or she might bring a mountain range down in a blind panic. I had no idea which.

I had no idea how much longer Fliss could survive the Tide or if she could resist the temptation to plunge into its depths, an act which would surely kill her and the fates alone knew how many people she'd take with her when she drowned. I had no idea if I could do anything to save her. No idea if Arryl's optimistic plan was even worth considering.

In fact, the only thing I was sure of, I decided, as we rode with Fliss chattering endlessly in front of Amaleta's saddle at the edge of my awareness, was that I had to find a way to get rid of Jaxyn before we reached Port Gallow.

Chapter 54

Cayal's voice had grown rough from his long tale and when he stopped, it took Arkady by surprise. Although sunlight was streaming in through the cracks in the shutters she had no idea what time it was. Yawning, she stretched her shoulders, wondering if there was enough water left in the pot for another cup of tea.

Cayal must have guessed her intentions, because without being asked, he climbed to his feet and walked over to the fireplace, swung the kettle back over the coals and then began stoking up the fire.

"Did you ever find out if Fliss was your child?"

Cayal shook his head, but didn't turn to look at her. "No. Although Arryl still insists she was."

"What abut Jaxyn?"

"What about him?"

"Where is he now?"

"Don't know." Cayal shrugged. "Don't particularly care, either."

"My husband has a . . . friend," she said. "Named for your precious Lord of Temperance. He's rather less than temperate, too."

"Now *there's* a good liar," Cayal said, standing up from the fire. He stretched his shoulders and then turned and smiled at her. "Jaxyn makes even you look like a rank amateur."

"The Tarot calls him the Lord of Temperance," Arkady told him. "You really did have him made the patron saint of every reformed drunk and virgin on Amyrantha, then?"

Cayal nodded, looking more than a little smug. "I'm not sure if virgins the world over still take oaths of celibacy in his name, but I do know he's rather pissed off with the notion of being known as the only Tide Lord with any real morals or self-control."

"You really do have an odd way of getting along with each other, you immortals."

"Who wants to get along with that little prick?" Cayal snorted. "The only reason I haven't killed him long before now is because I can't."

Arkady smiled sourly. "That's pretty much how I feel about the Jaxyn I know."

"Maybe the name itself is a curse," he suggested. "Didn't know I could do that, but then, Lukys often reminds me that true Tide Lords are only limited by their imaginations."

"Jaxyn certainly is," Arkady agreed. "Will you tell me the rest of it?"

"About Fliss and Amaleta?"

She nodded. "I'm still waiting to hear about this legendary love affair of yours."

"It wasn't much of a love affair, Arkady."

"So you say," she scoffed. "But if I believe your claims of how old you are, then the story has been passed down for over six thousand years. *Something* must have happened."

"Something did happen," Cayal agreed. "Just not what you think."

Chapter 55

We reached the coast about ten days after Marivale. I'd quite deliberately kept our pace slow, to give Arryl time to get ahead of us via the overland route so she would arrive in Port Gallow before us. By then Fliss and Amaleta were firm friends and I was ready to murder Jaxyn, if only such a thing were possible. He'd made it his mission to hint at my commission to kill Fliss at every opportunity, to the point where even Amaleta had begun to ask what he meant.

You're probably wondering why, with all the power I had at my command, I didn't just magically whisk her away to safety, aren't you? Believe me, I'd thought about it. But there wasn't much point. Jaxyn can surf the Tide as well as I can and does so with far fewer scruples, and that's saying something, because I don't have many. He'd follow us, if not now, then as soon as Fliss disturbed the Tide again and then I'd bring down the wrath of all the others upon us both, and any unfortunate mortals who happened to be in a thousand-mile radius of us at the time.

In hindsight, it was a futile notion, given what I ended up doing, but I think being around Fliss affected my judgement. She made me feel noble, paternal even. I couldn't go around destroying entire civilisations on a whim while she was with me.

She thought I was nice.

I didn't have the heart to disillusion her.

No, I needed to accomplish this the hard way. No magic. No cheating. For that I needed help, and the help I enlisted was Amaleta.

Arryl was waiting for us in Port Gallow. She had arranged for a ship to take her and Fliss back to Glaeba, where she intended to hide the child at the temple until we could work out what to do with her. It was a sound plan, in theory. The one place on Amyrantha where it was nigh impossible to sense a disturbance in the Tide was in close proximity to the Eternal Flame. Of course, it meant trusting Diala, but Arryl assured me she could handle her sister and, to be honest, I couldn't think of anything better.

The problem I had now was to lose Jaxyn long enough to make him think I'd killed Fliss.

I confided as much to Amaleta when we reached Port Gallow. I suppose that's how your "great love affair" story got started. I ordered her to my room in full view of everyone present in the taproom of the inn we'd commandeered, not in the least bit concerned what they might think about my intentions. Let them believe I was having my way with yet another mortal underling. It's not the worst thing I've been accused of. Fliss wasn't there to witness the scene. She was still with Jaxyn at the livery, settling in the horses. Oddly enough, I knew she'd be safe with him. Jaxyn's entertainment came from watching me sweat over my promise to kill her, not helping me wriggle out of it by doing the job himself.

Somewhat to my surprise, Amaleta came to my room as I commanded, her head held high, displaying more courage than I've seen from grown men on a battlefield. Amaleta thought as everyone else did, I'm sure. I can't begin to imagine what she thought I was planning to do to her.

"Shall I undress?" was the first thing she said to me when she closed the door.

"If it'll help you listen better."

"Pardon?"

"I'm not going to rape you, Amaleta. I need your help to save Fliss."

"Save her from who?" she asked in confusion.

"Me."

"Have you been drinking, Lord Cayal?"

She was fearless, Amaleta of Marivale.

"No. But I am supposed to kill Fliss on the orders of the Empress of the Five Realms and Lord Jaxyn is here to make sure I do. I need you to help me get Fliss to someone who can hide her, and then I need you to die."

"Sound plan, my lord," she agreed. "Right up to the point where I *die*."

Like I said, Amaleta didn't lack for courage.

I smiled. "I need you to give a good impression of it. Lots of blood, weeping . . . cursing me for murdering a small child . . . that sort of thing. If you can manage to slip in an eyewitness account of my foul deed, that would be helpful. Once you've gasped your dying breath, I'll arrange to have you taken away before you actually expire and I'll heal you, at which point you may leave town, ride back to your stableboy in Marivale and live happily ever after."

"What will happen to Fliss?"

"While you're faking your death, she'll be on a ship for Glaeba with Lady Arryl. She'll be safe at the Temple of the Tide."

"And what if I want no part of your plan, my lord?"

"Then I will kill you where you stand, Amaleta, and find somebody who *will* help me."

She smiled faintly. "That's a very persuasive argument, Lord Cayal."

"You'll do it?"

Amaleta nodded. "My mother always did say I was a good actress. I suppose now we'll find out how good."

Of course, getting Amaleta to help was easy. She was full of spunk and was rather keen to go on living. I still had to tell Fliss what I had planned for her and that wasn't going to be nearly as easy.

Amaleta brought her to my room the next day, while Jaxyn was downstairs eating breakfast. She left us alone and went to keep watch on the stairs. I didn't really need a lookout. I could feel Jaxyn's approach in the Tide long before I saw him if I was paying attention—which I hadn't been that day at the river ferry, which is how he managed to surprise me. But it gave Amaleta something to do while I spoke to Fliss.

"What's the matter, Cayal?" she asked as soon as we were alone. Amaleta's furtive manner must have warned her something was amiss. She'd dropped the *uncle* several days ago, although I'm not sure why.

"I have to tell you what's going to happen to you, Fliss."

"Am I in trouble again? I haven't done anything bad, Cayal, I promise . . ."

"No, Fliss," I hurried to assure her, mostly because I had no wish to deal with a distressed child. "You're not in any trouble. Lady Arryl is going to take you on a trip. She's taking you to Glaeba. To the temple where she guards the Eternal Flame."

I filled my voice with as much enthusiasm as I could muster, hoping to make it sound like a fine old time, but Fliss wasn't convinced. "I want to stay with you."

"You can't."

"Why not?"

"Because," I declared, thinking I sounded more like a real parent every day.

"Because why?"

"Because I said so."

"It's the Tide, isn't it?" Fliss's big blue eyes glistened with unshed tears. "What if I promise never to touch it again? Could I stay with you then?"

Her question puzzled me. "Why would you even want to?"

She looked away, biting her bottom lip, and then she turned those big tear-filled eyes on me again and I could feel myself being eaten alive by guilt, just from the way she was staring at me.

I despise children.

And I'm not very good at handling them. Jaxyn was right, you know. I should have killed her at the palace. It would have saved a lot of lives and a great deal of agonising about it on my part.

"If you stay with me, Fliss, I'll kill you."

She smiled wanly. "Don't make jokes like that, Cayal."

"I'm not joking. Syrolee wants you dead. They all want you dead, including Uncle Jaxyn. Arryl is taking you to safety and if you don't want to go with her, that's fine. I just want you to know what the alternative is."

She was crying uncontrollably by the time I was done, which made me feel a right bastard. I might have broken the news to her a bit more gently, I suppose, but I couldn't even think of a way to tell Medwen what had happened to her child. What was I going to say to Fliss?

She hugged me again, her thin arms squeezing me tight. "I love you, Cayal."

"I love you too, Fliss," I assured her, willing to say anything at that point to make her happy. I didn't see the harm in it. I truly believed Arryl would take her back to the temple in Glaeba and that proximity to the Eternal Flame would make it easier to teach Fliss enough control to stop the Tide from killing her.

It never occurred to me she meant what she said, or that she thought I meant what I said. It wasn't until it was far too late that I recalled our conversation and realised I was almost entirely to blame for what happened next.

There was one thing I didn't take into account in my grand deception to hide Fliss's escape from Tenacia. I forgot about Ven, Amaleta's aggrieved fiancé.

Unbeknownst to any of us, Ven had followed us to Port Gallow. News reached him quickly about the Tide Lords staying in the city and I suppose, on the heels of that, must have come the news that one of them was having his way with the servant girl in their company.

You can imagine the effect it had on him.

I had all my plans in place by then. I'd met secretly with Arryl and arranged to have Fliss delivered to her that evening. The ship was due to sail on the late tide. Amaleta was ready and had even procured a rather savage-looking dagger for me, so that I could inflict a convincing wound on her. She had enough confidence in me, apparently, to believe I would heal the wound before she died of it.

I didn't intend to kill her but she understood a fake wound would easily be discovered. Jaxyn had to see her and believe I'd killed Fliss and inflicted a fatal wound on Amaleta to be rid of them both. Once he was convinced, once Fliss was safe, I could magically undo the damage I'd done with the knife and Amaleta could be on her way home before midnight.

The plan worked, up to a point. We got Fliss aboard Arryl's ship about an hour after sunset and watched it slip its mooring lines, sliding across the dark water under the pull of the amphibious Crasii charged with seeing the ship safely through the heads.

Once I was satisfied they were out of Jaxyn's reach, I turned to Amaleta.

"Ready?"

She nodded, shivering in the cool night air. "Is it going to hurt?"

"Probably."

"But you will fix me up afterwards . . . before I die?"

"I give you my word."

She smiled trustingly. "I can see where Fliss gets her spirit from."

I scowled at her. "Fliss isn't really my child, Amaleta. She just told you that because she felt bad about not knowing who her father is."

"Whether she comes from your seed or not, my lord, you are the only father she has ever known. Fliss is the child of your heart, even if she's not the child of your loins."

I had no answer for that, so I turned and headed back toward the inn without even bothering to check if Amaleta was following.

I stopped in the street when we reached the inn and pulled Amaleta into the lane beside me. Jaxyn was inside. Even if the noise of the party going on in the taproom didn't give him away, I could sense his presence in the Tide.

"I'll go in first," I said in a low voice. "Give me a couple of minutes and then come in after me. Call me an evil child-killer, or something equally harsh. Just make sure it's loud and that you catch everyone's attention. You may not get to say much more before you pass out. As soon as you do, I'll have someone take you out of the taproom and then I'll come fix you up in a few minutes."

She nodded and then took a deep breath. "I know what to do."

I reached into my belt and withdrew the dagger. It was a wicked-looking beast with a blade near on a foot long, serrated along one side, designed to inflict as much damage as possible on its victim.

Amaleta saw my hesitation. "It'll be all right, Lord Cayal."

Sweet of her, don't you think, to imagine I had any qualms about taking her life?

She stood on her toes and kissed me lightly on the lips

and then wrapped her hands around mine on the hilt of the knife and pressed it against her blouse. "I trust you, Lord Cayal," she whispered.

"You filthy immortal bastard!"

Out of nowhere, Ven came at us, screaming like a berserker. He must have been waiting in the darkness, watched us talking in intimate whispers, seen Amaleta kiss me and gotten entirely the wrong idea.

There was no time to tell him that, though.

He slammed into us furiously, pushing Amaleta onto that savage blade, driving it far deeper than I'd intended to go. She cried out in agony, but I don't think Ven noticed, so intent was he on getting to me.

I brushed him off like an insect as Amaleta fell. Without a thought, I threw him across the street with a wave of my arm. His skull splattered on the stone facade of the building opposite, so loud I could hear it cracking open from where I stood on the other side of the street.

I spared the young man not another thought as Jaxyn burst out of the tavern, followed by everyone else in the taproom. Killing Ven by drawing on the Tide had jerked him out of his drunken torpor, while the mortals had followed out of curiosity. He was at Amaleta's side almost before I was.

"Tides!" he exclaimed. "You've killed her!"

"Did you think I wouldn't?" I managed to ask with a calm detachment I certainly didn't feel. What I *could* feel was Amaleta's life ticking away. I'd planned to stab her *near* the heart, not through it, which meant I'd have sufficient time to heal her wound after our little charade was done. Ven had robbed me of that option. The blade had gone right through her heart, right through everything, only a rib in her back stopping it scraping on the pavement.

If I was to save Amaleta, I had to do it now, not wait until we were alone.

If I saved her, Jaxyn would know the truth.

She opened her mouth to speak, but nothing came out. No accusations to convince Jaxyn I'd killed Fliss. No chance to show me what a good actress she was. Nothing but a burbling noise emerged from her blood-filled lungs.

I looked at Jaxyn, who was watching me expectantly. We have no telepathic ability to speak of, but I knew exactly what he was thinking. On this girl's death and my reaction to it rested the fate of Fliss.

The child of my heart, if not the child of my loins.

And then I looked down at Amaleta. Her eyes were fixed on me, full of hope. Full of trust.

In return for that trust I did nothing.

I knelt there in that cold, cobbled street of Port Gallow and let Amaleta die.

Chapter 56

A rkady was silent for a long time after Cayal finished speaking. The tea had long cooled; the fire had almost died out.

"Did Jaxyn never question you about Fliss's fate?" she asked, eventually.

He took a long time to answer, so long Arkady wondered if he'd heard the question.

"Given the dramatic nature of Amaleta's demise," he said, after a while, "and that he could no longer sense Fliss's presence on the Tide, he accepted I'd done it, I suppose, and moved on to more interesting entertainment."

"What did you do? Did you follow Arryl to Glaeba?"

He shook his head. "Not right away. Everyone had to believe I'd killed Fliss without remorse and the only way to do that was to resume my life seeding the Crasii farms and pretending I didn't have a care in the world."

Arkady stared at him, more than a little disturbed by his casual dismissal of the lives he'd ruined. "And when you were done?" she asked. "Seeding the Crasii farms and pretending you didn't have a care in the world?"

"I left," he replied, smiling thinly at her tone. "It was nearly a year before I could get away, though, and even then, I had to do it the old-fashioned way."

"The *old-fashioned* way?"

"I couldn't use the Tide because someone would have felt it and wondered what business I had there." He smiled wryly. "Ironic, don't you think, that the only way we great magicians can hide from each other is to *not* be great magicians?"

The irony wasn't lost on Arkady, but she was more interested in hearing the rest of the tale. "What happened when you got to the temple?"

"Arryl was there, but Diala was off on some business of her own, so for a time it was a very pleasant visit, indeed. Fliss was beside herself when she saw me, but I was shocked by her appearance. She was haggard. Black circles framed her eyes and she was thin to the point of emaciation. I couldn't believe the change in her."

"Was she ill?"

"Proximity to the Eternal Flame didn't seem to have made the slightest difference. The Tide was still killing her a little bit more each day. Even Arryl was starting to wonder if it might not have been kinder to let her die."

"Why doesn't the Tide affect you like that? Is it just because you're immortal?"

"It would almost have to be," Cayal agreed. "Maybe that's the true nature of the Tide. It ravages us the same way, but we heal up before we feel its effects."

"But Fliss didn't have your ability to heal," Arkady concluded. "Do you think she was the only one?"

Cayal shook his head. "The only mortal to wield Tide magic? Probably not. But any other child born as she is would have no notion of what was happening to them. I only know what happened to Fliss because there were others around with her ability to identify it for what it was. Any other mortal child with her talent would just wither and die and have it put down to bad blood or some mystery illness that miraculously nobody else in the village caught."

"Were you able to save her?"

"Far from it. I couldn't see any possible way to save her. Diala could, however. And when she returned to the temple a few weeks later, she was the one who suggested the solution."

"Which was?" Arkady asked, wondering at Cayal's reluctance. He'd been entirely forthcoming up until this point. Now she was having to drag the rest of the story out of him, one sentence at a time.

"She suggested we let the Eternal Flame decide."

"Surely not! Fliss was only . . . what . . . by then? Seven years old? That would doom her to eternity as a small child. That's a punishment cruel beyond description."

"I did point that out to Diala, you know. But I suppose Fliss must have known she was dying. I'd told her as much in Port Gallow and there was no way she could have been unaware of the effect the Tide was having on her. But I still wonder what was going through her mind that day. Did she stand there in the shadows, eavesdropping on a conversation between Arryl and Diala that she didn't really understand? Did she think if she was immortal she would still grow up? I don't know. I've wondered about it for thousands of years and I still can't fathom it. Whatever her reasons, Fliss sneaked into the temple after everyone had retired later that night and in an attempt to become immortal like us, she took the Eternal Flame down from the altar and set herself alight."

Arkady studied him across the table in the dusty sunlight coming through the shutters behind her, not sure what to say.

"Did she . . ."

"No. She died screaming and calling my name."

Arkady winced at the very thought of such a terrible thing. And while the memory obviously pained Cayal, she suspected the worst was yet to come.

"This is the part I'm not going to like, isn't it?"

He nodded grimly. "I felt as if I'd been ripped in two. If you've heard the expression *blind rage,* let me tell you, it's real. Everything I despised about the immortals, every moment of eternity I had suffered because of that wretched fire seemed to well up inside me with her screams. And it was High Tide." He hesitated, meeting Arkady's eye, his gaze an open challenge, as if he was daring her to despise him for what he'd done next. "I had only one thought, I swear, and it was to put an end to the Eternal Flame. I wanted it gone. So I reached for water, for all the water I could find. It began to rain. Then it deluged. And it didn't let up for a month or more."

"Didn't Arryl and Diala try to stop you?"

"They had no hope. I command more power than the two of them combined. But even if someone strong enough had been nearby, I doubt they would have been able to do anything to stop me. I was powered by rage; driven by unconscionable anger."

"Did you spare a thought for the people?"

He shook his head. "I didn't care what I was doing, Arkady, don't you understand that? My only thought was to smother that damned flame—with an ocean, if I had to. And that's what it took, in the end, before it finally sputtered and died. I'd dumped an ocean on it—or a sea, to be more accurate. The Great Inland Sea from Torlenia, actually, although I didn't realise it at the time. I was too angry to care where the water came from. I suppose I thought I was drawing it from the oceans, but freshwater is lighter than salt water, you see, and the largest body of fresh water nearby was in Torlenia. Of course, you have the Great Lakes to thank me for now, which weren't there until I happened along. I suppose that's how the legend of the Immortal Prince's tears creating your lakes got its start." He smiled, which chilled Arkady to the core. "Funny, when you think about it, there's actually a grain of truth in *that* legend."

"And how many innocent people died as a consequence of your wrath?"

Cayal shrugged, seemingly unconcerned. Was his lack of remorse because this had happened so long ago, or because he really was a monster? Arkady wished she knew the answer. It would have made her own emotions so much easier to deal with if the former was the case.

"Millions, I reckon," Cayal told her with a shrug. "Either in the flood or the years of drought and famine that followed afterwards while the world suffered the backlash of my storm. You can't mess with the weather on that scale without it having serious ramifications the world over for centuries after. This was worse than Magreth. With that one act I knocked human life on Amyrantha back to stone axes and face paint."

"You sound like you're proud of what you did."

"I am," Cayal told her without remorse. "I extinguished the Eternal Flame. For that reason alone, it was worth every life I destroyed to do it."

A part of her was horrified by the remorseless arrogance of this man responsible for the deaths of millions of people, while her heart bled for the father forced to witness the child he loved, screaming in agony as she burned alive.

"Did it ease your pain," she asked, "killing all those people?"

"Nothing ever eases the pain, Arkady. Not even the tincture of time, and the Tides know I've put *that* theory to the test."

For no reason she could name, she reached across the table, placing her hand over his. This man didn't deserve her pity. If she had any brains, she'd run screaming from him. He was arrogant, cruel and remorseless. Logically, Arkady knew that. But there was little logic here and what she was feeling had nothing to do with rational thought. "And this is why you want to die, or find oblivion? Because the pain never goes away?"

He stared at her hand for a moment and then slowly raised it to his lips.

For some reason, the temperature in the room rose

sharply, so much that Arkady half-expected the fire to reignite and flare up behind Cayal. It didn't, of course. The heat she felt didn't come from any external source.

"I think," he whispered against her fingers, "that I've finally convinced you I am who I claim."

"Don't gloat," she warned, knowing she should take her hand away.

He closed his eyes and turned her palm to his cheek, kissing the inside of her wrist. Her pulse hammered against his lips and she wanted to squirm in her seat with longing, but didn't dare move in case he took it as an invitation to go on.

Or worse, that he might stop.

"Please, Cayal . . . ," she whispered, trying to kid herself she was asking him to let her go.

He opened his eyes and stared at her. The naked ache in them made her want to cry.

"Please, *what*, Arkady?"

She was caught between fear and desire, trapped in the middle of her natural caution and the heat in her loins. No man had ever made Arkady feel like this. Desire was something to be feared; something that would cause her pain. She'd never felt so vulnerable, so fearful, so reckless.

Everything around her seemed frozen in time. The dust motes riding the beams of weak sunlight onto the table, the shadows darkening the walls of the tiny cabin, her heart halted between beats, even her breathing . . .

"I don't know," she told him softly, honestly.

"You can't make my pain go away, Arkady."

"You can do something about mine," someone Arkady didn't know replied.

They were alone, she knew that, but the woman who reached for Cayal wasn't anybody she recognised. He leant forward and kissed her, his lips soft and enticing, more gentle than she could have hoped, more dangerous than she dared acknowledge. He smelt of wood smoke and leather and tasted of ambrosia. Arkady was certain she might die from the tenderness of his caress. Carefully, achingly, he teased open her mouth with the tip of his tongue, his hands sliding through her tousled hair to draw her nearer.

Arkady couldn't breathe. The edge of the table pressed into her ribs, cutting off her air. It didn't matter, she didn't want to breathe.

"You know," he whispered through the kiss, "this would be a lot easier if there wasn't a table between us."

He couldn't have said anything worse if he'd asked her how much she charged.

She pulled away from him, jumping to her feet.

What a fool! she told herself angrily. *What a damned fool you are, woman!*

Cayal looked up at her, disappointed certainly, but perhaps not surprised.

"Arkady . . . ," he began apologetically, but he never got to finish what he was planning to say because at that moment the door opened and Maralyce stomped into the cabin, oblivious to the tension, complaining about the appalling quality of mining equipment these days.

There was no place to escape in Maralyce's tiny cabin. Arkady thought she might scream with the strain of saying nothing. Doing nothing. Sitting across the table listening to Maralyce curse and mutter about her equipment while trying to avoid Cayal's eye. He went out to chop wood for a while after lunch, which gave her some respite, but it was only temporary. Eventually he would come back inside. Eventually Maralyce would return to her underground tunnels.

Eventually they would be alone again.

Arkady was at war with herself. To have a man want her was nothing new, to feel his desire radiating from across the room was something she could recognise in her sleep. What made this different was her reaction to it. There was no snide remark at the ready, no deprecating smile, no patronising put-down she could think of. Just the desire, the *need* almost, to give in.

Tilly's stupid suggestion about having an affair was

starting to seem not just acceptable, but actually attractive. And how many times had Stellan said outright that he wouldn't mind if she took a lover?

But this wasn't about taking a lover or keeping marriage vows that had always been a sham. This was about letting go. This was about closing the doors on Fillion Rybank's rooms at the university, once and for all.

It shocked Arkady to realise how hard she was clinging to the pain of her growing years. *Is that why I so readily married Stellan?* she wondered. *Was it really about freeing my father or was it simply a convenient way of never having to confront my own fears?*

She couldn't find an answer and that disturbed her almost as much as the effect Cayal was having on her.

"He ain't worth it, you know."

Maralyce looked up from the pulley she was repairing on the table and frowned. Arkady had been staring out the window, watching Cayal chop wood. He'd discarded his shirt for the task and she was entranced by the dappled sunlight playing across the muscles of his perfectly formed back. Spellbound by the rise and fall of the axe, the strong arms that wielded it, rippling with the effort until the tendons stood out beneath the skin. . . .

She caught herself and turned to face Maralyce, certain she must be blushing crimson. "I beg your pardon?"

"Cayal," the old woman replied. "He ain't worth gettin' all worked up over. He's just a man, in the end. Pretty enough to look at, I'll grant, but in the end, just a man."

"Do you believe he's immortal?"

"Thought so the first time I met him," Maralyce agreed, returning her attention to the pulley. "Can't say he's done much in the past eight thousand years to change m'mind."

"Did he tell you what he did in Glaeba after Fliss died?"

"You mean that business with the rain? Didn't have to. Little bastard drowned two hundred years of my work with his tantrum. Only reason I forgave him was because it meant I had to take a different route through the mine and found another vein I didn't know about."

Arkady couldn't help but smile at the old woman's pragmatism. "You seem much more . . . accepting . . . of your immortality than he does," she remarked.

Maralyce looked up at her. "That's because I ain't tryin' to fight it. Cayal's never really come to terms with living forever, and he ain't the only one. He's just the most powerful of them that can't accept their lot in life, which makes him the most dangerous. He's a tenacious little bastard though," she added, thoughtfully. "If anybody can find us a way out of this hell, he will."

"You call it hell. Do *you* want to die?"

"Don't care one way or the other." The old immortal shrugged. "Don't mind livin', don't much care if I don't."

"I can't imagine what it must be like for you."

"Nobody's asking you to. You slept with him yet?"

Arkady drew herself up defensively. "No."

"Maybe you should. Rumour has it he's pretty good in the sack. Not that I've ever tried it for myself, mind you. Old enough to be his mother, I am. Old enough to be yours too, I'd say."

Arkady smiled. "If you're several thousand years old, Maralyce, I think that makes you old enough to be everybody's mother."

The old woman cracked a rare smile. "I like you, Arkady. You've got a bit of spunk. Don't let him get you killed."

"I'll make a point of it," Arkady promised and then she turned to stare out of the dusty window at Cayal chopping wood once more, letting her idle fantasies take her where she was far too afraid to go in real life.

Chapter 57

It was midafternoon and raining when Warlock and Boots left Shalimar's attic. By then both had eaten their fill, but decided nothing about what the Tide Lords might be up to. Shalimar had not volunteered the location of Hidden Valley nor given Warlock any indication that he intended to and had hurried them out of his small apartment as if the place was on fire.

Warlock spent little time dwelling on it, however. As the day progressed, Boots's scent had grown stronger and stronger until it was all he could do to concentrate on what Shalimar was saying.

Warlock wasn't the only Crasii male in the slums who could smell her. As they walked back to the Kennel via a much less circuitous route, a number of young males began to follow them, drawn by the irresistible scent Boots was giving off.

At first, Warlock tried to ignore them, telling himself they just happened to be going in the same direction, but when he and Boots turned down the lane between two old warehouses that led to the entrance of the Kennel, they discovered another male waiting for them, blocking their way.

They stopped and stared at the challenger. Without having to look behind him, Warlock knew three of the young males who'd been following them were closing in behind.

"Time to choose, Bootsie," the male in front of them declared. He was wet and bedraggled but there was no mistaking what he was after.

Warlock had no idea who the male was. He might have been one of the many residents of the Kennel who'd glared at him so suspiciously when he'd arrived last night. He might be another stray drawn by the irresistible allure of a female in heat. Whoever he was, he obviously knew Boots and had plans to be the one she chose when the time came for her to stand; a time that was distractingly close.

Before he could stop himself, Warlock growled low in his throat, warning the challenger off. Behind him he heard similar growls coming from the other three males. He glanced down at Boots, who stood beside him, alert, but unafraid.

Why would she be? Here she is, almost ready to stand, and she's confronted with five healthy males willing to kill each other for the privilege of standing with her.

The young canine smiled—flattered no doubt by the attention—and took a step backwards, until she was up against the decaying warehouse wall. "Why don't you boys decide this among yourselves, eh?"

Her words ignited bedlam. The male blocking the way to the Kennel was on Warlock before he could move, the other three charging at them with a roar. Warlock thrashed about with claws, teeth, fists, feet . . . anything he could use to fight off his attackers. Oddly, the males jumping him from behind actually helped his cause, because they hit the canine on his back first, taking him down, rendering him senseless within moments. That just left the three younger males, the closest of whom fled howling the moment Warlock's meaty fist connected with his cheekbone.

Warlock turned to face the last two. They'd scrambled clear of the melee, a little more cautious now that the first male was lying unconscious in the litter-strewn lane and their companion had abandoned them. Warlock was the bigger by far, but he was trained as a house steward and these were strays, used to living off their wits and their fighting skills. There wasn't much room to manoeuvre, either. The lane was cluttered with fallen boards and several generations of detritus.

All the while, Boots watched the exchange in silence from her vantage by the wall, her eyes wide, her scent enough to drive all of the three remaining males to acts of wild desperation in an attempt to win her favour.

"Reckon you can take the both of us?" the male on the left taunted through a grin revealing a number of missing teeth. His speckled grey pelt was pitted and scarred, a testament to the number of fights he'd survived.

"Reckon if I kill you, your little friend there is just going to run away like the other one did." Warlock shrugged, his chest heaving. It took every ounce of willpower he owned to resist the heady, musky scent filling the narrow lane. "Which means I really only have to kill *you.*"

In response, the male charged, growling savagely. He launched himself at Warlock, his mouth wide, clearly intending to go for his opponent's throat. A lesser creature might have baulked at such savagery. That's probably what the male was counting on. He wasn't counting on his opponent being more calculating than crazed, however. While the male was still in midair, Warlock bent down, swept up one of the fallen boards lying in the lane and swung it with all his might. The other male slammed into the plank so hard he almost wrenched Warlock's shoulders out of their sockets, and then he dropped like a sack. Warlock barely spared him, unconscious, a bloody mess where his nose had once been, a glance before turning on his last opponent.

The male turned and fled, tail between his legs, without so much as a backwards glance.

A triumphant grin cracked Warlock's face. He turned to face Boots.

She glanced down at the two unconscious contenders and then smiled. "My, my . . . aren't you just the hero?"

"I live only to protect your honour, my lady," he declared with a sweeping bow.

"Tides!" she exclaimed. "Court manners. There's something you don't see every day."

"It's not every day one is called on to defend a lady," he told her, daring to step a little closer.

Boots looked up at him, still smiling. Her dark eyes were wide as she ran her tongue over her lips to moisten them. "You know . . . right now . . . flattery probably isn't necessary . . ."

Warlock still hesitated. He'd seen a male killed by a female who wasn't ready, and despite her blatant provocation, despite the wild arousal of her scent, he had enough self-control, enough sense of self-preservation, to make sure he was very clear on what she wanted.

With a growl, she rolled her eyes. "Tides! What are you waiting for, you big lug? A written invitation?"

"Isn't that how you do things at the palace?" he asked with a grin, as she grabbed him by the ears and pulled his mouth down onto hers.

Warlock thought he might die for the wanting of her. Urgently, he slid his arms around her, pulling her to him. Pushed against the wall, she let out a low growl, and offered him her throat, throwing her head back and exposing her most vulnerable part in a sign of trust and desire that left him gasping.

There was little need for foreplay. A whole night and day of smelling her musky, tantalising scent was all the provocation he needed. Warlock couldn't believe how easily any pretence of civilisation abandoned them and instinct took over. It was broad daylight. A few feet away was a busy street on one side and the main entrance to the place several dozen canines called home on the other.

We may look human from a distance, Warlock thought in some part of his mind still civilised enough to be appalled by how easily his animal instincts could override a lifetime of careful self-control, *but in some things, we are still what we are made from.* He wanted to howl like a dog as he tore her shift away so he could bite down on her breast, his hand running over the knobbly line of fallow nipples under the soft pelt running down her taut abdomen—more proof of their canine ancestry—crying out in blessed agony as her claws raked down his back.

Boots is wrong, he decided, pulling away from her. He roughly spun her around, slamming her face first into the wall so he could take her from behind. Boots eagerly pushed out her buttocks to meet him with a gleeful yelp, lifting her bushy tail high, scouring deep scratches on the rotting warehouse wall, as he thrust himself inside her.

We are animals.

Chapter 58

By the fourth day of Arkady's disappearance, Stellan knew he had no choice but to confess her abduction to the king. The plans for Enteny's return to Herino were well underway and he was making noises about visiting Arkady in her rooms before he left, in the belief that an appearance by her king would perk her up and undoubtedly aid her recovery.

Stellan hadn't made any specific claims about what might be wrong with Arkady. The blanket description of "women's troubles" seemed to suffice, and was even enough to keep Declan Hawkes away. Queen Inala had never been fond of Arkady and seemed glad to be spared her company, although after the third day it became increasingly difficult to deter Enteny—who was quite enchanted by Arkady—from paying her a visit.

Stellan could think of nothing else sitting glumly at breakfast, paying little attention to the background chatter of his guests, the rattle of crockery or the patter of canine feet as the Crasii slaves hurried back and forth from the kitchens to keep the buffet loaded. He was too busy imagining all manner of dreadful fates awaiting him when he was finally forced to admit that far from being ill, Arkady had actually been kidnapped, and that he'd been lying to his king for days.

There wasn't likely to be a diplomatic posting at the end of this sorry little incident.

Fortunately, the betrothal of Kylia and Mathu had overshadowed even Arkady's absence. His niece was beside herself with happiness and Mathu seemed to feel the same. Stellan, for no reason he could put his finger on, wasn't nearly so enthusiastic. It might have been because Kylia was so young, but seventeen was a fairly common age for a Glaeban girl to marry, particularly one of noble birth.

It might have been because he doubted Mathu. The boy seemed sincere enough now, but how long would it be before Stellan was dragging the young prince out of brothels again? Once he and Arkady had left for Torlenia, who was there to perform that delicate function, anyway? Would Mat tire of Kylia as soon as he got her pregnant, a circumstance likely to occur sooner rather than later? How would Kylia cope with the pressure of being wife to the crown prince? Could she stand the constant scrutiny? The gossip and rumour? Once the blush of first love had faded would Mat bully her or ignore her? And how would she react? Would it crush her, or would the harsh reality of court life harden her and destroy that wide-eyed wonder that made her so alluring to Mathu in the first place . . .

"Your grace?"

Stellan looked up to find Tassie standing just behind him. She'd improved a great deal in the last few months to the point where she was now allowed to serve in the dining room with the king present.

"Yes?"

"Lady Ponting is here to see you."

Stellan nodded, hoping his relief was not too evident. He excused himself, pleading an urgent matter to attend to. Nobody really cared. The queen was describing her plans for the wedding which had Kylia and Mathu entranced and the king complaining loudly, but good-naturedly, about the cost.

Tilly was waiting for him in his office, studying the murals with interest. She looked around when she heard Stellan closing the door behind him and smiled broadly. She'd changed her hair colour. The widow was a redhead now, her hair a brassy orange colour that clashed badly with the fringed yellow shawl she was wearing over her green morning gown.

"Stellan, my dear! To what do I owe the pleasure of your summons?"

"Thank you for coming, Tilly."

"Always a pleasure to accept an invitation to the palace," she replied. "It keeps my catering bills down."

"I need your help, Tilly," he told her, indicating she should take a seat. He took the chair beside her, wondering if this desperate tactic he had planned was just going to plunge him deeper into the mire, rather than get him out of it.

Interesting, he thought, *how these days I always think of a lie to solve my problems first, before I even consider telling the truth.*

"You know I'd do anything for you, Stellan. And for Arkady."

"Does that include lying to the king?"

She seemed intrigued rather than shocked by the question. "Do you *need* me to lie to the king? What do you want of me, Stellan? To tell him I see his future in the cards? I could tell him he's known across the length and breadth of Glaeba as the beloved father of our nation instead of a pompous ass, I suppose. That would be a lie."

"I'm serious, Tilly."

"So am I," the old lady chuckled.

"Arkady is missing."

Tilly's smile faded. "Exactly what do you mean by missing?"

"She was last seen at Clyden's Inn four days ago with an escaped prisoner from Lebec Prison. I think he's kidnapped her."

"You don't sound too certain about it."

"I'm not," he confessed, guessing the only way to make Tilly a willing conspirator to this plan was to involve her fully.

"This prisoner wouldn't happen to be our Immortal Prince, by any chance?" she asked curiously.

Stellan frowned. "She told you about him?"

"Arkady wanted to know about the Tarot. His name . . . might have come up in conversation."

Suspiciously, he studied Tilly, wondering if she was also part of Arkady's plan to free Kyle Lakesh. "Do you know something about this, Tilly?"

"Specifically?" she asked, pulling off her gloves and laying them across her lap. "No. But your girl was mighty taken with the Immortal Prince, so it wouldn't surprise me if she didn't object too loudly when he tried to escape."

Stellan leant back in his chair and closed his eyes for a moment. *Tides, could this get any worse?* Then he opened them and stared at Tilly, wondering what her reaction would be to his next revelation. "She did more than *not object,* Tilly. She forged my signature on his release papers."

Tilly seemed impressed. "Resourceful sort of girl, isn't she?"

"This isn't a joke."

"I'm not joking," Tilly assured him.

Stellan hesitated and then asked the one question he'd been afraid to voice, even to himself. "Do you think she's run off with him?"

The old lady smiled. "Not on purpose."

"Not on *purpose*? What does that mean?"

"I mean, dearest, she might have been looking for a way to save him from Declan Hawkes, but Arkady has too much respect for you, and is far too cognisant of what's at stake, to throw it all away for a fling with a madman."

Stellan was unconvinced. "But if he didn't take her against her will . . ."

Tilly smiled. "Surely, you're not going to pretend you're jealous?"

He glared at her, not liking what she was implying. "I love my wife. How dare you suggest otherwise."

"I don't doubt you love Arkady, Stellan, just not the way most husbands do." She leaned forward and patted his knee. "Don't look at me like that. You might think I'm a silly old fool because I play with Tarot cards, but the truth is, I'm a lot wilier than I seem."

Her meaning was clear. Stellan's heart pounded as he realised how close to discovery he'd been all this time.

Tilly was a regular guest at the palace. Had he or Jaxyn done something foolish? Said something that might give them away? Had Arkady shared his secret, her frustration, with a trusted friend? And *was* she really a trusted friend? It was one thing to ask her to lie about Arkady, whom Stellan knew Tilly adored. It was quite another for him to expect her to keep *his* secrets.

"Then you're probably aware," he ventured cautiously, just so he was clear on where she stood, "of Jaxyn Aranville's position in my household?"

"Actual positions are something I don't care to dwell on," she replied with a wicked little smile. "But if you're asking me if I think you hired him simply because he's good at handling Crasii, then you're an idiot, Stellan Desean."

He shook his head, wondering how long she'd known. "Have you said anything to anyone about this?"

"And get myself struck off the palace invitation list? I'm old, Stellan, not stupid."

He sighed with relief. "Will you help us?"

"Of course, I will. What do you want me to do?"

"I need you to become a midwife."

"Are you pregnant?" she asked blandly.

"No, but we're about to be."

"I don't understand."

"Jaxyn is out looking for Arkady. He has my best Crasii tracker with him, so it's not an issue of *if* he brings her back, but when. The king doesn't know she's missing. I told him she's been unwell with women's problems."

Tilly nodded, understanding immediately. "And now you want me to announce that the problem isn't a problem at all, it's just that she's pregnant."

"Enteny is desperate for Arkady to produce a Desean heir," he added, filled with relief at Tilly's quick reading of the situation, "and the only thing that might keep him from disturbing her is the thought that he might be risking that heir by doing so."

"That's a pretty optimistic hope, Stellan."

"But all I have, short of confessing to the king that my wife aided a murderer to escape and is currently off in the mountains with him somewhere. Don't you see? Even if this maniac has her bound hand and foot, she forged the papers that got him out of prison and allowed him to escape. She looks guilty no matter what angle you view it from."

Tilly thought on that for a while and then nodded. "And if the king thinks she's pregnant, if he thinks she just needs rest until she's out of danger, he'll allow you to put off your journey to Torlenia and you can wait here until Jaxyn brings her home. That might actually work. I can see one problem, though."

"What's that?"

"What happens when you get Arkady back and she's not pregnant?"

Stellan shrugged. That was the least of his problems. "We'll tell Enteny she lost the child on the journey to Torlenia."

Tilly was silent for a moment and then she looked at him curiously. "Are you angry with her?"

"I'm worried about her, Tilly," he said. "The anger will come later, I'm sure, once I know she's safe."

"You're a good man, Stellan," she told him with a fond smile. "If a foolish one. When did you want me to make the happy announcement about your heir?"

"After breakfast, maybe? When everyone has other places to be. You'll have to bully the king a bit to stop him charging up the stairs to congratulate Arkady."

"Never you fear, dearest. I can handle Enteny Debree."

"I know you can," he agreed with a thin smile. "It's the reason I asked for your help."

She sighed and, picking up her gloves from her lap, rose to her feet. "And here I was, thinking it's because you fancied me."

Stellan stood up and took her hands in his, kissing her powdered cheek. "If I was that way inclined, I *would* fancy you, Tilly. I swear."

"Because I'm even more beautiful than your wife?"

"Because you're *much* more beautiful than my wife," he agreed solemnly. "And you cost me a whole lot less, too."

"After this favour, dearest," she promised, hugging him briefly, "believe me, *that* is going to change. In the meantime, I shall go upstairs to Arkady's rooms and wait there awhile before I come down and announce the happy news about your imaginary heir."

Stellan smiled with relief. "You're a good friend, Tilly."

The widow kissed his cheek again and let herself out of the office. Stellan turned to follow her but it wasn't until he had his hand on the doorknob that he stopped, frowning, as something disturbing occurred to him.

She might have been looking for a way to save him from Declan Hawkes, Tilly had said, trying to assure Stellan of Arkady's honourable intentions.

But how had she known that?

Stellan hadn't mentioned a word to her about the King's Spymaster or that Kyle Lakesh was going to be handed over to him.

Chapter 59

Maralyce didn't go back to the mine as Arkady was half-fearing, half-hoping she would. Instead the old lady pottered around the cabin for the rest of the day, fiddling with her equipment, muttering to herself and generally ignoring her houseguests as if they didn't exist. Cayal stacked the wood he'd chopped outside the cabin door and brought enough inside to see them through a blizzard.

Arkady prepared a meal, which wasn't much more than sausage and cheese, and midafternoon Chikita appeared in the yard unbidden, to report there was still no sign of pursuit, and then vanished again as soon as she was able.

Given the way Maralyce was glaring at her, Arkady didn't blame the poor feline one little bit.

The tension in the cabin was palpable, although Arkady wondered if she was the only one who could feel it. Maralyce acted as if there was nothing amiss, and to her, there probably wasn't. She patently didn't care what was going on between Arkady and Cayal and had no intention of letting either of them get in her way.

"Is the gemang gone?" Maralyce asked when Cayal came back inside after speaking with Chikita.

"She's gone."

"You just make sure she is," Maralyce grumbled. "Don't want those abominations hangin' around my place."

Cayal rolled his eyes but said nothing. Clearly this was a longstanding issue between them, which made Arkady curious. "Are you not one of the Tide Lords who helped create the Crasii, Maralyce?"

"I had nothing to do with that sordid little episode and I want nothing to do with the results. Ask your boy there what it took to make a Crasii. Abominations, they are, every last one of them, born of pain, perversion, rape and murder."

"I went to Tenacia to find out what happened to Medwen's child, remember?" Cayal pointed out, sounding a little wounded. "If I had to do a few things that weren't entirely . . . noble . . . while I was there, I had good reason."

"Bah!" she scoffed. "Listen to you and your excuses. You stayed with those shameless bastards for the better part of twenty years, Cayal, before you finally developed a conscience. And then, just when I thought you're on the brink of doing something decent, you pulled that stunt with the weather and ruined it for all of us. Don't expect me to pat you on the head and tell you what a brave lad you are, to suffer all those years of terrible torment, seeding the Crasii farms of Tenacia."

"You weren't there, Maralyce."

"No," she agreed. "I wasn't. That says something about both of us, don't you think?"

Arkady was beginning to wish she'd never broached the subject, but her curiosity drove her to probe further. "But surely, Maralyce," she said, "if the Crasii are now self-sustaining races, aren't they entitled to be treated like . . . real people?"

"Real *people* aren't slaves," the old lady argued. "And I don't mean that literally. The Crasii are slaves to their instincts; worse, they're slaves to our whim. I could walk down that path, find your Crasii and order every one of them to slit their own throats and they'd do it, because they have no choice. That's not a survival trait, lady."

"Yet they have survived."

"Only because the Tide goes out for hundreds of years at a time and their numbers breed up when the immortals aren't around to get them killed."

Arkady looked at Cayal, wondering if he was going to defend what he'd done to help create the Crasii, but he was leaning against the mantel, watching her, his expression thoughtful.

"Is that what *you* think?"

He shrugged. "Getting a lecture about the wickedness of my evil ways is the cost of Maralyce's hospitality. One of the reasons I tend not to visit her often."

"That," the old lady agreed, "and your aversion to honest hard work."

"I chopped your damned wood for you, you ungrateful old cow," he reminded her without rancour.

"Only because you didn't have a Crasii around to do it for you." She looked up from another piece of equipment she had dismantled and spread across the wooden table— Arkady had no idea what it was or its function—and frowned at her. "People who aren't averse to honest hard work usually don't feel the need to breed slave races to do it for 'em, ever noticed that?"

"Where I come from, we don't believe the Tide Lords created the Crasii at all. We believe the Crasii evolved the same way humans did."

"Then more fool them," the old lady sighed. "'Cause

the Tide is on the turn and it won't be long before your fancy academics in their sheltered, ignorant universities find out the hard way just how completely wrong they are about everything."

Later that afternoon, Maralyce stood up, let out a satisfied sigh, gathered up the thing she had been working on all day—Arkady was still in the dark about what it was exactly—and left the cabin without a word. Alone suddenly with both Cayal and her fears, she swallowed an unexpected lump in her throat, knowing the unresolved business between them could no longer be avoided.

Bracing herself, she turned to face him, forcing the distracting images of his sweat-sheened body wielding an axe in the dappled sunlight from her mind. *This wasn't about silly, idle fantasies,* she reminded herself. *This was real.*

Taking a deep breath, she discovered him—somewhat to her annoyance given how much she'd been agonising over him all day—staring thoughtfully out of the small dusty window, oblivious to her.

More than a little peeved by his lack of consideration, she snapped at him far more sharply than she'd intended. "Cayal?"

"Why did Chikita take the trouble to come up here and tell us there was no pursuit, do you think?"

If he noticed—or cared—that she was irritable, he gave no sign. Still, his distraction was something of a relief, in a way. Asking after a Crasii was the last thing she expected. Perhaps this wasn't going to be as fraught as she feared.

"Because," she ventured, "perhaps . . . there *is* no pursuit?"

Cayal wasn't amused. "Maralyce is right, you know. The Crasii are slaves to our whim."

"Which has what, exactly, to do with Chikita bringing us word that we're not being pursued?"

"I never asked her to report if there was no pursuit, only if there was."

She raised a brow at him. "You mean you didn't breed initiative into your slaves? How remiss of you, your highness."

He turned to her, frowning. "Don't take that tone with me."

"What tone?"

"That holier-than-thou tone you use when you think you own the moral high ground. You know nothing about me, Arkady, only what I choose to reveal."

She squared her shoulders defensively. "You can hardly blame me for thinking I own the moral high ground. By your own admission you're responsible for the deaths of millions of people and the total destruction of their civilisation."

"Then aren't you the lucky one," he replied sourly, "to be so without fault that you can judge me?"

"To judge you, I'd have to believe your lies first," she snapped.

He stared at her. "Tides, we're not going to start that whole *you can't possibly be immortal* routine, are we? I thought we were long past that."

"Maybe in the cold light of day, I've had a chance to come to my senses." Arkady said the words, but couldn't understand why. She believed him. He knew she believed him. It was absurd.

Cayal sat on the edge of the sill and folded his arms. "This is how you protect yourself, isn't it?"

"What?"

"This!" he said, waving his arm to encompass her. "Fight or flight. It's the first rule of mortal survival. Only you're too damned stubborn to run."

"I have no idea what you're talking about."

"I think you do, Arkady. Come here."

"No."

"Why not?"

"Because this cabin is about ten feet wide, Cayal, and

there is nothing you have to say to me that you can't say perfectly well with us that far apart."

"I can't kiss you from there."

"I have no intention of letting you kiss me again, so what difference does it make?"

He smiled. "Do you think you could stop me?"

"Given that you're a confessed rapist as well as a mass murderer, probably not."

That seemed to amuse him. "You're very beautiful when you're being irrational."

"You've had eight thousand years to work on your se- duction technique and that's the best you can come up with? Tides, I thought you immortals were supposed to be something special." She turned away with nowhere really in the tiny cabin to escape to, except Maralyce's small bedroom.

Before she could reach the door, however, it slammed shut in front of her.

Arkady jumped back in fright and spun around.

Cayal shrugged. "I warned you, my lady. The Tide's on its way back. Can't destroy civilisation as we know it, just yet, but I'll be a whiz at slamming doors for the next few days."

"Let me go, Cayal," she begged. She couldn't believe it of herself. Not since Fillion Rybank had Arkady begged a man for anything.

Fear tangled with apprehension, desire mixed with doubt, they all coloured her vision, blinding Arkady to anything but those tormented eyes. She closed her own eyes to shut out his anguish, but that just made her own torment worse.

How dare he make her feel like this? She hadn't felt so helpless since the first time she knocked on the door of Rybank's room at the university. As she realized that, anger replaced her fear. She had sworn she would never allow herself to be any man's victim, ever again.

Arkady's eyes flew open. It was as if her anger had set her free.

From the moment she acknowledged her newfound freedom, she discovered she had the power to decide her own destiny. It was her choice, now, to seize the moment or turn her back on it.

Arkady looked at Cayal through different eyes, no longer blinded by fear or guilt. She crossed the room in three strides and threw her arms around him, aghast at how badly she wanted this.

From somewhere deep inside Arkady, a dam seemed to burst, built of the bricks she'd placed around her emotions as a vulnerable child, the wall getting higher and higher after every visit to Fillion Rybank. The heat of her desire, the touch of Cayal's sure hands on her body as he undressed her, pushed her onto the rough wooden table, the chill bite of the air as the sun set, all served to sear away the last of her uncertainty.

She didn't remember moving to the bedroom, but with every thrust, Cayal drove the memories farther into the past. With every kiss, with every touch, with every cry of ecstasy as he drew her to the brink and back again, time and again, only the present, only the heat of their ardour remained, until finally, when she was sated and complete, Cayal collapsed against her, the weight of him almost as reassuring as her shattered wall had been.

Chapter 60

It was dark by the time Arkady woke to the unfamiliar feeling of another body beside her in the bed. For a long moment she lay there, her head resting on Cayal's chest, listening to his heartbeat, which beat like a distant battle drum heralding advancing danger.

Without warning, several fat candles on the shelf above the bed inexplicably flared into light, filling the bedroom with a soft yellow glow.

"Did you do that?" she asked, yawning.

"The Tide is coming in," Cayal explained, pulling her a little closer and tucking the furs under her chin. The air in the small cabin was icy. They must have let the fire go out.

"So you have your powers back?"

"Some," he agreed. "Can't do much more than light candles and slam doors just yet, but it's definitely on the way."

"And then what happens?"

"We pick up where we left off, I suppose," he replied. "Syrolee and Engarhod and their dreadful offspring will crawl out from whatever rock they're hiding under and try to find some hapless population they can bend to their will, which isn't much of a stretch for them, given both Elyssa and Tryan are Tide Lords and Pellys is never far away because he's too stupid to realise that Syrolee is never going to take him back."

"But I thought you said he'd lost all his memories? How would he even know he and Syrolee were once a couple?"

"Lukys told him. He thinks it's important we remember who we are."

Arkady frowned, wondering at the motives of this most enigmatic Tide Lord. Medwen's concern about what drove Lukys did not seem misplaced.

"Anyway," Cayal continued, unaware of the direction of Arkady's thoughts, "I suppose Brynden will give up contemplating his navel and wondering what he did to upset Kinta and start striding around the world trying to convince the rest of us we should be doing great deeds of derring-do for the betterment of mankind. Lukys will continue to ignore the rest of us because he's too busy trying to find a way to make the stars bang together. Jaxyn will already have his eye on the land he intends to rule once there's nobody around who can oppose him, and the rest of them . . . well, they'll flock to whoever looks like they're going to make the best go of it this time in the hopes they're on the winning side when we come to blows, as we invariably do."

Arkady pushed herself up on her elbow so she could see his face. "While I, on the other hand, who now knows that immortals actually exist, that the Tide Lords are real, that the Crasii were created magically and that everything we hold to be truth is a myth and that all our myths are true, will be helpless to do anything about it, because, of course, I can't prove a word of it."

"Such is the burden of all seekers of truth," Cayal agreed solemnly as she took a deep breath to recover from her outburst.

She punched his arm half-heartedly. "It's not funny, Cayal. I'm going to have to sit there grinding my teeth while that pompous misogynist, Harlie Palmerston, gets a peerage for his *Theory of Human Advancement*."

"Look on the bright side. The Tide's coming in. You'll all be enslaved by us evil Tide Lords before the year is out, anyway, so what does it matter?"

"Oh, well . . . what am I worrying about, then?"

"Shall I strike him down for you?" Cayal asked with a smile. "This pompous misogynist, Harlie Palmerston, and his wretched *Theory of Human Advancement*?"

She shook her head. "No. I think watching his world crumble around him when the Tide Lords reappear should be satisfaction enough. You will ask your evil and tyrannical immortal brethren to make a point of showing him how wrong he is, won't you?"

"It'll be my pleasure," he promised. "Besides, it's not the first time mortals have tried to will us out of existence."

"What are you talking about?"

"Your *Theory of Human Advancement*. It's one of the oldest tricks in the book. Educate everyone to the point where the existence of immortals appears completely irrational so that the next time the Emperor and Empress of the Five Realms try imposing their religion on an unsuspecting and credulous world, they're laughed at, rather than worshipped. It happened before the last Cataclysm, too. And it was surprisingly effective. It's been a long time since Syrolee got to be a goddess. A thousand years ago, they even had a secret society dedicated to ridding the world of us."

"If it was a secret society," Arkady asked, "how come you know about it?"

"Because humans can't keep secrets. The Cabal of the Tarot, they used to call themselves. That's where your wretched cards come from, you know, and the reason it irks me so much to hear you quote from them. The Tide Lord Tarot is just the last garbled remnant of a pitiful attempt by the mortals of Amyrantha to defy us."

"Maybe you should have paid more attention to them," she suggested. "If you want to die and they want to kill you, that kind of puts you on the same side, doesn't it?"

He stared at her in bewilderment. "That's the most idiotic suggestion I've ever heard."

"Right up there with 'let's kill seven people so they'll cut my head off and I won't have to deal with the pain any longer,' I guess?" Her smile faded as she studied him in the candlelight. "And what are you going to do now, Cayal?"

"Do? I don't understand what you mean?"

"What are you planning? Will the Immortal Prince look for some hapless population he can bend to his will, too?"

He shrugged. "I tried ruling the world once. It's a lot more work than you'd imagine."

"You haven't told me that story."

"I haven't told you a great many things, Arkady."

She fell silent, not certain how she should respond to that. "Maralyce was talking about you earlier, you know."

"Did she have anything nice to say about me?"

"Actually, she did."

"You see, I was right. The whole world order is on the brink of collapse."

Arkady smiled. "She says rumour has it you're . . . how did she put it? Quite good in the sack?"

"Like I said, Arkady. If you're alive long enough, you get to be good at everything, sooner or later."

"Even lovemaking?"

"Especially that," he told her. "Tides, you really *have* reached the bitter end when that bores you senseless."

"Does it bore you?"

He looked at her curiously. "Any particular reason you want to know?"

"You tried to have yourself beheaded, Cayal. How desperate does a man have to be to attempt that?"

"More desperate than you will ever comprehend, Arkady."

"Yet you have no choice but to go on." She fell silent, wishing there was something she could say that would help. There wasn't, of course, but that didn't stop her wanting to try. She kissed him again, revelling in the taste of him.

"Why don't you sleep with your husband?" Cayal asked, pulling away from her.

"Who says I don't?"

"You do," he told her. "You make love like a starveling. Does he not find you alluring?"

She laid her head against his chest again, snuggling into the solid warmth of him. "It's complicated, Cayal, and I really don't want to talk about my husband while lying naked in the arms of another man."

Cayal was undeterred. "Will he come after me, do you think? To avenge your honour?"

"Last time I checked he was after you anyway," she reminded him, "because you're an escaped convict. Having your way with his wife will just prove an added incentive to see an end to you, I imagine."

"Will you be in a lot of trouble when you go back?"

"None at all," she assured him, although the question pained her. There were no illusions in this bed. As world-shattering as it had seemed earlier, in the heat of their desire, this could not, *would* not last. This was the distant war-drum she could hear in her mind. Whatever Arkady felt for his man, her future lay with Stellan in Torlenia, not with a fugitive immortal.

She understood that and Cayal—to his credit—wasn't

trying to fool her into believing otherwise. "You kidnapped me. I'm the victim here."

She could hear the smile in his voice. "You're many things, Arkady, but believe me, a victim isn't one of them. Won't he know you're lying?"

"I'd rather we stopped talking about him."

"Tell me something else then."

"Like what?"

He shrugged. "I don't know. Something about yourself. Something from your childhood that doesn't involve dirty old men. A happy memory." He looked down at her with a frown. "You do *have* happy memories, don't you?"

"Of course I do. Don't you?"

"None that aren't rotting from old age."

She frowned, a little hurt by what he was implying. "Not even tonight?"

Cayal leaned forward and kissed her apologetically. "Tonight is still happening. It's not actually a memory yet."

Somewhat mollified, she smiled. "What do you want to know?"

"Anything. Just tell me something you've never told anyone else."

"Why?"

"Because that's the only gift you can give me that I can't take for myself."

That made a twisted sort of logic, actually, so Arkady settled down against him again and thought on it for a moment.

"When I was about eight," she began, recalling an incident all but forgotten over the years, "my father was called to the palace because the duke was ill and his physician was away. This was the old duke, Stellan's father, and my mother was still alive then, too, although heavily pregnant. The old duke had severe gout, poor man, and suffered with it terribly. There were plenty of other doctors in the city the duke could have called on, but my father and his personal physician were friends so as a favour to us he always arranged for Papa to cover for him when he was away. I think he knew my father would never accept charity—or payment from half his patients, which was half the reason we were so poor—and he knew how much we needed the money.

"Normally, I would have stayed at home for such a house call, but Mother was having a particularly bad day and she didn't want me underfoot, so my father took me to the palace with him. All the way there he admonished me about my manners and not saying anything and staying out of the way, which of course I promised to do, and which of course, I didn't.

"Anyway, as soon as we arrived, Papa was whisked away to attend the duke and I was left standing in this massive hall into which our whole house would have fitted. Naturally, I started poking into doorways until I found one unlocked. It led to a music room. I'd only ever seen musical instruments played by street performers before then, and we lived in the poorer part of the city, so they were pretty battered and worn. I'd never seen anything as beautiful as the dulcimer resting on a stand by the window. You should have seen it. It was shaped like a huge hourglass, enamelled in black and polished till it shone like a mirror. Its fretted fingerboard was inlaid with mother of pearl with a matching inlay scrolling down either side of the strings. I'd never seen anything so gorgeous. I reached out, and was just about to touch it, when this boy of about fourteen threw open the door and demanded to know who I was. Tides, he gave me such a fright, I nearly knocked the damn thing over.

"After I got over my shock, I explained why I was in the palace and then the boy walked across, picked up the dulcimer and asked me if I played. When I told him I didn't, he offered to show me what it sounded like. We must have spent the better part of the morning in that music room. Stellan played every song he knew, I think, and some of them more than once. He tells me he's not a particularly accomplished musician, but I was only eight, so what did I know? I just thought the instrument made the most beautiful sound I'd ever heard, and that the boy playing it was the nicest person I'd ever met.

"It wasn't until my father came looking for me in a panic a couple of hours or so later that I found out the boy was the duke's son, and even then I was too young to be impressed. He assured my father I'd been well behaved, bowed to me like I was a real lady and left the music room, after inviting me to come back and visit him again."

"*That's* the happiest moment of your life?" Cayal asked.

She shrugged. "It may not seem like much of a memory, but my mother miscarried and died a little more than a week later, and after that, things were never the same. It probably wasn't the happiest moment but that morning was the last time I can remember being truly and completely happy."

Arkady fell silent, letting the joy of that simple reminiscence envelop her. When Cayal offered no other comment, she looked up at him and discovered he wasn't even listening to her.

"Cayal?"

His attention was elsewhere, his eyes unfocussed, as if he was listening to something Arkady couldn't hear. He lay like that, still as a rock, for a few more moments and then he sat bolt upright, pushing Arkady out of his way without apology. Throwing the furs back, he cursed under his breath as he sprang out of bed and began fishing around for his trousers.

Arkady stared at him in alarm. "Cayal? What's the matter?"

"Jaxyn's here," he said, as he dressed hurriedly in his discarded prison uniform.

"How could you possibly know . . . ?"

"I can feel him on the Tide."

"But Jaxyn is . . ." Arkady's voice trailed off in horror as something awful, something almost too terrible to contemplate, suddenly occurred to her.

A sleazy little opportunist, Cayal had called him. *Jaxyn will already have his eye on the land he intends to rule once there's nobody around who can oppose him . . .*

"Cayal, wait!" she called after him, as he slammed the bedroom door open with a thought, so hard the whole cabin shook, and hurried into the main room to find his boots.

"I don't have time to wait," he told her. "Get dressed."

"But I think . . ." She never got a chance to finish the sentence because at that moment a chillingly familiar voice called to them from the yard outside.

"Cayal! O *Cay-al*! Come out, come out, wherever you are! Tide's turning, brother. It's time for you and me to have a little fun!"

Still naked, filled with a dread that left her nauseous, Arkady rushed to the window and looked out of the shutters, only to have her worst fears realised.

"Come on, Cayal! Be a sport! Don't make me come and get you!"

Standing in the yard, very much in command of the situation, surrounded by a force of nearly two dozen feline Crasii, including those Arkady had brought from the palace, was a Tide Lord. The torches the Crasii were holding illuminated the yard with fitful light, but there was no mistaking the figure standing out there, taunting Cayal.

It was the Lord of Temperance himself, Jaxyn Aranville.

Chapter 61

Cayal was more surprised by Arkady's reaction to the appearance of Jaxyn than he was by the arrival of his old enemy. Clearly, she recognised him. He sighed, thinking Jaxyn had more than a knack for finding himself the comfiest nest possible when the Tide was out. It bordered on a magical power.

My husband has a friend . . . Jaxyn, Arkady had told him.

Tides, a palace, a place full of secrets . . . Just the sort of bolthole Jaxyn has a nose for. Cayal should have realised then who she was referring to.

"You know him?" he asked, pulling his shirt on.

"It's . . ." She hesitated, obviously debating something within herself and then turned to look at him and said flatly "Jaxyn Aranville is my husband's lover."

Cayal wasn't surprised, not by the news Arkady's husband had a male lover (which explained quite a bit about Arkady), or that it was Jaxyn. Even older than Cayal, there was little left that he hadn't done, or people he'd done it to. The Aranville name . . . well, that was something he'd probably stolen either by killing the real Aranville or simply borrowing the family name to get a foot in the door at Lebec Palace. It wasn't a particularly difficult thing to do. Cayal had done it any number of times himself, in order to secure a comfortable niche to wait out a Low Tide. "He does get around, our Jaxyn, doesn't he? I take it you had no idea who he was."

"Are you kidding? I'm still getting my head around *you* being a Tide Lord. Trust me, I'm a long way from coming to grips with the notion I've been harbouring one under my roof for the past year." She shook her head and straightened up, probably unaware that her naked body was limned in firelight from the torches in the yard. "Still,

I suppose that explains why he was also so good at getting the Crasii to work for him."

Tides, she is beautiful, he thought, only half-listening to her. *And totally dismissive of it.*

In eight thousand years, Cayal had never met anybody less impressed by their own appearance than Arkady Desean. If she dressed like a duchess, it was only because she treated her role like a job, which to her it probably was, given what she had just revealed about her husband. She appeared to be totally without vanity, which fascinated Cayal.

Among the Tide Lords, vanity was more than just a common trait. It very nearly defined them.

"You said Jaxyn would already have his eye on the land he planned to take over . . . ," she began.

"I'd start practising my grovelling curtseys, if I were you," he advised and then he added in a less ominous tone, "but probably *after* you get dressed."

As if she'd only just realised she was still naked, Arkady wrapped her arms around herself, shivering.

"Come on, Cayal!" Jaxyn called from the yard. "I know you're in there!"

"Please, Cayal! Don't go out there!"

He was touched by her concern, which shocked Cayal, because he was rarely touched by anything, these days. It had been a very long time since anybody cared about what happened to the Immortal Prince. Perhaps that's what he found so beguiling about this woman. It wasn't just her beauty. Or even her intelligence. This woman had risked everything—her home, her title, perhaps even her husband's position in court—just to help him escape being tortured.

And it wasn't as if there was anything in it for Arkady Desean. While Cayal liked to imagine he was a competent lover, no woman would have risked what she had, just for the dubious pleasure of a night in his bed . . .

No . . . with eight thousand years of memories to call

on, Cayal couldn't remember the last time any living soul
had willingly risked so much to help him.

He stepped a little closer, taking her by the arms. "He
can't hurt me, Arkady. Well . . . that's not strictly true. He
can hurt me. But he can't kill me. And it's a while yet 'til
High Tide so I'm fairly certain it's in his best interests to see
you back to your husband in one piece. You really don't
have to worry." When he could see his reassurances were
having no effect, he kissed her forehead. "Get dressed. I'm
sure you don't want the sleazy little bastard finding you
naked."

Looking very cold and mightily unhappy, Arkady nodded and hurried back into Maralyce's bedroom. Cayal
turned to glance out the window. The Crasii who'd accompanied them from Clyden's Inn had all followed Jaxyn
here, which explained why Chikita had appeared earlier to
report on the lack of pursuit. She wasn't responding to
Cayal's command, but Jaxyn's. He would have sent her up
to the cabin to check that he and Arkady were still here.
Approaching himself—with the Tide on the turn—would
have alerted Cayal to his presence.

"You're only making this harder on yourself!"

Cayal felt no particular fear at the presence of his
nemesis. With the Tide so low there wasn't much either of
them could do that would cause the other trouble. Even at
High Tide, it was debatable who was the most powerful.
Cayal liked to believe it was he, just as he was sure Jaxyn
liked to imagine he was the stronger of the two. They'd
never really had reason to put the matter to the test until
now.

Perhaps, for the sake of every other living soul on
Amyrantha, it was a good thing the Tide was still on the
way in. This might get very nasty.

"Cayal."

He turned to discover Arkady had dressed in record
time, although she was still tucking in her blouse and her
tangled hair showed the evidence of their wild lovemaking. Maralyce probably didn't own a mirror, but even if

she had, with Arkady's lack of vanity she doubtless would have deemed it unnecessary.

"I'm sorry, Arkady."

"For what?"

"For dragging you into my world. You don't belong here."

She shrugged fatalistically. "Given that's my husband's lover out there, whom you assure me is planning to take over Glaeba and enslave us all as soon as he's strong enough, I think I was dragged into your world long before you came along."

"I'll burn it down if I have to, Cayal!" Jaxyn shouted, sounding a little impatient. "And then Maralyce will get mad. You know what happens when Maralyce gets mad."

Arkady glared at the door. "Why is he *doing* that?"

"You mean standing out there yelling, instead of breaking the door down?"

She nodded, obviously puzzled by Jaxyn's willingness to wait for Cayal to emerge in his own time. "He has a score of Crasii with him. They'd tear this place to shreds if he ordered them to."

"But then he'd have to explain to Maralyce why he destroyed her house," Cayal said. "Trust me, nobody in their right mind pisses that lady off. Not even a Tide Lord as strong as Jaxyn. Besides, this is all part of the game."

"You think this is a *game*?"

"Jaxyn does."

"I will never understand you."

He wasn't sure if she meant him or all Tide Lords in particular, but it didn't really matter. This was the end of the road for the Immortal Prince and the Duchess of Lebec. However pleasant an interlude they had shared, however beguiling she was, however selfless, there was no future for them.

Not now.

Maybe . . . The thought died almost before it was born. There was no *maybe*. Cayal had had enough of immortality and with the Tide on the turn, he might soon be in a position to do something about it. Getting himself beheaded wasn't the only plan he'd come up with to end his torment, just the only one that might have a chance of working at Low Tide.

Arkady wasn't a part of his suicidal dreams. If anything, she was a threat to them because she represented the only glimmer of hope in a life almost totally devoid of it.

Jaxyn turning up now is a good thing, he told himself, turning for the door.

"Aren't you even going to say goodbye?"

He glanced over his shoulder at her. "You're assuming I'm going to lose? Thanks for the overwhelming vote of confidence."

Arkady wasn't so easily fooled by his glib answer. "I don't think you care enough to win, Cayal."

"I care enough to wipe that smug expression off Jaxyn's insufferable little face."

She shook her head in amazement. "All the power you Tide Lords claim to command, and that's the best you can find to rouse you?"

"There might have been something else." He shrugged, looking away. "Once. Not any longer."

"No wonder you want to kill yourself," she said unsympathetically. "I would too, if that's all I'd been reduced to."

He was shocked by her callousness, and then suddenly he smiled. "Tides! Are you trying to *goad* me into wanting to live? That's incredible!"

"Why incredible?"

"That you'd care enough about a complete stranger to do anything so foolish."

"I rather thought we were beyond being strangers."

In answer, Cayal drew her to him, kissing her, surprised to find himself wanting her again, and wanting her to understand him. She slid her arms around his neck and kissed him back, stirring emotions in him he thought long dead, long forgotten.

For some reason, he wasn't just going through the motions with this woman. It wasn't even simple lust, the way he'd lusted for Gabriella. He'd only ever wanted Gabriella to love and admire him. He found himself wanting Arkady to *know* him, and that was about the most frightening thing that had happened to Cayal in the past eight thousand years.

To cover his uneasiness at the effect she was having on him, he pulled away from her. "This isn't goodbye, you know. We'll meet again."

She searched his face for a moment before answering. "As equals? Or when you and your kind have enslaved us all?"

"Slave or not," he told her, kissing her again, unable to resist the temptation, "I will never be your equal, Arkady. I could never aspire to anything nearly so lofty."

"I'm getting impatient, Cayal! Do I have to start killing things to get your attention?"

"Tides!" Arkady exclaimed in annoyance. "Whatever else you do this night, Cayal, will you shut him *up*?"

"Gladly." He took her arms from around his neck and held them by her sides, his eyes locked on hers. "But you have to wait until I leave the cabin. Don't come out with me. And don't *ever* give Jaxyn so much as a hint that you might feel something for me other than contempt. He'll find a way to use it against you, sure as the Tide's on the turn." *Or worse,* he added silently to himself, *he'll find a way to use you against me and once the Tide is up, that could prove catastrophic.*

"Will you be all right?" She studied him closely, more reflected on her face than she imagined. But then, Cayal was very good at reading faces, even closely guarded ones. He was eight thousand years old, after all. He was good at everything.

"I'm immortal, Arkady."

"That's not what I meant."

He shrugged. "I appreciate your concern, truly I do, but don't waste your time trying to fix what's wrong with me, Arkady. Believe me, I'm broken beyond repair."

"I don't believe that, Cayal," she replied, her eyes suddenly glistening. He suspected she was too proud to cry in front of him, and too smart to cry in front of Jaxyn, but that she had any faith in him at all left him speechless. "I *won't* believe it."

"Then you're a fool," he told her gently, kissing her one last time, with aching tenderness, fairly certain that the kindest thing he could do for Arkady Desean was to step out of her life completely and never see her or speak to her again. She would be safer. And probably happier.

Nothing good ever came of a Tide Lord loving a mortal.

The unbidden thought startled him and made him step away from her, as he realised just how close he was to allowing himself to feel something he'd long ago decided was more pain than it was worth.

"It's not going to be pretty if I have to come in after you, Cayal!" Jaxyn called, his impatience growing by the minute.

"Be careful, Cayal," she warned, softly.

He nodded dumbly, not trusting himself to speak, not sure what he might say if he replied.

So instead he turned his back on her and finally opened the cabin's small door. Squaring his shoulders to face down Jaxyn, he stepped outside, leaving Arkady, and all the conflicted emotions that came with her, behind him.

Chapter 62

The Immortal Prince finally emerged from the cabin, just as Jaxyn was seriously starting to weigh up the advisability of going in after him and risking Maralyce's wrath if anything was broken. But there was no need. Cayal stepped through the doorway, still wearing his linen prison garb, but otherwise unchanged since the last time the two of them had met, which was longer ago than he cared to recall.

Jaxyn was a little disappointed. Although he knew nothing could have changed about him, Cayal's greater height, his breadth of shoulder, even those sharp blue eyes of his, so rare in Jaxyn's country of birth, all combined to irritate Jaxyn in a way he couldn't explain. Perhaps his ambivalence toward Cayal *was* motivated by simple jealousy, as Diala had suggested once, but Jaxyn considered himself above such petty emotions.

The truth was far more simple and it boiled down to this: essentially, Cayal had ruined immortality for Jaxyn.

Until this wide-eyed princeling came along, Jaxyn had been the most noble of the immortals. Highborn and proud of it, *he* was the one the others looked to. When Syrolee and Engarhod decided to set themselves up as the Emperor and Empress of the Five Realms, it was Jaxyn they turned to for advice on how a royal court was run. The others looked up to him, their simple peasant minds taking their natural awe of the highborn into immortality with them.

And then the Immortal Bloody Prince came along. A mere accident of birth, that's all his wretched title was, and given Tryan had wiped Kordana off the face of Amyrantha eight thousand years ago, it was a pretty empty title at that.

But Cayal looked like people imagined a prince *should* look—Diala took great delight in pointing that out to Jaxyn every chance she got—garnering far more respect than he deserved on his appearance alone. And then, as if to rub salt into Jaxyn's open wound, it turned out the lucky dimwit was able to manipulate the Tide. Not just manipulate it. Master it. He was as strong a Tide Lord as any of the immortals. Probably rivalling Lukys, if the truth be told.

The unfairness of it all set Jaxyn's teeth on edge and meant the two of them had been at odds from the moment they'd first crossed paths and nothing much had happened in the intervening millennia to resolve the issue.

"Well, well, well," Cayal remarked, smiling condescendingly, a gesture Jaxyn was certain he meant purely to irritate. "Hear you're some nobleman's girlfriend, these days. My, how the mighty have fallen."

"Where's *your* girlfriend?"

"Who? Oh, you mean the duchess? Inside, waiting for you to rescue her. You should mark this day, Jaxyn. Your arrival was the first time I've ever seen anybody actually glad to see you."

Jaxyn was sceptical. "You mean you *haven't* been sampling the delights of the lovely Duchess of Lebec? I find that hard to believe."

"She talks too much." Cayal shrugged. "You're welcome to her. Ah . . . but your tastes lie in a different direction these days. What happened, Jaxyn? Run out of women who don't puke when you touch them?"

"You think you're so damned clever, don't you?" he snapped, a little surprised at how easily Cayal could rile him. "But at least nobody's trying to hang me, Cayal, and if you don't stop moving, I'm going to have one of the ladies here disembowel you."

Cayal had been inching his way around the yard as he spoke, moving away from the cabin. He stopped. "You think I'm going to let you take me back to Lebec?"

"I'm very much hoping you're going to resist, actually. I'd enjoy watching a couple of dozen Crasii tear you to shreds."

"Not on my claim you won't," Maralyce declared, emerging from the mine, her face filthy, eyes glittering angrily in the torchlight.

"Maralyce!" Jaxyn declared with mock enthusiasm. "How nice to see you again!"

She dumped the rope and pick she was carrying on the ground and glared at him. "Thought something on the Tide smelled rotten. What are you doing here, Jaxyn?"

"Come to collect your houseguest," he told her. He and Maralyce had never really gotten along, either. He wasn't sure why. That she would tolerate Cayal under her roof periodically when she rarely admitted any other immortal into her home—that alone was enough to irk him. "Cayal's been a naughty boy, Maralyce. Didn't you hear? They want him for murder. Already hanged him once. I think they're planning to keep on trying until they succeed, which should be entertaining, don't you think?"

"Get off my claim."

"Not without my prisoner."

Cayal actually laughed at him. "I'm not your prisoner, Jaxyn."

"We'll see about that." He took a step toward Cayal, but before he could do much more than that, the wind picked up, dust swirling about them, stinging his eyes and forcing the Crasii to cover their faces. The force of the unnatural gale extinguished a good half of the torches the Crasii were holding. Several others sputtered and died on the ground as the felines dropped them in a desperate attempt to protect their eyes from the swirling gravel.

"Don't take your eyes off him!" Jaxyn cried angrily, calling on his own power to quell the sudden gusts. Within a moment, the wind had died, but when the dust had settled, Cayal was gone.

"Idiots!" Jaxyn screamed, turning to backhand the nearest feline, who staggered under the blow but made no attempt to resist it. Cayal hadn't gone far. Jaxyn could still feel him on the Tide, and given the smug look on Maralyce's face, he'd probably taken refuge in the mine.

"Find the duchess and watch her!" Jaxyn ordered the Crasii. "I'm going after him."

"You wreck my mine, and I'll have your hide, Jaxyn," Maralyce warned, as he snatched one of the few remaining torches from another feline and turned toward the dark maw of Maralyce's endless tunnels.

"Go to hell," he told her as he stepped up to the entrance.

He bent down to enter the mine. *All that power to burn and she wastes it living like a pauper, digging underground in a mine that must be so big by now the whole damn mountain is in danger of caving in, hoarding gold she never bothers to spend.* Maybe that's why she and Cayal get along so well.

They're both fools.

Jaxyn was barely a hundred feet into the first tunnel when a length of rusty chain came hurtling along the passage, striking him in the forehead. He was dabbing gingerly at his bleeding temple as it healed when he heard a faint noise and glanced up, barely dodging the next missile, which flew past so fast he couldn't tell what it was.

It was then that he realised the torch was making him a perfect target in the darkness. Tossing it aside, he closed his eyes to give them time to adjust and to allow him to better sense Cayal ahead of him. He couldn't pinpoint him exactly—with the Tide so low he was barely able to sense the disturbance the other Tide Lord created—but he *was* there, some way ahead, probably setting traps at every turn.

It was stupid, Jaxyn realised at that moment, to have followed him into the mine. Cayal was the aggressor here. He held the high ground.

So we'll just have to change the lie of the land, Jaxyn decided, opening his eyes. Jaxyn waded into the Tide, weaving a wall of air around his body until it was almost solid. He wouldn't fall victim a second time to Cayal's flying debris.

Stepping forward, letting the silent darkness envelop him, Jaxyn concentrated on the Tide, rather than the mine, hoping to detect some warning surge that Cayal was drawing on it. It was an optimistic hope. At best, he'd get a fraction of a second's warning before something fell on him. On the other hand, once he located Cayal, who was already much deeper into the tunnels than he was, a fraction of a second might be all he needed.

A scraping noise ahead caught his attention. He ignored it, fairly certain it was Cayal trying to distract him. The Immortal Prince wasn't stupid. Foolish, sentimental and squeamish by Jaxyn's standards, perhaps, but hardly stupid. He was too clever to make a noise he didn't want Jaxyn to hear.

The darkness was suffocating the deeper into the mine Jaxyn went. The chill night air was soon replaced with warm, rancid dampness. The tunnel sloped down·for a time and then came to a junction. Three tunnels led off the main branch. He stopped, letting the Tide tell him where Cayal was hiding, rather than wait for a betraying sign. Cayal must be quite a bit ahead of him by now, the ripples in the Tide created by his passage were diminishing with every passing moment. Jaxyn hurried into the tunnel on the right, certain that's where he could feel him.

This tunnel plunged down sharply. Jaxyn took it at a run, partly in his haste to corner Cayal and partly because the slope of the tunnel allowed him no other option. Afraid he might plummet through some hidden vent, he tried to slow his progress by keeping his hands on the sides of the tunnel, scoring little more than a few spectacular splinters for his trouble.

The shaft went on and on, seemingly without end. Just when he was beginning to wonder if Maralyce had tunnelled to the very centre of the mountain, he almost tripped on a fallen beam as he rounded a corner to arrive at the next junction.

Lit by a score of sputtering torches, this was an unnatural cavern quite a bit larger and much lower underground than the first junction, with nearly a dozen tunnels leading off it. The walls had been magically wrought, the granite cut away in large slabs, the polished jagged surface glittering with mineral deposits of mica, pyrite and feldspar in the torchlight. The blocks cut from the cavern must have been huge, which made Jaxyn wonder what Maralyce had done with all the dirt and rock she'd been tunnelling out of this hollow mountain for the past few thousand years. Perhaps the next mountain over wasn't the result of natural formation but was actually Maralyce's slag heap. Jaxyn smiled at the thought and then froze as he caught a hint of

Cayal on the Tide, off to his left somewhere. With the extra tunnel entrances, it could have been any one of several down which he had vanished.

"Cayal!"

His voice echoed off the cavern walls but he received no response. That didn't surprise him. Cayal was hardly going to make this easy for him.

"I'll find you, Cayal!" he warned. "It's not as if we don't have the time!"

Again, there was no answer. Jaxyn frowned. He was lying about having the time to waste hunting his enemy through the mine. Truth was, he needed to get back to the surface before Maralyce took it upon herself to dismiss the Crasii and let Arkady go.

Cayal was still moving away from him. Jaxyn could feel him growing fainter and fainter, the ripples in the Tide less and less easy to detect. If Jaxyn didn't move soon, he'd lose Cayal altogether.

Perhaps that was Cayal's intention. Perhaps he'd led Jaxyn down here not to fight him, but to get him irretrievably lost. Right now, Jaxyn was fairly certain he knew the way back, but how much deeper did the mine go? How much longer would the chase go on?

Shaking his head, Jaxyn cursed himself for a fool as he realised he was walking right into Cayal's trap.

Still, a trap was only a trap when you didn't *know* it was a trap. And a smart prey could turn a trap around and use it on the hunter.

With a thin smile, Jaxyn abandoned his search for Cayal on the Tide. He was in one of the three tunnels to the left. That was near enough for his purposes. There wasn't enough power in the Tide to bring the mountain down on top of them, but there was certainly enough to weaken the supporting beams to all three tunnels and there were plenty of other potential hazards hanging from the cavern's ceiling. The weight of the mountain over their heads should do the rest.

Jaxyn dropped his air-wrought shield and drew every drop of power to him he could find, turning his attention to the beams at the entrances of the tunnels on the other side of the cavern. It was hard work, with the Tide still so tenuous, and he was sweating from both the effort and the underground heat by the time he heard the first creaks of collapsing timbers.

The ground rumbled as the tunnels to his left gave way. The mine belched a cloud of thick, choking dust, out of which soon emerged a figure covered in dirt and grime, bent over double, coughing up dust until he puked, wiping his streaming eyes. One arm hung uselessly at his side and there was blood pouring from a cut over his left eye.

"All hail the Immortal Prince!" Jaxyn declared with a sweeping bow.

"Go to hell, Jaxyn," Cayal replied, still bent double, his face contorted with pain as his broken arm began the painful healing process. Already the cut over his eye had stopped bleeding.

He didn't have long, Jaxyn guessed, bracing himself, before Cayal was recovered enough for this to get very, very nasty.

Chapter 63

"Did you want to be rid of them?"

Arkady looked up from her tea, which had gone cold from neglect, and stared at Maralyce blankly. She'd been too worried since Jaxyn followed Cayal into the mine to hear what the old woman was saying.

"What?"

"The Crasii," the old woman explained, waving her arm to indicate the three felines standing guard over Arkady.

"These wretched abominations. They'll follow my orders sure as they will them other two. I can send them all walking off a cliff if you'd like."

"Thanks," Arkady replied, fidgeting nervously. "But it's not their fault. And I do have to return home."

"You're assuming Jaxyn will emerge victorious."

Arkady hesitated, not sure what to say. She was being eaten alive by fear and anticipation, wondering what was happening underground. Who was winning? Was Cayal even bothering to fight back?

"I think Cayal intends him to," she said finally.

"Waste of effort, if you ask me, the whole damned thing. They fightin' over you, perchance?"

That suggestion almost made Arkady smile. As if she figured anywhere in the plans of two immortals. "Hardly. Jaxyn is more interested in my husband and Cayal . . ." Her voice trailed off. It wasn't because she was unsure about Cayal. It was because Arkady couldn't believe that in the space of an hour she had confided in two complete strangers a secret she'd kept from everyone she knew since before she married Stellan, even her best friends.

There was something about the weight of immortality that made her secrets seem insignificant.

"You could order them not to repeat what I just told you," Arkady suggested, a little uneasily, when she realised she'd not only confessed Stellan's secret, but done it with three Crasii in the room.

The old woman smiled. "You heard the duchess," Maralyce informed the felines. "You are never to repeat a word about what we discuss here, understand? Not among yourselves or to another Tide Lord. Is that clear?"

The three felines nodded without blinking, their eyes glittering in the candlelight.

"There," Maralyce assured Arkady. "They'll die before they say a word now, although I think you worry unnecessarily."

"How so?"

"You say Jaxyn's been living in your palace for nearly a year? If that's the case, the one Tide Lord with the power to destroy your husband by exposing his secret has known about him for a long time. The damage is well and truly done, I'd say."

Before Arkady could reply the ground began to tremble and they heard a faint rumbling in the distance. She gripped the edge of the table in fear and looked to Maralyce, wondering if the old woman knew what the tremor meant. It only lasted for a moment, but it was enough to have Maralyce cursing and on her feet.

"I warned those boys . . . ," she muttered as she slammed the cabin door open with a wave of her arm and stormed out into the yard.

Arkady glanced at the felines. "What *was* that?"

"I don't know, your grace," the tabby on her right replied. "A quake, perhaps?"

"Or a cave-in," she gasped, jumping to her feet to follow Maralyce. *Cayal . . .*

It must have been well past midnight by now, she realised, when she burst into the yard. The night was clear but her breath frosted as she ran to Maralyce's side. Surrounded by the remainder of the Crasii, who held up torches to light the entrance, the old immortal was staring intently at the mine, as if waiting for something else to occur.

"What happened?"

"Cave-in, probably," the old miner confirmed. "Just gotta wait awhile now, for the old girl to settle down, 'fore we disturb her again."

"Do you think . . . ?" Arkady began, afraid to give voice to her fears.

"Well, they ain't dead, I can guarantee that," Maralyce informed her. "Question is, who started it, and who's gonna have to spend the next five years diggin' himself out?"

"You have to go after them!"

"Not my business." Maralyce shrugged.

"No," Arkady agreed, thinking of the danger she might

have unleashed with her thoughtless need to set Cayal free. "It's mine."

The tunnel was dark and surprisingly warm. Arkady tried not to hear the deep rumbling ahead of her. With her hand on the rough tunnel wall, she felt her way forward, following her instincts as much as any path she could see. The whole mountain creaked in complaint around her as she ran, biting back a cry of agony as something banged against her shin.

Ignoring the pain, Arkady determined to press on. Somewhere ahead of her, Cayal might be trapped. Somewhere ahead of her, Arkady's entire future hung in the balance, even if, to the men responsible for it, she was nothing more than a distraction.

Arkady stumbled forward, almost falling on her face as the wall underneath her hand suddenly ended and she found herself tripping and skidding down a steep passageway toward a faint glimmer of light in the distance. The deep rumbling was more than a sound here. It was something she could feel. It reverberated through her very body, like a taut wire singing in a stiff breeze. It sang in concert with her fear.

Abruptly, the tunnel ended, opening into a large, torch-lit cavern Arkady knew instinctively wasn't natural. Grabbing the supporting beams holding up the tunnel roof, she managed to halt her headlong flight before she plunged into the large open space. Dust floated downwards, and she could hear voices, but it took a moment before she could make out the two figures standing in the centre of the glittering cave.

Arkady bit back a cry of relief when she saw Cayal. His left arm hung at his side and his face was obscured by blood. Worse than that, he was bent over and seemed to be in excruciating pain. There were perhaps five paces between the two men in the strange, polished cavern, and neither of them seemed aware of her presence. Dust from the earlier cave-in obscured the light and gave the cavern a surreal, unworldly atmosphere as it settled.

"That looks painful," Jaxyn was saying, as Arkady stepped back into the tunnel, her heart thumping. "Did it break? Think you would have learned by now that not even the great Immortal Prince can stop a cave-in with one hand."

"Your concern is heart-warming," Cayal gasped in pain. This was the accelerated healing he spoke of, she guessed, her heart constricting to see any creature in such torment.

"Ah, Cayal, I always worry about you," Jaxyn said with vast insincerity.

"You shouldn't . . . really," Cayal replied, straightening a little. He flexed his hand experimentally and although it was clearly causing him intense pain, his arm no longer seemed useless.

"But you leave me so little choice," Jaxyn said, moving cautiously to the right. "I turn my back on you for a couple of hundred years and look at you! Lost . . . on the run . . . about to be hanged . . . You're a wreck, old boy."

Still unaware of Arkady's presence, Cayal was completely focussed on Jaxyn, his eyes never leaving his foe. "And you're screwing a duke, I hear. Or being screwed by one." Cayal wiped the blood from his eye and smiled at Jaxyn in a way that made Arkady's blood run cold. "Tell me, is he always on top or do you take it in turns?"

Jaxyn refused to be taunted, however. He kept on moving, Cayal responding in kind until the two of them were circling each other like hawks getting ready to swoop down on a kill.

"Been talking to the lovely Arkady, I see. What else did she tell you?"

"About you? Not much. She didn't seem impressed by you, at all."

"Ah, but she was impressed by *you,* wasn't she, brother?" Jaxyn said, an edge to his voice Arkady had rarely heard before. "I hear you told her all about your tragic life. How you were tricked into becoming immortal. Did you tell her about poor Fliss? And what you did to Amaleta?"

"You killed Amaleta," Cayal countered.

"Whatever helps you sleep at night."

"It's the truth. I would have saved her, but for you."

"You sanctimonious bastard," Jaxyn spat in disgust, always moving, always circling. "Amaleta didn't die in some noble cause you were defending. She died because you drove a bloody great knife into her chest and then stood back and watched her bleed to death, just to get one up on me. And for what? To save some wretched mortal child who was dead a year later, anyway? Tides, you're a hypocrite, Cayal."

"Better a hypocrite than a monster."

Jaxyn laughed. "A monster? *Me*? Did you tell Arkady some of the other things you've done, while you were painting yourself as an immortal hero? Mention what happened to Kordana, perhaps?"

"Tryan destroyed Kordana," Cayal snarled.

"Only after you turned Lakesh into a molten slag heap," Jaxyn reminded him, as they continued to circle each other warily, their eyes never leaving the other's. "Did you tell her that bit? Or what you did in Verinia? Why Kinta left Brynden? Why there's nothing north of the Shevron Mountains but wasteland after you and Lukys were done with it? She might have been interested in what we did in Paradina, too. Who did win that nasty little altercation, by the way? I can never remember if it was you or me. What was the body count? Two hundred thousand? Or was it three? Damn," he added with a malicious smile, "old age must be making my mind slip."

"That would imply you had a mind to begin with."

"Temper, temper, Cayal," Jaxyn taunted. "Tide's not up far enough for one of your tantrums."

"Which would be why you're doing so well for yourself here in Glaeba with your boyfriend, I suppose," Cayal suggested. "I mean, it doesn't take any magical power at all to bend over and grab your ankles."

Jaxyn smiled. "Insulting me isn't going to get you out of this, Cayal."

"What were you planning, anyway, Jaxyn? Make yourself at home in Lebec and wait for the Tide to turn?"

"Good plan, I thought," Jaxyn agreed. "Particularly as it turns out I was right."

"Your standards are dropping. There was a time a country this small wouldn't have warranted your attention."

"There was a time the people of Amyrantha feared and respected the Immortal Prince, too," Jaxyn reminded him, as they continued to circle, matching each other pace for pace. Arkady couldn't tear her eyes away. It was like watching some strange dance for which only Cayal and Jaxyn knew the steps. "And look at him now . . . all pathetic and tragic and wanting to die."

"What do you want with these people, Jaxyn?"

"The same thing you want, Cayal. Somewhere to rest my weary head while the years tick away. I just happen to like doing it in a bit more comfort than you. With a lot less agonising over it, too, I might add."

Cayal shook his head. He was standing much straighter now, although he still seemed to be in pain. "It won't be easy, Jaxyn. Not this time. The Tide's been out a good long while. The human race has progressed. They've moved beyond folklore and worshipping gods. They've even explained away the Crasii. These people aren't going to fall at your feet the moment you announce you're a Tide Lord."

"I don't need them to." Jaxyn shrugged. "All I need is the Crasii. Once every gemang in the country turns their back on their human masters and starts following those they were bred to serve, just watch how quickly Glaeba falls."

Cayal had no argument with that, which terrified Arkady. If Jaxyn was right, taking Glaeba was going to be as easy as giving the command. What had Mathu said to her once? *If the Crasii ever took it upon themselves to revolt, we'd be in a lot of trouble.*

"Suppose one of the others has their eye on Glaeba?"

"Then they can fight me for it," Jaxyn replied, unconcerned. "Starting with you."

This was a side of Jaxyn she'd never seen before and it horrified Arkady. The idea this man—this amoral, unprincipled *monster*—not only could, but probably *would,* destroy everything she loved, everything she knew, filled her with anger. And an overwhelming sense of helplessness. How could anybody fight something so insidious, so ephemeral? So unbelievable . . .

Cayal shook his head, wincing with the pain he was so desperately trying not to show. Arkady didn't blame him, understanding that to show weakness in front of a man like Jaxyn was to expose one's throat to the wolf. "I don't want to rule your wretched little country."

"Let me guess . . . all you want is Arkady . . . how sweet."

Cayal laughed so derisively, it cut Arkady to the core. "Tides, what would I want with her? She's so full of the importance of her own opinions it's a wonder her spine doesn't snap under the pressure. You want her? Take her. I don't give a toss."

Jaxyn shook his head, frowning. "You know, it irks me that I can never really tell if you're lying."

"Try to imagine how much sleep I'm going to lose over that news, Jaxyn."

They were still circling each other, but the circle had gotten smaller as they talked. Arkady wasn't sure if Cayal realised Jaxyn was closing in on him. Perhaps the pain was distracting him.

"Try to imagine how little I *care,* Cayal," Jaxyn replied, and then he moved, so quickly his arm was a blur. Arkady cried out a warning, but it was too late, the knife Jaxyn wielded plunging into Cayal before he had a chance to react.

His eyes glittering with malice, Jaxyn glanced over his shoulder at her cry, and she realised she'd given herself away.

The instinct for self-preservation took over, without consciously thinking about it, Arkady turned and ran. Her last sight as she fled up the steep tunnel was Jaxyn thrusting the knife into his immortal companion over and over again until there was nothing but blood and dust and the rumbling protests of a mine on the brink of collapse.

Arkady ran. Her heart pounding with fear as much as the exertion, she bolted back the way she'd come. The mine rumbled around her, the creaking replaced by the sharp crack of splintering rock. The mine was breaking up behind her, taking the cavern and probably Cayal and Jaxyn with it. She didn't have time to dwell on what that meant, but her eyes blurred with tears as she stumbled out of the mine and into the ring of torch-bearing felines.

Before she had time to even register that fact, someone barrelled into her from behind and she was knocked to the ground.

Winded, and gasping for air, she was forced onto her back, looking up to find Jaxyn sitting astride her, covered in dust and Cayal's blood.

He smiled maliciously. "Good evening, your grace."

"What have you done to my mine, Jaxyn?" Maralyce demanded of him, hands on her hips.

"Why do you assume I've done anything?" he asked still astride Arkady, looking a little peeved as he tried to brush off the dust and debris the cave-in had coated him in. He could do nothing about the blood, however, and the sight of it made Arkady want to weep. "For all you know, it was Cayal's handiwork."

"Cayal has too much respect for other people's property."

"Funny, that's not what you said after he drowned your mine last time."

"That wasn't deliberate malice," Maralyce reminded him grumpily. "This was. You just wrecked *how* many years' work? And for what, you fool? You ain't killed him. All you've done is slow him down for a bit."

"Maybe that's all I wanted to do." He shrugged. He studied Arkady for a moment and then climbed off her. "I do, after all, have a rescue to perform and he really was getting in my way." He offered Arkady his hand.

With a great deal of reluctance, she accepted his help and he pulled her up.

"I see you've fared quite well despite your ordeal, your grace?"

"It's been very . . . informative," she replied, forcing herself to stand tall. She wanted to weep for Cayal, she wanted to run away screaming, but even if she'd been able to, there was nowhere to go.

Jaxyn studied her curiously. "Perhaps the damsel isn't in quite as much distress as she'd like her husband to believe?"

"I rather think that's between me and my husband, don't you?"

He seemed amused and in remarkably good spirits. Was this how Jaxyn reacted to death and destruction? *Tides, we're in so much trouble.*

"Cayal certainly didn't knock any of the stuffing out of you, did he, your grace? I wonder what he did knock out of you then."

"You are beyond disgusting, Jaxyn," she told him, wondering why she was bothering to keep up the fiction that she considered him nothing more than her husband's lover. "And I fully intend to report everything to Stellan when we return to Lebec. Including what you really are. And what you intend to do."

Jaxyn was singularly unimpressed by the threat. "Good luck getting him to believe you. He already thinks you've lost your mind, Arkady. By all means, go home and tell him *I'm* a Tide Lord, along with the prisoner you helped escape. That should convince him you haven't been out in the sun too long." Without waiting for her to reply, he turned on Maralyce. "We'll be gone at first light, Maralyce. I promise."

"Bah! What's your promise worth?" she spat, turning her back on him. "Just get them abominations off my claim, Jaxyn, and don't you bother comin' back for a good long time, neither."

"Stupid bitch," Jaxyn muttered at her retreating back,

and then he turned on Arkady. "Enjoy your little adventure, did you?"

She met his eye evenly and said nothing.

Jaxyn wiped away more of the blood-soaked dirt streaking his face, before ordering one of the Crasii to find him something to wash with. One of them hurried off to do as he bid as he turned his attention back to Arkady. "The Tide's turning, you know."

"So Cayal and Maralyce inform me."

"If you keep fighting me, you'll be on the wrong side of the line when the Tide Lords return and take their rightful place as the Gods of Amyrantha."

"And what's the right side of the line, Jaxyn? Standing on the same side as you?"

"I'll be ruling Glaeba before the year is out," he assured her with a quiet confidence that chilled her to the bone. It wouldn't have once. Once she would have laughed off his boast as the idle dreams of a reckless young man. But now . . . after all she'd seen and heard . . . "You don't want me as an enemy, Arkady."

"I think that might be rather less dangerous than being your friend, Jaxyn."

He studied her for a moment in the flickering torchlight and then nodded. "So be it," he said with unsettling finality. "You've chosen which side you're on, Arkady Desean. Don't say I didn't warn you."

Chapter 64

Just as Jaxyn promised Maralyce they would, Arkady left the mine on foot with the Crasii and the Tide Lord at first light the following morning, returning to the camp farther down the trail where the horses were tethered. Once mounted, they headed down the mountain at an almost leisurely pace. The Crasii obeyed Jaxyn unquestioningly, and for the most part he acted no differently than he had before Arkady discovered he was an immortal.

For the first day or so, Jaxyn seemed content to leave her alone with her thoughts, but after a barely adequate meal of cheese and jerky on the evening of the third day, Jaxyn came and sat opposite the fire from her.

"You really don't get who I am, do you?"

"I get it, Jaxyn. I'm just not impressed by it."

"You will be," he predicted. "Then you may wish you hadn't been quite so dismissive of me."

"Jaxyn, I don't care who you are, or who you *think* you are, because it doesn't alter *what* you are. Immortality might give you power, it may even make people afraid of you, but it can't make people like you."

"You'll live to regret not liking me," he warned. "So will Stellan."

Arkady shook her head, refusing to be intimidated by his threats. She'd thought about this a lot over the past two days and was fairly certain she knew the way this would play out. The Tide Lords might be on the rise, but there was time yet, before they were ruling the world again.

Time, perhaps, to find a way to prevent it.

"You won't expose Stellan," she told him confidently. "Not yet, at least. To expose my husband means exposing yourself as his partner in crime. Until your power has returned fully, you can't afford to lose your position in our household. Even with us going to Torlenia, you still have access to the corridors of power in Glaeba through Kylia. You're not going to risk losing that until you're ready. By then, I suppose it won't matter what you say about Stellan, will it?"

"You really are too clever by half, aren't you, Arkady?"

She shrugged, privately pleased she'd been able to out-think him, at least this once. "That remains to be seen, I suppose."

"You really don't understand it, though," he warned. "You think you know what's coming, but you don't realise what it means. You don't appreciate the truly unique relationship between the immortals and the Crasii, and that's a pity."

"They're your *slaves*," she replied impatiently. "I get it, Jaxyn, really, I do."

"No, you don't. Nobody gets it. Not until they've witnessed it for themselves."

"I've witnessed your power over the Crasii plenty of times, Jaxyn. I'm even moderately impressed by it. Does that make you feel better?"

He smiled. "I think you need a demonstration."

"You can make them jump through hoops, I get it."

"Who's your favourite?"

"What?"

"There's a score of Crasii here with us and you know most of them by name. Which one do you like the most?"

She shivered, hoping it was the icy darkness that made her shudder. "That's an absurd question."

"Very well, which one is the most loyal? Which one would you trust with your life?"

Arkady didn't want to play this game but she was fairly certain there was no way to avoid it. "Chelby, I suppose."

"The canine? He's your best tracker, isn't he?"

"You know that. It's why you brought him along, isn't it?"

"Be it on your own head then," Jaxyn said, rather ominously. He turned and called over his shoulder, "Chelby! Come!"

Obedient as ever, the canine hurried across their small camp to the fire. "My lord?"

Jaxyn withdrew the knife he carried from his belt. The knife he'd used to mutilate Cayal—not to kill him, so much, as slow him down, Arkady realised now. He held the knife out to Chelby, who accepted it with a puzzled look.

"Sire?"

"Cut your throat," Jaxyn ordered calmly.

The canine blinked, but made no objection.

"No!" Arkady cried, leaping to her feet.

Chelby looked at her, his eyes glistening, shaking his head, but he didn't even hesitate before raising the knife. Around them, the felines stopped to watch, every one of them staring at the canine with dark, questioning eyes. Chelby was visibly distressed by Jaxyn's command, yet inexorably, his hand was moving upwards, the knife getting closer and closer to his throat.

"Jaxyn, stop this!"

"You wanted proof, didn't you?"

"You can't do this! Make it stop!"

Jaxyn watched her closely, apparently amused by her distress. The knife Chelby held was pressing against his throat, a bead of blood already forming around the tip.

"Tell you what, I'll stop him, if you'll make a deal with me."

"Whatever you want! Just stop it! Now!"

Jaxyn studied her for a moment longer and then turned to the canine. "Halt."

With a great deal of relief, Chelby dropped the knife. He was visibly shaking, his ears flat against his head, his tail hanging limply between his legs, and obviously in a great deal of distress.

"What deal?" she demanded, wishing she could comfort the poor creature, but she suspected any sympathy on her part toward the Crasii would just make it harder on them.

"I'll not tell your husband you were a willing accomplice to Cayal's escape, if you don't say anything about who I am."

"What would be the point of making a promise like that? As you said, if I tell Stellan you're a Tide Lord, he'll just think I'm crazy."

"On the off-chance he actually thinks you're not, I'd like to cover myself. As you say, it doesn't suit me to rock the boat just yet."

"Do you truly have your eye on Glaeba's throne?" she asked. "Is that why you singled Stellan out? What were you planning, Jaxyn, to kill the other heirs ahead of Stellan and rule through him?"

"More or less." He shrugged. "Of course, things are a little different now. I've realised there are other ways to the throne besides through your husband. They may even prove quicker. I *can* navigate the corridors of power without magical help, you know."

She glared at him suspiciously across the fire. "What are you up to, Jaxyn?"

He smiled. "As if you didn't already know! Weren't you listening in while Cayal and I were discussing my evil plans for Glaeba?"

"You actually *have* an evil plan, then? How foresighted of you."

"You can mock me all you want, Arkady," he told her, scooping the knife Chelby had discarded off the ground. "Sooner or later, you'll be kneeling at my feet, begging for my mercy, remembering there was a time when I was actually willing to give it, and you rejected me."

He turned his back on her but had only taken two steps before she called him back. "Jaxyn!"

"Your grace?" he enquired, looking over his shoulder.

"I'll do it."

"Do what?" he demanded as he turned to face her again, making sure he was extracting the promise he wanted.

"Keep your confidence. For now." He looked so smug Arkady wanted to throw something at him. "I'm not doing this for you, idiot. Stellan loves you, although I can't for the life of me imagine why. It would destroy him to learn you were using him to gain the throne. The idea that by inviting you into his home, by trusting you . . . he might well have betrayed his king . . . it would probably kill him faster than the realisation he was conned by an immoral, ruthless killer with no scruples about sleeping his way to power."

Jaxyn beamed at her as if she'd paid him a huge compliment. "My, you *have* been talking to Cayal, haven't you?"

"Well? Do we have a deal?"

"Indeed we do, your grace."

"Then let that be the end of it," she agreed. "For now."

He eyed her up and down suggestively. "Not interested in sealing our pact with a kiss?"

Arkady squared her shoulders, glaring at him across the fire. "Don't push me, Jaxyn."

"Push you?" he laughed. "You're threatening *me*? Tides, but you've got balls, Arkady."

She lifted her chin defiantly. "I believe you were the one who said he didn't want to rock the boat? I may not be able to stop you in the long run, but trust me, I can capsize your cosy little rowboat for you now, Jaxyn, and long before you get a chance to navigate anywhere near the halls of power you seem so fond of."

He studied her for a moment in the firelight, and then, somewhat to Arkady's surprise, he bowed in acknowledgement of her power—however fleeting—over him.

"Then we have a truce, Arkady. For the time being."

"For the time being," she agreed, with a bad feeling that, far from helping her cause, she had just made a pact with the devil.

"Don't even think of crossing me," he warned.

"I wouldn't dream of it."

He studied her for a moment and then shook his head ruefully. "Actually, I suspect you'll be dreaming of little else," he concluded. "Maybe you *do* need reminding about what I can do, after all."

Before she could stop him, Jaxyn turned on Chelby. He handed the knife back to the canine, hilt first, with a brusque command. "Do it. Now."

Without hesitating, without a single objection, Chelby accepted the knife and—despite the anguish in the young canine's eyes—with a single sweep of his arm he slashed himself across the throat. Blood sprayed both Jaxyn and Arkady as Chelby fell. Arkady screamed, stumbling backwards, soaked in the blood of the dead Crasii.

Even worse, the felines stood and watched as if frozen in place.

Jaxyn flinched distastefully and stepped back as Chelby lay twitching on the ground, his anguished eyes staring up at them as he silently bled to death at her feet. The immortal turned to Arkady. She had fallen to her knees, sickened by what she'd seen, numb at the thought of what it meant.

"Now," Jaxyn predicted with satisfaction, "you begin to understand."

Chapter 65

Three days after the King and Queen of Glaeba and their entourage left for their own palace in Herino with Mathu and Kylia in tow, Declan Hawkes formally requested an audience with the Duke of Lebec. Although he remained outwardly calm, Stellan was panic-stricken by the request. There was only one reason Stellan could think of that would attract the attention of the King's Spymaster. Guilt about the lies he'd told, the lies he'd arranged for Tilly to tell . . . all of it had settled into an uncomfortable lump in the centre of his chest that simply refused to go away.

There was no possibility he could deny the King's Spymaster an audience. Any attempt to delay it, the slightest hint that the Duke of Lebec had something to hide, may be all that was needed to throw suspicion on himself. Declan might have no solid evidence at all of Stellan's guilt. Any attempt to avoid him, however, could easily be the proof the spymaster was looking for to implicate the duke in all manner of treasonous activities, ranging from his affair with Jaxyn right up to lying about the whereabouts of his wife and concealing the fact that she had forged the release papers for a convicted murderer.

Hawkes stepped into his office at the appointed time, looking around at the murals with interest. Stellan indicated he should sit and took his own seat behind his desk, laying his palms flat upon the polished desktop so that Declan wouldn't see them shaking.

"Interesting room, I've always thought," the young man remarked, making himself comfortable in one of the ivory-legged chairs. "Artwork's quite impressive."

"My great-grandmother had the murals done long before I was born," Stellan explained, relieved to be talking about something harmless. "The artist was quite a character, I hear. Used to have tantrums and run screaming through the place claiming he couldn't possibly work under such trying conditions. According to my father, they ended up locking him in here and refusing to let him out until the job was done."

Declan smiled. "It's a good story. Do you think it's true?"

"I don't know," he replied. "There's probably a grain of truth there somewhere."

"Lot of myths are like that."

"Do you think so?" Stellan asked, not sure of the purpose of the discussion. He wasn't fool enough to believe that Declan was making idle conversation.

"I *know* so," Declan chuckled, and then he sobered a little. "Dangerous things though."

"Myths?"

"Aye. They make people forget."

"I would have thought their purpose quite the opposite," Stellan disagreed. "Aren't myths the reminder of things we shouldn't forget?"

"You're confusing myths with morality tales," Declan told him. "They're the parables you want to pass on to your children. You know . . . it's bad to steal, lying will bring you nothing but trouble, you'll get devoured by hairy spiders if you don't eat all your vegetables . . . that sort of thing."

"I remember the hairy spider tale," Stellan laughed.

"When I was a small child, I had a Crasii nanny with a knack for storytelling. First time I refused to eat my vegetables, she had me too scared to sleep."

"Well, I never had a Crasii nanny, but I grew up quite convinced there was a family of tiny assassins living under the floorboards, ready to scuttle out in the dead of night while I was asleep and do me in if I so much as thought about sneaking out the window of my bedroom."

"Your *grandfather* told you that?" Stellan asked in surprise. Although he'd never met Shalimar Hawkes, to hear Arkady speak of him, Stellan had always thought the old man a candidate for sainthood.

Declan smiled at Stellan's expression. "I was a bit of a handful, back then. I think Pop decided scaring me into staying put was the most expedient way to get a good night's sleep."

"I can't imagine you being afraid of anything, Declan."

"Ask Arkady, if you don't believe me," he suggested. The spymaster seemed amused. And far more relaxed than Stellan was expecting. "Even now, memories of those tiny assassins will do me in, every time."

"I'll have to remember that the next time I want to intimidate the King's Spymaster." The pleasant, nonthreatening nature of their conversation was straining Stellan to breaking point. Declan did nothing without cause. He certainly wasn't the sort to indulge in this kind of idle chatter.

"Now myths are another thing altogether," Declan mused. "They're the stories we don't believe are true because they seem too fantastic to be real."

"Did you have a particular myth in mind?"

"The Tide Lords are a good example," Declan replied, and then he added calmly, "and there's a particularly good one I heard recently about a duchess letting a murderer go free."

Stellan stared at Declan trying to determine if the man was fishing for information or if he actually knew something. If he suspected anything at all, a lie now might be fatal.

But if the spymaster was only guessing . . .

Stellan couldn't risk it. He swallowed the lump in his throat and shrugged. "Things are not always what they seem."

"I couldn't agree more."

"You want an explanation, I suppose?"

"Let's start with the facts," Declan suggested. "Arkady isn't upstairs resting as you and Lady Ponting assured the king, is she?"

Fighting to keep an outward air of calm, Stellan hesitated and then decided that for once, he'd be better served by the truth. Or at least part of it. "No, she's not."

"So she's not pregnant then, either?"

"She may be. I haven't asked her recently."

"And the prisoner she had released from Lebec Prison with your authorisation? Where is he?"

"If I'm lucky, he's wherever Arkady is, she is still alive and he'll let her go when he no longer feels threatened."

Declan seemed a little surprised. "You mean you knew about this?"

Stellan raised a brow at Declan. "Did you think I wouldn't?"

"His release was more than a little irregular, your grace."

"It was a little irregular," Stellan agreed. "But you know Arkady better than anyone. She was convinced she was close to exposing him. When the king ordered him to be handed over to you, she begged me for one last chance to question him. I saw no harm in it, so I sent her to the prison with a release order and a Crasii escort, so that she could question him on the return journey, before handing the prisoner over to you. They stopped to water the horses at Clyden's Inn and the prisoner escaped, taking Arkady hostage and somehow subverting the escort. As soon as I learned about it, I sent Jaxyn Aranville and another dozen Crasii after them. If you don't believe me, speak to the owner of Clyden's Inn."

"I already have," the spymaster admitted.

Almost faint with relief that he'd chosen to tell most of the truth, Stellan shrugged. "What more can I tell you?"

"You can tell me why you lied to the king about Arkady."

That charge was much harder to dodge, but Stellan hadn't entirely wasted the time since Declan asked to see him just fretting about it. He had his answer at the ready; didn't even hesitate before providing it. "I'm surprised you have to ask," he said with a smile that spoke much about what he thought of the spymaster's reputation. "You must be aware I have arranged for Mathu to marry my niece. There have been some very delicate negotiations going on between me and the king. I wasn't about to jeopardise them by letting him know I'd done anything as foolish as putting my own wife in the power of a madman. The king gets distracted easily, Declan. You know that. I didn't want anything to get in the way of the betrothal."

Declan nodded, apparently accepting his explanation as a perfectly legitimate reason, which, for any other noble family in Glaeba, it probably was. Fortunately, only Arkady had any idea Stellan wasn't happy about Kylia's engagement.

"Do you need help finding her?" he offered.

"Thank you, but I'm still hoping Jaxyn will prevail. He's a resourceful lad, knows the area quite well and is very fond of Arkady. I'm sure he won't rest until he's brought her home."

"And what of Kyle Lakesh?"

"Lord Aranville has orders to take whatever actions are necessary to rescue Arkady. If that includes killing an escaped convict, then so be it."

"I admire your restraint, your grace," Declan remarked, watching him closely. "I think—in your place—I'd be climbing the walls with worry."

"If only I had the luxury," Stellan replied. "It's considered weakness among the highborn to display emotional extremes, you know. The idea is drummed into us from infancy. Apparently, letting on that we own even the most basic human feelings makes us appear weak in front of the peasants."

"Then I'm glad I'm a simple peasant," the spymaster said. "Not sure I've the courage to maintain a stiff upper lip."

"I'm not sure any of us have," Stellan agreed. "One just has to learn to fake it."

"And how much faking are you doing, your grace?" Declan enquired.

The lump in Stellan's chest relocated itself in his throat. "I beg your pardon?"

"You lied to the king about your wife. You've lied about her being pregnant, which means you're going to have to lie to him again when her belly fails to swell. Seems to me, you're pretty good at this game. Makes a man start to wonder where you got the practice."

"I don't like what you're implying, sir."

"Any more than I like what I'm seeing here," the spymaster replied. "In my experience, where there's one lie, there's a whole raft of others beneath it and it's my job to bring such lies to the attention of the king, not to mention the fact you are married to a woman I consider one of my closest friends. If there's something going on here, that jeopardises either one of them . . . well, I'm sure you can see my dilemma."

"If you're trying to insinuate that I'm somehow involved in some plot against the king . . . ," he sputtered with convincing indignation.

Declan held up his hands in a conciliatory gesture. "I'm insinuating nothing of the sort. I'm concerned, that's all. You're an important man, Duke Stellan, a close friend—and relative—of the king. I find it disturbing to think you might be involved in deceiving him. For whatever reason. A man can lie to his liege for purposes other than treason, you know."

Stellan felt the blood drain from his face, certain there was no way Declan Hawkes could miss such a blatant sign of his guilt. Did he know everything? About Jaxyn? About the others before him? About the sham of his marriage to Arkady? Had she told him? And if she had, why wait until now before saying anything about it?

"Exactly what are you implying, Master Hawkes?"

The spymaster opened his mouth to speak, but before he got a word out, the door flew open and Arkady stepped into the room. Stellan jumped to his feet in shock, followed by Declan, who rose a little less abruptly from his chair. Looking travel-stained and weary, her normally perfectly coiffed hair in a long, loose braid, her clothes splattered with something that looked disturbingly like dried blood, she didn't even glance at Declan. Instead, she rushed to her husband, threw herself into his arms and kissed him full on the mouth.

"Oh, Stellan!" she cried, after a delivering a kiss most storybook lovers would have been proud of. "I feared I'd never see you again!"

He held her tightly, glancing up to see Jaxyn standing at the door. Stellan smiled at them both, relief warring with surprise, as Jaxyn stepped into the room.

The young man beamed at them, obviously pleased he had been instrumental in facilitating this reunion. He looked upon Stellan and Arkady indulgently and then turned to Declan Hawkes. "I do love a happy ending, don't you, Master Hawkes?"

"Certainly do, Lord Aranville," the spymaster agreed, obviously a little puzzled. "I'm glad to see you safe and sound, Arkady."

"It's only thanks to Jaxyn," she informed him breathily, gushing in a manner anybody who knew her well would know immediately was an act—a fact that worried Stellan a great deal, because Declan *did* know her well. "He tracked us to an abandoned mine in the mountains and was able to free the Crasii and then trap the fugitive in a cave-in. You must reward him, dear, for his heroism. I don't know what that wretch would have done to me if I'd been his prisoner much longer."

Stellan studied her face, searching for answers Arkady

was too smart to give him with Declan Hawkes in the room. "He didn't hurt you then?"

She smiled; a genuine smile, not a fake one. "Truly, Stellan, I'm fine."

"There's blood on your clothes . . ."

"Not mine, thankfully. There was . . . Chelby was killed."

"I would sacrifice every Crasii I owned if it meant seeing you safe." He hugged her again, looking over her shoulder at Jaxyn. "Thank you."

"You're welcome," Jaxyn replied. "Believe me, nothing gave me more pleasure than settling the score with the madman calling himself the Immortal Prince."

"And what of the Crasii?" Declan asked.

"What?" Stellan and Jaxyn both asked simultaneously.

"Lady Desean said you freed the Crasii. How did this fugitive wagon builder manage to subvert an entire squad of felines in the first place?"

"He told them he was a Tide Lord," Arkady replied, while Jaxyn was still trying to come up with a plausible answer. "As I predicted when I was first brought in to interrogate this man, Declan, news that he had survived the noose and was claiming to be the Immortal Prince took very little time to spread to the Crasii. Between that, a commanding tone and a bit of sleight of hand with an axe at the inn, he had them all purring at his feet in a remarkably short time." She turned to Stellan and added, "I warned you he was dangerous, didn't I, darling?"

"But that doesn't explain how Lord Aranville freed them," Declan insisted. "That is what you said, isn't it, Arkady? Jaxyn freed the Crasii?"

"You make it sound far more sinister than it warrants, Master Hawkes," Jaxyn said with a laugh. "He'd left them at a camp a few miles below the mine her grace spoke of. I untied them, that's all. What do you think I'd done? Told our sadly deluded felines that *I* was a Tide Lord too and I was countermanding the Immortal Prince's orders?"

"Forgive me, Lord Aranville," the spymaster said with an apologetic bow. "I did not mean to lessen the heroic nature of your deed." Declan then turned to Stellan and bowed to him also. "I should withdraw, your grace, and let you see to your wife."

"Wasn't there something else you wanted to discuss?"

Declan studied Arkady for a moment, who was still standing in the circle of Stellan's embrace, her eyes focussed on her husband as if there was no other man in the world, and then he shook his head. "No, I don't think so. Now that Arkady is back, I'm sure you'll be able to smooth things over with the king. Perhaps the next time something like this happens, you might come to me for help, though, instead of lying about it?"

Stellan nodded. "I will. Thank you for your forbearance, Declan."

"I'm just glad to see Arkady safe, your grace." He bowed politely. "And now if you will excuse me? Arkady. Lord Aranville."

Nobody said another word until the King's Spymaster had left the room and closed the door behind him.

Chapter 66

Arkady took a decadently long time to finish her ablutions. When she finally emerged from her rooms several hours after she returned to the palace she felt properly clean for the first time in nearly two weeks. Dressed in fresh clothes, her hair back in its customary chignon and looking every inch the duchess again, she returned to Stellan's office. Opening the door without knocking, Arkady walked in on her husband and his lover locked in an intimate embrace that could have ruined them all if it had been Declan Hawkes at the door.

The men jumped apart, although Jaxyn seemed more amused than startled by her appearance.

"Are you *trying* to destroy us all?" she asked, directing her question at Jaxyn, who she was convinced was the instigator of anything so foolish behind an unlocked door with the King's Spymaster still a guest in the palace.

Stellan, on the other hand, was quite pale. "Tides! You gave me a fright, Arkady."

"If you don't like nasty surprises, Stellan, perhaps you should ask Jaxyn to check if the door is locked first."

"Now, now . . . it was my fault—," Stellan began apologetically.

"If you don't mind, Jaxyn," Arkady cut in, before Stellan could take all the blame. "I'd like to speak to my husband. Alone."

Jaxyn smiled in a way that made Arkady's blood run cold. "Of course. I'm sure you have a great deal to talk about."

"I'll see you later?" Stellan asked, almost hopefully.

"Count on it," Jaxyn promised as he took his leave of them. He stopped and bowed to Arkady as he passed her. "Just remember our discussion, your grace."

"I'm not likely to forget it, Jaxyn."

"Good girl," he said, softly enough that Stellan wouldn't catch the words, and then he left, closing the door behind him.

Stellan looked at Arkady curiously. "What discussion is he talking about?"

Arkady shrugged. "It's nothing really. We had a chance to talk on the way back. I promised I'd be more accepting of him, if he promised not to irritate me so much."

Stellan smiled. "I appreciate that. It's very difficult when the two people you love the most don't get along."

"Do you really love Jaxyn?" she asked, taking the seat so recently occupied by Declan Hawkes.

"Yes, I do."

"And do you honestly think he returns your affection?"

Stellan studied her thoughtfully. "Clearly *you* don't.

Did he say something to you that would make you believe such a thing?"

Yes, she wanted to yell at him. *He's* using *you. He's using us. Can't you see that?*

But of course, she didn't. She couldn't. "No. It wasn't anything he said. I'm just naturally suspicious, Stellan. You know me."

"I thought I did," he said, taking the seat behind his desk. "And then you forged my signature, released two prisoners without my permission, pardoned one of them and let the other escape. That's not the Arkady I thought I knew."

It wasn't until that moment it occurred to Arkady just how difficult it was going to be to justify what she'd done without telling him the whole truth. "Are you very angry with me, Stellan?"

"I'm prepared to hear you out," he told her. "But I have to warn you, I'm not feeling particularly well disposed toward you at the moment, Arkady. You have no idea the trouble I've had covering for you with the king."

"I'm sorry, Stellan. Truly, I am."

Stellan seemed to accept her apology, but it was hard to tell. She'd never seen him in this mood before.

"Did this man hurt you?"

"No."

"He didn't force himself on you?"

"No."

"You slept with him." It wasn't a question.

"You wanted me to take a lover," she pointed out.

He didn't appreciate the reminder. "I assumed you'd exercise somewhat better judgement, Arkady. What was it about this man? That he was a killer? A convict? A peasant? Are you angry at me because of Jaxyn and looking for a way to get back at me so you chose the most inappropriate man on Amyrantha to prove your point?"

She shook her head. "This wasn't about you, Stellan."

"Then explain it to me, Arkady, because the Tides know I haven't been able to explain it to myself."

She looked down at her hands, surprised at how hard this was proving to be. "You'll think I'm crazy."

"Believe me, we're *long* past that point, my dear."

Arkady took a deep breath. "Kyle Lakesh wasn't lying, Stellan. He truly is a Tide Lord. He is Cayal, the Immortal Prince."

Stellan stared at her. "I see."

"I'm quite sure you don't. And I know what this sounds like, but it's true. I swear. You have to trust me in this. I saw his fingers grow back in front of my eyes, Stellan. Even if the stories he told me hadn't seemed too real to be made up, I know what I saw at the inn."

"You said he was dead."

"I said Jaxyn trapped him in a cave-in, which is quite true. I never actually said he was dead."

"Do you know for certain that he isn't?"

Only in my heart, she felt like saying, but realised it wouldn't help her cause. "No, I don't know for certain."

"And you don't allow for the possibility he tricked you?"

"This was no parlour trick," she assured him, shaking her head. "I saw him cut his fingers off, and I witnessed them grow back. But even if I hadn't seen that, the Crasii reaction to him was enough to convince me."

"You're the one who told Declan Hawkes it was all a lie. What was it you said . . . *a commanding tone and a bit of sleight of hand with an axe, he had them all purring at his feet in a remarkably short time*? That scenario sounds much more likely than you—or the Crasii—seeing a man wielding Tide magic."

"Doesn't that tell you something, Stellan?" she said. "I'm not a fool. I don't believe in magic. At least I didn't. But I've seen it. I've felt it. And I've watched a man cut off three fingers and regrow them. I'm not imagining this, and I'm not crazy. What I am is worried, *desperately* worried, because the Tide is turning. The immortals are among us and they'll soon regain their powers. Then the whole world will be in danger from them."

"*Danger*? What danger?"

"Stellan, please, you must believe me. These immortals . . . these Tide Lords . . . they're monsters. They use volcanoes as weapons and play with human lives the way you'd play a board game and with just as little compassion for the pieces. We have to do something before their power returns fully."

"Can you hear yourself, Arkady?" he asked in wonder. "You speak of immortals and Tide magic and things that can't possibly be real as if you truly believe them."

"I wish they weren't real," she sighed. "But they are, Stellan, and we need to start thinking about how we're going to deal with them."

His eyes went wide. "*Deal* with them? I'm sitting here wondering if I shouldn't have you sedated until you come to your senses."

She sighed. "I feared this would be your reaction."

"Then why try such a ridiculous tale on me?" he asked. "Arkady, if you love this man—that I could understand. I may not approve of it, may not even understand your infatuation, but I could deal with it. I realise I've only myself to blame for placing you in his power, but please, respect my intelligence enough not to try blinding me with stories of Tide magic and immortals."

She leant forward in her chair, hoping she sounded rational, fearing she sounded quite the opposite. "Stellan, if I could prove this, don't you think I would? If there was *any* other explanation, no matter how implausible, don't you think I would latch on to it with both hands and cling to it for dear life? Tides! How hard have I fought to be taken seriously as a historian? Do you think I would jeopardise that for a moment if I didn't believe this is real?"

He accepted the truth of her words, she could see that, but he still didn't believe her. Arkady didn't blame him. Cayal had had to chop three fingers off before she was willing to admit the truth, and even then she'd fought it every inch of the way.

"Where are they then?"

"Where are who?"

"These immortals, these dangerous Tide Lords you want me to worry about. Do you know where they are?"

"No," she was forced to admit, even while knowing there was a viper in their midst. Not that it made much difference. Even if she hadn't made a deal with Jaxyn, even if the memory of Chelby cutting his own throat on a word from Jaxyn weren't so fresh in her mind, her husband was too blinded by his love to see the truth. If she accused Jaxyn of being a Tide Lord, Stellan would think she was making all this up just to get rid of him.

"So, what action do you suggest I take, Arkady, to defend us from this looming peril?"

She hesitated and then shrugged helplessly. "I don't know."

"Well, you will let me know when you come up with a plan, won't you, my dear?"

"Don't be like that, Stellan."

"Like what?" he demanded, as close to anger as she had ever seen him. "I had to have Tilly Ponting tell the king you were pregnant, Arkady, just to stop him asking questions about where you were. And then I had to agree to my seventeen-year-old niece being betrothed to a reckless young man I know is going to break her heart because I couldn't afford to rock the boat while my wife was off in the mountains having a fling with the killer she busted out of gaol. So I'm sorry if my patience and understanding are close to their limit, dear, but I do seem to have been awfully put upon lately."

Arkady could have cried to see Stellan like this. In all the time she'd known him, they'd never fought. Not once. Not so much as a raised voice between them. "I never meant any of this to hurt you, Stellan. I don't want to make you angry."

"I'm not angry, Arkady, I'm disappointed, which I think actually hurts more."

She rose to her feet, nodding in acknowledgement of

her contribution to that pain. "I'll do whatever I must to make it up to you, Stellan."

"Then get yourself pregnant," he said bluntly. "Assuming you're not already."

She stared at him in shock. *"What?"*

"I've told the king you're with child, Arkady. Worse, I had to involve Tilly in my deception and make her just as culpable as me. So we'll *make* this a truth—we have that much in our power—and that will be one less lie I have to deal with."

"You cannot be serious."

He shrugged heartlessly. "Sleep with Jaxyn. Take Declan Hawkes to your bed and put him out of his misery. Pull a labourer out of the fields if you must—that seems to be your taste these days—just get yourself knocked up. We're leaving for Herino in three days for the royal wedding. I expect by the time we get there, your condition will be a fact and not just wishful thinking on Enteny's part."

"You can't just order me to sleep with someone!" she gasped in horror.

"That was our deal, Arkady," he reminded her. "I pardon your father, you give me an heir."

"My father died in prison."

"Of consumption, Arkady, and after I signed his pardon," he pointed out. "Not because I didn't keep up my end of the bargain."

She glared at him suspiciously. "Did Jaxyn put you up to this?"

Stellan shook his head, almost as if he pitied her. "You can't keep blaming him for everything, Arkady. It's not Jaxyn's fault. You've brought this on yourself."

"Do you even care who fathers your heir?"

He looked down at his desk and picked up a quill, as if he had other, better things to do with his time than discuss this with her. "Given there's a reasonable chance my heir has already been fathered by a convicted killer who's somehow managed to convince my wife he's immortal, I don't know that I'm in a position to be all that picky. Now . . . if you don't mind . . ."

His callous dismissal of her cut Arkady to the core. "Stellan . . . please . . ."

"Three days, Arkady," he reminded her coldly, turning his attention to the papers on his desk. "I'll understand if you're not at dinner this evening."

Arkady stared at him, the depth of the betrayal she felt only just beginning to dawn on her. "I've lied for you every day for six years, Stellan. I've kept your secrets. I've done everything you ever asked of me and more. I protected you. I've protected your damned lovers, too, including Jaxyn Aranville, who is not what he seems, I can assure you. And the first time I falter . . . you turn on me? Like this?" She drew herself up, squaring her shoulders, forcing herself not to give into the tears she could feel welling up behind her eyes. "Tides, I may not be the woman you imagined, Stellan Desean, but you're certainly not the man I thought I knew, either."

With that, Arkady turned on her heel. Blinded by the tears she was too proud to shed, she left him at his desk, unable to bear the look of distrust and disappointment in Stellan's eyes which must surely be reflected in her own.

Chapter 67

Arkady took breakfast on the terrace the following morning, her eyes gritty from lack of sleep. She had tossed and turned all night, trying to think of a way to make things better between her and Stellan. All night she had lain awake trying to think of a way to expose Jaxyn—a moot point given that even if she told Stellan what his lover was, he'd never believe her.

And for much of the night she'd been trying not to think of Cayal.

In the end, Arkady had given up. Just on dawn she had come down to the terrace to watch the sunrise on the lake. As she was facing west, the sun climbed across the sky behind her, painting a golden path along the still waters, tinting the faint mist pink and gold as it rose off the rushes near the water's edge.

Nature's glory on display, she thought, *while buried somewhere in a mine in the Shevron Mountains is one of her abominations. Another is chiselling her way through eternity looking for gold.*

Yet another was living under Arkady's roof, trading on the credulity of a good and decent man with the misfortune to have been born with a nature that social convention deemed perverted.

"Did you want another pot of tea, your grace?"

Arkady glanced up, pulling her shawl a little closer against the cool morning. "Thank you, Tassie. That would be lovely."

The canine hurried away to fetch a fresh pot of tea, leaving Arkady alone with her morose thoughts.

"You never used to be such an early riser, Arkady."

Arkady sat up sharply, alarmed to find Declan Hawkes climbing the terrace steps. He was coming from the right, from the direction of the Crasii village. "Declan!"

He bowed politely. "Good morning, your grace."

She forced a smile, although she certainly didn't feel like it, indicating the other side of the table. "Please, won't you join me? Tassie has just gone to fetch a fresh pot."

"Breakfast on the terrace with the Duchess of Lebec, eh?" Declan lowered his tall frame into the chair and leaned back, admiring the view of the lake. "I'm honoured."

"You accuse me of being an early riser," Arkady remarked, ignoring his tone, more concerned about what he was doing roaming the estate so early in the morning. "And yet you've obviously been up for quite some time."

"I like to stretch my legs in the mornings," he explained. "It helps me think."

"Well, I hope you enjoyed the gardens," she replied. "They really are quite spectacular." Arkady hesitated, and then added, "Why are you still here, Declan? Doesn't the king require your presence in Herino?"

"I have family here in Lebec," he said. "And this friend of mine gave me a right ticking off the other day about my appallingly bad behaviour toward them, so I decided to take her advice."

Arkady was shocked. Declan and Shalimar hadn't spoken in years, as far as she knew. "You've been to see your grandfather?"

"That I have."

"How is he?"

"Very well, actually. He says you bring him food parcels."

"Someone has to look after him."

"And I do appreciate your efforts, Arkady, but truly, Pop isn't nearly as helpless as he likes to make you think."

"You're just saying that to make yourself feel better for neglecting him. When are you leaving for Herino?"

"Your husband has kindly offered to let me join your party when you sail for the capital in a couple of days."

"That was very thoughtful of him."

"I thought so," he agreed, smiling. He studied her closely for a moment. "Are you feeling better? After your harrowing ordeal."

"Much, thank you."

"Can't have been easy for you. I hear the Immortal Prince can be rather . . . trying. Arrogant, they say. A bit full of himself."

Arkady smiled. She wasn't so foolish or tired that she would walk into such an obvious trap. "You're not buying this wild story about immortality and Tide Lords too, are you, Declan?"

"The Crasii believe the Tide Lords are real."

"Do *you*?" she asked, eyeing him curiously.

Declan smiled. "I rather think, Arkady, it's more a question of whether or not *you* believe in them."

She laughed dismissively. "What's my belief got to do with anything?"

"Not much," he admitted. "Not while the Tide is out. But it's on the turn, so I'm told. We're about to have a world of trouble rain down on us and there's not many mortals in a position to appreciate what that means."

Arkady stared at her oldest friend in shock. "What do you mean, the Tide is turning?"

He eyed her carefully, cautiously, as if he was testing her. "I think you know."

Arkady shivered, certain it wasn't the cool breeze coming off the lake that prickled her skin with goose bumps. "Has Jaxyn accused me of something?"

"If he had, Arkady, I'd not be paying it any mind. I'm under no illusions about Lord Aranville."

He knows, Arkady thought, her heart in her mouth. *Tides! He knows about Stellan and Jaxyn.*

"Well," she said, trying to sound as light-hearted as possible. "I know why *I* don't like him. What's your problem with him?"

Declan wasn't smiling. "Same problem I've got with all the immortals."

Arkady stared at him for a long time. Finally she forced a smile she didn't feel and shook her head dismissively. "I'm sorry; my hearing must be failing me. I thought you just said Jaxyn was an immortal."

Declan was watching her closely. "There's nothing wrong with your hearing, Arkady."

"Then there is clearly something wrong with your mind, Declan Hawkes."

He studied her for a moment and then nodded in understanding. "You fear I'm trying to trap you into saying something I can use against you."

"I can't imagine *why* you'd be looking for something to use against me," she replied, "but I think it's a reasonable fear, given you're the King's Spymaster now."

"I beg to differ," he replied. "I think, if I was planning to bring you down, I could have done it long before now."

Arkady frowned. "You swore to me you'd never say a word about Fillion Rybank to anybody."

"Nor have I," he assured her. "Your father went to his grave in ignorance of what was done to you, just as you requested. I promised I wouldn't reveal your secret, and I've had no reason to break my vow."

"So you say . . ."

He smiled. "How do you think the man who murdered Rybank knew where and when to find the old pederast indulging his sick fantasies with his assistant's thirteen-year-old son?"

Arkady stared at him in surprise. "Rybank was killed by one of his junior colleagues the year after I was married." She shook her head, wondering why she'd never suspected Declan had a hand in his demise. "Tides, I just thought it luck that he was finally caught. I never imagined it was your doing."

"I told you I'd kill the monstrous bastard." His smile widened and he was looking more than a little smug. "Sometimes, it's very useful being me."

Almost faint with relief, Arkady smiled weakly. "You promised me you wouldn't do anything foolish."

He leant back in his seat and smiled. "Nor did I. In fact I think I managed the whole affair rather nicely. Unfortunately, I wasn't the spymaster back them, so I didn't have the power to countermand an arrest order issued by a Prefect and have your father released, but rest assured, your father died believing you were safe and innocent and would be taken care of, regardless of what might happen to him."

"Would that the messenger carrying his pardon had ridden a little faster," Arkady lamented. "He might also have died a free man." She drained the last of her tea and smiled at him. "I am grateful for your silence, Declan," she said. "And that you were able to put an end to Rybank. Truly, I'd help you if I could. But do you really expect me to admit I believe in magic and Tide Lords and all that nonsense?"

"You and I both know it's not nonsense," he said softly, and then he sat a little straighter in his seat as Tassie appeared with the fresh pot of tea they were waiting on.

"We do, do we?" Arkady asked in a noncommittal tone.

"Ask your canine here, who her real lord is," Declan suggested. "I'm quite sure you won't like the answer."

Arkady stared at him for a moment and then turned to Tassie. "You heard Master Hawkes, Tassie. Who is lord here in Lebec?"

"Duke Stellan, of course," she answered.

Arkady gave Declan an "I told you so" look, rather relieved by the answer.

"But who is your *master*?" Declan asked.

"Lord Jaxyn," the Crasii replied without hesitating. "Was that all, your grace?"

"You may go," Declan told the Crasii before Arkady could say a word. Once they were alone again, he turned to Arkady. "You see?"

"That proves nothing." She shrugged. "Jaxyn has been Kennel Master for almost a year. It's only natural they think of him that way."

"Arkady, please don't play games with me," Declan warned, a little impatiently. "My job is hard enough, without people like you actively working against me."

"I wasn't aware that I *was* working against you, Declan."

"If you're going to sit here pretending you know nothing about the Tide Lords then that's exactly what you're doing," he informed her. "I've spent a lifetime tracking these bastards down. You had one in your grasp, and you let him go."

"Kyle Lakesh escaped," she insisted, still not convinced this wasn't an elaborate trap for some nefarious purpose of his own that Arkady couldn't fathom. "That's all there is to it."

Declan shook his head. "Tides, Arkady! You stopped at

Clyden's Inn and let a prisoner talk to your Crasii. You may have permitted it, just to satisfy your own curiosity, or it may have been a mistake, but you let him talk to them and they changed sides faster than you could blink."

Arkady didn't reply, not sure what she could say. At the same time, a glimmer of hope began to awaken in her. It was possible Declan knew of the Tide Lords. He was the King's Spymaster, after all. If anybody in Glaeba knew the immortals were real, it might be her old friend. She hesitated for a moment longer and then nodded slowly. If she couldn't trust Declan Hawkes, she couldn't trust anyone. "I witnessed Jaxyn order Chelby to kill himself for no better reason than to prove a point to me."

Declan seemed unsurprised. "Then imagine what will happen if he starts to order all the Crasii around. Our entire civilisation is built on the backs of their race. If they were to change allegiance, at best we'd face economic ruin, at worst he might order them to turn on their human masters and massacre every one of us."

Arkady nodded, as he gave voice to the nameless fears that had kept her awake since returning to Lebec last night.

"You know they're real," Arkady said flatly.

"I've always known, Arkady," he replied.

"Who else knows?"

"Besides the Crasii?" he asked. "Maybe a handful of people in all of Glaeba and not much more beyond. Many Torlenians believe in them still, but it's mostly wishful thinking on their part. They have no proof the Tide Lords still exist, although the new Imperator seems to be quite keen on reviving their worship, which may prove problematic when you get there. The Caelish are like us, they've either forgotten the Tide Lords or believe they're nothing more than a fanciful myth. Most of the nations in the north believe the same. The Senestrans don't remember them at all, probably because the only Crasii they have in any great numbers are the amphibians and they don't tend to mingle much with the human population."

"And how is it that you know?" she asked.

He shrugged evasively. "My family has a long history of protecting the truth about the Tide Lords."

"Then your grandfather knows about them, too?"

"Yes."

"How many others?"

"There are pockets of believers all over the world, but few who know for certain outside of the Crasii."

"I mean how many other people that *I* know?"

He looked at her oddly. "You want names? Why?"

"You're asking me to believe you've known about the Tide Lords all along, Declan. I've known you all my life. Why didn't you say something sooner?"

"Oh, yes, what a good idea," he agreed. "Confess to Arkady the Academic that I believe in magic. There's a plan."

Arkady shook her head, feeling a little winded. "Tides, you think you know someone all your life and they turn out to be quite the opposite of what you thought. It's frightening."

He frowned. "I remember thinking the same thing the day you told me you were getting married."

Arkady glared at him. "Don't try to get out of this by changing the subject."

"I don't want to change the subject," he assured her. "I want to know if you're willing to help."

"Help who, exactly?"

"Me. And a few others who want to protect humanity from the next High Tide." When he could see she still wasn't convinced, he added, "Tilly's one of us."

"Tilly Ponting?"

He nodded. "You were foolish to scoff at the Tarot, you know. Tilly knows more about it—and the Tide Lords—than anyone else alive."

"*Tilly* is a part of your . . . ?" She stopped, remembering something Cayal had told her, and how oddly protective of the Tarot Tilly had been. *Some of us go to a great deal of trouble to ensure this record of the true nature of the Tide Lords never fades from memory,* Tilly had told her that day she went to Tilly's house to learn about the Tarot. *It's a solemn trust that we take very seriously.*

"The Cabal of the Tarot."

Declan's eyes narrowed dangerously. "Where did you hear that name?"

"Cayal mentioned it. He said the Cabal was a secret society before the last Cataclysm dedicated to destroying the Tide Lords."

"So you and the Tide Lord found plenty of time to chat, then?"

His tone cut her to the core . . . but there was no way to explain what she was feeling. Or what had happened between her and Cayal. Declan would not understand, of that much she was quite certain. "What is it you want, Declan?"

"Finding the bastards is the first problem."

"Do you know where they are?"

"A few of them," he explained, helping himself to more tea. "We always know where Maralyce is. She never moves from her mine up in the mountains around the Valley of the Tides. We're pretty sure Brynden and Kinta are in Torlenia. Medwen is living in a village in Senestra. Arryl was last heard of in Senestra, too, although where her sister, Diala, is . . . well, that's anybody's guess. Krydence and Rance are running a circus in Tenacia. Jaxyn's here in Lebec. And until you let him go, we had the Immortal Prince right where we wanted him."

"And what of the others?"

"We have no idea."

"Can't the Crasii sense them?"

"Of course, but any immortal worthy of the name forbids the Crasii from revealing who they are as soon as they encounter them, so unless you've got a Scard in the mix, we're never going to hear about it."

"*Could* you stop them?" she enquired. "I mean . . . once the Tide returns . . . once their powers are restored . . ."

"We have a year," he told her. "Maybe less, before the

Tide is strong enough to cause us real problems. We need to find them before then, and find ways to prevent them gaining influence. Your experience with the Immortal Prince places you in a unique position, Arkady. You know him better than any other mortal alive. And—I'm relieved to see— you appear to have survived the experience unharmed. Given Cayal's reputation and your obvious fascination with him, I feared you might fall victim to his charms."

Arkady swallowed a nervous lump in her throat. "How can you be sure I haven't?"

"I'm not." He shrugged. "I'm taking a chance on the fact that you'd rather side with your own kind than a bunch of immortal homicidal megalomaniacs."

She smiled thinly. "You know, Stellan thinks I'm insane to believe Cayal was anything other than a wainwright turned killer."

"More likely a killer turned wainwright," Declan corrected. "I'll put him straight, if you want. For a price."

Arkady sighed. This was the hammer blow she'd been expecting. "What price?"

"Firstly, I want you to stop Jaxyn Aranville's access to the Lebec Crasii."

Is that all? she groaned silently. "That may not be as easy as you think without tipping him off that you know what he is. Stellan thinks very highly of his ability to work the Crasii. Accuse his Kennel Master of being a Tide Lord and my husband will likely laugh at you and, worse, turn straight around and share the joke with Jaxyn."

"I'm aware of the risks involved, Arkady, which is why I'm relying on you to deal with this for me. You have to encourage your husband to find him another position in your household. In a perfect world, you'd have him appoint Jaxyn his ambassador at court where I can keep an eye on him while you're in Torlenia. At least there, all he'll be doing is hanging around the Herino Palace playing cards with all the other freeloaders."

"In a perfect world, Declan, there wouldn't be any Tide Lords to begin with."

"True. For now, I'd settle for keeping Jaxyn away from the felines. Lebec has an army of Crasii that could threaten the throne and you've got them being trained by a Tide Lord."

Although what Declan was saying made a great deal of sense, Arkady still wasn't ready to commit to anything. "You said *firstly,*" she reminded him. "I'm assuming there's more?"

"I want you to help me find Cayal."

"He's trapped in the mountains somewhere," she told him. "Buried under a cave-in."

"That won't stop him. He's immortal."

"Even so . . ."

"You know him, Arkady. You know what he looks like."

"So do any number of other people," she pointed out. "The warders at the prison, for instance, his cellmates in Recidivists' Row. The Crasii in the cell opposite him could *smell* him."

"The canine, Warlock?" Declan asked. "The one your husband pardoned?"

Tides! He actually believes Stellan signed those papers. She smiled, although not for the reason Declan thought. "Warlock's input was very helpful. He was one Crasii not overawed by a Tide Lord."

Declan studied her curiously. "Do you know where he is now?"

"Warlock? I have no idea. I haven't seen him since he was released."

"I should probably find this fearless canine of yours," he said. "I believe the Scards may well be our only allies if things go the way I suspect they will."

"That places you in a very small minority, Declan."

He nodded. "That's why I'm asking for your help. To face this threat the Cabal will need people like you. People who have faced down a Tide Lord and walked away from it unscathed."

Arkady took a sip of rapidly cooling tea from her cup, hoping the delicate china would hide her uncertainty at

Declan's optimistic and entirely incorrect assumption that she had emerged from her confrontation with a Tide Lord unscathed.

She had been marked by Cayal far deeper than she cared to admit. It was just that nobody but Arkady could see the scars.

Chapter 68

With the callous disregard common to all canine females, the day after Boots and Warlock mated so savagely and irresistibly in the lane outside the Kennel, she was all business again, acting as if nothing had happened between them. While the change in her attitude did not surprise Warlock, it did disappoint him. Intellectually, he understood the primal urges that drove his race to procreate, while in his heart, he resented mightily the immortals who had so thoughtlessly created them. The Tide Lords had wanted slaves and cared nothing for the way canine society might happen to evolve.

Warlock lamented the lack of opportunity for a meaningful relationship with a female. There were no anniversaries celebrated by their kind. No rewards to mark a marriage that had stood the test of time. There was affection between them and the urge to mate. Love as it existed for humans was unknown to them, and Warlock thought the Crasii poorer for the lack. Canines made friends and formed family groups for protection of their young, they cohabited, even married, but when it came time to rut, all bets were off and the strongest male won, regardless of what had gone before or might happen in the future.

The musky, maddening scent of Boots had faded significantly by the following day and was gone completely after a few days, which made it much easier for Warlock to concentrate when she was around. The males who attacked them in the alley returned to the Kennel, showing no interest in continuing the fight, once the female was no longer in heat. Had the memory of their sharp, savage coupling not been imprinted so vividly in Warlock's memory, he might have begun to believe he'd imagined it.

Every day they made the trek through the crowded, dirty streets of the Lebec slums to Shalimar's attic, and every day—at least once—they ate like noblemen while Warlock tried to recall everything Cayal had said to Lady Desean in his hearing. He told them about Gabriella and Planice, the Queen of Kordana. He told them of Arryl and Diala, Syrolee and Engarhod, Tryan and Elyssa, Krydence and Rance and the enigmatic Lukys, who even among the Crasii remained something of a mystery. He told them of the suzerain's dark moods, his assertion that Warlock was probably a Scard and Cayal's promise—which had seemed so empty at the time—to settle the score once the Tide returned.

Shalimar took copious notes as he spoke, and then questioned Warlock extensively, probing for details he may have overlooked or not recalled in the first telling. Warlock found the interrogations quite exhausting, but he suffered through them willingly enough. Not only was it an opportunity to eat like a civilised being, but it meant Boots stayed with him, listening intently to every word, adding her questions to Shalimar's, revealing a sharp intellect and a remarkable eye for detail in the process.

"Did Cayal never speak of the destruction of Kordana?" Shalimar asked one afternoon, following another intensive session of questions.

Warlock shook his head. "He spoke of it only in passing. He blamed Tryan for it, I know that much, but he never said exactly what happened. Is it important?"

"Knowing what drives these monsters is always important," Shalimar said, putting down his notes. "If we could define some pattern in their behaviour . . . some trigger that sets them off . . . perhaps we could find a way to stop them."

"Be more use to us to find a way to kill them," Boots grumbled, picking at the bones of a chicken she had all but sucked dry. Warlock liked to kid himself she was hanging around because she fancied him, even though she was no longer in the grip of her mating instincts, but he suspected she was driven by the need for decent food just as much as he was.

"Then you and the Immortal Prince are of one mind," Warlock remarked. "He'd very much like to find a way to kill himself, I suspect."

"Would that we could aid his quest," Shalimar lamented, stretching his tired shoulders. It was hot in the attic and his face was damp with sweat, but he didn't seem to notice. "What a torment Cayal must be suffering, to want death so desperately while knowing it can never be."

"Tides, Shalimar!" Boots complained. "You sound as if you feel sorry for him."

"I do a little," the old man replied. "Not enough to want to be enslaved by him, mind you, but I pity any creature in pain." Suddenly he smiled, revealing a row of uneven teeth, yellowed with age and cowberry juice. "In fact, I'd *like* to help the poor sod find a way to kill himself. I'd then like to apply the same remedy to the rest of his merciless brethren and be rid of the whole flanking lot of them."

"Do you think there is a way to kill an immortal?" Boots wondered without looking up, too busy picking over the bones of the chicken for any tiny morsel that may have escaped her notice to give the others her full attention.

"Maybe." Shalimar shrugged. "I suppose the one thing the immortals don't lack is the time to look for it."

"Are they all like Cayal?" Warlock asked. "Do they all seek an end to their endless existence?"

Shalimar looked thoughtful. "To be honest, I have no idea. Until you shared your incarceration with him, we didn't even know any of them *wanted* to die. And it could just be some sort of temporary insanity brought on by the long Low Tide. First hint of the Tide turning and for all you know the Immortal Prince is fair bouncing with glee at the prospect of another millennium lording it over the rest of us."

"Might get interesting if it isn't temporary," Boots remarked.

"Why?" Warlock asked.

She pushed the plate away and rubbed her greasy hands on her shift to clean them. "Suppose he finds a way to die and the others aren't interested in joining him in oblivion? The Tide Lords are bad enough, by all accounts, when they can only *hurt* each other. What happens if they find a way to start murdering each other, too?"

"It may not be such a bad thing," Warlock speculated. "It'd thin their numbers down at the very least."

"Might also take the rest of us with them," Shalimar reminded him with a frown. "But it's an interesting problem and one I will dwell on much in the coming weeks, I suspect. Will you come back and see me again tomorrow?"

Warlock glanced at Boots, who nodded. "If you want."

"I'd like to know more of what Cayal told you about the Eternal Flame."

Warlock was going to say that he'd already told him everything he knew, but then he glanced at the laden table and nodded. "I'll try to make sure I remember everything," he said.

"Then I'll see you tomorrow," Shalimar declared, rising to his feet to usher them toward the door. "And we'll see if we can't learn all about becoming an immortal, eh?"

"What does Shalimar do?" Warlock asked Boots a little later, as they strolled past the beggars and the whores of the slums toward the Kennel. It was almost sunset and the streets were even busier than they had been earlier. They passed slaves and workmen, indentured servants and free

Crasii of every sub-species, even a pair of canines mating up against the wall of one of the many taverns scattered through the city outskirts, in full view of the passers-by. He looked away in disgust, his disapproval tempered by the knowledge he was no better than they were. At the thought, his disgust turned to a measure of self-loathing, the faces of the couple against the wall blurring in his mind, his tormented imagination replacing them with himself and his companion against that wall . . .

Boots noticed his expression and the copulating couple and because she had no notion of the direction of his thoughts, she smiled. Warlock looked away, embarrassed by his own weakness as much as her amusement.

Despite the noise and the smells, Warlock was a little surprised to find he was growing accustomed to the hordes of people and had discovered the hang of shouldering his way through a crowd. He still wasn't used to the libertine attitudes of the slum Crasii, but was growing a little more accepting of the idea that instinct was a harsh mistress. She didn't like to be ignored.

"What do you mean?"

"Pardon?"

"You asked about Shalimar."

Warlock forced himself to forget the couple and tried to concentrate on the matter at hand. "I was wondering where all the food comes from? He has to pay for it somehow. How does he make his living? As a healer? A scribe? A fortune teller?"

Boots thought about it for a moment and then shrugged, stepping over an oily puddle exuding a smell that made Warlock want to retch. Between the endless spring rains and summer fast approaching, stinking, unidentifiable sludge regularly clogged what passed for gutters here.

"Don't really know. Maybe he gets by on donations."

"From whom?" he asked, wondering how Boots could negotiate these streets so oblivious to the smells and the refuse that polluted them. "This is the Lebec slums, Boots.

There's nobody here with the coin to keep their own bellies full, let alone give it away to set a table as full as Shalimar's."

"From the Scards he helps, perhaps?" she suggested, clearly worried now that Warlock had brought the matter to her attention. "Maybe he charges passage to Hidden Valley and puts a percentage on top."

"That would make him a scavenger who lives off Crasii misery," he said. "Not the great man you seem to think he is."

Boots looked up at him curiously. "What are you trying to say, Warlock? That Shalimar is some sort of evil charlatan trading on Crasii misfortune?"

"Do you *know* where Hidden Valley is?"

"No."

"Have you ever spoken to anybody who's been there? Seen anybody come back from there?"

She frowned. "Well . . . no . . ."

"So for all you know, Shalimar is getting rich pretending to help our people, when in fact, he could be taking their money, slitting their throats as soon as they leave the city and burying them in an unmarked trench somewhere, just outside the city."

Boots stopped and looked up at him for a moment and then shook her head, rolling her eyes at him. "You're crazy."

"I was just asking how he can set a table like that, that's all."

"Why don't you ask him?"

"I might, tomorrow."

"You do that," she said, obviously annoyed. "I'll look forward to Shalimar's reaction to what you're insinuating."

Warlock sighed. He hadn't meant to make her angry. "Boots . . . I wasn't trying to insinuate anything. I was just thinking, that's all, how it seems a little odd—"

"Halt!"

Instinctively, Warlock froze at the shouted command. Boots, being much more used to freedom than he was, had the opposite reaction. She ran—a futile ambition in these narrow crowded streets—only to slam straight into the arms of a pair of City Watchmen. She yelled at the men, struggling violently as they tried to restrain her, scratching one on the cheek, biting the other on the arm. Warlock growled low in his throat and moved to help.

"Not another step, dog boy!" someone yelled behind him. "Not if you and the bitch expect to live!"

Warlock hesitated and glanced over his shoulder to discover a crossbow aimed squarely at his torso. There were a dozen or more Watchmen behind them and even more moving in behind the pair who held Boots. Completely surrounded, the Watchman with the bow trained on him was almost close enough to touch, certainly close enough to shoot before Warlock could reach him, and near enough to be confident he wouldn't miss.

After a tense moment while Warlock debated the wisdom of trying to free Boots and make a break for it, he slowly lowered his tail and raised his hands. The officer visibly relaxed.

"Wise decision, dog boy." He turned to his men. "Take him back to the Watch-house."

"What about the female?" one of the Watchmen asked.

"Take her, too," he ordered.

The men moved in closer, and quite warily, probably because of Warlock's size.

"What am I being arrested for?" he called after the officer, who was ordering the remainder of his men to clear the street of the curious onlookers who had gathered to gawk at this unusual event. "I have done nothing wrong! I have a pardon from the Duke of Lebec."

The officer glanced over his shoulder at Warlock. He seemed singularly unimpressed by the news.

"It's not the duke who wants you, dog boy," the officer told him with a shrug. "It's the king."

Chapter 69

I t was late in the evening on the day before they were due to depart for Herino before Stellan saw his wife again. Certain she was deliberately avoiding him, he finally decided to visit her room as she was preparing for bed, knocking as he entered although he didn't wait for permission.

Dressed in a long pale blue nightgown, Arkady was folding down the covers as he opened the door. She turned to face him, but he was unable to read her expression in the inadequate light coming from the single candle on the bedside table.

"Come for your regular conjugal visit, husband?" There was an edge to her voice, the ritual greeting a cruel parody of their former easy companionship.

Stellan closed the door and leant against it. He'd been expecting her to be angry, but not so cold. Not so distant. "Actually, I came to apologise."

She shrugged and turned back to the bed covers. "As you wish."

"I truly am sorry, Arkady," he said, walking toward her. He stopped when he reached the bed, reaching out to her, hoping to convey his remorse. She ignored the gesture.

Disappointed, he dropped his hand. "What I said the other day . . . you didn't deserve that. I was angry. Declan Hawkes scares the life out of me, and with you disappearing like that, forging my signature . . . him breathing down my neck . . ."

She stopped arranging the bed covers and turned to face him. "It's all right, Stellan. You don't have to explain."

"He came to see me about you."

She didn't seem surprised. With a sigh, she sat on the edge of the bed.

He sat down beside her. "He told me I was being a fool."

Arkady smiled thinly. "Really? How did he know?"

"I'm not sure. You do know he's in love with you, don't

you? It's one of the reasons he frightens me so. I took you away from him."

"That's crazy," she scoffed. "Declan's my oldest friend. There was never anything between us."

Stellan shook his head, wondering why people never saw what was right in front of them. "You married me before Declan had a chance to declare himself, I fear, which is why every time he steps foot in my palace I start to worry. He's the King's Spymaster, Arkady, and even for a man without my secrets, that makes him a very dangerous enemy."

"Declan doesn't suspect a thing and if anything, our marriage brings you an added layer of protection. To bring you down, Declan would have to bring me down too, and he wouldn't do that."

Stellan nodded slowly. "I hope you're right. Did you say something to him . . . about your kidnapping?"

She hesitated, which made him wonder how much of her crazy theory about immortals she had shared with Declan. Not much, he concluded, given Declan had done nothing but praise her courage.

"We had a very . . . enlightening . . . discussion at breakfast a few days ago," she admitted finally. "He's very interested in tracking down Cayal."

Stellan nodded. "Yes, he told me that. Said you were to be admired for your bravery, actually, and that your contribution to his eventual recapture will be vital."

"You didn't tell him your suspicions about me having an affair with the Immortal Prince, then," she remarked. He had the feeling she was still not quite ready to forgive him.

"I'm truly sorry, Arkady," he assured her, taking her hand. "You've stood by me without complaint for six years. I should never have suggested anything so callous. I don't know what I was thinking. If you're not with child, then so be it. We'll tell the king you miscarried, as I originally intended."

"I slept with Cayal once, Stellan. Don't get your hopes up."

"Do you love him?"

The question took Arkady by surprise. She thought about it for a moment and then stunned him with her answer. "I don't know, Stellan. Is longing a sign of love? The inability to concentrate? The inability to think of anything else but those haunted blue eyes?"

He looked at her as if seeing her for the first time. Was it really like that for her? He knew all too well the agony of a love that could never be acknowledged, never even suspected. Stellan would never have wished the same pain on Arkady. "There's no future for you down that road, Arkady," he warned gently.

Arkady smiled and nodded. "Now that I *do* know." She squeezed his hand apologetically. "Never fear, Stellan, I'm not planning to run off with my immortal lover anytime soon."

He frowned. There was love, and there was blind foolishness. He had never thought Arkady likely to fall victim to a confidence trickster, not even one as accomplished as this one apparently was. "You're still insisting he's immortal."

"And I fear you'll find out the hard way I'm not as deluded as you imagine," she predicted, almost defiantly.

Stellan let it go. He didn't come here looking for another fight. Instead, he put his arm around her, hugging her gently. "We're a fine pair of fools, aren't we? You fall for a convicted murderer and me for a blatant fortune hunter."

"Speaking of your blatant fortune hunter," Arkady asked abruptly, "what will happen to him when we go to Torlenia?"

And just when I thought we were going to be friends again . . . "I was planning to leave him here in Lebec."

"He'll die of boredom a week after we're gone," she warned. "And he'll likely go looking for his fun elsewhere."

"I'm surprised you care."

She looked at him, her expression serious. "I care about *you*, Stellan. And despite how undeserving I might think

Jaxyn Aranville is of your affection, I know there's nothing I can do to prevent you loving him."

Well, that's something. Arkady wasn't usually so willing to accept the inevitability of his relationship with Jaxyn. "What do you suggest I do with him? He can't come to Torlenia with us."

"Actually, I've been thinking about it quite a bit," she said, shifting on the bed so she was facing him. "Why not send him to court?"

"To Herino?"

She nodded. "With you out of the country, Reon Debalkor will be looking for any opportunity to diminish you in the eyes of the king. I know you have friends at court, Stellan, but you need someone there whose job it is to look out for your interests specifically."

Her suggestion astounded him, as much for its brilliance as its unexpectedness. "You would trust Jaxyn with such a role?"

She hesitated and then nodded. "Yes, I would."

"It would mean I'd have someone there to keep an eye on Kylia, too," he mused, which was an angle Arkady probably hadn't even considered. With everything else going on lately, she'd barely spared his niece a second thought since she got back from the mountains, he suspected.

"Will you give it some consideration?" she asked.

He nodded. "It's not a bad idea, actually."

"I'm not entirely blinded by my infatuation, Stellan."

He looked at her oddly. "Are you suggesting I am?"

"I don't know. Are you?" she asked with a raised brow.

He hugged her gently and let her go, rising to his feet. "I think we'd be doing ourselves a favour by staying out of each other's affairs. Neither of us seems to approve of the other's tastes."

"I'm sorry if I caused you any trouble, Stellan. I didn't mean to." The apology was genuine, the edge gone from her voice. Things might yet be all right between them.

"I know you didn't," he assured her. "Fortunately, there

appears to be no lasting harm done. That canine you released hasn't caused any problems and your immortal—even if he isn't dead—is apparently no longer a threat. Declan Hawkes is satisfied I was only lying to protect Kylia's engagement and Jaxyn is a hero. Things could be a lot worse."

"Yes," she agreed. "They could be."

"Are you all ready for the trip to Herino?"

"Pretty much."

"It should be a pleasant enough trip. The weather's been very nice of late."

"Yes, it has, hasn't it?"

Tides, we've been reduced to discussing the weather! Is this how it's going to be from now on? "Smooth sailing all the way, I suspect."

They were travelling by boat rather than on horseback. From Herino they would be sailing down the Lower Oran after the wedding, through the lock to the Upper Ryrie and then down the Lower Ryrie to Whitewater City in the south. From there they would travel through the dangerous Whitewater Narrows to the coast, where they would take another ship for Torlenia.

He smiled, hoping for a sign that things really were back to normal between them. "Well . . . I guess I'll see you in the morning."

She nodded. "Goodnight, Stellan."

He hesitated for a moment longer, wondering if Arkady had something else to say, but when she offered nothing further he turned and left the room, leaving her alone with the one thing he couldn't make better with an apology—her pain.

Stellan found Jaxyn with Declan Hawkes in the library. The two of them had liberated a decanter of his best brandy (Jaxyn's idea no doubt) and were discussing the relative merits of punishment and rewards when it came to training Crasii.

Jaxyn was lamenting his inability to get any sense out

of a canine before they were fifteen years old, which was rather ingenuous of him—he got remarkable results with all the Crasii. Better than anybody Stellan had ever seen. In fact, Stellan had never witnessed Jaxyn so much as raise his voice to a Crasii, who all seemed to hunger for his approval in a way that made Stellan quite envious.

"Don't listen to him, Master Hawkes," Stellan warned with a smile as he took the seat opposite Declan. The men were sitting in the deep leather chairs by the hearth but the night was warm enough that it remained unlit. "Jaxyn has a remarkable way with the Crasii."

"I don't doubt it, your grace," the spymaster agreed, taking an appreciative sip of his brandy. "Lord Aranville's reputation as a Crasii handler has reached even the salons of Herino."

"I really don't do anything special," Jaxyn said with a self-deprecating shrug. "Anybody could get the Crasii to respond to them if they took the time to study their behaviour."

"Have you been studying them long, Lord Aranville?"

"Longer than you'd imagine," he replied with a smile. "I'm older than I look, you know."

"And wiser too," Stellan agreed. "At least you are, according to my wife."

"How is dear Arkady?" Jaxyn asked. "Still recovering from the trauma of her kidnapping?"

Stellan frowned. He didn't need Jaxyn taking that tone in front of Declan Hawkes. "She seems to have weathered it very well. And she suggested something by way of a reward that I'm rather inclined to grant you."

"Really, Stellan, I didn't do it for payment," he assured him. "Seeing Arkady safe in your arms again was all the reward I needed."

"I'm curious what Lady Desean thinks her rescue was worth," Declan said. If he had any suspicion there was a double meaning to their conversation, he gave no sign of it.

"She suggested I appoint Jaxyn as my ambassador to court while we're away in Torlenia."

Jaxyn looked stunned. "*Arkady* suggested that?"

Stellan nodded. "You don't like the idea?"

"No!" he objected. "Quite the opposite, in fact. I'm just surprised that . . . after all the trouble she's had lately, and the ordeal she's been through, that her grace would take the time to think of such a thing."

"I imagine she had plenty of time to be impressed by your abilities when you rescued her and on your return journey to Lebec, Lord Aranville," Declan remarked. "Perhaps she saw a side of you she hadn't previously suspected."

An odd expression flickered over Jaxyn's handsome young face and then he smiled. "Perhaps she did at that. And if you're offering, Stellan, I'd be delighted to represent Lebec's interests in Herino while you're away."

"Are you sure?" he asked, a little surprised at how quickly Jaxyn had jumped at the opportunity. Given his initial reaction to the news they were leaving soon for Torlenia and his ambivalence toward Arkady, he was expecting a lot more resistance to any plan conceived by his wife.

"Quite sure," Jaxyn insisted. "Besides, who else is there to look out for Kylia while you're gone?"

"I rather think that would be the concern of her new husband, my lord," Declan suggested.

Jaxyn smiled. "You know what I mean. But it's an excellent idea for any number of other reasons. You don't want your enemies benefiting from your absence."

"What enemies would those be?" Declan enquired curiously.

"I imagine I'll find out soon enough," Jaxyn said with a laugh, neatly dodging the question. "Besides, while at court I might even find myself a wife. I'm getting to that age, I suppose, where a man needs to think of these things." He turned to Stellan with an innocent expression. "Do you suppose I could find myself one like Arkady?"

Arkady is right, Stellan decided. *Sometimes, Jaxyn is a fool.*

"I'm sure the young ladies will be flocking to you in

Herino, my lord," Declan remarked. "A man with your prospects . . . and an ambassador to boot."

"Well, that settles it!" Jaxyn declared with a grin. "I'll take the job!"

Stellan smiled, not sure if he was worried or relieved. "You'd better get packing then," he suggested. "We're leaving tomorrow morning."

Jaxyn nodded and rose to his feet. "I suppose I should," he agreed. "And I'd better get it done tonight. Goodnight, Master Hawkes. Stellan."

Declan waited until Jaxyn had left the room before nodding his approval of Stellan's decision. "I think Lord Aranville will do well at court."

"I'm glad you approve."

"It's not my place to approve or disapprove of your appointments to the king's court, your grace. I was merely expressing a personal opinion."

"Nonetheless, I would rather have your endorsement than your censure, Declan. The only problem I can foresee is Jaxyn and Mathu deciding to go looking for entertainment together. That may prove problematic."

"I'll keep an eye on his highness," the spy promised. "And a close eye on Aranville. I'll make sure they stay out of trouble."

"I'd appreciate that," Stellan said. He smiled, as if the idea had a great deal of merit, while privately panicking at the thought of the King's Spymaster watching his lover while he was gone.

And realising that even if he wanted to, there was nothing he could do to prevent it.

Chapter 70

"He betrayed us," Warlock announced, gripping the unmoving bars on the window and shaking them in frustration to absolutely no effect. "Shalimar betrayed us."

Boots stopped pacing their small Watch-house cell long enough to glare at him. It was dark and raining outside and the cell reeked of stale urine. All he could make out was the glittering orbs of her dark eyes and the faint silhouette of her shadow on the opposite wall. "Don't be ridiculous!"

"Then how else did the Watch know where to find us?"

"More to the point, farm dog," she retorted, "is why they were looking for you at all."

That was a question to which Warlock had no answer. "Did they say anything to you?" he asked.

"You mean other than *sit, stay,* and *there's a good doggie*? Not a lot. They certainly never said why they were looking for you."

"The officer who arrested us told me it wasn't the Duke of Lebec who ordered it, but the king."

"Well, aren't you just the lucky one, having all these impressive enemies?"

Before Warlock could answer that accusation, the lock rattled and the cell door swung open. Squinting in the sudden flare of torchlight, he felt rather than saw Boots backing up until she bumped into him, and then the soft feel of her pelt as her hand clutched his for reassurance.

The man holding the torch wasn't a Watchman. He was younger than Warlock was expecting, tall and powerfully built, dressed well, but not remarkably so. His jacket was well cut but his rumpled shirt was open, and his eyes—even in the torchlight—seemed to miss very little. He studied the pair of them for a moment and pointed to the door.

"Come with me," the man ordered.

"Where are we going?"

"Somewhere we can sit down," the stranger informed them. "It's very late and I'm too tired to question you for hours on my feet."

Warlock drew himself up to his full height, which made him only a little taller than their visitor. "You must let my companion go. She has nothing to do with any of this."

The human squinted at Boots and then shook his head. "As you have no idea what *this* is even about, how do you know she's not a part of it?"

Warlock could feel Boots's tight, desperate grip on his hand. Whatever trouble he was in, Boots was an innocent bystander. He would do whatever he had to, to keep her free of it. "I will cooperate if you let her go."

"You'll cooperate because I damned well tell you to cooperate," the man told him impatiently. "But before you start getting all tetchy and biting people, let me assure you I'm not interested in anything you've done in the past. I'm far more interested in what you can do in the future." He studied Boots for a moment and then nodded. "As for your little friend there, seems to me she fits the description of an escaped canine wanted for killing a feline at the Lebec Palace compound a few months back."

Warlock looked down at Boots in surprise. "You *killed* a feline?"

"Like I'm going to admit anything like *that* while I'm standing in the middle of the Lebec City Watch-house," she retorted.

"You see," the man said. "Your girlfriend's got more sense than you have. Now, are you going to come without a fight, or do I have to send to the palace for someone to identify your friend there as their runaway slave?"

"How do I know you haven't sent someone to the palace already?"

"You don't," he replied. "You're going to have to believe I haven't turned her in, and I have to believe you're not going to rip my throat out, first chance you get. It's called trust, my large and hairy friend. Something that tends to be in short supply between your kind and mine, these days."

By now, Warlock was thoroughly confused. This man clearly held authority here, but he spoke like no human he'd encountered before, with the possible exception of Shalimar. "I don't understand."

"Then come with me," the man insisted. "Won't be long, believe me, before you understand all too well what I want of you."

"You've spoken to Cayal," the man said once the introductions were done with.

Somewhat to Warlock's surprise, rather than an interrogation cell, he and Boots had been escorted to the Watch Commander's office. They were alone, the Watch Commander having been ordered to vacate the room while they made use of it. It was cluttered and stuffy in the office but a veritable palace compared to the torture chamber Warlock had been expecting. The man had introduced himself as Declan Hawkes. He said he worked for the king. He failed to specify exactly what he did in the king's employ, however.

Whatever he did, he had the authority to evict the Watch Commander of the Lebec City Watch from his office.

"I beg your pardon?" Warlock asked, not sure if he'd heard the man right.

"Cayal," Declan Hawkes repeated. "The Immortal Prince. You shared a cell block with him until recently."

Warlock was amazed. "Does *everybody* know about the Tide Lords?"

"Everybody knows about them, my friend," Hawkes agreed, leaning back in the Watch Commander's chair. "There're only a few of us who understand they're a real threat. Reckon you'd know him if you saw him again?"

Warlock nodded slowly, glancing at Boots to see what her reaction was to this startling revelation, but she was just sitting there, arms crossed, scowling at Hawkes, probably wondering if she was about to be sent back to Lebec Palace.

"Any Crasii could tell you who he is if they met him,"

Warlock told him. "We can sense the suzerain the same way you can smell the difference between fresh milk and sour."

"Yes, I know that. But how many of them could walk away from him if he commanded them to stay?"

Warlock frowned. "You've been speaking to Shalimar."

"Good one, farm dog!" Boots exclaimed, punching his arm. "Tell him all about Shalimar. Why not name every stray in the Kennel while you're at it? Give the Watch something really useful to do."

Hawkes looked at the two of them, shaking his head. He seemed amused. "Do you seriously think a man like Shalimar can operate in a city the size of Lebec and us not know about him? Tides, I always credited the canines with more intelligence than that."

"He's your agent," Warlock concluded, meeting Hawkes's eye evenly. "That's how he lives as well as he does."

Hawkes didn't bother to deny the accusation, which didn't surprise Warlock, although it clearly disturbed Boots.

"I don't believe that! Shalimar is our friend. He wouldn't betray the Crasii."

"Nor has he," Hawkes assured her. "That's not his job."

"What is his job, then?" Warlock asked. "To lure runaway slaves into his trust and then send them unsuspectingly back into the arms of their masters while they assume they're fleeing to safety?"

Declan Hawkes smiled. "Hardly."

"Hidden Valley is just a myth, isn't it?" Warlock accused. "It's a story made up to lull the wary into a false sense of security."

"On the contrary, Hidden Valley is very real," the man informed them. "And just like the legend says, it's full of Scards. Real Scards, mind you, not the human definition, which is basically just a runaway slave. These are all Crasii we're certain can defy the Tide Lords. Lady Desean assures me you're one of them, Warlock. The only reason your little friend here isn't in chains and on her way back to Lebec Palace right now is because she defied Jaxyn when she killed that feline and fled the palace compound, so it's a fair bet she's a genuine Scard too. That makes both of you more valuable than you realise."

"Valuable *how*?" Warlock asked, still not convinced this wasn't some sort of elaborate trap.

"The Tide is turning. Shalimar must have told you that."

"Then you know . . . what Shalimar is?"

"A Tidewatcher?" Hawkes said without blinking. "Of course."

"But . . . ," Warlock began, feeling more and more lost by the moment. "I still don't understand . . ."

"He's building a Scard army," Boots said. "That's why he wants us. That's what Hidden Valley is. It's where they're hiding their Scard army against the return of the Tide Lords."

Declan said nothing. He made no attempt to deny or confirm Boots's conclusion, and his silence on the matter spoke volumes.

"The legend of Hidden Valley has been around since before I was born," Warlock pointed out. "Have you been building a Scard army for that long? How could you know when the Tide will turn? Even the immortals don't know that."

"A Tidewatcher can sense it long before the Tide Lords are even aware of it. Shalimar's known it was coming back since he was a child and he's over sixty now. We've had plenty of time to prepare."

The scope of such a plan left Warlock a little breathless. "Shalimar has been planning this since he was a *child*?"

"Grand schemes are usually constructed on even grander scales," Hawkes replied. "If we're to defeat the Tide Lords, if we're to have any hope of protecting Glaeba from them, we need to think on the same timescales they do."

"You speak of saving Glaeba. What of the rest of Amyrantha?"

Hawkes shrugged. "Not my concern. The other nations

can bow down and worship the Tide Lords when they return or not, as they see fit. I'm only interested in protecting my home. Your home too, coincidentally."

"You said you worked for the king," Warlock reminded him. "I'm curious. Does the king know about your Scard army in Hidden Valley?"

"Are you suggesting I'm working behind the king's back?"

"I'm suggesting that most humans believe the Tide Lords are nothing more than a children's bedtime story. At best, the characters on a deck of cards. I'm just wondering at King Enteny's reaction when you told him of your plans to spend a considerable amount of his fortune building a force in the mountains to fight off these mythical creatures, if and when they return. He must have been well convinced if he's spent the sort of resources it takes to build an army in secret."

The man's expression didn't change. Declan Hawkes wasn't a man who flinched from much, Warlock decided.

"Let's just say the king financially supports our endeavours and that it's not always necessary to burden him with the details of how his money is spent."

"Siphoning off funds from the royal purse to build an army in secret," Warlock mused. "That could be considered treason, in some circles, Master Hawkes."

"In most circles, I would imagine," Hawkes agreed with a thin smile. "There's a reason it's called *Hidden* Valley, you know."

"What do you want of me?"

"I'd like you and your friend here to join the rest of your compatriots in Hidden Valley. The Tide's turning. We're beyond the notion that it *might* return. It *has* returned. Within a few months, the immortals will start to feel confident enough to reveal themselves. We plan to be ready for them."

"But even if you know where they are, and who they are," Boots asked, "how do you plan to stop them? They can wield Tide magic. You can't fight that."

"We're not the ignorant fools our forefathers were, just waiting for the immortals to come along and show us the way. They've been gone a very long time. We're smarter now, more capable of defending ourselves against them. And I believe we can, provided we're prepared for them. Tide magic is elemental. They can't conjure armies out of thin air and, fortunately for us, they're usually more interested in fighting each other than their human pawns. We're nothing to them really—just one of their weapons. Just something else to use in their own, endless, internecine battles. I plan to use that against them."

"You seriously expect to stop the rise of the Tide Lords?" Warlock said, shaking his head.

"Probably not." Hawkes shrugged. "Truth is, we may not have to. All we really need do is make taking control of Glaeba more trouble than it's worth. Let them find easier pickings. It's my job to protect Glaeba. Don't much care what happens to the rest of the world."

Warlock didn't doubt for a moment that this man was telling the truth. He smelled of quiet confidence, not fear or deception. But the level of trust he was displaying in a couple of stray canines he'd never met until half an hour ago was disturbing.

"I'm curious," Warlock said. "What will happen to us if we refuse to join your Scard army? With what you've told us, I could go to the king and have you arrested for treason and probably receive a hefty reward for my loyalty."

Hawkes smiled indulgently. "Warlock, you strike me as being an intelligent creature. You can't seriously believe you have a choice here."

"Yeah? Well, maybe I'd *rather* be arrested than sent back to Lebec Palace!" Boots suggested defiantly.

"That's not the alternative he's offering, Boots," Warlock warned softly, not taking his eyes off Declan Hawkes.

Hawkes nodded slowly. "You are a clever dog, aren't you?"

Boots's gaze swung between the two of them, aghast, as

she realised what Warlock was suggesting. "They'd *kill* us?"

The man shrugged. "A convicted murderer and a runaway slave who's already torn the throat out of one feline? I'd get a medal for it."

He would too, Warlock knew. That was the trouble with being thought of as animals. No human cared about your death the way they grieved for their own. "Will you guarantee our safety if we agree?"

Hawkes shook his head. "I can't guarantee anything of the sort. You know that."

Warlock nodded. That answer was more reassuring than having Hawkes make a promise he knew he couldn't keep. "What would you have us do?"

Boots glared at him. "You're going to go along with this absurd plan?"

"I'm not ready to die."

"Good answer," Hawkes remarked. He turned to Boots with a questioning look. "And what about you? What's it going to be? Hidden Valley or the opportunity to discover firsthand if Crasii have souls?"

"If I go with Warlock, will I get a chance at that bastard Jaxyn, someday?"

"More than likely," Declan agreed. "Given he's heading for Herino as we speak, there's a good chance we'll have to deal with him first."

Slowly, almost reluctantly, Boots nodded. "Guess I'm in, then. I just have one question."

"I'll answer it if I can."

"This Hidden Valley of yours . . . is the food any good?"

Chapter 71

The day of their departure dawned bright and blustery and brought with it news that sometime during the night, after he'd left her room, Stellan had taken his wife's advice and asked Jaxyn to accompany them to Herino and remain at court as Lebec's ambassador while they were in Torlenia.

Arkady learned of the decision at breakfast from Declan, who complimented her on her wise decision to cooperate, as well as her remarkable ability to make her husband see reason. Arkady accepted the compliment distractedly, still thinking about what Stellan had told her last night about Declan's feelings for her. If he was wasting away from unrequited love, however, he was showing no sign of it at breakfast.

Watching Jaxyn stride confidently up the barge's gangway, joking with the crew as they manhandled his luggage aboard and generally behaving as if he thought his new position at court was the best thing that had ever happened to him, she began to wonder about the wisdom of suggesting such a thing. Jaxyn's jovial demeanour worried Arkady. If they had thwarted any plans the immortal had for the Lebec Crasii, why was he so happy to be leaving?

Have I saved Glaeba from the threat of a Tide Lord with a Crasii army at his back, or let loose the fox in the chicken house?

"Are you sure this was a good idea, Declan?" she asked softly, as she and her old friend watched Jaxyn embarking from the upper deck. "The Lord of Temperance doesn't appear unduly bothered by his removal from Lebec."

"Could be he's fairly good at hiding his true feelings."

"They're good at everything," Arkady said.

"Pardon?"

"Something Cayal said—after eight thousand years, you get good at everything."

"Well, he'd know."

Arkady didn't reply but remained at the railing of the upper deck, watching the amphibian Crasii prepare the ship for launch. More a floating palace than a sailing ship, the boat was two decks high above the gunwale and another three below, not including the holds. Painted red and gold, its cabins appointed with a level of luxury even the king envied, the ship would be their home until they reached the coast. On their way south they would stop in Herino long enough to witness Kylia's marriage to Mathu and then after the wedding they would sail to the coast where the king's own flagship awaited them, ready to take them south to Torlenia.

Across the bow of the ship was a complicated rigging system that stretched upwards through a forest of ropes and pulleys connecting the ship's main mast to the harness which currently rested in the water, but which would soon be occupied by the school of twenty-five amphibians—five deep and five abreast—who would tow the ship, riding the current and assisted by the wind. The design was unique to Glaeba, although Arkady had heard it said that the Senestrans were the ones who came up with the idea of towing sailing ships using amphibian Crasii.

She could see a few of them diving into the water near the jetty, ready to take up their position in the harness. Although magically blended with humans in the same way the felines and the canines had been, there was less human and more salamander about the amphibians. They had long tails, hanging down between their oddly proportioned legs, which finished in webbed hands and feet. Their double-lidded eyes were set in dark, shiny faces that seemed more a parody of humanity rather than a member of the same race.

"Do you think he's free yet?" Arkady asked abruptly.

"Who? Cayal? I suppose that depends on how deep he

was buried and how much help Maralyce was willing to give him."

Arkady glanced at Declan in surprise. She hadn't mentioned a word about Maralyce.

He smiled. "It wasn't a hard conclusion to jump to, Arkady. Cayal fled into the mountains and the only refuge he's likely to find there is with Maralyce."

"Do you know the location of her mine?"

He shook his head. "Other than a general, rough idea of the area, not really. I was hoping you could fill in the details. Truth be told, finding her isn't a priority. Maralyce hasn't moved out of her lair in thousands of years. It would take something fairly spectacular to shift her now, I suspect."

It was a fair assessment, Arkady thought. Maralyce was quite happy in her isolation and wouldn't stir out of her mine for anything trivial.

"Will Cayal come back, do you think?"

Declan smiled reassuringly. "We'll see you're protected from him."

"That's good to know," she said, fairly sure that if Declan knew what she was thinking he'd brand her a traitor to humanity.

"And what of the Lord of Temperance," she asked, looking down at the main deck where Jaxyn stood talking with Stellan, who had finally come aboard and was ordering the ship to cast off. "What plans do you have to protect us all from him?"

"You'll just have to trust me on that, Arkady. Suffice to say there are plans in place and that you need know nothing about them to do what is required of you."

Arkady looked at him in surprise, and more than a little offended. "You don't trust me enough to tell me, is that it?"

He smiled apologetically. "As you so rightly pointed out, Cayal may yet return. It would be dangerous to give you information he might find a way to extract from you."

"Do you *expect* him to come after me?" *Tides, what kind of hopeless fool am I for hoping that he will?*

And will your spies be watching me to see if he does?

"Who's to say?" Declan shrugged. "You may have intrigued him enough to catch his attention for a time, or you may be just another forgotten memory in a long life filled with countless forgotten memories. If I knew that much about the Tide Lords I'd be another step along the way to finding a way to be rid of them."

"I'm curious, Declan, at your passion for this cause," she remarked, watching the last of the amphibians slip into the harness and the ropes tossed aboard by the three Crasii remaining on the docks. "What did the immortals ever do to you?"

"It's a family matter." He shrugged, as the amphibians took up the slack in the harness and began to pull the great ship from the dock.

"An immortal hurt your family?"

"An immortal is responsible for it," he told her cryptically. "But it's nothing you need fret about. You have a royal wedding to attend and Torlenia to prepare for. For the time being you're safe from the immortals, although if you happen to stumble across Brynden or Kinta while you're in Torlenia, I'd be grateful if you'd let me know."

"We have a long road ahead of us, I fear," she agreed, waving to Stellan when he glanced up at her. She really wanted to yell at him. She wanted to tell him about Jaxyn, warn him away from his lethal charms, but she knew there was no point. So she waved and smiled and pretended she didn't see the threat, hoping they could think of something before the Tide returned completely and the humans of Amyrantha were lost forever.

"That we do, Arkady," Declan Hawkes agreed.

"I know you said you know where some of the immortals are, but according to the Tarot there are twenty-two of them, aren't there?"

"Not all of them wield the sort of power Cayal and Jaxyn are capable of, fortunately," Declan reminded her. "Some have more nuisance value than they are a threat. There's one or two who may even be considered reasonable, under the right circumstances."

"So where are they, Declan?" Arkady asked with a frown, as Jaxyn looked up at her also with a sly, knowing smile.

"What do you mean?"

"The lesser immortals? Do we need to worry about them the way we fear the Tide Lords? Will they try seizing power on their own or will they be allying themselves with the others? Who are they? *Where* are they? Will they try to stay hidden? Will they help *us*!"

"That's what the Cabal is here for," Declan said. "Because we have to find out."

Chapter 72

Short engagements were the norm in Glaeba and the crown prince's betrothal to Lady Kylia Debrell was no exception. Within three weeks of Stellan, Arkady and Jaxyn arriving in Herino, the wedding was over. Being something of a cynic, Jaxyn suspected the custom stemmed from a lack of trust rather than any inherent streak of romanticism or sentimentality in the Glaebans. Once a man had his virgin bride selected, one did their best to get the wedding over and done with while she remained in that condition.

Not that Jaxyn blamed Mathu for wanting Kylia in his bed as soon as he could manage it. She looked breathtaking in her dark blue wedding gown, her face alight with happiness, as she and Mathu danced the night away to the strains of Glaeba's finest musicians playing songs that were older than any of them realised.

Jaxyn watched the party from the balcony, smiling at Kylia's obvious delight.

I take my hat off to you, my lady. You accomplished in a couple of months what I hadn't been able to do in a year.

The ballroom was packed, as one would expect for the wedding of a crown prince. The actual wedding ceremony, conducted earlier today in the throne room with far fewer guests in attendance, had been quite dull by comparison. But the reception, to which anybody with even the slightest pretension to grandeur had managed to wrangle an invitation, was the place to be this stormy evening. Even the Caelish Ambassador—no doubt still smarting over the fact that this wedding put paid to any hopes of a union between Caelum and Glaeba—seemed to be enjoying himself.

Turning his attention from the newlyweds, Jaxyn scanned the crowd, looking for Arkady. He spied her eventually by the food tables, sipping a glass of punch while discussing the Tides knew what with that crafty old bitch, Tilly Ponting, who'd also come to Herino for the wedding. Her hair was blue today, the same shade as her ball gown, a garment with far too many frills and flounces for a woman her age. Still, nobody expected Tilly Ponting to set the standard of fashion and good taste in Herino. Not while ever she was able to tell their fortunes.

Jaxyn smiled. There was a future ahead that Tilly Ponting knew nothing of. One she would be hard-pressed to even imagine. *What will she do,* he wondered, *when the Tide Lords of her wretched Tarot begin to come to life?*

Arkady leant forward and said something to Tilly that made the old woman laugh. She looked ravishing, as usual, dressed in a deep crimson gown and the Lebec family rubies gracing her long creamy neck.

What is she talking to Tilly about? The wedding? The dresses of the other women? The foolishness of some of the guests who'd drunk too much of the king's wine?

Cayal, perhaps? Her kidnapping? Or maybe her bleak future in Torlenia?

It had been awkward for Arkady since they'd arrived in the capital. The king was still convinced she was pregnant and insisted on treating her as such, a fact Jaxyn could see irked the duchess no end. There was nothing she could do about it, however. Stellan had decided to keep up the fiction for a little longer, fearing the announcement of a miscarriage might start the king worrying that Arkady was unable to carry a child to term and set him thinking about alternative ways to ensure an heir to Lebec. It was good practice for her, Jaxyn thought spitefully. Arkady and Stellan were leaving for Torlenia in two days' time and there would be no chance for her, in that restrictive and miserable place, to indulge in her academic pursuits. Torlenian women were rarely even seen in public. She certainly wouldn't be allowed the same sort of freedom she enjoyed here in Glaeba.

It still irked Jaxyn that he didn't know what had gone on between Arkady and Cayal while they were in the mountains. Logic told him something must have happened. He knew Cayal well enough to be certain of that. Yet Arkady displayed none of the symptoms of a woman pining for a missing lover, or a shred of guilt over anything she may have done.

She carried on as normal, which annoyed Jaxyn no end.

It would have been nice to think he had something on Arkady. Even better to think he might have found some leverage over Cayal. *Has he dug himself out of that cavein yet, I wonder?* Was he on his way to Herino, even now, looking to even the score, or would he give up the fight and look for greener pastures elsewhere, now the Tide was turning and he realised Jaxyn already had his claim staked on Glaeba?

And the Tide *was* coming back. Fast.

Jaxyn could feel it swelling a little more every day. Already he had the ability to affect the elements around him, although he was a long way from commanding them yet. That sort of power only happened with the Tide at its peak. But it was rising and rising rapidly. It wouldn't be long now . . . a few months until they could risk revealing themselves fully, and maybe a year or two before their power was really something to inspire awe.

Trouble was, the same thing was happening to all the

Tide Lords. Somewhere out there, Syrolee and Engarhod—
and their dreadful offspring with them—were on the move.
Brynden would be stirring out of his torpor.

And Lukys . . . he might reappear too, which was something even Jaxyn had reason to be wary of . . .

But that was in the future. Right now, Jaxyn was more
interested in Arkady Desean and what might have tran-
spired between her and the Immortal Prince.

Somewhat to his surprise, she had kept her end of the
bargain, saying nothing to Stellan. Or if she had broken
their confidence, he didn't believe her. The posting to
Herino worried Jaxyn a little, but then he thought about it
and decided she was probably trying to get him away from
the Lebec Crasii and thought sending him to Herino was
the safest way to do it.

Fool woman. She had unwittingly played right into his
hands. With Stellan in Torlenia, Lebec—and her duke—
were of no interest to Jaxyn any longer. Jaxyn needed to
be here. Needed to be close to Kylia.

Allies they might be, but he didn't trust Diala as far as
he could throw her.

Jaxyn still hadn't quite got over the shock of Diala arriving unannounced at the Lebec Palace several months
ago, posing as Stellan's niece. The real Kylia was dead,
of course, just as the real Jaxyn Aranville was rotting in
a ditch alongside a hunting trail around Darra. Neither
Jaxyn nor Diala could risk their namesakes turning up at
an awkward time to expose the impostors and ruin their
plans.

Diala had been just as shocked to find Jaxyn in residence
and after ordering the Crasii to keep their secret and several
heated, albeit very guarded, exchanges late at night or on the
rare occasions they could manage a moment alone, they'd
eventually agreed to become allies. They'd hammered out
the final details the day Arkady agreed to let them go boating
alone on the lake.

You'd better make sure she comes back a virgin, Arkady
had warned him that day.

Jaxyn had almost choked. A *virgin*? Tides, this was the Minion Maker. She'd seduced more men than Arkady could count. She might be able to pass for seventeen—Diala was only nineteen, after all, when she stepped into the Eternal Flame with her sister, Arryl—but she'd been alive for the better part of nine thousand years and spent a sizeable portion of that time sleeping with anything that took her fancy.

Diala had no morals at all. Not a one. Jaxyn knew that for a fact. He was one of the first men she'd coaxed into the flames.

Poor Mathu really hadn't stood a chance.

Their agreement was simple. One of them would find a way to take the Glaeban throne, and share it with the other. Jaxyn's plan had been to remove the other contenders standing between the throne and Stellan Desean, but then Mathu arrived in Lebec and all Diala had to do was smile and flutter those long dark lashes at the boy and he was done for.

While Jaxyn admired Diala's skill, he'd known from the moment Mathu Debree stepped into the Lebec Palace dining room that Diala was going to seduce him. Getting him to marry her was a refinement that had taken Jaxyn by surprise, but he'd countered that with his unexpected posting to Herino, where he could keep an eye on her.

He smiled, remembering how annoyed she was when he informed her Stellan had appointed him Lebec's ambassador and that he would be staying here at court, after all.

If Diala thinks I'm going to let her loose in Herino as the wife of the crown prince without me there, she is sadly mistaken.

"What's so amusing?"

Jaxyn looked up to find Stellan walking toward him on the balcony, carrying a glass of wine, no doubt looking for some relief—as Jaxyn was—from the crush of people in the ballroom below them. Being in Herino had forced the cessation of any overt exchanges of affection between them, but Stellan was still convinced the two of them were lovers and that Jaxyn intended to wait here in Herino for his return from Torlenia. He'd probably have to spend the night with Stellan again before they left, just to ease the duke's mind about leaving his companion, but then he was done with Stellan Desean. Jaxyn's only interest in the Duke of Lebec now was what his impostor niece could do for him.

And what his wife had got up to with the Immortal Prince.

"I wasn't aware that I was laughing."

"You were smirking," Stellan informed him with a smile.

Above them, the dull rumble of thunder announced yet another storm breaking over the city. *Stellan's trip down to the coast is going to prove eventful,* Jaxyn thought idly, *if this weather doesn't let up.*

"I was just thinking how happy Kylia looks."

Stellan smiled and came to lean on the balcony next to Jaxyn, looking down over the crowded reception. "You will watch over her for me, won't you?"

"Like she was my own," he promised.

"And don't let Mathu lead you astray. Or worse . . . you lead him astray."

"I wouldn't dream of it."

"We might only be away a few months, you know," Stellan suggested.

Jaxyn was amused. He knew what Stellan was trying to say. *Wait for me. I won't be gone long.* The Duke of Lebec didn't understand that ship had already sailed. Any future Stellan Desean might have imagined he had with Jaxyn Aranville vanished with the first glimmerings of the returning Tide.

"How do you think Arkady will like it?"

Stellan's smile faded. "I think you already know the answer to that."

"She may find it very interesting, you know," Jaxyn suggested with a nasty little smile. "I hear the Imperator's

Consort is always looking for fascinating companions. Perhaps your lovely wife can befriend the lady and make your job a little easier once she has her ear."

"Arkady will do what is required of her."

"Doesn't she always?"

Stellan frowned at him. "You owe her as much as I do, Jaxyn. She keeps your secret along with mine."

Ah, Stellan, if only you knew how true that was.

"I'm sorry," he said. "I suppose I'm just a little peeved, that's all. I still think I should be allowed to go with you."

"I thought you were quite pleased to be staying here in Herino as my ambassador?"

"Only as a consolation prize," he replied, and then added softly, "I'd rather be with you."

Stellan kept his eyes fixed on the crowd, as aware as Jaxyn was that anybody looking up would see them. To the casual observer they appeared no more than two guests surveying the festivities from afar.

"I'll be back for you, Jaxyn," he promised. "As soon as I can sort this business out in Torlenia. I swear."

"I'll be here," Jaxyn assured him.

Diala and I have a throne to take and an entire country along with it, after all.

The Tide is coming in.

Epilogue

The Immortal Prince stood on one of the high bluffs overlooking the Whitewater Narrows, wondering at the foolishness of mortals. Through the rain, he could just make out the shape of Arkady's ship as the amphibians towed it toward the rapids. The rain had swelled the rushing waters, making them cloudy and perilous to navigate. A human sailor standing on the deck of a ship had no hope of navigating the dangerous narrows and surviving. It was only the presence of the amphibians, swimming ahead of the craft, towing it in their wake, which made the journey through the Whitewater Narrows possible at all.

What had possessed Arkady—or perhaps her husband— to set sail in this weather?

As the waves tossed it closer and closer to the gap in the rocks, Cayal pondered the wisdom of letting the ship go. Although it was weeks since he'd last seen Arkady in Maralyce's cabin, on board that ship was the only woman who'd managed to get under his skin since Gabriella.

Perhaps she was even more dangerous, because she had made no promises she didn't intend to keep, had offered Cayal nothing she wasn't willing to give.

Nor had she asked for anything in return, which made her the most remarkable woman he had ever met.

Even before he was immortal, Cayal had been plagued by the fear that people—women in particular—were interested only in the political advantage his friendship might bring them, a fear cruelly realised when Gabriella revealed her true colours the day he was exiled by his sister. For a Tide Lord, the problem was infinitely worse. Despite the incredible magic he could command at High Tide, there was no power in the universe able to truly know the heart of a woman, no magical ability to peer into the mind of a man.

Cayal had been alive too long to believe in love as a pure and unsullied force, able to triumph over all adversity. There were no happily-ever-afters in his world. His view of love and all its attendant baggage was much darker, far more cynical. Love was at best an excuse for stupidity, at worst a destructive, dangerous emotion that drove men to acts of annihilation which defied logic. It was a twisted, insidious sentiment used to justify everything from spoiling a child to destroying entire civilisations.

That's what made Arkady truly dangerous to him, he knew. He recognised the feeling in himself, the constriction in his chest at the thought of losing her. The horror of watching her wither and die while he remained unchanged . . .

The fear of never seeing her again . . .

Worse, the fear that he *might* actually be able to find a way to have her—the Tide was on the way back, after all. It wouldn't be long now before he could compel the world to do as he commanded if the mood took him, Arkady along with it.

Cayal shook his head at his own pathetic predictability. Already he was contemplating world domination just for the sake of having one woman.

That's love for you.

And what if she'd changed her mind? It was more than a month since she'd left Maralyce's mine with Jaxyn. What if she didn't still want him the way Cayal wanted her? What if the memory of Maralyce's cabin had faded to an embarrassing interlude she'd rather forget?

Arkady was a duchess, after all, hugely conscious of her husband's position. And protective of it. That she'd kept his secret while they were married, even to the point of putting up with Jaxyn under her roof, was proof of her loyalty. And she certainly went back to her husband quickly enough when she thought Cayal was defeated . . .

Tides, it's enough to make a man crazy just thinking about it.

The rain was falling harder now, as the ship moved closer to the dangerous narrows. He hadn't caused this storm. Although he could affect its course, his power had yet to reach the point where he could harness this much energy out of thin air and force it to do his bidding.

Arkady might die in the next hour, he thought, *through no fault of mine.*

Which would solve his problem rather neatly.

And Arkady *was* his problem. She had made him hope. She made him want to live again, even if only for the length of her tragically short life span.

Cayal was in no mood to be hopeful. He was done with immortality and determined to find a way to end it.

*How dare you come into my life and threaten my re-
solve, Arkady Desean.*

The ship was in the clutches of the current now, the
efforts of the harnessed amphibians having little effect.
Lightning streaked overhead as the storm moved closer,
the thunder prickling along Cayal's forearms as the Tide
magic returning to him responded to the elemental display. They were close enough now that he could just make
out the cries of the crew as they desperately fought to
bring the ship under control. Their efforts were futile. The
cumbersome vessel had been swept up by the pull of the
white water and was heading far too quickly into the narrows.

*There will be no hope, no pain, once you're dead,
Arkady.*

Over the years he had come to understand Pellys's fascination with killing things. The guilty pleasure of watching something expire, the envy, the almost sensual delight
of witnessing a life go where an immortal had no hope of
following.

I'd be doing you a favour, letting you die, my love.

That was the logic Cayal's endless existence had forced
him to adopt. He lived in a world where life was pain and
death was a welcome release for some . . . a door locked
to him and his kind forever.

*Are you frightened aboard your silly, dangerously top-
heavy ship, Arkady? Are you clinging to the railing, blood
racing through your veins as your heart pounds in anticipation of death, certain this is the end?*

Thunder rumbled overhead. Below him in the raging
straits, the amphibian harness became tangled as one of
the outriders was thrown against the rocks. It was too late
to turn back. The vessel had no choice but to move on.

Is your life flashing before your eyes, Arkady?
Are you thinking of me?

Another amphibian was torn from their harness by the
rocks, its scream drowned out by the storm. If the ship lost
any more of them, that would be the end of it.

When you're gone, there will be no more uncertainty.
I can go back to being sure I want to die.

The ship would break up on the rocks. Arkady would drown, more than likely, which as deaths went was probably one of the better ways to go . . .

How I envy you, my love.

Another crack of lightning, the rain falling so hard he was all but blinded by it, the rumble of thunder making the ground shake . . .

And then it stopped abruptly as Cayal lost his nerve. Cursing his own cowardice, he waved his arm across the water, stilling it instantly.

The storm seemed to hold its breath as it halted on his command.

On the ship below him, the shouts of panic turned to shouts of astonishment, carried clearly now across the still water, echoing off the sheer cliff walls enclosing the White-water Narrows. The rain stopped, the raging white water calmed to a gentle flow.

Hastily, the remaining amphibians pulled the ship into the centre of the waterway and towed it forward. They could probably feel his presence. At the very least, unlike the humans on the barge, the Crasii would know there was magic at work.

The barge sailed past the dangerous entrance and through to the wider, deeper waters farther downstream, heading for the coast.

Cayal stood on the edge of the cliff, watching the ship sail past, knowing he was a fool but unable to find it in himself to regret saving Arkady.

Perhaps it was a good idea, not an act of rank stupidity, he consoled himself. She was smart. Intelligent. Resourceful. Maybe, if he sought her out again, she could help him find a way to die . . .

Cayal smiled sourly at his own foolishness. What a pathetic justification to go looking for her. And as if any mortal could even understand, let alone be a willing accomplice to, such an endeavour.

But then another thought occurred to him. What if she feared him? If she felt threatened, perhaps, or believed humanity was threatened?

Would that be enough to enlist her cooperation?

Is that what I have to do?

The thought made a twisted sort of logic.

If you won't help me die, my love, then perhaps I'll have to make you want to kill me.

Turn the page for a preview of

The
GODS *of*
AMYRANTHA

JENNIFER FALLON

Available July 2009

TOR® A TOR HARDCOVER

ISBN-13: 978-0-7653-1683-7   ISBN-10: 0-7653-1683-8

Prologue

T *hree thousand years ago. Prior to the Fourth Cata-*
clysm . . .

The hardest thing about torturing someone, Balen decided, was trying not to empathise with your victim's pain.
You had to distance yourself from it. Detach that part of
you which was human and make sure it stayed detached.

Most of all, you had to remind yourself the creature you
were torturing wasn't really human.

The latter wasn't easy. Lyna looked human. With her
long dark hair and her soulful dark eyes, she looked more
like Balen's married daughter than a monster.

Balen closed his eyes for a moment, trying to shut out her
screaming. *I'm doing this because I have to,* he reminded
himself, tossing the severed hand on the forge's glowing
coals. *There must be a way to kill these creatures.*

The disembodied hand browned and burned, the leaking blood hissing and spitting. It smelt horribly reminiscent of last night's roast.

It's not logical to think something cannot die.

Logical or not, they'd had no luck killing their captive
immortal so far.

Perhaps they'd used up all their luck just finding her. But
with the Tide on the rise, and the immortals with it, they
were much less careful, these days, about hiding their iden-
tities. Balen and his compatriots would never have had a
chance of capturing a true Tide Lord. Lyna, fortunately, was
one of the lesser immortals. She didn't have the power to do
the sort of damage someone like Cayal or Pellys or Tryan

could do. She could touch the Tide, sure enough—all the immortals could—but she didn't seem to be able to do much with it.

That was fortunate. If she'd been a Tide Lord . . . if the Tide had peaked . . . well, given what they'd done to her these past few weeks, if she'd been able to wreak any sort of vengeance on them, they'd all be dead.

And probably everyone within a hundred-mile radius, as well.

Bracing himself, Balen turned to look at her. Naked and filthy, Lyna lay on the floor of her cell, curled into a foetal position, weeping with the pain of her amputation. Despite the burns, the stab wounds, even the hand he'd just amputated to see if she would bleed to death, the rest of her body was whole and unmarked. Everything he'd done to her had healed, and the more traumatic the injury, the faster she seemed to recover from it.

Tides, what's it going to take?

Perhaps these unnatural creatures truly *were* immortal. Perhaps there *was* no end for them. Ever. Perhaps, some unimaginable time in the future when the universe grew cold, they would still be here, alone and alive, with nothing but their endless existence to sustain them . . .

It's not possible, Balen assured himself. *Besides, until we reach the end of time, how will we know if they can survive that long?*

"Has she recovered again?"

Balen looked up to find his son standing at the entrance to the smithy. The boy was morbidly fascinated by what his father was doing. A little *too* fascinated, perhaps. He feared the young man didn't see the monster lying in the cage regrowing a hand his father had just hacked off, he only saw the tormented young woman. At seventeen, Minark was too young to appreciate the danger immortality presented to the mortals of this world.

"It would appear so."

"Can I see her?"

Balen frowned. "Why?"

"I . . . I just can't believe she's not hurt."

Balen glanced over his shoulder at the pathetic, weeping young woman. He didn't know how old she was exactly— five thousand . . . ten thousand years old? She looked little more than twenty-five; more than young enough for an impressionable youth to find her appealing. Already the bleeding had stopped and there was new bone and flesh taking shape. "She's hurting, sure enough, Minark. But she just keeps healing up."

"Can I see . . . ?"

"No," he said, concerned Minark was taking far too much interest in the tortured immortal's plight. The last thing he needed was the lad sneaking back here in the dead of night to offer her sympathy. Or worse. Lyna had been a whore, after all, before she was made immortal. She'd not hesitate to use her wiles on someone as wide-eyed and credulous as his son. "What are you doing here, anyway, boy? I thought I told you to stay away from this place."

Minark ventured a few steps further into the smithy, straining to see past his father. "Vorak sent me."

Balen took a step sideways to block his son's view of the naked young woman with her regrowing hand. "What does he want, Minark?"

"He's just got back from the markets in L'bekken. He said there was someone asking around in the village. About her," he added, pointing to the immortal.

"Did he say who it was?"

Minark shook his head. "Just that he was asking. And he was heading this way when he left."

Balen cursed silently. *Surely they hadn't come for her yet?* And if they had, was it one of the other lesser immortals, which would be bad enough? Or was it one of the Tide Lords themselves? He shuddered at the thought. If someone like Cayal, or Tryan or Kentravyon discovered Lyna caged and tortured like this, everyone in this village and the neighbouring village of L'bekken would, in all probability, soon be dead.

"This man was a stranger, yes?"

"That's what I said, wasn't it?" Minark leaned a little to the left so he could catch sight of the immortal. "Did you try cutting her into smaller pieces? Vorak thought that if you fed the meat to the dogs . . ."

"She heals too quickly," he said, wishing Vorak would stop discussing his wild theories with Minark. "And the faster you cut, the faster she heals. Did Vorak think this stranger was an immortal?"

Minark shrugged. "He didn't say. Just to tell you some-one was asking about Lyna."

Balen glanced over his shoulder at his prisoner, won-dering if he should just let her go. She'd been blindfolded when she was overpowered in the streets of L'bekken and brought here in chains. If they took her far away from their village before they dumped her, it was unlikely she would know how to find this place again.

But how often did one get a chance like this? How often did one capture an immortal? How often had they been able to put their theories on how to put an end to them to the test?

The opportunity against the risk . . . that was Balen's problem.

"I warned you," the young woman said, pushing herself up on her elbows.

He looked over his shoulder. Lyna's face was tear-streaked and filthy. On hearing the news someone was ask-ing after her, she rallied her strength. A fresh stump had already formed on the end of her arm, even though it had only been minutes since he'd cut off her hand. "You'll die for what you've done to me, you pathetic mortal *pig*."

"It was probably just one of your regular customers," Balen said, hoping he sounded unafraid. "Good whores have repeat customers, I'm told, and I hear you were a *very* good whore."

She smiled, which Balen found disturbing. Three days ago, he'd beaten her so badly, most of her teeth had bro-ken. Yet her smile now was white and even, mocking him with its unnatural perfection.

"My brothers will level this place," she warned, pushing herself to her feet. "They will take apart your pitiful village, kill you, your son, your wife, your grandchildren and everyone else in this valley."

"They have to find you first, you immortal whore!" Minark retorted gamely.

Lyna smiled through the pain of her regenerating hand. "*Find* me? Tides, boy, that's the easy part."

"What do you mean?"

"I mean we can sense each other on the Tide, you fool. If there's another immortal around, he'll feel my presence and there's nothing you can do to stop him finding me, short of killing me. But you've tried that, haven't you? I'll bet you're sorry now, that none of your brilliant little plans worked."

Balen had no reason to doubt her. If anything, he began to get nervous. Her growing defiance was at such odds with the lack of resistance she'd shown thus far, he had to wonder at the cause of it.

Was her confidence brought on by the news that one of her immortal brethren was nearby?

We can sense each other on the Tide, she'd said, which meant if another immortal could feel her presence, then she would be able to . . . *Tides*!

"Get to the house, now!" he ordered Minark. "Tell your mother and your sister to take only what they can carry. We must flee. *Now*!"

"Flee?" Minark asked in confusion. "Why must we flee? Vorak said the stranger asked about her and then moved on. Nobody told him anything."

"Nobody had to, Minark," Balen said, shoving him toward the entrance to the smithy. "Didn't you hear what she said? They can sense each other on the Tide. He'll know she's here. Which means he's probably on his way. And if he finds us with her . . ."

"But it might only be one of the lesser immortals, like Taryx or Rance . . ."

"Are you willing to risk your mother's life on that, son?"

The boy hesitated for a moment longer, staring at the immortal woman, and then he turned and fled. Balen grabbed one of the hammers from his forge, shoved it into his belt in case he needed a weapon, and then turned to face Lyna. She was standing at the bars of the cage they'd fashioned to contain her. Already, short stubby fingers were protruding from the stump. Although still in pain, he guessed she was improving by the minute, her recovery accelerated, no doubt, by the sense that there was another of her kind nearby.

"It wasn't anything personal," he said, as if an explanation or an apology was going to make the slightest difference at this point.

She glared at him and held up her mangled wrist. "Trust me, Balen. You *made* it personal."

He shook his head, wondering what he hoped to achieve by lingering here, trying to explain himself. He had tortured this creature relentlessly for weeks. It was too late now to ask for forgiveness. "You must tell them . . . I am the one at fault here. Not my family."

"I'm sure that will be a great comfort to them as they're dying."

Balen stared at her, only now, perhaps, realising the enormity of what he'd done. "Is there no chance of mercy?"

Lyna studied him for a moment and then nodded. "Despite what you think, we're not monsters, Balen. You want mercy for you and your family?" The immortal smiled coldly, showing her perfect teeth. "Then I shall see you get it."

"Really?"

"*Really,*" she said. "It will be my pleasure, in fact when my friends arrive to free me, to recommend they show you all the *mercy* you showed me."

"*If* your friends arrive," he replied gamely.

"Oh, I think you can be sure they will," a deep voice behind him announced.

Startled, Balen turned to discover a stranger standing in the entrance to the forge. He was a big man, wearing leather armour, a dark crimson cloak caught up in a jewelled brooch on his right shoulder.

"Kentravyon!" Lyna called as soon as she saw him, although Balen needed no introduction.

He backed up against the forge. There was no hope he could defeat an immortal, certainly not a Tide Lord as powerful as Kentravyon, but he might be able to distract him long enough for the others to get away.

"You have hurt my friend," the immortal said, walking toward him.

"It was . . . We only meant . . ."

"I know what you meant to do," Kentravyon said. He didn't sound angry. He sounded calm. Almost disinterested. "You were trying to find a way to kill us, weren't you?"

Balen nodded as he felt the warm stone of the forge against his back. It was too late to run now. He had nowhere else to go.

"It must be hard for you to deal with the notion of immortality," the Tide Lord said as he moved closer. "I can appreciate that."

His tone was far more reasonable than Balen might have expected. He allowed a glimmer of hope to flicker in his soul. Perhaps the rumours he'd heard about Kentravyon were just that. Rumours . . . nothing else . . .

The Tide Lord stopped before him. He smiled, and reached up with both hands. Balen leaned back from him, but the immortal didn't try to strike him. He took Balen's face between his hands with a gentleness that shocked him, smiling beatifically.

"Poor, poor mortals," he whispered softly, seductively. "You so badly want what we have, don't you?"

Balen couldn't answer. Kentravyon's gloved hand caressed his face. The world seemed to retreat. Even Lyna's whimpering faded into the background . . .

Kentravyon leaned forward and kissed him on the mouth and then he pulled back and smiled at Balen. "I forgive you."

Balen sagged with relief. "My lord . . ."

"And because I forgive you, I will save you from witnessing what I'm going to do to your family. And your village. And anybody else who thinks they can torment their gods."

It was the look deep in the immortal's eyes as much as his words that panicked Balen. There was forgiveness, sure enough, but it was forgiveness without reason. Balen struggled to break free, but the Tide Lord held him fast, moving his hands until his thumbs pressed against his eyelids.

Slowly, Kentravyon pushed down against Balen's eyes, until the pressure was unbearable. Balen heard someone screaming and realised it was his own voice. The pressure grew worse until he could stand it no more. The left eye collapsed a moment after the right, blood streaming from his eye sockets, his screams tasting salty as the blood mixed with his tears.

Kentravyon let him go and he collapsed to the floor, sobbing not only for his own torment, but the pain of impending death.

This was just a precursor, he knew. He did not have much longer to live.

In the distance he heard a lock rattle and realised Kentravyon must have released Lyna from her cage. A moment later a foot slammed into his ribs. He grunted with the force of it, rolling onto his side to avoid a second blow. The world remained black, his ruined eyes nothing more than a gelatinous goo leaking out of his bloody eye sockets.

"Bastard!"

"Now, now, Lyna . . . that wasn't very nice." Kentravyon's voice was still calm . . . soothing even . . .

"I'm going to kill the sadistic little prick."

"No, my dear, you're not."

"He cut off my hand!"

"And you *will* be avenged," the Tide Lord promised. "But your tormenter must *know* you are being avenged, my dear, or he cannot achieve redemption."

"How's he going to know anything?" she demanded of her saviour impatiently. "You put out his eyes."

"But he can still hear us," Kentravyon said.

Balen whimpered in fear, but not for himself.

Tides, please let my family be safely away from here . . .

The Tide ignored his plea. His family were still in the house, he soon discovered; the villagers asleep in their homes, unaware of the danger he had brought down upon them in his arrogance.

He couldn't see them, of course.

But as he lay by the forge, feeling it grow cold, he discovered Kentravyon was right.

He could—and did—hear their screams as they died.

TOR

Voted
#1 Science Fiction Publisher
20 Years in a Row
by the *Locus* Readers' Poll

Please join us at the website below
for more information about this
author and other science fiction,
fantasy, and horror selections, and to
sign up for our monthly newsletter!